PRAISE FOR THESE AWARD-WINNING AUTHORS

New York Times bestselling author
ELIZABETH LOWELL

"For smoldering sensuality and exceptional storytelling Elizabeth Lowell is incomparable."
—*Romantic Times Magazine*

"I'll buy any book with Elizabeth Lowell's name on it!"
—*New York Times* bestselling author Jayne Ann Krentz

❤ ❤ ❤

New York Times bestselling author
HEATHER GRAHAM

"Heather Graham knows what readers want."
—*Publishers Weekly*

"Ms. Graham is a true artist at blending historical detail, excitement, high drama, sensuality and romance."
—*Romantic Times Magazine*

❤ ❤ ❤

Award-winning author
MIRANDA JARRETT

"A sparkling talent!"
—*Romantic Times Magazine*

"Miranda Jarrett knows how to put life and love into her pages and make you believe every word."
—*Rendezvous*

Elizabeth Lowell, *New York Times* bestselling author, has won countless awards, including the Romance Writers of America Lifetime Achievement Award. She also writes mainstream fiction as Ann Maxwell and mysteries with her husband as A.E. Maxwell. She presently resides with her husband in Washington State.

Heather Graham considers herself lucky to live in Florida, where she can indulge her love of water sports, like swimming and boating, year-round. Her background includes stints as a model, actress and bartender. She was once actually tied to the railroad tracks to garner publicity for the dinner theater where she was acting. Now she's a full-time wife, mother of five and, of course, a *New York Times* bestselling writer of historical and contemporary romances under the names Heather Graham, Shannon Drake and Heather Graham Pozzessere.

Miranda Jarrett was an award-winning designer and art director before turning to writing full-time. A descendant of early settlers in New England, she feels a special kinship with her popular fictional family, the Sparhawks of Rhode Island. Miranda admits herself that it's hard to keep track of all the Sparhawk family members, and she has prepared a family tree to help, including which characters appear in each book. She loves to hear from readers, and you can write to her and enclose a self-addressed stamped envelope; she'll send you a copy of the family tree along with her reply. Her address is P.O. Box 1102, Paoli, PA 19301-1145.

ms

RECKLESS HEARTS

ELIZABETH LOWELL

HEATHER GRAHAM
AND
MIRANDA JARRETT

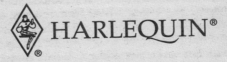 HARLEQUIN®

TORONTO • NEW YORK • LONDON
AMSTERDAM • PARIS • SYDNEY • HAMBURG
STOCKHOLM • ATHENS • TOKYO • MILAN • MADRID
PRAGUE • WARSAW • BUDAPEST • AUCKLAND

ISBN 0-373-83484-5

RECKLESS HEARTS

Copyright © 2001 by Harlequin Books S.A.

The publisher acknowledges the copyright holders of the individual works as follows:

RECKLESS LOVE
Copyright © 1990 by Two Of A Kind Inc.

DARK STRANGER
Copyright © 1988 by Heather Graham Pozzessere.

COLUMBINE
Copyright © 1992 by Susan Holloway Scott.

CONTENTS

Reckless Love

Elizabeth Lowell

Chapter One

Heart pounding, body flattened to the hot earth, Janna Wayland peered down the brush-covered slopes and watched the tall stranger run naked between a double line of Cascabel's renegade Ute warriors.

He'll never make it, Janna thought. Her heart turned over in pity for the man as blow after blow rained onto his powerful body, staggering him, sending him to his knees. *No matter how big or how strong he looks from here, they'll kill him. They always kill the white men they catch.*

Crimson streaks appeared on the man's broad back as he struggled to his feet and began to run once more, doubled over in pain, lurching from side to side between the two lines of half-drunk warriors. When he reached the end of the gauntlet he straightened unexpectedly and surged forward, his legs driving hard, his head up, running with the power and grace of a wild stallion.

The laughing, jeering Utes remained unconcerned about their prey's apparent escape. Other men had run the gauntlet before. Most of them never reached the end before being knocked unconscious and clubbed to death. The few prisoners who managed to survive the gauntlet had provided great sport for the renegades as they tracked their bleeding quarry through the rugged canyons, plateaus and mountains of the lower Utah Territory. Whether they found their prisoner a hundred yards away or a mile, the end was always the same—torture and a death that was no more merciful than the red-rock desert itself.

Go to the left, Janna prayed, her slender body vibrating with intensity. *Don't take the first side canyon that offers itself. It's a death trap. Go left. Left!*

As though he heard her silent pleas, the man passed up the brush-choked entrance of a small ravine and ran on. For a few more moments Janna watched him through her spyglass, assuring herself that he was running in the correct direction. Despite the crimson blood staining his skin, the man ran smoothly, powerfully. Janna's breath caught and then wedged in her throat as she watched the stranger run. Every line of his body proclaimed his determination to survive. She had seen nothing so beautiful in her life, not even Lucifer, the black stallion every man pursued and every shaman said no man would catch.

The stranger disappeared around a bend in the dry wash, still running hard. Janna collapsed the spyglass, stuffed it into her hip pocket and began wiggling backward out of the brush that had concealed her from the warriors below. As she moved, she automatically smoothed out signs of her passage and replaced stones or twigs that her body overturned. She had survived for years alone in Indian country by being very, very careful to leave few traces of her presence.

Once Janna was out of sight of the warriors below—and of the guard on the rimrock at the head of Raven Canyon, where Cascabel's renegades had their camp—she began running on a roundabout course that skirted one of the many prows of rock that jutted out from the sloping base of Black Plateau. She crossed a dry wash by leaping from boulder to boulder, leaving no trace of her passage. Then she set off on a course that she hoped would cut across the stranger's trail within a few hundred yards.

If he got that far.

Despite her urgency, Janna used every bit of cover along the way, for she could do the man no good if she were caught by renegades herself. After five minutes she stopped, held her breath and listened. She heard nothing to suggest that the renegades had begun pursuing the stranger. Hope rose a little higher in her heart. She resumed running, moving with the grace and silence of fire skimming over the land. It was the silence of her movement as well as the rich auburn blaze of her hair that had caused the natives to call her Shadow of Fire.

Just before Janna reached another dry wash, she saw the stranger's trail. She veered left, following him, wondering which hiding place the man had chosen of all those offered by the tiny finger canyons and rugged rock formations that riddled the base of the plateau. Not that hiding would do him much good. He tried to conceal his trail, but he was bleeding so much that every few feet bright crimson drops proclaimed his passage.

Janna slowed and began rubbing out the telltale drops, using sand or dirt or brush, whatever was near at hand. When his blood trail began to climb up the slope, she noted with approval that the man had passed up obvious hiding places where the renegades would be sure to look. In spite of injuries and the certain knowledge of pursuit, the man hadn't panicked. Like the elusive Lucifer, the stranger relied on intelligence as well as raw strength for his survival.

Yet it was the man's determination that impressed Janna while she followed his twisting trail up the steep, rocky flank of the plateau. She realized that he was hiding in the most unexpected manner. He was taking a route up the plateau's north face that was so difficult the warriors wouldn't believe their prey could possibly have gone that way. The renegades would search the easier escape routes first, perhaps wasting enough time that darkness would fall before the stranger was discovered.

It was a long chance, but it was the only one he had, and he had been smart and tough enough to take it.

Janna redoubled her efforts, moving quickly, wiping out signs of the man, doing everything she could to help him elude the warriors who were sure to follow. The farther up the flank of the plateau she climbed, the more her admiration for the stranger's determination and stamina increased. She began to hope that he knew of an ancient footpath to the top of the plateau, a path that had been abandoned by the Indians, who now rode horses.

The farther up she climbed, the more she allowed herself to believe that the stranger would make it to the top. Up there was water, cover, game, all that a man would need to survive. Up there she could hide him easily, care for his wounds, nurse him if he required it.

Hopes high, Janna levered herself over a rockfall, only to find a stone cliff cutting off all possibility of advance or escape. At the base of the cliff, piñon and rocks grew in equal profusion.

There was no one in sight.

But there was no way out of the rugged little canyon except the way he had come, and she certainly hadn't seen anything bigger than a rabbit. He had to be somewhere in the piñon- and rock-filled hollow behind the landslide—unless he had spread spectral wings and flown from this trap like a shaman.

A frisson went over Janna's skin at the thought. If any man could have flown like a pagan god, this one could have. He had taken a beating that would have killed most men, then he had run three miles and threaded his way to the head of a nameless rocky canyon over land that had tried even Janna's skill.

Don't be foolish, Janna told herself firmly. *He's as human as you are. You've looked at enough of his blood in the last mile to swear to that on a stack of Bibles as tall as God.*

Intently Janna stared at every foot of the sloping hollow. Despite her sharp eyes, it took two circuits of the ground before she spotted the stranger lying facedown amid the low, ragged piñon branches. She approached him cautiously, unwilling to make any unnecessary sound by calling out to him. Besides, he could be playing possum, waiting for her to get within reach of those powerful hands. He wouldn't expect to be followed by anyone but a renegade Indian out to kill him.

A few minutes of silent observation convinced Janna that the stranger wasn't lying in ambush. He was too still for too long. Janna began to fear that the man was dead. He lay utterly motionless, his limbs at very awkward angles, his skin covered by blood and dirt. In fact it was the slow welling of blood from his wounds that told her he was still alive. She crawled beneath piñon boughs until she was close enough to put her mouth next to his ear.

"I'm a friend. Do you hear me? I'm a friend."

The man didn't move.

"Mister?" Janna whispered, touching his naked shoulder, shaking him lightly, calling to him in her low, husky voice.

There was no sign that he heard.

Carefully Janna sat on her heels next to the man, letting fragrant piñon boughs brush over her. She slid her hand around his neck until she could press against the jugular…and breathed out. Her first impression was of fiery heat, then of the strength in his muscular neck, and then finally she felt the slow, somewhat ragged beating of his heart. From the size of the lump on the side of his head, she was surprised that he had remained conscious long enough to get this far.

"You're not going another inch, are you?" she asked very softly.

The man didn't disagree.

With gentle fingers Janna probed his head wound. Though it was puffy, there was no softness of crushed bone beneath. Nor was blood pooling in the dirt anywhere around his big body, which meant that none of his wounds were bleeding him to death.

Once Janna assured herself of that, she didn't waste any more time checking injuries. The stranger's extraordinary efforts had ended up defeated by a dead end against a stone cliff, but his original plan was still good—take such a difficult route up the side of the plateau that Cascabel wouldn't think to look there for an injured man. All Janna had to do was backtrack, thoroughly wiping out the man's trail as she went. Then she would lay a false trail in another direction and sneak back up to the stranger to make sure that he kept quiet until Cascabel tired of the game and went back to camp.

Slowly Janna worked back down the man's trail, doing a thorough job this time of removing all signs that anyone had come this way. Where blood had fallen onto loose stone, she picked up the stained rock and substituted another of like size. Where the man's feet had disturbed earth, she brushed it flat once more and sifted dust and plant debris over the surface.

She worked in this manner past several places where he could have chosen other routes to the left or right, up the slope or down. When she came to another place where he had a choice of directions, she pulled a knife from the sheath at her waist, gritted her teeth and cut her arm until blood flowed.

Using her own blood, Janna laid a false trail, concealed it so hastily that it could be detected readily by a warrior with sharp eyes, and began a long, slanting descent to the base of the plateau, heading away from the renegades' camp. As she went, she made more obvious attempts to conceal her direction each time there was a logical choice in routes to make. The closer to Mustang Canyon she came, the less blood she left behind, for she wanted to suggest to the renegades that their quarry wasn't badly wounded; that, in fact, he was bleeding less and less with each moment. Hopefully, when the blood spoor disappeared, the Indians wouldn't be suspicious.

Just as Janna reached the broad mouth of Mustang Canyon, she heard Cascabel's men. They were behind her—and they had just discovered the trail of their prey.

Chapter Two

Trapped by Mustang Canyon's high rock walls, the cries of the renegades echoed eerily, making Janna feel surrounded. She redoubled her speed, running hard toward the head of the wide, deep canyon. As she ran, she pulled the bandanna from her neck and wrapped her arm so that no more drops of blood would fall to the ground.

By the time Janna found the tiny side canyon she had been headed for, she was breathing raggedly. Even so, she took great care to mask her trail when she turned into the twisting slot that opened onto the floor of Mustang Canyon. The feeder canyon she had chosen was extremely deep and narrow. The creek that lay in the tiny canyon's bottom was dry, for it carried water only in the wet season or after summer cloudbursts.

No more than six feet wide as it opened onto Mustang Canyon's broad floor, the slot was a hundred feet deep. Only if the sun were directly overhead did any light reach the bottom of the finger canyon. Thirty feet up the sides were marks of previous floods—brush and small trees wedged into crevices, water stains, small boulders perched precariously in water-smoothed hollows. The floor of the feeder canyon was a dry wash paved with boulders and fine deposits of silt and dried mud, all of which angled steeply back into the body of the plateau.

Leaving no trace of her passage, Janna leaped from boulder to boulder up the slot canyon's floor until it became so narrow that she couldn't extend both arms out from her sides at the same time. At this point the top of the canyon—which was the surface of the plateau itself—was only fifty feet away. Farther on, when the red stone walls pressed in even more tightly, she turned sideways, put her back against one wall and her feet against the opposite wall and inched up the chimney-like opening. The top was only thirty feet away, but her progress was dangerously slow. If one of Cascabel's men should happen into the tiny side canyon, she would be discovered within minutes.

In the distance came shouts from the renegades. Janna ignored them, concentrating only on climbing out of the slot canyon and onto the relative safety of the plateau beyond. By the time she reached the top, she was trembling with the effort of levering her body up the narrow opening. She heaved herself over the edge and lay flat, breathing in great gasps, trembling all over and stinging from the scrapes and cuts she had gotten from the stone walls.

What am I complaining about? she asked herself tartly. *He suffered a lot worse and kept going. And if I don't do the same, he's going to come to and thrash around and groan and Cascabel will find him and spend the next four days torturing him to death.*

The thought galvanized Janna. The stranger was too strong and too courageous for her to permit him to die at Cascabel's cruel hands. She pushed herself to her feet and began trotting across the top of Black Plateau, whose rumpled forests, meadows, and crumbling edges she knew as well as any human being ever had. The plateau was part of the summer grazing territory of Lucifer's band.

Janna had spent five years following Lucifer's band, caring for the sick or the lame, taming those animals that hungered for human companionship or easy food, leaving free those horses that could not accept anything from man's hand, even safety. One of those horses had become Janna's only companion in the plateau's wildness, coming to her freely, staying with her willingly, carrying her on wild rides across the rugged land. It was that horse Janna hoped to find now. The band often grazed this part of the plateau in the afternoon.

She found Lucifer and his harem grazing along one of the plateau's many green meadows, some of which ran like a winding river of grass between thick pine forests. A tiny creek trickled down the center of the sinuous meadow.

Janna lifted her hands to her mouth. Moments later a hawk's wild cry keened over the meadow. She called three times, then went to one of the small caches she had scattered across the plateau and surrounding countryside for the times when Cascabel amused himself by pursuing her. From the cache she took a canteen, a handful of rawhide thongs, a leather pouch that was full of various herbs, a blanket and a small leather drawstring bag that contained some of the gold that Mad Jack insisted was her father's share of his gold mine. As her father had been dead for five years, Mad Jack simply paid her instead.

After a moment of hesitation, Janna removed a knife as well, the last item in the small cache. It took just seconds and a few lengths of rawhide thongs to transform the blanket into a makeshift pack. She slung the pack diagonally across her back and looked over to where the wild horses grazed. Lucifer was staring in her direction with pricked ears, but he was not alarmed. Though he had never permitted her to come within fifty feet of him, he no longer ran from or threatened to attack her. He had come to accept Janna as a particularly slow and awkward horse that showed up from time to time carrying delicacies such as rock salt and grain—certainly no threat to his band despite the man odor that accompanied her.

By the time Janna filled her canteen at the small stream, one of Lucifer's mares had come over at a trot, whinnying a welcome. Zebra was dust colored with black mane, tail, stockings, ears, muzzle, and a black stripe down her back. Cowboys called such horses zebra duns and prized them above all others for stamina, intelligence, and the natural camouflage that allowed them to pass unnoticed where other horses would be spotted by hostile Indians or equally hostile outlaws.

"Hello, Zebra," Janna said, smiling and stroking the dust-colored mare's velvety black muzzle. "Ready for a run? It won't be far today. Just a few miles."

Zebra nudged her muzzle against Janna with enough force to stagger her. She grabbed a handful of mane and swung onto Zebra's back. A light touch of Janna's heels sent the mare into a canter, which rapidly became a gallop. Guided only by Janna's hands, heels and voice, the mare took a slanting course across a corner of the plateau, then plunged down the hair-raising trail used by the wild horses to climb up or down the plateau's north side.

This particular route was one of the most difficult ways to ascend or descend the plateau. That was why Janna chose the route. To her knowledge, none of Cascabel's men had ever used it. They gained access to the plateau through one of the two western trails or from the southern edge, leaving the northern and eastern areas of the plateau pretty much alone. That suited Janna very well; a slot canyon that opened up from the plateau's eastern face was as close to a home as she could ever remember having.

Twenty minutes after Zebra attacked the precipitous trail down into Mustang Canyon, she slid to the canyon's floor and stretched out for a good run. Janna let her go until she was as close to the stranger's hiding place as she could come without making her destination obvious.

"That's it girl. Whoa, Zebra. This is where I get off."

Reluctantly Zebra slowed. Janna leaped off and smacked the mare lightly on her dust-colored haunch to send her on her way.

The mare didn't budge.

"Go on," Janna said, smacking Zebra again. "I don't have time to play anymore today. Next time, I promise."

Abruptly the mare's head went up and her nostrils flared. She stood motionless, drinking the wind and staring off down the canyon. Janna didn't need any more warning; she faded back into the rocks and clumps of brush. Zebra stood for a few moments more, then quietly withdrew back up the canyon. Within minutes she was all but invisible, protected by her natural camouflage.

Moving quickly, silently, camouflaged by her own dusty clothes and earth-colored hat, Janna retreated along the canyon bottom until she could turn and climb up to the small hollow. Wiping out her traces as she went, she approached the stranger's hiding place from a different, even steeper angle, scrambled over the rock slide at the hollow's entrance and immediately looked toward the tangle of piñons and rocks at the base of the cliff.

The stranger was gone.

Janna ran across the hollow and went into the piñons on her hands and knees. There was blood still fresh on the ground, as well as signs that the man had dragged himself deeper into cover. She followed his trail, wiping it out as she went, crumbling and scattering earth and the debris that piled up beneath the piñons. She found him in a dense thicket that crowded up against the cliff. Bloody handprints on the stone told her that he had tried to climb, only to fall. He lay where he had fallen, facedown in the dirt, his hands still reaching toward stone as though he would awaken at any moment and try to climb once more.

She bit her lip against unaccustomed tears, feeling as she had once when she had found a cougar with its paw wedged into a crack in the rocks. She hadn't been able to approach the cat until it was nearly dead with thirst. Only then had she been able to free it—but she would never forget the agony of waiting for the magnificent cat to weaken enough to allow her close.

"Pobrecito," Janna murmured, touching the man's arm as she settled into place beside him. *Poor little one.*

The swell of firm muscle beneath her fingers reminded Janna that the man was hardly little; he was as powerful as the cougar had been, and perhaps as dangerous. He had shown a frightening determination to survive, driving himself beyond all reason or hope. Perhaps he was like Cascabel, whose ability to endure pain was legendary. As was his cruelty.

Was this man also cruel? Had it been savage cunning and coldness that had driven him to survive rather than unusual intelligence and courage and determination?

Shouts floated up from the canyon bottom as renegades called to one another, searching for the man who had run their gauntlet and then disappeared like a shaman into the air itself. Janna shrugged out of her pack, untied the rawhide thongs and spread the army blanket over the stranger. An instant later she removed it. The solid color was too noticeable in the dappled light and shadow of the piñons. As long as there was any chance of Cascabel finding the hollow, the man was better off camouflaged by random patterns of dirt and dried blood.

Slowly, silently, Janna shifted position until she was sitting next to the man, his face turned toward her. She looked at him intently, trying to guess what kind of man lay beneath the bruises and dirt. If she hadn't already had ample evidence of his strength, his body would have convinced her of his power. His shoulders were as wide as the length of an ax handle, his back was a broad wedge tapering to narrow hips, and his legs were long, well muscled, and covered in black hair that was repeated in the small of his back and beneath his arms.

Gradually Janna realized that the stranger was very handsome and intensely male. There was a regularity of feature in his face that was pleasing. His forehead was broad, his eyes were set well apart and thickly lashed, his cheekbones were high and well defined beneath the black beard stubble, his nose was straight, his mustache was well trimmed, and his jaw fully reflected the determination he had already shown. She wondered whether his eyes were dark or light, but his skin gave no clue. Faint lines of laughter or concentration radiated out from the corners of his eyes. Beneath the dust and blood, his hair was thick, slightly curly, and the color of a raven's wing. His hair tempted her to run her fingers through it, testing its depth and texture.

More voices floated up from the canyon, freezing Janna in the act of reaching out to stroke the stranger's hair. Cascabel's men were closer now—much too close. They must have seen past her efforts to obscure the trail.

The man's eyes opened. They were a deep, crystalline green, and they burned with the savage light of his determination to live. Instantly Janna put her fingers over his lips and shook her head. Her other hand pressed down on his back, urging him not to move. He nodded his understanding that he must not speak or make any motion that might give away their hiding place.

Frozen, barely breathing, they waited and listened to the sounds of Cascabel's renegades searching the rugged land for their prey.

Gradually the sounds withdrew. Apparently the Indians hadn't believed that their wounded prey could climb the steep side of the canyon. When the voices failed to come back again, the man let out a long, broken breath and fell unconscious again.

Janna bent and stroked the stranger's hair in a silent reassurance meant to soothe the animal awareness that had awakened him at the first sound of pursuers. She understood the kind of life that resulted in a division of the mind where part slept and part stood guard. It was how she slept, alertly, waking often to listen to the small sounds of mice and coyote, the call of an owl and branches rustling against the wind. She accepted the dangers of a wild land, thinking no more about their presence than she did that of the sun or the wind or the brilliant silver moon.

After it had been silent for an hour, Janna cautiously opened the leather pouch she had brought. One by one she unwrapped the herbs she had collected at different times and places as she roamed the Utah Territory. Some of the herbs had already been made into unguents. Others were whole. Working quickly and quietly, she treated the wounds she could reach without disturbing the stranger's sleep. His feet were a collection of cuts, thorns and bruises. She cleaned the cuts, removed the thorns, applied a thick layer of healing herbs and wrapped his feet in strips she cut from the blanket. Not once did he stir or show any signs of waking. His stillness would have worried her had it not been for the strong, even beating of his heart and his rhythmic breathing.

When Janna could do no more for the stranger, she pulled the blanket over him, sat next to him and watched the sky catch fire from the dying sun. She loved the silent blaze of beauty, the incandescence and the transformation of the sky. It made her believe that anything was possible—anything— even her fierce, silent hope of someday having a home where she could sleep without always waking alone.

Only when it was full dark and the last star had glittered into life did Janna put her arms around her knees, lower her forehead to them and sleep, waking every few minutes to listen to the small sounds of the living night and the breathing of the man who trusted her enough to sleep naked and weapon- less at her feet.

Chapter Three

Tyrell MacKenzie awoke feeling as though he had slept beneath a herd of stampeding steers. Despite the pain lancing through his head with every heartbeat, he didn't groan or cry out; his instincts were screaming at him that he had to be silent and hide. The Civil War had taught Ty to trust those instincts. He opened one eye a bare slit, just enough to see without revealing the fact that he had returned to consciousness.

A pair of moccasins was only inches away from his face.

Instantly memories flooded through Ty's pain-hazed mind—Cascabel and his renegades and a gauntlet of clubs that had seemed to go on forever. Somehow he had gotten through it and then he had run and run until he thought his chest would burst, but he had kept on running and trying to find a place where he could go to ground before the Indians tracked him down and killed him.

Another memory came to Ty, that of a thin boy with ragged clothes and steady gray eyes warning him to be silent. Ty opened his eyes a bit more and saw that the moccasins belonged to the boy rather than to one of Cascabel's killers. The boy had his head on his knees and was hugging his long legs against his body as though still trying to ward off the chill of a night spent in the open.

The angle and direction of the sunlight slanting between the towering black thunderheads told Ty that it was early afternoon rather than early morning, which meant that he had slept through yesterday afternoon, all of the hours of darkness, and most of the day, as well. He was surprised that the cold hadn't awakened him during the night. Even though it was still August, the countryside wasn't particularly warm once the sun set behind Black Plateau.

The boy turned his head until his chin rested on his knees. Ty found himself staring into the clear gray eyes he remembered. Such a steady glance was unusual in a boy so young that he wouldn't need a razor for a few years. But then, Ty had seen what war did to children. The ones who survived were old far beyond their years.

The youth raised his index finger to his lips in a signal for Ty not to make a sound. Ty nodded slightly and watched while the boy eased through the underbrush with the silence of an Indian. Despite the aches of his bruised and beaten body, Ty didn't shift position. That was another thing the war had taught him. The man who moved first died first.

While Ty waited for the youth to return from reconnoitering, he noticed that there was a blanket covering his body, protecting him against the chilly air. From the look of the corner covering his arm, the blanket was as ragged as the boy's clothes. Ty realized that the blanket must belong to the boy, who obviously had stood guard throughout the cold night and the long day as well, protecting a helpless stranger, giving him the only cover.

Hell of a kid, Ty thought. *Wonder what he's doing out here alone?*

It was the last thought Ty had before he drifted off into a pain-filled, fitful sleep.

He was still dozing when Janna returned through the brush as silently as she had come. Even so, his eyes opened. Like a wild animal, he had sensed that he was no longer alone.

"You can move around, but we can't leave yet," Janna said in a low voice. "Cascabel and his men are still searching for you, but they're on the east side of Black Plateau."

"Then you better get out while you can," Ty said hoarsely. He shifted position with cautious movements, grimaced with pain and kept moving anyway. He had to find out what his body would be good for if he had to run again. And he would have to run if Cascabel were still searching. "I left a trail a blind man could follow."

"I know," Janna said softly. "I wiped it out as I followed you."

"Won't do any good," Ty said in a low voice that was more like a groan. He forced himself into an upright position despite dizziness and the excruciating pain in his head. "Once Cascabel sobers up, he'll find your sign. He could track a snake over solid rock. Go on, kid. Get out while you can."

Janna saw the stranger's pallor and the sudden sweat that covered his face. She wanted to tell him to lie down, not to move, not to cause himself any more pain; but she knew that he might have to move, to run, to hide. Better that they find out now how much strength he had so that they could plan for his weakness rather than being caught by surprise.

"I laid a false trail to a blind keyhole canyon way back up Mustang Canyon," she said softly. "Then I climbed out. I'd stopped bleeding by then, so I didn't leave any sign of where I went."

"Bleeding?" Ty looked up, focusing on the boy with difficulty because pain had turned the world to red and black. "Are you hurt?"

"I cut myself," Janna said as she unwrapped the bandanna from her arm. "Cascabel knew you were bleeding. If there weren't any sign of blood, he wouldn't believe the trail was yours."

The last turn of the bandanna was stuck to Janna's skin by dried blood. She moistened the cloth with a small amount of water from the canteen, gritted her teeth and pulled the bandanna free. The cut oozed blood for a moment, then stopped. There was no sign of infection, but she dug in the leather pouch and sprinkled more herb powder over the cut anyway.

"You all right?" Ty asked thickly.

Janna looked up and smiled. "Sure. Papa always told me that cuts from a sharp knife heal better than cuts from a dull one, so I keep my knives sharp. See? No sign of infection."

Ty looked at the long red line on the back of the unmuscular forearm and realized that the boy had deliberately cut himself in order to leave a trail of blood for Cascabel to follow.

"Your papa raised a brave boy," Ty said.

Janna's head came up sharply. She was on the edge of saying that her father had raised a brave *girl*, when she caught herself. Other people had mistaken her for a boy since her father had died, especially after she had done everything she could to foster the impression. She bound her breasts with turn after turn of cloth to flatten and conceal her feminine curves. For the same reason she wore her father's old shirts, which were much too big, and his old pants rode low on her hips, hiding the pronounced inward curve of her waist. She wore her hair in thick Indian braids stuffed beneath a man's hat, which was also too big for her.

Being taken for a boy had proven useful when Janna went to the few ranches around to trade her writing and reading skills for food, or when she went to town to spend a bit of Mad Jack's gold on store-bought clothes or rare, precious books. Being a boy gave her a freedom of movement that was denied to girls. Because she loved freedom as much as any mustang ever born, she had always been relieved when strangers assumed she was a boy.

Yet it galled Janna that this particular stranger had mistaken her sex. Her first reaction was to make him look beyond the clothes to the woman beneath. Her second reaction was that that would be a really stupid thing to do.

Her third reaction was a repeat of her first.

"Your papa didn't do badly, either," Janna said finally. "Cascabel has killed more men than you have fingers and toes."

"Don't know about the toes," Ty said, smiling crookedly as he sat upright and examined his feet. The sight of the bandages made him look quickly at Janna.

"Oh, you've still got ten of them," she said. "A bit raw, but otherwise intact. It's going to hurt like the devil to walk on them, though."

Ty hissed softly through his teeth as he crossed his legs and sat Indian-style. "Don't have to wait until I walk. Hurts like hell right now."

Janna said nothing because her mouth had gone dry. When he had sat up and crossed his legs, the blanket had fallen away, revealing a broad, bloody chest and muscular torso. Crisp black hair swirled around his flat nipples, gathered in the center line of his body and curled down to his loins. There the hair became thick and lush as it fanned out, defining and emphasizing the essential difference between male and female.

Abruptly Janna looked away and forced herself to drag air into her aching lungs, wondering if she were going to faint.

Why am I being such a goose? she asked herself fiercely. *I've seen naked men before.*

But somehow cowboys washing off in lonely water holes and dancing Indians wearing little more than strings and flapping squares of cloth weren't the same as the powerful man sitting naked and unconcerned just a few feet away from her.

"Hey, kid," Ty said softly. "You sure you're all right? You look kind of pale."

Janna swallowed hard, twice. "I'm fine," she said huskily. "And my name is…Jan, not 'kid.'"

"Jan, huh?" Ty said, unwrapping his right foot carefully. "My mother's father was called Jan. He was a big Swede with a laugh you could hear in the next county. Mama used to say I took after him."

"Well, you're big enough," Janna said dryly, "but I'd keep a tight rein on the laughing until Cascabel gives up."

Ty hissed an obscenity under his breath when the strip of blanket refused to come off the sole of his foot. After a moment he added, "My name's Ty MacKenzie." He looked up at the long-legged, thin youth and smiled. "As for big, don't worry, ki—Jan. You'll start putting on height and muscle about the same time you think you need to shave."

"And pigs will fly," Janna muttered beneath her breath.

Ty heard anyway. He smiled widely and gave Janna a brotherly pat on the knee. "I felt the same way when I was your age. Thought I'd never catch up with my older brother, Logan, but I finally did. Well, almost. No one's as big as Logan. I've had one hell of a lot more luck with the ladies, though," Ty added with a wink.

The news didn't sweeten Janna's temper. She could well imagine that women would swoon over a cleaned-up version of Tyrell MacKenzie, because the beaten, dirty, naked version was giving her pulse a severe case of the jump and flutters. And that irritated her, because she was certain that she hadn't had the least effect on Ty's pulse.

You'll start putting on height and muscle about the same time you think you need to shave.

Grimly Janna told herself that one day she would think back on this and laugh. Someday, but definitely not today.

A small sound from Ty made Janna glance up—way up, all the way to his eyes, which were narrowed against pain. He was sweating again and his hands were pressed against his forehead as though to keep it from flying apart. Instantly she forgot her pique at not being recognized as a woman and reached to help him.

"Lie down on your back," she said, pushing against Ty's chest and supporting his head at the same time.

It was like pushing against a sun-warmed cliff.

"If you lie down, it will be easier for me to tend your cuts," Janna pointed out. "I could only get to your back last night. If I don't clean up your front, you'll get infected and feverish and be no more use in a fight than a half-starved kitten."

Ty shook his head slowly, then grimaced again.

"How's your stomach?" Janna asked, giving up for the moment on making him lie down. With deft fingers she re-wrapped the bandage on his right foot. "Do you feel sick?"

"No."

She stared into the crystalline green of his eyes. Both of his pupils were the same size.

"Look into the sun for a second," she said.

Ty gave Janna a long look, then glanced overhead, where a piece of sun was peeking between thunderheads. When he looked away, she stared at his pupils intently. Both of them had contracted in response to the sun's light.

"Well? Do I have a concussion?" he asked, his voice low and amused.

"With a skull as thick as yours, I doubt it," she retorted.

"Is that a professional opinion, doctor?"

"Pa was the doctor, but he taught me a lot before he died." Janna looked at Ty's pupils again, fascinated by the clear midnight circles surrounded by such a gemlike green. "It's a good thing Indians collect scalps, not eyes. Yours would be a real prize."

Ty blinked, laughed softly, then made a low sound of pain as his own laughter hit his skull like a hammer.

"You sure your stomach is all right?" she asked.

"Yes," he said through clenched teeth. "Why?"

"You should drink to replace the blood you lost, but if you're going to throw up there's no point in wasting water. The nearest seep is a quarter mile from Cascabel's camp."

Silently Ty took the canteen Janna held out to him. He drank slowly, savoring the cool glide of water over his tongue and down his throat. After several long swallows he reluctantly lowered the canteen and handed it back. Janna shook her head, refusing the canteen. "Unless you're nauseated, drink more."

"What about you?" he asked.

"You need it more than I do."

Ty hesitated, then took a few more swallows and handed the canteen back.

"Here, chew on this while I clean the cuts on your chest," Janna said.

As she spoke, she dug a piece of beef jerky from her shirt pocket. Ty took the tough strip of dried meat, automatically reached to his waist for a knife with which to cut off a bite and realized all over again that he was naked. Before he could say anything, Janna handed him the long-bladed hunting knife she had taken from the cache. He tested the edge, nodded approvingly and sliced off a chunk of jerky with a swift, controlled motion that spoke of real expertise in using knives.

Janna cut off the cleanest corner of the blanket she could find, moistened it carefully with water from the canteen and reached toward the broad expanse of Ty's chest. At the last instant she hesitated.

"This will hurt."

Ty gave her a sidelong, amused glance. "Boy, there isn't a square inch of me that doesn't hurt."

Boy.

The corners of Janna's mouth turned down in displeasure, but her hands were careful as he cleaned the blood-encrusted cuts on Ty's chest. Two of them were ragged, puffy and already inflamed. She bit her lip against the pain she knew she must be causing Ty despite all her care.

"Sorry," she whispered helplessly when he grimaced.

Ty heard the distress in the youthful voice and felt like gathering that slender body into his arms and giving comfort. The thought both surprised him and made him uncomfortable. He definitely wasn't the type of man who liked boys. Abruptly he grabbed the narrow wrists and held them away from his body.

"That's good enough," he said brusquely.

"But I'm not fin—"

Janna's words ended as though cut off by a knife. Into the taut silence came the sound of a rock bouncing and rolling down the slope.

Ty's hands shifted with shocking speed. In an instant Janna found herself jerked over his body and then jammed between his broad back and the face of the cliff.

Naked and weaponless but for the knife, Ty waited to see what scrambled up over the rockfall and into the piñon-filled hollow.

Chapter Four

A soft nicker floated through the air as a horse scrambled over the last of the rockfall and into the hollow.

"What the hell?" whispered Ty.

Janna peeked over his back. "Zebra!"

"Boy, can't you tell a horse from a zebra!"

"Better than you can tell a girl from a boy," Janna muttered.

"What?"

"Let me out," she said, pushing against Ty's back.

"Ouch!"

Instantly Janna lifted her hand and apologized. Ty grunted and moved aside so that she could crawl out over his legs. Zebra walked up to the edge of the piñon grove, pushed her head in and nickered again.

"Hello, girl," Janna said softly, rubbing the velvet muzzle. "Did you get lonesome without me?"

Zebra whuffled over Janna's fingers, nudged her hands, and kept a wary eye on Ty all the while. When he moved, her head came up and her nostrils flared.

"Be still," Janna said. "She's not used to people."

"What does she think you are?"

"A bad-smelling horse."

Ty laughed softly. The sound made Zebra's ears twitch. He began talking in a gentle, low voice.

"You've got a better nose than my daddy's best hound ever

did,'' he said. Without looking aside he asked Janna, ''How long have you owned her?''

''I don't.''

''What?''

''I don't own her. She likes me, that's all. Some horses enjoy people, if you approach them the right way.''

''And some horses damn near get people killed,'' Ty said. ''I was about ten seconds away from dropping my loop on Lucifer's neck when Cascabel jumped me.''

Janna's heart hesitated, then beat faster. Despite Lucifer's refusal to approach her, she thought of him somehow as her own horse. ''How did you get so close to him?''

''I'm a fair tracker when I'm not half-dead,'' Ty said dryly.

''The shamans say that no mortal man will ever capture Lucifer. He's a spirit horse.''

Ty shook his head. ''That old boy is pure flesh and blood, and he sires the best colts I've seen west of the Mississippi. Lucifer's my ticket to the future that the Civil War took away from the MacKenzie family. With him I'm going to found the kind of herd that my daddy always wanted. He would have had it, too, except for the war. The four MacKenzie brothers rode off to battle on his best horses. They saved our lives more than once.''

Janna saw Ty's mouth harden. He shrugged as though to throw off unhappy memories. Into the silence came the rumble of distant thunder and the scrape of branches stirring beneath a wind that smelled of moisture.

''Hope it rains soon,'' Ty said, looking up at the massed thunderheads. ''Otherwise that big dog's tracks are going to lead Cascabel right to us.''

''It will rain.''

The confidence in Janna's voice made Ty turn and look at her intently.

''How do you know?'' he asked.

''I just…know,'' she said slowly. ''I've lived with the land so long that I know a lot of its secrets.''

''Such as?''

''Such as—when the air over the Fire range gets an odd

sort of crystal shine to it and then clouds form, it always rains about two hours before sundown. It rains hard and cold and sudden, like an ocean turned upside down and pouring back to earth. After an hour or two some of the finger canyons run twenty feet deep with water.'' Janna pushed away the mare's muzzle and looked at Ty. ''Are you still dizzy?''

Ty wasn't surprised that his occasional dizziness had been noticed. He was discovering that not much escaped those clear gray eyes.

''Some,'' he admitted. ''It comes and goes.''

''Do you think you can get over that rockfall if I help?''

''Count on it, with or without your help.''

Janna looked at the determined lines of Ty's face and the latent power in his big body and hoped he was right. The rocky hollow had been useful, but it would become a lethal trap the instant Cascabel scrambled up and found his prey. The sooner they left, the better it would be.

There was only one haven Janna could think of. It lay on the southeast side of Black Plateau, at the edge of Cascabel's ill-defined territory. It was a spirit place avoided by Indians, whose legends told of a time when the mountain had roared in anguish and split open and thick red blood had gushed forth, spirit blood that made everything burn, even stone itself. When the blood finally cooled it had become the dark, rough rock that gave Black Plateau its name. There, at the foot of ancient lava flows and sandstone cliffs, Janna had found a keyhole canyon snaking back into the solid body of the plateau. Once past the narrow entrance, the canyon widened out into a park-like area that was thick with grass and sparkling with sweet water. It was there she wintered, secure in the knowledge that no warriors or outlaws would see her tracks in the snow.

It had been her secret place, as close to a home as she had ever known. She had shared it with no one. The thought of sharing it with Ty made her feel odd. Yet there really was no other choice.

''Soon as I get you patched up,'' Janna said, turning to her bag of herbs, ''we'll go to a keyhole canyon I know about.

Nobody else has any idea that it exists, except maybe Mad Jack, and he hardly counts.''

"Mad Jack? I thought he was a legend."

"He's old enough to be one."

"You've actually seen him?"

Janna dug out the herbal paste she had made during the long hours of daylight while Ty had slept. "Yes, I've seen him," she said, and began dabbing the paste on the worst of Ty's cuts.

"I've heard he has a gold mine hidden somewhere on Black Plateau."

Her hands paused, then resumed slathering on medication. "Whatever Mad Jack has or doesn't have is his business."

Ty's black eyebrows lifted at Janna's curt words. "Ouch! Watch it, boy, that's not stone you're poking."

"Sorry," she said in a tight voice.

For several moments Ty watched the gray eyes that refused to meet his.

"Hey," he said finally, catching Janna's chin in his big hand, forcing her to meet his eyes. "I'm not going to hurt that old man no matter how much gold he might have found. I'm not a thief or a raider. I'm not going to build my future on bloodstained gold."

Janna searched the green eyes that were so close to hers and saw no evasion. She remembered Ty telling her to leave him and save herself, and she remembered how he had put his own body between her and whatever danger might have been coming into the hollow. Abruptly she felt ashamed of her suspicions.

"I'm sorry," Janna said. "It's just that I've had men follow me out of town when I buy supplies with a bit of gold I've found here and there. It's usually easy enough to lose the men, but it hasn't given me a very kind opinion of human nature."

The surge of anger Ty felt at the thought of a child having to lose white men in the rocks as though they were Indian renegades surprised him. So did the protectiveness he felt toward this particular child. Uneasily it occurred to Ty that beneath the shapeless old hat and the random smears of dirt, the youth's face was...extraordinary.

My God, I've seen women a hell of a lot less beautiful than this boy. Maybe the men weren't following gold, after all.

Ty snatched his hand back as though he had been burned. The sudden movement made Zebra shy away violently.

"That damn horse is as spooky as a mustang," he said, rubbing his hand against his chest as though to remove the tactile memory of soft skin and delicate bone structure.

Janna blinked, wondering what had made Ty so irritable. She wished that he would put his hand beneath her chin again. His palm was warm and firm, his fingers were long and gentle, and it had been years since she had felt a comforting touch from another human being.

"Zebra is a mustang," Janna said huskily. "When she's not with me, she runs free."

Ty's head turned toward the mare with renewed interest. He studied her carefully, especially her hooves. They had been trimmed by stony ground rather than by a pair of steel nippers. She was sleek without being fat, strong without being big. Nowhere did she show the marks of man—no brand, no ear notch, no shoes, no rubbed places on her hide where bridle or saddle had rested.

"Do you ride her?" he asked.

"Sometimes, when it's safe."

"When is that?"

"When Cascabel isn't around," Janna said simply. "He's been around a lot the past six months, which is why Zebra is so lonesome. I guess the Army is making life hard for Cascabel."

"Or Black Hawk is tired of being blamed for Cascabel's raids and is clamping down," Ty said. "Black Hawk is a war chief and a leader. Cascabel is a butcher and a raider. Hell, I'm surprised that renegade hasn't tracked you down and cooked you over a slow fire just for the sport of it."

Janna shrugged off the implicit question. She had no intention of telling Ty that to most Utes she was Shadow of Fire, *una bruja*, a witch who walked with spirits. Ty thought of her as a boy, which was both irritating and quite useful—especially as long as he was sitting around stark naked while she rubbed medicine into his cuts.

The renewed realization of Ty's nudity brought heightened color to Janna's cheeks. It took every bit of her willpower to keep her hands from trembling as she smoothed the herb paste over his skin.

Ty noticed the fine tremor in the slender fingers and swore under his breath.

"Sorry, boy. I didn't mean to scare you," he said gruffly. "Once we get free of Cascabel, I'll take you to the Army post at Sweetwater. You'll be safe there."

Janna shook her head and said nothing, concentrating on keeping her hands from revealing the uncertain state of her emotions.

"Don't be silly," Ty said. "You might have survived out here in the past, but it's different now. The Army has been fighting Black Hawk for nearly three years, since the end of the Civil War. They've had a bellyful of fighting Utes. There will be a big campaign before winter. The Army figures to have it all wrapped up by Thanksgiving and to have Cascabel's ears in the bargain. Between Black Hawk and the soldiers fighting each other, and Cascabel killing everything that moves, it won't be safe for man nor beast here, much less a boy who's as skinny as a willow switch."

"If it's so dangerous, why are you here?"

"Lucifer," Ty said simply. "I figured this was my best chance. Once the Utes are quiet, every man with an eye for prime horseflesh will be trying for that stallion. Even if no one gets him, sure as hell some money-hungry mustanger will put a bullet through his black head just to get at his colts." Ty looked at Zebra again. "He sired her, didn't he?"

"Yes."

"It shows in her long legs and well-shaped head. The barb blood in Lucifer comes through no matter what he breeds with. Does she run with his bunch?"

"Yes."

"How did you get close to her?"

Janna wiped her fingers on her pants as she looked critically at Ty's cuts. "Her mother was a runaway ranch horse. She liked salt and grain and human company. Zebra grew up with me petting her. There are others like her in Lucifer's bunch. They accept me. After a time, so do some of the true mustangs. I take care of their cuts and scrapes and scratch the places they can't reach, and they tell me when there are men around. That's how I've kept away from Cascabel. Lucifer can smell him a mile off."

"Does Lucifer let you pet him?" Ty asked intently.

"He's as wild as a storm wind," Janna said, not answering the question.

"So is that one," Ty said, looking at Zebra, "but she followed your trail like a tame old hound dog. Will the next horse through that gap be Lucifer?"

"No. I've survived by being inconspicuous. Anyone standing next to Lucifer would be as conspicuous as lightning."

Thunder belled suddenly, but Ty didn't look away from Janna's face.

"Have you ever tried to get close to Lucifer?"

"No."

"Why not? Is he a killer?"

Janna shrugged. "Wouldn't you try to kill a man who wanted to put you in a cage?"

"Horses have been bred by men for thousands and thousands of years. It's a partnership, like men and dogs."

"Not to a lot of men."

"Those same men are cruel to other men. I'm not. I don't fight for the pleasure of it, but to get the job done."

Janna looked at her knife, which Ty kept within easy reach at all times. She remembered how he had held the knife—as a weapon, not as a tool. There was no doubt in her mind that he could "get the job done" better than any man she had ever seen, except Cascabel.

The realization should have frightened her, for despite Ty's injuries he was far stronger than she was. Yet she was no more frightened of him than she was of Lucifer. In the past her instincts had proven to be very good at picking up the presence of senseless viciousness or cruelty; she sensed none in either Ty or the big black stallion so many men longed to own.

But what if I'm wrong this time? What if Ty is just another man greedy for whatever he can get from those weaker than he is?

There was no answer to Janna's silent question but the obvious one—if she took Ty to her private refuge and discovered there that she had been wrong about his essential decency, she would have made the worst mistake of her life.

And probably the last, as well.

Chapter Five

The sudden downpour of cold rain was like a blow. In spite of that, the rain was welcome, for it would wash away Ty and Janna's trail.

"Ready?" Janna asked.

Ty nodded grimly. He was still angry at having lost the battle of the shrinking blanket. Over his objections Janna had cut the blanket up into a breechcloth, bandages for his bruised ribs and a makeshift poncho. He hadn't objected to the breechcloth, had given in on the bandages, but had been damned if he would wear a blanket while a child ran around with no more protection against the thunderstorm than a ragged shirt and pants.

Yet here he was, wearing the blanket; and there the kid was, wearing only a shirt and pants.

"Stubborn as a Missouri mule," Ty snarled, but his words were drowned out by thunder.

Zebra took the lightning, thunder and pelting rain with the indifference of a horse born and raised out in the open. She watched with interest as Ty and Janna negotiated the rocky rubble at the head of the hollow. While the mustang wasn't completely relaxed around Ty, she no longer shied at his every movement.

It was a good thing. Ty made some very sudden movements as he clawed over the rockfall, hobbled by his injuries and the increasing slickness of the rocks. Though he said nothing, he was grateful that his ribs were bound, despite the fact that it made breathing deeply impossible. He was also grateful for the small, surprisingly strong hands that helped to lever him over the tricky places—although he had nearly yelped with surprise the first time he had received a firm boost from behind.

Janna passed Ty just beneath the crest of the rockfall. She motioned with her hand for him to wait. When he sank into a sitting position, she peered through a crevice between two rocks. All but the first two hundred feet of the slope was veiled in sheets of rain. In the stretch of land that she could see, nothing moved but rain itself. She turned and went back to Ty.

"How do your feet feel?"

He gave her a slanting glance. "You saw them. How do you think they feel?"

"Worse than your ribs and better than your head," Janna said succinctly.

Ty grunted and began to struggle to his feet once more.

She bent, put both of her hands around his right arm just beneath his shoulder and steadied him as he came to his feet. The hissing intake of his breath, the pallor of his skin and the clenched iron of the muscles beneath her hands told Janna just how painful it was for Ty to stand on his raw feet. There was no help for it, though. There would never be a better time to exit the hollow without attracting Cascabel's notice.

By the time Janna and Ty had climbed up and over the rockfall, both of them were sweating in spite of the cold rain pouring over their bodies. Though Ty was breathing hard and fast, he didn't suggest a rest. The slope was too exposed. One of Cascabel's renegades—or a bolt of lightning—could find them at any moment.

Behind Ty and Janna came the clatter and slide of stones as the mustang scrambled over a slope Ty would have sworn a donkey would refuse. But then, he had watched in disbelief while Lucifer's band took worse countryside at a dead run in order to escape from men, including one Tyrell MacKenzie. The horses that weren't fast enough were caught. The remainder ran free to give birth to another generation of fleet, agile mustangs.

When the steepest part of the slope had been negotiated, Janna stopped and looked over her shoulder. Zebra was following close behind, watching the humans' progress with interest, pausing from time to time to sniff the strange mixture of sweat and herbal odors that Ty gave off. On the whole, the mare was rather intrigued by his smell.

"She likes you," Janna said.

"She ought to. I smell like the warm mash Daddy used to give his favorite brood mares."

Janna smiled. "Can you ride bareback?"

Ty gave Janna a disbelieving look. "What do you think I am, a greenhorn? Of course I can ride bareback."

"Let me rephrase that. Can you ride Zebra without a saddle or a bridle?"

"Boy," Ty said, shifting his position in a vain attempt to ease the searing pain in his feet and the throbbing in his head and ribs, "this is a piss poor time for me to be breaking a mustang."

"I've ridden Zebra a lot. She likes it."

Ty looked skeptical.

Janna made an exasperated sound, dropped her hold on Ty and went to the mare. She grabbed a double handful of thick mane and swung onto Zebra's back. The horse didn't even switch her tail, much less offer to buck. When Janna urged her forward until she stood next to Ty, the mustang responded as placidly as a plow horse.

"Pet her," Janna said.

Zebra flinched at the strange hand reaching up to her neck, but Ty's low, reassuring voice and gentle touch soon calmed the mare. After a few minutes she sighed and lowered her head until she could use Ty's chest as a shield against the cold rain. Smiling slightly despite his pain, he rubbed the base of the mare's ears, scratching all the itchy spots a horse couldn't reach for itself.

As Janna watched Ty's big, careful hands caressing the mare so skillfully, an odd feeling shimmered in the pit of her stomach. She wondered what it would be like if he stroked her half as gently as he was stroking Zebra. The thought brought a tingling that spread out from her stomach to her fingertips, making her shiver. With a quick motion she slid off the horse. In her haste she landed so close to Ty that she had to catch her balance against his bare, rain-chilled thigh. Instantly she snatched back her hand.

"I'll help you on," Janna said, then added quickly, "I know you could do it alone, but there's no point in putting any more strain on your ribs than you have to."

"Five will get you ten that your mustang bucks me off into the rocks," Ty said.

"She's never bucked with me."

"She's never had a man on her back instead of a skinny boy."

Boy.

"Listen," Janna said through gritted teeth, very tired of hearing herself described as a boy, "it's at least twenty miles to my winter camp. You can walk, you can ride, or you can freeze to death right here while you make smart remarks about my lack of muscle."

"Easy, girl," Ty said softly.

For an instant Janna thought he was talking to her; then she realized that he had taken a good grip on Zebra's mane and was looking over his shoulder toward the "skinny boy."

"Well?" Ty asked. "You waiting for me to freeze to death?"

"Don't tempt me," Janna muttered.

She braced herself, cupped her hands to make a stirrup and prepared to help Ty onto the mare. A few seconds later Janna was looking up at him in surprise. He had moved so quickly that she had barely felt his weight before it was gone. Zebra looked around in surprise as well, for she had been expecting Janna's light weight. But instead of mounting the horse, Janna stood with her hand on Zebra's muzzle in a steady pressure that was a signal to stand quietly. The mare snorted uneasily, then stood still, adjusting to the strange weight on her back.

"You're very quick for such a big man," Janna said.

For the space of a few breaths Ty was in too much pain to answer. When he did look down he had to fight the impulse to cup his hand caressingly beneath that delicate chin. The eyes looking back up at him were as clear as rain and a lot warmer…the eyes of a woman experiencing the slow unfolding of desire.

Pain is making me crazy, Ty told himself in disgust. *That's a boy looking up at me, not a girl, and he's got a bad case of hero worship. Poor kid must be lonely as hell, living with only wild horses for companionship.*

"And you owe me ten dollars," Janna added.

"What?"

"Zebra didn't buck you off into the rocks."

"You'll have to collect from Cascabel. He stole my money along with my hat, boots, guns and clothes."

"And your horse."

Ty's mouth flattened. "He shot Blackbird out from under me. That was the only way Cascabel caught me. Blackbird was half-thoroughbred and all heart."

"I'm sorry," Janna said, resting her hand on Ty's leg in an impulsive gesture of comfort.

At first touch his skin was cold, yet within moments the vital heat of him flowed up and warmed her palm. After a time Janna realized she was staring up at Ty, and had been for too long. She snatched back her hand and turned away, heading down the steep slope to the flatter land beyond the plateau's face. She would have to take a looping route to her secret canyon, for the base of the plateau itself was too rugged to travel along in anything approaching a straight line.

Zebra followed Janna without guidance, which was just as well. After the first four miles Ty was no longer in shape to give directions. The pounding in his head alternated with twisting strikes of agony from his ribs. The blanket was some protection against cold, but not nearly enough. He was shivering before a mile had passed beneath the mustang's agile, untrimmed hooves.

During the first hours Janna turned and looked over her shoulder every few minutes to reassure herself that Ty was all right. The farther they went, the more he slumped over Zebra's neck. Janna kept on going because there was no other choice. She had to get Ty to a place of safety.

Rain pelted down in an unceasing, cold barrage. Behind the clouds the sun slowly set, its passage marked only by a gradual lowering of the level of light. A wind sprang up soon after sunset, tearing apart the storm until only brief, hard showers remained. Through great rents in the clouds a brilliant half-moon shone forth. The wind concealed and then revealed the moon again, weaving intricate patterns of darkness and light.

Shivering, tired, worried about Ty's strength and his ability to endure any more pain, Janna forced herself to keep going, knowing that that was all she could do to help him. She walked quickly despite her own weariness, using the familiar silhouettes of buttes and mesas looming against the night sky as her landmarks. The moon had crossed more than half of its arc before she stopped and looked toward the bulky, ragged outline of the plateau whose north and east flanks she had been skirting through the long hours of darkness.

The long, sloping outwash plain glittered with rills and shallow streams as Black Plateau shed water from the recent storm. A branch of that network of shifting, gleaming temporary streams led to her hidden canyon. She hoped that there would be enough water in that temporary stream to hide her tracks, but not so much that it would be dangerous to go through the narrow slot that led to the concealed valley. She hoped, but she had no way of knowing until she got there. Everything depended on how much rain had fallen on this side of Black Plateau.

Until now Janna had made little effort to conceal her trail, hoping that the violent, intermittent showers would wash out enough of her tracks to confuse any pursuer. But now she was within four miles of her hidden valley. She could take no chance that a wandering renegade would come across her tracks and follow them to the tiny slot carved by time and water into the side of Black Plateau.

Resolutely Janna turned toward the nearest shallow wash and began wading. Zebra watched, then calmly paced along-

side—beyond the reach of water. Janna waded farther out.
Zebra kept walking along the edge of the runoff stream. Finally Janna waded back toward the horse.

"Ty?"

There was no answer.

For an instant Janna's heart stopped. She ran up and saw
Ty slumped over Zebra's neck, his hands twisted into her
mane. He seemed to be asleep.

"Ty?" she asked, pressing against his arm. "Zebra has to
walk in the water."

Slowly he straightened. She looked up at him anxiously. As
she watched, he began to slump again. Obviously he wouldn't
be able to guide the mustang. Nor could Janna lead her; she
had never put a rope on Zebra, so the mare wouldn't have the
least idea how to respond.

"I hope you don't mind riding double," Janna said to Zebra. "Stand quiet, girl. It will be a big load for you, but it's
the only way I'll be able to hide your tracks."

Janna grabbed the horse's long mane in her left hand and
tried to swing around Ty and up onto the mare's back. It was
an awkward mount that was saved from disaster only when
Ty wrapped his arm around Janna and heaved her into place.
The groan that ripped through him at the effort told her more
than she wanted to know about the condition of his ribs.

Zebra sidestepped, almost unseating both riders. Janna
spoke reassuringly and sat very still, letting the mare become
accustomed to the added weight. When Zebra settled down,
Janna nudged her lightly with her heels. The horse moved
awkwardly for a few minutes, then settled back into her normal rhythmic walk. Ty slumped forward once more, keeping
his seat by instinct, experience and sheer determination.

"Hang on, Ty. We're almost there."

It was a lie, but it was more helpful than the truth, which
was that they had a lot of hard going left—and no assurance
at all that the slot wouldn't be choked with floodwaters when
they finally arrived.

Chapter Six

Ty awoke with the sun shining right onto his face and the familiar sound of a horse cropping grass nearby. As he turned to check on Blackbird, pain brought back all the memories—his horse's death and his own capture, Cascabel and the gauntlet, pain and running endlessly, and the gray-eyed waif who had patched up his wounds. Vaguely Ty remembered getting on a zebra dun and riding until he was quite certain he had died and gone to hell.

Except that this wasn't hell. True enough, the overhang he lay beneath was hot red stone, but the canyon floor was lush with the kind of vegetation that only came from water. Definitely not a flaming hell. In fact, with the sun's warmth and the lazy humming of insects and the calling of birds, this could only be a slice of heaven.

Automatically Ty sat up to have a better look around. Pain and dizziness struck, chaining him in place, forcing him to revise his opinion of where he was. Eyes closed, his weight braced on his elbows, he decided that the valley might be in heaven, but his body was indeed in hell.

"Lie down, Ty. You've been sick."

He opened his eyes. Gray eyes watched him with concern. Without thinking, Ty shifted his weight until he could raise his hand to touch the cheek that was so close to his. The skin was smooth and fine grained, as soft as an angel's wing.

"It's all right," he said fuzzily. "I'm fine now."

"Lie down," Janna said, pressing against his bare shoulders.

It did no good. He remained as he was, propped half-upright on his elbow.

"Please, Ty," Janna said, her voice husky with emotion. "Lie down. The fever's broken and you're much better, but you need to rest."

"Thirsty," he mumbled.

Instantly Janna grabbed a canteen, poured a stream of amber, herbal-smelling tea into a tin cup and helped Ty to drink. The taste of the liquid brought back other memories. He had drunk from this cup many times, with slender hands holding him upright and then easing him back down and stroking him until he fell once more into feverish sleep.

Sighing deeply, Ty allowed Janna to help him to lie down again.

"How long?" he asked.

"How long have we been here?"

He nodded slightly.

"Four days."

His eyes opened.

"You've been sick," Janna explained. "You caught a chill riding through the rain. That, plus your injuries from the gauntlet..." Her voice died. Automatically she reached forward and brushed back the slightly curly lock of black hair that had fallen over Ty's forehead.

Ty flinched from the touch and looked Janna over with narrowed green eyes. "You don't look so good yourself. You're skinnier than ever. If you don't take better care of yourself, you'll never get tall and put on muscle."

"Not all men are built like a side of beef," Janna retorted, hurt because Ty had refused her touch. She reached into the herb pouch, brought out a twist of paper and sprinkled the white powder into another cup of the herbal tea. "Here. Drink this."

"What is it?"

"Poison."

"Fresh as paint, aren't you, boy?"

"You're half-right," Janna muttered, but she said it so softly that Ty couldn't hear. She silently vowed that she would make him see which half of the truth he knew—and that he would be crazy with desire before he figured it out.

Ty drank the contents of the cup, grimaced and gave his companion a green-eyed glare. "Tastes like horse piss."

"I'll take your word for it, having never tasted that particular liquid."

Ty laughed, grabbed his left side and groaned. "Damn. Feels like a mule kicked me."

"It won't be so bad in a few minutes," she said, standing up. "Then I'll unwrap the bandages and take another look."

"Where are you going?"

"To check on the soup."

The thought of food made Ty's salivary glands contract in anticipation.

"Hungry?" she asked wryly, recognizing the look.

"I could eat a horse."

"Then I'd better warn Zebra to stay away from you."

"That old pony would be too tough to eat," Ty drawled, smiling slowly as he relaxed against the folded blankets beneath him.

Janna watched from a distance while Ty's eyelids closed and the taut lines around his eyes relaxed as he drifted into sleep. Only then did she return to his side, kneel and pull up the blanket so that his shoulders were covered once more. Even with the overhang of red rock to reflect back the sun's heat, she was afraid of his catching another chill. She didn't know what she would do if he became ill again. She was exhausted from broken sleep or no sleep at all, and from worrying that she had helped Ty to escape from renegades only to kill him by dragging him through a cold rain into the secret valley.

These had been the longest days of Janna's life since her father had died five years before, leaving his fourteen-year-old daughter orphaned and alone at a muddy water hole in southern Arizona. Watching Ty battle injury and fever had drained Janna's very soul. He had been so hot, then drenched in cold sweat, then hot and restless once more, calling out names of people she didn't know, fighting battles she had never heard of, crying out in anguish over dead comrades. She had tried to soothe and comfort him, had held him close in the cold hours before dawn, had bathed his big body in cool water when he was too hot and had warmed him with her own heat when he was too cold.

And now Ty flinched from her touch.

Don't be foolish, Janna told herself as she watched Ty sleep for a few moments longer. *He doesn't remember anything. He thinks you're a skinny boy. No wonder he didn't want you petting him.* And then, *How can he be so blasted blind as not to see past these clothes?*

As Janna went to the small campfire to check on the soup, she couldn't help wondering if Ty would have responded differently if he had known she was a girl.

Her intense desire that he see her as a woman caught her on the raw. She knew she was becoming too attached to the stranger whom chance had dropped into her life. As soon as Ty was healed he would leave with as little warning as he had come, going off to pursue his own dreams. He was just one more man hungry for gold or for the glory of being the person to tame the spirit horse known as Lucifer.

And he was too damned thickheaded to see past the skinny boy to the lonely woman.

Lonely?

Janna's hand froze in the act of stirring the soup. She had been alone for years but had never thought of herself as lonely. The horses had been her companions, the wind her music, the land her mentor, and her father's books had opened a hundred worlds of the mind to her. If she found herself yearning for another human voice, she had gone into Sweetwater or Hat Rock or Indian Springs. Each time she went into any of the outposts of civilization, she had left after only a few hours, driven out by the greedy eyes of the men who watched her pay for her purchases with tiny pieces of raw gold—men who, unlike Ty, had sometimes seen past Janna's boyish appearance.

Gloomily Janna studied the soup as it bubbled and announced its readiness in the blended fragrances of meat, herbs and vegetables. She poured some soup into her steep-sided tin plate and waited until it cooled somewhat. When she was sure the soup wouldn't burn Ty's mouth, she picked up her spoon and went to the overhang.

He was still asleep, yet there was an indefinable change in his body that told her Ty was healing even as she watched. He was much stronger than her consumptive father had been. Though Ty's bruises were spectacular, they were already smaller than they had been a few days before. The flesh covering his ribs was no longer swollen. Nor was his head where a club had struck.

Thick muscles and an even thicker skull, Janna told herself sarcastically.

As though he knew he were being watched, Ty opened his eyes. Their jeweled green clarity both reassured and disturbed Janna. She was glad that he was no longer dazed by fever, yet being the focus of those eyes was a bit unnerving. He might have been just one more gold- and horse-hungry man, but he had the strength, intelligence and determination to succeed where other men never got past the point of daydreaming.

"Are you still hungry?" Janna asked, her voice low and husky.

"Did you cook up poor old Zebra for me?"

The slow smile that followed Ty's words made Janna's nerve endings shimmer. Even covered with beard stubble and lying flat on his back, Ty was one of the most handsome men she had ever seen.

"No," Janna said, smiling in return. "She was too big for my pot." With unconscious grace, Janna sank to her knees next to Ty, balancing the tin plate in her hands without spilling a drop. "A few weeks back I traded a packet of dried herbs, three letters and a reading of *A Midsummer Night's Dream* for thirty pounds of jerked beef."

Ty blinked. "I beg your pardon?"

Janna laughed softly. "I'll tell you while I feed you soup. Can you sit up?"

Cautiously, then with greater assurance, Ty sat up. He started to say that he could feed himself before he realized that he was light-headed. He propped his back against the gently sloping stone cliff that was both wall and, eventually, ceiling to the natural shelter. The blanket covering him slid from his shoulders, down his chest, and finally rumpled across his lap.

Janna's pulse gave an odd little skip at the sight of the dark, masculine patterns of hair curling out from beneath Ty's bandages and down his muscular body. The temptation to trace those patterns with her fingertips was almost overwhelming.

Don't be a goose, she told herself firmly. *I've been washing, feeding and caring for Ty like a baby for four days. I've seen him wearing nothing but sunlight and soapy water, so why on earth am I getting all foolish and shivery now?*

Because he's awake now, that's why.

Ty looked down at his own body, wondering why he was being stared at. What he saw made him wince. Spreading out from beneath his rib bandage were bruises every color of the rainbow, but the predominant hues were black and blue with garish flourishes of green.

"I'm a sight, aren't I?" Ty asked wryly. "Looks worse than it feels, though. Whatever medicine you've been using works real well."

Janna closed her eyes for an instant, then looked only at the plate of soup in her hands. The surface of the liquid was disturbed by delicate rings, the result of the almost invisible trembling of her hands while she had looked at Ty.

"Don't go all pale on me now, boy. You must have seen worse than me."

Boy.

And thank God for it, Janna reminded herself instantly. *I have no more sense than a handful of sand when he looks at me and smiles that slow, devil-take-it smile.*

But, God, I do wish he knew I was a woman!

She took a deep, secret breath and brought her scattering emotions under control.

"Ready?" she asked, dipping the spoon into the soup.

"I was born ready."

She put the spoon into Ty's mouth, felt the gentle resistance of lips and tongue cleaning the spoon, and nearly dropped the plate of soup. He didn't notice, for the taste of the soup had surprised him.

"That's good."

"You needn't sound so shocked," she muttered.

"After that horse piss you've been feeding me, I didn't know what to expect."

"That was medicine. This is food."

"Food's the best medicine save one for what ails a man."

"Oh? What's the best?"

Ty smiled slowly. "When you're a man you won't have to ask."

The spoon clicked rather forcefully against Ty's teeth.

"Sorry," Janna said with transparent insincerity.

"Don't look so surly, boy. I felt the same way you did when I was your age. You'll grow into manhood with time."

"How old do you think I am?"

"Oh…thirteen?"

"Don't try to be kind," she said between her teeth.

"Hell, boy, you look closer to twelve with those soft cheeks and fine bones, and you know it. But that will begin to change about the time your voice cracks. It just takes time."

Janna knew that there would never be enough time in the whole world for her to grow into a man, but she had just enough common sense and self-control to keep that revealing bit of truth to herself. With steady motions she shoveled soup into Ty's mouth.

"You trying to drown me?" he asked, taking the soup from her. "I'll feed myself, thanks." He crunched through a pale root of some kind, started to ask what it was, then decided not to. The first thing a man on the trail learned was that if it tastes good, don't ask what it is. Just be grateful and eat fast. "What's this about herbs and Shakespeare and letters?" he asked between mouthfuls of soup.

"My father and I used to divide up a play and read parts

to each other. It helped to pass the time on the trail. I still have a trunk of his books,'' Janna said, helplessly watching the tip of Ty's tongue lick up stray drops of broth. ''When I need supplies, I'll go to the Lazy A or the Circle G and write letters for the cowhands. Most of them can't read anything but brands, so I'll also read whatever letters they've saved up until someone like me happens by.''

Ty looked at the thick, dark lashes, crystalline eyes and delicately structured face of the youth who was much too pretty for Ty's comfort. ''Where did you go to school?'' he asked roughly.

''On the front seat of a buckboard. Papa had a university degree and a case of wanderlust.''

''What about your mother?''

''She died when I was three. Papa told me her body just wasn't up to the demands of her spirit.''

The spoon hesitated on the way to Ty's mouth. He pinned Janna with an intense glance. ''When did your Daddy die?''

Janna paused for an instant, thinking quickly. If she told Ty her father had died five years before, he would ask how a kid under ten had survived on his own. If she told Ty that she was nineteen, he would realize that the only way a nineteen-year-old boy could lack a deep voice and a beard shadow and muscles was if said boy were a girl wearing men's clothing. She wanted Ty to figure that out for himself—the hard way.

''Papa died a few seasons back,'' she said casually. ''You lose track of time living alone.''

''You've lived alone since then?'' Ty asked, startled. ''The whole time?''

Janna nodded.

''Don't you have any kin?''

''No.''

''Wouldn't any of the townspeople let you trade room and board for work?''

''I don't like towns.''

''Surely one of the ranches would take you on as a cook's helper or fence rider. Hell, if you can tame a mustang, there isn't a ranch anywhere that wouldn't take you on as a mustanger,'' Ty added, disturbed at the thought of an orphaned child wandering homeless over the land. "You could make a decent living catching and breaking horses for the rough string.''

"I don't catch mustangs," Janna said flatly. "Too many of them refuse to eat once they're caught. I've seen them starve to death looking over a corral fence with glazed eyes."

"Most mustangs accept men."

Janna simply shook her head. "I won't take a mustang's freedom. I've gentled a few ranch-bred horses for women's mounts or for kids, but that's all."

"Sometimes a man has to do things he doesn't want to in order to survive," Ty said, his eyes narrowed against painful memories.

"I've been lucky so far," Janna said quietly. "More soup?"

Slowly, as though called back from a distance, Ty focused on Janna. "Thanks, I'd like that," he said, handing over the plate. "While I eat, would you mind reading to me?"

"Not at all. Anything in particular you want to hear?"

"Do you have *Romeo and Juliet*?"

"Yes."

"Then read to me about a woman more beautiful than the dawn." Ty closed his eyes and smiled. "A well-bred lady of silk, softer than a summer breeze, with pale hair and skin whiter than magnolias, and delicate hands that have never done anything more harsh than coax Chopin from a huge grand piano…"

"What's her name?" Janna asked tightly.

"Who?"

"The silk lady you're describing."

"Silver MacKenzie, my brother's wife." Ty's eyes opened, clear and hard. "But there are other women like her in England. I'm going to get one."

Abruptly Janna came to her feet. She returned a few minutes later with a heavy book tucked under her left arm and carrying a bowl of soup with her right hand. She gave Ty the soup, opened the worn book to *Romeo and Juliet*, Act II, Scene II, and began to read:

"'But, soft! What light through yonder window breaks?

It is the East, and Juliet is the sun...'"

Chapter Seven

That day set the pattern for the next two weeks. When Janna thought Ty had been pushing himself too hard in his efforts to regain full strength, she would bring out the Bible or the Shakespearean plays or the poetry of Dante, Milton or Pope, and she would read aloud. Ty saw through what she was doing, but didn't object. He had too much fun teasing "the boy" over the real meaning of the words in *The Song of Solomon* or Pope's *The Rape of the Lock.*

"Read that verse to me again," Ty said, smiling. "You ran over it so fast I missed most of the words."

Janna tilted her head down to the worn pages of the Bible and muttered, "'Vanity of vanities…all *is* vanity.'"

"That's Ecclesiastes," Ty drawled. "You were reading *The Song of Solomon* and a woman was talking about her sweetheart. 'My beloved is gone down into his garden, to the beds of spices, to feed in the gardens…' Now what do you suppose that really means, boy?"

"He was hungry," Janna said succinctly.

"Ah, but for what?" Ty asked, stretching. "When you know the answer, you'll be a man no matter what your size or age."

Janna looked at Ty's long, muscular arms and the smooth give-and-take of his skin over his chest and torso and vowed again that she would go into Sweetwater first thing tomorrow and get Ty some clothes. She wasn't going to be able to look at him running around in a breechcloth much longer without reaching out and running her hands over all that tempting masculine hide.

The thought of Ty's shocked expression if she gave in to temptation restored her humor. It would be worth almost anything to see him shocked. Until that time came, she would have to be satisfied with watching his unease when she leaned too close or casually brushed against him, making him uncomfortable because of ''the boy's'' closeness.

When Ty saw Janna's full lips curve into a slow, almost hidden smile, he felt a jolt of something uncomfortably close to desire lance through him.

That boy is too damned feminine for my self-respect, much less for my peace of mind. I think I'd better take another long soak in that hot pool in the head of the valley. Doubt that it will take the starch out of me, though. I haven't been this hungry since I was fourteen. Dammit, but I need a woman.

Disgusted with himself, Ty came to his feet in a muscular rush. Janna was so surprised by the abrupt movement that she dropped the book she was holding. A sheet of paper that had been held safely between the pages fluttered out. Ty scooped it up before Janna could. He looked at the paper and let out a low whistle of admiration.

''Now there is a real lady,'' Ty said, gazing at the drawing of a woman in long, formal dress and elaborately coiffed hair. ''Elegance like that is damned rare. Where did you get this?''

''Papa drew it when Mother was alive.''

''This is your mother?''

Janna nodded.

''I see where you get your fine bones and...''

Ty's voice died. There was no point in telling the kid that his mouth would have done credit to a courtesan and his eyes were too big and too expressive to belong to a boy of any age. So Ty kept his mind on the drawing and off the fey creature whose skin and hair smelled like a meadow drenched in sunshine and warmth.

''Your daddy was a lucky man,'' Ty said after looking at the drawing for a long time. ''This is a woman to dream on.

All silk and sweet softness. After I catch Lucifer and build my own horse herd, I'm going to Europe and court a fine lady just like this. I'll marry her and bring her home, and we'll raise strong sons and silky daughters.''

"Silk doesn't last long on the frontier," Janna said stiffly.

Ty laughed. "That's why I'm going to build my fortune first. I'd never ask a true lady to live in a dirt-floored shack and ruin her soft hands on scrub brushes and the like."

Janna looked at her hands. While not rough, they weren't exactly silky, either. "Soft isn't everything."

Ty shook his head, seeing only his dream. "It is in a woman. I'll have my silken lady or I'll have none at all for longer than it takes to pleasure myself."

The words sliced into Janna like knives, wounding her. The pain she felt shocked her, and the rage, and the sense of... betrayal.

"What makes you think that a silken woman would have a man like you?" Janna asked coolly.

Ty smiled to himself. "Women kind of take to me, especially when I'm cleaned up a bit."

"Huh," she sniffed. "I don't think there's enough cleaning time between now and Christmas to make any fancy woman look at you twice."

Before Ty could say anything, Zebra whinnied in alarm. Even as he turned toward the sound, Ty yanked Janna to the ground and pulled out the hunting knife he wore at his waist. An instant later his big body half covered hers, pinning her against the earth.

"Don't move," Ty breathed against Janna's ear, his voice a mere thread of sound.

Janna nodded slightly. She felt Ty's weight shift as he rolled aside. There was a flash of tanned skin in the tall grass, a suggestion of movement in the streamside willows, and then nothing more. Ty had vanished. A shiver went over Janna as she realized how very quick Ty was now that he was well, and how powerful. She thought of wiggling backward until she was in better cover, then discarded the idea. Ty would expect her to be where he had left her—and he would attack

anything that moved anywhere else. That thought was enough
to rivet her in place.

The willows slid soundlessly past Ty's nearly naked body
as he eased through the streamside thickets. The creek was no
more than a few feet wide and still slightly warm from its
birth in a hot springs back at the head of the small valley, a
place where lava and red rock and lush greenery entwined in
a steamy Eden whose water contained a sulfurous whiff of
hell.

Nothing moved in the willows around Ty, nor was there
any sound of birds. The silence was a warning in itself. Nor-
mally small birds darted and sang in the valley, enjoying the
rare presence of water in a dry land. If the wildlife were quiet,
it meant that an intruder was nearby.

Fifty yards away, belly-deep in grass, Zebra snorted. The
sound was followed by a drumroll of hooves as the mare fled.
The mustang's flight told Ty that the intruder was either a
cougar or a man. Nothing else would have sent the horse racing away in fear. Without disturbing the thick screen of willow
branches, Ty looked out into the valley. Zebra was standing
seventy yards away with every muscle quivering and poised
for flight. Her head was high and her black ears were pricked
forward. She was looking at something that was well downstream from Ty.

*Something just came out of the slot. Which direction is the
intruder going, girl? Is he going for the hot springs at the
north end or the Indian ruins at the south end?*

Motionless, Ty watched the mare, knowing that she would
track the intruder better than he ever would have been able to
with mere human senses. Zebra kept her head and ears up,
watching something that he couldn't see. Slowly her head
turned toward Ty.

All right. The intruder is coming toward me.

Mentally Ty reviewed the small, irregularly shaped valley.
Barely more than a mile long, never more than a quarter of a
mile wide, the valley was walled in by red sandstone on one
side and black lava on the other. The hot springs at the north
end fed the small stream. Other watercourses joined the stream

at various points of the valley, but they held water only after
heavy rains, when cliffs wore lacy waterfalls that were as
beautiful as they were short-lived.

Ty decided that the best point for an ambush was right
where he was. A very faint trail wound between the edge of
the willows and the ancient lava flow that all but cut the valley
in two. Anything trying to reach the head of the valley would
be forced to walk between the willow thicket and the cliff. All
Ty had to do was be very still and watch what passed within
reach.

Motionless, poised for attack, Ty waited as he had waited
too many times before.

*Wish Logan were here. A man's unprotected back gets real
itchy at times like this.*

But Logan was in Wyoming with Silver. As for his other
brothers, the last Ty had heard, both Case and Duncan were
looking for gold with Blue Wolf, trying to repair the Mac-
Kenzie family fortunes and make a future for themselves. At
least, that's what Duncan was doing. No one but God—more
likely, the devil—knew what went on in Case's mind. Fighting
in the war had closed Ty's youngest brother up tighter than
bark on a tree.

A few minutes later Ty heard the faint sounds of a man's
progress through the tall grass. When the sounds passed the
willows where Ty hid, he came out in a silent rush. One arm
hooked around the intruder's neck from behind as the knife
sliced upward in a lethal arc.

At the last instant Ty realized that the man was old and
unarmed. He pulled the knife aside.

"Who are you?" Ty asked quietly, holding the blade across
the man's throat.

"John Turner. And I'm right glad you ain't an Injun or a
bandit. I'd be dead by now."

Ty didn't bother to make welcoming sounds. "Walk ahead
of me toward that red cliff. Don't hesitate or turn around. If
you make a wrong move I'll kill you."

Chapter Eight

Ty followed close behind the intruder, but not so close that a sudden turn and lunge would have caught him off guard. A few minutes later they walked up to the edge of Janna's hidden camp.

"All right, kid. Come on out," Ty said.

Janna stood up. "How many times do I have to tell you that my name isn't kid, it's—oh, hello, Jack. Did you run out of stomach medicine already?"

The old man didn't answer, because Ty's knife was resting once more against his throat.

"You told me your name was John Turner," Ty said.

"'Tis, but most folks call me Mad Jack."

Ty looked over at Janna.

She nodded. "It's all right, Ty. Jack was Papa's friend."

Ty lowered the knife. Mad Jack turned and spat a thin stream of brown liquid toward a nearby bush.

"Her pa staked me. We was partners," Mad Jack said, shifting the cud of tobacco to the other side of his mouth. "He cashed in his chips a few years back, but I ain't done with the game yet." He looked at Janna. "Brung you some more gold, but you wasn't in any of the old places."

"It wasn't safe anymore. Cascabel's new camp was too close."

"Yeah, them pony soldiers have made that old rattlesnake's life pure hell this summer." Mad Jack shucked off his backpack, untied a flap and pulled out a fat leather bag that fit in his hand. "Figured you'd need to lay in some winter supplies. From the size of your young buck, I shoulda brung two pokes of gold."

"How has your stomach been?" Janna asked hurriedly, wanting to get off the subject of her "young buck."

"Middlin'," Mad Jack said, shifting the wad of tobacco again. "How 'bout you, Janna? You be all right? You come early to your winter-over place."

"Ty was injured," Janna said. She glanced briefly at him and prayed without much hope that he would ignore the difference between the names Janna and Jan. "He ran Cascabel's gauntlet and got away."

Mad Jack turned and looked at Ty as though for the first time. "So you're the one, huh?" The old man's chuckle was a dry, rustling sound. "Made Cascabel the laughing-stock of the Utes. Black Hawk ever finds you, he'll like as not give you a medal 'fore he lifts your hair. How'd you hitch up with Janna?"

The second time Ty heard the name Janna, he knew it hadn't been a slip of the old prospector's tongue. Ty turned and looked at the "boy" with narrowed green eyes. After an instant the "boy" began to study the ground as though it were alive and likely to start nibbling on toes at any instant.

"Janna, huh?" Ty asked. "Is that your real name, kid?"

She threw him a quick, sideways glance, looked away and nodded very slightly.

Ty's right hand flashed out as he yanked off the floppy old hat Janna always wore. Two long, thick, Indian-style braids fell down her back. The braids were tied with leather thongs. An Indian band went around her forehead and tied in back, keeping any stray locks from escaping the hat's confinement. Her hair was a dark auburn that shimmered with unexpected fire whenever her head moved. In contrast with the darkness of her hair, the pale, crystalline depths of her eyes looked as brilliant as diamonds. The delicacy of her bone structure and the fine-grained texture of her skin seemed to taunt him for his blindness.

"Well, kid," drawled Ty, narrow eyed, furious with himself for having been deceived and with her for having deceived him, "I'll say this—you made a prettier boy than you do a girl."

Mad Jack's rustling chuckle did nothing to make Ty feel better. He flipped the hat over Janna's head and pulled down hard, covering her to her nostrils.

"Fooled ya, did she?" Mad Jack asked, slapping his hands together in pleasure. "Don't feel bad, son. That's a right clever gal. She's got the Indians believing she a *bruja*—a witch—and the mustangs believing she's just a funny kind of two-legged horse."

Ty grunted.

"'Course," Mad Jack continued, looking at Ty's nearly bare, tanned body, "a body what runs around near naked and sneaks up on folks might be accused of tryin' to make folks think he's an Injun. Might also explain why a young lady might want to be taken fer a boy."

"Lady?" Ty asked sardonically, looking up and down Janna's ragged length. "That might indeed be a female, Jack, but it sure as hell isn't a lady. A lady wouldn't be caught dead in that outfit."

Janna ignored the hurt caused by Ty's caustic comments and let her anger bubble forth instead. She turned to Mad Jack and spoke in the cool, cultured voice that her father had taught her was appropriate for reading Shakespeare.

"Of course, you have to understand that Ty is an expert on ladies. You can tell that just by looking at him. Note the fashionably cut pants and the spotless linen shirt. His suit coat is obviously handmade from the finest blend of silk and wool. His boots are fine examples of craftsmanship raised to the level of art. His own skin couldn't fit him better."

Long before Janna had finished her sarcastic summary of Ty's attire, Mad Jack was laughing so hard he nearly swallowed his cud of tobacco. Ty's smile was a bleak warning curve carved out of the blackness of his beard.

"There's more to a man than his clothes," Ty said.

"But not to a woman, hmm?"

"Kid, you don't have enough curves to be a woman." Ty turned away before Janna could say anything more. "I'm going to the Tub," he said, using Janna's nickname for the deep pool in which they both bathed—separately. "Don't worry about hurrying along to scrub my back. I can reach it just fine."

Careful to show no expression at all, Janna watched Ty stalk from the camp. Then she turned and began preparing an herbal tea for Mad Jack.

"Sorry, gal," Mad Jack said, watching her work. "If I'd thunk about it, I wouldn't've opened my trap. You want I should stay with you?"

Janna shook her head. "It's not necessary. I know how restless you get after you've been in camp for a few hours. Ty's mad, but he'll get over it."

"That wasn't what I meant. Now that he knows you're a female, maybe you won't be wanting to be alone with him."

"There won't be any problem," Janna said unhappily. "You heard him. He thinks I'm about as appealing as a fence post." She shrugged, trying to appear casual about her lack of feminine allure.

Mad Jack's faded eyes watched Janna shrewdly. "And you be kinda wishin' it was otherwise," he said after a moment.

She opened her mouth to object forcefully, then realized there was no point in denying the truth, no matter how painful that truth might be.

"Yes, I'd like to be attractive to him. What woman wouldn't? He's all man," Janna said. She added a pinch of herbs to the tiny pot. "And he's a good man. Even when he was half out of his head with pain, his first instinct was still to protect me rather than himself. He'd never force himself on me." She grimaced and added wryly, "Not that he'd ever have the chance. I'd probably say yes so quick it would make his head spin."

Mad Jack hesitated, then sighed. "Gal, I don't know how much your pa told you about babies and such, but more women have spent their lives wishin' they'd said no than otherwise. When the urge is ridin' a man, he'll talk sweet as molasses and promise things he has no damn intention of giving."

"Ty wouldn't lie to me like that."

"You can't rightly call it lyin'. When a man's crotch is aching, he don't know lies from truth," Mad Jack said bluntly. "It's natural. If menfolk stood around wonderin' what was right instead of doin' what come natural like, there wouldn't be enough babies to keep the world goin'."

Janna made a neutral sound and stirred the herbal tea. Despite the faint suggestion of red on his weathered face, Mad Jack forged ahead with his warning about the undependable nature of men.

"What I'm tryin' to say," Mad Jack muttered as he dug around in his stained shirt pocket for a plug of tobacco, "is that's a big stud hoss you found, and he's getting right healthy again. He'll be waking up hard as stone of a mornin' and he'll be lookin' for a soft place to ease what's aching."

Janna ducked her head, grateful for the floppy brim of the hat, which concealed her face. She didn't know whether to throw the steaming tea at Mad Jack or to hug him for trying to do what he was obviously ill-suited to do, which was to be a Dutch uncle to a girl who had no family.

"Now, I know I'm being too blunt," Mad Jack continued doggedly, "but dammit, gal, you ain't got no womenfolk to warn you about a man's ways. Next thing you know, you'll be gettin' fat, and I can tell you flat out it won't be from nothing you et."

"Your tea is ready."

"Gal, you understand what I been sayin'?"

"I know where babies come from and how they get there, if that's what you mean," Janna said succinctly.

"That's what I mean," Mad Jack mumbled.

Janna glanced up and made an irritated sound as she saw Mad Jack sawing away on a plug of tobacco with his pocketknife. "No wonder your stomach is as sour as last month's milk. That stuff would gag a skunk."

Dry laughter denied her words. "I'm at the age when a good chew is my only comfort. That and finding a mite of gold here and there. I done right well for myself since your pa died. I been thinking 'bout it, and I done decided. I want you to take some gold and get shuck of this place.''

The immediate objections that came to Janna's lips were overridden by Mad Jack, who didn't stop speaking even while he pushed a chunk of tobacco into his mouth and started chewing with gusto.

''Now you just listen to me, gal. Territory's gettin' too damn crowded. One of these days the wrong man's going to cut your trail, the kind of man what don't care about sweet talkin' or protecting or any damn thing but his own pleasure. And I don't mean just renegades, neither. Some of them pony soldiers is as bad as Injuns, an' the scum selling rifles to Cascabel is no better than him.''

Mad Jack looked at Janna as she worked gracefully over the fire, every line of her body proclaiming both her femininity and her unwillingness to listen to his advice.

''It's gettin' too damn dangerous out here for any woman a'tall, even one wearing men's clothes. You be too good a woman to go to waste out here alone.''

''I've done fine for five years.''

He snorted. ''Fine, huh? Look at you, thin as a mare nursing two foals. You want to get a man, you gotta put meat on them bones.''

''My mother wasn't built like a butter churn,'' Janna muttered. ''Papa didn't mind one bit.''

And neither had Ty, if his reaction to the drawing were any guide.

Mad Jack cursed under his breath and tried another tack. ''Don't you get lonesome chasing mustangs and living so small you barely cast a shadow?''

''Do you?'' Janna countered.

''Hell, I'm different. I'm a man and you ain't, never mind the clothes you wear. Don't you want a man of your own an' kids to pester you?''

Janna didn't answer, because the answer was too painful. Until she had found Ty, she hadn't really understood what life had to offer. Then she had met him—and now she knew the meaning of the word *lonely*.

"The mustangs are all I have," she said.

"And they're all you'll ever have if'n you don't leave."

"If I leave, I'll have nothing," Janna said matter-of-factly. "I'm not the kind of woman to catch a man's eye. Ty has made that real plain, and he's the 'stud hoss' who should know." She shrugged, concealing her unhappiness. "I'd rather live with mustangs than cook at a boardinghouse where men grab at me when they think nobody's looking."

"But—"

"I'm staying, and that's that."

Chapter Nine

The Tub's slick-walled pool was far enough from its hot-spring source to have lost the scalding edge of its temperature and nearly all of its sulfurous smell. The water was a clear, pale blue that steamed gently in the cool hours of night and gleamed invitingly all the time. Though safe to drink, the water was too hot for plants to grow in it. Nothing but sand and stone ringed the pool. The high mineral content of the water had decorated the rock it touched with a smooth, creamy-yellow veneer of deposits that had rounded off all the rough edges of the native stone, making a hard but nonetheless comfortable place for Ty to soak out the last legacy of Cascabel's cruel gauntlet.

Usually Ty enjoyed the soothing heat of the pool, but not today. Today he simmered from more than the temperature of the water. Knowing that "the boy" was a girl made him want to turn Janna over his knee and paddle her until she learned some manners. When he thought how she had let him run around wearing nothing more than a few rags of blanket...

A flush spread beneath the dark hair on Ty's chest and face. The realization that he was embarrassed infuriated him. It was hardly a case of his never having been nearly or even completely naked around a woman; of all the MacKenzie brothers, Ty had been the one who had caught women's eye from the time he was old enough to shave. What bothered Ty was that he must have shocked Janna more than once. The thought of a girl of her tender years being subjected repeatedly to a full-grown man's nakedness made Ty very uncomfortable.

She must have been dying of embarrassment, but she never let on. She just kept on washing me when I was delirious and putting medicine all over me and reading to me while I teased her in a way I never would have teased a girl. A woman, maybe, but not a girl. Why, she can't be much more than... Abruptly Ty sat up straight on the stone ledge, sending water cascading off his body. *Just how old is she? And how innocent?*

Ty remembered the look of desire he had once seen in Janna's eyes. Instantly he squelched the thought. He was nearly thirty. He had no damned business even looking at a thirteen-year-old, no matter how soft her cheeks were or how her gray eyes warmed while she looked at him when she thought he wouldn't notice. Besides, boy or girl, at thirteen a case of hero worship was still a case of hero worship.

If she was, indeed, thirteen.

She can't be much older than that. I may be blind but I'm not dead. If she had breasts, I'd have noticed. Or hips, for that matter. Even under those flapping, flopping, ridiculous clothes, I'd have noticed...wouldn't I?

Hell, yes, of course I would have.

The reassuring thought made Ty settle back into the pool. A kid was still a kid, no matter what the sex. As for his own body's urgent woman-hunger, that was just a sign of his returned health. It had nothing to do with a gray-eyed waif whose delicate hands had touched nearly every aching inch of his body.

But it was the aching inches she hadn't touched that were driving him crazy.

"Dammit!" Ty exploded, coming out of the water with a lunge.

He stood dripping on the stone rim of the pool, furious with himself and the world in general, and with one Janna Wayland in particular. Viciously he scrubbed his breechcloth on the rocks, wrung it out and put it on, concealing the rigid evidence of his hunger.

Then he turned around and got right back into the Tub
again. This time he remembered the bar of camp soap that
Janna always left in a nearby niche. Cursing steadily, he began
washing himself from head to newly healed feet. When he
was finished he rinsed thoroughly, adjusted the uncomfortably
tight breechcloth once more and stalked back to camp.

Janna was calmly tying twists of greenery to branches she
had laid between two tall forked sticks. The stems of the plants
turned slowly in the sun and wind as the leaves gave up their
moisture. In a week or two the herbs would be ready to store
whole or to crumble and pound into a powder from which she
would make lotions, pastes, potions and other varieties of medicine.

"How do your feet feel?" Janna asked without looking up
from her work.

"Like feet. Where's Mad Jack?"

"Gone."

"What?"

"He was worried when he didn't find me in any of the usual
places, so—"

"Where are the usual places?" Ty interrupted.

"Wherever Lucifer's herd is. Once Jack found out I was all
right, he went back."

"To where?"

"Wherever his mine is."

Ty reached to readjust the breechcloth again, remembered
that Janna wasn't a boy and snatched back his hands, cursing.

"Do you think that zebra dun of yours would take me to
Sweetwater?"

"I don't know. She likes you well enough, but she doesn't
like towns at all."

"You two make a fine pair," Ty muttered, combing through
his wet hair with long fingers.

"Catch."

Reflexively Ty's hand flashed out and grabbed the small
leather poke Janna had pulled from her baggy pants pocket.

"What's this?" he asked.

''Mad Jack's gold. You'll need it when you get to town. Or were you planning to work off whatever you buy?''

''I can't take gold from a thirteen-year-old girl.''

Janna looked up briefly before she went back to arranging herbs for drying. ''You aren't.''

''What?''

''You aren't taking gold from a thirteen-year-old. I'm nineteen. I only told you I was thirteen so that you wouldn't suspect I was a woman.''

''Sugar,'' drawled Ty, giving Janna a thorough up-and-down look, ''you could have walked naked past me and I wouldn't have suspected anything at all. You're the least female female I've ever seen.''

Janna's fingers tightened on the herbs as the barb went home, but she was determined not to show that she'd been hurt.

''Thank you,'' she said huskily. ''I just took a leaf from Cascabel's book—hide in plain sight. The pony soldiers caught him way down south last year. He escaped from them. They went looking for him, expecting to run him down easily because there was no cover around. It was flat land with only a scattering of stunted mesquite. No place for a rabbit to hide, much less a man.''

Ty listened in spite of his anger at having been deceived. As he listened, he tried to figure out why Janna's voice was so appealing to him. Finally he realized that she no longer was trying to conceal her voice's essentially feminine nature, a faintly husky music that tantalized his senses.

And she was nineteen, not thirteen.

Stop it, Ty told himself fiercely. *She's all alone in the world. Any man who would take advantage of that isn't worthy of the name.*

''Because the soldiers knew there was no place to hide, they didn't look,'' Janna continued. ''Cascabel is as shrewd as Satan. He knew that the best place to hide is in plain sight, where no one would ever look. So when he was convinced that he couldn't outrun the soldiers and they would catch him in the open, he rolled in the dust, grabbed some mesquite branches and sat very still. The branches didn't cover him, but they gave the soldiers something familiar to look at—something they would never look at twice. And they didn't," Janna concluded. "They rode right by Cascabel, maybe a hundred feet away, and never saw him."

"Probably because Cascabel looks a hell of a lot more like a mesquite bush than you look like a woman."

"That's your opinion," Janna retorted, "but we both know how trustworthy your eyes are, don't we?"

Ty saw the reaction that Janna tried to hide. He smiled, feeling better than he had since he realized how badly he had been fooled. If his brothers ever found out what had happened, they would ride him until he screamed for mercy. Ty had always been the one the MacKenzie men turned to for advice on the pursuit and pleasuring of the fair sex.

He laughed aloud and felt his temper sweeten with every passing second. He was going to get some of his own back from the gray-eyed chameleon, and he was going to enjoy himself thoroughly in the process. She would rue the day she had fooled him into believing she was an effeminate boy.

"If you'd been any kind of a woman," Ty drawled very slowly, "I'd feel right ashamed of being fooled. But seeing as how you only *say* you're a girl, and I'm too much of a gentleman to ask you to prove it...I guess I'll just have to keep my doubts to myself."

"You? A gentleman?" Janna asked in rising tones of disbelief. She looked pointedly at his half-grown beard and soggy breechcloth. "From what I can see—and there's darn little I *can't* see—you look like a savage."

Ty's laugh wasn't quite so heartfelt this time. "Oh, I know I'm a gentleman for a fact, *boy*. And so do a lot of real ladies."

Mentally Janna compared herself to the sketch of her mother—loose, ragged clothes against stylish swirls of silk, Indian braids against carefully coiffed curls. The comparison was simply too painful. So was the fact that Ty had been taken with her mother's image and couldn't have been more blunt about the daughter's lack of feminine allure.

Unshed tears clawed at the back of Janna's eyelids, but the

thought that Ty might catch her crying appalled her. Without a word she dusted off her hands and brushed past Ty, refusing even to look at him, knowing that for all her scathing comments to the contrary, his eyes were uncomfortably sharp when it came to assessing her mood.

When Janna was at the edge of the grassy area of the valley, she cupped her hands to her mouth and called out to Zebra, using the keening cry of a hawk. To human ears there was almost no difference in the sounds—to Zebra, it was a call as clear as a trumpet's. Within moments the mare was cantering through the grass towards Janna.

"Hello, pretty girl," Janna murmured. She stroked the mare's neck and pulled weeds from her long mane and tail. "Show me your hooves."

She worked slowly around the horse, touching each fetlock. Zebra presented each of her hooves in turn, standing patiently while Janna used a short, pointed stick to worry loose any mud or debris that had become caught between the hard outer hoof and the softer frog at the center.

"It would be easier with a steel hoof pick," Ty said.

Janna barely controlled a start. On the meadow grass Ty's bare feet had made no more sound than a shadow.

"If I bought a pick, people would wonder what I was planning to use it on. Only one other human being knows that I've tamed..." Janna's voice died when she realized that Ty as well as Mad Jack knew that she mingled with Lucifer's herd. "Could it be our secret?" she asked as she looked at Ty, her voice aching with restraint. "It's bad enough that I turn up from time to time with raw gold. If some of the men around here knew that I could get close to Lucifer, they'd hunt me down like a mad dog and use me to get their hands on him."

Ty looked at the face turned up toward him in silent pleading and felt as though he had been kicked in the stomach. The idea of using Janna to get close to Lucifer had been in the back of his mind since he had realized that Zebra was part of the big black stallion's harem.

They'd hunt me down like a mad dog and use me...

Before Ty realized what he was doing, he cupped Janna's chin reassuringly in his hand.

"I won't tell anyone," he said quietly. "I promise you, Janna. And I won't use you. I want that stud and I plan to have him—but not like that, not by making you feel you had betrayed a trust."

The heat of Janna's tears on his hand shocked Ty, but not as much as the butterfly softness of her lips brushing over his skin for an instant before she turned away.

"Thank you," she said huskily, her face hidden while she resumed working over Zebra's hoof. "And I'm sorry about what I said earlier. You're very much a gentleman, no matter what you're wearing."

Ty closed his eyes and fought against the tremor of sensation that was spreading out from the palm of his hand to the pit of his stomach and from there to the soles of his feet. Before he could prevent himself, he had lifted his hand to his lips. The taste of Janna's tears went to his head more quickly than a shot of whiskey, making him draw in a sharp breath.

You've been without a woman too long, he told himself as he fought to control a combination of tenderness and raw desire.

Yes—and the name of the cure is Janna Wayland.

"No," Ty said aloud harshly.

"What?" Janna said, looking up.

Ty wasn't watching her. He was standing rigid, his face drawn as though in pain. When she spoke, he opened his eyes. She wanted to protest the shadows she saw there, but he was already speaking.

"I'm not what you think," Ty said, his voice rough. "I'm too woman hungry to be a gentleman. Don't trust me, Janna. Don't trust me at all."

Chapter Ten

Under Janna's watchful eyes, Ty sprang onto Zebra's back with a flowing, catlike motion. The mare flicked her ears backward, then forward, accepting Ty as her rider without a fuss.

"I told you she wouldn't object," Janna said. "You've ridden her before."

"Don't remind me," he said. "I've had nightmares about that ride every night since." He leaned down and offered Janna his left arm. "Grab just above the elbow with your left hand, pretend I'm a piece of mane and swing up behind me."

Janna followed Ty's instructions and found herself whisked aboard Zebra with breathtaking ease. She lifted her hand instantly, too conscious of the heat and power of Ty's bare arm. She found herself confronted by an expanse of naked shoulders that seemed to block out half the world.

"H-how is your back healing?" she asked.

"You tell me," Ty said dryly. "You can see it better than I can."

She bit her lip, irritated by her inane question and his goading response. On the other hand, asking that question had been safer than following her original impulse, which had been to run her hands over his tanned, supple skin. Taking a deep breath, Janna forced herself to concentrate on the shadow bruises and faint, thin lines of red that marked recently healed cuts. She traced the longest line with delicate fingertips. He flinched as though she had used a whip on him.

"Don't do that," he snapped.

"I'm sorry. I didn't know it was still painful. It looks healed."

Ty's lips flattened, but he said nothing to correct Janna's assumption that it had been pain rather than pleasure that had made his body jerk. Her fingertips had been like that single touch from her lips, a brush of warmth and a shivering hint of the feminine sensuality concealed beneath men's clothing.

"When we get back from town, I'll put more salve on," Janna continued.

His mouth opened to object, but he closed it without making a sound. The temptation to feel her soothing hands on his body was simply too great for him to deny himself the opportunity of being cared for by Janna.

Silently Ty nudged Zebra with his left heel. The mare turned obediently and headed toward the cleft in the rocks that surrounded the tiny valley. Each motion of the horse's buttocks, combined with the natural forward slope of Zebra's back, gently moved Janna toward Ty's warm body. He flinched again when the brim of her floppy hat touched his skin.

"Sorry," muttered Janna, pulling her head back.

He grunted.

Zebra kept on walking and Janna kept sliding closer to Ty. Before they came to the cleft that led from the valley, she was flush against his body. Only by leaning back at an awkward angle could she prevent her hat—or her lips—from brushing against his skin.

The fifth time Janna felt compelled to apologize for the contact she could not avoid, she wriggled away from Ty until she could put her hands on the horse's back between their bodies. Cautiously she pushed herself backward a fraction of an inch at a time, not wanting to alarm Zebra.

As Janna's weight settled farther back on the mare's spine, her tail swished in warning, sending a stinging veil of hair across Ty's naked calf.

"Damn, what is her tail made of—nettles?"

Janna didn't answer. Instead, she eased herself backward another inch, then two.

Zebra balked and humped her back in warning.

"What's wrong with her?" Ty asked, turning to look over his shoulder at Janna. "What the hell are you doing way back there? Don't you know a horse's kidneys and flanks are sensitive? Or maybe you're trying to get us both bucked off in the dirt?"

"I was trying not to hurt your back."

"My back? My back is just fi—" Abruptly Ty remembered what he had said about his back being hurt by Janna's light touch. "I'll live," he said grimly. "Scoot on up here where you belong before this mustang bucks us both off."

"I'd rather not," Janna said through stiff lips.

Ty kicked his right leg over Zebra's neck and slid off onto the ground. "Get up there where you belong," he said in a curt voice. "I'll walk."

"No, I'll walk," Janna said, dismounting in a rush, landing very close to Ty. "I'm used to it. Besides, I haven't been hurt and you have."

"I'm all healed up."

"But you said your back—"

"Get on that mustang before I lose my temper," Ty said flatly, cutting across Janna's protest.

"Lose your temper? Impossible. You'd have to find it first."

Ty glared into Janna's gray eyes. She didn't flinch. With a hissed curse he grabbed her and dumped her on her stomach across Zebra's back. He had plenty of time to regret the impulsive act. Janna's scramble to right herself and assume a normal riding position pulled the fabric of her pants tightly across her buttocks, revealing to him for the first time the unmistakable curves of a woman's hips.

At that instant Ty abandoned all thought of climbing on Zebra behind Janna. The feel of those soft curves rubbing between his thighs and against his aching male flesh would quickly drive him crazy.

Cursing steadily beneath his breath, Ty reached up to drag Janna off the mare. He told himself it was an accident that his hands shaped Janna's buttocks on the way to pulling her down, and he knew that it was a lie. He could have pulled on Janna's feet or even her knees. He didn't have to grab her hips and sink his fingers into her resilient flesh, sending a wave of heat through his body.

Even as Ty withdrew his hands, he wondered if he had been as wrong about Janna's breasts as he had been about her hips—she had more than enough curves to fill a man's hungry hands. The realization that the ride into town would probably tell him just how soft and tempting her breasts were was enough to make Ty groan and swear even more. The amount of control he had to exert to drag his hands away from Janna's body shocked him. He had never been the kind of man who grabbed at what a woman wouldn't freely offer to him.

"Stand still," Ty said harshly as Janna twisted against him, trying to regain her balance.

"Now listen, you son of—"

A broad, hard palm covered Janna's mouth. Green eyes stared into furious gray ones.

"No, you listen to me, *boy*," snarled Ty. "We're going to get on that horse and you're going to ride far enough forward that Zebra's spine isn't hurt. She's a good-sized mare, but carrying double is still a lot of weight for her, especially when one of her riders is my size."

Janna stopped fighting. She hadn't thought that her foolish scooting about might have hurt Zebra. With a small cry she turned toward the mare. The horse looked back at her with an equine's patience for crazy humans.

"I'll walk," Janna said.

"Like hell you will. It's too far."

"I've walked a lot farther in a morning."

"And left footprints every step of the way. If you take time to hide your trail, it'll take a week to get to town. If you don't hide your trail, the next man through that gap won't be Mad Jack. It will be Cascabel."

There was a moment of silence while Janna digested the unpleasant truth of what Ty was saying. Signs left by an untrimmed, unshod horse wouldn't attract much attention, particularly after they crossed their trail with that of any of the several wild horse herds in the area. Tracks left by a trimmed, shod horse, or a human, would bring down Cascabel quicker than the strike of his namesake reptile—the rattlesnake.

"It won't hurt Zebra to carry double," Ty said, "especially without a saddle. Just don't ride so far back."

"What about you? I don't want to hurt your back, either."

He closed his eyes so as not to see the unhappiness in Janna's at the thought of hurting anything, even the man who was presently making her life very difficult.

"I'm ticklish, that's all," Ty said grimly. "My back is fine."

"Oh."

Ty swung up onto Zebra, helped Janna swing up behind him and gritted his teeth at the feel of her breath against his naked skin. When Zebra walked once more to the cleft that led out of the valley, the gentle rubbing pressure of Janna's thighs against his own was an even worse distraction than the heat of her breath washing over his spine.

Think of her as a boy.

Ty tried. All he could think of was the lush resilience of Janna's hips. The smooth, curving heat of them could never have belonged to a boy.

Be grateful she doesn't have big breasts to rub against you.

Ty tried to be grateful. All he could think of was pulling off Janna's tentlike shirt and finding out just how soft her breasts were, and if her nipples were as pink as her tongue, and if they would pout hungrily for his mouth.

The reflexive tightening of Ty's body in response to his thoughts was communicated to Zebra. Sensing his agitation without understanding its source, she began to shy at the breeze stirring through the belly-deep grass as though it were a yellow-eyed cougar stalking her.

Janna talked to the mare in a soothing, husky voice that worked on Ty's aroused senses like repeated, silky caresses. He clenched his teeth when she shifted position and leaned around him in order to stroke Zebra's neck soothingly.

"I don't know what's wrong with her," Janna said, keeping her voice low and reassuring. "She's only like this when there are Indians or cougars around. I haven't seen any sign of cats in the valley. Maybe Mad Jack didn't cover his trail out of here well enough and Cascabel followed it.''

"Doubt it," Ty said in a clipped voice. "That old man has been outsmarting trackers for more years than I've been alive. Zebra's probably just nervous about having two riders.''

Janna made a sound that had no meaning except to soothe the restive mustang.

By the time they approached the slit in the cliffs that surrounded the valley, Zebra no longer shied at every shadow, Janna had relaxed so that she no longer jerked back from the inevitable contact with Ty's nearly naked body—and Ty's jaw ached from being clenched against the hot sensations radiating through his body from every accidental, brushing contact with Janna.

And it seemed that she touched him everywhere, except in those places where he ached to the point of pain.

Chapter Eleven

Silently Ty endured the continual brush of Janna's body against his as they went toward the cleft. They rode alongside the stream until it spread out into a small slough and vanished, leaving not even a trickle to enter the stone slot that was the valley's only outlet. There was nothing about the mouth of the cleft to suggest that it was any different from the hundreds of other narrow, barren gouges in the eroded flanks of the huge plateau. That, and the fact that the narrow, twisting passage was both difficult and uninviting for a horse, were why the valley had remained Janna's secret.

The slit in the rocks looked like the entrance to hell, but Ty watched it approach with a feeling of relief. When the opening was thirty yards away, he could bear Janna's unintentional sensual torment no longer. With a feeling of relief, he slid off Zebra and away from the fiery brush of Janna's body.

"Wait here," Ty said curtly. "I'll check out the trail."

He was gone before Janna could put her objections into words.

Inside the cleft it was cool, damp, dusky. A few shallow pools left by recent rain showers reflected the dark red, oddly stained cliffs that towered above the floor of the narrow canyon. Overhead the sky was reduced to a thin blue string thrown carelessly between the cliffs. In the places where black lava replaced sandstone, the cleft darkened until it was both somber and eerie, as though night had condensed and taken a solid form on the face of the land itself.

There were no tracks at all in the dry watercourse, not even those of wildlife. Ty wasn't surprised by the lack of animal signs. He had expected to find nothing. Wild animals had an instinctive abhorrence of small openings, of being trapped somewhere that lacked room to run or places to hide. What did surprise Ty was that Mad Jack had left no more trail than if he had flown from the secret valley.

In fact, Ty found it impossible to believe that Mad Jack had gone through the cleft at all.

The passage itself was familiar to Ty. He had made it a point to familiarize himself with the slit that was the difference between the valley being a haven for them or a trap with no exit. Yet each time he walked the cleft he felt a deepening admiration for Janna, who had found and used a passage whose secret had been lost to the Indians for hundreds of years, perhaps even thousands. He doubted that any Indian had used the cleft at all since the coming of the horse several hundred years before.

Or perhaps the valley hadn't been lost by the Indians but simply avoided as a spirit place where mortal men shouldn't go, a place of the People who Came Before. Within the twilight confines of the slot canyon, it would be very easy to imagine malevolent spirits waiting in ambush for anything foolish enough to stray inside the black stone jaws.

The narrowest point of the cleft was not at the entrance to the valley but about a third of the way toward the open land beyond. At the stricture, both canyon walls were of a dense, black, fine-grained stone that cracked in long parallel columns. Water had polished the stone into a slick, shiny mass that, with the addition of a layer of fine mud, was almost as slippery as ice. Unlike Mad Jack, Janna had never found a way to avoid leaving tracks over that segment of the slot, which was why she had always taken on the passage just before or just after a rain, when any tracks she left would be washed completely away by the runoff stream.

That was another thing Ty admired. Few people who knew

the country would have had the courage to test the stone slit when clouds massed over the plateau and water was running down its sides in rushing veils. Fewer people still would have had the skill to read the land and weather correctly enough to survive negotiating the narrow slot. He wondered how many times Janna had waited, eyeing the muddy rush of water and calculating her best chance to pass through without leaving a sign or being drowned.

Warily Ty looked up the uneven walls where debris lodged twenty or thirty feet higher than his head. The thought of the risk Janna had taken to get him into the hidden valley made sweat start on his body. He remembered the black clouds, the pelting rain…and nothing more. He only knew that she had taken an enormous risk while getting him to a safe place to heal. In fact, she had taken one hell of a risk for him, period, since the first moment she had begun wiping out his trail so that Cascabel would lose his prey. If the renegade ever found out how his prisoner had truly escaped, Janna's life wouldn't be worth a handful of cold spit.

Ty half walked, half slid over the cleft's slick bottom. Once he was past the place where black walls pinched in, the cleft opened out slightly again. He moved quickly, leaving very little trace of his passage. There was no other sign of life within the steep canyon. When the gloom brightened, announcing the end of the slot, Ty went to the deepest area of shadow and eased forward until he could look over the fan of debris that washed down from the plateau's edge, creating a sloping skirt that led to the flatlands beyond.

For several minutes Ty remained motionless, studying the landscape for any sign of movement. There was no motion but the ragged race of cloud shadows over the earth. No bird was startled into flight. No raven scolded an intruder in hoarse tones. No shape of man or horse separated from cover to ghost over the land. If there were anyone about, he was even better hidden than Ty.

After ten minutes Ty withdrew from the entrance to the slot and returned to Janna. She was waiting precisely where he had left her, for she knew the importance of keeping the secret of the slit canyon and the hidden valley beyond.

"All clear," Ty said, answering the question in Janna's eyes. "Nothing has been in or out since the last shower."

Even though Janna had expected nothing else, she couldn't conceal her relief. Without the secret valley she would have no place to hide, no sanctuary in which to live during the wild country's cold winters.

Ty saw Janna's relief, guessed at its source and had to restrain himself from telling her not to worry, she wasn't going to have to spend another winter hiding in the valley, she was leaving Indian country and that was that. But he said nothing, because she would have argued with him, and arguing against the inevitable was a waste of time. As far as he was concerned, it was inevitable that Janna would no longer live alone. No white woman should have to exist like a savage, fearful of every shadow and without even the company of other human beings when danger threatened.

Ty had decided that he would take Janna to Sweetwater or Hat Rock or Santa Fe or even all the way to Denver, if it came to that. It was the least he could do for the orphan girl who had saved his life.

To Ty's surprise, Janna slid down from Zebra and walked to the cleft. As always, the mare followed her.

"Aren't you going to ride?" he asked.

"Too dangerous. That narrow stretch must still be slick from the last rain."

"We rode in double that way."

"Someone had to keep you astride Zebra. We'll mount after the canyon widens again."

Ty didn't argue. No matter how important it might be not to leave human footprints, he had dreaded the thought of going over the slippery black rock while mounted bareback and double on an unbroken mustang.

In the end it was the very narrowness of the canyon that kept Ty from falling. He simply levered himself along by acting as though he were trying to push the two sides of the canyon farther apart with his hands. Janna, more accustomed to the tricky stretch, knew where there were handholds and niches to use in maintaining her balance. Zebra had the advantage of four feet—if one slipped, there were three to take its place.

"How did you manage on horseback?" Ty asked as he reached a wider point in the slit and Janna came alongside.

"There was no other choice."

He thought about that for a moment, then nodded slowly, understanding that that was how Janna had managed to survive out here on her own: she believed that there was no other choice.

But there was.

"With all your books, you could be a teacher," Ty said as he swung aboard Zebra once more and scraped his knee against the canyon wall in the process.

Janna grabbed his arm and swung up behind him. "Not enough kids except in towns."

"So?"

"I don't like towns. They seem to bring out the worst in people."

Ty opened his mouth to argue, realized that he agreed with Janna and felt trapped. "Not all the time," he muttered.

She shrugged. "Maybe I just bring out the worst in towns."

"Do you really plan on spending the rest of your life out here?" he demanded.

"Unless you keep your voice down, the rest of my life won't amount to more than a few hours," Janna said dryly. "These walls make a dropped pin echo like a landslide."

Ty turned around and glared at her but said nothing more, except for a muffled word or two when his legs scraped against narrow points in the cleft. Janna's slender legs were in no such danger, and in any case were enveloped by protective folds of cloth. Even so, Ty had an acute appreciation of the warm flesh beneath the folds, especially when she rubbed against him as she adjusted to Zebra's motions.

Cautiously Ty urged Zebra out of the cleft, keeping to shadows and high brush wherever possible, trying to break up the telltale silhouette of horse and rider. They had gone no more than a mile when they cut across tracks left by a group of unshod ponies. The horses had moved in a bunch, not stopping to graze or to drink from the few puddles that remained after the previous thunderstorm. From the distance between sets of prints, Janna guessed that the horses had been cantering.

"That's Cascabel's horse," Janna said in a low voice.

She pointed to a set of larger hoofprints that had been all but obliterated by the rest of the group. Though the horse had once been shod, it had no shoes any longer. All that remained were vague traces of nail holes around the rim of the un-trimmed hooves.

"He stole two Kentucky horses from an officer at the fort over by Split-rock Springs," she continued. "One of the horses used to be the fastest horse in Utah Territory."

"Used to be? What happened?"

"Cascabel ran it to death trying to catch Lucifer. He takes better care of the second horse. It won't last much longer, though. It's a paddock horse, bred for grooming and grain. All it has out here is grass and a big renegade with a whip."

"Yeah, and that big renegade is too damn close for comfort."

Janna chewed silently on her lip for a moment before agreeing. "Yes. This is only the third time I've found his tracks on the east side of Black Plateau. I wonder what happened to make him come this far. The ranches he usually raids are in the opposite direction."

"I'll bet the soldiers are closing in. They have a real mission where Cascabel is concerned. They're going to see him hang or know the reason why."

She closed her eyes and shook her head, trying to throw off the uneasy feeling that had been growing in her day by day since the beginning of the summer, when she had discovered that Cascabel had been forced to move his camp. He had chosen to make his new camp on the Raven Creek watershed, a place that was perilously close to Mustang Canyon. Whether Black Hawk had driven Cascabel south, or the soldiers had, or Lucifer had lured him to the red buttes and high plateau and brooding Fire Mountains, it didn't matter. Janna knew that she couldn't remain hidden for long once so many eyes started scrutinizing every shadow.

Yet she couldn't leave, either. She had no place to go. A woman alone among men was the subject of snickers and speculation and blunt offers of sex in exchange for money or safety. The closest thing she had to a home was the wild land itself. She couldn't bear to lose it and her freedom in the same blow.

Unfortunately, it was becoming clear that she had no other choice.

Silently Janna guided Zebra in a circuitous route to Sweetwater. When Ty realized where they were going, he turned questioningly to her.

"Hat Rock is closer," he said.

"I know. I went to Sweetwater last time."

"So?"

"So Joe Troon won't be looking for me there."

"What?"

"I never go to the same town or ranch twice in a row," Janna explained. "Except for the hidden valley, I never go to the same places at the same time of year or in the same order. If you don't have a pattern, no one can guess where you're going to be and lay a trap for you."

Ty sensed the apprehension behind Janna's calm words. "Did this Troon character try to trap you?"

"Once or twice."

"Why?"

"Mad Jack's mine, Lucifer or..." Janna's voice died as she remembered overhearing Troon bragging about how he would break her in right and then sell her south to a Mexican whorehouse after she led him to Lucifer and Mad Jack's gold mine. She cleared her throat. "I didn't wait around to find out."

The surge of anger and adrenaline that went through Ty's body surprised him, but it didn't keep him from demanding roughly, "Did he lay a hand on you?"

"He never even saw me that time," Janna said evasively. "I hung back in the brush and listened long enough to figure out how he had found me, and then I swore never to be predictable again. I haven't been, either.''

"You said you follow Lucifer's bunch in the summertime."

"Yes."

"Then you're predictable. Every mustanger knows Lucifer's territory. All any man would have to do is to lie in wait at the water holes his herd uses. Lucifer is fast enough to get away from that kind of ambush. You aren't.''

"Cascabel is keeping the mustangers away."

"He didn't keep me away. Nothing will. I'm going to have that stud no matter what. I need him too badly to let a few renegades get in my way.''

"You plan to use Lucifer to buy your silken lady?"

"Yes," Ty said, his voice flat, inflexible. "The war took everything but my life and my dreams. I'll have that silken lady or die trying.''

Janna held herself tightly, trying not to flinch against the pain she felt.

"Then you understand," she said huskily.

"What?"

"You understand why I can't live in a town as a kitchen maid or a saloon girl. I have my own dream.''

There was a surprised silence while Ty digested the idea that the ragged waif had a goal beyond simple survival. "What is it?''

Shaking her head, eyes tightly closed, Janna said nothing. There was no point in telling Ty that she had begun to dream of having him turn to her and discover within her the silken lady he sought. It was a dream that would never come true and she was practical enough to know it.

But it was the most compelling dream Janna had ever had. She could no more turn away from it than she could transform herself into the lady of Ty's dreams.

Chapter Twelve

A mile outside of town, Ty shifted his weight and spoke softly to the mare. Zebra stopped obediently no more than two feet from a clump of boulders and brush.

"Get down," Ty said, handing Janna the big knife she had given him. "I'll be back as quick as I can."

"I'm going with you."

"No."

"But—"

"No!" Hearing the roughness in his own voice, Ty winced. "Janna, it isn't safe. If you're seen with me on a mustang—"

"We'll tell them you tamed her," Janna interrupted quickly.

"They'd have to be dumb as a stump to believe that," he retorted. "I'm going to have enough trouble making them believe I survived without help as it is. You know damn good and well if Cascabel finds out you were responsible for making him the laughingstock of the Utah Territory, he'll come after you until he gets you and cooks you over a slow fire."

Without another word Janna slid down from Zebra. She vanished into concealment between one breath and the next. For a moment Ty couldn't believe that she had ever been with him at all. An odd feeling shot through him, loneliness and desire combined into a yearning that was like nothing he had ever known.

"Janna?" he called softly.

Nothing answered but branches stirring beneath a rain-bearing wind. The scent of moisture reminded Ty of the urgency of the situation. They had to be back at the hidden valley before the storm broke or they would spend a miserable night out in the open, unable even to have a fire to warm them for fear of giving away their presence.

Thunder rumbled in the distance, causing Zebra to throw up her head and snort. Ears pricked, nostrils flared, the horse sniffed the wind.

"Easy, girl," Ty murmured. "It's just the summer rains."

He slid from Zebra's back, landed lightly and pulled off his breechcloth. His foot wrappings came off next. After he poked the scraps of blanket into an opening between two boulders, he turned east and began working his way over the rocky surface of the land toward a wagon trail a half mile beyond. He was very careful not to leave any signs of his passage, for he had been into Sweetwater once before, riding Blackbird and armed with two pistols, a rifle and a shotgun. He had been glad for each weapon; the only thing sweet about the town was the name and the tiny spring that bubbled to the surface nearby, watering stock and men alike without regard to their individual natures.

As Ty walked toward town, he wished heartily for one of the new repeating carbines that loaded as fast as they fired. Even a pistol would have been nice. Two revolvers and extra cylinders loaded with bullets would have made him feel a lot better about going in among the canted shacks.

Though Janna seemed not to realize it, Sweetwater was an outlaw hangout, and the two ranches she bought supplies from had a reputation for branding "loose" cattle that was known from the Red River to Logan MacKenzie's ranch in Wyoming. Some of the Lazy A's and Circle G's cowhands were doubtless reasonably honest men who had been forced to make a living any way they could after the Civil War had ruined their farms and homes. Other cowhands on those ranches were men who would have been raiders in heaven itself, because they plain enjoyed riding roughshod over people weaker than themselves.

How the hell did Janna ever survive out here? Ty asked

himself for the hundredth time as he walked quietly into the collection of ramshackle, weathered shacks that constituted one of the few towns within several hundred miles.

No answer came back to Ty but the obvious one, the uncomfortable memory of women in a war-ravaged land, women selling themselves for bread or a blanket, women who in peacetime wouldn't have dreamed of letting a man touch them outside the boundaries of love and marriage.

Is that how you survived after your father died, Janna? Did you sell yourself until you had the skill and the strength to survive alone?

Again there was no answer but the obvious one. She had survived. The thought of Janna's soft body lying beneath rutting men both sickened and angered Ty; for a woman to sell herself like that in order to survive was simply another kind of rape.

In the past, Ty had surprised more than one woman caught within the ruins of war by giving her food or shelter or blankets and taking nothing in return. He would never forget one girl's combined look of shock, relief and gratitude when he had refused her thin, bruised body as payment for a plate of beans. She had eaten quickly and then had vanished into the night as though afraid he would change his mind and take her after all.

And when Ty had finally fought his way home, he had discovered that his sister, Cassie, hadn't been so fortunate in the strange men who had crossed her path. Taken by raiders, she had been a captive until she became too ill to service the men; then she had been abandoned to die. She would have, too, if Logan and Silver hadn't caught up with her and gentled her back into sanity and health.

Ty's grim thoughts were a match for the town that he finally reached. There were no men loitering in front of Sweetwater Mercantile when Ty walked by. There were no horses tied to broken railings. No dogs slept in sun-warmed dust. The first person Ty saw was a boy who was emptying slops out the saloon's back door. The boy took one look at Ty and ducked back inside. Instants later the door creaked open again. The bartender stood with a shotgun cradled in his thick hands. A single glance took in Ty's muscular, naked body covered with healing bruises.

"Well, you be big enough and the right color," the bartender said. "Maybe you be Tyrell MacKenzie."

Ty nodded slowly.

The bartender stepped aside. "Come on in. Name's Ned. A breed by the name of Blue Wolf was looking for you 'bout two weeks back."

When he heard Blue Wolf's name, Ty almost laughed aloud. "Wondered how long it would take him to catch up with me."

"Friend of yours?"

"Yeah."

"Good thing, too. From the look of that buck, he'd make a powerful bad enemy. He's damn near as big as Cascabel and white-man smart into the bargain. Talks English better than me."

"He's a dead shot, too."

Ned grunted, reached behind the door and pulled a ragged shirt off a nail. He threw the cloth to Ty. "Wrap up and sit down."

Within moments Ty had the shirt wrapped around his hips and between his legs in a semblance of a breechcloth. He sat down, enjoying the unfamiliar sensation of a chair after months on the trail. Ned went to a sooty corner of the small room and pulled a pot off a broken-legged stove. He wiped a spoon on his britches, stuck it into the pot and shoved it in front of Ty.

"Reckon you're hungry."

Ty wasn't, but admitting that would raise too many questions, so he dug into the cold beans and ate quickly, trying not to remember how much better Janna's food had been. Cleaner, too. Living in the camp with the hot springs had spoiled him. A bath every day, clean dishes, and clean company. It would take him a long time to get used to the smell of a sty like Ned's saloon.

"Thanks," Ty said, shoving away the empty pot.

"Smoke?"

Ty shook his head. "Gave it up the night I saw a man get killed lighting a pipe when he should have been holding still and looking out for enemies."

Ned grinned, revealing teeth about the color the beans had been. "Yep, war can be hard on a man. Worse 'n robbin' banks or rustlin'."

The oblique question about his past was ignored by Ty.

"Don't mean to jaw your arm off," Ned said quickly, "but it's been nothin' but me and Johnny for two weeks now. Rest of 'em went to the fort. Old Cascabel's got 'em pissin' their britches. Hear tell he killed two white men a week ago."

"I wouldn't know about that. I've been too busy hiding and healing. Did Blue Wolf say when he'd be back here?"

Ned opened a stone jug and thumped it onto the table. "Don't know as he's comin' back. I told him you'd been took by Cascabel. He said you wouldn't stay took. Left a poke of gold for you over to the fort. Said you'd be needful of it when you got shuck of Cascabel. From the look of you, he was right."

"Did he say where he was going?"

"He was meetin' up with your brothers north of here. Looking for gold." Ned grunted. "Probably'll find it, too, if'n Black Hawk don't lift their hair first."

"With Wolf on scout, no one will even know they're around." Ty paused, then added casually, "When my brothers come back here looking for me—and they will—tell them I headed for Mexico. I'm going to finish healing up in some *señorita*'s bed."

Ned's smile was as crooked as a dog's hind leg as he absorbed Ty's gentle message: Ty might be naked and alone, but if he were killed his brothers would come hunting for the killer. So Ned poured cloudy liquid from the jar into a dirty tin cup and put it in front of Ty.

"Drink up."

"If it's all the same, I'd rather have water," Ty said. "My daddy always told me not to mix liquor with an empty stomach or a knot on the head."

Ned chuckled, picked up the cup and drained it. His harshly expelled breath made Ty glad there wasn't an open flame nearby. Sure as hell, the alcohol on Ned's breath would have caught fire and burned down the saloon.

"Damn, but that's good 'shine," Ned said, wiping water from his eyes. "A man couldn't get from dawn to dusk without it."

Ty could have gotten from birth to death without moonshine, but he said nothing. He had known a lot like Ned, men for whom the savage bite of homemade liquor was the sole joy of life. With outward patience, Ty waited while Ned's hands stroked the cold curves of the stone jar, lifted it and shook it to gauge the amount of liquor left within.

"You say you and the boy are the only ones left in Sweetwater?" Ty asked after a few moments.

Ned poured another half cup of pale liquid, belched and sat down opposite Ty. Though it was daytime, the interior of the saloon was gloomy. If there had ever been glass windows in the slanting walls, the panes had long since been replaced by oiled paper.

"Yep. Just me and that useless whelp. He's so scared he's gonna run off first time I turn my back." Ned took another swig of liquor, shuddered deliciously and sighed. "And Joe Troon. That sidewinder ain't never far off. Used to keep a Mex gal stashed somewhere off in the rimrock to the north, but she run off with Cascabel's renegades. Ol' Troon's real lonely these days, less'n he caught that *bruja* again."

"What?"

"That red-haired gal the renegades call Sombra, cuz she leaves no more sign than a shadow. Lives with the mustangs, and she's a wild 'un just like them." Ned took another huge swallow, grimaced and sighed out the fumes. "Troon had her once a few years ago but she got away. Gals don't cotton much to Joe Troon. Mean as a spring bear, and that's gospel. Wish he'd kept her, though. I get right tired of squaws."

When Ty understood that the *bruja* under discussion was Janna, it was all he could do not to hurl himself over the table and hammer the half-drunk bartender into the floor.

"But now Troon's decided to make hisself rich off of that old black stud," Ned continued. "He took his rifle and went to Black Plateau. Gonna crease that stud bastard, break him and take his colts while every white man in the territory is too scared to butt in."

Ty grimaced. "Creasing is a chancy thing. A lot more horses are killed than caught that way."

"One mean stud more or less won't make no never mind in this world. If'n it was me, I'd kill the stud, grab the best colts and light a shuck clean out of the territory before the Army finds Cascabel and the whole shootin' match goes up in smoke."

Ty thought of Lucifer as he had last seen the stallion—ears pricked, neck arched, muscles gleaming and sliding beneath a shiny black hide. The thought of someone killing that much animal just to grab his colts made Ty both disgusted and angry. But he had no doubt that Troon would do just that, if he got to Lucifer first.

"Is the mercantile closed?" Ty asked, interrupting Ned's monologue.

"What? Oh, you mean the Preacher's store. Naw, he didn't close up when he went to the fort. Ain't no man would steal from him. Sooner steal from Satan hisself. Even the renegades leave the Preacher alone. Cunning as a coon and snake-mean into the bargain. Troon gave up on the red-haired gal after the Preacher told him to leave her be. See, she gave him a Bible once. So when you see her again, you tell her it's safe to come into Sweetwater. Troon won't bother her."

A cold breath of caution shivered over Ty's skin. The bartender was no more drunk than Ty was.

"Who?" Ty asked, scratching his beard.

"The red-haired gal."

"Don't know her. She live around here?"

Ned squinted at Ty with pale, watery eyes. "Nobody knows where she lives. 'Cept maybe you. She pulled your tail out of a mighty tight crack."

"Mister, the only crack my tail has been in lately was with Cascabel's renegades, and I got shuck of them by running my feet to the bone, hiding in brush, drinking rainwater and eating snakes. Not a one of them had red hair.''

Ned stared at Ty for a long time and then nodded slowly. ''If that's the way you want it, mister, that's the way it is.''

''Wanting has nothing to do with it,'' Ty drawled coolly, standing up. ''I'm telling you the way it was. Thanks for the beans. I'm going over to the Preacher's store. I'll leave a list of what I take. He can get his payment out of the gold Blue Wolf left at the fort.''

''I'll tell Preacher when I see him.''

''You do that.'' Ty started for the door, feeling an acute need for fresh air, then realized he wasn't through with Ned yet. ''I need to buy a horse.''

''The Circle G has right fine horseflesh. Best in the territory. Course, if'n a man was to ride one out of the territory, he might run into a cowpoke what lost a horse just like it.''

Ty smiled wryly as he got the message. ''I'll settle for a town horse.''

''Ain't none,'' Ned said succinctly. ''Took 'em all to the fort.''

''Where's the closest homestead that might have an animal to sell?''

''Ain't none left for a hundred miles, 'cept renegade camps and wherever that redheaded gal lives. But you don't know nothin' about her, so it don't help you none.''

Ty shrugged. ''I'll find a horse between here and Mexico. Thanks for the beans, Ned.''

The door shut behind Ty, but he still felt Ned's narrow, calculating eyes boring into his naked back. It made Ty's spine itch and his palms ache for the cool feel of an army rifle.

Janna didn't know it, but she wasn't coming back to Sweetwater again. Ever.

Chapter Thirteen

Janna awoke when a man rose up from the ground in front of her, blocking out the sun with his body. She was grabbing for her knife when Zebra snorted and the man turned and sunlight caught the emerald glint of his eyes.

Hardly recognizing Ty beneath his store-bought clothes, Janna could do no more than stare. The slate-gray shirt and hat, black bandanna, and black pants emphasized Ty's size and masculine grace. He looked as handsome as sin and twice as hard. His beard was shaved off, leaving his face clean but for a midnight slash of mustache that heightened the pronounced planes of his cheekbones and made his teeth gleam whitely. In that instant, with fright still vibrating in her body and her defenses awry, Janna's response to him was so intense that she could scarcely breathe.

"Ty?" she asked huskily. "Is that really you?"

"You better hope it is," Ty snapped. "What the hell were you doing asleep? It could have been Joe Troon who cut your trail rather than me. Or maybe you'd like to be kept by him again?"

Janna's heart was beating too rapidly for her to make sense out of Ty's words. "You scared the life out of me, sneaking up like that!"

"Sneaking up? Hell's bells, Janna, you expect Cascabel to march in here with a band playing 'Onward Christian Soldiers'?'' Ty demanded. "You should have been on guard and seen me coming half a mile away!"

"Zebra was on guard," Janna said, standing and wiping her palms on her baggy pants. "Yell at her. She must have recognized your smell and not made a fuss."

Ty looked over at the mustang. Zebra was cropping at wisps of dry grass, lifting her head to scent the wind, then relaxing once more for a few moments before sniffing the wind again.

"Scented me, huh?" Ty said, feeling his anger slide away as he realized that Janna had been well guarded after all. "Are you saying I need some more time in your hot spring?"

"Ask Zebra. Her nose is better than mine," Janna retorted, forcing herself to look away from the hard, handsome planes of Ty's face. She closed her eyes, braced her fists in the small of her back and knuckled the tight muscles. "Lordy, there was a root beneath me the size of my arm. No matter how I lay I couldn't avoid it."

Whatever Ty had been going to say was forgotten beneath the impact of the supple reach and sway of Janna's body while she worked out the kinks of lying in cover for several hours.

"Here," he said gruffly. "This will help."

Janna's eyes flew open when she felt Ty's strong hands knead down her spine to her hips and back up again, lingering at the curve of her waist, rubbing the muscles in the small of her back, then caressing her waist once more before probing at the bands of cloth that wrapped her rib cage beneath her shirt. When he discovered the knotted muscle in her shoulder, he pressed down firmly, smoothing away the knot, making her knees loosen with relief.

"Oh, that feels good," Janna said huskily, her voice catching with pure pleasure. "Yes, there. Ahhh… You're unraveling me like a snagged mitten."

With a low sigh that was almost a moan of pleasure, Janna let her head slowly drop back until it rested on Ty's chest. His hands hesitated as his heart slammed suddenly, sending blood rushing through his body, making him feel both heavy and powerful. Taking a discreet, deep breath, he resumed the leisurely, gentle massaging of Janna's back. Each murmur of her pleasure was like flames licking over him, tightening every muscle in his big body, flushing him with sensual heat.

The piñon-and-sunshine smell of Janna's hair intoxicated Ty. The curve of her neck above her clothes tantalized him. The sounds she made inflamed him. He wanted to bend over and taste the clean skin rising above her collar; then he wanted to peel her clothes away and taste soft skin that had never seen the sun. Yet she felt so fragile beneath his big hands, almost frail.

She's just a girl, Ty reminded himself harshly.

The memory of what Ned had said about Joe Troon and Janna went into Ty like a knife.

Poor little thing, Ty thought, moving his hands up to her shoulders and rubbing very gently before he released her with a reluctance he couldn't disguise. *She's known little of kindness from men. I can't take advantage of her just because she comes undone at a gentle touch.*

Janna turned her head, brushing her lips lightly over Ty's fingers as they moved away from her shoulder.

"Thank you," she murmured, her eyes closed and her voice a sigh of pleasure. "That felt as good as sunlight on a cold day."

Head still turned toward Ty, Janna opened her eyes—and felt her breath wedge tightly in her throat. He was so close, his eyes a glittering green that was both beautiful and savage. Tiny shards of black acted to deepen and define the vivid green surrounding the pupils. The dark gleam at the center of his eyes was repeated in the dense midnight of his eyelashes. His pulse beat full and strong at his temple and his lips were a flat line, as though he were angry or in pain.

"Ty? Did...did everything go all right in Sweetwater?"

Janna's question sounded very far away to Ty. Slowly he realized that he was staring into the depths of her rain-clear eyes while his fingertips traced and retraced the soft curve of her cheek.

"You're never going back there, Janna. That damned greasy bartender..." Ty's voice died. He could think of no delicate way to put into words what he had seen in Ned's eyes when he talked about women.

"Ned?" Janna asked, shrugging. "I stay out of his way. I'm careful never to be in town more than a few minutes at a time. Even if someone sees me, the Preacher makes sure I'm left alone."

"The Preacher pulled up stakes and went to the fort along with everybody else except Ned. Renegades from all over the territory are drifting down to Black Plateau to join Cascabel."

She frowned. "Why would Ned stay in town? Nothing in his dingy old shack is worth dying for."

"Before Cascabel caught me, I spent some time in Hat Rock. The folks there think Ned is the one selling guns to the Indians. If that's true, he wouldn't be too worried about getting his hair cut by a renegade barber."

"Pity," she said. "He could use a trim."

Ty smiled and Janna's stomach did a little dip and curtsy. She looked away hastily.

"Guess we'd better get back to Black Plateau," she said, clearing her throat. "It will be—"

"You're going to the fort," Ty interrupted.

"What?"

"It's too dangerous for a woman out here. On the way in to Sweetwater I cut the trail of three different groups of Indians. Two or three braves to a group. No sign of women or kids."

"Utes?"

Ty shrugged. "If they are, they're renegades. Black Hawk is trying to keep a short rein on his young warriors."

"Where were the tracks headed?"

"Sweetwater," Ty said succinctly. "I'll bet they bought rifles from Ned and then hit the trail for Cascabel's new camp."

Frowning, Janna looked at the sky over toward Black Plateau. The thunderheads were a solid, blue-black mass that trailed dark curtains of rain. The Fire Mountains had been buried in storm clouds when Ty left for town, which meant that several hours of rain had fallen on top of Black Plateau.

The finger canyons would be filling with runoff before too long.

"Don't even think about it," Ty said, following Janna's glance. "The crack leading to your camp is probably up to a horse's fetlocks by now. Even if Zebra galloped all the way back, the water would be hock-high for sure. Chest-high, more than likely. But it wouldn't matter."

"It wouldn't?" Janna asked, surprised.

"Hell, no. We'd be dead before we got there, picked off by renegades and staked out for the ants to eat."

"But—"

"Dammit, Janna, don't you see? Cascabel must have passed the word that he's getting ready for one last push. Every renegade Indian west of the Mississippi is jumping reservation, stealing a horse and riding hard for Black Plateau. The only safe place for you is at the fort."

"For me?" she questioned.

Ty nodded tightly.

"What about you?" she asked.

"I'm going after Lucifer."

"What makes you think Cascabel won't get you?"

"If he does, that's my problem."

"Then we agree."

"We do?" asked Ty, surprised.

"We do. We'd better get going. I know a good place to camp on the northeast slope of the plateau."

"The fort is to the west of the plateau. Won't you be taking us the long way around?"

"I'm not going to the fort."

"The hell you aren't."

"That wasn't our agreement," Janna said quickly.

"What?"

"Our agreement was that it's your problem if Cascabel gets you, correct?"

"Yes."

"Then it follows that it's my problem if Cascabel gets me."

Ty opened his mouth, closed it, grabbed Janna in his powerful hands and lifted her until she was at eye level with him.

"You," he said coldly, "are going to the fort if I have to tie you and carry you belly down over my saddle."

"You don't have a saddle."

"Janna—"

"No," she interrupted. "You can tie me up and haul me from one end of the territory to the other, but the second you turn your back or take off the ropes I'll be gone to Black Plateau."

Ty looked into Janna's unflinching gray eyes and knew that she meant every word. Her body might have been slender but her will was fully the equal of his own.

Ty looked from Janna's wide gray eyes to her lips flushed with heat and life. He could think of many, many things he would like to do at that moment, but none would be quite as sweet as sliding his tongue into her mouth until he could taste nothing but her, feel nothing but her, know nothing but her.

Yet he shouldn't even touch her. Even if she didn't have the sense to realize it, she was a nearly helpless girl whose life was at risk every hour she spent running free with her mustangs.

"What am I going to do with you?" he asked huskily.

"Same thing I'm going to do with you," she retorted.

Ty smiled slowly. "What are you going to do with me?" he asked, his voice deep, his mouth frankly sensual.

"Hunt L-Lucifer," Janna said, stammering slightly, wondering what had given Ty's green eyes their sudden heat and intensity.

"I thought you didn't want to help anyone catch Lucifer."

"I said 'hunt,' not 'catch.'"

"Little one, what I hunt, I catch."

Janna tried to breathe, couldn't, and tried again. "Ty..." she said, her voice ragged.

The word sounded more like a sigh than a name. She licked her lips and prepared to try again.

Ty's hands tightened almost painfully around Janna's rib cage as he watched the pink tip of her tongue appear and disappear, leaving behind lips that were moist, soft and inviting. Knowing he shouldn't, unable to help himself, he slowly brought Janna closer to his own mouth.

Just beyond the shelter of the brush, Zebra threw up her head and pricked her ears, staring upwind. Her nostrils flared, fluttered and flared again. Abruptly her ears flattened to her head.

Ty dropped to the ground, taking Janna with him.

Moments later, no more than two hundred feet away, a group of four Indian warriors rode out of a shallow ravine.

Chapter Fourteen

Stomach on the hard, uneven ground, Janna lay wedged between a boulder on one side and Ty's body on the other. Very slowly she turned her head until she could see beneath Ty's chin. He had a pistol in his left hand and was easing his right hand toward another boulder, where he had propped his new carbine before he woke her up. From the corner of her eye she saw his long fingers wrap around the stock of the weapon. Without making a sound he lifted the carbine and slowly, slowly eased it into firing position at his shoulder.

Screened by brush and rocks, Janna and Ty watched the warriors cross a small rise and angle back toward the cover of another dry wash. For long minutes after the Indians vanished, Ty lay unmoving. The weight of his body ensured that Janna stayed motionless, as well. Not until Zebra snorted, rubbed her muzzle against her knee and then resumed grazing did Ty release Janna. Even so, when he spoke to her, he laid his lips against her ear, and his voice was a mere thread of sound.

"Ready to go to the fort now?"

Janna turned until she could see his eyes, so close they all but filled her world.

"No," she said distinctly.

"You're a fool, Janna Wayland."

"Then so are you."

"I'm a man."

"You support my argument," she shot back in a fierce whisper.

Thunder broke and rumbled over the land.

"We should go as far as we can before the storm breaks," Ty said. "That way our tracks will be washed away before any wandering renegades can find us." He came to his feet, pulling Janna after him. "Get on Zebra. I'll ride behind you."

Janna swung up on the mare and looked back at Ty. He was shrugging on a big, heavy backpack stuffed with clothes, bedding and supplies. The carbine was strapped to the back of the pack, muzzle down, riding in what would have been a saddle holster if Ty had had a saddle; but he didn't. He was his own pack mule for the moment.

Ty handed Janna an oilskin slicker, jerked his new hat into place and swung up behind her, heavy backpack and all.

Fat, cold drops of rain began to fall.

"Put on the slicker," he said.

"What about you?"

"Put on the damned slicker!"

Janna shook out the drab, canvas-colored cloth, saw that it was no more than a tarpaulin with a slit for a man's head, and promptly widened the slit with her knife.

"What are you doing?" Ty demanded.

"Making it big enough for two. Hang on to your hat."

Janna turned around enough to pull the slicker over Ty's head. Facing forward again, she put her own head through the slit and tucked flapping folds beneath her legs. Ty's motions told her that he was doing the same thing, although while he did it, he was muttering a lot of words she preferred not to overhear.

When Janna settled into place to ride, she realized that she was sitting quite close to Ty. In fact, she couldn't have been sitting closer unless she had been on his lap rather than surrounded by it. She felt the rub of his thighs along hers, the small movements of his hips and the supple swaying of his torso as he adjusted his body to Zebra's stride. Janna was doing the same—rocking slightly, rubbing gently, swaying, cocooned in oilcloth and wrapped in warmth.

Once she got used to the novelty of being so close to Ty, she realized that it was deliciously warm and comfortable, except for the shivery sensations that uncurled along her nerve endings at odd moments when his hands brushed her thighs or his breath rushed over her neck. And even those unexpected quivers of heat within her body were—intriguing. With an unconscious sound of pleasure, she settled more deeply into the warmth and muscular resilience of Ty's body.

Ty set his teeth until his jaw ached, barely resisting the impulse to rip off the oilcloth and free himself from the innocent, incendiary rock and sway of Janna's body. The wind gusted, bringing cold splashes of sensation that only made the shared intimacy of the oilcloth more vivid.

After a time it began to rain in earnest, as though the descending sun had somehow freed the water drops from their cloud prisons. The oilcloth turned away much of the rain, but not all. Although it became increasingly damp beneath the poncho, neither Janna nor Ty suggested stopping, for there was no cover nearby worthy of mention. When lightning bolts became closer and more frequent, Janna said something that Ty couldn't catch. He bent forward, bringing his mouth against her ear.

"What?"

She turned toward him, so close that her warm breath washed over his lips. "Hang on."

The belling of thunder drowned out Ty's response, which was just as well. Instinctively his legs clamped around Zebra's barrel as the mare went from a walk to a gallop. The rhythmic rocking motion intensified the friction of Janna's body rubbing against Ty's. The resulting heat was a bittersweet pain. Each time the mare climbed a small rise, Janna's buttocks pressed more snugly into his lap, stroking his aroused flesh. Each time the mare descended, he slid harder against Janna, their bodies separated by only a few folds of cloth, until he wanted nothing more than to imprison her hips in his hands and move with her until he burst.

"How much farther?" asked Ty through gritted teeth.

"Two miles."

Ty wondered if he would survive. He couldn't decide if the stimulation would have been easier to bear at half the pace and twice the time of suffering, or if twice the stimulation and half the time was indeed the easier course.

Oblivious to Ty's masculine discomfort, Janna guided Zebra into what looked like a simple thickening of brush. It turned out to be a narrow trail snaking up the base of a nameless mesa. Soon Ty had to reach around Janna and grab the mare's mane with both hands to keep his slippery seat.

Partway up the mesa, the trail ended in a shallow overhang of red rock stained with streaks of very dark brown. There was no way out and no other trail but the one they had just come up. Obviously this was the shelter Janna had chosen.

Ty didn't wait for an invitation to dismount. He ducked out of the shared slicker and slid from Zebra's back, barely biting off a savage word when the shock of landing jolted through his aroused body. He eyed the narrow shelter with a mixture of relief and anger. There was just enough room for the mustang and two people to stay reasonably dry—if the mustang weren't restless and the two people occupied the same space at the same time.

Bitterly Ty told himself that at least staying warm without a fire wouldn't be a problem. All he had to do was look at Janna, or even think about looking at her, and his new pants fit way too tightly. He told himself that it was because the pants were too small, and he knew he lied. He could count his heartbeats in the hard flesh that had risen between his legs, and every beat made him want to draw up in pain.

What the hell is the matter with me? he asked himself savagely. *I've never gotten this hot over a full-grown woman wearing silk and perfume. Why am I getting in a lather over a ragged little waif with no more curves than a fence rail?*

The only answer that came to Ty was the memory of Janna's uninhibited response when he had rubbed her back. If such an impersonal touch made her breath shiver and break, what would happen if he touched her the way he wanted to, no holds barred, nothing between them but the sensual heat of their bodies?

Biting back a curse, Ty fought to subdue the demands of his own flesh. He forced himself to ignore the sexual urgency that grew greater with each of his rapid heartbeats, reminding him that he was very much a man and that Janna, despite her ragged men's clothes and slender body, was way too much woman for his comfort.

Without a word to Janna, Ty began exploring the dimensions of the ledge that would be his prison for the night. From the corner of her eyes, Janna watched Ty prowl while she dismounted and checked Zebra's hooves for stones. There were none. She caressed the mare's curious, nudging nose for a few minutes, tugging from time to time on the horse's soft lips in a gentle kind of teasing that Zebra enjoyed as much as Janna did.

"Go find dinner," Janna said finally, pushing Zebra's velvet muzzle away.

Apparently the mare had grazed enough while waiting for Ty to return. She showed no inclination to go back down the steep trail to look for food.

"Then get out of the way," Janna said, exasperated.

Zebra looked at her.

Janna laced her fingers in the mare's mane and tugged. Obediently Zebra moved forward, allowing herself to be led to the opposite end of the ledge, where it angled down to the nearly invisible trail.

"It's all yours, girl."

Thunder rumbled heavily, making the ground quiver. Zebra flicked her ears and sighed.

"Have you ever hobbled her?" Ty asked, eyeing the narrow space they all had to share.

Janna shook her head.

"Hope to hell she doesn't walk in her sleep," he muttered, unloading his backpack. The burden hit the ground with a *thump* that spoke eloquently of weight.

"We spent three days up here in the spring, when Cascabel was trying to catch Lucifer," Janna said. "Zebra never stepped on me once. I think she has me confused with a foal. When I lie down to sleep, she'll move off to graze, but she always keeps her eye on the place where I'm sleeping. If anything happens, she gives me a warning.''

"Are all your mustangs like that?"

She shook her head again. "No, just Zebra. Most of the time she really likes my company."

"Most of the time?"

"When she's in season, she stays close to Lucifer and I stay away."

Ty glanced over at Zebra. "Is she in season now?"

"It's early. But if she isn't pregnant by winter, it won't be Lucifer's fault," Janna said dryly.

Ty's smile gleamed for an instant and he drawled, "I'm sure Lucifer takes good care of his mares. I'm surprised he lets her wander, though."

"He's too busy running from men and driving off other stallions to worry about a stubborn bunch quitter. Besides, he's figured out that Zebra always comes back."

"How long have you been following Lucifer's bunch?"

"Since Pa died."

"Has Lucifer always kept to the same territory?"

"It's bigger than it was in the beginning, but otherwise Lucifer is like all wild animals. He sticks to what he knows is safe unless he's forced to change. When that happens, he goes into hiding with just a few of his wildest mares."

"Do you know where he goes?"

Janna gave Ty an unhappy look and said nothing. He knew that she was protecting the big stud's secrets. He didn't blame her, but he intended to have those secrets just the same.

"You know Joe Troon," Ty said. "How good a shot is he?"

The change of subject surprised Janna. "Pretty good, unless he's been drinking. Then he's only fair."

"Is he a good tracker?"

"Not as good as you or me."

"You're sure?"

"Once he spent a whole afternoon looking for me, and I was only fifteen feet away most of the time."

Ty closed his eyes against the sudden rush of adrenaline

that came when he thought of Janna alone, hiding in the brush, and a man like Troon searching for her with tight britches and pure lust in his blood.

"Can Troon get within rifle range of Lucifer?"

Janna froze. "What are you saying?"

"Ned told me that Troon took his rifle and went hunting. He's going to crease Lucifer. Unless Troon is a damn fine shot, he'll end up killing Lucifer by mistake."

A shudder ran through Janna's clenched body. Her greatest fear had been that some greedy mustanger would give up trying to catch the elusive stallion and simply kill him instead, thereby making the job of capturing the herd much easier.

"If Troon catches the mustangs in one of the pocket canyons, he could shoot from the cliffs above. But Lucifer's been chased so much lately that he's stayed away from the east side of Black Plateau. He's pushed north and west, into the slick rock country that only the Indians know."

"Will he stay there?"

Janna wanted to say yes, but she knew Lucifer too well. He had been driven from his preferred range in the past; he had always returned to Black Plateau, often with new mares he had run off from ranches or other wild herds. The stone canyons, year-round seeps and untrammeled space of the land spreading out from the plateau seemed to have an indelible allure for the big stallion. Year after year he returned, no matter how hard man chased him. But this time he would be chased by bullets that even his strong legs couldn't outrun.

The thought was unbearable to Janna. There was only one way she might be able to prevent Lucifer's death—by betraying him to a man who wouldn't use a gun.

Janna looked up into Ty's steady green glance and prayed that she was making the right decision.

"The best grazing and water for a hundred miles in any direction is around Black Plateau," she said, her mouth dry. "I know every seep, every bit of cover, every place where grass grows lush and thick. I'll take you to each secret place until we find Lucifer, but first you have to promise me one thing."

The unhappiness and determination in Janna's face made Ty wish for a moment that he had never heard of the big black stallion. But he had heard of Lucifer, and so had every other man from the Rio Grande to the Snake River. The stallion's time as a free-ranging mustang was rapidly coming to an end, and Janna knew it as well as Ty did. That was why she was blinking back tears and trying to speak.

"I'll be as gentle as possible with him," Ty said in a low voice, taking Janna's hand between his own. "I don't want to break Lucifer's spirit. I just want to breed him with some fine mares. I'll take him to Logan's ranch in Wyoming and let him run with the remuda while I build my own ranch. For Lucifer, it will be almost as good as running free down here. He'll be safe, Janna. No man will come after him with a rifle or a whip.

"And if he can't accept capture," Ty continued, stroking Janna's hand with his fingertips, "I'll turn Lucifer loose myself. I'd rather that he die free than live in a cage with eyes as dull as stones. Is that what you wanted me to promise?"

She drew a shaking breath. "Thank you, but I already knew those things about you or I'd never have spoken in the first place and offered to help you."

"Then is it money you want? I don't have much, but I'll be glad to—"

"No," she interrupted swiftly. "I'd never take money for Lucifer. I want you to promise that you'll let me try to gentle him first. I couldn't bear to see him brought down by a rope and broken by force."

Ty thought of the stallion's raw power and his hard, flashing hooves. "No. It's much too dangerous."

For a long moment Janna looked at Ty's face. The dying rays of the sun revealed a determination as great as her own. Without a word she eased her hand from his grasp, tossed the rain poncho aside and went about smoothing out a place to sleep for the night. As she worked Ty watched her in silence, wondering what she was thinking.

Finally the lightning barrage ended, leaving only a hard, steady rain. Ty looked over at Janna, who was half-reclining against the stone wall. In the darkness he couldn't be sure whether she was asleep. He thought she was.

"Janna?" he called softly.

No answer came.

Ty pulled on the rain poncho and walked from the protection of the ledge. If he had been camping with one of his brothers, he wouldn't have gone more than ten feet before relieving himself. As it was, he went considerably farther.

When he came back Janna was gone.

Chapter Fifteen

The cold rain made Janna shiver and long for the bedroll she had left in her winter camp, but no matter how much it rained, she didn't stop to find shelter from the downpour. As long as it rained her tracks would be washed out. Besides, she was less than three miles from one of her Black Plateau caches. By morning she would be warm and dry and sleeping in a place no man would ever find.

Not even Ty MacKenzie.

When the clouds finally dissolved into streamers of mist buffeted by a playful wind, Janna was beginning to wish she hadn't left Zebra behind. But she hadn't been able to bring herself to leave Ty afoot in a land teeming with Indian renegades. Zebra would at least take him as far as the thousand hidden canyons and secret springs of Black Plateau before she trotted off to look for Lucifer's herd once more.

And Janna had no doubt that it would be toward Black Plateau that Ty headed, rather than toward the safety of the fort. He wouldn't leave the territory until he had what he had come for—Lucifer.

The cold light of a new moon gave small illumination and less comfort to Janna as she walked steadily toward the dark bulk of the plateau, which rose from the land until it shut out the stars along the horizon. When she could see the faint notch she called Wind Gap, she turned west. Alternately running and walking, she came closer to the place that was as much a home as she had ever had.

In the darkness before dawn, it took Janna three tries to find the mound of broken boulders where she had stashed a spare canteen, blanket, knife and matches. The blanket was mouse chewed and musty but dry. She wrapped it around her and filled her canteen from a hole that had been worn in solid stone, creating a bowl that held rainwater after a storm.

Canteen and knife on her hip, dry matches in her shirt pocket, Janna climbed farther up the canyon until she came to a place where water from runoff streams had long ago worn out a room-size hole in the canyon wall. Water no longer reached the hollow; even in the highest flood it remained safe and dry. By the time she scrambled up the last steep pitch of rock to the east-facing hollow, Janna was trembling with hunger, cold and exhaustion.

Because the wind was from the north, only the hardest gusts reached her. She thought longingly of the hot spring in her winter camp, and of sunlight and of beds fragrant with piñon. Then she thought of the warmth of Ty's big body, and the sweet friction of his chest against her back, his thighs against her thighs, his arms like warm steel around her as he hung on to Zebra's long mane.

The curious, fluttering warmth returned to the pit of Janna's stomach, making her shiver with something more than cold. She remembered Ty's strength, the feel of his flexed muscle when he had lifted her and she had balanced herself by hanging on to his arms. The memory made her palms tingle as though she had been rubbing them along his sleeves. She thought of the strained, intent look on his face when he had bent down to her in the thicket where he had startled her from a deep sleep; and she wondered what would have happened if Zebra hadn't scented the renegades on the wind, ending the hushed expectancy of the moment.

After a time Janna finally fell asleep. Her dreams were as restless as the wind.

* * *

Ty slept until the wind swept the sky free of clouds, allow-ing the moon's narrow silver smile to illuminate the land.

"How about it, girl?" Ty said very softly. "You afraid of the dark?"

Zebra tugged impatiently against the hand restraining her nose. She wanted to be free to go down the trail.

"Yeah, that's what I thought. Which will you go after, Janna or that big black stud?"

Zebra snorted.

"Well, I'll tell you, girl," Ty said, swinging onto the mare's warm back, "I hope it's Janna. When I find her, I'm going to…"

Ty's voice faded. He didn't know what he was going to do when he found Janna. His dreams had left him restive and aroused, and as surly as a bear with a broken tooth. He was furious that Janna had slipped out into the stormy night with-out so much as a makeshift poncho to turn away the rain. No matter how many times he told himself that she had earned whatever her stubbornness brought her—or that she was ob-viously able to take care of herself in any case—the thought of her being wet and cold and hungry haunted him.

"Hell, why didn't she at least ride you?" muttered Ty to the horse. "Did she figure your tracks wouldn't wash out well enough? Or did she figure you would run off and I'd follow and miss her tracks completely?"

Zebra didn't even pause at the sound of her rider's muttered questions. She picked her way down the slope with the swift, clean poise that only a mustang could achieve over the rugged land.

Ty didn't bother trying to guide Zebra. He didn't know where he was going. Besides, in the dark the mare's senses were much more acute than his own. His only advantage over the mustang was his brain.

Some advantage, Ty told himself sardonically. *I can't even outwit a slip of a girl.*

The thought didn't improve his disposition. Nor did the fact that every time he closed his eyes, he saw the utter stillness of Janna's face when he had refused to promise that she would be the one to capture Lucifer.

Hellfire and damnation, Ty seethed silently. *What kind of a man does she think I am to let her risk her scrawny little ass fighting that stud?*

A vivid memory of Janna's body condensed in Ty's mind, reminding him that her bottom wasn't scrawny at all. It had been smooth and resilient beneath his hands when he had pulled her from the horse. Her hips had curved enticingly below her slender waist, curves that sheltered feminine secrets, curves that invited a man's hands to follow them, then his mouth, his lips, his tongue....

Ty shifted to relieve the pressure on his burgeoning, hardening flesh. He ached with every heartbeat, an ache that had become all too familiar since his mind had discovered what his body had known all along: Janna was a woman, not a boy.

Did she know how much I wanted her? Is that why she ran out into the storm?

Uneasiness flattened Ty's mouth into a hard line. Janna had saved his life, risking her own in the process. The thought that he, however unintentionally, had driven her away from the protection he could offer in this troubled land made him disgusted with himself and his unruly body.

Ty's reaction to Janna baffled him. He had never pursued women in the past; he had never had to. They came to him like moths to a naked flame. He took what they offered, gave them pleasure in return and avoided virgins because he was determined not to marry until he could have a fine silk lady for a wife. He had made no secret of his intention to remain free, but the women who came to him either hadn't believed him or hadn't cared.

But none of them ran from me, by God. Hell, often as not I was running from them!

The cold wind swirled down from Black Plateau's rumpled heights, reminding Ty of how miserable Janna must be—on foot, no real jacket and probably soaking wet, as well. He glared out at the pale rose dawn as though it were responsible for all that had gone wrong since he had been within moments of catching the big black stud, only to find himself caught by Cascabel instead.

The dawn sky passed from pale pink to a pale, rain-scrubbed blue. There was little real warmth in the early-morning sun, but as Zebra trotted toward the crest of a long rise, the light was strong enough to allow Ty to find out where he was. He halted Zebra just below the top of the rise, dug a new spyglass out of his backpack and looked out over his trail. Nothing moved behind him but a few ravens flying blackly through the hushed air.

Ty shifted position, looking to the right and the left. It was the same everywhere he could see. Nothing moving. He couldn't have been more alone if he had been the first man on earth.

Zebra snorted and shifted her weight, telling Ty that she wanted to be on her way.

''Easy girl. Let me look around.''

No matter where Ty looked, the countryside was daunting. It was also beautiful to anyone who appreciated the naked form of mountains and mesas, stone pinnacles and steep canyons, long crests and ridges of rocks devoid of gentle greenery. The plants that existed were spread out over the rugged countryside so thinly that the stone substructure of the land was visible in many places. Against the deepening blue of the sky, rock ridges and cliffs and gorges gleamed in every color from white through pink to rusty red and black. On the lower slopes juniper stood out like deep green flames burning at random on the fantastic rock formations.

The only familiar-looking part of the landscape to someone who hadn't been born west of the Mississippi was the pile of stone known as Black Plateau; from a distance, it rather resembled a ruined mountain. Other than that, the stark combination of sheer red or white cliffs and rumpled rivers of black lava were like nothing Ty had ever seen. He could still remember the excitement and visceral sense of danger that the land had called forth from him at first look. Harsh, beautiful, beguiling in its secrets and its surprises, the vast country threatened his body even as it compelled his soul.

Frowning, Ty looked out over the land behind him once more, letting his gaze go slightly unfocused. Even using that old hunter's trick to reveal movement in a vast landscape, Ty saw nothing new. If Janna were somewhere behind him, he couldn't see her. Nor could he see any renegades, soldiers, mustangs or rabbits. He put the spyglass away.

"All right, girl. Let's go."

Zebra moved out smartly, hurrying over the crest of the rise as though she understood that to silhouette herself against the sky was to ask for unwanted attention. The mustang had taken a straight line beginning at the place where they had sheltered from the worst of the rain and ending at the long, broken line of cliffs that marked the eastern margin of Black Plateau. Ty knew of no way up onto the plateau from the east side, unless there was a game trail. In any case, he wouldn't want to try such a path riding bareback on a mustang that might take a notion to unload him at any time.

"I can ride you or track you," Ty muttered. "Which would be better?"

If personal safety were the most important consideration, Ty knew he should let the mustang go and track her. But he wasn't worried about his own safety half as much as he was about finding Janna quickly; and for speed, riding beat tracking six ways from Sunday. If Zebra unloaded him, then he could worry about tracking her through the afternoon thunderstorms that occurred as often as not in the canyon country. Until then, he would stay with her like a cactus thorn and hope to get to Janna before she caught lung fever from running around in the rain.

And Ty would also hope that Troon poured enough rotgut down his throat to ruin his aim, so that Lucifer lived to be captured by Tyrell MacKenzie.

Chapter Sixteen

The track was as perfect and as unexpected as a diamond in a handful of mud.

"Whoa, Zebra."

Ty might as well have saved his breath. Zebra had already stopped and lowered her nose to the footprint. She sucked in air, blew it out and sucked it in again. Unlike the mare, Ty didn't have to rely on his sense of smell; he had no doubt that the line of slender footprints was Janna's. What baffled him was that the tracks appeared from nowhere and vanished within thirty feet.

Bruja. Witch.

Skin shifted and prickled on Ty's neck. He wasn't a superstitious man, but it was easier to believe in witches than it was to believe that something as generous and gentle as Janna had survived unaided in this land.

Atop Zebra, Ty quartered the land where the prints had vanished. Beyond them he spotted a narrow tongue of stone coming in from the right. The toe of the last track was more heavily imprinted, as though Janna had dug into the wet ground in the act of leaping toward the stone. Zebra whuffed over the stone tongue for a minute before she looked back at Ty as though to ask, *Well, what now?*

"Good question," Ty muttered.

The runner of rock led to a rugged, narrow ridge that was nothing but wind-smoothed stone. Someone as agile as Janna might have been able to use the ridge as a trail, but it would be rough going for the mustang and her rider.

Like all good hunters, Ty had learned long ago that tracks weren't the only way to follow prey. A better way was to know where the prey was going. He had seen the dismay and fear in Janna's face at the thought of Lucifer being hunted with a rifle. It took no particular prescience on Ty's part to decide that she would head for Lucifer by the shortest possible route. Unfortunately, nothing of the country ahead of him looked passable by man, much less by horse.

Then Ty remembered what Janna had said: *I know every seep, every bit of cover, every place where grass grows lush and thick.*

Sitting motionless, Ty looked at the land ahead of him. It wasn't simply luck that had led him to cut across Janna's trail. In fact, luck had had little to do with it. Despite the vastness of the land itself, there were relatively few places where people and animals could move freely, and fewer still where they could pass from one mesa or canyon to another. The jutting mesas, deep stone ravines, and unfailing ruggedness of the land limited movement to the broad washes between Black Plateau and the mesas or to snaking around the plateau itself. Everything—deer, wild horses, Indians, cattle and cowhands alike—was forced to follow pretty much the same course over the face of the land.

Hiding was another matter entirely. There were literally thousands of places for a person to hide. But eventually every rabbit had to come out into the open to find water or to find food or simply to find a safer place to hide.

Janna was no different.

Janna bit her lip and tugged her hat lower over her auburn hair, concealing any telltale flash of color. The sun's heat had strengthened to the point that cold was no longer a problem for her. Her canteen took care of her thirst. Her stomach, however, was unhappy. It reminded her ceaselessly that it was past time for breakfast and lunch, not to mention that she hadn't had so much as a snack after her midnight walk in the rain.

Yet hunger wasn't Janna's biggest problem. Ty was. Barely a half mile away, he sat on stone outcropping that gave him a commanding view of the countryside. A rugged piñon that grew in the crevices gave concealment to his body; if Janna hadn't caught a glimpse of movement when he had climbed up to his present position, she would never have spotted him in time to go to ground.

Now she was trapped. She had to move across bare rock in order to get to the sole path up Black Plateau's steep eastern side. The instant she broke cover Ty would be on her like a hungry coyote on a rabbit.

Why didn't you just ride Zebra up onto the plateau when she became restless? Janna silently demanded of Ty. *Why did you turn her loose? She could lead you to Lucifer as fast as I could, so why are you staked out over there looking for me instead of for that stallion?*

Nothing answered Janna's silent questions. She shifted her weight carefully, rubbing her hip where a loose rock had been digging into tender flesh. With an impatient sound she turned her head just enough to look across the distance separating her from Ty.

He was still there.

Ordinarily Janna would simply have settled deeper into cover and outwaited her hunter. She had done it many times before, when Cascabel's men had come across her tracks and given chase. Always her patience had proven to be greater than that of her pursuers.

But no longer. Janna's patience was evaporating even more quickly than rain puddles beneath the hot sun. Every minute she stayed in hiding was one minute closer to Lucifer for Joe Troon. The thought was agony to Janna, especially when she knew that she wasn't in any real danger from Ty. Even if he caught her, he wouldn't beat or rape or torture her. In fact, Janna couldn't think of anything painful he would be likely to do to her, except to remind her of how far she was from his ideal of a silken lady.

The thought deepened the unhappy downward curve of Janna's mouth. Beyond being certain that she didn't stand out against the rugged landscape, she had never thought much about her appearance one way or another. Now she did. Seeing Ty in his new clothes with his cheeks smooth shaven had driven home to her just how handsome he was, and by how great a margin she missed being the fragile silken lady who could attract and hold him.

Janna looked across the wild land at Ty and admitted to herself how much she wanted to be his dream. And at the same time she admitted to herself how impossible it was for her to be that dream.

If she had been the silken lady of Ty's desire, she would have died at the same lonely water hole her father had, for there had been no one to depend on but herself. If she hadn't died there, she would certainly have starved, because she would not have been able to catch and kill her own food. Instead of feeling wretched because she was self-sufficient, she should be thanking God for her ability to adjust to the harsh demands of surviving in the wild land.

Do I really want to be all soft and useless just so I can attract Ty? she asked herself scornfully.

Yes.

The prompt, honest reply didn't improve Janna's humor. She glared out across the ground separating Ty from herself.

If I'd been all simpering and soft in the head, Cascabel would have tracked Ty down and killed him. But did Ty ever think of that? No. He just mooned over a will-o'-the-wisp that would probably faint combing tangles out of her own hair.

Janna glared across the space separating herself from Ty. *Move, dammit! I've got better things to do even if you don't.*

Ty remained in place.

Another half hour crawled by, marked by no more motion than that of the shadows responding to the slow arc of the sun across the empty sky. Ravens called across empty ravines. Rabbits nibbled on brush. Lizards whisked across hot rock, towing the racing black shape of their shadows behind. A hawk circled overhead, sending its keening cry to the earth like a thrown lance. Janna felt like calling out in return, venting her growing frustration.

Another sound came—a rifle shot rather than the call of a hawk. The sound was distant and wasn't repeated.

Three things occurred to Janna simultaneously. The first was that no white man was crazy enough to call down the attention of Cascabel's renegades by shooting at game. The second was that Joe Troon had taken a shot at Lucifer. The third was that Ty would be looking in the direction of the shot rather than at the open space between herself and the route up the east side of Black Plateau.

No sooner had the thought occurred than Janna acted. She popped out of the crevice in which she had hidden and began running swiftly.

Ty had heard the sound of the rifle shot at the same instant Janna did. Like her, he had thought of several things simultaneously while he strained to hear other shots and heard only the wind. But he didn't look in the direction of the shot. He knew that whatever had happened or was happening over there was too far away for him to affect. His attention never wavered from the broken land between himself and the plateau.

He spotted Janna instantly. He had spent the past few hours memorizing the possible approaches to the vague trail he had spotted up onto Black Plateau, so he didn't even hesitate to choose his own route. He came to his feet and hit top speed within a few strides, running hard and fast and clean, covering ground with a devouring speed, closing in on Janna with a diagonal course.

Janna caught the motion from the corner of her eye, recognized Ty and redoubled her own efforts to reach the plateau trail. It was as though she were standing still. She had seen Ty run once before, but he had been injured then, reeling from the effects of running Cascabel's gauntlet. Ty wasn't injured now. He ran with the speed of a wolf, closing the space between himself and his prey with every leaping stride.

One instant Janna was in full flight—the next instant she was brought down on the hard earth. Only it wasn't the ground she fell upon, it was Ty, who had turned as he grabbed her so that it would be his body that took the impact of the unforgiving land.

Even so, Janna was knocked breathless. By the time she could react, it was too late. She was flat on her back, pinned to the hot earth by the weight of Ty's big body. He caught her wrists and held them above her head, imprisoned in his hands.

"Don't you think it's time that you and I had a little chat?" Ty drawled.

"Let go of me!"

"Promise you won't run?"

Janna twisted abruptly, trying to throw Ty off. He simply settled a bit more heavily onto her body.

"I'm bigger than you are, if you hadn't noticed," Ty said. "A little thing like you doesn't have a chance against a man of any size, much less one as big as I am."

Janna started calling Ty the same names her father had used when the wagon mule wouldn't move. "You misbegotten whelp of a cross-eyed cow and the stupidest stud son of a bitch that God ever—"

A big hand clamped over Janna's mouth, cutting off the flow of her invective.

"Didn't anybody ever tell you a girl shouldn't use such language?"

The muffled sounds from beneath Ty's hand told him that Janna wasn't listening to him. She flailed against his shoulder and chin with the hand he had freed in order to cover her mouth. He lifted that hand and grabbed her wrist again.

"Bastard son of a one-legged whore and a one-eyed, flea-brained—"

Abruptly Ty's hard mouth covered Janna's. Her lips were open, her breath hot, the taste of her as fresh as rain. He shuddered heavily and thrust his tongue deep into her mouth again and again, wanting to devour her.

The fierceness of Ty's mouth and the wild penetration of his tongue shocked Janna into complete stillness. She trembled helplessly, overpowered by his strength and by her awareness of his body moving over hers, rubbing urgently, as though he were trying to push her into the ground.

Janna couldn't move, couldn't breathe, and still the contact went on and on, his big body crushing hers, showing her how futile it was to fight him. She tried to speak and found she couldn't even do that. Twisting, writhing, she tried to fight him but he was too big, his body was everywhere; she was as helpless as a mouse caught in the talons of a hawk.

Chapter Seventeen

When Ty finally tore his mouth away and stared down at Janna, he was breathing in deep, ragged bursts and her pupils were wide, dark, enormous, magnified by tears.

"Don't you ever run from me again," Ty said, his voice hoarse and his eyes almost black from the dilation of his pupils.

Janna felt the violent shudder that shook his body, felt the quick force of his breaths against the tears on her cheeks, felt the savage power of his clenched muscles. She should have been terrified, yet at some deep, subconscious level she knew that Ty wouldn't truly hurt her. Even so, she trembled, not understanding the feelings that were coursing through her body—and through his.

"You can let me g-go," she said shakily. "I w-won't run."

For the space of several breaths there was only silence and the wild glitter of Ty's eyes. Abruptly he let go of Janna and rolled aside into a sitting position, drawing his legs up to his body as though he were in pain.

"Christ," Ty said through clenched teeth. "I'm sorry, little one. I've never forced myself on a woman in my life."

Janna let out one long, ragged breath and then another. "It's all right."

"Like hell it is," he snarled. He turned his head and looked at her with eyes as hard as stone. "You don't belong out here, Janna Wayland. You're a walking temptation to every man

who sees you all alone and unprotected. I'm going to take you
to the fort and that's final.''

"If you do that, Joe Troon will kill Lucifer, assuming he
hasn't already. That could have been the rifle shot we heard.''

Ty said something savage beneath his breath, then added,
"You don't understand.''

"No, it's you who doesn't understand,'' Janna said quickly.
"At the fort or in any town or at one of the ranches, I'm a
girl without kin, fit only for washing clothes or dishes or feeding men or...well, you know.'' Janna shook her head fiercely.
"I don't want that. Out here I'm free of their sly looks and
pawing hands. The only man out here is you, and you don't
think of me that way.''

"I don't? What the hell do you think just happened?'' Ty
demanded, hardly able to believe his ears.

"I made you mad and you got even.'' Janna shrugged. "So
what? I've taken a lot worse from men and survived.''

Ty started to ask what Janna meant, then realized that he
didn't want to know. He had heard his sister's broken cries
when she relived in nightmare the time of her captivity at the
hands of white raiders. The thought of Janna being brutalized
like that was unendurable. She was so fierce in her desire for
freedom, so terrifyingly fragile beneath the heavy clothes that
muffled her.

"God,'' Ty groaned, putting his head in his hands, hating
himself. "Janna...little one...I didn't mean to hurt you.''

"But you didn't.'' She looked at him anxiously when he
didn't respond. She put her hand on his wrist where the shirt
ended and his warm flesh began. "Ty? Honest. You scared
me a little and confused me a lot, but you didn't hurt me at
all. And I've changed my mind. I'll help you get Lucifer before Joe Troon does.''

For a long moment Ty stared at the hand resting on his
wrist. The fingers were long and delicate, gently browned by
the sun, the nails beautifully formed and pink with health, the
skin supple and warm. He wanted to pick up that feminine
hand and kiss the hollow of her palm, lick the sensitive skin
between her fingers, bite gently at the pad of flesh at the base

of her thumb until her breath broke and her hand curled around his touch like a sleeping flower....

"Stop looking at me like that," Janna said, snatching her fingers back. "I know my hand isn't lily-white and soft and stinking of perfume, but it's a good hand all the same. It helped to save your stupid masculine hide, remember?"

Ty opened his mouth to tell Janna that she had misunderstood, that he had been thinking how alluring her hand was rather than the opposite. At the last instant common sense held his tongue in check. She refused to leave the country, and he couldn't leave until he had Lucifer. He needed her help with the stallion and she needed him to guard her back; but he was so woman hungry that he barely trusted himself to keep his hands off her. Keeping her irritated with him would go a long way toward maintaining a safe distance between them. Knowing what her experience with men must have been like, he simply couldn't have lived with himself if Janna thought he were demanding sex in return for safety or anything else he could give her.

"And I've been trying to thank you for saving my hide by saving yours in return," Ty drawled, "but to hell with it. You want to run around here risking your scrawny little self, you go right ahead. Me? I'm just thanking God that He made you so damned unappealing to men. Any other woman and I'd be tempted to find out what was beneath all the rough clothes. But you? You're like a baby quail, all eyes and mouth and frizzled features. With you I'm as safe from the temptations of the flesh as any monk in a monastery."

"Why, you—"

Ty's hand shot out, covering Janna's mouth and cutting off her words.

"You should be down on your knees thanking God that I feel that way," Ty said savagely. "If I ever put my hands on you, it wouldn't be violins and roses. I'm too woman hungry to stop short of taking what I need. And that's all it would be. Taking. No promises, no soft words, no wedding vows, nothing but male hunger and a handy female."

Janna heard every word but only cared about Ty's admission that he was woman hungry. It gave her the weapon she needed. It appeared that her efforts at proving she was a woman had been having some effect.

She smiled rather bitterly and decided that she would make him eat every one of his cutting words about her lack of womanly allure. From that moment on she would redouble her efforts to remind him that she was a woman and he was a hungry man. She would bring him to his knees with desire...and then she would laugh in his face and walk away, leaving him as miserable and unhappy as she was now.

"Now that we understand each other," Janna said tightly, "could we possibly get going so that Joe Troon doesn't kill Lucifer before we can stop him?"

Ty told himself that the hurt and anger he saw in Janna's eyes were better than the bigger hurt that would come if he couldn't keep his hands off her. From what he had heard, at best she had been roughly treated by men; at worst she had been brutalized. If he took advantage of her, he would be no better than Joe Troon.

Ty told himself that, but he wasn't sure he believed it. He would be gentle with Janna even if it killed him...wouldn't he? Surely he would. He wasn't an animal to take what a woman wouldn't freely give him.

Oh, sure. I'm a real Southern gentleman. That's why I was grinding Janna beneath me into the dirt as though I'd never had a woman and never would unless I had her right there. I can't trust myself with her any farther than I can throw myself uphill.

Ty looked at Janna's gray eyes watching him with too many shadows, waiting for his answer.

"Hell of an idea," Ty said curtly. "Wait here while I get my pack."

Janna watched him get up and leave without a backward look. She didn't move. She knew that he was testing her, finding out if he could trust her. If she were going to run off at the first opportunity, better that he discover her untrustworthiness now than when it came time for her turn at night guard while he slept. Approving his pragmatism almost as much as she approved his lithe, muscular stride, Janna watched until Ty disappeared. She waited for his return without moving one inch from her cross-legged position on the ground.

When Ty returned and saw Janna precisely where he had left her, he understood her silent message: he could trust her. He nodded approvingly and held out his hand to help Janna to her feet.

It was the opportunity she had been waiting for. She allowed herself to be pulled upright, then stumbled and fell against Ty's body, letting him take her full weight. His arms closed around her automatically, supporting her.

The impact of Janna's weight was negligible to a man of Ty's size, but the warmth of her body wasn't. When his arms tightened around her to keep her upright, he knew a lightning stroke of pleasure at how perfectly she fit against him. Supple, slender, smelling of piñon, she was like an armful of sunlight.

"Janna? What's wrong?"

For a moment longer she savored the delicious warmth and strength of Ty's body before she slowly began to take her own weight again. Even then, she held on to his muscular arms, bracing herself against his strength.

"Sorry," Janna said, eyes downcast as she flexed her fingers into the swell of Ty's biceps and very slowly released him. "I guess I'm a little...hungry."

Ty was glad Janna wasn't looking at him when she confessed her hunger, because she would have seen the naked statement of his own need in the tension of his face. In the next instant he understood that Janna wasn't talking about the elemental hunger of sex but the equally basic hunger of the stomach. Hers was growling audibly as she rested her cheek against his chest, leaning as though she were too tired to stand entirely by herself. He smiled despite the desire snaking through his loins. He tapped the bridge of Janna's nose gently with his index finger.

"Poor little baby bird," Ty said sympathetically. "Come on. As soon as we get in better cover, I'll feed you."

His voice was a deep rumble beneath Janna's cheek, but the indulgence in his tone was unmistakable. *Baby bird.* Her mouth drew down unhappily. Her attempt to arouse desire in him had resulted in a brotherly pat. The temptation to bite the hard, warm chest that lay beneath her cheek almost overwhelmed her. She sensed that would have been a serious mistake in her campaign of "accidental" seduction, so she contented herself with pushing away from the shelter offered by Ty's arms.

"Thank you," Janna said politely. "I'm fine now."

She turned away and began walking quickly toward the rugged wall of black lava and red sandstone that formed the east face of Black Plateau. Ty stood and watched the almost concealed sway of Janna's hips beneath the men's clothing and prayed that she would find Lucifer and find him very soon; the more he looked at Janna, the harder it became to ignore her unconscious, utterly feminine allure.

Yet he had to ignore it. He had to forget how good it had felt to rock his hips hard against the softness beneath her clothes.

He had to...but he couldn't.

Chapter Eighteen

Anger helped Janna to hold to a good pace despite her growling stomach. Without looking back to see how Ty was doing with his heavy pack, she attacked the steep, winding trail that led to the top of Black Plateau. As she climbed, she looked for signs of anyone else using the trail.

She found no traces of man and very little of beast. There were no signs that anything had used the trail recently other than herself. There were no hoofprints in the rare patches of dirt, nor scars where hooves had slipped or scraped across stone. She had never seen signs of any hoofed animal on the trail except occasional deer—and once, just once, tracks that indicated that Lucifer had skidded down over the precipitous path in order to shake off mustangers who had gotten too close.

The idea of any horse taking the trail down the plateau's east face made Janna's heart stop. She herself used the route only when she was afoot and wanted to go to Sweetwater by the shortest possible route. There were other, safer routes up onto the plateau. One route was on the north side, one on the south, and there were several on the western side. All of them were far easier than the eastern trail.

Climbing at a rapid rate, Janna worked her way up the trail until it dipped into one of the many runoff ravines that channeled the plateau's east face. Safe from observation from any angle but directly overhead, Janna sat on a stone seat and awaited Ty's arrival. She didn't wait long. He had walked only far enough behind her to avoid the shower of pebbles disturbed by her passage.

Ty grunted and shucked off the heavy pack, using it as a seat while his breathing returned to normal.

"Hell of a path," he said after a bit. "I didn't see any sign of Zebra coming up, but she sure headed straight here like she had something in mind."

"She did—avoiding a river of black rock about a quarter mile south of here," Janna explained. "It's too rough to climb over. To avoid it, you have to go several miles away from the plateau until the rock sinks into the dirt, or you have to climb partway up the east face of the plateau to go around the head of the rock river. That's what Zebra usually does. Then she goes up onto the top by the southern route, which is easy."

For several minutes there was silence while Ty looked out over the land from his new perspective, checking his memories against Janna's words.

"Does the lava flow—the river of black rock—begin there?" he asked, pointing to what looked like a dusty black creek running out from the base of the plateau.

Janna leaned out to look, taking the opportunity to brush against Ty's outstretched arm.

"Yes."

Ty grunted. "I can see why Zebra goes around it. A lot of jagged rock and nothing much else."

He looked for a time longer, waiting for Janna to withdraw the tantalizing brush of her body. She didn't. He shifted slightly, ending the intimacy, for his blood was still running hotly. Even worse, he suspected that it was going to be a permanent condition around the ragged, too-feminine waif.

"How deep are those canyons?" Ty asked, pointing toward the shadows that looked rather like a network of black lightning fanning out from the base of the plateau.

For a few moments Janna considered moving closer to Ty in order to brush against him again, but then she decided against it. Next time she would choose her moment better, so that retreat would be impossible. In a place as narrow as this crevice, she shouldn't have to wait long for her opportunity.

"The canyons are deep enough that the wild horses go around them," Janna said. "The countryside is full of ravines and washes and canyons like that. Most of them are dry, but nearly every butte and mesa has at least a tiny seep or rock tanks that hold water almost year-round. Black Plateau is different. It's big enough to have water all year up top as well as seeps and springs at the base. That's why there's so much grass and game."

Saying nothing, Ty smoothed a patch of dirt with his hand, then began drawing on the surface with his fingertip. Knowing that the plateau was Lucifer's preferred range, Ty had spent weeks scouting the area before he had decided on the best way to capture the wild stallion. Unfortunately Ty had ended up captured by Indians before he could try out his plan. Janna, however, had spent years on and around Black Plateau. If there were anything wrong with Ty's plan, she would spot it.

"This outline is Black Plateau," he said, pointing to the very rough rectangle he had drawn in the dirt. He added sides to the rectangle, showing depth as well as area. Only the western side remained untouched, suggesting the relative flatness where the plateau's surface blended into the rumpled front of the Fire Mountains. "From what I've seen, the closer you get to Black Plateau from the east, the steeper and deeper the canyons, gullies and ravines get."

Janna shifted position, brushing against Ty's thigh as she did so. When she leaned forward to look at what he had drawn, she braced her hand on his thigh. Ty's hand, which was drawing lines in the dirt, jerked. He said something beneath his breath and changed position until Janna's hand was no longer resting on his thigh.

"That's right," she said. "The plateau's east face rises very steeply from the flatlands." She leaned forward again, and again braced herself on Ty's leg, ignoring his attempts to evade her touch. "Black Plateau is really part of the Fire Mountains," she added, drawing a series of pyramids along the plateau's western flank to represent the mountains. "According to Indian legends, the spirits fought each other until the earth cracked and bled and everything the blood touched became fire. Long after the earth healed, the angry spirits roared and spit fire among the peaks of the Fire range, and sometimes new blood flowed over the plateau and dripped down into the desert, where it turned into black rocks. The angry spirits still live beneath the earth around here, turning water so hot that there are springs that cook food faster than a campfire.''

Ty tried to concentrate on Janna's words, but the presence of her hand on his leg was burning hotter than anything in the Indian legend. He would have retreated to the side again if he could have. He couldn't. The crevice in the plateau's side where they had taken shelter was simply too small. He was up against a black boulder right now—and her hand had slipped around to the inside of his thigh. She was so involved in the map he had drawn that she didn't seem to notice.

Talk about being between a rock and a hard place... Ty told himself, disgusted because the hard place was in his own lap. He pulled off his hat and dumped it between his legs, hiding the growing evidence of his discomfort in the only way he could.

''There are two good trails up on top of the plateau on its western side,'' Janna continued, flexing her fingers slightly as she shifted position. Now that she had discovered it, the heat and resilience of Ty's leg fascinated her. ''The first trail is here, about two miles from the southern boundary. It's called the Long View Trail.'' She leaned down and forward until her ribs brushed Ty's leg as she marked the trail on the map he had drawn in the dirt. ''That's the easiest way up. The Indians have used it for as long as anyone can remember. The second trail is here.'' She made another mark. ''The trails are about twenty miles apart as the crow flies. Walking it doubles the distance. The second route up is called Raven Creek Trail. It isn't as easy as the Long View Trail, and it doesn't lead immediately to water or good grazing, so Raven Creek Trail isn't used except by Indian hunting parties.''

''Or war parties?''

Janna nodded. "Cascabel has his camp at the base of the plateau, where Raven Creek empties into Santos Wash. Mustang Canyon," she added, pointing to the northern edge of the plateau, where a large notch had been cut into the stone foundations of the land, "is here. There's good grazing all year and a trail to the top of the plateau that only deer and mustangs use, and occasional crazy mustangers."

"And you?"

She smiled. "And me. But Zebra grew up on that trail. Sometimes I think her mama was a goat. Zebra is as sure-footed as one. Besides, most of the time I get off and walk. There's one slick rock patch that gives me nightmares."

Ty smiled thinly. "You? Nightmares?" he scoffed. "You're too tough to be afraid of anything."

Janna said nothing, though she couldn't help remembering all the nights after her father had died when she had jumped at the smallest sound, biting off screams that would have given away her position rather than summoning the help she needed. Even years later, certain combinations of sounds and smells could set her heart to hammering hard enough to break her ribs.

"Is your keyhole canyon about here?" asked Ty, pointing to a place near the southeast corner of the plateau.

"Yes."

Steadfastly ignoring the gentle crowding pressure of Janna's body, Ty looked at the map and mentally began turning the plateau's neat edges into a fringe of varying lengths, for that was closer to the truth of the landscape. The plateau's north, east and south edges were fringed with sheer-sided stone promontories and cliffs, as well as canyons and ravines of varying sizes and depths; and the larger canyons had side canyons, which in turn branched into finger canyons, which branched into runoff crevices.

The result was a maze in which a person could stand on one canyon edge and look at the opposite edge only a few thousand feet away—and it would take a day of circling around to get to the other side. Most of the hundreds of nameless canyons that fringed the plateau were blind; ultimately they had only one outlet, and that was down onto the flatlands rather than up onto the top of Black Plateau itself.

"Do you know of any other trails up to the top?" Ty asked, marking the ones Janna had already mentioned. "What about all these fringe canyons? Could a man on foot climb out of some of them and up onto the plateau itself?"

Janna shrugged. "Ask Mad Jack the next time you see him. He knows things about Black Plateau that even the Indians don't. But the canyons I've seen end in sheer cliffs, the kind you'd have to be crazy or running for your life to try to climb."

"Does Lucifer graze in blind canyons?"

"The biggest ones, yes. The narrow ones, never. Some mustangers must have trapped him once. He won't even go near the entrance of any canyon that isn't at least a quarter mile across. He's smart and wild as they come."

"No wonder he's still running loose," Ty said, admiration and disgust mixed equally in his voice. "I was lucky to get as close as I did before Cascabel nailed me. What are the chances of startling Lucifer and getting him to run headlong into a small blind canyon before he knows what's happening?"

"It's been tried by every mustanger who ever came here."

Ty didn't ask what the result had been. He didn't need to. The stallion still ran free.

"No wonder Troon decided to try creasing that black devil," Ty muttered.

Janna thought of the rifle shot they had heard and bit her lip.

Ty saw and had to look away. The idea of gently biting Janna's lip himself was too tempting. In fact, everything about her was too tempting. Though she was no longer leaning over to add marks to his rough map, her hand was still resting on his leg, sending heat spreading out in all directions through his body, tantalizing him with how close those slender fingers were to the very part of him that ached for her touch.

Cursing silently, viciously, Ty tried to ease away from the intimate contact. Half an inch away he came flat up against the crevice's stony limits. Close beside him, Janna's stomach growled audibly in the taut silence, reminding Ty that she hadn't eaten since they had left Keyhole Canyon yesterday morning.

"Scoot over so I can reach my pack," Ty muttered.

Even if Janna didn't move, the pack was within a long arm's length of Ty—if he were willing to press against her in order to increase his reach. She gave him a sideways look and decided not to point out how close the pack was. Without a word she eased backward and to the side an inch or two.

"More."

Ty's curt command irritated Janna. "Haven't you noticed? There's not much room in this crack."

"Yeah, and you're taking up at least three-quarters of it," he retorted. "Quit crowding me."

"Crowding you? My God, you'd think I had fleas or something," Janna muttered beneath her breath. "Seeing as how you're the one who's been to Ned's saloon recently, you're more likely to have fleas than—"

"Janna," Ty interrupted, his voice threatening. "Move!"

"All right, all right, I'm moving." She pushed herself to the far side of the crevice and hugged the wall as though there were a cliff inches away from her feet. "This better?"

Ty snarled something Janna chose not to hear. A pocket-knife appeared in his hand. He grabbed his pack and began rummaging through it. A few moments later he pulled out a tin can. He punched the point of the blade twice into the top of the can. The second time he rotated the knife, making a wider opening. He handed the can to Janna.

"Here. Drink this."

Janna lifted the can, tilted, sipped and made a sound of disbelief as the thick, sweet, peach-flavored liquid trickled across her tongue. She took two long, slow swallows before she reluctantly handed the can back to Ty. He refused to take it with a shake of his head.

"Finish it," he said.

"I can't do that. Preacher charges a dollar a can for his peaches."

A look at Janna's clear eyes told Ty that arguing over the peaches would be futile. He took the can, drank two small sips and handed it back over.

"Your turn," he said flatly.

She said nothing, but she took the can and drank slowly, savoring each drop. Her undisguised pleasure made Ty smile with the knowledge that he had given her a real treat. He had spent more than enough time on the trail to know how much a person began craving something sweet and succulent after weeks or months of dried meat and biscuits and beans.

The can was passed back and forth several times, and each time Ty swore that the metal became warmer to his touch. He tried not to think about the lips that had been pressed against the rim before his own lips drank. In fact, he was doing fine at controlling the direction of his thoughts until Janna tipped the can up and waited for several seconds for the last sweet drop to fall from the rim onto the tip of her outstretched tongue. The temptation to suck that drop from her tongue with his own lips was so great that he had to turn away.

"Now what?" she asked, holding the can under Ty's nose.

Hell of a question, he thought savagely. *Wish I had an answer I could live with.*

Using swift, vicious strokes of the pocketknife, Ty cut the lid from the rim, speared a peach half and held it out to Janna. She took the lush golden fruit with her fingertips, ate with delicate greed and waited her turn for another. They traded turns eating until only one piece of fruit was left, a piece that stubbornly eluded Ty's knife. Finally he speared it and held it out to Janna. As she slid the fruit from the knife blade she sensed Ty's intense interest. She looked up to find him watching her mouth. His eyes were a smoky green that made frissons of heat race over her skin. Without thinking she took a bite of the succulent fruit and held out the remainder to him with her fingertips.

"Your turn," she said huskily.

For a long, aching moment Ty looked at the sweetness dripping from Janna's slender fingers. Then he stood up in a controlled surge of power, grabbed his pack and strode out of the crevice without a word.

Chapter Nineteen

A late-afternoon storm had swept across Black Plateau, making the rocks and trees shine as though freshly polished. The slanting golden light transformed the winding meadow into a river of glistening gold. Once Janna would have felt the beauty of the land like a balm over her hungry soul; today she only saw what was absent rather than what was present. Lying on her stomach, using a row of evergreen seedlings for cover, she scanned the length of the long meadow in front of her once more, staring through the spyglass until her arms trembled with fatigue.

Ty didn't bother to go over the land again with his own glass. He knew he would see what he and Janna had seen for the past five days—grass and water and wind in abundance, but no Lucifer standing guard over his herd. Cascabel's renegades had been present, however. They were the reason that Ty and Janna had had to tiptoe around the plateau like thieves, able to get only as close to the mustangs as the tracks they had made yesterday or even the day before.

"I don't understand it," Janna said, finally lowering the spyglass and wiggling backward deeper beneath the cover of the pines that grew right to the meadow's edge. "Even if Lucifer had been caught, wouldn't we at least see some of his herd wandering around? No mustanger is going to want the older mares or the spring foals. Besides, we haven't seen or

heard any sign of Troon or any other mustanger since we came
up the east trail.''

''Except for that flurry of rifle shots yesterday,'' Ty said.
''That didn't sound like the hunting parties we've been hearing. Troon could have run afoul of Cascabel.''

Janna frowned and said reluctantly, ''I suppose I should
scout Cascabel's camp.''

''What?'' Ty asked, astonished.

''That's how I found you,'' she explained. ''I heard gunfire,
ran over, saw where the tracks of two shod horses were
crossed by a bunch of unshod Indian ponies. The ponies turned
to follow your horses and so did I. Eventually the tracks led
to Cascabel's camp. I couldn't get to you right away to free
you, so I hid and waited for a chance to help. It finally came
when you got through the gauntlet and were still able to run.''

Ty thought of the danger Janna had risked to save a total
stranger and shook his head in wonder. That deceptively slender body hid a lot of plain old courage, but there was no need
to spend it on a swamp Yankee like Joe Troon.

''Is Troon a friend of yours?'' Ty asked.

Janna gave Ty a startled look. ''Joe Troon? I wouldn't cry
one tear at his funeral,'' she said in a low, flat voice. ''In fact,
he…''

Her voice died. She didn't like to remember the time Troon
had trapped her and started stripping off her clothes before she
managed to break free and run. He had spent hours searching
for her. The whole time he had yelled just what he would do
when he caught her.

The combination of fear and dislike on Janna's face told Ty
more than he wanted to know about Janna and Joe Troon.

''Janna,'' Ty said softly, pulling her out of her unhappy
memories, ''from what I've heard in towns where I bought
my supplies, Troon is a drunk, a thief, a coward, a woman
beater and a back shooter. He deserves whatever Cascabel
feels like giving to him. Besides, you don't even know if
Troon has been captured. He could be back in Sweetwater
right now, getting drunk on Ned's rotgut. There's no point in

either of us risking our butt to scout a renegade camp for a no-good bit of swamp gas like Joe Troon.''

"I know," Janna said. "I just hate to think of anyone caught by Cascabel. He's so cruel."

Ty shrugged. "Cascabel doesn't see it that way. He's a warrior who has stood up to the worst the country, the pony soldiers and his fellow Indians can offer in the way of punishment. He's never given quarter and he's never asked for it. And he never will.''

"You sound like you admire him.''

There was a long silence before Ty shrugged again. "I don't like him, but I do respect him. He's one hell of a fighter, no matter what the weapon or situation. He has knowledge of how to use the land and his limited arms to his own advantage that many a general would envy.''

"Do you have any idea what he does to the captives who don't escape?''

"Yes," Ty said succinctly. "I didn't say I admired him, Janna. But I learned in the war that honor and good table manners don't have a damned thing to do with survival. Cascabel is a survivor. Black Hawk knows it. He hasn't pressed a confrontation because he hopes that the U.S. Army will take care of the renegades for him.''

"Black Hawk is lucky that Cascabel hasn't lured the whole tribe away from him," Janna grumbled. "Cascabel must have half of Black Hawk's warriors down here by now, and they're still coming in by twos and threes every day.''

"Cascabel is half-Apache. The elders in the Ute tribe would never let him be a headman. As for the younger men, they still believe that they're invincible. They haven't had time to learn that the same army that flattened the South sure as hell won't have too tough a time ironing out a few renegade wrinkles in the Utah Territory.''

Janna started to speak, then caught a flash of movement at the far edge of the meadow. Ty had seen the movement, too. As one they flattened completely to the earth, taking advantage of every bit of cover offered by the slight depression in which they had lain to watch the meadow.

Four hundred feet away, five Indians rode out into the wide river of meadow grass that wound between the two evergreen forests. The men rode boldly, without bothering about cover or the possibility of ambush, because they knew that Cascabel ruled Black Plateau. The only reason they weren't laughing and talking among themselves was that human voices carried a long way in the plateau's primal silence, and the deer they were hunting had excellent hearing.

Peering cautiously through the dense screen of evergreen boughs, spyglass shielded so that it wouldn't give away their position by reflecting a flash of light, Ty watched the hunting party ride along the margin of forest and meadow. Usually in any group of Indians, barely half the men were armed with carbines, rifles or pistols, and there were rarely more than a few rounds of ammunition for each weapon. Part of the problem for the Indians in getting arms was simply that it was illegal to sell weapons or ammunition to Indians. What they couldn't take as the spoils of war they had to buy from crooked white traders.

But most of the problem the Indians had in staying well armed was that none of the tribes had any experience in the care and repair of machines or in the art of making reliable bullets. The weapons they acquired through war or bribery quickly became useless either because of lack of ammunition or because of mechanical failure.

Cascabel's men were well outfitted. As well as the traditional bow and arrows, each man had a carbine and a leather pouch bulging with ammunition. Ty was relieved to see that the carbines were single-shot weapons of the type that had lost the Civil War for the South. None of the five Indians had a weapon that could compete with the new Winchester carbine he had discovered in an otherwise empty box at the store Preacher had rather hastily abandoned. Ty's new carbine was the type of weapon Johnny Rebs had enviously insisted that a Yank "loaded on Sunday and fired all week long." With his new Winchester, Ty could reload as fast as he could fire, an advantage the Indians didn't have unless they used their bows and arrows.

Ty went over the details of the Indians' gear with the experienced eye of a man to whom such knowledge had meant the difference between continued life and premature death. The presence of good weapons explained some of Cascabel's allure for young warriors—on a reservation, these men would have barely enough to eat, no weapons beyond what they could make with their own hands, and no freedom to roam in search of game. With Cascabel, the young men would have a chance to gain personal fame as warriors, they would be well fed and well armed, and they could live the roving life celebrated in tribal legends.

The fact that the young men would also find themselves the target of every white man with a gun simply added spice to the Indians' lives. After all, there weren't that many white men.

Ty knew that the situation would change, even if the Indians didn't. Since the end of the Civil War, footloose and disenfranchised white men had pressed west in greater and greater numbers. Most of them had already been in shooting battles, so the prospect of occasional skirmishes with Indians wasn't much of a deterrent. Ty himself was one of those men, as were his brothers. There were hundreds and thousands more men like the MacKenzies, drawn by the West's wild horizons and seductive promises of a better life for anyone who had the courage and stamina to withstand the hardships. Not all the promises of the new land would be kept, but each man was certain that, for him, the dreams would indeed come true.

And a lot of those men would be armed with repeating rifles and carbines and as many bullets as they could wear without dragging their belts down to their boot tops. The Indians would take some of those weapons and put them to deadly use, but more white men would come west, and then more and more, and their superior arms would always be enough to offset the Indians' superior knowledge of the land.

Ty had no doubt about the eventual outcome of the battle between Indian and white; he just wasn't sure he would be alive to share in the celebration when the renegades were defeated.

Abruptly the five Indians stopped their mounts. One of the warriors leaped from his horse, landed lightly and sat on his heels while he examined something on the ground. After a time he stood again, walked a few steps and then bent over the ground once more, looking at everything from a different angle.

Ty lay without moving, going over in his mind once more what he would do if he and Janna were discovered. With his new carbine he could cause as much damage in one minute as ten men with single-shot guns. Even allowing for the fact that he hadn't had time to accustom himself to the Winchester's action, he should be able to put two warriors out of the fight before the others took cover. That would give Janna plenty of time to slip away while he played cat and mouse with the remaining warriors. With a little luck, he might even get away himself.

With a lot of luck, he and Janna wouldn't be discovered in the first place.

When the warrior finally remounted and the five continued along the far edge of the meadow without looking in the direction where Janna and Ty lay concealed, he breathed a quiet sigh of relief. He had known some men who loved fighting and killing. He wasn't one of them. He was quite pleased to see the Indians disappear into the trees without a single shot having been fired from his shiny new carbine.

Neither Ty nor Janna stirred from their prone position. Something had piqued the Indians' curiosity enough to deflect them from their original course of hunting. If the curiosity were quickly satisfied, the Indians would come back to the meadow and resume hunting deer.

Besides, Janna was lying quite close to Ty, able to feel him all along her right side, able to move subtly against him, reminding him of her presence. She had done a lot of that in the past five days, leaning over him by the campfire, brushing his hand when she gave him a plate of food, tripping and falling against him when the trail permitted it.

She had seen the green intensity of his glance and had known that her presence was felt, but she was no longer cer-

tain that she would laugh and walk away if she brought him
to his knees with desire. The thought of being close to him,
truly close, brought her to her own knees with an answering
desire that burned just beneath her skin, silently reaching out
to him even as his own male heat radiated out to her, caressing
and calling to her.

The bronze light of very late afternoon burnished the
meadow. Soon deer would be emerging from cover to feed.
At first they would graze only along the western margin of
the meadow, where the descending sun pushed thick shadows
out of the dense pines. As the shadows stretched across the
grassy clearing, the deer would follow until finally the
meadow would be dotted by graceful shapes grazing upon
moon-silvered grass.

That was when it would be safest for Ty and Janna to move,
when the much more acute senses of the deer would give
warning of other men roaming around in the night. Not that
Ty expected to run across any Indians on the move in full
darkness, but he had learned that allowing for the unexpected
was the best way to survive life's lethal little surprises.

Besides, it was very pleasant to lie in the warm aftermath
of day on a thick bed of pine needles and listen to birds settling
into cover for the night, calling and singing to one another as
though they had a lifetime of information to pass on and only
a few minutes until the last golden sunlight faded, bringing
with it darkness and night.

It was also pleasant to feel Janna's warm body pressed
against his left side.

After a moment's thought, Ty conceded to himself that perhaps pleasant wasn't the right word to describe the combination of sensuous heat and mental torture she had inflicted on
him in the past days. He couldn't turn around but she was
there, touching him in the most casual ways, never forward or
aggressive, just...*there*. Always. A smile or a fleeting brush
of her body over his, a look from gray eyes as clear as spring-
water, a soft laugh that made his loins tighten. He sensed that
she was getting even with him for belittling her feminine al-

lure, but he couldn't prove it. There was always a logical reason for her touches.

And her touches were driving him crazy, sending fire licking over his skin, heat whispering to him, telling him that beneath those flapping clothes was a woman. With each second that passed, the chance of the Indians returning became less likely, and the fragrance of her body became more compelling. He sensed each of her breaths, knew that she felt him as well, and he wanted nothing more than to turn toward her and mold her along the aching length of his body.

Ty kept remembering that single, penetrating kiss he had given to Janna. He could recall the feeling of her body beneath his with a vividness that sent blood rushing hotly, hardening his male flesh until it ached.

But she hadn't enjoyed that kiss. She had taken it as a punishment.

Yet it was Ty who was being punished. He owed Janna his life. He had sworn to himself that he wouldn't repay that debt by frightening or hurting her as other men had. The only way he could keep his promise to himself was to keep his hungry hands off her. And his hungry mouth. And most of all, his hungry—

"Ty?" Janna whispered softly.

Her body was shaking. So was her voice. Though she made no more noise than a sigh, Ty heard her. He heard every breath she took, saw every time she licked her lips, tasted her in his memory. He didn't know how much longer he would be able to admire her without touching the easy sway of her hips as she led him along the plateau's secret byways.

"Ty?" she said, a bit more loudly.

"What?" he groaned, wondering how much longer he could lie next to her without grabbing her.

"There's a snake crawling along my leg."

Chapter Twenty

"*Don't move.*"

Ty knew as soon as he whispered the urgent words that his command was unnecessary—Janna knew better than to make a sudden move around a snake. She also must know that all she had to do was lie quietly until the snake slithered off into the late afternoon and she would be all right.

"Can you see the snake?" he whispered.

Janna's answer was more a whimper than a "no."

"Just stay quiet," he repeated. "The snake isn't interested in you and he won't be as long as you don't move."

But Janna couldn't remain still. Tremors of sheer terror were rippling through her. She could face almost anything without losing her head, but not a snake. She remembered all too well the nightmare of awakening to her father's shouts and frantic flailing about as he tried to shake off the rattlesnake that had crawled into his bedroll. He had been bitten on his feet and his calf, his wrist and his cheek.

At the time they had been deep in Indian country, chasing one of her father's dreams of gold. There had been no one to help. None of the herbs or balms or potions her father knew had managed to pull the poison out of his body. Nor had lancing the oozing wounds helped.

She would never forget the endless death throes of the big snake after she had cut off its triangular head with her sheath knife. Nor would she forget the long days of her father's agony and delirium before he finally died.

Without realizing it, Janna began whimpering softly with every shallow breath she took. Ty heard and realized that she wouldn't be able to lie still until the snake moved on in search of its normal evening meal of mice or young rabbit. She was terrified. In the grip of such mindless fear she might scream, and then the snake would be the least of their worries.

"Janna," Ty whispered urgently. "You'll be all right. Just lie still. I'll take care of it. Whatever happens, *don't move*."

The increasingly violent trembling of Janna's body was her only answer.

Slowly Ty eased onto his right side, lifted himself on his elbow and reached to his waist for his sheath knife. The way he and Janna were lying, he had no choice except to use his left hand, but that fact didn't slow him down. The first thing the elder MacKenzie had taught his boys was that a left-handed knife fighter had an advantage in a brawl, and a two-handed fighter would win every time.

Ty's movements and Janna's trembling had made the snake freeze in place as it tried to decide whether the movement represented food or danger or simply a neutral presence such as the wind. In the dying light the motionless snake blended so well with its surroundings that Ty had a hard time seeing it. When he did, he swore silently.

It was a timber rattlesnake, and it was as thick around as his forearm. There would be enough venom stored up in that big mouth to kill a man, much less a girl the size of Janna.

When nothing came of Janna's quaking movements, the rattler lowered its head and continued on its evening hunt. The snake was so close that Ty could easily make out the flickering tongue and the triangular head darting from side to side with the forward motion of the coils. He could even distinguish the third "eye" that identified the deadly pit viper.

The rattlesnake's body made an odd rubbing-rustling sound as it progressed slowly along the length of Janna's pant leg. Ty watched with the poised patience of a predator, knowing that he had no choice but to wait for an opening. Until the snake's head was drawn away from Janna's body by the sinuous movements of reptilian coils, there was nothing Ty could do that the snake couldn't do quicker—and it would be Janna rather than Ty who suffered from any miscalculation on his part.

Speaking softly and reassuringly to Janna, telling her that there was nothing to fear, Ty waited until the snake's undulating forward motion finally pulled its head to the left, away from Janna's leg. Ty struck swiftly, cleanly, severing the rattlesnake's head from its body. Then he struck again with savage speed, using the knife point to pick up the deadly head and fling it far away from Janna. He grabbed the writhing coils and threw them away, as well. Then he went down beside Janna and pulled her into his arms.

"It's all right, little one," Ty whispered, holding her shaking body. "It's all right. The rattlesnake is dead."

The soothing rumble of Ty's voice and the gentle stroking of his hands over Janna's back calmed her more than his words. Unable to control the trembling of her own body, she clung to him, whispering incoherently about a water hole and a rattlesnake that had struck again and again, and the long days and nights before her father had finally died.

When Ty finally understood what Janna was saying, emotion went through him like a burst of dark lightning. He couldn't bear the thought of Janna alone with her dying father, watching him swell and blacken as the poison slowly destroyed his flesh. It could so easily have been her bedroll the snake had chosen, her tender skin pierced by fangs, her life draining away between labored breaths; and then Ty never would have known Janna, never held her, never breathed kisses over her tear-streaked face.

The realization of how close he had come to losing Janna caused a surge of emotion that was both tender and fierce. The thought of almost having been deprived of her presence made it impossible to deny himself the sweet luxury of holding her now.

The warmth and comfort of Ty's big hands rubbing slowly down Janna's back gradually penetrated her panic. His gentle,

brushing kisses brought heat back to skin that had been chilled
by fear. Turning her face up to his lips, she gave a long, shaky
sigh and snuggled even closer to him, needing the reassurance
of his body in a way that she couldn't put into words. Nor did
she have to. He needed her physical proximity in the same
way, the warm pressure of her body against his telling him
that they both were alive and safe.

When Ty's arms tightened around Janna and he whispered
her name, her hands crept up his chest to his stubble-
roughened cheeks and beyond. Her fingers sought the thick
black hair she longed to caress as she had in the days when
he had been too ill to object to her touch. She slid her hands
beneath his hat, dislodging it, and she shivered with pleasure
when her fingers knew again the silky textures and fullness of
his hair. She moved her hands slowly, flexing them gently,
caressing him and the sensitive skin between her fingers at the
same time.

The intimate, changing pressure of Janna's hands on Ty's
scalp made his breath catch, break and emerge as an almost
silent groan. He moved his head slowly, increasing the pressure of her caressing hands, and the sound he made seemed
to Janna more like a purr from a very large cat than any noise
a man might make. Smiling, she closed her eyes and concentrated on the delicious sensations radiating out from her hands
to envelop her whole body.

Janna's small, almost secret smile was irresistible to Ty.
Knowing he shouldn't, unable to help himself and no longer
caring, he bent his head until he could trace the curve of her
mouth with the tip of his tongue. The unexpected caress startled a soft cry from her.

"Hush," Ty breathed against her lips, moving his head
slowly from side to side, gentling her with soft kisses.
"You're all right, little one. You're safe with me. I won't let
anything hurt you."

Janna parted her lips to explain that she wasn't frightened
any longer, but the gentle glide of Ty's tongue into her mouth
stole from her both the ability and the desire to speak. This
was totally unlike the kiss he had given her before. His mouth

was seductive rather than demanding, his tongue tempting rather than overwhelming. The sliding, hot, almost secret touches were unbearably sweet. Without realizing it, she began to return his caresses. At first the movements of her tongue were tentative, but when his arms tightened, bringing her even closer to his body, she knew that he was enjoying the kiss as much as she was.

Ty felt the hesitant touch of Janna's tongue as though it were a soft flame. The knowledge that she wasn't frightened of him both reassured Ty and tightened every muscle in his body with the anticipation and hunger that had been growing in him since he had first looked through a haze of pain into her clear, compassionate eyes. Even though he had been beaten, bloodied, half-dead with exhaustion, some elemental male level of awareness within himself had seen past her clothes and recognized the essential female presence beneath.

''Janna,'' Ty sighed. He nuzzled her lips, trying to part them again, knowing he shouldn't. He was too hungry, blood rushing too hotly, the aftermath of danger and adrenaline mixed wildly with his need of her. ''Let me kiss you, really kiss you. It won't be like the other time. I won't hurt you,'' he whispered, licking her lips gently, feeling her tremble. ''Do you trust me not to hurt you?''

The sweet glide of Ty's tongue over Janna's sensitized lips made her shiver again. She knew that her moment had finally arrived, the moment when she could get even with him for making fun of her lack of allure. He wanted her now. He couldn't deny it. It was there in the tension of his body, in his ragged breath, in the heat of his flesh hard against her hip.

Trembling, she breathed her answer into his mouth, tasting him. ''I trust you.''

With gentle, inevitable movements of his head, Ty fitted his mouth more deeply to Janna's. She felt herself tasted and enjoyed in the sensuous rhythm of penetration and retreat, advance and withdrawal, the cycle repeated endlessly, like flames dancing up from a campfire. Each caressing movement of their joined mouths brought more and more pleasure until her whole body trembled in anticipation of the next touch, the next intimate tasting, the next languid tangling of warm tongues.

Heat stole beneath Janna's skin, flushing her face, shortening her breath. Bubbles of sensation grew slowly inside her, expanding with each warm movement of Ty's tongue until she shivered and a bubble burst, drenching her with golden heat; and then pleasure gathered again, burst sweetly, made her shiver and moan Ty's name. The slender hands buried in Ty's hair flexed and relaxed in the same rhythms of Janna's tongue—seeking, stroking, finding, mating with the slow, deep motions he had taught her.

The sensuous, searching caresses brought a violent hardening of Ty's flesh that both shocked and dismayed him, telling him that he was very close to the edge of his self-control. With an effort he turned aside from Janna's mouth.

"Little one," he whispered, grabbing her hands, stilling them. "Don't."

When Janna felt Ty's withdrawal, she was unable to control a soft cry of protest. "I thought—I thought you wanted—"

Her voice broke. She didn't try to speak again; the loss of his warmth was devastating to her. Even the hushed light of dusk couldn't conceal the hurt twisting through her at his abrupt rejection. Just as she gathered herself to turn away from him, he shifted his hands and pinned her in place.

"Hell yes, I want you!" Ty whispered fiercely, looming over Janna. "I want your hands all over me. I want to take off your clothes and put my hands all over you, and then I want to open your legs and slide into that soft body of yours and feel you take every bit of me. I want it so much I couldn't stand up straight right now to save my soul."

The look of stunned disbelief on Janna's face made Ty want to laugh and swear at the same time.

"Can't you feel me shaking?" he demanded, barely remembering to keep his voice low. "Do you think it's because of that fool snake? Hell, I've eaten bigger snakes than that and looked around for seconds. It's you that's making me shake. You've been driving me crazy since I first came to after hiding from Cascabel and saw your beautiful gray eyes watching me.''

''You th-thought I was a boy,'' Janna accused in a low voice.

''I thought you were too damned sexy, girl *or* boy, because my britches had a better grip on the truth than my eyes did. My eyes kept telling me that you were a boy and I was some kind of crazy to get all hot and bothered when you touched me. My britches kept telling me that you were as female as they come and I was some kind of moron not to peel off your clothes and get better acquainted.''

The hands that had been tightly gripping Janna eased and began rubbing her shoulders with gentle, circular motions.

''I know you've been hurt in the past,'' Ty said, his voice low, carrying no farther than her ears. ''And I want you so bad that I can't even think, but I would cut off my fingers rather than hurt you. And the way you were kissing me…'' He closed his eyes as a sensual echo resonated through his body, tightening his loins until he had to clench his teeth against the bittersweet ache. ''Do you want me, little one?''

Janna tried to speak but she had no breath. Her heart was wedged in her throat, blocking the passage of air. Seeing Ty's need turned her inside out. She wanted to hold his head against her body and comb her fingers soothingly through his hair; and she wanted to kiss and be kissed again, teasing his tongue with her own and tasting him in a slow, secret kind of dance that made pleasure expand and softly burst deep within her body. Her need to experience that again was so great it was pain.

Was that what was drawing Ty's face into taut lines? Did he feel the same aching need?

''Ty?'' she whispered.

His eyes opened. In the fading light they were a green as deep as the forest itself.

''I…'' Janna's voice died. She licked her lips and felt the sudden tension in Ty's body as his glance followed her tongue. ''Did you like kissing me?''

Ty almost laughed in the instant before he remembered that any knowledge Janna had of men was brief and brutal.

"Yes," Ty murmured, brushing his open mouth over hers. "I liked it. Did you?"

He felt her breath hesitate, catch, then flow over his face in a sweet sigh of agreement. Smiling, he gently caught her lower lip between his teeth, testing the warmth and resilience of her flesh. She went very still in the instant before she trembled and made a small sound.

"I'm sorry," Ty said, releasing her. "I didn't mean to frighten you."

"You didn't," Janna said quickly. "I don't know what's wrong. It just felt so good it made something burst inside me and I went all shivery. I'm sorry."

Ty's breath caught and his eyes narrowed in sensual response to her words. Whatever might have happened to Janna in the past, she was a total innocent when it came to the pleasure a woman could find in the arms of a loving man. The thought of teaching Janna the secrets hidden within her body made Ty feel hot, heavy, thoroughly masculine.

"Don't be sorry," he said huskily. "I like knowing that I've pleased you."

"You do?" she whispered, looking at his lips, wanting to taste him again, to feel his tongue moving within her mouth.

"Yes." Ty smiled and nuzzled the slanting line of Janna's cheekbones until he came to the silky edge of her hair. He stripped off her hat and headband, untied the rawhide thongs holding her braids and unraveled them until his hands were full of the cool fire of her hair. He made an inarticulate sound of pleasure as he searched blindly with his mouth for the tempting curves of her ear. "I want to please you, little one. Will you tell me if I do?"

"Y-yes."

"Yes," Ty breathed as he found Janna's ear with the tip of his tongue, teased the rim and then penetrated the hidden, sensitive core.

Frissons of pleasure tightened Janna's skin, sending telltale parades of goose bumps up and down her arms. She made a startled sound and her hands tightened on Ty's shirt in sensual reflex. When his tongue repeated the penetration again and then again, she felt a sensation like wires tightening deep within her body, making her feel languid and restless at the same time.

"More?" Ty whispered, biting Janna's ear delicately.

He felt her helpless shiver of response and his lips shifted into a very masculine smile of approval and triumph. Before she could speak he softly devoured her ear, his tongue pressing into its core with the same rhythmic movements that had made pleasure swell and burst within her before. Her husky, barely audible moan made him feel as though he were being bathed in golden fire.

With a swift movement of his head Ty captured Janna's mouth. There was no surprise this time when his tongue slid between her teeth, filling her mouth with the taste and feel and textures of his hungry kiss. She answered him by spearing her fingers into his hair and holding his mouth hard upon her own, moaning softly at the sensual heat of him, wanting to take that heat within her own body. The rhythmic caress of tongue against tongue was reinforced by the unconscious movements of her body against his as she tried to ease the heaviness and aching that had condensed in her tightly bound breasts and between her restless legs.

Making a sound halfway between a curse and a prayer, Ty gently disengaged from Janna's hot embrace.

"Before you ask," he said, breathing quickly, audibly, keeping his voice low, "I liked having your body rubbing over mine. I liked it too damn much. I don't want to hurt you, little one. That means we have to take it slow for a bit longer, until you're ready." He closed his eyes and wondered how the hell he would manage it. "Which means that you'll have to give me a minute or two to catch my breath."

"Can I talk while you breathe?" she asked hesitantly, keeping her voice as low as his.

Ty laughed softly despite the savage ache between his legs. Leaning down, he brushed his lips over Janna's mouth, tasting her with a single quick stroke of his tongue before straightening and smiling down at her.

"What do you want to talk about?" he murmured.

"I wish it were darker. Then you wouldn't see me blush when I ask you."

"I'm glad it isn't darker," Ty whispered, nibbling on her chin. "I want to see you, blushes and all. Especially the 'all.' What's your question?"

"Will it—will you hurt me?"

"Oh, God," Ty whispered, gathering Janna into his arms and rocking her gently against his body. "No, little one," he said, kissing her hair, her ear, her flushed cheek, her eyelids, her lips, butterfly brushes that reassured her as no words could have. "If I go slow and you try to relax and not be afraid, it won't hurt you at all. And I'll go slow, Janna. I'll go slow if it kills me."

Slowly her arms came up and around his neck. She pressed her face against the hot skin at the opening of Ty's shirt.

"Will going slow spoil it for you?" Janna whispered. "I don't want to make it bad for you. I want to please you, Ty. I want that so much I ache."

"Going slow won't spoil it. In fact, it can make it so good you feel like dying."

"It can?"

Janna's voice was husky with the conflicting emotions racing through her, passion and nervousness and a hunger to touch and be touched that was completely new to her.

"It can," Ty said. "At least, that's what I'm told. I've never known that kind of pleasure myself."

Janna tried to speak but had no voice. She licked her lips and tilted her head back until she could look into the darkly luminous green of Ty's eyes.

"I want to pleasure you like that," she whispered. "Will you teach me how?"

Chapter Twenty-One

The husky intensity of Janna's voice and her honesty made Ty want to ravish and cherish her in the same instant. The thought of teaching her how to tease and ease and pleasure him was more heady than any liquor he had ever drunk. He traced the lines of her face with his fingertips before caressing the taut curve of her neck and the warm flesh inside her collar. Inevitably his fingers found and undid the first button of her shirt. He bent and pressed his lips against the pulse beating rapidly just beneath her skin.

"Janna," Ty said, breathing her name as much as saying it, "I hope to God I can set fire to you half as hot as you set fire to me. If I can, we'll burn down the whole damn plateau."

"Is that—is that good?"

"Ask me tomorrow," he said, barely stifling a groan as he felt the leap and quickening of her pulse at the touch of his tongue.

Then Ty could deny himself no longer the minor consummation of Janna's mouth. He kissed her slowly, deeply, hungrily, as he finished unbuttoning her shirt. When the cloth parted he expected to find the warmth of her flesh beneath. Instead he found thick layers of fabric and no buttons at all. Even after he took Janna's arms out of the sleeves of her shirt, he could see no way of removing the layers of cloth that bound her.

"What the hell?" muttered Ty.

Belatedly Janna realized that her shirt was unbuttoned and Ty was looking at the wrapping she used to flatten her breasts, disguising her feminine outline.

"Do you sew yourself into that thing?" Ty asked, giving her a crooked smile that made her toes curl.

Janna laughed helplessly, torn between embarrassment and the delicious feeling of having Ty's hands caressing her bare arms. His palms stroked her from her wrists to her shoulders, caressing her inner arms with his long fingers. As he softly probed, he discovered the place beneath her left arm where she tucked in the tail of the cloth, securing the wrapping.

"So that's how you do it."

Pulling the end of the cloth free, Ty turned it back upon itself several times, rolling it loosely. When he had unrolled the fabric across her chest and under her other arm, he put his hand just below Janna's shoulder blades and arched her back enough that he could reach beneath, continuing the slow unwrapping.

With each complete circuit of her body, an inch of previously hidden skin was revealed. Both the cloth and her skin had an elusive fragrance that was a compound of herbs and wildflowers and warm femininity that made his head spin. When he could bear it no longer, he bent and kissed the smooth band of flesh he had just unwrapped.

The feel of Ty's lips skimming below her collarbone made Janna tremble. She slid her hands into his thick hair and rubbed his scalp, smiling when she felt the answering movement of his response. After a few moments the temptation of her still-covered breasts overcame Ty and he resumed unwrapping the long length of cloth.

Gradually the pressure of Janna's bindings eased as more and more layers of fabric were removed. As always, the relief was exquisite. She arched her back, trying to make the unwrapping go more quickly, eager to be able to breathe easily once more, to be free of the cloth restraints.

Ty refused to be rushed, for he was finding an unexpected, intensely sensual pleasure in the slow revelation of Janna's body. As the turns of fabric moved down her chest, the first curves of her breasts were unveiled. There were long lines of red pressed into her skin, legacy of the tight bindings. He smoothed his thumb over the lines as though to erase them, then brushed his lips over the marks and traced them with the tip of his tongue.

Eyes closed, Janna made soft sounds of pleasure as Ty soothed her skin. She was still breathless from the unexpected caress of his tongue when he arched her back, lifting her so that the cloth could unwind beneath her. He circled her body once and then twice, three times; and then the unwrapping stopped again. But instead of gently lowering her to the ground as he had before, he held her suspended over his powerful forearm, the graceful line of her back like a drawn bow. Slowly Janna opened her eyes and saw Ty staring at her as though what he saw was totally unexpected.

And it was. He never would have guessed at the presence of full, firm curves and lush pink tips hidden beneath turn after turn of tight cloth.

"Ty?" Janna whispered, not understanding why he was so still, so intent. "What's wrong?"

He looked up and her eyes widened at the harsh lines of his face.

"Don't ever," Ty said distinctly, "punish yourself like that again."

Before Janna could speak he bent over her breasts and soothed each mark that had been left by the cloth, working from the first smooth swell of flesh toward the deep pink crowns. The feel of his tongue laving the small marks the bindings had left was indescribable. She wanted to twist slowly in his arms like a flame, offering every bit of her breasts to his mouth. When he came to the margin between the satin of her skin and the velvet of her nipple, he circled her with exquisite care, ignoring her startled cry and her broken breath and the fingers tightening reflexively in his hair.

And then Ty could bear the temptation no longer. He took Janna's offering into his mouth, sucking on the velvet nipple until it was tight and hard, and still he tugged on her with slow, sensual rhythms that made small cries ripple from her.

When the nipple could be drawn out no more, he slowly released it, admiring the taut, glistening peak. He cupped the breast in his hand and made tight circles with his palm, rubbing the hard nipple as he bent and caressed her other breast with lips and tongue, drawing her out, shaping her, pulling sensuously until her breath was quick and broken with the lightning strokes of sensation streaking through her body.

Dizzy, breathless, lost in a hushed, shimmering world she had never known existed, Janna felt pleasure expand and burst and radiate through her. Ty felt it too, the flush of sensual heat spreading beneath her skin, the small movements of her hips as she sought the pressure of his body, the tiny cries when his teeth and tongue brought new heat to her.

Finally Ty lifted his head, releasing the nipple he had so lovingly shaped. Janna whimpered very softly, wanting more of the pleasure that had grown in her with each movement of his mouth. She opened her gray eyes and looked at him with silent pleading.

"More?" Ty asked, smiling, his voice as heavy as the blood beating in his veins.

Janna shivered helplessly as Ty's hand closed over one of her breasts and slowly pleasured her.

"Yes," she whispered.

He smiled, enjoying her open pleasure and the growing flush of arousal beneath her skin. "Where else would you like to be kissed?"

The shocked look that came to Janna's face told Ty that she had never thought about such things.

"Never mind, little one," Ty said. He circled the erect tip of each breast with his tongue and whispered, "I'll think of something."

With a speed and power that surprised Janna, Ty turned and lay on his back and in the same movement lifted her, pulling her over his body like a living blanket. When her hips pressed against the hard ridge of flesh that waited impatiently beneath the thick cloth of his pants, he made a low sound of pleasure-pain.

Not understanding, Janna pulled away. Ty's legs parted and

her own legs sank between his. He moved quickly, lifting his legs just enough to trap hers beneath, twining his legs with hers at the ankles, forcing their bodies into an intimate match, hard against soft, consummation no more than a few layers of cloth away.

"Unbutton my shirt," Ty said in a thick voice. "You'll like the feel of my bare skin against your breasts. And so will I."

The slight movement of Janna's body when she reached for Ty's collar button made her hips rock against the hot cradle he had made for her between his legs. He groaned in a kind of exquisite agony, for he had never needed a woman so much as he needed Janna at that instant.

"Again," he whispered. "Move against me just once more. Just once."

Hesitantly Janna moved her hips against Ty again, feeling the hard bulge of his erection like a brand against her abdomen. The sound he made deep in his throat could have come from agony or undiluted pleasure. His hand came between their bodies. Unerringly he found the most sensitive part of her and pressed, rocking his hips slowly beneath her. The sudden heat that radiated out from his hand made her gasp. His name came from her lips in a husky, urgent, questioning cry.

"Yes," Ty said, his voice low and thick. "You can feel it, too, can't you?" Gently he released Janna's ankles and lifted her into a sitting position astride his waist. Her breath caught and her hips moved helplessly as he teased her nipples again with his fingertips. "It's going to be good. It's going to be so damn good. Unbutton my shirt, sugar. I want to feel your hands on my bare skin."

With fingers that trembled, Janna undid the buttons on Ty's shirt. She had seen him naked before, but it hadn't affected her one-tenth as much as watching his powerful body emerge from the shirt. In the dusk, the curling pelt of black hair was very distinct, as was the dark center line of his body where the hair narrowed to pencil width and vanished behind his belt. The heat and resilience of him were as alluring as his dark smile. With catlike pleasure Janna kneaded the muscular flesh she had so often bathed or medicated but had never caressed.

And she had wanted to. She realized that now. She understood that her hands had quivered to know every texture of Ty, the satin smoothness where skin stretched over muscle, the power inherent in him, the thick silk of his chest hair, the finer silk of the hair beneath his arms, the flat disk and hard nubbin of his nipples. Just as she had become lost in the discovery of her own body beneath his mouth, she became lost in the discovery of his body beneath her hands.

Ty watched Janna through eyes narrowed with passion. Her transparent pleasure in exploring his body was violently exciting to him. It was unlike anything he had ever known. It put him on an exquisite rack, which pulled him in two conflicting directions. Part of him wanted to grab Janna and thrust into her and end the pulsing ache of his body.

And part of him wanted to keep his hands off her and learn more about himself and her and the sweet torment of being suspended between anticipation and ecstasy.

Again and again Janna's fingers combed through the hair covering Ty's chest, tracing his nipples and then following the quickly narrowing pelt down to the cold of his belt buckle. She knew that slim line of hair would continue down his body for a hand span and then radiate out into a thick, curling thatch. She wanted to see that too, to run her hands over him without any boundaries on the touching. She wanted that so much she couldn't breathe.

Not stopping to think or to question, Janna reached for Ty's belt buckle.

"Not yet," he said huskily, grabbing Janna's hands and pulling them back up to the safer territory of his chest. "It will be too quick that way. I want to enjoy you first."

"I thought you had enjoyed me," she whispered, bending to kiss his hands.

His smile made her heart turn over. "Just part of you, sugar. There's some very sweet territory I haven't unwrapped yet, much less enjoyed."

Ty reversed their positions with one of the swift, powerful movements that always caught Janna off guard but no longer frightened her. Whatever came next, she was certain Ty would

164   *Reckless Love*

be careful with her. She lay quietly, watching him as he knelt at her feet and removed her knee-high moccasins and his own boots with quick motions. He tugged open his belt but left his pants untouched. When he unfastened Janna's belt she trembled.

"It's all right," Ty said, kissing Janna's lips. "I won't hurt you."

Janna took a shaky breath and nodded. "I know. It's just…"

Before she could explain that she had never been naked in front of anyone, it was too late. Her ability to speak deserted her as leather slipped from the buckle with an easy movement of Ty's hand. Without the belt, her oversize men's pants slid easily from her body, and with them her underpants.

When Janna lay completely nude before Ty, his breath came out in a slow, unraveling groan.

"It's like seeing a satin butterfly emerge from a mud cocoon," Ty whispered, running his fingertips over the pale curves and velvet shadows of Janna's body.

When he reached the dark delta at the base of her torso, she made a surprised sound and moved as though to evade his hand, pressing her legs together reflexively.

"Hush, little one," Ty murmured, kissing her lips. "I know you've been hurt there but I won't hurt you. I know how delicate you are, how soft, how warm. Even you don't know how soft you can be or how warm. Let me show you."

"What d-do you want me to do?" Janna's voice broke as she shivered in a combination of nervousness and surprise at the presence of Ty's fingers searching gently through the dense triangle of hair that shielded her most sensitive flesh.

"Don't be so stiff. I won't hurt you," Ty murmured. He kissed Janna coaxingly until her lips parted and he could love her with slow, deep strokes of his tongue. He lifted his mouth and whispered against her lips. "Open your legs just a little, sugar, just a little. I'll be very gentle."

His voice became a husky sigh of triumph and discovery when Janna relaxed enough to allow his fingertip to skim over the soft, hot folds between her legs.

"Just a little more," Ty whispered, caressing her, seeking the heated well of her femininity, finding just its soft, burning edges. But it was enough. It told him that her blood was running as hotly and hungrily as his own. He probed lightly and was rewarded by a hint of the smooth, sultry sheath that awaited him. "My beautiful satin butterfly," he said huskily. "So hot, so sleek. Open a little more for me, butterfly. I won't force you. I just want to love all of you. Let me…"

Janna tried to speak but her voice broke over Ty's name. The gliding, skimming caress of his finger had changed into a gentle penetration that took her breath away. He bent to her mouth and his tongue echoed the tender movements of his hand between her legs. The heat and tension that had been gathering deep within her body flared suddenly, wildly, claiming her in a gentle convulsion that took her wholly by surprise.

But not Ty. He had been coaxing Janna toward just such a minor peak of ecstasy since he had first discovered the sensuality hidden within her body. He repeated the twin, gentle assaults on her body, his tongue gliding over hers in a deep kiss as his finger slid between her legs in a slow, teasing dance of penetration and withdrawal that brought soft whimpers from her throat. Passion shimmered and burst within her again, heat and pleasure overflowing.

Janna moaned softly as Ty withdrew from her sultry center and caressed the bud of her passion with fingertips still slick from her own response. Heat speared through her, tightening her body. She cried out into his mouth and her hips moved beneath his hand, asking for something she had never known. She sensed his hesitation, felt as much as heard him groan, and bit back a cry of protest when he withdrew his caressing hand.

"Hush, little one," Ty murmured, freeing himself of his clothes in a few swift movements. "It won't be long."

"Ty?"

"I'm right here," he said, gently pressing Janna's legs farther apart, making room for himself.

Delicately he teased the nub he had coaxed from her soft, humid folds. She trembled and her knees flexed instinctively, allowing him greater access to her body. Her passionate response spilled over him as he probed her softness with his own aching flesh. The moist, welcoming heat of her body was unmistakable, a silent command that he come deeply within her; but she was so tight that he was afraid of hurting her.

Shivering with the harshness of his self-imposed restraint, Ty began taking Janna as gradually as evening took the day. Her eyes opened in sensual surprise and she looked up into the face of the man who was slowly, so slowly, becoming part of her. Each time the pressure of him within her became almost painful, he sensed it, withdrew and gradually came to her again.

The exquisitely gentle penetration made waves of heat gather and burst within her, showering him with her pleasure. She heard him groan and push more deeply inside and then felt the harsh tension shaking his body as he forced himself to stop.

"You're a virgin!"

Chapter Twenty-Two

Ty's accusing voice was hoarse as he fought against his deepest needs and tried to force himself to retreat from Janna's moist, clinging heat. But he couldn't. He wanted only to continue taking her a bit at a time; and when he caressed her to ecstasy once more he wanted to thrust past the frail barrier separating their bodies from total unity. She would feel no pain at the instant he took her because she would be too deeply enmeshed in her climax to know or care that for the first time in her life a man would be fully sheathed within her.

Virgin.

"Christ," Ty groaned, "if I'd known, I never would have touched you."

"Then I'm glad you didn't know," Janna said huskily. She shivered and melted over him again, moving her hips helplessly, in the grip of a passion she had never expected and had no idea how to control. All she wanted was more of him, more of the sweet friction as she stretched around him. "I want this, Ty. Please. You're not hurting me. I love…feeling you." She moved her hips slowly, caressing him and herself in the same motion. "Oh, that's so good," she whispered raggedly, rocking, moving as much as he would allow, "but it's not enough…not…enough."

"Stop it!" Ty said roughly as he felt the last shreds of his self-control slipping away. "You're a virgin!"

Janna's nails dug into the flexed power of Ty's buttocks

and her body twisted wildly beneath his as she whispered
again and again that what he had given her was good but not
enough. With each movement she became more seductive,
more demanding, more welcoming, so hot and sleek that he
found himself pressing again and yet again at the fragile flesh
that barred total consummation.

Ty groaned and forced himself to move just slightly while
his fingers sought and claimed the slick, delicate nub of
Janna's passion. He controlled the instinctive rocking of her
hips by settling more of his weight between her legs, pinning
her in place while he caressed her, bringing her closer and
closer to ecstasy.

When he felt the sudden mist of passion flush her skin and
her breath broke and her cries came quickly, rising urgently,
he covered her mouth with his own and began to move again
within her, trying to hold back from the elemental consummation that awaited him in the depths of her virginal body. A
groan racked him as he thought what it would be like to
sheathe every bit of his need in her, to pierce her virginity and
feel her pleasure flow over him in a hot, ecstatic rain.

And then it was happening, the hot rain and the sheathing,
ecstasy bursting with each movement of Ty's hips; and Janna
wept at the perfection as he let go of control and locked himself so deeply within her that she felt the certainty of his climax as the most intimate kind of caress, a pulsing presence
that sent her spinning into ecstasy once again, her body caressing him rhythmically in the quivering aftermath of his own
release.

Janna's tiny, ecstatic cries pierced Ty like golden needles,
reaching past the flesh to the soul beneath. Violent pleasure
racked him until his muscles stood out like iron. The endless,
shuddering release that followed overwhelmed him. Unable to
see, unable to think, unable to speak, he spent himself again
and again in the virgin who had touched a part of him no other
woman ever had.

When Ty was at last quiet once more, Janna clung to his
powerful, sweat-slicked body, savoring the intimacy of lying
beneath him and feeling him inside her as evening condensed

soundlessly into night around them. She hadn't known what to expect from the act of love, but she hadn't anticipated anything so hot, so sweet, so violently complete.

"I love you," Janna whispered, kissing Ty's shoulder.

The words were very soft, barely a whisper, but Ty heard them. A combination of guilt and anger raced through him when he remembered the irrevocable instant when he had taken Janna's virginity. Silently he raged at himself and his baffling lack of control where she was concerned. He had been able to keep himself tightly reined while he seduced her, yet he hadn't been able to pull back after he had discovered she was a virgin.

He didn't understand that. He should have been able to turn away from her; she wasn't the first woman to try that particular marital trap. He had eluded the others in the past, and those girls had been much more accomplished in their snares and lures.

But Janna had been a handful of fire and beauty, and her ecstatic cries as he pierced her virginity would haunt Ty until he died.

"I never should have taken you," he said in a low, bitter voice.

Janna's gently stroking hands became still. "Why?"

"Because I discovered that you were a virgin and I had no intention of marrying you, that's why. But I had a lot of help getting past your innocence, didn't I? First you tell me you're not a virgin—"

"I never said that," Janna interrupted in a fierce whisper.

"What about when you ran and I brought you down and kissed you too hard, and you said you'd taken a lot worse from men and survived?"

"I only meant that you hadn't really hurt me. And you hadn't."

"What about Joe Troon?"

"What about him?"

"Ned said that Troon 'kept' you for a while."

"Ned is a drunk and a liar. Troon caught me but he never kept me."

"Well, sugar, you sure as hell didn't act like any virgin I'd ever met. Ever since I came to after Cascabel's gauntlet you've been rubbing up against me and sighing and smiling and looking at me out of those smoky gray eyes like I'd spilled honey in my lap and you couldn't wait to lick off every bit of it," Ty said in a low, angry voice. "It would have served you right if I'd backed you up against a tree, opened my pants and had you standing up like the lowest kind of camp follower."

Janna thought of the ways she had tormented Ty without truly understanding the elemental force of his need...and her own. The thought of how often she had smiled when he had turned away to hide the evidence of his arousal made her ashamed now.

"I'm so sorry," Janna said, touching Ty's face tentatively. "I didn't know what I was doing to you. I didn't know the power of what you were fighting, how much you needed me."

"It was a woman I needed, not you," snarled Ty, jerking away from Janna's gentle touch.

All the movement accomplished was to remind him that he was still held within the satin sheath of her body; and she felt even better now than in his hottest memories. He told himself to roll aside, to separate himself from her, but his body refused to respond. He was drinking her heat, growing inside her, and his blood was beating heavily, urging his hips to move in primal rhythms.

"*Virgin,*" Ty said, and it was a curse. "But you wanted it as much as I did, didn't you? Hell, you damn near burned me alive with your cries and your hips sliding, pushing me deeper and deeper..."

Ty shuddered unexpectedly, memories bursting inside him, sensuality lancing through his body, tightening him, making him feel every bit of the hot perfection of being locked inside Janna.

The knowledge of his own helpless response to her shocked Ty. He shouldn't feel this way. The sweat wasn't dry on his body from the first time he had taken her. He shouldn't want her again the way he did right now—need knotting his guts, his body hard and heavy and hot, filled to bursting once more.

He fought to remain still, not to respond, not to move, but the knowledge of the ecstatic consummation he would find within Janna's body was too new, too overwhelming for him to deny or control it. With a low, raw cry, he fought against the lure of her, but even as he cried out he was moving slowly, surrendering himself to her one hard inch at a time.

Janna's breath caught as Ty deliberately measured himself within her once, then twice, then three times. She didn't understand his rejection of her apology or his anger with her, but she understood the need that was making him tremble; it was her own need, doubling and redoubling with each heartbeat, a flame burning up from their joined bodies, heat delicately melting and ravenously devouring her at the same time. She shivered and arched beneath him in sensual abandon.

Ty groaned and felt fire eat ever more deeply into him, burning away thought, burning away reluctance, leaving only the elemental union of male and female, a joining that was deeper than flesh, hotter than desire, two living flames leaping higher as they touched, overlapped, entwined. He swore in a mingling of awe and savage triumph as he felt his lover's fluid grace rise to match his own savage need.

"Satin...butterfly," Ty said hoarsely, more accusation than affection in his voice. "Did you think that I'd marry you once I found what it was like to have you?"

He thrust his tongue into Janna's mouth, muffling whatever her answer might have been. Before the kiss ended she was moaning softly and moving in languid counterpart to the slow, circular dance of his hips.

"It won't work," he said, his breath coming quickly, heavily. "I'll take every bit of your body. I'll give you every bit of my body in return. But that's all. Just two bodies giving and taking. Do you hear me?"

Janna moaned brokenly and closed herself around him in a deep, instinctive caress.

"Do you hear me?" Ty demanded, clenching himself against the unbearable seduction of her body.

"Yes," she whispered. Her hips lifted slightly, then circled,

seducing him, loving him. "I heard you the first time you told
me in the valley."

"What?"

Ty's past words echoed cruelly within Janna's mind: *I'll
have my silken lady or I'll have none at all for longer than it
takes to pleasure myself.*

"I know that I'm not the silken lady of your dreams," Janna
said, her voice a whisper of unquenchable hope and a foretaste
of despair. "You're pleasuring yourself. That's all."

Ty didn't argue or protest her words.

Janna had expected no more, yet she had to bite her lip not
to protest aloud the emotions tearing through her, passion and
grief and the shivering precursors of wild ecstasy. When Ty
moved within her again, she wept silently, grateful that it was
too dark for him to see her tears, feeling his breath as cool,
quickening gusts over her wet cheeks.

"But you still want me?" Ty persisted. "No games, no
secret plans, no regrets?" He locked their bodies together suddenly, a joining so deep and hot and complete that it tore a
low cry from his throat, a cry that was her name. He rocked
against her with tiny, intense motions, burning up, buried in
fire and wanting it, all of it, *burning*. "Do you still want this?"

"I want…" Janna whispered, but could say no more because tears drowned her voice and the truth was too bitter to
speak aloud. She wanted to be loved by him in all ways, not
just one.

"Janna?" Ty asked, holding himself motionless but for the
helpless shuddering of his aroused body. "Answer me!"

She tried to move, to take from him what he was withhold-
ing. It was impossible. He was too strong, too skilled, and she
loved him.

"Yes, damn you," she whispered achingly. "Yes!"

Ty heard only the agreement, not the pain. He let out his
pent breath in a ragged groan.

"I need you," he said in a low voice. His hips began to
move in quickening rhythms as shudder after shudder of tension went through his powerful body. "God help me, I've
never needed any woman like this."

Janna heard the bafflement and strain in Ty's voice and felt herself swept up in his overwhelming need. Crying silently, loving him and knowing that he would love no one but the silken lady of his dreams, Janna took all that Ty could give to her of himself and in return gave all of herself that he would take.

The sensual generosity of Janna's response washed over Ty, bathing both of them in fire. She heard his broken groan, felt the power of him within her redouble, felt the hungry, rhythmic penetration as his body drove against hers again and again and again. His urgency excited her, overwhelmed her, shattered her, and still he moved hard within her, drinking her rippling cries, rocking, rocking, rocking...burning, she was burning and there was no end to the wild, consuming flames.

Janna's breath broke and a low cry was torn from her throat as she surrendered to savage ecstasy. Ty drank that cry and silently asked more of her, fierce in his demands of her body, wanting something he couldn't name, driving into her as though she were the last woman he would ever have, wanting at some deep, inarticulate level of his consciousness to leave his imprint upon her very soul.

Her legs twisted around his waist and her body shivered, her mouth bit into his, her nails scored his back; and he smiled and spoke dark words to her as he slipped his arms beneath her knees and slowly pulled her legs up his body, over his shoulders, opening her to him fully.

With deep, shuddering pleasure Ty drove again and again into the satin heat of Janna's body, smothering her abandoned cries with his mouth, penetrating her completely, repeatedly, powerfully, until she was racked by ecstasy; and still his potent movements continued, as though he would become a part of her or die in the effort. She thought she could know no greater pleasure without dying, and she tried to tell him but suddenly she had no voice, no will, for she was transfixed by a savage rapture.

Janna would have screamed her pleasure then, heedless of the danger, but Ty's mouth was consuming hers. He took the ecstatic scream into himself as passionate convulsions swept his body, burning him to his soul, ecstasy racking him with every heartbeat.

And he thought he was dying as he poured himself into her wildly shivering, welcoming body.

Chapter Twenty-Three

Utterly spent, Ty groaned softly and laid his head next to Janna's. He kissed her very gently, feeling an almost overwhelming tenderness toward the woman who had accepted him without restraint or regret or promises, bringing him the most intense, consuming union he had ever known.

When his lips brushed her cheek he tasted tears. The thought that his ecstasy had caused Janna hurt made pain lance harshly through Ty, an agony as surprising to him as the endless, hot, violent upwelling of his need for her had been.

"I'm sorry," Ty said, kissing Janna's face blindly, gently, finding everywhere the taste of tears. "Little one, I'm sorry. I didn't mean to hurt you."

Janna tried to answer but could not, for emotion had closed her throat.

Ty held her, rocking her in his arms, hating himself for hurting the girl who had saved his life at such great risk to her own.

"I owe you so much more than this…" he whispered, and he was haunted by the silken lady of whom he had dreamed so long, the wife who would be the greatest adornment of the life he would build to replace what war had taken away. "Oh God, what have I done to you, to myself?"

Janna shook her head silently, fighting for control of herself, not understanding what had caused the pain in Ty's voice. After a few moments she was able to speak.

"You didn't hurt me."

"Like hell I didn't."

"Ty, you didn't. I felt nothing but pleasure."

He heard Janna's words, felt her hands stroking his hair, soothing him, and felt a cold rush of self-contempt. He had wanted her, he had taken her despite her innocence, and in doing so he had left her suited only for the life of a prostitute or a nun.

"You're so innocent. My God, you don't even understand what has happened, do you?"

"I understand that you didn't hurt me."

"I didn't hurt…" Ty's laughter was low and as harsh as the guilt clawing at him. His hands tightened on Janna as he realized the extent of his folly. "You little fool, I ruined you! You have no family, no profession, no wealth. All you had of value for a husband was your virginity, and now that's gone. I've left you suited to be nothing except a man's mistress, but you lack the social graces for even that profession. You'll end up locked in a nun's cage or you'll be the toy of many men, not one."

Janna flinched and tried to draw away from Ty's cruel summation of her value as a woman, a mate, but she was too securely held to retreat. He drew her closer, not even noticing her futile attempts to free herself from his embrace.

"Never mind, little one," Ty said, his voice low and empty, echoing with despair at the death of his personal dream, the silken lady who now would forever be beyond his reach. "It was my fault, not yours. I'll marry you as soon as we get to the fort."

It took Janna a minute to absorb what he had said, what he had implied—and when she understood, she was wild with hurt.

"Like burning hell you'll marry me," Janna said in a low, savage voice.

"What?"

"I may be suited only to be a saloon girl, but I keep my word."

"Janna, I didn't mean—" Ty began, only to be cut off.

"No! I said that I wouldn't ask for any promises or have any regrets or any secret plans," she whispered angrily, telling herself that hopes weren't the same as plans.

Not that it mattered. Ty had taken care of the hopes, as well. *No family. No profession. No wealth. No social graces.* And no emotion in his voice but guilt and despair and anger at being trapped into marrying such a poor specimen of femininity.

"I've never trapped a living thing in my life," she said fiercely, "and I'll be damned to hell for eternity if I take your freedom now. Do you hear me, Tyrell MacKenzie? Do you?"

"You didn't take my freedom. I gave it away the same way men always have, thinking with my crotch instead of my brain."

"You can have it right back—freedom, brain, crotch, all of it! I want nothing that isn't freely given."

"The world doesn't work that way, sugar," Ty said wearily, releasing Janna and rolling over onto his back. "The only virgin a decent man takes is the girl who becomes his wife. We'll be married as soon as—"

"They'll be picking cotton in hell before I marry you," Janna interrupted, her voice shaking, her body cold and empty without him.

It was as though Ty hadn't heard. "I'm responsible for you. I live up to my responsibilities."

"I'm responsible for myself. I've lived on my own for five years. I can do it for another—"

"Christ!" hissed Ty, cutting Janna off. "Are you so naive that you don't know you could get pregnant after this? How would you take care of yourself, much less a baby, too?" He waited, but there was no answer except the small sounds Janna made as she searched for her clothes in the darkness. "We'll be married at the fort and you'll stay there while I hunt for Lucifer."

"No."

"Janna—oh, the hell with it," Ty whispered harshly. "We'll be married at the fort and then we'll hunt Lucifer together. Does that satisfy you?"

"No."

Janna thrust an arm through a shirtsleeve and fished around for the other opening. Even if it hadn't been dark, the tears streaming down her face would have blinded her. None of her emotions showed in her constrained whisper, for which she was grateful. Having marriage offered to her out of guilt was bad enough; having it offered to her out of pity would be unbearable.

"Janna, be reasonable. I'll need Lucifer to build a good horse herd," Ty said as patiently as he could manage. "Otherwise I'll have no way to take care of my family."

"I said I'd help you catch Lucifer and I will. Marriage was no part of the bargain."

Ty's patience evaporated. With uncanny speed he grabbed Janna, flattened her beneath him once more and began whispering furiously.

"Listen to me, you little fool. You have no idea how the world works."

"Then teach me," she whispered defiantly. "Teach me how to please a man, how to be good enough to be a mistress rather than a whore. That's all I ask of you. Education, not marriage."

"But if you're preg—" he began.

"I stopped bleeding two days ago," she interrupted. "There's little chance you've made me pregnant."

Ty should have been relieved, but the scent and feel of Janna beneath him was driving everything else from his mind. Even as he told himself he must be crazy, he realized that he wanted her again.

"This time, yes," he agreed huskily, "but what about the next time I take you, and the next, and the times after that? Because if I'm around you, I'll take you every damned chance I get." His hand slid down her body until he could feel once more her intimate heat. "Satin butterfly," he whispered, unable to control the faint trembling of his fingers as he skimmed the edges of her softness. "Don't you understand yet? When I see you, hear you, smell you, touch you, taste you…"

A threadlike groan vibrated through Ty. "You're killing

me. I can't leave you alone if I'm around you. I can't live
with myself if I get you pregnant. And I need you around so
that I can track down Lucifer before he gets killed or this
whole damned territory blows up in our faces. We have to get
married, Janna. There's no other way.''

''No.''

Janna clamped her legs together, trying to deny Ty the softness only he had ever touched.

It was futile. All she succeeded in doing was imprisoning
his hand between her thighs. He made a sound of pleasure and
despair as one finger slid gently into her and he felt her sleek,
humid warmth surrounding him once more.

''I won't marry you,'' Janna whispered, her breath breaking.
''Do you hear me? I won't spend my life having you look at
me and long for a silken lady.''

Ty hesitated, then slowly probed Janna's sensuous warmth.
''I hear you. But what are we going to do about this? I meant
what I said, little one. Having had you, I can't leave you
alone.''

She tried not to give voice to her pleasure, but a husky
sound escaped her lips. ''Teach me. That's all I ask of you.
A mistress, not a whore.''

The words went into Ty like knives, twisting even as they
sliced into him. ''I can't live with that. It's not enough. You
deserve much more. Come back to Wyoming with me,'' he
said in a low voice, caressing Janna because he was helpless
to stop. ''Silver and Cassie can teach you how to sit and speak
and smile like a lady. They'll teach you how to dress and I'll
see that you have enough dowry to attract a good man, a man
who won't berate you for what I took from you. Then you'll
be a married woman, Janna, not any man's mistress or every
man's whore.''

''I'll marry no man,'' she whispered. ''Ever.''

''Janna…''

Her only answer was a husky cry and her warmth reaching
out to Ty, silently promising oblivion within her body. The
heat and scent of her filled his nostrils, sending a wave of
desire through him. Suddenly he wanted to bend down and

immerse himself in Janna, tasting her essence, drinking the very secrets of her body. The thought shocked him, for he had never wanted that kind of intimacy with a woman before.

"You're so sweet to touch," Ty whispered, stroking Janna with slow, hidden motions. "I never knew a woman could be so responsive, so perfect. Satin butterfly, more beautiful to me each time I touch you."

"Ty..." Janna said, moaning his name softly, feeling her tumultuous emotions condense into pure burning desire.

She knew she should tell him to stop but she was unable to form the words. She wanted his touch too much. She had never known such ravishing closeness with anyone, had never even dreamed it was possible. The knowledge that he, too, found something special in her made it impossible to turn away from his need.

Ty heard the telltale break and quickening of Janna's breath and didn't know whether to curse or laugh as he felt himself hardening, succumbing to her sleek satin trap once more. She was a handful of fire, a sensuous dream, so recently a virgin and yet so generous and unafraid as a lover.

Janna's small hands found his in the darkness and she held them motionless, trying to still the secret movements within her body.

"Stop," she whispered, yet even as she spoke she felt her own heat overflowing in silent contradiction.

"Why?" Ty murmured, slowly penetrating and withdrawing from her body despite her clinging fingers. "Am I hurting you?"

"N-no."

To Ty the sensual break and shiver of Janna's voice was as arousing as her heat welling up at his touch.

"You're too innocent to understand how rare you are, how extraordinary this is," he whispered, feeling the vital hardening of his flesh as he bent down to her. "But I'm not innocent. I know. I'd agree to anything in order to keep on touching you. I've never been like this with any woman. *Bruja*, sweet fire witch. You burn me alive and I tremble and spend myself within you…and then you renew me with a breath, a kiss, a touch.''

Janna whispered Ty's name helplessly, moved beyond words that she could affect him so deeply.

"Renew me," Ty whispered, lifting her hand and kissing it before placing it over his swelling male flesh.

She felt the helpless, sensuous jerk of his body as her fingers curled around him in answer to the pressure of his own hands.

"Teach me?" she whispered.

"Yes," he said. "Every chance I get. All the way from here to Wyoming. And then—"

"No," she interrupted, arching up to meet him. "No tomorrows. Just teach me. Teach me now."

He started to speak, then forgot what he was going to say when her hands moved.

"Like this?" Janna whispered, measuring and caressing him with the same slow, sensuous motion.

"Sweet…God…yes," Ty said. His whole body tightened and moved with her hands in a sinuous dance that made him tremble. He lowered his head until he could feel her breath against his lips. "And like this," he whispered, fitting first his body and then his mouth to hers, thrusting deeply into her generous warmth. "And this…and *this*…"

Even as Janna shivered and softly cried out, Ty bent and drank ecstasy from her lips, sinking wholly into her, wondering who was the teacher and who the student in the hushed intimacy of the meadow night.

Chapter Twenty-Four

The brutal crack of rifle fire at the northwest end of Raven Creek's meadow jerked Janna and Ty awake in a heart-pounding instant.

Neither one moved.

No more sounds came. After a few minutes Ty eased away from Janna, grabbed his carbine and crawled to a vantage point where he could look out across the meadow. There was nothing in sight. A moment later he sensed Janna coming up behind him. He turned and shook his head. She retreated as silently as she had come. So did he.

Without talking, they withdrew to the place where they had slept. Ty reached for his backpack at the same instant that Janna reached for the cloth she had used to bind her breasts. Although she and Ty had been forced by the cold to put on their clothes in the hours before dawn, he hadn't allowed her to wrap up in the cloth again. Instead, he had curled spoon fashion along her back, slid his hands up beneath her loose shirt and caressed her gently until they both fell asleep.

As soon as Janna's fingers closed on the binding, she realized that she wasn't going to be allowed to use it this morning, either. Ty snatched the cloth from her fingers, rolled it tightly and jammed it into his backpack. Then he pulled her to her feet.

"I'd kiss you," he said very softly, looking hungrily at her mouth, "but if I did, I'd undress you and lie between your legs again. That wouldn't be a very smart thing to do right now.''

Janna's mind agreed, but her body swayed hungrily toward Ty. He let go of her as though he had grabbed something too hot to hold. Saying nothing, Janna turned and began threading through the forest, circling toward the northeast corner of the meadow. After a few minutes she looked at Ty and gestured toward the meadow. He nodded. Together they walked, then crawled and finally wiggled snake fashion toward the edge of the meadow.

In the clear yellow light of morning, the signs were unmistakable—a group of unshod horses had grazed the meadow within the past few days. The presence of small hoofprints and diminutive manure piles told Ty and Janna that the horses were wild, for hunting or raiding parties didn't use mares whose foals were unweaned. Overlaid on the random tracks of grazing animals were those of a shod horse walking across the meadow and into the dense pine forest beyond. It was those prints that had attracted the Indian hunting party the previous night.

''Troon,'' Janna whispered, looking at the prints.

''How can you tell?''

''See how worn the shoe is on the left front hoof? Troon's too cheap to get his horse shod regularly.''

''Wasn't bothering to hide his trail, was he?'' Ty muttered.

''He was probably drunk.''

''Then he's probably dead. Was it Lucifer's bunch he was following?''

''I can't tell from the tracks around here. I'd have to go to the center and check the muddy spots along Raven Creek. Besides, Lucifer never mixes with his herd when the mares graze. If this is his bunch, his tracks will be off to the side somewhere.''

Both Janna and Ty looked out over the empty, inviting meadow that Troon had crossed sometime yesterday. The ground beneath their bodies was still slightly damp with dew, but they were in no hurry to stand up and expose themselves to any watchers who might have been posted by the meadow.

Raven Creek's watershed had become all but overrun by Cascabel and his growing band of renegades.

Ty's hard green eyes searched the boundary between forest and meadow, seeking any sign that Indians were about. Birds called and flew naturally, landed in low branches or on the meadow itself. No bird flew up with a startled outcry, indicating that danger lay hidden somewhere around Raven Creek's meadow itself.

Janna watched the area as carefully as Ty. She saw nothing that should disturb her, yet she was reluctant to cross the meadow in pursuit of either Lucifer's tracks or those of Joe Troon. She looked at Ty and gestured toward the meadow in silent question. He shook his head in a slow negative. She didn't disagree. Together they eased backward deeper into the small trees and sun-hungry bushes that ringed the meadow. When both of them were within the cover of the forest once more, Ty gestured for Janna to choose the best route around to the opposite side of the meadow.

Moving quickly and quietly, Janna set off into the forest. Within the fragrant, hushed cover beneath the trees, the going became easier. The tall pines screened out much of the sunlight, making it impossible for plants to thrive on the forest floor. Even so, fallen trees and branches forced Janna to make many small detours. Every few minutes she stopped and stood motionless, watching and listening to the forest with the consummate grace and stillness of a wild deer.

Ty never became impatient with Janna's detours or her seemingly random stops. Watching her blend with the land was a pleasure for him. Though he took second to few people in his ability to track or to hunt, Ty knew that here on Black Plateau, Janna was at home in a way that only a wild animal could equal.

It's a good thing she didn't get up here before I found her, Ty thought as he watched Janna merge with the shadows beneath the trees. *I never would have caught her.*

Part of Ty wondered if that wouldn't have been better for both of them, but even as the question occurred to him he denied it. The thought of never having known such intense, consuming pleasure was unbearable to him. Memories of the night before licked like scented fire over his body. For an instant he savored the sensuous rush of images, tasted again in memory Janna's mouth and breasts, felt again the tightness of her body as she accepted him into her satin heat. Then he put memories aside with a skill he had learned during the war, dividing his mind into compartments like a dresser; and like a man dressing, he had learned to open only the drawer that contained what he needed at the moment.

Making no sound, Janna walked forward once more, a gray-eyed shadow among shadows. With an unconscious movement Ty shifted his carbine into carrying position again, holding his right hand around the stock in such a way that it would take only an instant to pull the trigger and keeping the muzzle pointed so that an accidental firing wouldn't hit anyone in front of him. The buttoned pocket of his wool shirt bulged with a box of bullets. Similar boxes made his backpack heavier than its size would have indicated.

He didn't notice the extra weight, much less complain of it. There had been too many times in the past when he would have sold his soul for extra ammunition. He felt the same way about the beef jerky that he was chewing on at the moment— it might have been tougher than leather, unsalted and stone dry, but it was food and he had been hungry too many times in the past to be fussy about what he ate now.

The wind breathed softly over Janna and Ty, bringing with it the smell of pine resin and sun. Off in the distance a raven jeered at something concealed within pine boughs. Janna and Ty froze as one. The raven's harsh cries rang in the silence, then faded as the bird flew farther away. Both of them remained motionless, wondering if it had been another bird or a man that had disturbed the crow.

The breeze sighed over Janna's face, stirring wisps of auburn hair. The delicate brushing movement reminded her of Ty's gentleness when he had first taken her into his arms to calm her after her encounter with the snake. An odd frisson of sensation raced through Janna's body from her breasts to her thighs as she remembered what had followed the first soft kisses.

And on the heels of hot memories came the icy knowledge that Ty was hers for only a short time, just long enough to find and tame Lucifer. Then Ty would go in search of the silken lady he was determined to have. A yearning to be that lady twisted through Janna with such painful intensity that she couldn't breathe.

Don't be a fool, she told herself harshly. *I know all about silk purses and sows' ears. A man like Ty does, too. He was raised in a grand house with servants and tutors and people to tell him how to speak and eat and dress and write a fine hand. I had my father and a wagon seat and a trunk full of old books. I can read and write…and that's all. If I ever wore a dress, I've forgotten what it feels like. The only shoes I remember having are the moccasins I make for myself. The only perfume I know is what I make from crushed flowers. The only salves I have are for healing, not for making me beautiful. The only thing my hands are good for is surviving, not for playing grand songs on a piano.*

Then Janna remembered one other thing her hands had proven to be good for—arousing Ty until he was as hot and hard as sun-warmed stone. If she closed her eyes she could still feel him changing within her grasp, becoming full and tight and heavy, moving blindly between her hands, seeking more of her.

Will he want me like that again tonight, nothing but the two of us locked together and pleasure like a fire burning between us?

Without thinking, Janna turned and looked over her shoulder where she knew Ty would be. He was standing as motionless as she was, and he was watching her with eyes that glittered like green gems. She sensed in that moment that he knew her thoughts, her memories, for they were his thoughts, his memories.

The breeze blew softly, caressing Janna's face. Ty could see the stirring of soft auburn hair. He knew what those silky wisps felt like on his lips, knew what her skin tasted like along her hairline, knew that she trembled when the tip of his tongue traced her ear or found the pulse beating in her neck. And he knew from the sudden, slight parting of her lips that she was remembering what it had felt like to have his tongue slide between her teeth to probe and caress the passionate softness of her mouth.

Janna made no sound as she turned away from Ty, but he knew why she had retreated. If they had looked at each other for even one more second, he would have pulled her down to the ground and taken her and to hell with the risk. It would have been worth it to die of ecstasy and then to be reborn and die again, sheathed so perfectly within her body.

The small, normal sounds of the forest surrounded Janna as she moved from shadow to shadow, all senses alert. A squirrel scolded a trespassing cousin, two ravens called as they flew overhead, and needles whispered secretively as they combed through the erratic breeze. Through the massed, dark trunks and dead lower branches of the pines, Janna caught occasional views of the sunny meadow.

There were game trails crisscrossing the forest and the meadow itself. Whenever Janna came to such a path, she stopped and read the signs left by passing animals. The damp earth held tracks for a long time, telling of the passage of deer and coyote, cougar and bear, men and horses. The first few game trails were little more than faint threads winding around deadfalls and between trees. The fourth path she discovered was much more obvious, for it was frequently used by wild horses. The trail began at the west end of the meadow and took a reasonably straight line toward the northwest corner of the plateau, where Raven Creek cut through the land on its way to joining the warm, shallow waters of Santos Wash— and Cascabel's sprawling renegade camp guarding the north-west approach to the plateau.

Suddenly Janna went to her knees, her heart pounding. There, alongside the main trail, was a partial track left by a large, unshod horse.

"Lucifer," she said, spreading her fingers, measuring the huge print.

"Are you sure?" Ty asked, quickly kneeling beside her. "There's not much of a track to go on."

"No other horse but Cascabel's is so big. But there's no sign that this horse has ever been shod, and Cascabel's has."

Silently Ty began casting for a sign on either side of the trail. He wasn't long in finding it.

"Janna."

She came to her feet instantly and ran to his side.

"He was coming out of the meadow and something spooked him," Ty said softly, pointing to the place where Lucifer's hooves had dug abruptly into the trail, gouging out clots of dirt and debris as he sprang to one side. "He took off running through the trees."

Janna looked from the churned earth to the forest beyond. A faint trail of disturbed pine needles showed as lighter marks against the forest floor. She bent and studied the damp, undisturbed ground and the tracks themselves.

And then she saw the blood.

Joe Troon took off with his rifle. Swore he was going to crease or kill Lucifer.

With a trembling hand she touched the blood spoor. It was neither fresh nor old.

"The tracks were left within the past few hours," Ty said. "So was the blood."

Janna sensed rather than saw Ty's head jerk toward her. Within seconds he was squatting on his heels next to her, rubbing a bit of the dark, thumbnail-size spot between his fingers. He stared at the results and cursed the man who hadn't drunk enough to miss entirely.

"I'll bet it happened just after dawn," Ty said.

"We heard more than one shot."

Ty grunted. "There's more than one renegade riding around here looking for trouble. Maybe one of them found Joe Troon."

Ty rubbed his hand clean on his pants and stood. The idea of the magnificent stallion slowly bleeding to death made him sick. But before they followed Lucifer's trail, they had to know if it were Joe Troon or a renegade party they were likely to run into.

"I'm going to cast around back toward the meadow and see if I can find what spooked Lucifer," Ty said. "You follow his tracks. I'll follow you. If you lose the trail, stay put until I catch up." He looked into her clear eyes. "Do you want the carbine?"

She shook her head. "Keep it. I haven't shot a long gun in years. Snares or a bow and arrow are much more quiet for hunting game."

"At least take my pistol."

Janna hesitated, then gave in. She wouldn't do either Ty or herself much good if she stumbled across renegades and all she had to throw at them was a handful of pine needles.

Frowning uneasily, Ty watched Janna push his big revolver behind her belt. He knew it was irrational of him not to want to leave her alone—after all, she had survived for years on her own in this very country—but he still didn't like it.

"You're coming with me," he said without warning.

Startled, she looked up. "Why?"

"My backbone is itchy as all hell, that's why, and I'm a man who listens to my instincts."

"Lucifer's bleeding. If I hurry—"

"A few minutes more or less won't make much difference," Ty interrupted. "Besides, there's no way we can be sure that it was a bullet that hurt him. Could have been a sharp branch he shied into. Could have been another horse. I've seen him fight more than one eager stud and they both walked away dripping blood." Ty turned back toward the meadow. "Hurry up. We're wasting time talking when we could be tracking."

Mouth open, Janna watched Ty trot off along the game trail, covering ground at a good clip while looking for signs of other horses or other men. If he noticed that she wasn't following, he gave no indication of it.

Without a word Janna turned and began running in a different direction, following the trail Lucifer had left during his panicked flight away from the meadow.

Chapter Twenty-Five

Head down, his attention focused on the wild horse trail, Ty trotted rapidly through the forest toward the meadow. Tracks and signs abounded, but he could see without slowing that nothing was less than a few days old. He was looking for much fresher marks.

He found them less than two hundred feet from the meadow itself.

The empty rye bottle glittered on top of the pine needles. The bottle hadn't been there long, for when Ty picked it up and sniffed, the smell of alcohol was strong in his nostrils. Nearby was a tree stained with urine from chest high to the ground. There were hoof tracks left by a shod horse next to the tree.

From that point the trail was easy to reconstruct. Troon—for Ty was certain that the empty bottle had belonged to Joe Troon rather than to a solitary Indian—had been relieving himself from the saddle when something had surprised him.

"I'll bet he was hot on Lucifer's trail and had to piss so bad that his back teeth were floating," Ty said very softly, believing that Janna was right behind. "So there he was, still in the saddle and pissing up a storm when he saw Lucifer through the trees, dropped everything and grabbed for his rifle. Lord, what a mess that must have been."

When Janna made no comment, Ty turned and looked at his own trail. Janna was nowhere in sight.

The uneasiness that had been riding Ty crystallized in an instant of stabbing fear. He ignored his first impulse, which was to backtrack along his own trail until he found Janna. That would take too long, for he had come nearly half a mile. Obviously Troon's trail and Lucifer's crossed somewhere ahead. If Ty followed one and Janna followed the other, they would meet much quicker than if he retraced his own tracks and then hers, as well.

If both of them were really lucky, none of Cascabel's renegades would ride over to find the cause of the single rifle shot. But Ty really didn't expect that kind of luck.

Swearing savagely to himself, he began trotting along the trail left by the shod horse. Within ten yards he spotted the brass from a spent cartridge gleaming among pine needles. The shine of the metal told Ty that the cartridge hadn't been long out of a rifle barrel. He had no doubt that it was the debris of the shot that had awakened Janna and himself less than half an hour ago. He also had no doubt what the intended target had been.

You drunken, greedy swine. If you've murdered that stallion I'll roast you over a slow fire and serve you to Cascabel with an apple in your mouth.

Rifle shots split the silence, followed by the wild cries of Indian renegades hot on a human trail. Fear splintered through Ty like black lightning, for the sounds were coming from ahead and off to his right, where Troon's trail was going, where Lucifer would have gone if he had followed a straight course through the forest—and where Janna would be if she had been able to follow Lucifer's trail.

Ty had no doubt that Janna could track Lucifer anywhere the stallion could go.

Running swiftly and silently, Ty traced the twisting progress of Troon's horse through the forest. The animal had been moving at a hard gallop, a pace that was foolhardy under the conditions. Stirrups left gashes across tree trunks where the horse had zigzagged between pines. Farther down the trail low-growing limbs showed signs of recent damage. Bruised clus-

ters of needles were scattered everywhere. A man's battered
hat was tangled among the branches.

Ty had no doubt that he would find blood if he wanted to
stop and check the bark on the limb that was wearing Troon's
hat, but at the moment it wasn't Troon's blood that interested
Ty. It was the palm-sized splotches that had suddenly appeared
along with the hoofprints of a huge, unshod horse.

Lucifer.

Like the rifle cartridge, the blood hadn't been exposed to
air for more than a half hour. The spots glistened darkly in
the shade and were near-crimson markers in the occasional
patches of sun. From their position, they could only have come
from the stallion.

Breathing easily, running quietly, Ty followed the bloody
trail. He knew that he should be sneaking from tree to tree in
the thinning forest. He knew that at the very least he should
be hunting cover in case he literally ran up on the heels of the
renegades. He also knew that Janna was somewhere up ahead
alone, armed with a pistol good for six shots and no spare
cylinders or ammunition within reach. He didn't know how
many renegades there were, but he doubted that six shots
would get the job done.

*Janna's too clever to be spotted by renegades. She'll go to
ground and pull the hole in after her. They'll never find her.*

The reassuring thought was interrupted by a flurry of rifle
fire. The sounds came from ahead, but much farther to the
right than Ty would have expected from the trail he was following. Either Lucifer or Troon—or both—must be hoping to
escape by making a break for the steep northern edge of the
plateau.

There were a few more sporadic shots and eager cries, then
silence. Ty ran harder and told himself it was good that he
hadn't heard any pistol shots, for that meant Janna hadn't been
spotted. He refused to consider that it could also mean she had
fallen in the first outbreak of shooting before she even had a
chance to defend herself. He simply ran harder, carrying his
carbine as though it were a pistol, finger on the trigger, ready
to shoot and fire on the instant.

The hoofprints, which had been a mixture of shod and un-shod, abruptly diverged. The unshod prints continued without interruption. The shod hoofprints veered starkly to the right. Ty had no doubt that he was seeing traces of the instant when the renegades had spotted Troon; the prints of Troon's horse were inches deep in the ground at the point where the horse had dug in and spun away from the renegades. Troon had chosen to flee along the rumpled, downward sloping land that led to the plateau's northern edge. There the land was rocky, broken, full of clefts and hollows and sheer-sided ravines where a man could hope to hide.

If Troon were lucky, he might even survive. Ty hoped he didn't. Any man who would shoot at a horse like Lucifer out of greed deserved to die. Without a further thought, Ty veered off after the stallion, leaving Troon to whatever fate luck and the renegades would visit upon him.

The stallion's tracks showed no sudden gouges or changes in direction as Troon's had. When the renegades had spotted Troon, apparently Lucifer hadn't been within sight. The wild horse had cannily chosen a route that looped back toward the eastern end of Raven Creek's long, winding meadow. From there Lucifer could head for the northeast edge of the plateau and slide on his black hocks down into Mustang Canyon or he could run southeast and then straight south, using the entire surface of the plateau, losing himself among the pines, meadows, ridges and ravines that covered the land's rugged surface.

Assuming, of course, that Lucifer was in any shape for a long, hard run. It was an assumption Ty wasn't prepared to make. The stallion's tracks were becoming closer together. His strides were shortening as though he were winded, and the blood splotches were bigger and more frequent. Part of the horse's slowed progress might have been simply that the land was broken and rolling here, with more uphill than down as Lucifer headed straight toward the eastern lip of the plateau. And the shortening strides might also have been the result of injury.

Ty remembered Janna saying that she had once seen signs that Lucifer had skidded down the steep trail on the plateau's east edge in order to evade mustangers. He wondered if the stallion had remembered his past success and was laboring toward the east trail in hope of another such escape.

But Ty didn't think Lucifer would make it. The path on the east face was too far, too steep, and the blood sign along the stallion's trail was almost continuous now. The land here was steep, rising sharply into one of the many low ridges that marked the plateau's rumpled surface.

I hope they catch you, Troon. I hope they cut off your—

Ty's bitter thoughts of vengeance were wiped from his mind the instant he saw over the crest of the ridge to the land below. Less than a quarter mile away, Janna was running flat out down the slope. Her course paralleled a narrow, steep ravine that cut into the body of the ridge. Lucifer was forty feet ahead of her, veering toward the ravine as though he were planning to jump it, but it was too wide a leap for an injured horse. A half mile off to the right, all but concealed in another fold of land, a dust cloud of renegades was in wild pursuit of Joe Troon, who apparently had abandoned the idea of making a run to the northwest and Raven Creek Trail. Instead he was spurring his horse toward the east, leading the renegades toward Janna, who couldn't see them yet but almost certainly could hear their chilling cries.

Turn around and hide, Janna! Go to ground, Ty commanded silently. *Don't get yourself caught trying to help Lucifer.*

The stallion reached the edge of the ravine and threw himself toward the far side. His forelegs found purchase on the opposite bank of the ravine, but his left rear leg gave way when it should have provided support. He was too weak to struggle over the lip to safety. Kicking and screaming in a mixture of fear, pain and rage, the black horse skidded and rolled into the narrow, brush-choked bottom of the ravine twenty feet below. There he lay on his side, thrashing wildly in a futile attempt to regain his feet and scramble to safety.

Without pausing, Janna threw herself over the edge of the ravine, hurtling down into the tangle of brush and flailing hooves.

There was only one way Ty could save Janna from being injured or killed by the trapped stallion. Even as he whipped the carbine to his shoulder and took aim at Lucifer's beautiful black head, he saw hooves glance off Janna's body. At the precise instant he let out his breath and took the last of the slack from the trigger, Janna's back appeared in the gun sight. She had thrown herself over the stallion's head, pinning it to the earth, ensuring that the horse wouldn't be able to struggle to his feet.

Get out of there, you little fool! Ty screamed silently. *You can't hold him. He'll beat you to death with those big hooves.*

The ravine Lucifer was trapped in was a long crease running down the side of the ridge at whose top Ty waited. It would be an easy shot, no more than three hundred feet. He had made more difficult shots with a pistol. A savage fusillade of shots and triumphant shouts came from the direction of Troon and the renegades. Ty's attention never wavered from the bottom of the ravine, nor did the tension of his finger lift on the trigger.

A man's screams told Ty that either Troon or a renegade had just been wounded. Ty's glance remained fixed on the ravine bottom where Janna struggled to master the big horse. Ty knew that sooner or later Lucifer's struggles to free his head would throw Janna aside. When that happened, Ty's finger would tighten on the trigger and the stallion would die.

What the hell...?

Janna had one knee pinning the stallion's muzzle to the ground and the other knee just behind his ears. She was literally kneeling on the horse and ripping her shirt off at the same time.

A crescendo of triumphant whoops and shots told Ty that the chase was over for Joe Troon. Ty still didn't look up from the ravine; he wouldn't have walked across a street to aid the man who had captured Janna once and bragged to a bartender about what he would do when he caught her again. As far as Ty was concerned, Troon had gone looking for trouble and he had found more than he wanted. It often happened that way to a man who drank too much and thought too little. Ty's only regret was that Troon hadn't bought it sooner, before he had led the renegades back to within a quarter mile of Janna.

Over the carbine's steel barrel, Ty watched while Janna turned her torn shirt into a makeshift blindfold and struggled to secure it around Lucifer's eyes. Abruptly the stallion stopped thrashing around. With rapid movements Janna whipped a few turns of cloth around the horse's muzzle. When she was finished, Lucifer could open his mouth no more than an inch. She bent over him once more, holding him down while she stroked his lathered neck.

Ty could see the shudders of fear that rippled over the stallion with each stroke of Janna's hand. Ty could also see that the horse was no longer a danger to her; blindfolded, muzzled, pinned in place by Janna's weight, Lucifer was all but helpless.

Very slowly Ty eased his finger off the trigger and sank down behind the cover of a piñon tree that clung to the rocky ridge top. Screened by dark green branches, Ty pulled out his spyglass and looked off to the right. A single glance confirmed what his ears had already told him: Joe Troon had made his last mistake.

Ty looked around carefully and decided that he had the best position from which to protect the ravine. Pulling his hat down firmly, he chose a comfortable shooting position, shrugged out of his pack and put two open boxes of ammunition within easy reach. Stomach against the hard earth, green eyes sighting down the carbine's metal barrel, Ty settled in to wait and see if the renegades were going to come toward the ravine when they were finished looting and mutilating Troon's body.

Chapter Twenty-Six

"Easy now, boy. Easy...easy."

The ceaseless murmur of Janna's soft voice and the gentle pressure of her hands finally penetrated the stallion's pain and panic. With a long, groaning sigh, Lucifer stopped fighting. Janna rewarded him by shifting her knee from his muzzle to the ground, praising him with a flow of sentences and nonsense sounds, knowing that it was her voice rather than the meaning of her words that reached past the horse's fear.

Very slowly Janna slid her other knee from Lucifer's neck, leaving him able to lift his head, which was the first thing a horse did before it came to its feet. Lucifer made no attempt to take advantage of his freedom in order to stand up. As Janna had hoped, the blindfold held him more quietly and more surely than any rope could have. Even so, she reluctantly bound his left hind foot to his right foreleg. When she began cleaning and treating the bullet wound on his left rear leg, she didn't want him to lash out at the pain. She was already bruised enough as it was. A broken bone wouldn't do either of them any good.

Ignoring her own pain, Janna kept one hand constantly on Lucifer's head, talking incessantly and softly, letting him know where she was. When his ears were no longer flattened against his head, Janna leaned over and snaked her own makeshift backpack to a place within easy reach. While she sorted one-handed through her herbs and salves, she told herself that

Ty was all right, that the shots had been from Troon or the renegades, not from Ty's carbine, that he and she were safe even though they were separate....

"God, please let him be safe," Janna prayed softly, stroking the powerful, lathered neck of the stallion.

Though Lucifer was no longer fighting her, he groaned with each heaving breath he took, for the cloth muzzle restricted his breathing. In the silence, the sound of the horse's labored breaths were like thunder. After a few minutes Janna opened her pocketknife and cut the cloth free, allowing the stallion to open his mouth and nostrils fully. Immediately his breathing eased.

"You weren't going to bite me anyway, were you?" Janna murmured, stroking Lucifer's nose.

The stallion's ears flicked but didn't flatten against his head. He was too tired, too weak or simply not fearful enough to attack Janna.

Wondering if anyone had been attracted by the stallion's labored breathing, Janna glanced anxiously up and down the crease in the earth that was their only hiding place. She heard no one approaching. Nor did she see any movement along the ravine's rim.

It was just as well, for there was no way to hide from anyone. The brush through which Lucifer had fallen had been bruised and broken beyond all hope of concealment from any trackers. Nor was there any real cover within the ravine itself. Janna had no illusions about what her chances of escape would be if the renegades found her in the bottom of the ravine with the wounded, blindfolded stallion.

After a last look at the rim of the ravine, Janna pulled out Ty's big pistol, rotated the cylinder off the empty chamber and cocked the hammer so that all it would take was a quick pull on the trigger to fire the gun. Very carefully she laid the weapon out of the way yet within easy reach. Then she turned back to Lucifer.

"This is going to hurt," Janna said in a low, calm voice, "but you're going to be a gentleman about it, aren't you?"

She wet the last torn piece of her shirt with water from her canteen and went to work cleaning the long furrow Troon's bullet had left on Lucifer's haunch. The blindfolded stallion shuddered and his ears flattened, but he made no attempt to turn and bite Janna while she worked over him. She praised the horse in soothing tones that revealed neither her own pain from her bruises nor her growing fear that Ty hadn't been able to evade the renegades.

Lucifer flinched and made a high, involuntary sound as Janna cleaned a part of the wound that had picked up dirt in his slide down into the ravine.

"Easy, boy, easy...yes, I know it hurts, but you won't heal right without help. That's it...that's it...gently...just lie still and let me help you."

The low, husky voice and endless ripple of words mesmerized Lucifer. His ears flicked and swiveled, following Janna's voice when she turned from her backpack to the wound on his haunch.

"I think it looks a lot worse than it is," Janna murmured as she rinsed out her rag and poured more water into its folds. "It's deep and it bled a lot, but the bullet didn't sever any tendons or muscles. You're going to be sore and grouchy as a boiled cat for a while, and you'll limp for a time and you'll have a scar on your pretty black hide forever, but you'll heal clean and sound. In a few weeks you'll be up and running after your mares.

"And you'll have a lot of running to do, won't you? Those mares will be scattered from hell to breakfast, as Papa would have said. I'll bet that chestnut stud you ran off last year is stealing your mares as fast as he finds them."

Lucifer flicked his ears, sucked in a long breath through his flaring nostrils and blew out, then took in another great breath.

"Easy now, boy. Easy...easy... I know it hurts but there's no help for it."

Janna reached for her backpack again and winced. Her left arm was beginning to stiffen. By the time she was finished doctoring Lucifer, she'd have to start in on herself. With only one hand, it was going to be difficult.

*Ty, where are you? Are you all right? Did you get away?
Are you lying wounded and—*

"Don't think about it!" Janna said aloud, her voice so savage that Lucifer, startled, tossed his head.

"Easy, boy," she murmured, immediately adjusting her
voice to be soothing once more. "There's nothing to worry
about. Ty is quick and strong and smart. If he got away from
Cascabel he can get away from a bunch of hurrahing renegades who were looking for a man on horseback, not one on
foot. Besides, I'll never get a better chance to tame you," she
said, stroking the mustang's barrel, where lather was slowly
drying. "If you accept me, you'll accept Ty, and then he'll
have a start on his dream, a fine stallion to found a herd that
will bring money enough to buy a lady of silk and softness."

Janna's mouth turned down in an unhappy line, but her hand
continued its gentle motions and her voice remained soothing.

"Anyway, boy, if I leave you and go looking for a man
who is probably quite safe, who will take care of you in three
days or four, when your wound gets infected and you get so
weak you can hardly stand?"

Lucifer's head came up suddenly and his ears pricked forward so tightly that they almost touched at the tips. His nostrils
flared widely as he took in quantities of air and sifted it for
the scent of danger.

Watching him closely, Janna reached for the pistol. Being
blindfolded was no particular handicap for the stallion when
it came to recognizing danger—a horse's ears and sense of
smell were far superior to his eyes. But when it came to dealing with danger, a blind horse was all but helpless.

Janna looked in the direction that Lucifer's ears were pointing. All she saw was the steep side of the gully and the brushy
slope rising to the ridge top beyond. She hesitated, trying to
decide whether it would be less dangerous to crawl up out of
the ravine and look around or to simply lie low and hope that
whatever Lucifer sensed wouldn't sense them in return.

Before she could make up her mind, Janna heard what was
attracting the horse's attention. There was a faint chorus of
yips and howls and cries followed by the distant thunder of

galloping horses and the crack of rifle fire. The sounds became louder as the renegades galloped closer to the ravine. For a few horrible minutes Janna was certain that the renegades were going to race straight up the slope above the ravine—and then she and Lucifer would be utterly exposed, with no place to hide and no way to flee.

The sounds peaked and slowly died as the Indians galloped off to the northwest, where Cascabel had his camp.

Heart pounding, Janna set aside the pistol she had grabbed and went back to tending Lucifer with hands that insisted on trembling at the very instant she most needed them to be still. She watched Lucifer's ears as she worked on his wound, for she knew that his hearing was superior to hers.

"I hope they're not coming back," she said softly, stroking the horse's hot flank as she examined the long furrow left by the bullet. "Well, Lucifer, if you were a man I'd pour some witch hazel in that wound to keep it clean. But witch hazel stings like the very devil and I don't have any way of telling you to hold still and not make any noise, so—"

Janna froze and stopped speaking as Lucifer's ears flicked forward again. Concentrating intently, she heard the faintest of scraping sounds, as though a boot or a moccasin had rubbed over loose rock, or perhaps it was no more than the friction of a low branch against the ground. Then came silence. A few moments later there was another sound, but this time that of cloth sliding over brush. Or was it simply wind bending the spring brush and releasing it again?

The silence continued with no more interruptions. Very slowly Janna reached for the pistol again, listening so intently that she ached. She didn't breathe, she didn't think, she simply bent every bit of her will toward hearing as much as possible. The stallion remained motionless as well, his ears pricked, his nostrils flared, waiting for the wind to tell him whether to fight or freeze or flee whatever danger existed beyond the ravine.

"Janna?"

At first the whisper was so soft that she thought she had imagined it.

"Janna? Are you all right?"

"Ty? Is that you?"

"Hell, no," Ty said in disgust. "It's Joe Troon's ghost come to haunt you. Stand back. I'm coming down."

A pebble rolled down the side of the ravine, then another and another as Ty chose speed over caution in his descent. Crossing the open spots from the top of the ridge to the gully's edge had taken years off his life span, even though there was no reason for him to think that the renegades would come back right away. Nor was there any reason to think that they would *not*. The sooner he was under even the minimal cover of the gully, the better he would feel.

Janna watched Ty skid down the last steep pitch into the ravine. He braced himself on a dead piñon trunk, looked toward her and smiled in a way that made her heart turn over.

"Sugar," Ty drawled, "you are a sight for sore eyes."

His glance moved over her like hands, reminding her that she was naked from the waist up. Blushing, she crossed her arms over her breasts but couldn't conceal the pink tide rising beneath her skin.

Ty's breath caught and then stayed in his throat at the picture Janna made, the pale perfection of her body rising from the loose masculine pants. Her arms were too slender to hide the full curves of her breasts. The hint of deep rose nipples nestled shyly in the bend of her elbows.

"Ty...don't."

"Don't what?"

"Look at me like that."

"Like what?" he said huskily. "Like I spent most of the night licking and love biting and kissing those beautiful white breasts?"

Janna couldn't conceal the shiver of sensual response that went through her at Ty's words.

"Put your arms down, sugar. Let me see if you remember, too."

Very slowly Janna's arms dropped away, revealing breasts whose rosy tips had drawn and hardened at his look, his words, her memories.

"God," breathed Ty, shutting his eyes, knowing that it

didn't matter, the vision was already burned into his memory. Blindly he dug into his backpack, found the roll of cloth he had refused to let her wear, and dropped the cloth on her lap. "Here. Wrap up before you make me forget where we are. Do it fast, little one. A man never wants a woman so much as when he's come close to dying."

"Does it work that way for a woman, too?" Janna asked as she snatched the cloth and began wrapping it over her breasts.

"I don't know. How do you feel right now?"

"Shivery. Feverish. Restless. And then you looked at me and I felt hot and full where you had touched me...and yet empty at the same time."

"Then it works the same for a woman, if the woman is like you," Ty said, trying to control the heavy beat of his blood. "Satin butterfly. God, you don't know how much I want to love you right now. I saw Lucifer jump and fall into the ravine and then you threw yourself after him and I couldn't get a clean shot at his head and—"

"What?" Janna interrupted, appalled. "Why did you want to shoot Lucifer? He isn't that badly injured."

"I know. That's why I was afraid he'd beat you to death with those big hooves."

"You would have killed him to save me?"

Ty's eyelids snapped open. "Hell, yes! What kind of a man do you think I am?"

Janna tried to speak, couldn't find the words and concentrated on wrapping herself tightly.

"For the love of God," Ty said in a low voice. "Just because I seduced you doesn't mean that I'm the kind of bastard who would leave you to be killed when I could have saved you!"

"That isn't what I meant. It's just that...that..."

"What?" Ty demanded angrily.

"I'm surprised you would have killed Lucifer without hesitation, that's all," Janna said, her voice shaking. "Lucifer is your best chance of building a fine horse herd. He's your best hope of getting enough money to buy your silken lady. He's

the beginning of your dreams. He's…everything. And I'm…''
She drew in a deep breath, looked away from Ty's harsh,
closed expression and continued quietly. ''I'm not your blood
or your fiancée or anything but a…a temporary convenience.
Why should you kill your dream for me?'' She glanced
quickly at him. ''But thank you, Ty. It's the nicest thing anyone has ever done for me.''

Chapter Twenty-Seven

"How bad is he hurt?" Ty asked.

Janna jumped in surprise. It was the first thing Ty had said to her in the hour since she had thanked him for being prepared to sacrifice his dream in order to save her life.

After that, Ty had gone to Lucifer's head, knelt and put himself between the horse's teeth and Janna. He had spoken gently to the stallion, stroking Lucifer's powerful neck with slow sweeps of his hand until the horse relaxed and accepted the strange voice and touch. Except for those murmured reassurances to the big horse, Ty had said nothing as he watched Janna tend Lucifer. Ty moved only to stroke the stallion or to hand her a packet from her leather pouch or to rinse the rag she was using to clean Lucifer's cuts and abrasions.

"He's strong. He'll be fine," Janna said, smiling tentatively at Ty.

"That's not what I asked. I've treated horses for sprains and stones in their shoes and colic and such, but bullet wounds are new to me. It's not a deep wound, but I've seen men die of shock with wounds not much worse than that. Do you think Lucifer can walk?"

Janna turned and reached for the stallion's muzzle, only to have Ty quickly intervene.

"I can't answer your question until I've looked at Lucifer's mouth," she explained.

Ty gave Janna an odd look and reluctantly moved aside.

She bent over the stallion's muzzle and spoke in low, even tones as her fingers lifted his upper lip. His ears flattened warningly and he jerked his head away. Patiently Janna worked over him until he tolerated her fingers around his mouth without laying back his ears.

"What the hell are you doing?" Ty asked quietly.

"Papa said you can tell a lot about men or animals by the color of their gums. Lucifer was real pale when I first checked him, but he's nice and pink now. He'll be able to walk as soon as I untie his feet, but it would be better if he didn't move around much. That wound will start to bleed all over again at the first bit of strain."

Ty looked at the long gash on Lucifer's haunch and muttered something beneath his breath.

"What?" asked Janna.

"We can't stay here. Those renegades could come back or some of their friends could come prowling to see if anything was missed the first time around. Lucifer left a trail a blind man could follow." Ty glanced at the sky overhead. "No rain today and probably not any tonight, either. And if there was enough rain to wash out the trail, we'd be washed right out of this gully, too. There's no food, no water and no cover worth mentioning. The sooner we get out of here the longer we'll all live."

Janna looked unhappily at the stallion but didn't argue with Ty. What he had said was true and she knew it as well as he did. She just didn't want to have to force the wounded stallion to walk.

"I wish he were human," Janna said. "It would be so much easier if we could explain to him."

"How far do you think he can go?"

"As far as he wants to, I guess."

"He moved fast enough getting here," Ty said dryly.

"He was running scared then. I've seen frightened mustangs gallop on sprained ankles and pulled hamstrings, but as soon as they stop running, they're finished. They can barely hobble until they heal."

Ty said nothing. He had seen men in the heat of battle run

on a foot that had been shot off; after the battle, those same men couldn't even crawl.

"The sooner we get going the better our chances are," Ty said finally. "At the very least we've got to get to decent cover and wipe out as much of our trail as we can. Do you know any place near the meadow?"

Janna shook her head. "Not where a horse could hide long enough to heal. The only place Lucifer would be safe is my keyhole canyon, and I don't know if he'd make it that far. By the time we got over to the Mustang Canyon trail and down into the canyon and then clear out away from the plateau to the Santos Wash trail…" She shook her head again. "It's a long way from there to my winter camp."

"And the renegades are real thick in Santos Wash," Ty added. "We've got no choice, Janna. We'll have to take Lucifer down the east face of the plateau. From there it's only a few hours to your hidden canyon."

Janna's objections died before they were spoken. She had come to the same conclusion Ty had; she just hadn't wanted to believe it was their best chance. The thought of taking the injured stallion down the precipitous eastern edge of the plateau, and from there through the tortuous slot canyon, made her want to cry out in protest.

But it was their best hope of keeping Lucifer—and themselves—safe while his bullet wound healed.

"I know how you feel about restraining a horse, so I won't ask you to do it," Ty said firmly. "I don't think Lucifer's going to take too kindly to it, either, but there's no damn choice." He looked at Janna. "Get your medicine bag packed and stand lookout up on the ridge."

"I'll help you with Lucifer."

"There's not room enough for two of us."

"But I'm used to mustangs."

"You're used to coaxing mares into gentleness when they have all the room in the world to run. Lucifer is a stud and trapped and hurting and probably of no mind to be meek about wearing his first hackamore. I don't blame him a bit. I'll be as gentle with him as I can, but I want you a long way away when I pull off that blindfold. Besides, someone has to stand watch. That someone is going to be you.''

Janna looked into the crystalline green of Ty's eyes and knew that arguing would get her nowhere. ''I'll bet you were an officer in the war between the North and the South.''

Ty looked surprised, then smiled. ''You bet right, sugar. Now shag your lovely butt up onto that ridge. If you see something you don't like, give me that hawk cry you use to call Zebra. And don't forget my pistol.''

Without a word Janna tucked Ty's pistol in place behind her belt and began climbing out of the ravine. When she was safely up on the rim, Ty turned to Lucifer once more.

''Well, boy, it's time to find out if all your piss and vinegar is combined with common sense, or if you're outlaw through and through.''

Speaking gently and reassuringly, Ty reached into his backpack and pulled out a pair of sheepskin-lined leather hobbles that he had taken from the Preacher's store in hope of just such an opportunity to use them. When the hobbles were in place on Lucifer's front legs, Ty cut through the cloth that joined the stallion's hind and foreleg. Lucifer quivered but made no attempt to lash out with his newly unbound feet. Ty stroked the horse's barrel and talked soothingly until the stallion's black hide no longer twitched and trembled with each touch.

''You did real well, boy. I'm beginning to think you're as smart as you are handsome.''

Ty went to the backpack for the length of braided rawhide and the steel ring he had also bought. A few quick loops, turns and knots transformed the ring and rawhide into a workable hackamore.

''You're not going to like this, but you'll get used to it. Easy, son. Easy now.'' As Ty spoke, he slipped the makeshift hackamore onto the stallion's head.

Lucifer snorted and began trembling again as soon as he felt the rawhide against his skin. Patiently Ty rubbed the horse's head and neck and ears, accustoming him to the pressure of human hands and hackamore on his head. Lucifer calmed quickly this time, as though he were losing the ability to become alarmed—or questioned the necessity for alarm— at each new thing that happened. Ty hoped that it was common sense rather than weakness that was calming the stallion, but he wouldn't know until he got Lucifer up on his feet how much strength the wound had cost the horse.

"Well, son, this is the test. Now you just lie still and show me what a gentleman you are underneath all that bone and muscle and wildness."

With slow, smooth motions, Ty eased the blindfold down Lucifer's nose until the horse could see again. For a moment the stallion made no movement, then his ears flattened and he tried to lunge to his feet. Instantly Ty pinned the horse's muzzle to the ground and held it there, all the while talking soothingly and petting the rigid muscles of the stallion's neck as he struggled to get to his feet and flee.

Ty never knew how long it took to get through Lucifer's fear to the rational animal beneath. He only knew that he was sweating as hard as the stallion before Lucifer finally stopped struggling and allowed himself to be calmed by the voice and hands whose gentleness had never varied throughout the pitched, silent struggle.

"How the hell did she ever hold you long enough to get the blindfold on?" Ty wondered aloud as he and Lucifer eyed each other warily. "Or were you just used to her smell?"

The stallion's dark, dark eyes regarded Ty with an intelligence that was almost tangible. There was no malevolence, no sense of a feral eagerness to find an opening and strike. There was simply an alertness that had been bred into the horse's very bones and had been honed by living in the wild.

"Wonder who your mammy was, and your daddy, too. They sure as hell weren't bangtail ridge runners. You've a lot of the great barb in you, and maybe some Tennessee walking horse thrown in. My daddy would have traded every stud he ever owned to get his hands on you, and he would have considered it a bargain at twice the price. You're all horse, Lucifer. And you're mine now."

Lucifer's ears flicked and his eyes followed each motion Ty made.

"Well, you're half mine," Ty amended. "There's a certain stubborn girl who owns a piece of you whether she admits it or not. But don't worry, son. If you can't take the tame life, I'll set you free just like I promised. I don't mind telling you, though, I hope I don't have to. I left some fine mares with Logan. I'd love to take you up to Wyoming and keep you long enough to have at least one crop of foals from you."

While Ty talked he began to shift his weight off the stallion's muzzle a bit at a time until very little was left to hold the horse down.

"Ready to try getting up again? Slowly, son, slowly. Real nice and gentle. You lunge around this little gully and you're going to hurt both of us."

Once Lucifer realized that his head was free, he rolled off his side and got his feet underneath him. He quickly learned that the same man who could pin his muzzle to the ground could also help getting him to his feet with a few judicious pulls on the halter rope. Very shortly the stallion was standing again, unblindfolded and trembling all over at the strangeness of being close to a man.

"I was right. You're as smart as you are handsome. It's a shame you ran loose so long. You would have been a fine partner for a man, but after all these years I doubt you'd accept a rider. But that's all right, son," Ty said, slowly coiling the rawhide lead rope until he was right next to Lucifer's head. "I don't need to strut and show off how grand I am by breaking you. There are a thousand horses I can ride, but you're the only one I want covering my mares."

The words meant nothing to the stallion, but Ty's calm voice and gentle, confident hands did. Lucifer gave a long snort and stopped rolling his eyes and flinching at every touch. Slowly he was accepting the fact that although man in general had been his enemy in the past, this particular man was different. Lucifer had been pinned and blinded and helpless, but the man hadn't attacked him. Obviously he wasn't going to, either.

As the stallion slowly relaxed, Ty let out a long, quiet breath. "You're going to make it easy on both of us, aren't you? I'm sure glad that bullet and a few miles of running took the starch out of you. I've got a feeling you wouldn't have been nearly so civilized about this if I'd caught you fresh. But then, if you'd been fresh, we'd never have caught you, would we? The Lord works in strange ways, Lucifer. I'm glad He saw fit to give you to us, if only for long enough to heal you and set you free."

Ty stood and praised the stallion for a long time, until at last the horse let wariness slide away and weariness claim his big body. With a huge sigh, Lucifer allowed his head to drop until it all but rested against Ty's chest. Standing three-legged, favoring his injured hip, the stallion took no more notice of Ty than if he had been a foal.

Slowly Ty bent until he could release the hobbles on Lucifer's front legs. The stallion's shoulder muscles flinched and rippled as though shaking off flies, but that was all the notice he took of being free.

"That's real good, son," Ty murmured, stroking the stallion's black hide. "Now let's see if you're going to try to kill me the first time I tug on that hackamore."

Chapter Twenty-Eight

As Ty slowly tightened the lead rope, Janna watched with breath held and her hands so tightly clenched around the spyglass that her fingers ached.

"Be good, Lucifer," she prayed. "Don't go crazy and hurt Ty when that hackamore gets tight."

Lucifer's head came up sharply when the hackamore began to exert pressure behind his ears and across his upper neck. He snorted and shook his head, but the gradually increasing pressure didn't diminish. Trembling, sweating nervously, ears swiveling forward and then away from the man's gentle voice, the stallion tried to understand what was happening, how to meet the new threat. When he attempted to back away from the pressure, it got sharply worse. When he stood still, it got slowly worse.

But when he limped forward, the pressure lifted.

"That's it," Ty murmured, slacking off on the lead rope immediately. He petted Lucifer, praising the horse with voice and hands. "Let's try a few more steps, son. We've got a long way to go before we're safe."

It didn't take Lucifer more than a few minutes to understand that a pressure urging him forward meant walk forward and a pressure across the bridge of his nose meant stop.

"You're not an outlaw at all, are you?" Ty asked softly, stroking the horse's powerful, sweaty neck. "Men have chased you, but thank God no man ever had a chance to ruin you with rough handling.''

Lucifer flicked his ears as he followed the calm sounds of Ty's voice while the man backed up, paying out lead rope as he went.

''All right, son. It's time to get you out of this hole.'' Slowly Ty tightened the lead rope. ''Come on. That's it... that's it. One step at a time, that's all.'' His mouth flattened as he saw the stallion's painful progress. ''That hip sure is sore, isn't it?'' Ty said in a low voice. ''Well, son, it's going to get worse before it gets better, I'm afraid. But you'll live, God willing.''

Ty coaxed the limping stallion along the bottom of the ravine until they came to a place he had spotted from the ridge above, a place where the sides of the gully were less steep. Ty climbed halfway out, turned and began applying a steady pressure on the lead rope once more.

''Up you go. It will be easier to walk once you're on sort of level land again. Come on...come on...don't go all mulish on me now, son. It's not as steep as it looks.''

Lucifer disliked the idea of climbing the gully, but he disliked the slowly tightening vise of the hackamore even more. Suddenly he lunged forward, taking the side of the ravine in a hurtling rush. Ty leaped aside just in time to avoid being trampled and scrambled up the slope after the stallion. Once on top, Lucifer came to a stop and stood three-legged, trembling from nervousness and pain.

Janna left her lookout place on the ridge and ran down to meet Ty, slowing to a walk for the last few yards so as not to frighten Lucifer.

''No one in sight,'' she said quietly.

''All right.'' Ty lifted his hat, wiped his forehead and resettled the hat with a hard tug. ''How's your arm?''

Surprised that Ty had noticed, Janna hesitated and then shrugged. ''Better than Lucifer's haunch.''

''Hand over your pack.''

She tried not to wince as he helped her out of the rawhide straps, but she couldn't conceal her left arm's growing soreness. With gentle fingertips he traced the dark bruise where one of Lucifer's hooves had struck a glancing blow.

"Any numbness?" Ty asked.

She shook her head.

"All your fingers work?"

Silently she wiggled each of them in turn.

"Can you scout for us?" Ty asked, releasing her arm, caressing her all the way to her fingertips.

Suddenly breathless, Janna nodded.

"Cat got your tongue?"

She smiled and stuck her tongue out at Ty.

"Is that a promise?" he drawled. He smiled and touched her lips with his fingertip. "Stick it out again, sugar."

"I don't think—"

That was as far as Janna got before Ty bent and took what she had promised to him a moment before. Surprise stiffened Janna for an instant before she sighed and invited Ty into the softness and warmth of her mouth. Almost shyly she touched his tongue with her own, retreated, then returned to touch fleetingly again and again, until there was no more retreat, just two mouths in a seething, seamless mating.

When Ty finally lifted his head he was breathing too hard, but he was smiling.

"It occurred to me when that stallion was doing his best to trample me into the dirt," Ty said, "that a man shouldn't die without tasting a woman on his lips. You taste good, like Christmas and Thanksgiving and my birthday all rolled into one. And if you don't turn around and get busy scouting, I'm going to be walking bent over double and in damn near as much pain as Lucifer."

Janna smiled up at Ty, showing him the same near shyness with which she had begun their kiss. His eyelids lowered and desire changed his expression, making it both harder and more sensual. For an instant she thought that he was going to kiss her again, and she longed for it. Then he reached out, turned her around and swatted her lightly on the rear. She would have said something about the trail she was going to take to the east, but the swat had ended with Ty's hand tracing the curve of her buttocks with loving care and suddenly she found herself breathless and aching.

"I'll head east and a little bit south unless you come and tell me otherwise," Ty said. Quickly he removed a handful of bullets from his pistol belt. "Take these."

The bullets felt smooth, cool and heavy in Janna's hand. She put them in her pocket and prayed she wouldn't need them. While she could shoot a pistol, she couldn't hit much at any range greater than a few hundred feet. If she were forced to use the weapon at all, its greatest benefit would probably be as a warning to Ty that he had better take cover.

And he would need that warning. Unable to hide his tracks, forced by Lucifer's injury to go slowly and to take the easiest—and therefore most open—way available, Ty would be a sitting duck in a pond surrounded by hunters. Both he and Janna knew it.

Janna set off to the southeast at a steady trot. Her knee-high moccasins made almost no sound over pine needles and grasses, and she left few marks of her passage. She ran without pausing except to listen for any wind-carried conversations or for the sound of distant gunfire. She heard nothing but the normal calling of birds, the scolding of squirrels, and the restless murmuring of the wind as it tried to herd together enough clouds for a storm.

Behind her, Ty talked to the black stallion, praising him as he limped over the land. For his part, Lucifer moved as quickly as he could. A lifetime of running from man had given the stallion a relentless wariness that worked to Ty's benefit; the horse was as intent upon reaching a safe place as Ty was. And like Ty, the stallion knew instinctively that safety wasn't to be had in the wide-open spaces of the plateau. Space was useful only if you could outrun your enemies. At the moment, Lucifer couldn't outrun anything that was worth fleeing from in the first place.

Initially Ty walked ahead of Lucifer, encouraging him with a steady pressure on the hackamore. After the first hour, the horse no longer needed to be reminded that he was supposed to keep walking. When Ty moved, so did Lucifer. When Ty stood, Lucifer stood. When Ty walked, Lucifer walked with his head even with Ty's left shoulder. The hackamore's lead rope remained slack.

"You're some kind of special," Ty said, talking to Lucifer as they walked. "You're as gentle as a lady's hack. Makes me wonder if maybe you weren't paddock raised and then got free somehow. Of course, it simply could be that we both want the same thing right now—a safe place to hide. You might be a lot harder to get along with if you wanted one thing and I wanted another."

Lucifer's only answer was a brisk swish of his long black tail as he drove off flies attracted to his wound. Ty checked the gash, saw that it was bleeding again and knew that nothing could be done for it.

"Better a wound that bleeds than one that festers," Ty reminded himself, drawing on his battlefield experience. "As long as it doesn't bleed too much."

He kept an eye on the stallion's injury. After a few miles it became apparent that the bleeding was more of a steady oozing than a serious flow.

Janna, using her spyglass, had reassured herself on the same subject; Lucifer was bleeding, but it wasn't a problem yet. Despite his limp he was moving at a good walking pace. With luck they would reach the edge of the plateau before dark. Otherwise they would have to find a place to sleep, because nothing short of the most extreme emergency would force Janna to take on the east trail in full darkness while leading an unbroken, injured mustang.

Ignoring the steady throbbing of her arm, Janna trotted across the plateau's wild surface, scouting both for enemies and for the easiest, quickest way to reach the trail down the east face. She used what cover she could find but didn't waste time trying to be invisible. It was more important that Lucifer and Ty reach the east edge of the plateau before dark than that she leave no trail.

As the day wore on, Janna ranged farther and farther ahead, checking on Ty and Lucifer less and less often. They had agreed that if she didn't check back before Ty reached the east rim, he would take Lucifer down the trail and keep on going toward the keyhole canyon. He was reluctant to stop for a rest, much less for a whole night, because he knew that Lucifer would stiffen up badly once he stopped moving.

By the time Janna reached the last, long fold of land that lay between her and the eastern edge of the plateau, it was late afternoon. She climbed the long ridge at a diagonal, heading for two tall pines. From the top she knew she would be able to see out across several hundred square miles of plateau, including the eastern edge and a bit of the low country beyond. She hoped that she would see only the usual things—pines, grass, sky, rivers of black rock spilling down ragged slopes, wild horses grazing, perhaps even an antelope or two. What she hoped *not* to see was any sign of man.

Just below the crest, Janna dropped to her stomach and wormed her way up until she could see over without giving away her own presence to anyone who might be on the other side. The first thing she saw was a hawk patrolling just below the ridge top. The second thing she saw was Zebra grazing with a scattering of Lucifer's mares.

Immediately Janna put her hands to her mouth. A hawk's wild cry floated from her lips. Zebra's head came up, her ears pricked and her nostrils flared. A soaring hawk cried in fierce answer to Janna's call, but Zebra didn't even turn her head toward the bird. Janna's high, keening cry came again. Zebra spun and cantered eagerly toward the ridge, whinnying her welcome.

"Hello, girl," Janna said, standing up, as pleased as the mare was. "Did you know that you're the answer to a prayer? Now I'll be able to cover three times the ground and not have to worry about tracks."

Zebra nickered and whuffled and pushed her head against Janna's body, nearly knocking her off her feet.

"I hope you're as eager for a run as you look, because you're going to get one. Hold still, girl. My arm is as stiff as an old man's knees."

Janna's mount wasn't very elegant, but she managed to finish right side up on the mare, which was all that counted.

"Come on, girl, let's check on your lord and master."

Eagerly Zebra responded to the pressure of Janna's heels. Cantering swiftly, the horse ate up the distance between Janna and Ty. Janna guided the horse in a long, looping curve, wanting to check more of the land on the way back to Ty. The mare sped quickly through the open country, going from tree shadow to full sun and back again, a kaleidoscope of light and darkness flowing over horse and rider, and always the earth flying beneath the mare's hooves.

Janna was only a few minutes away from where she had left Ty when she saw the renegades.

Chapter Twenty-Nine

Zebra spun aside and leaped into a full gallop in the same motion. Janna didn't try to slow or turn the horse back toward the place where Ty was. She simply grabbed a double handful of flying black mane and bent over the mare's neck, urging her on to greater speed. Behind her the Indians shouted and fired a few shots as they gave chase.

Janna had ridden Zebra at a gallop before, but nothing like this frantic pace. The mare's speed would have been frightening to Janna if it hadn't been for the fact that she was fleeing an even greater danger. As it was, Janna flattened down against Zebra's sleek, driving body, urging greater speed and trying to make herself as light a burden as possible.

Zebra stretched out her neck and ran as though fleeing hell. The force of the wind raking over Janna's eyes made tears stream down her face. Her hat was ripped from her head. One of the chin strings snapped and the hat sailed away. Soon her braids had unraveled and her long hair was streaming out behind her like darkly burning, wind-whipped flames.

The sudden appearance of Janna's distinctive hair cooled the urgency of the chase for the Indians. There was little sport and even less glory or booty in capturing a homeless girl. There were also the uncomfortable whispers about the true nature of that girl. *Bruja.* Witch. Shadow of Flame. That was what she looked like as she bent over the wild horse she rode with neither bridle nor saddle, her body all but lost in the flying mane and her own unbound hair streaming behind her in the wind like a warning flag.

And surely only a spirit horse ridden by a spirit woman could be so fleet.

Janna didn't try to guide Zebra, for the mare knew the plateau's twists and turns and traps as well as Janna did. All that she cared about was that the horse was racing away from the eastern trail and therefore away from Ty and the injured stallion. She made no attempt to use the revolver that was digging into her body as she rode the wildly galloping horse. Drawing the weapon would have been difficult enough; shooting accurately would have been impossible.

With every passing minute it became more obvious that Zebra was outrunning the renegades. Well fed, well rested, carrying only Janna's insignificant weight, Zebra not only had more speed than the renegades' horses, she had more stamina, as well. After a few miles the renegades became certain that they were spending their horses in a losing cause. First two warriors dropped out of the chase, then a third, then a fourth, until finally only one man still pursued the bright banner of Janna's hair. Finally he, too, gave up and stopped whipping his laboring horse.

Zebra knew before Janna did that the chase was over. Even so, the mare kept galloping for a time, putting more distance between herself and her pursuers. Janna sensed the difference in Zebra's pace and knew that the immediate danger had passed. Cautiously she shifted her grip on the mane, wiped her eyes and looked over her shoulder. There was nothing behind her but Zebra's tracks across an empty land.

When Zebra breasted a ridge, Janna urged the mare into the cover of some trees and then checked her trail very carefully, using the spyglass. The renegades weren't anywhere to be seen. What she could see of the land ahead of her looked equally empty.

For a few minutes Janna considered the various ways and means of hiding Zebra's tracks in order to confuse any followers. Every way she thought of, including dismounting and letting the mare go free once more, would make it impossible for Janna to get to the east rim of the plateau before dark. She would have to keep Zebra with her and count on the mare's speed to thwart any more pursuit.

"All right, girl," Janna said, "let's go back and see if Ty and Lucifer are all right."

At a touch from her rider, the mustang turned and began cantering at an angle to her old trail. Though Janna watched warily, she saw no sign that any human had been along recently. Wild horses grazed undisturbed until Zebra appeared, and then the horses spun and raced away. Janna urged Zebra to detour into the three groups of horses she found, mixing the mare's tracks with those of her mustang kin, making it all but impossible for anyone to follow Janna from that point on.

By the time Janna spotted Ty and Lucifer, it was midafternoon and she was only a mile from the eastern trail. Clouds that had been frail and white earlier in the day had matured into towering, seething billows, which were creamy on their curving tops and blue-black on their flat bottoms. The Fire Mountains were already obscured beneath dense clouds. Distant thunder rumbled down from the invisible peaks. Soon the plateau would be engulfed by sound and fury and tiny, icy hammer blows of rain. Lightning would strike the plateau's promontories and lone trees would run the risk of being transformed into torches.

It would be no different for a man caught in the open on the exposed, eastern face of the plateau. If they hoped to get down the east trail today, they would have to move quickly.

As though sensing her rider's urgency, Zebra cantered to the edge of the plateau. There, wind and rain had unraveled the land into countless crevices, gullies, ravines and canyons. There, at the head of an insignificant ravine, began the sole path down the plateau's rugged east face. There, too, were Ty and Lucifer.

Ty didn't wait for Janna to dismount. Before Zebra had come to a full stop, he plucked Janna off and held her close while the two horses nickered and nuzzled each other in friendly greeting.

"What the hell happened to you?" Ty demanded harshly, but the hands stroking her unbound hair were gentle.

"I found Zebra and we were coming back to check on you and we popped up over a rise and found a bunch of renegades." Janna felt Ty's arms tighten abruptly.

"I knew it," he said, his voice rough. "I heard those damned shots and I just *knew*."

"The renegades were as surprised as I was," Janna said, trying to reassure Ty. "They only got off a few shots before I was out of range. None of the bullets even came close."

"Then how did you lose your hat?"

"Wind," Janna said succinctly. "Zebra ran like hell let out for a holiday. I couldn't see for the tears in my eyes."

Ty thought of the rugged land and the wild mustang and Janna riding her with no stirrups to support and balance her, no bridle to help her control her mount, nothing to help her stay in place if the horse should stumble; and injury or death awaiting her if she fell.

"Dammit, Janna…!"

Ty's voice trailed off. He knew that it was unreasonable of him to be angry with her for having been in danger. She could no more help her position in the wild land than he could.

"This can't go on," Ty said beneath his breath. "I've got to get you to a place where you'll be safe."

Thunder muttered across the plateau, reminding Ty that danger wore many faces, and another one was looking at them right now. Reluctantly he turned and measured the hair-raising trail that awaited the injured stallion.

The path began at the head of a narrow ravine that rapidly branched sideways and downward, threading a tortuous zigzag route across the crumbling east face of the plateau. After the first quarter mile the path became less steep. After a mile the trail merged with the sloping outwash plain that began several thousand feet below the plateau itself. At that point the path became no worse than any other game trail in the rugged land.

But that first quarter mile was a nightmare, and the last three quarters were little better. It had been difficult enough to scramble up onto the plateau via that trail. Climbing down was always more dangerous. Ty didn't see how they were going to negotiate the steep path without losing the tug-of-war with gravity and falling a long, long way down.

"The first part is the hardest," Janna said.

"Is that supposed to make me feel better?"

"Well, it shouldn't make you feel worse."

For an instant Ty's smile flashed whitely beneath his black mustache. He brushed his lips over Janna's answering smile before he released her.

"Keep Zebra back until Lucifer is through with the worst of it," Ty said. "I'm going to have enough trouble staying out from under the stallion's hooves. I sure don't need to be looking over my shoulder for the mare, too." He turned to Lucifer and pulled gently on the hackamore's lead rope. "Come on, son. Might as well get it over with. As my daddy used to say, 'We can't dance and it's too wet to plow.'"

Lucifer walked to the beginning of the path, looked down the slope and refused to take another step.

"Don't blame you a bit," Ty said soothingly, "but it has to be done." He increased the pressure on the lead rope. "Come on, you big black stud. Show Janna what a well-behaved gentleman you've become during our walk today."

The stallion's head came up sharply, counteracting the pressure that tended to pull him toward the steep, dangerous path. Thunder rolled and muttered. A freshening wind brought with it the scent of rain, warning that the possibility of a storm grew greater with every passing minute.

"Come on," Ty said, increasing the pressure on the lead rope until he could pull no harder. "If you think that little bit of a path looks rough now, wait until it's raining fit to put out the fires of hell. When that happens we want to be long gone from here."

Lucifer's ears went back as he set himself more firmly, pulling hard against the pressure on the hackamore.

"Your daddy must have been Satan's own black mule," Ty said, but his tone was still mild and reassuring. "Come on, son. You heard the lady. The first part is the hardest. After that it's as easy as licking honey off a spoon."

Lucifer's ears flattened against his head.

Ty had several choices. He could keep pulling and hope the stallion would give up. He could keep pulling and have Janna make a loud noise, stampeding the stallion over the rim—and right onto Ty. Or he could lure the stallion onto the trail using the oldest bait of all.

"Janna, do you think that cat-footed mare of yours will go down this trail?"

"I don't know. It's worth a try."

"Easy, son," Ty said as he went up to Lucifer and put pressure on the horse's black nose to make him back up. "If you don't want to be first you'll just have to get out of the way and let your lady show you how easy it is."

Lucifer willingly backed away from the trail. Wind gusted suddenly, bringing with it a foretaste of the chilly storm. The stallion pricked his ears and snorted, feeling an instinctive urge to seek shelter.

Ty wrapped the lead rope and secured it around Lucifer's neck, freeing his own hands and at the same time making sure that the stallion didn't get all tangled up in loose rope. When Ty was finished he led the stallion aside, making room for Janna and Zebra to approach the rough path. When Zebra was pointed in the right direction—straight down—Janna smacked the mare on her warm haunch.

"Down you go," she said hopefully.

Zebra turned and looked at Janna.

"Shoo, girl! Go on, get on down that trail. Get!!"

The mustang shook her head as though ridding herself of persistent flies. Deliberately she backed away from the trail.

"Dammit," Ty said. "Maybe if we—Janna, don't!"

It was too late. Janna had already darted around in front of Zebra and started down the trail herself. She picked her way down the first steep pitch, found a relatively secure place to stand and turned to call to Zebra.

"No," Ty said urgently. "Don't take the trail in front of Zebra. If she slips she'll roll right on over you and leave you flatter than a shadow!"

"I'll stay out of her way," Janna said, but her voice was

tight. She knew even better than Ty the danger of being on the downhill side of a horse on a precipitous slope. "Come on, girl. Point those black hooves in this direction. Come to me, Zebra. Come on."

As always, Janna's coaxing murmur and her outstretched hands intrigued the mare. She edged as far forward as she could without committing herself to the trail. Neck outstretched, nostrils flaring, ears pricked forward, Zebra leaned toward Janna. Her hooves, however, remained firmly planted.

Without hesitation, Janna retreated farther down the trail. When she reached another relatively level patch of ground, she was fifty feet away. She put her hands to her mouth and a hawk's wild cry floated up. Zebra nickered nervously and shifted her feet. The hawk cry came again, reminding the mare of all the times she had answered the call and found Janna waiting with her backpack full of treats.

One of the mare's black hooves lifted, then set down barely a few inches away. Another hoof lifted. Another few inches gained. Ears pricked, skin flinching nervously, Zebra literally inched her way down the trail. Janna melted away in front of the mustang, calling softly, praising Zebra with every breath.

As Ty watched, his body ran with sweat. A single hesitation, a loose stone, any miscalculation on the mare's part and Janna quickly would be engulfed in a flailing, lethal windmill of horse and human flesh. There was no place for her to leap aside, no place to hide. If Zebra fell, Janna would be killed.

Unknowingly Ty prayed in low tones, never lifting his glance from Zebra's mincing progress, feeling as though his soul were being drawn on a rack.

If you get out of this alive, Janna, Ty vowed silently, *I'll make sure you stay out of danger if I have to tie you up and stuff you in my backpack and never let you out.*

Lucifer whickered nervously, calling to Zebra. The mare ignored him, intent on the trail and on the girl who kept retreating down the dangerously steep slope. The stallion's next call was louder and more urgent but it had no more effect than the first. He whinnied imperiously. Zebra's ears swiveled and her tail swished. She lifted her head to look, began slipping and sat down on her haunches. For the space of several breaths the mare simply remained motionless, then she slowly gathered herself and resumed her inching progress down the trail.

The stallion's barrel swelled as he took in air for another whinny.

"Shut up, son," Ty said.

Long, powerful fingers closed gently and completely over the stallion's nostrils, making it impossible for the horse to whinny. Lucifer threw up his head but Ty hung on, talking calmly the whole time.

"Yelling at her won't do any good right now," Ty assured the stallion. "That little mare no more listens to you than Janna listens to me. Later I'll be glad to let you give your woman a royal chewing out—and I plan to do the same to mine—but first let's get them to a safe place."

The firm hands and reassuring voice held Lucifer quiet, though his half-flattened ears told anyone who cared to look that the stallion wasn't very happy about the situation.

Ty didn't notice. The farther the mare got down the trail, the more impossible it seemed that a horse had descended it at all. But Zebra had. The evidence was everywhere, in clumps of dirt gouged out by hooves and in hoofprints elongated by skids. Beneath his breath Ty counted out the steps remaining on the last steep pitch before the trail leveled out to the point where Zebra didn't have to go down half-sitting and braced on her stiffened forelegs.

"Seven, six, fi—"

Zebra skidded the last fifteen feet and then stood quietly, absorbing Janna's praise. Ty let out a long breath as he released his grip on Lucifer's muzzle.

"All right, son. It's our turn. And this time I'm not taking no for an answer."

Chapter Thirty

Lucifer went to the edge of the plateau, whinnied loudly and was answered by Zebra. He whinnied again. Zebra looked up the steep path but didn't move one step in the stallion's direction.

"She's not about to scramble up to you," Ty said calmly. He stood to the side of Lucifer's head and pulled steadily forward on the hackamore. "If you want her, you're going to have to do it the hard way."

The stallion stood at the trailhead, laid back his ears...and began climbing down.

Janna found it more unnerving to watch Ty descend alongside the stallion's big hooves than it had been for her to climb down the plateau's face in front of Zebra. The first quarter mile was especially dangerous, for there really wasn't enough room for Ty to stand alongside the horse on the path without being under Lucifer's feet half the time.

Let go, Ty. Let Lucifer do it alone, Janna urged silently. *He won't back out now. He can't. The only thing he can do is keep coming down and he knows it.*

Snorting, mincing, sliding, sweating, the muscles in his injured leg trembling at the strain, the stallion negotiated the first quarter mile with surprising speed. More than once it was Ty's timely jerk on the hackamore that saved Lucifer from a fall by levering his head up, which helped the horse to regain control when his feet started sliding. Under normal conditions the mustang's own agility would have been sufficient to get him down the trail, but his injury made the difficult footing all but impossible had it not been for Ty's help.

Without warning the stallion's injured leg gave way and he lost his footing. Ty threw all his muscle behind the hackamore, forcing Lucifer back onto his haunches. Front legs braced, hooves digging into the path, the horse slid about twenty feet before he came to a stop. Sitting up like a big black hound, the stallion sweated nervously while displaced pebbles bounced and rattled down the slope. Right beside him, Ty sweated just as hard. It had been much too close to disaster. Someone with less strength than Ty wouldn't have been able to prevent the horse from falling.

Janna held her fist against her teeth as she forced back a scream. Ty had taken a terrible gamble, for if his weight and leverage hadn't been enough to counteract gravity, he would have been swept away with Lucifer in a long, lethal fall.

"That's it, son," Ty said, his voice soothing despite the hammer blows of his own heart. "You rest and get your wind back. That old leg just keeps fooling you. You expect it to be there for you and it isn't, not the way you need it to be. That's the problem with strength. You get to counting on it and then it lets you down. So use your head instead. You can't just rush the path and scramble and slide and get it over with the way you would if you had your usual muscle and coordination. You have to take it nice and slow."

When Lucifer's skin no longer rippled with nervous reaction, Ty gradually released his pressure on the hackamore. Gingerly the stallion shifted his weight forward and began descending once more. As though he had understood Ty's words, the mustang moved more slowly now, demanding less of his injured leg.

Even so, by the time Lucifer reached the end of the steepest portion of the path, Janna was trembling with a fear she had never known for herself. When both man and horse were on safe ground, she let out a shaky breath and ran to Ty, throwing herself at him, holding on to him with fierce strength despite her bruised arm.

"I was so frightened," Janna said against Ty's neck. "All I could think of was what would happen if Lucifer got to sliding too fast or lost his footing completely and you couldn't get out of the way in time."

Ty's arms closed around Janna, lifting her off her feet. "The same thought occurred to me about every other step," he said roughly, "but worst of all was watching you stand in front of Zebra and knowing there wasn't a damn thing I could do if things went to hell." He held Janna hard and close, savoring the feel of her in his arms, her living warmth and resilience and the sweet rush of her breath against his neck. "God, little one, it's good to be alive and holding you."

A cool wind swirled down the plateau's face, trailing the sound of thunder behind. Reluctantly Ty released Janna and set her back on her feet. A moment later he fished the crumpled rain poncho from his backpack. Without a word he tugged the waterproof folds over Janna.

"That should do it," he said. "Now let's get off this exposed slope before lightning has better luck at killing us than that damn trail did."

With the casual strength that kept surprising Janna, Ty tossed her onto Zebra's back.

"Don't wait for me. Just get off the slope," Ty said to Janna. He stepped back and smacked Zebra lightly on her haunch. "Get to it, horse. And you keep your rider hair side up or I'll skin you for a sofa covering."

Zebra took to the path again with an eagerness that said more plainly than words that the mustang understood the danger of being caught out in the open during a storm. Lucifer was just as eager to see the last of the exposed trail leading from the foot of the plateau to the lowlands beyond, but his injury forced a slower pace. Limping heavily, the stallion started off down the rocky decline.

Out in the distance to the east, blue-black buttes and localized thunderstorms were intermixed with golden cataracts of light where sunshine poured through gaps between squall lines. Overhead, lightning played through the massed clouds and the wind increased in power.

By the time Lucifer and Ty reached the place where the plateau merged with the lower canyon lands beyond, the last luminous shafts of sunlight had slowly merged with the thunderstorm gathering overhead, leaving behind an odd, sourceless gloaming that made every feature of the land stand forth as though outlined in pale gold. The effect lasted for only a few minutes, until the first sweeping veils of rain came down, blending sky and land into one seamless whole. Lightning danced across the land on incandescent feet, while thunder rumbled behind its shimmering, elusive mistress.

"Well, son," Ty said, pulling his hat down tighter against the wind and pelting rain, "this cloud's silver lining is that no self-respecting renegade is going to be out chasing around in the rain."

If that fact cheered Lucifer, the horse didn't show it. He limped along with his ears half-laid-back in warning of his surly temper. Ty felt the same way himself. With luck the storm would turn out to be a small, fast-moving squall line. Without luck, the rain would last for hours. With bad luck, the slot leading into Janna's hidden canyon would be too deep with runoff water from the thunderstorm for them to enter and they would have to spend another night in the open.

Janna was worrying about the same thing. If she were alone, she would have hurried Zebra toward the miles-distant slot. But she wasn't alone, and despite Lucifer's best efforts, his shuffling, painful walk meant that it would be several hours before they reached the haven of her hidden canyon.

The rain quickly limited visibility to a few hundred yards, making scouting both impossible and unnecessary. Janna turned Zebra and retraced her steps until she saw Lucifer and Ty. She slid off Zebra and fell into step beside Ty.

"Go ahead on to the canyon," he said. "No sense in you catching your death out in the rain."

"It will be dark an hour before you get to the slot. You'll miss it. Besides, you know how it is with misery. I was feeling like a little company."

Ty thought of objecting more forcefully to Janna's presence but didn't. Part of him agreed with her that he would have

trouble finding the narrow slot in the dark in the rain, because
the only other time he had been through it from this direction
he had been more dead than alive. But the real reason he didn't
object was that he enjoyed having Janna beside him, her fingers laced through his, their hands slowly warming with
shared body heat.

"Janna?" Ty asked after a long time of rain and silence,
voicing a thought that had been nagging at him for hours.

"Yes?"

"Why did you risk your life holding on to Lucifer in that
ravine?"

"I didn't want Troon to get him again."

"But you heard the renegades. You had to figure that Troon
was as good as dead. You could have let Lucifer go, but you
didn't. You hung on despite the danger to yourself."

Janna said nothing.

"Sugar? Why?"

"I promised you a chance to gentle Lucifer," Janna said
simply. "There would never be a better chance than in that
small ravine."

Ty swore very softly. "I thought it was something crazy
like that. Listen to me. You're free of that promise you made.
Do you hear me? If Lucifer decides to take off in twelve different directions, that's my problem, not yours. You just get
the hell out of the way where you won't get hurt." Ty waited
but she said nothing. "Janna?"

"I heard you."

"Do I have your word that if Lucifer bolts or goes loco,
you'll get out of the way instead of trying to help?"

"Ty—"

"Give me your word," he interrupted, "or so help me God
I'll turn around right now and walk back to Wyoming and to
hell with that damned black stud."

"But he's your future, the only way you'll get a chance to
buy your silken—"

Ty interrupted with a burst of language that was both savage
and obscene. It was a mile before Janna had the courage to
break the silence that had followed.

"I promise," she said finally. "I don't understand why you won't let me help you, but—"

"You don't understand?" Ty demanded fiercely, cutting off Janna's words once more. "You must have a damned poor opinion of me if you think I'd build my dream on top of your dead body!"

"I never meant anything like that!" Janna said instantly, shocked that Ty had misunderstood her words. "I know you'd never do something that awful. You're much too kind and gentle and generous."

Ty's laughter was as harsh as his swearing had been, for he knew that a man who was kind or gentle or generous wouldn't have eased his violent hunger at the cost of Janna's innocence. But Ty had done just that and now she was no longer innocent…and worst of all, he couldn't bring himself to truly repent his action. The ecstasy he had known within Janna's body was too great, too consuming, to ever be repudiated.

If he had it to do all over again, he would no more be able to preserve Janna's virginity than he had been the first time. She was wildness and grace and elemental fire, and he was a man who had hungered a lifetime for all three without knowing it. She had sensed his needs, given herself to him and had required nothing of him in return. Not one damn thing.

And he felt the silken strands of her innocence and generosity twining more tightly around him with each moment, binding him.

"Do you do it on purpose?" Ty demanded angrily.

"What?"

"Give everything and ask nothing and thereby chain me to you tighter than any steel manacles could."

Janna felt as though she had been struck. The cold rain that had been making her miserable became her friend, for it hid the tears and disappointment she was too tired to conceal. When Ty had swept her up in his arms and held her as fiercely as she had held him, she had begun to hope that he cared more for her than simply as a sexual convenience. When he had held her hand and walked in companionable silence with her through the storm, she had been certain that he cared for her.

What she hadn't realized was that he would resent that caring, and her.

"Well, you're by God going to take something from me," Ty continued. "Lucifer is half yours."

"I don't want him."

"I didn't want you to risk your neck, either," Ty shot back, "and a lot of good my wanting did me."

Janna jerked her hand free of his. "Did you ever think that the reason I didn't ask for anything from you was that there was nothing you had that I wanted?"

"Nothing?" Ty asked sardonically. "You could have fooled me."

The tone of his voice told Janna that he was remembering her hands caressing him, her lips clinging, her hips lifting in silent pleading that his body join with hers. Shame coursed through her.

"Don't worry," she said, her voice strained. "You won't have to lose any sleep on my account tonight. I won't seduce you again."

"Seduce me? Is that what you think happened? You seduced me?" Ty laughed. "Sugar, you don't have the least idea how to seduce a man. A woman seduces a man with rustling silks and secret smiles and accidental touches of her soft, perfumed hands. She seduces a man with her conversation and the sweet music of her voice when she greets her guests for a fancy ball. She seduces a man by knowing fine wines and elegant food, and by her special grace when she enters a room knowing he'll be there." Ty shook his head and added, "You well and truly bedded me, but you sure as hell didn't seduce me."

Janna remembered what Ty had said about her last night... *suited to be nothing except a man's mistress, but you lack the social graces for even that profession.*

Without a word Janna turned away from Ty and swung onto Zebra's warm back, ignoring the pain that mounting the horse without aid gave to her bruised arm.

"Janna? What the hell...?"

She didn't answer. Her heels urged Zebra forward until Janna could see and hear only the rain.

Chapter Thirty-One

"Come on, it's just a little bit farther," Ty said to the stallion, hoping he wasn't lying. Neither Ty's voice nor the steady pressure he put on the hackamore revealed the weariness that had settled into the marrow of his bones, turning his muscles to sand.

For a moment Ty was afraid that the stallion wouldn't respond, but the pressure on the hackamore eased abruptly as the horse resumed his awkward walking gait.

"That's it, son," Ty said encouragingly. "She said the slot was at the top of a little rise."

And that was all Janna had said through the long hours of intermittent rain and wind. When it wasn't raining she rode far ahead of Ty and Lucifer. When it rained she rode in close enough that her tracks were always clear for Ty to follow. When it became dark she rode closer still, ensuring that Lucifer wouldn't get lost.

Ty was certain that it was the stallion's welfare rather than his own that concerned Janna. Not once since she had mounted Zebra had she said anything to Ty. He missed her conversation. In the past weeks he had become accustomed to her insights into the land and its animals, her uninhibited response to the wind and sun, and her shy smile when he touched her. He missed her laughter when she talked about hiding from Cascabel in the same way the renegade had once hidden from the soldiers—out in plain sight. Ty missed the snippets of plays and poetry and essays she liked to talk about with him, drawing from him the missing parts of her education. Most of all he missed the warm, companionable silence they had shared while they walked hand in hand in the cold rain.

The silence Ty and Janna had shared since she had ridden off was anything but companionable. It was as chill and empty as the night.

"Maybe you can tell me," Ty said to Lucifer. "Why would a woman get all upset because I told her it isn't her fault that she's not a virgin anymore? Because it sure as hell isn't her fault. Janna didn't have the faintest idea of what waited for her at the end of that primrose path. She could no more have known when to say no to me than she could have walked down the plateau trail carrying Zebra on her back.

"But I knew where we were going. I knew the first time I kissed Janna that I should stop myself right there or I wouldn't be able to quit short of burying myself in that sweet young body. But I didn't stop. I wanted her the way a river in flood wants the sea. Just plain unstoppable. And God help me, I still want her just like that.

"I knew what I was doing every inch of the way…and it was every inch the best I've ever had. I'll die remembering the beautiful sounds she made while I was inside her, pleasuring her with my whole body."

Ty's voice thickened as memories poured through him in an incandescent tide. Despite his exhaustion, his blood beat heavily at the thought of being sheathed within Janna's fire and softness once more.

"She didn't have a chance to refuse me," Ty continued, his voice rough. "Not a single damned chance in hell. It should have made her feel better to know that what happened was my fault, not hers.

"So why won't she speak to me?"

Lucifer didn't have any answer for Ty. Not that he had expected one. If the stallion had known how to handle the supposedly weaker sex, Zebra wouldn't have been racing around the plateau with Janna for the past few years. Muttering to himself, Ty walked up the rise, urging the limping stallion along with a steady pressure on the hackamore.

At last a low nicker came floating out of the darkness in front of them. Lucifer nickered in return. No verbal welcome came to Ty, however. Nor did Janna say anything when she dismounted and walked around the stallion. Frowning, peering into the coldly brilliant moonlight that had replaced the wind-frayed clouds, she tried to gauge Lucifer's condition.

"Is there too much water in the slot for us to get through?" Ty asked.

"No."

He waited, but Janna had nothing more to say on that subject—or any other, apparently. At least, not to him. But it seemed she had nothing against talking to the stallion.

"You poor, brave creature. You've really been put through it today, haven't you?" Janna said in a gentle voice as she reached out to pet Lucifer.

Ty opened his mouth to warn Janna that the stallion was feeling surly as hell, but the words died on his tongue when Lucifer whickered softly and stretched his muzzle out to Janna's hands. Slender fingers stroked his muzzle and cheeks, then searched through the stallion's thick, shaggy forelock until she found the bony knob between his ears. She slid her fingers beneath the hackamore and rubbed away the unaccustomed feel of the leather.

Lucifer let out a breath that was almost a groan and put his forehead against Janna's chest, offering himself to her touch with a trust that first shocked Ty, then moved him, making his throat close around all the emotions he had no words to describe. Seeing the stallion's gentle surrender reminded Ty of the ancient myth of the unicorn and virgin. But as Ty watched Janna, he wondered if it weren't some elemental feminine quality that had attracted the unicorn to the girl, rather than her supposedly virginal state.

That poor unicorn never had a chance, Ty told himself silently. *He was born to lay his head in that one maiden's lap and be captive to her gentle hands.*

The insight made Ty very restless. Though Janna had done

nothing to hold him, he felt himself somehow confined, caught in an invisible net, tied with silken threads; and each thread was a shared caress, a shared smile, a shared word, until one thread became thousands woven into an unbreakable bond, and the silken snare was complete.

"Ready, boy?" Janna asked quietly. "It's going to be hard on your poor leg, but it's the last thing I'll ask of you until you're healed."

Janna turned and walked toward Zebra. Lucifer followed, silently urging Ty forward with a pressure on the lead rope he still held. The reversal in their roles gave Ty a moment of sardonic amusement. He wondered what would happen if he tied the rope around the stallion's neck and then turned and walked away, leaving everything behind.

I'll tell you what would happen, Ty thought to himself. *You'd spend the night hungry and freezing your butt off in the cold and Lucifer would spend it belly-deep in food with Janna's warm hands petting him. So who do you think is smarter—you or that stallion?*

With a muttered curse Ty followed Lucifer over the wet, rocky ground to the invisible opening in the plateau's wall. The face of the plateau at this point was made of broken ranks of sheer rocky cliffs punctuated by dark mounds of black lava. As though to make up for the precipitous nature of the land, the cliffs were only a tenth of the height of the heavily eroded wall Janna and Ty had descended earlier.

Even so, Janna had discovered no trail up onto the plateau itself from this area. If she wanted to go back up on top, she had to walk much farther south, following the ragged edge of the plateau as it rose and fell until she reached the gentle southern ascent. That would have been a full day's ride on a good horse. The east path, while steep, was only a few hours by foot.

Ahead of Ty both horses stopped abruptly. Zebra snorted nervously when Janna waded into the water gushing from the slot, but the mare didn't balk. She followed Janna into the ankle-deep runoff stream, for she had done this before and not been hurt by the experience. Lucifer hesitated, lowered his head and smelled the water, then limped into the stream in the manner of an animal who was too exhausted at the moment to do more than go where he was led.

Inside the slot, moonlight was reduced to a pale glimmering over the surface of the water. The horses were better off than the humans, both by reason of four legs and the superior night vision of equines. Even with those advantages, the horses didn't have an easy time of it. Janna, with her greater experience in negotiating the slot, managed not to slip and fall more than twice. Ty fell four times and considered himself fortunate that it wasn't a lot worse.

When they emerged into the valley, humans and animals alike were soaked by a combination of rain, runoff water and sweat.

"That's it, girl," Janna said tiredly, slapping the mare on her muscular haunch. "We're home."

Zebra trotted off into the moonlight, heading for the sweet grass and clover she had discovered on her previous visit. Ty considered hobbling Lucifer, then rejected the idea. Even if the stallion wanted to leave Zebra, Lucifer was too tired to take on the slot again. With a few smooth motions Ty removed the hackamore. When it was off, he rubbed away all the marks the leather had left on the horse's head. Lucifer leaned into the touch, obviously enjoying it.

"Yeah, I know. It doesn't take long to get spoiled, does it?" murmured Ty, thinking of Janna and the night before. "Tomorrow I'll give you a good rubdown, but right now you need food more than you need petting. Go follow Zebra, son. She knows where all the sweet things are in this place."

After Ty removed his hand, it took a moment for the stallion to realize that he was free. When he did, he snorted, shook his head and limped off after Zebra. Ty looked away just in time to see Janna vanish into the willows that grew alongside the stream.

By the time Ty got to the cliff overhang Janna called home, a small glow of flame was expanding into the darkness. Sitting on her heels next to the fire, Janna fed in fuel from the supply she kept dry in one corner of the overhang. Once the fire took hold she added wet wood from the pile that was stacked beyond the protection of the rock.

Only when water was warming over the fire did Janna turn away and go to the small trunk she had laboriously tugged through the slot three years before, when she had discovered the secret canyon. Most of the trunk was filled with books. A small part of it was taken up with the last of her father's clothes. Only one ragged shirt remained, one pair of Sunday pants, three socks and the moccasins she had traded medicines for last spring.

"I took three shirts from Preacher's store. Do you want one of them?"

The sound of Ty's voice startled Janna. She hadn't realized that he was in camp. But there he was, standing on the other side of the fire, stretching muscles that were tired from carrying the heavy backpack that now rested against the stone cliff. Ty peeled off his hat and slapped it against his thigh, driving water from the hat rim in a fine spray.

"No," Janna said, turning away from Ty again, refusing more than his offer of a shirt.

She unlaced her soggy moccasins and set them aside to dry. With cold hands she worked beneath the poncho, unwinding the cloth that bound her breasts. The motions sent stabbing pains through her bruised arm. She set her teeth and continued. She had suffered worse injuries in the past; she would probably suffer more in the future.

Ty didn't bother to ask if Janna wanted any help, for he knew she would refuse him. Without a word he lifted the cumbersome poncho from Janna's shoulders and threw it aside. The sight of the bruise on her arm made his breath come in with an audible hiss. Even though experience told Ty that the bruise looked much worse than it actually was, he hated seeing the dark shadow of pain on her skin.

"Don't you have something for that?" he asked.

"Yes."

Janna tried to step away. Ty's hands closed around her lower arms in a grip that was gentle but unshakable.

"Hold still, sugar. Let me help you."

Afraid to trust her voice, Janna shook her head in a negative.

"Yes," Ty countered instantly. "You've patched me up often enough. Now it's your turn to be patched."

Janna looked up into Ty's glance. His eyes were very dark yet alive with flames reflected from the campfire. The warmth of his hands on her chilled skin was shocking, but not as shocking as the heat that uncurled in her loins at the thought of being cared for by him. She shivered in a combination of cold and remembered desire.

And she hated it, both the memory and the desire, hated wanting a man whose feelings for her teetered between pity and contempt, lust and indifference.

"You're chilled through and through," Ty said, frowning as he saw Janna shiver violently. With quick motions he began unwrapping the cloth that bound her chest. "Where's the medicine you need?"

She shook her head, refusing him, refusing her memories, refusing everything.

"Janna, what in hell is the matter with you?"

Ty didn't wait for an answer. Janna felt cloth being stripped from her body by his big hands. Suddenly she couldn't bear the thought of her naked breasts being revealed to Ty again. He would touch them, kiss them, and the heat that was spreading from the pit of her stomach would flare up, burning away everything, even the knowledge that she loved a man who loved only his own dream...and she was not that dream.

With an inarticulate cry Janna tried to push away Ty's hands. It was like pushing on warm stone.

"It's too late to be shy," he said flatly, ignoring her attempts to stop him from unwrapping her breasts. "Hold still while I get this wet stuff off you."

"Let go of me."

The quality of Janna's voice was chilling. Ty's hands froze in the act of unwrapping her.

"Janna, what's wrong?"

His voice was gentle but Janna didn't hear that, or the emotions churning just beneath his control. She heard only her own memories, Ty's voice echoing and reechoing in her mind as he listed all her shortcomings as a woman—nothing to offer a husband, too unskilled to be a mistress, good only for the male need that built up inexorably when no other woman was around.

"Little one?" Ty asked, tipping Janna's chin up and brushing a kiss over her lips. They were as cold as her voice had been. "What did I do to make you so angry with me?"

When he would have kissed her again, she jerked her head away. "Don't touch me. I don't feel like being your whore tonight."

Chapter Thirty-Two

Ty's tightly held emotions exploded into a fury that was unlike any he had ever felt. He stopped trying to peel off layers of wet cloth and grabbed Janna's shoulders instead.

"Don't say something like that about yourself! Do you hear me, Janna Wayland? *You are not a whore!*"

Angry, ashamed, defiant, Janna stood shivering within Ty's grasp. "Just what would you call it?"

"We're...lovers."

"I don't think so," she said distinctly. "To be someone's lover suggests a certain affection mixed in with the lust. I'm not your lover. I'm a convenience until you take Lucifer and go off to buy your silk—"

"Don't say it," Ty interrupted savagely. "I'm sick to death of having those words flung in my face."

"Then stop flinging them in mine."

"I've never—"

"The hell you haven't!" Janna interrupted, her voice as savage as his. "'I'll have my silken lady or I'll have none at all for longer than it takes to pleasure myself,'" Janna quoted, each word clipped. "'You're the least female female I've ever seen.' Then you said that Cascabel looked more like a mesquite bush than I looked like a woman, and the comparisons didn't stop after you had me, either. You couldn't wait to tell me that it was a woman you'd needed, not me."

Janna's voice broke, then steadied as words rushed out.

"And then you told me that my virginity was all I had to offer
to a husband because I had no family, no profession, no
money. You said that you had ruined me, because now I
wasn't good enough to be a wife and wasn't educated enough
to be a mistress and that meant that I wasn't good enough to
be anything but a 'toy of many men, not one.' That's a whore
in any man's language."

"Janna—my God, I never meant—"

"I'm not finished," she said, cutting across Ty's shocked
words. "Or maybe I should say *you're* not finished. You've
had a lot to say about my shortcomings as a woman. As
woman hungry as you were, I couldn't even seduce you. You
said, 'Sugar, you don't have the least idea how to seduce a
man. A woman seduces a man with rustling silks and—'"

Ty's hand clamped across Janna's mouth, cutting off her
bitter recitation of his words.

"You don't understand," Ty said urgently. "I didn't mean
any of that to belittle you. Especially after we made love."

The mute defiance of Janna's eyes and the hot rain of her
tears said that she had understood him all too well.

"Janna," he whispered, kissing her eyelashes, tasting her
tears, "please believe me. I never meant the words as an insult
to you. You're a young girl alone in the world and I seduced
you, knowing I shouldn't. That's all the words meant. My
shortcomings, Janna, not yours."

She trembled as she felt Ty's caresses and soft words stripping away her anger, revealing the despair that was the other
side of her fury. Nothing he had said or could say would
change the heartbreaking reality: she was not the silken lady
of her lover's dreams.

"Do you believe me?" Ty asked, the words as soft as the
repeated brush of his lips over Janna's eyelids, her cheeks, her
mouth. "I never meant to belittle you. Satin butterfly...believe
me...I never meant..."

Gentle words became tender kisses, which lingered and
deepened until Ty's tongue touched Janna's for just an instant.
Then he withdrew.

"You're so cold you're shivering," he said huskily.

With a volatile mixture of despair and tenderness and desire, Janna waited for Ty to suggest the obvious way to warm her.

Ty looked from Janna's clear, fathomless eyes to the fire whose flames were licking against a huge wall of stone. "And that fire has a lot of rock to warm before it will do us any good." Suddenly he smiled. "But there's a better way."

Janna's answering smile was bittersweet as Ty's hands went to the soggy material that was still wrapped around her breasts. She could refuse him when she was in the grip of anger, but she could never refuse the man who had kissed her so gently just moments before.

When Ty saw the sad acceptance of Janna's smile, he felt as though a knife were turning within his body. He knew that he could have her now, that she would give herself to him once more with all the sensual generosity that had been such a marvel each time he had experienced it; but this time, after the shattering ecstasy had passed, she would believe herself a whore once again.

Nothing he could say would change her mind, for he had said too much already, heedlessly, not knowing that his words were wounding her. He had never meant to strip her pride away. But he had, and he finally knew it.

Too late.

Janna felt the world tilt as Ty picked her up and carried her away from the fire. She made a startled sound and threw her arms around his neck.

"It's all right, Janna. I won't drop you."

Although Ty's voice was as gentle as his kisses had been, in the moonlight his face was a portrait composed of harsh planes and angles, and the line of his mouth was as sad as Janna's had been. At first the clammy fabric of his shirt made Janna shiver with renewed chill. Caught between two bodies, the cloth quickly warmed, and so did she.

Neither of them spoke while Ty walked down the path that led to the hot spring. As the stone ramparts closed in and the valley narrowed, the temperature rose due to the heat radiated by the hottest pool. Ty stopped well short of the first pool, choosing instead the one they called the Tub. There he knelt and lowered Janna into the water without bothering to remove the rest of her clothes. She made a long sound of pleasure as the water's heat penetrated the chill that had come from hours of riding through the storm with only the haphazard protection of the poncho to turn aside the cold rain.

"That feels wonderful," Janna murmured.

With a sigh she sank up to her chin in the water, all but disappearing beneath the veils of steam lifting from the pool's surface. Automatically she searched out the water-smoothed ledge that she usually half floated and half lay on while she soaked in the pool's heated water. Closing her eyes, she eased down the ledge to make room for Ty to join her. When minutes passed and there was no splash or displacement of water from his entry into the pool, she opened her eyes.

She was alone.

"Ty?" she called softly.

No one answered.

"Ty?" This time Janna's call was louder. "There's room here for both of us. You don't have to wait to get warm."

Words that Janna couldn't distinguish came from the direction of camp. She listened intently but no other sounds came. She started to get out of the pool, only to begin shivering immediately. Experience told her if she stayed in the pool for a long enough time her body would absorb so much heat that the walk back to the campfire wouldn't chill her, even in the middle of winter.

Janna took off her remaining clothes, slid back into the pool and let the hot water claim her body once more. Eyes closed, half-floating in the gently flowing water, she wondered why Ty hadn't gotten into the pool with her. Surely he had to be as cold as she was, for he hadn't even had the protection of the makeshift poncho against the rain and wind.

Gradually Janna realized that she was no longer alone. She opened her eyes and saw Ty sitting cross-legged at the edge of the pool, fully clothed, smiling as he watched her. She didn't know that her answering, half-shy smile was another knife of regret turning within him; she only knew that for an instant he looked so sad that tears burned behind her eyes.

"Ty?"

"I'm here, little one."

Janna didn't hesitate or withdraw when Ty bent over the pool. She turned her face toward him, expecting to be pulled into his arms for a kiss that was as steamy and deep as the hot spring itself.

"Close your eyes and hold your breath," he said huskily.

She blinked in surprise, then did as he asked.

"Now go under the water."

Saying nothing, Janna moved down the ledge until she slipped beneath the veils of mist and water. When she surfaced again Ty was waiting for her with a mound of soft, fragrant soap in his palm. The haunting scent of summer roses expanded through the steamy air.

"No wonder your backpack was so heavy I could hardly drag it," Janna said. "You must have cleaned Preacher out."

The white curve of Ty's smile gleamed in the moonlight. "It had been a long time since I'd been in a store with a poke of gold to spend."

Soon Ty's strong fingers were working the soap through Janna's hair until soft mounds of lather gathered and dropped to the water, only to float away downstream like tiny ghost ships in the moonlight. Janna closed her eyes and luxuriated in the unprecedented pleasure of having someone wash her hair.

"Ready to hold your breath again?"

She nodded even as she sank beneath the gently steaming water once more. When she emerged he was waiting with more fragrant soap. He lathered her hair again, working slowly, enjoying the feel and scent of the soap, savoring the pleased curve he had brought to her lips, a smile that was untinged by sadness. It was many minutes before his fingers reluctantly released her soft, rose-scented hair.

"Hold your breath."

Smiling, Janna held her breath and slipped into the pool's seamless embrace. When she came up again her hair was free of soap, yet the fragrance of roses lingered. Ty inhaled deeply, letting the scent caress his senses. He dipped into the pot of soft soap once more before he began washing the rest of Janna as gently as though she were a child. The hard rise of her nipples beneath his palms told Ty that she was a woman, not a child, but he forced himself to continue bathing her without lingering over the breasts that were silently begging for his caresses.

Ty's hands didn't hesitate in their slippery travel from her ribs to her hips. He tried to bathe her sleek legs with the same, almost impersonal touch he had used on her shoulders. He succeeded until he came to the triangle of hair that was glittering midnight now but had been brushed by fire in the hushed twilight when he had first undressed her.

As Ty's long fingers began washing the warm mound at the apex of Janna's thighs, she trembled and made a broken sound.

"Hush, little one," he murmured, ignoring the doubled beating of his own heart. "At least you won't have to hold your breath to rinse off. I'll be able to do it for you."

Janna's answering smile lasted only an instant before the intimacy of Ty's touch called another small cry from her lips. He made the same kind of meaningless, reassuring, almost purring sound he had so often used on Lucifer.

"It's all right," he said softly. "I'm not going to take you again. I'm just bathing you. Do you mind that so very much?"

"It's...no one has ever..."

Janna's words fragmented into an involuntary sound of pleasure as Ty's fingers moved between her legs, washing and setting fire to her in the same sliding motions.

Despite his fierce desire, Ty's smile was gentle. "I'm glad. I've never bathed a woman before." He started to add that he had never wanted to, but Janna cried out and he remembered the past night, her innocence ripped away, and his repeated, urgent penetrations of her untouched body. "Are you sore, darling? Am I hurting you now?"

Janna tried to speak, couldn't and shook her head instead, sending wavelets lapping against the sandy rim of the pool.

"Are you sure?"

She nodded, making more tiny waves.

"Cat got your tongue?"

The lazy, sensual humor in Ty's voice made Janna smile just before she stuck out her tongue. As she had hoped, he pulled her halfway from the pool even as he bent to kiss her; and the kiss was what she had longed for, a sharing as hot and deep as the pool itself.

"I'm getting you wet," Janna said when Ty finally released her, letting her slide back into the heated water.

"The rain already took care of that. Open your legs, satin butterfly. I don't want to leave any soap on that soft, soft skin."

The swirling motions of the water as Ty rinsed Janna made heat shimmer up through her body. She smelled the haunting fragrance of roses again when Ty scooped a bit more soap onto his palm.

"Wash your hair once for cleanliness, twice for beauty. Isn't that what mothers tell their daughters?" Ty asked.

"Is that what mothers tell daughters?"

"Yes."

"Yes," Janna whispered, shivering in anticipation.

Again Ty's hand slid and pleasured, skimming over Janna, sensitizing her until her breath was a husky sigh. When he pressed apart her thighs, she gave herself willingly, shivering with each hot swirl of water rinsing her, crying out helplessly when his finger began to ease into her warmth. Instantly he stopped.

"Was that a cry of pain?" Ty asked huskily.

"No."

The word became a moan as he stole tenderly into Janna. The satin flutter of her response tore a barely throttled groan from him. He didn't know how he had borne being without her all the long hours of the day—or how he would be able to bear not having her again day and night without end.

"Satin butterfly," Ty whispered, withdrawing from Janna, his hand trembling.

He lifted her from the water and laid her in the center of the blanket he had brought back to the pool. Steam rose from her body even as it did from the water itself, veiling her in silver mist. He folded over the sides of the blanket until she was covered snugly. With long, leisurely sweeps of his hands over the blanket, he dried her. When she would have helped, he captured her hands, kissed them and tucked them along her sides beneath the blanket once more.

"Let me," he said huskily, peeling back the edges of the blanket until her nipples were just barely uncovered.

"Yes," Janna whispered, feeling herself tighten as she remembered the pleasure of Ty's mouth loving her.

But it was his hands that came to her breasts, caressed them, plucked at their rosy tips until her back arched in response to the currents of pleasure pouring through her. She closed her eyes and gave herself to the shimmering sensations her lover's hands called from her body. Her teeth sank into her lower lip, biting back the cries that came when his mouth caught one nipple and suckled until a bubble of pleasure burst within her. When his hands skimmed down her body and pressed between her legs, she shifted, allowing him the freedom of her body.

Janna's reward was a love bite that made pleasure expand through her until she could hold no more and sultry heat overflowed, merging her scent with that of roses. Ty groaned beneath the redoubled violence of his own arousal. He would have given his soul to take her while she melted around him, but he knew it wasn't his soul that would be forfeited. It would be hers.

Janna trembled as Ty kissed and licked and nuzzled the length of her torso, smoothing her legs apart as he had in the pool. This time there were no hot swirls of water to caress her, only the heat and textures of her lover teasing the humid softness that his fingertips had first discovered.

The first gliding touch of Ty's tongue brought a startled cry from Janna. It was answered by a reassuring murmur and a kiss both tender and hotly intimate. She tried to say his name, but all that came out was a whimper of shock and pleasure. She started to sit up, only to be impaled by a shaft of ecstasy when her lover captured and teased the violently sensitive nub that had been hidden between soft folds of skin. A sound came from deep in her throat, protest and extraordinary pleasure combined.

Ty's hands flexed, holding Janna captive and sensuously kneading her thighs at the same time.

"Don't pull away," he said in a low voice. "I won't hurt you. I just want to…love you." Slowly he turned his head from side to side, caressing Janna with his breath, his stubble-roughened cheeks, his mouth. "You're so sweet, so soft, so warm. I'll be gentle with you. Let me…"

Janna didn't answer, for the hunger and passionate intimacy of Ty's caresses had taken from her the ability to think, to form words, to speak. Her breathing disintegrated into ragged gasps as she felt her body begin a slow, sensual unraveling that had no end, no beginning, just a timeless, ravishing moment in which pleasure burst and grew and burst again, incandescent sensations rippling through her body until she moaned and moved helplessly, totally captive to the man and the ultimate instant of pleasure.

And still the moment and the unraveling and the sweet ravishment continued. Ty's name burst from Janna's lips in a cry of protest and pleasure, for she hadn't known that ecstasy was the mythic phoenix, rising newborn from the steamy ashes of sensual completion. She rose with the phoenix, spiraling higher and higher until she screamed at the violent currents of pleasure searing through her, burning through flesh and her mind, leaving her soul as naked as her body.

And then he touched her so perfectly, so gently, so hotly that she wept his name and died.

For a long time Ty held Janna's trembling body against his own, ignoring the violent demands of his own hunger, stroking her slowly until she could take a breath that didn't fragment with the aftershocks of ecstasy. When she stirred and sighed and began sliding from ecstasy into sleep, he tilted her face up and brushed her lips with his own.

"You're not a whore, Janna Wayland."

Chapter Thirty-Three

Lucifer cantered across the valley toward Ty and Janna. His ears were pricked alertly, his tail was held up like a black banner and his stride was both muscular and effortless. It was only in the chill of morning that he walked stiffly, revealing the injury that was almost, but not quite, healed.

"Hard to believe he's the same horse that stumbled into this valley three weeks ago," Janna said.

"More like a month," Ty corrected.

She said nothing, although she knew that it had been precisely twenty-four days since Ty had carried her to the steamy pool and then had brought such intense, exquisite pleasure to her. Twenty-four days, each one longer than the one before, because he hadn't touched her since then. Not once. Not even in the most casual way. It was as though she stood behind an invisible wall too thick and too high for him to reach across.

Lucifer came to a stop a few feet away from Janna and Ty, tossed his elegant black head and watched both of them. Then he nickered a soft welcome and stretched his neck toward Ty's hands. Janna smiled to see the big stallion's trust. Although he often looked to her to be petted, it was to Ty the stallion came first. An unusual, deep bond had been forged between man and horse on the painful trip from the plateau to the keyhole valley. The bond had been reinforced in the weeks that followed, weeks when Janna had deliberately stayed away from Lucifer much of the time, wanting it to be Ty whose touch and voice and medicines both healed and tamed the stallion.

With a hunger Janna couldn't conceal, she watched Ty's long-fingered hands smooth over Lucifer's black coat. She didn't realize how much her stare revealed until she sensed Ty's attention and looked up to find him watching her in the same way that she had watched him. Hastily she looked away, not knowing what else to do, unable to slow the sudden hammering of her heart.

Each time she had begun to think Ty didn't want her anymore, she would turn around suddenly and see him watching her with hunger blazing in his green eyes. Yet he never moved toward her, always away. He would not touch her.

You're not a whore, Janna Wayland.

The words Ty had spoken that first night in the valley echoed in Janna's soul every hour of every day. She believed Ty, but it was the way he had made love to her that had instilled that belief; without his healing touch, the words would have been but a thin balm over a deep wound.

When a week had gone by and Ty had made no move to touch Janna in any way, she had tried to tell him that she understood why he couldn't love her, that she had accepted not being his dream, that it was all right if he touched her, that she wanted to be his lover; but he had turned away and walked out into the meadow, leaving her alone, ignoring the words she called after him in her futile attempt to make him understand that she wanted him without vows or pledges or guarantees of anything beyond a sharing of selves within the hushed stone boundaries of the secret valley.

He still would not touch her.

Janna would have tried to seduce Ty, but she didn't know how. She had no silks to wear, no grand home in which to throw parties, no room to enter gracefully knowing that he waited within to see her. She knew nothing about such civilized rituals of seduction. She only knew that she awoke in the middle of the night with her hands clenched into fists and her body on fire and her heart beating so harshly that her head felt as though it would split with the pain and force of her rushing blood.

But that wasn't the worst.

The worst was the emptiness growing inside Janna, the feeling of having lost something unspeakably rare and beautiful. It was the certainty that where she had once gone through life alone and content, now she would go through life alone and lonely. She was doomed to remember a time when she had touched love and had had it slide like sunlight through her outstretched fingers, leaving bleak night behind to pool in her palms until it overflowed and kept on overflowing, consuming the remaining light, consuming her.

A velvety muzzle nudged Janna gently, then more insistently. She started and realized that she had been staring at Ty once more, her breath held in anticipation of…something. Yet there was nothing to anticipate now but one more day, one day worse than yesterday, more light sliding through her outstretched fingers, more darkness pooling in her empty soul.

With a stifled cry Janna looked away from Ty again. She tried to make herself breathe deeply. It was impossible. Her body was so taut that she vibrated like a bow being drawn by too powerful an archer, the wood bent so harshly that breakage was only a breath away…so she refused to breathe.

I can't be with Ty like this. I can't bear it. It's worse than being alone. It's like watching Papa die all over again, all the life, all the possibilities, all the laughter, all the love, everything sliding away beyond my reach.

Something thumped soundly against Janna's chest. She made a startled noise and looked down. The thump had come from Zebra's muzzle. The mare was getting impatient for her mistress's attention.

"H-hello, girl," Janna said, stammering slightly, unable to prevent the telltale trembling.

The catch in Janna's voice made Ty feel as though a knife had flicked over an open wound. Like her body, her voice said that she wanted him until she shook with it. He wanted her in the same way, wanted her until he felt as if his guts were being drawn through the eye of a red-hot needle.

And he wouldn't take her.

"Easy, son," Ty said, making his voice as gentle as he could under the circumstances.

Lucifer eyed Ty warily, telling the man that his attempt to be reassuring hadn't been very convincing.

"Let's take a look at that wound," Ty murmured, smoothing his hands over the stallion's warm hide. "Easy, son, easy. I'm not going to hurt you."

The echo of Ty's reassurances to Janna by the pool pierced the silence between the two of them with uneasiness. He refused to look at her, knowing that if he did he would see in her eyes the sweet, consuming wildfire of her passion. He had never touched a woman as he had Janna that night; even the memory of it brought an almost shocked disbelief...and a searing hunger to know her that way again, to bathe in her like a warm pool, washing away the impurities of the years in which he hadn't known that he could touch his own soul by soaring deep within Janna's sensual generosity.

"You'll have a scar," Ty said tightly, looking at Lucifer's haunch, "but that's little enough for a bullet wound to leave as a calling card."

Silently Ty wondered what wound would be left on his own life by the much softer, much more agonizing brush of a satin butterfly's wings.

"Soon Lucifer will be strong enough to go to Wyoming," Janna said, speaking her worst fear aloud.

"Yes." Ty's tone was curt. "You won't be able to take much except clothes, but your books should be safe enough here. When things settle down in the territory, you can..." His voice died. "I'll see that you get your books. I'll see that you get everything you need for the kind of life you deserve."

Janna turned away from Ty, hiding her face, not letting him see in her expression the decision she had made not to go to Wyoming. She really had no choice but to stay. Instinctively she knew it would be easier to live alone in the valley than anywhere on earth with Ty always within reach, never touching her.

"Janna?" he asked roughly.

After a few seconds she said calmly, "I'll do what has to be done."

It sounded like agreement, yet...

Ty stared at the back of Janna's head and wished that he could read her mind as easily as she seemed to read the animals and the clouds. And himself.

"The sooner we start, the better," he said.

Janna said nothing.

"We should get out of here before the Army decides to move against Cascabel."

She nodded as though they were discussing nothing more important than the shape of distant clouds.

"We'll have to take it slow until I can find a horse to ride. Even if Lucifer would accept me as a rider—which I doubt—he should have another week or so without any strain." Ty waited. Janna said nothing. "Janna?"

Auburn hair flashed in the sun as she turned to face him. Her eyes were as clear as rain—and haunted by elusive shadows.

"Yes, it would be better for Lucifer not to have to take the strain of a rider for a few more days."

"That's not what I meant and you know it."

Janna hesitated, then shrugged. "The first days will be slow and dangerous. Walking is always slower than riding."

"You're coming with me," Ty said bluntly.

"Of course. Lucifer would never leave the valley without Zebra," Janna said, turning away again, stroking the mare's dust-colored hide with loving hands.

"And Zebra won't leave the valley without you," Ty said.

"She never has before."

Ty's scalp prickled. Every instinct he had told him that Janna was sliding away from him, eluding his attempts to hold her nearby. She was vanishing as he watched.

"Say it," he demanded.

"Say what?"

"Say that you're coming to Wyoming with me."

Janna closed her eyes. Hidden beneath Zebra's mane, her hands clenched into fists. "I'm leaving the valley with you."

"And you're coming to Wyoming with me."

"Don't."

"Don't what?"

"Force me to lie to you."

"What does that mean? You can't stay here forever and you know it!"

"I can't stay on your brother's ranch in Wyoming, either."

"You won't have to stay there forever."

"Just long enough to set a marriage snare for some man who's too stupid to know the difference between true silk and an ordinary sow's ear?" Janna offered bitterly.

"Dammit, that's not what I said!"

"You don't have to say it. I did." She swung onto Zebra's back with a quick motion that was eloquent of wild emotions barely restrained. "I promised to help you get your stallion. You promised to teach me how to please a man. Those promises were made and kept on Black Plateau. Wyoming was no part of it."

Abruptly Zebra exploded into a gallop.

In seething silence Ty watched while the mare swept toward the far end of the valley where Indian ruins slowly eroded back into the stony land from which they had come. Janna had spent a lot of time in the ancient place since they had brought the stallion into the valley. Ty had thought Janna's sudden interest in the ruins was an attempt to remove Zebra's distracting presence while he spent hours with Lucifer, accustoming the wild stallion to a man's voice and touch.

But now Ty suspected that Janna had been trying to wean Lucifer of Zebra's company so that the stallion wouldn't balk at being separated when the time came for Ty to head for Wyoming—without Janna.

"It won't work!" Ty called savagely. "You're coming to Wyoming with me if I have to tie you over Zebra's back like a sack of grain!"

Nothing answered Ty but the drumroll of thunder from the mare's speedy, fleeing hooves.

Ty's words echoed mockingly in his own ears. He knew that all Janna had to do was ride off while he slept or worked with Lucifer. On foot he couldn't catch her. Even if she didn't ride Zebra, Ty wasn't much better off. Black Plateau was an open book to Janna; she could hide among its countless ravines the way a shadow could hide among the thousand shades of night.

He would find her eventually, of course. Assuming Cascabel didn't find them first.

Chapter Thirty-Four

The stallion's clarion call resonated through the valley, echoing and reechoing from stone walls, telling anything with ears that an enemy had appeared in the tiny, concealed Eden.

Ty dropped his dinner plate, grabbed his carbine and sprinted for the willows. Within seconds he was under cover, but he didn't slow his speed. Running, twisting around slender limbs, leaping roots and rocks, heedless of noise, Ty raced toward the entrance of the valley.

When he arrived at the edge of the willows' dense cover, he stopped and watched the meadow for signs of man. Nothing moved near the cleft, which was the valley's only access to the outer world. Carbine at his shoulder, Ty stared down the metal barrel at the expanse of grass. Nothing moved in the emptiness but the wind.

Lucifer's wild, savage call to arms came again, making the skin of Ty's scalp ripple in primal response. The stallion was far up the valley, out of sight in the narrow bend where the Indian ruins were hidden. Neither Zebra nor Janna was in sight.

Desperately Ty wanted to call out to Janna and reassure himself that she was safe. He kept silent. He didn't want her to give away her position to a skulking renegade.

Ty had no doubt that the stallion's savage cry had been triggered by the presence of a strange human being. In the weeks since he had come to the valley, Ty had never seen signs of anything larger than a rabbit within the valley itself. Of all the animals in the vast land, only man had the curiosity—or the need—to follow the narrow, winding slot through stone-lined darkness into the canyon's sunlight.

Stay down in the ruins, Janna, Ty prayed silently. *You'll be safe there. The Indians avoid the spirit places.*

The birds that usually wheeled and darted over the meadow were silent and hidden. Ty's narrowed glance raked the valley again, looking for any sign of the intruder.

Suddenly Lucifer burst out from the area of the ruins into the larger meadow. Zebra was running at his side. When the stallion dug in and stopped, the mare kept galloping, stopping only when she was several hundred feet beyond. Lucifer reared and screamed again, hooves slashing the air, putting himself between the mare and whatever danger threatened.

As the stallion's feral challenge faded, the cry of a hawk soared above the silence, followed by Janna's voice calling what could have been Ty's name. He turned toward the sound. Over the metal barrel of the carbine, he saw Janna coming from the area of the ruins. A man was walking behind her. Reflexively Ty took slack from the trigger, let out his breath and waited for the trail to turn, giving him a view of the stranger.

It was Mad Jack.

Gently Ty's finger eased from the trigger as he lowered the carbine from his shoulder. When he emerged from the cover of the willows and trotted out into the open and across the meadow, Lucifer neighed shrilly, as though to warn him of danger. Ty turned aside long enough to reassure the stallion.

"Thanks for the warning, but it's just a crazy old prospector," Ty said, talking soothingly to the stallion.

Lucifer snorted and stamped nervously but permitted Ty to stroke his neck. Even then the stallion never stopped watching the two figures that were coming out of the ruins. When the people began walking toward him, Lucifer spun and ran away, sweeping Zebra before him. Ty turned and waited for Janna and Mad Jack.

"Right fine lookout you have there," Mad Jack said, holding out his hand for Ty to shake.

Smiling, Ty took the old man's hand. He was surprised at how fine Mad Jack's bones were beneath his scarred, leathery skin. The prospector's grip was a quick, light pressure, as though any more would be painful.

"Run out of stomach medicine again?" Ty asked, although he suspected that medicine was the last thing on the other man's mind.

Mad Jack laughed. He knew what Ty was thinking—that he had come to check up on Janna, not to replenish his supply of medicine.

"You be half-right, son. I come to check on my gal."

"Well, you can see that she's bright eyed and bushy tailed," Ty said dryly.

Mad Jack's faded eyes appraised Janna with a frankness that made her flush.

"You be right," he said, fishing in his pocket for his chewing tobacco. "'Course, mares in foal look right sassy for the first few months, too."

"Don't beat around the bush," Janna said in a combination of embarrassment and exasperation. "Just say anything that's on what passes for your mind."

"I make it a habit to do just that. So are you?"

"Am I...?"

"Pregnant."

Red flags burned on Janna's cheeks. "Jack!"

"Well, are you?"

"No."

"You sure?"

"Yes," she said succinctly. "As sure as I am that water runs downhill."

Jack rubbed his face and sighed. "Well, durn it all anyway. That's gonna fuss things up considerable."

"Have you been drinking?" Janna demanded.

"No." He sliced off a big hunk of tobacco, stuffed it in his mouth and said, "I been thinkin', which is a horse of another color entirely. Both of 'em make my head hurt, I'll give you that.''

"What," Ty asked, "is going on?"

"Mad Jack has been thinking," Janna said. "That's a serious matter."

"Damn straight it is," Jack agreed. "Last time I got to thinkin', I took old Jimbo—he was my mule—out of the traces, hiked my leg across his back and headed west. Nary a word to my wife since then, nor my kids, neither. Thinkin' is right hard on a man."

"Sounds like it wasn't real easy on your wife, either," Ty said dryly.

"That's what I got to thinkin' about," Mad Jack agreed. "I been pokin' in rocks for years, tryin' to find the one glory hole what's got my name on it. Well, I don't rightly think I'm gonna find it this side of heaven and more 'n likely I'm a-headed straight for hell." Jack spit, wiped his mouth and continued. "Now, ol' Charity—that's my wife—probably died of some woman's complaint or another by now, but my kids was right healthy grasshoppers. Some of 'em are bound to be alive, or their kids. An' that's why I'm unhappy that you ain't pregnant," he added, pointing at Janna.

Ty looked sideways at Janna. She was watching Mad Jack as though he had just sprouted horns or wings or both.

"I don't understand," she said flatly.

"Hell, gal, it's as plain as the color of the sky. I got gold to give to my kids, an' I ain't gonna leave this here country and you can't get out the gold alone, an' if you ain't pregnant, you ain't got no stud hoss to protect you, an' my gold won't get delivered an' my kids won't know their pappy ever thought about 'em."

Janna opened her mouth. Nothing came out. She swallowed and tried again, but it was too late. Ty was already speaking.

"Let me be sure I understand," Ty said smoothly, seizing the opportunity with both hands. "You have gold you want taken to your children. You thought if Janna were pregnant, we'd be leaving the valley and we could deliver the gold to the fort for you."

Mad Jack frowned. "I had in mind something more… friendly like than the fort. See, I ain't sure where my kin are no more. Now, if'n I go hire some man at the fort I don't know from Adam's off ox, how can I be sure my gold gets to my kin once I turn my back?"

Ty tried to say something. It was impossible. Mad Jack had been thinking, and the result of that unusual exercise had made the future clear to him.

"I can't be sure," Mad Jack said forcefully, answering his own question. "But if'n I give the gold to a friend, I can rest easy. You get my drift, son? Now, you ain't my friend. No offense, just the God's truth. Janna here, she's my friend. If'n she told me she'd get the gold to my kids, I know she would or die trying.

"And that's the crux of the matter. She's game but she ain't real big. Ain't mean, neither. Carryin' gold needs someone who's mountain big and snake mean."

"Like me?" Ty suggested.

"Yep."

"But I'm not your friend. No offense."

"None taken, son. It's the God's truth. But if'n you was Janna's man, an' she took the gold, you'd go along to protect her. Then she'd be safe and the gold, too. But she ain't pregnant so you ain't her man an' that means my gold ain't got no man protectin' it once it leaves here."

"The fact that I'm *not* pregnant should reassure you that Ty is an honorable man," Janna pointed out quickly. "If he agreed to take your gold, you could be sure that he wouldn't keep it for himself."

Mad Jack made a sound that was a cross between a mutter and a snort. "Hell's bells, gal, if you ain't pregnant, it ain't because you was sayin' no, it's because he weren't askin'. That may say somethin' about his honor right enough, but it sure as hellfire don't reassure me none about his manly, er, notions."

A wave of scarlet humiliation went up Janna's face as she realized that Mad Jack knew how much she had wanted Ty to notice her as a woman. When the blood ebbed Janna was very pale. All that kept her from turning and walking away was the need she sensed in Mad Jack, a need that was driving the old man far beyond the boundaries of even his customary bluntness. She looked at the prospector's face and saw the yellowish pallor underlying the weathered skin. Although he had always been wiry, now he seemed almost frail. He looked...desperate.

Thinking could be hard on a man, especially when he was old and ill and had only one chance to right past wrongs.

Janna gathered her courage, ignored her own raw feelings and touched Mad Jack's arm reassuringly. "There's nothing wrong with Ty's sense of honor or his 'notions' or anything else," she said with a fierce kind of calm. "He took what I was offering and decided it wasn't for him, that's all."

"Janna—" Ty began.

"What?" she demanded, interrupting without looking away from the old man. "I didn't say it as fancy or as long-winded as Ty did, but that doesn't change what happened, does it? I wanted him. He took me. He doesn't want me anymore. It's an old story. From the books I've read, I'd say it's the oldest story on earth. But that doesn't mean one single thing against Ty's honor, Jack. He didn't lie to me, not even the way you said a woman-hungry man would. No pretty words, no fancy promises, nothing but Ty and me and the night."

Mad Jack was quiet for a long moment before he sighed and patted Janna's hand. "I'm sorry, gal."

"Don't be. I'm not. When I go back and read that trunk full of books again this winter, I'll understand them better. That's nothing to be sorry over. It will make spring come faster for me. Then Zebra will have a foal for me to fuss over and by the end of summer I'll be riding Zebra again and we'll fly over the plateau like a hawk's shadow and then autumn lighting will come again and thunder and the mustangs' breath will be like earthbound clouds and snow will turn the night silver and I'll make up stories about the shadows my campfire throws against the stone cliff, people and places and memories coming to life..." Janna's voice faded into a whisper. "Don't be sorry."

Ty tried to speak and found he had no voice. Janna's words were in his own throat, crowding out speech, filling him until he ached. He clenched his teeth against a sadness as piercing as it was unexpected.

"You can't stay," Ty said hoarsely.

It was as though he hadn't spoken. Janna didn't look away from the old prospector, who was watching her and shaking his head slowly.

"He's speakin' God's truth," Mad Jack said. "You can't stay here, gal. Not no more. I been thinkin' about that, too. Spent a lot of time on it. A lot of my gold belongs to you."

"Don't be ridic—" began Janna.

"No, young'un," Mad Jack said, cutting across her objections. "You jest button up and listen to an old man what's seen more of this here world's good an' bad than you have. Your pappy gave me money more times than either of us counted."

"And you've given us gold as long as I can remember," Janna said quickly.

Mad Jack grunted. "What about the time you found me all broke up at the bottom of a gulch and you set my bones and patched me up and you were no more than a kid in men's britches? You saved my life, you keep my stomach from eatin' a hole in itself, and you listen to my stories no matter how often I tell 'em. Half my gold is yours and that's flat. Should of give it to you years ago so you could get out and get a life for yourself, but I liked knowin' there was one soul in this godforsaken land that wouldn't kill me for my gold."

"Thank you, but I enjoyed your company as much as you enjoyed mine," Janna said. "Any gold you have is yours."

"You ain't been listening, gal. It ain't safe for you here no more." Mad Jack turned to Ty. "Beggars can't be choosers, son. I got a proposition. You be willin' to listen?"

"I'm willing."

"This here gal is game, but game ain't gonna get the job done. Injuns been comin' into the country like rain. Soldiers' scouts been comin', too. Everybody's sayin' that the Army is gonna clean out that rattlesnake's nest once an' for all. Cas-

cabel's been fastin' an' prayin' up a storm. A few days back
a vision come to him. He's gonna lead his renegades to a big
victory—but not until Janna's hair hangs from his war lance.''

Ty's whole body changed subtly, as though Cascabel himself had just appeared at the slot entrance to the valley. Mad
Jack measured the change and smiled beneath his ragged
beard; Ty might not be Janna's man, but he wasn't about to
go off and leave her to fend for herself against the likes of
Cascabel.

"Well, she was right about the honor," Mad Jack said.
"An' I'll take her word about the rest of you bein' man
enough. Here's the deal, son. You get her out of here and to
a safe place, and my gold with her, and a quarter of my gold
is yours.''

"Keep your money, old man," Ty said savagely. "I'll get
Janna out of here and to a safe place. You've got my word
on it.''

Mad Jack chewed for a few moments, turned aside and spat
a brown stream into the grass. Turning back, he wiped his
beard on his frayed shirtsleeves.

"Suit yerself. Just so's you get her shuck of this place, and
my gold with her. She'll need her quarter so's she won't have
to marry no mean lard-butt town widower nor sell her company to strangers just to put beans on the table.''

"I'm not going to leave just because you—" Janna began
hotly.

"Shut yer mouth, gal," Mad Jack said, giving her a fierce
glare. "You ain't dumb so don't get to actin' like it. Only
reason Cascabel ain't caught you is he ain't took a hard notion
before now. Well, he done been took somethin' fierce. Long
as that evil son of a rattlesnake is alive, this country ain't safe
for chick nor child.''

Janna closed her eyes and fought against the ice condensing
in her stomach. "Are you sure that Cascabel is after my hair?"

"Dead sure. Sound carries right good in some of these canyons. He bragged on his intentions to Ned.''

"The saloon keeper?" Ty asked. "What was he doing with
Cascabel?''

"Sellin' rifles, same as always. But don't worry, son. He won't be doin' it no more. He upped the ante once too often. Cascabel took Ned's rifles, then he took his liver, lights and hair."

Janna shuddered.

Mad Jack turned aside, spat and straightened, pinning Ty with a shrewd glance. "You break that stud hoss yet?"

"No."

"Better get to it, son. Man on foot carryin' gold ain't gonna do nothin' out there but die."

Chapter Thirty-Five

"**M**y God." Ty knelt in the dirt and gritty dust of the ruins and looked up at Janna for a long moment. With hands that were none too steady, he refastened the old saddlebags. "It's gold. All of it. Sweet Jesus. When Mad Jack talked about gold, I thought he meant a few pokes, not two big saddlebags jammed full to overflowing." Ty looked at his hands as though hardly able to believe the wealth that they had held. "Pure. Gold."

Ty lifted the bags and stood with a grunt of effort. Janna watched him with wide gray eyes. His words had meant little to her. Even the sight of the gold hadn't made it seem real to her; but watching the saddlebags make Ty's muscular arms bunch and quiver made the gold's weight all too real. She had tested that male strength, seen Ty's power and stamina and determination; and she knew that it wouldn't be enough.

Man on foot carryin' gold ain't gonna do nothin' out there but die.

"You can't take it all," Janna said.

"Doesn't weigh much more than you," Ty said, "but dead weight is the hardest kind to carry." He shook his head in continuing disbelief. "When I get back to camp and get my hands on that crazy old man, I'm going to ask him how the hell he got these saddlebags into the valley."

"Maybe he's been bringing the gold in a poke at a time."

Ty grunted. "If so, he didn't leave any more tracks between

here and the slot than the wind. Anyhow, it doesn't matter. I'm not taking a quarter of his gold and he's not staying behind to get spitted and roasted by Cascabel. Like it or not, that old man's coming out with us.''

Janna didn't argue or point out the difficulties in taking a third person when there was only one horse to ride. She felt as Ty did about leaving Mad Jack behind.

Finally Janna had realized that staying in the valley was the equivalent of a death sentence. Mad Jack was correct: the only reason she had been safe during the past years was that she had been more trouble to track down than she was worth to Cascabel. That was no longer true. Cascabel now believed that she was all that was standing between himself and the conquest of the Utah Territory.

Unhappily Janna followed Ty as he picked his way out of the crumbling ruins that filled the small side canyon. Once out in the meadow again, the walking was easier. Lucifer and Zebra waited out in the middle of the grass. The stallion was restive. He kept watching the willows that fringed the valley as though he expected a predator to leap out. Zebra was calmly grazing, not nearly as upset by Mad Jack's presence as Lucifer was.

''We could rig a surcingle for Zebra,'' Janna said, spotting the mare. ''That way she could carry the saddlebags and your pack while we walked.''

Ty gave her a sideways look that was little more than a flash of green.

''Zebra can't carry both of us and the gold, too,'' Janna pointed out.

''She can carry you and the gold if it comes to that. All you have to do is get her used to a hackamore and a surcingle.''

''But what about you?''

''That's my problem.''

White teeth sank into Janna's lower lip as she bit off her retort. She closed her eyes and silently asked for Lucifer's forgiveness. But there was really no choice. If he could be broken to ride, it had to be done.

"Be as gentle with Lucifer as you can," she said in a low voice, "but don't hurt yourself in the process, Ty. Promise me that you'll be careful. He's so strong and so quick." She looked at the stallion standing poised in the meadow, his big body rippling with strength, his ears erect, his head up, sniffing the wind. "And he's so wild. Much wilder than Zebra."

"Not with you. He comes up and puts his head in your hands like a big hound."

"Then why won't you let me be the one to break him?" Janna's voice was tightened by fear and exasperation. She and Ty had argued about just this thing since the moment Mad Jack had pointed out that a man on foot didn't have much chance of surviving.

"God save me from stubborn women," muttered Ty. "I've spent the last half hour telling you why. That stud's big enough to buck you into next week and you know it. I sure as hell know it! You're quick and determined as they come, but that's no substitute for sheer strength if Lucifer goes crazy the first time he feels a rider's weight."

Impatiently Ty shifted the slippery leather connecting the saddlebags. When the bags were in a more secure position over his shoulder he continued his argument. "Besides, you'll have your hands full talking Zebra into a hackamore and surcingle. She's not going to like that belly strap worth a damn. I'm going to rig stirrups for you, too. She won't like those, either, but it's the only way you and that old man stand a chance of staying on if we have to run for it. One of you has to be stuck on tight enough so the other has something to hang on to."

Janna opened her mouth to object but didn't. She had lost this argument, too, and she knew it. She hadn't wanted to put restraints on Zebra, yet there was little rational choice. If their lives were going to depend on their mounts, the riders had to have more than intangible communication with their horses. Particularly if she and Mad Jack were going to be riding double.

"Once we get to Wyoming, you can go back to riding Zebra any way you want," Ty said. "Hell, you can let her run wild again for all of me. But not until then, Janna. Not until you're safe.''

Closing her eyes, she nodded in defeat. "I know."

Ty gave Janna a surprised look. He had expected a fierce battle over the necessity of introducing any real control over Zebra. Janna's unhappy expression told him just how much the concession cost her. Without thinking about his vow not to touch her again, he took Janna's hand and squeezed it gently.

"It's all right, sugar. Even with a hackamore and surcingle, you aren't forcing Zebra to obey you. You aren't strong enough to force an animal her size. Anytime Zebra lets you up on her back, it's because she wants you there. All the hackamore will do is make sure Zebra knows where you want her to go. After that, it's up to her. It's always that way, no matter what kind of tack the horse wears. Cooperation, not coercion."

The feel of Ty's palm sliding over her own as they walked was like being brushed by gentle lightning. Janna's whole body tingled with the simple pleasure of his touch.

"Thank you," she said, blinking back sudden tears.

"For what?"

"For making me feel better about putting a hackamore on Zebra. And—" Janna squeezed his hand in return "—for understanding. It's frightening having to give up the only home I've ever known."

Knowing he shouldn't, unable to prevent himself, Ty lifted Janna's hand to his face. The long weeks during which he hadn't shaved had softened his beard to the texture of coarse silk. He rubbed his cheek against her palm, inhaled her scent and called himself twelve kinds of fool for not touching her in the past four weeks—and fifty kinds of fool for touching her now.

She wasn't a whore or a convenience. She was a woman who appealed to him more with every moment he spent in her company. Her sensuality was like quicksand, luring him deeper and deeper until he was trapped beyond hope of escape. But she didn't mean to be a trap any more than he meant to

be trapped. He was sure of it. That was what made her feminine allure all the more irresistible.

With aching tenderness Ty kissed Janna's palm before he
forced himself to let go of her hand. The loss of her touch
was a physical pain. The realization appalled him.

*God in heaven. I'm as stupid as that damned unicorn being
drawn to his captivity and not able to pull away to save his
life, much less his freedom.*

Abruptly Ty shifted the heavy gold to his other shoulder,
using the saddlebags as a barrier between himself and Janna.
She barely noticed. She was still caught in the instant when
his hand had been sharply withdrawn. It had been like having
her sense of balance betray her on a steep trail, leaving her
floundering. She looked at Ty questioningly, only to see a
forbidding expression that promised unhappiness for anyone
asking questions of a personal nature, especially questions
such as *Why haven't you touched me? Why did you touch me
just now? Why did you stop as though you could no longer
bear my touch?*

"Will you take the gold on Lucifer?" Janna asked after a
silence. She forced her voice to be almost normal, although
her palm still felt his caresses as though Ty's beard had been
black flames burning through her flesh to the bone beneath.

"He's strong enough to take the gold and me both and still
run rings around any other horse."

"Then you'll have to use a surcingle on him, too, either for
stirrups or to hold the saddlebags in place or both."

"The thought had occurred to me," Ty said dryly. "First
time he feels that strap bite into his barrel should be real interesting."

Ty shifted the gold on his shoulder again and said no more.
In silence they continued toward the camp beneath the red
stone overhang. Janna felt no need to speak, for the simple
reason that there was little more to say. Either Lucifer would
accept a rider or he wouldn't. If he didn't, the odds for survival
against Cascabel were too small to be called even a long shot.

"We have to talk Mad Jack into leaving the gold behind,"
Janna said finally.

Ty had been thinking the same thing. He also had been thinking about how he would feel in Mad Jack's shoes—old, ill, eaten up with guilt for past mistakes, seeing one chance to make it all right and die with a clean conscience.

"It's his shot at heaven," Ty said.

"It's our ticket straight to hell."

"Try convincing him."

"I'm going to do just that."

Janna's chin came up and she quickened her pace, leaving Ty behind. But when she strode into camp, all that was there of Mad Jack was a piece of paper held down by a stone. On the paper he had painfully written the closest town to the farm he had abandoned so many years ago. Beneath that were the names of his five children.

"Jack!" Janna called. "Wait! Come back!"

No voice answered her. She turned and sprinted toward the meadow.

"What's wrong?" Ty demanded.

"He's gone!"

"That crafty old son of a bitch." Ty swore and dropped the heavy saddlebags with a thump. "He knew what would happen when we found out how much gold there was to haul out of here. He took our promise to get his gold to his children and then he ran like the hounds of hell were after him."

Janna raised her hands to her mouth. A hawk's wild cry keened across the meadow. Zebra's head came up and she began trotting toward them.

"What are you going to do?" Ty asked.

"Find him. He's too old to have gotten far in this short a time."

Ty all but threw Janna up on top of Zebra. Instants later the mare was galloping on a long diagonal that would end at the narrow entrance to the valley.

By the time they arrived at the slot, Zebra was beginning to sweat both from the pace and from the urgency she sensed in her rider. Janna flung herself off the mare and ran to the twilight shadow of the slot canyon.

Heedless of the uncertain footing, she plunged forward. She

didn't call Mad Jack's name, however; she didn't want the call to echo where it might be overheard by passing renegades.

No more than fifty feet into the slot, Janna sensed that something was wrong. She froze in place, wondering what her instincts were trying to tell her.

There was no unexpected sound. No unexpected scent. No moving shadows. No sign that she wasn't alone.

"That's what's wrong," Janna whispered. "There's no sign at all!"

She went onto her hands and knees, but no matter how hard she examined the ground, the only traces of any passage over the dry stream course were those she herself had just left.

Zebra's head flew up in surprise when Janna hurtled back into the valley from the slot.

"Easy, girl. Easy," Janna said breathlessly.

She swung onto the mare. Within moments a rhythmic thunder was again rolling from beneath Zebra's hooves. When she galloped past Lucifer, he lifted his head for an instant, then resumed biting off succulent mouthfuls of grass, undisturbed by the pair racing by. In past summers, Zebra and Janna often had galloped around while he grazed.

"Well?" Ty demanded when the mare galloped into the campsite.

"He's still in the valley. You take the left side and I'll take the right."

Ty looked out over the meadow. "Waste of time. He's not here."

"That's impossible. There's not one mark in that little slot canyon that I didn't put there myself. He's still here."

"Then he's between us and Lucifer."

Janna looked to the place where the stallion grazed no more than a hundred feet away. There wasn't enough cover to hide a rabbit, much less a man.

"Why do you say that?" she asked.

"Wind is from that direction. Lucifer stopped testing the wind and settled down to graze about ten minutes ago."

Janna's urgency drained from her, leaving her deflated. If

the stallion didn't scent Mad Jack it was because Mad Jack wasn't around to be scented.

Grimly Janna looked at the heavy saddlebags, an old man's legacy to a life he had abandoned years before. It was too heavy a burden—but it was theirs to bear. Her only consolation was that Ty's share, plus her own, should be enough to buy his dream. She didn't know how much silken ladies cost on the open market, but surely sixty pounds of gold would be enough.

Ty's expression as he looked at the saddlebags was every bit as grim as Janna's. His consolation, however, was different. He figured that Janna's thirty pounds of gold, plus his thirty, would be more than enough to ensure that she would never have to submit her soft body to any man in order to survive.

Chapter Thirty-Six

Lucifer's ears flattened and he screamed his displeasure, lashing out with his hind feet. Ty made no attempt to hold the mustang. He just ducked and ran for cover. The stallion exploded into wicked bucking as he tried to dislodge the surcingle Ty had cut from the buffalo robe in Janna's trunk. When bucking didn't work, the stallion tried outrunning the strap and the flapping rope stirrups.

By the time Lucifer realized that he couldn't outrun the contraption clinging to his back—and that he wasn't being attacked by whatever was on him—the stallion's neck and flanks were white with lather and he was breathing hard. Janna wasn't surprised at the horse's signs of exertion; Lucifer had been racing flat out around the valley for nearly half an hour.

"Lord, but that's one strong horse," she said.

Ty grunted. He wasn't looking forward to the next part of the stallion's education, the part when he felt a man's weight on his back for the first time. Ty approached the big mustang slowly, speaking in a low voice.

"Yeah, I know, it's a hell of a world when you can't outrun all of life's traps and entanglements. But it isn't as bad as it seems to you right now," Ty murmured, stroking the stallion. "Ask Zebra. She took to the surcingle and stirrups like the good-hearted lady she is."

Lucifer snorted and butted his head against Ty as though to

draw the man's attention to the irritation caused by the un-wanted straps.

"Sorry, son. I'll rub away the itches but I'm not taking off that surcingle. I had enough trouble getting the damned thing on you in the first place."

Janna had a hard time not saying a heartfelt "amen." Watching Ty risk his life under Lucifer's hooves in the process of getting the surcingle in place had been the most difficult thing she had ever done. She had both admired Ty's gentle persistence and regretted ever asking him not to use restraints on the powerful stallion.

Ty continued petting and talking to Lucifer until the horse calmed down. Gradually Ty's strokes became different. He leaned hard on his hands as he moved them over the horse, concentrating mainly on the portion of Lucifer's back just behind the withers, where a man would ride. At first the stallion moved away from the pressure. Ty followed, talking patiently, leaning gently and then with more force, trying to accustom the mustang to his weight.

Again, Janna watched the process with a combination of anxiety and admiration. Most of the men she had known would have snubbed Lucifer's nose to a post, twisted his ear in one hand and then climbed aboard in a rush. Once the rider was in the saddle, the horse would have been released and spurs would have begun raking tender hide. The bucking that would have followed was inevitable. So was the fact that some horses broken that way weren't trustworthy. They tended to wait until the rider was relaxed and then unload him with a few wicked twists of their body.

Yet Ty had to be able to trust Lucifer with his life, and he had promised Janna to treat the stallion as gently as possible and still get the job done.

Breath came in sharply and then stuck in Janna's throat while she watched Ty shift his weight until his boots no longer touched the ground. Lucifer moved nervously, turned around in a circle rapidly several times, then accepted the fact that Ty's soothing voice was coming from a new direction. After a few minutes the stallion began grazing rather irritably, ignoring the fact that Ty was draped belly down over his back.

By the time two more hours passed, Ty had gotten Lucifer to the point of not flinching or even particularly noticing when Ty's weight shifted from the ground to the horse's back. Janna had seen Ty creep into position, moving so slowly that every muscle stood out as he balanced against gravity and the mustang's wary, mincing steps. When Ty finally eased from his stomach to a rider's normal seat, Janna wanted to shout a cheer. All that kept her quiet was an even bigger desire not to spook the mustang.

For the stallion's part, Lucifer simply twitched his ears and kept grazing when Ty sat upright. The horse's whole stance proclaimed that the bizarre actions of his human companion no longer disturbed him.

Elation spread through Ty when he felt the calm strength of the stallion beneath him. More than ever, Ty was certain that Lucifer had been gently bred, raised by humans, and then had escaped from his owners to run free before any brand of ownership had been put on his shiny black hide.

"You're a beauty," Ty murmured, praising the stallion with voice and hands. "Does part of you know that you were born and bred to be a man's friend?"

Lucifer lipped grass casually, stopping every few minutes to sniff the wind. Ty made no attempt to guide the stallion with the hackamore. He simply sat and let the mustang graze in a normal manner. When Lucifer moved in the course of grazing, he walked a bit awkwardly at first, unaccustomed to the weight settled just behind his withers. But by the time the sun was tracing the last part of its downward arc in the west, Lucifer was moving with his former confidence, adjusting automatically to the presence of a rider. Occasionally he would turn and sniff Ty's boot as though to say, "What, are you still here? Well, never mind. You're not in the way."

Ty's answer was always the same, praise and a hand stroking sleek muscles. When Lucifer responded to a firm, steady pull on the hackamore by turning in that direction, the praise and the pats were redoubled. When the pulls were accompanied by gentle nudges with Ty's heels, Lucifer learned to move forward. When the pressure on the hackamore was a steady pull backward, the stallion learned to stop.

"That's it for now, son," Ty said, sliding carefully from Lucifer's back. "You get the rest of the day off."

The stallion snorted and sidestepped at the release of the pressure from his back, but that was all. When Ty raised his hands and tied the hackamore lead rope securely around the black neck, Lucifer didn't even flinch.

"You're a shining wonder," Ty murmured.

Lucifer promptly put his head against Ty's chest and rubbed hard, trying to dislodge the hackamore. Laughing softly, Ty began soothing away the itches that came from wearing leather against hot, sweaty hide.

"Sorry, son. I'm going to leave all this gear in place. It won't hurt you and it will save me a hell of a lot of trouble come tomorrow, when the lessons resume. But right now you've earned a good graze and I've earned some time in the Tub. Get along, son. Go over and berate Zebra about the crazy humans she sicced on you."

A few minutes later Janna looked up from sorting herbs and saw that Lucifer was riderless. For a moment her heart turned over in fear. Then she realized that Ty had probably dismounted of his own accord, giving both himself and Lucifer a rest. Janna turned back to her herbs, testing the leaves' dryness. Fragrances both pungent and mild rose from the rustling herbs as she set some aside to be taken from the valley and designated others to be made into tinctures or lotions or balms. She knew that she wouldn't have time to properly prepare more than a fraction of the herbs and seeds she had collected, but that didn't stop her. Working with them gave her hands something to do besides remember how it had felt to touch Ty and her mind something to do besides think about leaving the valley behind...and then leaving Ty behind, as well.

Stop thinking about it, Janna told herself urgently. *And don't think about Mad Jack probably being sick or Cascabel probably waiting to kill me. Don't think about anything but these herbs. I can't affect Mad Jack or Ty or that cruel renegade.*

I can make lotions, though. I can make a batch of stomach medicine and leave it behind. I can do the same with the other medicines. I can do anything I want while I'm still here.

Except seduce Ty.

Herbs and seeds tangled and fell to the ground as Janna's hands jerked at the thought of seducing Ty. She bit back unhappy words and picked up the mess. The second time she thought of making love with Ty the same thing happened. Her fingers were just too shaky to deal with anything as finicky as preparing medicines.

"Well, I can at least get some of that sulfur water from the high spring," she muttered to herself. "Surely that shouldn't be too difficult for my clumsy hands."

Janna grabbed a small metal pot and set off toward the Tub. In the past weeks the trail had become rather well beaten. Both she and Ty loved to float in the warm water and watch the clouds change shape overhead. They did their floating alone, but the thought of what had happened the one time she and Ty had been together in the Tub nearly made Janna drop the small pot. She would have given a great deal to be allowed again to touch Ty so tenderly, so intimately, so wildly. Just once more.

Just once before they left the valley and never saw each other again.

When Janna entered the narrowest part of the valley, the hot springs' steamy silence brought an onslaught of memories. The lush profusion of soft-leaved plants, the sparkling condensation of water on black rock, the vague sulfur odor underlying that of earth and sun and greenery, everything combined in her mind to create a dizzying mixture of memory and desire.

And then she saw Ty rise out of the nearest pool and stand naked on the sandy shore. Silver streamers of mist lifted from his hot skin, moving as he moved, their fragile grace in sharp contrast to the bunch and ripple of his powerful muscles. Unable to move, Janna simply stared at Ty, transfixed by the pagan beauty of the man, memorizing every pattern of water curling down through the dark hair of his chest and torso and thighs.

Janna didn't have to look at Ty's face to know that he had seen her. The visible evidence of his maleness stirred into life, growing rapidly, insistently, rising from its dark nest of hair as inevitably as Ty had risen from the steaming pool.

The pot Janna carried made a sharp sound as she dropped it onto a rock. She didn't even hear the noise. She had attention for nothing but the man who stood naked before her. Without knowing it she began walking to him.

The expression on Janna's face was the most potent aphrodisiac Ty had ever known. A savage, elemental need twisted through him, black lightning tightening his body until he could barely speak; and with the lightning came an even blacker despair. He had fought so hard to keep from touching Janna, from taking her, from making her feel like a convenience with no value beyond the passionate moment. He had lain awake night after night in the willows, his body on fire, his mind determined not to allow himself the surcease he knew waited within her generous, sensuous body. But he had also known that whatever private hell of deprivation he suffered would be worth it if he never again had to listen to Janna describe herself as a whore.

Yet there she was, inches from him, and her gray eyes blazed with reflections of the need that burned within him.

"Janna," Ty said hoarsely. "No."

Chapter Thirty-Seven

Janna's slim fingers covered Ty's lips, preventing him from saying any more.

"It's all right," she murmured. "I just want to…" Whatever Janna was attempting to say was lost temporarily when she bent her head and kissed the hard swell of Ty's biceps. "Yes," she breathed, shivering with the exquisite pleasure of brushing her lips over his naked arm. "Let me…"

When the tip of Janna's tongue traced the shadow line between Ty's arm and the flexed muscles of his chest, he made a sound as though he were in pain; yet she knew that it was need, not pain, that had dragged the sound from his body. The cry sent piercing needles of pleasure through Janna, making her tremble with the intensity of her response. She turned her head and found the dark, flat disk of Ty's nipple with her tongue and lightly raked the erect nub with her teeth.

Ty's hands closed suddenly around Janna's upper arms as though to push her away, but the attempt never was made. His hands refused to take the commands of his mind. He simply couldn't force himself to push her away. He had wanted her too much for too long. He held her closer and shuddered as though each gliding caress from her tongue was a harsh blow rather than the most tender kind of caress.

"Yes," Janna whispered, feeling the lightning strokes of desire racking the man she loved. "Yes, you need this. You need…" She shivered and her teeth pressing into the hard muscles of his torso became less gentle. "You need to...be tasted. And I need to taste you. Please, Ty. Let me. Please."

Janna didn't wait for an answer before she flowed down his body. The flesh beneath her caressing mouth was hot, misted with sweat, tasting of salt and passion and the indefinable flavor of masculinity. Touching Ty was a pleasure so great it was nearly pain. A shivering ripple of sound came from her lips, for she had dreamed of being given the gift of his body once more.

Ty's clenched thigh muscles barely gave beneath the testing of Janna's teeth. Feeling the intense strokes of desire that shook him with each of her moist caresses was intensely arousing to her, but she was too consumed by her sensual explorations to realize that her own body was as hot as his. She only knew that bursts of pleasure went through her when she rubbed her breasts over his hard thighs and brushed her cheeks over the rigid evidence of his desire.

"Janna," Ty said raggedly. His voice when she turned her head and her lips brushed over him in a caress that nearly undid him. "Sweet God, you're killing me. Love, don't, I've never...you'll make me..."

The intimate touch of Janna's tongue was a liquid fire that burned away Ty's words, burned away his thoughts, burned away everything but the incandescent instant when she first tasted him.

Speech unraveled into a cry that was torn from deep in Ty's throat. The harsh sound made Janna stop. She looked up. The green blaze of his eyes made her tremble.

"Did I hurt you?"

"No."

"But you...cried out," she said hesitantly.

"So did you when I touched you that way."

Janna's eyes half clouded as sensual memories burst inside her, drenching her with heat. She looked at Ty and remembered what it had been like to feel his mouth loving her, enthralling her, devouring her in steamy intimacy. She looked again at the potent male flesh that had felt so hard and smooth and intriguing to her tongue just a moment ago.

"Don't," Ty said huskily, biting back a raw sound of need. "You'll make me lose control."

"But I'm not even touching you," she whispered.

"You are in your mind. And in mine. Satin butterfly, hot and sleek and perfect. When you took me into your body it was like being taken into a fiery paradise. You burned me to my soul. You're still burning in my soul, burning in my body, everything burning. You don't know what you do to me."

Ty saw Janna's shivering response to his words and thought he would lose what little control remained to him.

"You burned me the same way," she said, touching him with the tip of her tongue. "I'm still burning."

Restlessly Janna stroked her hands over Ty's clenched leg muscles, trying to tell him something for which she had no words, seeking something she couldn't name. One of her hands caressed the inside of his thigh until she could go no higher. She felt him shudder, heard his ripping intake of breath and knew she had found another way to touch him with fiery paradise. Fascinated by the tangible variation between his body and her own, she caressed the very different flesh suspended so tightly between his thighs.

Ty watched Janna with eyes that were no more than green slits set against the stark tension of his face. He had thought he could want her no more without losing control. He had been wrong. He wanted her more now than he ever had; yet he made no move to take her, for he was learning more about himself and her with every instant, every caress, each sweet glide of her tongue as she discovered the changing textures of his masculinity.

The sight of Janna loving him, enjoying him, pleasuring him and herself at the same time was unlike anything Ty had ever known. Slowly his legs gave way, unable to bear the weight of his passion any longer. He sank to his knees, then onto the grass; and she moved with him, loving him in silence, displaying that love with every caress.

When her mouth circled him, accepting and cherishing him with a shattering intimacy, a cry was ripped from him once again. This time she didn't stop loving his hot flesh, for she knew that he had but given voice to the savage, overwhelming pleasure that was shaking his body.

"*Janna...*"

Her answer was silent, a changing pressure of her mouth that dragged a hoarse sound of ecstasy from his throat. He tried to tell her what she was doing to him, consuming and renewing him with each clinging movement of her lips and tongue. Despite his efforts no words came, for he had none to describe the shattering beauty of being loved without inhibition, without bonds, without expectations, nothing but the sultry heat of her mouth cherishing him.

"Janna," he said hoarsely. "Don't. I'm going to..." Words became a groan of ecstasy dragged from Ty as his hips moved in helpless need. "For the love of God...stop."

"Am I hurting you?" Janna asked, knowing the answer, wanting to hear it anyway.

Ty laughed brokenly, then made a low sound when her hands and mouth slid over him once more, caressing him, burning through his control, burning him alive.

"Love...stop. I can't take any more without losing control."

He felt the shiver that overtook Janna in the instant before she stroked him and whispered, "Yes, I'd like that."

Ty clenched against the pulses of ecstasy that were bursting through his body, not knowing how to give himself in that elemental way.

"Please," Janna whispered. She touched the tip of her tongue to the blunt masculine flesh that was no longer a mystery to her. "You taste like life itself."

Watching her, Ty made an anguished sound as he fought the tide of ecstasy that was surging through him. Deep within his soul he realized that he would never forget the picture she made as she loved him with a generosity that was a kind of ecstasy in itself, a giving and a taking that became a profound sharing he had never imagined possible. She accepted and cherished him without restraint, teaching him that he had known nothing of true intimacy before he had known Janna.

Ty felt his control being stripped away with each loving

instant, each sweet and wild caress. Pleasure convulsed him, shaking his body and soul with each primal pulse of rapture; and the word he cried out at the shattering peak of ecstasy was Janna's name. The cry pierced her soul, bringing tears that were both hot and sweet, an overflowing of her joy in the certainty that she had given the man she loved such intense pleasure.

When Ty could again control his own body, he caught Janna between his hands and pulled her into his arms, needing the feel of her close to him. She closed her eyes and held him as strongly as he was holding her, savoring the closeness and the sound of her name repeated over and over by her lover as the aftermath of ecstasy shuddered through his powerful body. When he finally tilted her face up to his own, she smiled and nuzzled against the masculine lips, which were resilient and soft and…insistent.

"Ty?"

Her husky voice was like a caress on his hot skin.

"I need to be part of you," he said simply. His hand slid from Janna's cheek, skimmed down her shirtfront, below her waist, seeking and finding the soft mound at the apex of her thighs. He made a deep sound of discovery and satisfaction when he felt the sultry heat of her. "And you need me, too. I can feel it even through all the clothes you use to conceal your beauty. My own satin butterfly, waiting to be freed of your cocoon."

The pressure of Ty's strong hand cupping her so deliberately made a shimmering tension gather in the pit of Janna's stomach.

"You need me, butterfly," Ty said, flexing his hand, feeling Janna's alluring heat calling to him. He bent to take her lips, then stopped just short of that goal. "You need me, but do you want me, too?"

Janna tried to answer. All that came out was a breathless sound when Ty's tongue touched her lips and she realized how hungry she was for his kiss. Vaguely she felt a shifting pressure at her waist, but she barely noticed, for Ty's teeth had caught her lower lip and were holding it captive for the slow

probing of his tongue. He released her soft lip by tiny incre-
ments.

"Do you want me?" he asked huskily while his hand
flicked open buttons, pushed aside cloth, slid beneath fabric,
seeking her feminine core. "Will you let me undress you,
touch you, tease you until you're hot and wild and you can't
breathe without calling my name?"

Janna couldn't answer, for his hand had claimed her and
the blind searching of his fingertip was making her tremble in
anticipation of the ecstasy she would know again at her lover's
hands.

"Janna," Ty said in a low voice. "Tell me what you want."

"Touch me," she said raggedly.

"I'm already touching you."

She shivered and shifted her legs unconsciously, silently
telling him what she wanted.

"Say it," he whispered. "I want to hear it. I need to know
that I'm giving you something as sweet and powerful as you
gave to me."

"I...I..."

Janna turned her face against Ty's chest in a gesture of trust
and shyness that made him smile despite the need clenching
fiercely within him. She had been so abandoned in her seduction of him a few moments before that he had forgotten she
was new to sensuous play.

"Then I'll tell you what pleases me," Ty said, and as he
spoke, his fingertip barely brushed the dark auburn triangle
that both defined and concealed Janna's softness. "I love seeing you this way, with your clothes opened and your breasts
bare and my hand between your beautiful thighs. I love watching your nipples rise and tighten even though nothing of me
is touching you but my words. I love watching your breath
shorten and your legs move restlessly until you open for me,
asking that I touch what no other man has."

Smiling with frank sensuality, Ty watched the effect of his
words on Janna. He encouraged her movements with teasing
hesitations and tiny touches on her breasts, her navel, the

heavy auburn silk at the apex of her thighs; and she moved beneath his touch, response and plea at once.

"Yes, like that. Just like that," Ty said, his voice thickening. His hands moved, caressing and revealing her in the same motions. "I love parting your soft lips and sliding into you. So warm…"

A ragged cry came from Janna as she felt a bubble of sensation expand wildly within her and then burst, heat spilling over at her lover's words, his touch, his clear enjoyment of her body.

"Yes, I love that, too," Ty said.

He advanced then withdrew his touch from her, teasing her and pleasuring her in the same motions, feeling the increase in her heat and softness with each caress. His voice changed with the heavy running of his own blood, becoming dark, deep, as elemental as the endless hunger he felt for the woman whose body became his at a touch.

"The way you respond to me makes me feel like a god. Hot satin butterfly…" Ty's voice broke as he felt the sudden constriction in Janna's satin depths, heard her breath hesitate and then come out in a low moan. "Love," he whispered, bending down to her, "tell me what you need. I'll give it to you, all of it, and then I'll begin all over once more, touching you, pleasuring you again and again until neither one of us has the strength to speak…if that's what you want. Tell me what you want."

Ty's name came from Janna's lips in a ripple of small cries marking the rings of pleasure expanding and bursting sweetly within her body. Blindly her hands moved over his hot skin until she found the flesh that she had come to know so intimately. He was hard and smooth to her touch, as tight as though it had been weeks rather than minutes since he had known release. Having tangible proof of her ability to affect Ty was like another kind of caress, deep and hot and unbearably sweet.

"I want you," Janna said, her voice breaking beneath an unexpected, wild burst of pleasure at feeling him so thick and heavy in her hands. "I want to be joined so closely with you that I can feel each heartbeat, each pulse of life..."

Her words shattered into rippling sounds, tiny cries called from her very core as Ty swept her loose pants from her body and merged their bodies with a single powerful motion, giving her all that she had asked for and more, for he had wanted the joining as intensely as she had.

The swift fulfillment was like lightning searching through Janna's flesh, creating an incandescent network of fire, burning through to her soul. She didn't know that she called Ty's name even as ecstasy transfixed her, but he knew. He heard his own name, felt the satin convulsions deep within her body, and he smiled in a mixture of triumph and passionate restraint as he bent to drink from her lips the taste of ecstasy.

Only when the last of Janna's cries had faded and the final echoes of passionate release had stilled in her body did Ty begin the slow dance of love, penetration and withdrawal, sliding deeply, retreating, sheathing himself within her once more, retreating, sheathing.

Janna's body gave no warning; suddenly she was in the grip of something unknown, something hot and vital coiling relentlessly within her, tighter with each movement, tension dragging breath from her lungs and strength from her limbs.

"Ty."

His answer was an even more complete sheathing followed by husky laughter when he felt Janna's back arch in helpless reflex to his presence deep within her body. Her cries unraveled into a moan as she joined with Ty in the sinuous dance of love, her body driven by the pressure coiling within her. He encouraged her with dark words whispered into her ear and the strength of his arm circling beneath her hips, sealing their bodies tightly together. He felt the tension vibrating within her satin depths as surely as she did; the realization that she was poised on the brink of violent rapture slammed through him, nearly wrenching away his own control.

Ty fought against his own climax, dragging himself back from the brink. He didn't want release yet. Not before he had drunk the wine of Janna's passion to the last glorious drop.

The feel of her nails against his buttocks was like being burned by sensual fire. He groaned and gave her what she was demanding, what she needed, the elemental joining of his body to hers, no barriers, no calculation, nothing but heat and sweet friction and the driving rhythms of life.

The tightness within Janna increased until she would have screamed, but her voice was paralyzed. Her body twisted and her legs wrapped around Ty's lean hips as she strained toward something she both feared and needed, something so powerful that having it might destroy her; but not having it would certainly destroy her. She began to call Ty's name with each breath, broken sounds; she was being pulled apart by the tension that had no end, no release, nothing but a need that drove her relentlessly higher.

And then the tension doubled and redoubled with each heartbeat. She screamed his name and burst into a thousand blazing pieces, each one of them a separate ecstasy consuming her all the way to her soul.

Ty held Janna and himself, drinking her passion, feeling her climax to the marrow of his bones and beyond, kissing her with both gentleness and hunger, holding himself still despite the tension still hammering in his body with each breath, each heartbeat; and he didn't move because he wanted it to last forever.

There had never been a woman for him like Janna. He had learned in a twilight meadow on Black Plateau Janna's rare gift for ecstasy. Now he was driven to learn the boundaries of that gift. He began to move again, caressing and probing and filling her once more, each motion inciting flesh still quivering from the height of sensual stimulation and wild release.

"Ty?" she asked, opening dazed eyes.

"Yes," he said, bending down to Janna's mouth. "To the last drop of passion. Until we can't breathe. Until we die."

Chapter Thirty-Eight

Janna looked at the stone overhang that had been the only home she had ever had. Only scattered ashes remained of the campfire that had always been carefully tended. The pots and pans had been washed, upended and set aside. The trunk had been filled with herbs that would discourage insects or mice from settling in. All that she had kept out was a small pack consisting of her bedroll, herb pouch and canteen…and the sketch of her mother, a silken lady who hadn't survived the rigors of frontier life.

"We'll be able to get the books once the Army takes care of Cascabel," Ty said, putting his arm around Janna.

For an instant Janna leaned against Ty, savoring his strength and the knowledge that for once she didn't have to stand alone. Then she straightened and smiled up at him, but she said nothing about their coming back to the secret valley. If she kept her portion of Mad Jack's gold, she could build a home anywhere she wished, save one—wherever Ty was. That she would not do. She had been lucky enough to have her dream of a home made possible. The fact that she now wished for Ty to share that dream was unfortunate, but it was her misfortune, not his. She had taken advantage of his natural woman-hunger by teasing him until he was beside himself with need. She hadn't realized the power of the weapon she had turned on him. He had tried to resist, but he hadn't been able to, not entirely. That was her fault, not his.

Especially yesterday, when she had thrown herself at him with utter abandon, touching him in ways that made it impossible for him to turn away. Even now the memories made her tremble with the aftershocks of what he and she had shared.

But to Janna, her wantonness was no reason for Ty to give up his own dream. Requiring him to give up his deepest desire just because he had been the first man to show her ecstasy; that would be an act of hatred, not of love...and she loved Ty so much it felt as though she were being pulled apart by claws of ice and fire and night.

Silken lady, wherever you are, whoever you are, be kind to the man I love. Give him the dream he has wanted for so many years.

"Janna?" Ty asked, his throat aching with the sadness he felt twisting through her, the bleak shadow of night just beneath her sunny smile. "We'll come back. I prom—"

She put her fingers over his lips, sealing in the unwanted promise before it could be spoken. "It's all right," she said. "I knew I would have to leave someday. Someday...is today."

Ty lifted Janna's hand and pressed a kiss into her palm. "Wyoming is beautiful, too. If you don't like it there we can go anywhere."

Tears Janna couldn't conceal came to her eyes. Ty's words were agony to her, for they weren't the words she had longed so much to hear, the words he only spoke to her in her dreams, the words his silken lady would someday hear from his lips.

I love you.

But Ty didn't love Janna. He was amused by her, he liked her, and he was enthralled by her sensuality without realizing that passion's wellspring was her own deep love for him. He talked about their future together, but it was a future decreed by his unbending sense of honor and duty, not his desire to make Janna his mate, his lifetime companion, the mother of his children.

Honor and duty weren't love. Neither was kindness. Janna would rather live the rest of her life in the wild than watch

Ty become bitter and ground down by regrets for the freedom and the dream he had lost.

And Janna would rather die than live to see the day when Ty stood like a captive mustang, his head down and his eyes as dead as stones.

"Go ahead and cry," Ty said, folding Janna into his arms, rocking her. "It's all right, sugar. It's all right. You'll have the home you've dreamed of if it's the last thing I do. It's the very least that I owe you."

Janna closed her eyes to conceal the wave of pain his words had caused. Very gently she brushed her lips over his shirt-front, savoring for the last time his heat, his scent, his strength, the male vitality that radiated from him.

"You owe me nothing at all."

Ty's laugh was harsh and humorless. "Like hell I don't. You saved my life, and all I've done since then is take from you. When I think of you throwing yourself under Lucifer's hooves just to catch him for me, I..."

Ty's words faded into a hoarse sound. Strong arms tightened almost painfully around Janna, as though Ty were trying to convince himself that she was all right despite all the dangers she had endured for him.

"I didn't catch Lucifer to make you feel obligated to me," Janna said quietly. "I did it so Lucifer wouldn't be killed by some greedy mustanger or be caught by a man too cruel to do anything but make Lucifer into a killer. You were the one who gentled Lucifer. You were the one who taught him to trust a man. Without that, what I did would have been worse than useless. Thank yourself for Lucifer, not me."

Ty tilted up Janna's chin and stared at her translucent gray eyes. "You really believe that, don't you?"

"I know it. *You don't owe me anything.* Not for your life, not for Lucifer, and not for the pleasure we shared. Not one damn thing. Once we get to the fort we're quits. You're as free as Lucifer once was. And so am I."

A chill came over Ty, making his skin tighten and move in primitive reflex. Janna's voice was calm and precise, lacking in emotion, as bleak as the darkness underlying her smile. She was systematically pulling away from him, cutting the ties that had grown silently, powerfully between them during the time they had spent in the hidden valley.

"No."

Ty said nothing more, just the single word denying what Janna had said. Before she could say anything in argument, Ty turned away and whistled shrilly.

Moments later Lucifer came trotting over and began lipping at Ty's shirt in search of the pinch of salt Ty often had hidden in a twist of paper. There was no salt today, simply the voice and hands Lucifer had come to enjoy.

Ty petted the stallion for a few moments before he picked up the heavy saddlebags Mad Jack had left behind. Ty had cut slits in the leather that joined the saddlebags. Through the slits he had threaded the surcingle. Once the strap had been tightened, the saddlebags would stay in place on the stallion's back.

Lucifer didn't care for the surcingle around his barrel, but he had become accustomed to it. He did nothing more than briefly lay back his ears when the strap tightened just behind his front legs. Ty praised the stallion, shrugged his own backpack into place and vaulted onto the mustang's back. It was a heavy load Lucifer was carrying, but Ty wasn't worried. Lucifer was an unusually powerful horse. Even if Ty had added a saddle to the load, the stallion wouldn't have been overburdened for normal travel.

"I'll scout the area beyond the slot," Ty said. "Get Zebra over there and wait for my signal."

"Ty, I won't let you—"

"Let me? *Let* me!" he interrupted, furious. "To hell with 'letting'! You listen to me and you listen good. You might be pregnant. If you think I'll run off and leave an orphaned girl who could be carrying my child to fend for herself in Indian country, there's no damned point in even talking to you! I'll try hammering my message through that thick skull of yours after we get to the fort. Maybe by then I'll have cooled down or you'll have grown up. Until then, shut up and stop distracting me or neither one of us will live to see tomorrow."

Lucifer leaped into a canter before Janna had a chance to speak, even if she had been able to think of something to say.

By the time the stallion reached the exit to the valley, Ty had gotten his temper under control. He didn't permit himself to think about Janna and the immediate past, only about Cascabel and the immediate future.

Ty dismounted and looked at the area right in front of the cleft. No new tracks marked the meadow. A vague, telltale trail had been worn through the grass despite his and Janna's efforts never to take the same way twice into the cleft.

It doesn't matter now. By the time we come back the grass will have regrown. And when we do come back, we won't have to try to live so small we don't even cast shadows.

Beyond the ghostly paths there were no signs that anything had ever passed through the cleft to the outer world. Ty picked his way over the narrow watercourse and through the shadowed slot between rock walls. The afternoon light glowed overhead, telling him that the sky was nearly cloudless. Until the sun went down they would be vulnerable to discovery, for there would be no rain to conceal their presence while they crossed the wild land.

Yet they had no choice but to move in daylight. There was simply too much risk that one of the horses would injure itself scrambling over the cleft's treacherous watercourse in the dark. Besides, even if they got through the slot safely at night and then traveled until dawn, they would still be deep within Cascabel's preferred range when the sun once more rose, exposing them to discovery.

Their best chance was to sneak out of the slot and take a long, looping approach to the fort, hoping that Cascabel would have been driven to the southern edges of his territory while the two of them traversed the northern part. The fort itself was a hard three-day ride, and there was no haven short of the stockade walls.

Standing well back from the sunlit exit to the cleft, Ty pulled out his spyglass and examined as much of the land as he could see beyond the stone walls. A quick look showed nothing. A long look showed no more. A point-by-point survey revealed no sign of renegades.

Wish my backbone didn't itch.

But it did, and Ty wasn't going to ignore his instincts. There was danger out there. His job was to find out where and how much. Unconsciously he fingered the hilt of the big knife he always carried at his belt. He waited for fifteen minutes, then lifted the spyglass and studied the land again. Again he saw nothing to alarm him. He took off his backpack, checked the load in his carbine, grabbed a box of bullets and went out to have a closer look at the land.

He was no more than thirty feet from the cleft when he cut the trail of three unshod ponies. The hoofprints stayed together and marked a purposeful course, telling Ty that the horses had been ridden; they had not been grazing at random as wild horses would. The horses had come out of Cascabel's usual territory.

As Ty followed the traces he hoped that the Army had been successful in driving the renegades away. That hope died when he saw other tracks meet those that he was following. The two sets of tracks mingled, then split once more, heading in all directions, as though the riders had exchanged information and had then separated and gone to search for something.

Ty had a terrible suspicion that what the renegades were searching for was a *bruja* called Janna Wayland.

Keeping to cover as much as possible, crawling when he had to, walking when he could, Ty followed the tracks that crisscrossed the flatlands in front of the cleft. Everything he saw brought him to the same conclusion: the renegades were going to beat the bushes and ravines until their auburn-haired quarry burst from cover. Then they would run her down and bring her back to Cascabel. There would be medicine chants and dances, celebrations of past victories and future coups; and then Cascabel would lead his renegades into war with Janna's long hair hanging from his lance like a flag, proving to the world that his spirit was the greatest one moving over the wild face of the land.

For a moment Ty considered simply sneaking back to the

cleft and waiting until Cascabel got tired of searching for his elusive quarry. That was what Janna had done in the past— hide. But in the past, Cascabel hadn't been so determined to catch her. If Ty and Janna retreated to the valley and then were found, they would be trapped in a stone bottle with no chance of escape. Better that they take their chances in the open.

Retreating silently back toward the cleft, Ty made a brief side trip to the top of a rise. From there he hoped to get a better view of the rugged land they had to cross. Just before he reached the edge of the rise, he took off his hat and went down on his stomach, presenting as little human silhouette as possible.

An instant later Ty was glad he had taken the trouble to be very cautious. On the far side of the rise, four warriors sat on their heels, arguing and gesticulating abruptly as they divided up the area to be searched for the Shadow of Flame, the witch who had been stealing Cascabel's spirit. Just beyond the warriors, seven horses grazed on whatever was within reach.

Four renegades. Seven horses. And my backbone is on fire.

The only warning Ty had was a slight whisper of sound behind him. He rolled onto his back and lashed out with his booted feet as the renegade attacked.

Chapter Thirty-Nine

Ty's kick knocked the air from the Indian's lungs, preventing him from crying out and alerting the others. Even so, Ty had no sooner put his hand on his knife hilt than the renegade was on his knees and trying to bring his rifle to bear. Ty threw himself forward, pinning the Indian to the ground with a hard forearm across his throat. A knife flashed and blood burst silently into sunlight. The renegade jerked once, twice, and then lay motionless.

For a few instants it was all Ty could do to breathe despite the screaming of his instincts that the danger had just begun, not ended, and he should be running rather than lying half-stunned. He rolled off the dead renegade and began collecting himself, relying on the survival reflexes he had learned in war. He cleaned his knife blade and put it back in its sheath. He picked up the carbine, checked it for dirt or mechanical damage, found none and made sure the weapon was ready for instant use.

Only then did Ty retreat silently, pausing long enough to close the dead warrior's eyes.

Ashes to ashes, dust to dust... And may God have mercy on both our souls.

Three hundred feet away Janna sank slowly to her knees, feeling as though her own heart had burst. The barrel of the pistol she was holding clanked softly against stone. She took a deep breath, then another, trying to quiet her body's trembling as she watched Ty glide from brush to boulder, retreating toward the cleft's uncertain shelter.

It had been nerve stretching for Janna to stay within the slot's narrow shadow, knowing as she did from Ty's actions that he must have cut the trail of renegades. She had been watching him for the past half hour while he reconnoitered. Her eyes ached from staring out and trying to guess what Ty was reading from various signs crisscrossing the earth.

Then an Indian had risen up out of the very ground and launched himself at Ty, choosing the greater glory of personal combat to the sure kill offered by picking off Ty with a rifle. Even though the range had been too far for Janna to use the pistol with real accuracy, she had reached for the gun. The fight had ended before she could even lift the weapon above her waist to take aim. She had never seen a man so quick as Ty, or so deadly in that quickness. She realized at that instant just how much of his strength he held in check when he was with her.

And Ty could have died despite all his power and speed, his blood a crimson stain bursting from his body to be drunk by the thirsty earth. All that was Ty, the passion and the laughter, the anger and the sensual teasing, the silence and the silken dream, all of it gone between one breath and the next.

Janna watched each of Ty's movements hungrily, needing the reassurance that he was alive. She scanned the land behind him as well, and she did it from over the barrel of the pistol, wanting to be able to shoot quickly at anything she saw.

Despite Janna's alertness, she didn't see the second renegade until the sun glinted off a rifle barrel as the warrior shifted position to shoot at Ty. Not even bothering to aim, Janna triggered a shot in the direction of the Indian.

At the sound of the shot, Ty dived for cover in a shallow ditch left behind by storm water fanning out from the cleft's narrow mouth. A few instants later he had his hat off and his carbine barrel resting on the lip of the ditch as he searched for the source of the attack. He didn't have to search long. The Indian shifted his aim again, sending more sunlight off his rifle barrel and drawing another shot from the cleft.

Janna's second bullet came much closer than the first had. The renegade's answering shot sent rock chips flying not four feet from her.

Despite the heavy pack Ty wore, he was up and sprinting for the next bit of cover while the renegade reloaded. Ty halfway expected to draw more fire from the other Indians, but none came. He hit the dirt a second before Janna fired at the rifle barrel that was once more poking out from a low mound of rocks and brush. The sharper *crack* of a rifle shot occurred a split second after Janna triggered her pistol.

Ty scrambled up and began running again, counting off the seconds he had before he must throw himself to the ground again. As intently as a hawk, Janna watched the cover that concealed the renegade. Steadying the heavy pistol with both hands, she waited for the renegade to reload and poke the rifle barrel out again, giving her a target.

Suddenly a flash of human movement off to the side caught Janna's eye. She screamed at Ty to take cover as she spun to the left and fired. Two rifle shots rang out, kicking dirt just in front of Ty. He flattened out into another shallow runoff ditch while Janna fired a shot at the orginal attacker.

Five, Ty counted silently to himself. *That's it. She has to reload.*

The pistol in Janna's hand clicked loudly twice before she realized that she was out of ammunition.

"Reload!" yelled Ty without looking away from his right, where the new attacker was hidden. *Come on, come on,* he silently urged the second renegade. *Show yourself.*

Reloading was much easier said than done for Janna. White lipped, she worked to eject the spent casings, fumble bullets from her pocket and shove them one by one into the six waiting chambers. This time she wouldn't leave one chamber empty as a precaution against accidentally discharging the revolver; she wanted all six shots and she wanted them right now.

But first she had to get the bullets into the chambers.

Four hundred feet away and to the right of Ty, a thrown pebble bounced harshly on the hard ground. Knowing it was a feint, Ty fired in that direction anyway, then turned quickly toward the position of the first attacker.

Come and get it, he urged silently.

As Ty had hoped, the first renegade assumed he was facing an enemy armed with a single-shot rifle. The Indian broke cover and stood up, striving for a clean shot before his prey could reload or find better cover. Smoke puffed from Ty's carbine and the renegade died before he could even realize what had gone wrong. Ty levered another bullet into the firing chamber even as he whipped around to confront the second renegade, who had had time to reload and was taking aim.

Ty threw himself to the side, spoiling both his own shot and the renegade's. Ty's second and third shots were dead on target. He rolled to a new position of cover and waited. No more shots came. Either the other renegades hadn't had time to take position yet or the speed with which Ty could "reload" and fire his carbine had made them cautious.

"Janna," called Ty. "Are you all right?"

"Yes." Her voice was oddly thinned but strong.

"Tell me when you've reloaded."

Swearing shockingly, Janna worked at the unfamiliar task of putting cold, slippery bullets into the warm cylinder. She dropped two bullets before she managed to get all six chambers full. Cocking the revolver, she looked out over the land once more.

"Ready," she called.

"I'm coming in from your right."

"Go!"

An instant later Ty was on his feet and running toward the slot, dodging and turning every few seconds, doing everything he could to spoil a hunter's aim. Janna's gray eyes scanned the countryside to the left of the slot, alert for any sign of movement. At the edge of her side vision she watched Ty's long-legged stride eat up the distance between himself and safety.

Only twenty yards to cover. Then ten, then—

There was no time to warn Ty, no time to aim, no time to do anything but fire at almost point-blank range as a renegade sprang from cover just outside the cleft and came at Janna with a knife. Her first shot was wild. Her second shot hit the renegade's shoulder a glancing blow, knocking him backward. The third and fourth shots were Ty's. No more were needed.

"Get back," Ty said harshly, dragging Janna farther inside the cleft. "There are three more out there and God knows how many will come in at the sound of the shots."

Breathing hard, Ty shrugged out of his backpack and took up a position just inside the slot. He began refilling the carbine with quick, sure motions. As he worked he looked up every few instants to scan the landscape. What he saw made him swear tonelessly. There was a distant swirl of dust, which was probably a rider going off for reinforcements. One of the remaining renegades was taking up a position that would cover the mouth of the cleft.

The second Indian wasn't in sight, but he was within rifle range, as a screaming, whining, ricocheting bullet proved. Rock chips exploded, showering Ty with dust and stinging shards.

"Get farther back," he yelled as he blinked his eyes and took aim.

Ty fired several times at the most likely patches of cover from which the renegade might be shooting. Then he lowered his carbine and waited. A few moments later another shot whined past. This time he saw where it had come from. He answered instantly with closely spaced shots, sending bullets raking through the cover. There was a startled yell, then silence. Methodically Ty shoved bullets into the carbine's magazine, replacing those he had spent.

No more shots came.

"Janna?"

"I'm back here," she said.

The odd acoustics of the canyon made her sound close, though she was thirty feet away.

"We're going to have to get out on foot and try to steal horses from the Indians," Ty said.

Janna had arrived at the same conclusion. Getting Lucifer

and Zebra out without being spotted by the Indians would be impossible.

"There's no moon tonight," Ty continued without looking away from the bit of cover where the Indian had hidden. "We'll go out an hour after full dark. Try to get some sleep until then."

"What about you?"

"I'll guard the entrance."

"But the ricochets—"

"If I get out of range of a ricochet," Ty interrupted impatiently, "I won't be able to see the mouth of the slot to guard it." Ty's expression softened for a moment when he looked at Janna. "Don't look so worried, sugar. He doesn't have a very good angle from where he is. I'll be all right."

Turning back to the slot, Ty fired six times in rapid succession, stitching bullets on either side of the place where the renegade had taken cover, forcing anyone who might still be in range to get down and stay down. Janna hesitated, then went quickly to Ty. She threw her arms around him and hugged him fiercely. He returned the embrace with a strength and a yearning that made tears burn against Janna's eyelids. In tones too soft for him to hear, she whispered her love against his neck before she turned away and retreated toward the meadow.

But Ty had heard Janna's words. For an instant he closed his eyes and felt the exquisite pain of having been given a gift he didn't deserve.

With automatic motions Ty propped his backpack against a stone, sat on his heels and loaded the carbine to full capacity once more. The angle of the shadows on the canyon walls told him that he had several hours to wait until sunset came, much less full dark.

Leaning against the wall, carbine at the ready, Ty tried to convince himself that when dawn came he and Janna would still be alive.

Chapter Forty

The meadow's sunlight seemed blinding after the cool, dim passage into the secret valley. Janna stood on the edge of the opening and sent a hawk's wild cry into the still air. A second call brought Zebra at a trot, her head high, her ears pricked. Lucifer followed after the mare, for the two horses had become inseparable during the weeks when the stallion was healing.

Janna mounted Zebra quickly and turned the mare toward the ancient ruins where Mad Jack had hidden his gold. She had never pried into the old prospector's secrets before—but then, she had never been trapped in a stone bottle before, either.

"Jack must have had a way in and out of this valley without coming through the slot," Janna said aloud to Zebra, "because I never saw a mark in that creek bed. If he had been coming and going from my end of the valley, I'd have heard him or you would have or Lucifer would have."

Zebra flicked her ears back and forth, enjoying the sound of Janna's voice.

"But you didn't hear Jack, and that old man was too weak to carry more than a few pounds of gold at a time, which means there was a lot of coming and going before those saddlebags were full. He had to have left some kind of trail, somewhere. He just had to."

And Janna had until dark to find it.

She urged Zebra into a canter, watching the rocky walls and

lava flows, probing light and shadow for any sign of a faint trail. The valley narrowed in at the south end, where the ruins were. Beyond ascertaining that there was a clear spring welling up at the base of the ramparts that were just before the ruins, Janna had never really explored this part of the valley. The ruins were eerie by daylight and unsettling by night. She much preferred the clean reach of the stone overhang at the opposite end of the valley to the cramped and broken rooms of a people long dead.

But Janna wasn't looking for a campsite now, or even for temporary shelter. She was looking for the ancient trails that the vanished Indians must have left if they came and went from their home by any route other than the dark cleft. It was possible that the Indians might have built their fortress in a blind valley with only one exit, but Janna doubted it. A tribe that took so much trouble to hide its home was a cautious people, and cautious people knew that the only difference between a fortress and a trap was a bolt hole.

In the country outside the valley, Janna had spotted ancient trails in the past simply by standing on a ridge and allowing her eyes to go slightly unfocused. When she lost the finest edge of visual acuity, other patterns came to light, vague lines and odd shadows. Most often they were simply random lines in a wild land, but sometimes they were ghost trails no longer used by man.

Crisscrossing the area around the ruins, Janna searched for any trail, new or old. She found nothing on the ground but grass, brush, rocks, sunlight and signs of her own passage. She urged Zebra farther into the ruins. The angle of the sun made shadows spill out from crumbling stone rooms, as though darkness had breached stone dams and was welling up to fill the valley beyond.

A frisson of uneasiness ran through Janna. She had always avoided the ruins in the hours beyond midafternoon, when the descending sun played odd tricks with light and shadow and stone. All that drove her farther into the ruins now was the certainty that nothing a ghostly Indian had to offer could be worse than what waited beyond the cleft in the form of flesh-and-blood renegades.

No matter how Janna focused her eyes or didn't, tilted her head or held it straight, narrowed her eyelids or widened them until her eyes ached, she saw nothing on the ground to suggest an ancient, forgotten trail. Working out from the room in which Mad Jack had stored his gold, she quartered the open space. She found nothing she could be sure was Mad Jack's sign rather than her own or a random displacement of pebbles.

The farther back into the ruins Janna went, the narrower the canyon became. Stone rubble covered the ground. At first she assumed the rocky debris was the result of stones falling from the surrounding cliffs, but the farther back into the narrow throat of the canyon she went, the more she was struck by an odd thing—in some places the rubble looked as though it once had been level, as though broad steps or narrow terraces had once climbed up the throat of the valley.

With growing excitement Janna followed the frayed remnants of what might once have been a well-built path snaking back and up the broken ramparts of stone that surrounded the hidden valley. Behind Zebra a pebble rolled under Lucifer's feet. The mare snorted and shied at the sound, giving vent to her nervousness at being asked to take a trail that showed every evidence of getting more and more narrow while going nowhere at all.

"Easy, girl," Janna said soothingly, stroking the mare. "There's nothing around but you, me, Lucifer and a lot of rock. The shadows just look scary, that's all. There's nothing in them but air."

Under Janna's urging Zebra climbed the steepening path. The farther along she went, the more Janna's hopes sank. What had once looked like a wide path was rapidly degenerating into a jumble of stone that resembled nothing so much as the debris that always built up at the foot of stone cliffs.

Janna's hopes sank when Zebra scrambled around a tight corner and was confronted by a rock wall. Nothing that in any way resembled a trail broke the sheer rise of stone. Apparently

Janna had been following a random chute paved with fallen rocks rather than a ghost path left by an ancient people.

For a long time she simply sat, staring at the end of her carefully constructed and entirely false logic of hope. However Mad Jack might have come into the valley, it wasn't this way; and this had been by far the best hope of finding his path. The other possibilities—the random ravines and slender runoff gullies and crevices that opened into the narrowest end of the valley where Janna was—were much less likely to lead to the top of the plateau than the ground she had just covered.

But Janna had no choice except to try the other possibilities. No matter how small they were, they were better than the chance of sneaking past Cascabel and his renegades while they were camped outside the valley's only exit like a horde of hungry cats waiting at a mouse hole.

There was barely enough room for Zebra to turn around in order to head back where she had come from. Lucifer saw Zebra turning and followed suit. He led the retreat over the rough ground at a brisk trot, relieved to be free of the narrow passage between broken walls of stone. Zebra was equally relieved. She followed after the stallion eagerly.

They had retreated no more than a hundred feet when Janna noticed a small ravine that she hadn't seen before, for it joined at an oblique angle to the main passage and was walled off by a pediment of stone. Immediately she turned Zebra toward the side ravine. The mare tossed her head, not wanting to leave Lucifer and enter the narrow gulch.

"Come on, girl. There's nothing up this trail but stone and shadows and maybe, just maybe, a way out of here."

Zebra didn't budge.

Janna stopped using pressures of her hand to guide the mare. Instead, she pulled on the knotted hackamore reins Ty had insisted that Zebra be trained to wear. Reluctantly the mare turned away from Lucifer and walked into the gulch. Once past the rocky outcropping that guarded the ravine's narrow mouth, the passage opened out again, becoming wider than the slot where Ty waited for a renegade who was brave or foolish enough to show himself.

Janna didn't know if it were wishful thinking or truth, but it seemed to her that the new path had once been made more level by a series of broad steps composed of stony rubble, which followed the steep rise of the ravine farther and farther back into the body of the plateau. The steps, or ramps, had since largely crumbled and been washed away beneath torrential rains, but enough remained to give a mustang adequate footing.

To Janna's surprise, Lucifer followed, as though determined not to lose sight of Zebra in the midst of echoing stone ravines. The path snaked higher and higher, sometimes scrambling over stony ridges to follow a different runoff course up the broken walls that constituted the western side of the valley.

There were places where Janna was certain that rock must have been hammered away to make passage possible. In other places she was just as certain that nothing had touched the trail but wind and water, sun and storm. Then she would see gouge marks on the stone and wonder if they weren't the result of intelligence rather than past landslides.

The trail came to yet another narrowing of the branching network of runoff channels that covered the eroding face of the western ramparts of the valley. Without being urged, Zebra scrambled and lunged over the small rise, for there had been many such changes of direction in the past half mile.

There was sun shining on the rise, for they had climbed far enough to be beyond the reach of lengthening shadows. Janna shaded her eyes and looked ahead, confidently expecting to find an obvious way to proceed. She saw nothing except a lateral crack in the stone cliff, but the crack was too small to be called a passage. Turning slowly, she looked over her trail. Her breath came in with a sharp sound. She was nearly to the top of the stone ramparts that surrounded her hidden valley.

"There has to be a way to get out from here," Janna said aloud as she stroked Zebra absently.

For several minutes Janna looked at the dubious lateral crevice that angled up and across the remaining cliff. The narrow ledge she saw might or might not lead to the top of the plateau. If the ledge ended short of the top, she would be stuck; there was no place for a horse to turn around. If the mustangs entered the crack they would be committed to going up, not down.

Janna slid off Zebra, then pressed the mare's nose in a signal for her to stay behind. Ears pricked, nostrils flared, the mustang watched her mistress take the narrow trail. Janna looked back only once to assure herself that Zebra wasn't going to stray.

After Janna had gone fifteen feet, she was certain that she was going the right way. The crack became a very narrow ledge, too narrow for a horse to pass safely. Marks that could have been left by a chisel or hammer showed in the stone. Apparently the ancient tribe had widened and leveled a natural split in the rock face until it became a ledge just wide enough to take a man on foot. With overhanging rock on her left, a path no more than twenty inches wide at her feet—and sometimes less, if the rock had crumbled away—and a sheer drop to the valley floor on her right, she scrambled the length of the crack.

When Janna vanished around a column of rock on the far end of the ledge Zebra nickered as though to call a foal back to her side. When that didn't work, the mustang neighed loudly. Lucifer added a ringing, imperious command that carried from one end of the hidden valley to the other.

Janna popped back into view, sliding and skidding down to the ledge, desperate to calm the stallion before he alerted half of Utah Territory. Despite the need for haste, Janna slowed to a very careful walk while she negotiated the dangerous ledge. Zebra whickered softly in encouragement or warning, then nuzzled Janna when she was within reach once more. Having achieved his purpose in calling back a straying member of his band, Lucifer made no further noise.

"Lord, what a bugle you have," Janna said to Lucifer, who ignored her irritation. She looked back at the ledge and shook her head. "I know, that's a scary path even for humans. I can imagine what it must look like to you. But you didn't give me a chance to find out if the rest of the trail—if it really is a trail—goes all the way to the top."

After a few moments spent reassuring the horses, Janna started toward the ledge again. She had taken no more than two steps when she heard a barrage of rifle fire.

She froze, listening intently, trying to decide where the shots were coming from. The lighter, rhythmic barks of Ty's Winchester resolved the issue beyond a doubt. The sounds were coming from the cleft that Ty had remained behind to guard. The Indians must have decided to try rushing the cleft's entrance, or perhaps it was only a feint.

Either way, Janna wasn't comforted. The number of shots that were being fired told her that renegade reinforcements must have arrived. If they timed their attack carefully, they could provide cover for one another while they reloaded their rifles. But Ty was alone in the rocky cleft with no one to cover him while he reloaded.

Chapter Forty-One

The trip back down the ancient trail took much less time than the trip up had, but it seemed like an eternity to Janna. The instant it was safe to demand speed from Zebra, she kicked the mare into a hard gallop that ended only at the shadowed entrance to the cleft. Heart hammering, Janna leaped from Zebra and ran into the dark opening just as there was a renewed fusillade of rifle fire. The cleft distorted sounds, making them seem to come from nearby and far away all at once. She kept hoping to hear the carbine's lighter sound but heard only her own breath and the erratic bark of renegade rifles.

Just as Janna rounded the last bend before the exit, Ty's carbine resumed its rhythmic, rapid firing. She slowed slightly, almost dizzy with relief.

Ty heard her footsteps and looked over his shoulder. "You're supposed to be sleeping."

"Not likely with all the racket you're making," she said breathlessly.

His smile was rather grim as he turned his attention back to the land beyond the cleft. He fired quickly three times and was answered by a scattering of shots.

"I'm having a little help making noise, as you can see."

"How many?" Janna asked.

"I saw enough dust for an army, but I don't think there are more than ten rifles out there right now, and all of them are single shot."

''For these small blessings, Lord, we are thankful,'' Janna said beneath her breath. ''I think.''

Ty's smile was little more than a hard line of white beneath his black mustache. He wasn't sure that it made a difference what kind of rifles the renegades were shooting. The chance of Janna and himself slipping past the Indians—much less of stealing a horse or two on the way by—had dropped to the point that it would be frankly suicidal rather than probably suicidal to try escaping through the cleft.

But there was no other way out.

''I think I found a way out,'' Janna said.

Her words echoed his thought so closely that for a moment Ty wasn't sure that she really had spoken. His head snapped around.

''What did you say?''

''I think I found how Mad Jack got his gold into the ruins without our seeing him.''

A movement beyond the cleft commanded Ty's attention. He turned, got off two quick shots and had the satisfaction of knowing that at least one of them had struck home. There was a flurry of return fire, then silence. As he watched the area beyond the cleft he began reloading methodically.

''How did he do it?'' Ty asked.

''You know how the valley narrows out behind the ruins?''

''Yes.''

''I followed it,'' Janna said.

''So did I about two weeks ago. It ends in a stone cliff.''

''There's a ravine coming in before that.''

''There are at least ten ravines 'before that,' and those ravines branch into others, which branch into others. And they all end against a stone cliff,'' Ty concluded flatly.

''Even the one with the ledge?'' Janna asked, trying to keep the disappointment from her voice.

''What ledge?''

''The one that goes along the western lip of the valley almost to the rim.''

''Are you certain?''

''I was on it until I heard rifle fire.''

Slowly Ty lowered his carbine and turned toward Janna. "You said 'almost to the rim.' How close is 'almost'?"

"I don't know. Zebra started whinnying when I got out of sight and then Lucifer set up such a ruckus that I came back to calm him down. Then I heard rifle fire and was afraid they were rushing you and you didn't have anyone to cover you while you reloaded." Janna closed her eyes briefly. "I got back here as quick as I could."

"How close is almost?" Ty repeated calmly.

"A hundred feet. Maybe a hundred yards. Maybe a quarter mile. I couldn't see."

"Would you bet your life on that path going through?"

"Do we have a choice?"

"Probably not. If Cascabel isn't out there soon, he will be when word gets to him. Until then, there are at least eight able-bodied warriors and two wounded renegades under cover out there, just waiting for something to show at the cleft."

"What if we wait until dark?"

"We can try it."

"But?" Janna prodded.

"Our chances of getting out alive through that cleft are so slim they aren't worth counting," Ty said bluntly. "The same darkness that would cover our movements also covers theirs. Even now the renegades are moving in closer, finding cover, covering each other, closing in on the cleft. By dark they'll have the cork well and truly in the bottle. After that, it's just a matter of time until I run out of ammunition and they rush me."

Ty said nothing more. He didn't have to. Janna could finish his bleak line of thought as well as he could.

"There's something else to consider," Ty said. "If you can find that trail from this end, sure as God made little green apples, a renegade can find it from the other end if he has a good enough reason to go looking—and your hair is a good enough reason, thanks to Cascabel's vision."

Janna nodded unhappily. The same thought had occurred to her. "We can take the horses most of the way."

"But not all?"

"The ledge was made for men, not horses."

Ty had expected nothing more. He bent, put his arms through the straps of his heavy pack and shrugged it into place. "Let's go. We only have a few hours of light left."

Janna turned to leave, then was struck by a thought. "What happens if the Indians rush the cleft while we're still in the valley?"

"I've made the renegades real wary of showing themselves. But if they do—" Ty shrugged "—I can hold them off in the ruins almost as well as in the cleft. You'll have plenty of time to follow the path."

"If you think I'd leave you to—"

"If I tell you to take that trail," Ty interrupted flatly, *"you damn well will take that trail."*

Without another word Janna turned and began working her way rapidly back through the cleft. Ty was right on her heels. When they came out into the little valley, Zebra and Lucifer were standing nearby, watching the opening attentively. Janna mounted and waited while Ty pulled the saddlebags full of gold out of a hiding place and secured them on Lucifer's muscular back. As soon as Ty had mounted, Janna urged Zebra into a gallop.

The mustangs quickly covered the distance to the ruins. Janna didn't slow the pace until the valley narrowed and the rubble underfoot made the going too rough for any speed greater than a trot. The sounds of stones rolling beneath the horses' hooves echoed between the narrowing walls of the valley. Walking, trotting, scrambling, always pushing ahead as quickly as possible, Zebra climbed up steeper and steeper byways, urged by Janna through the twisting web of natural and man-made passages. Lucifer kept up easily despite the double load of Ty and the gold. The stallion was powerful, agile and fully recovered from his brush with Joe Troon's rifle.

More than once Ty thought that Janna had lost her way, but each time she found a path past the crumbling head of a ravine or through places where huge sheets of rock had peeled away from the ramparts and smashed to pieces against stone outcroppings farther down the cliff. When Zebra scrambled over

a ridge of stone and came to a stop, Ty wondered if Janna
had finally lost her way. He hoped not; he had begun to believe there was a way out of the hidden valley that had been
first a haven and then a deadly trap.

Janna turned and looked back at Ty. "This is as far as the
horses can go."

Before Ty could answer, Janna slid from Zebra's back, adjusted the small pack she wore and set off to traverse the
narrow ledge. Ty dismounted, scrambled up the last few feet
of trail and saw the ledge—and the sheer drop to the valley
below.

"Sweet Jesus," he whispered.

Ty fought against an urge to call out to Janna to come back.
All that made him succeed was the fear of distracting her from
the trail's demands.

The sound of rifle fire drifted up from the direction of the
cleft, telling Ty that the renegades were on the move once
more. He turned and looked toward the east. He couldn't see
the spot where the cleft opened into the meadow. He could,
however, see that once the renegades spread through the valley
looking for their prey, it would be just a matter of time until
a warrior looked up and saw Janna poised like a fly on the
wall of the valley's western ramparts.

Zebra called nervously when Janna vanished around a bulge
of stone. The stallion's ringing whinny split the air, reverber-
ating off rocky walls. Ty went back to Lucifer and clamped
his hand over the horse's nostrils. The stallion shook his head
but Ty only hung on harder. He spoke softly, reassuring the
mustang, hoping the horse's neigh hadn't carried over the
sound of rifle fire.

"Easy, boy, easy. You and Zebra are going to be on your
own again in just a little bit. Until then, shut up and hold still
and let me get this surcingle undone."

Lucifer snorted and backed away, tossing his head even as
his nostrils flared. Ty threw himself at the stallion's head, just
managing to cut off Lucifer's air before he could whinny
again.

"What's wrong with you?" Ty asked soothingly. "You've

never been this jumpy. Now hold still and let me get this strap off you."

Without warning Lucifer lurched forward, shouldering Ty roughly aside.

"What the hell?"

Ty regained his balance and followed Lucifer up the last few feet of trail. Ty was fast, but not fast enough. Lucifer's demanding bugle rang out. Reflexively Ty lunged for the stallion's nose. The horse shouldered him aside once more. Cursing, Ty scrambled to his feet, wondering what had gotten into Lucifer.

"Dammit, horse, where the hell do you think you're going?"

The stallion kept walking.

Then Ty looked past the stallion and realized what had happened. "God in heaven," Ty whispered.

Zebra had followed Janna out onto the ledge—and the stallion was going out right after her, determined not to be left behind.

Chapter Forty-Two

Afraid even to breathe, Ty watched Zebra and Lucifer picking their way over the narrow ledge with the delicacy of cats walking on the edge of a roof. The worst part of the trail was halfway along the ledge, where rock had crumbled away to make an already thin path even more skeletal. All that made passage possible was that the cliff at that point angled back from the vertical, rather than overhanging as it did along much of the ledge.

When Zebra reached the narrow place where rock had crumbled away, she stopped. After a moment or two her hooves shifted restively. Small pieces of rock fell away, rolling and bouncing until there was no more stone, only air. The mare froze in place, having gone forward no more than an inch or two.

"Go on," Ty said under his breath. "You can't turn around and you can't back up and you can't stay there forever. There's only one way out and that's to keep on going."

Zebra snorted. Ears pricked, she eyed the ledge ahead. Her skin rippled nervously. Sweat sprang up, darkening her pale hide around her shoulders and flanks. Trembling, she stood on the narrow ledge.

And then she tried to back up.

A hawk's wild cry keened across the rocks. The sound came once, twice, three times, coaxing and demanding in one; Janna had returned to the far side of the ledge to see what was taking

Ty so long. A single glance had told her what the problem was, and how close it was coming to a disastrous solution. She began speaking to Zebra in low tones, calming the mare, praising her, promising her every treat known to man or mustang if Zebra would only take the few steps between herself and Janna.

Slowly Zebra began to move forward once more. Holding out her hands, Janna backed away, calling to the mustang, talking to her, urging her forward. Zebra followed slowly, placing each hoof precisely—and on her right side, part of each hoof rested on nothing but air.

Gradually the ledge became wider once more, allowing Zebra to move more quickly. She completed the far end of the trail in a subdued rush, barely giving Janna a chance to get out of the way.

Ty had little time to be relieved that Zebra was safe, for now it was Lucifer's turn on the crumbling stone. The stallion liked it even less than the mare, for he was bigger and the saddlebags tended to rub hard against the overhang along the first part of the ledge, pushing the horse outward and toward the sheer drop to the valley floor. Unlike Zebra, Lucifer didn't stop on the narrow section of the trail. He simply laid back his ears and placed each hoof with excruciating care, sweating nervously until his black coat shone like polished jet.

Just as he reached the far end of the ledge, a piece of stone crumbled away beneath his great weight. His right rear hoof lost purchase entirely, throwing him off balance.

Janna bit back a scream as she watched Lucifer scramble frantically to regain his balance and forward momentum. For long seconds the stallion hung poised on the brink of falling. Without stopping to think of the danger, Janna darted past Zebra, grabbed Lucifer's hackamore and pulled forward as hard as she could, hoping to tip the balance.

"Janna."

Ty's horrified whisper was barely past his lips when Lucifer clawed his way over the last of the ledge and lunged onto the wider trail, knocking Janna down and aside in his haste to reach safe footing. The stallion crowded against Zebra, nipping at her haunches, demanding that she keep going up the trail.

Ty barely noticed the narrowness of the ledge or the rub of his left shoulder against the overhang. He covered the stone pathway with reckless speed, wanting only to get to Janna. With fear like a fist in his throat, he knelt next to her and touched her cheek.

"Janna?"

She tried to speak, couldn't and fought for air.

"Take it easy, sugar," Ty said. "That fool stud knocked the breath out of you."

After a few more moments air returned to Janna in an aching rush. She breathed raggedly, then more evenly.

"Do you hurt anywhere?" Ty asked.

Janna shook her head.

"Have enough air now?"

She nodded.

"Good."

Ty bent and pulled Janna into his arms, hugging her hard, then taking her mouth in a kiss that was both savage and tender. After a long time he lifted his head.

"Don't ever do anything like that again," Ty said roughly. "Nothing's worth your life. Not the stallion. Not the gold. Not *anything*. Do you hear me, Janna Wayland?"

She nodded, more breathless from Ty's searching, hungry and gentle kiss than from her skirmish with Lucifer.

Ty looked at Janna's eyes. They were clear and warm as summer rain, radiant with emotion, and he felt his heart turn over in his chest. He closed his own eyes, unable to bear the feelings tearing through him, pulling him apart.

Two feet away from Ty's left leg, stone chips exploded, spattering both of them with shards. From the valley below came the sound of rifle fire.

Ty dragged Janna up the trail and around an outcropping of rock until they were out of view of the valley. From ahead came the sound of stones rolling and bouncing as the mustangs scrambled on up the trail.

"When you get to the top, wait ten minutes," Ty said. "If

I don't come, get on Zebra and ride like hell for the fort. Don't come back, Janna. Promise me. Don't come back. There's nothing you can do here but get killed.''

"Let me stay," she pleaded.

"No," he said. Then he added in a low voice, "Please, Janna. Let me feel that I've given you something. Just once. Just once for all the things you've given to me. Please."

Janna touched Ty's cheek with fingers that trembled. He turned his head and kissed her fingertips very gently.

"Now go," he said softly.

Janna turned and walked away quickly, trying not to cry. She had gone no more than a hundred feet before she heard the harsh, evenly spaced sounds of Ty's carbine firing down into the valley below.

The remaining trail to the top of the plateau was more of a scramble than a walk, for the ravine that the path followed was filled with stony debris and a few hardy evergreens. The mustangs had left ample signs to follow—broken twigs and overturned stones and shallow gouge marks along solid rock.

The few steep pitches were mercifully brief. Within fifteen minutes Janna was standing on top of the plateau. She hadn't heard any sounds of shooting for the last ten minutes as she had climbed upward. She had told herself that that was good, that it meant Ty was on his way up the trail. She also had told herself he was all right, but tears kept ruining her vision and fear made her body clench.

From where Janna stood on the plateau there was no hint that there might be a trailhead nearby, or even that the long, shallow gully she had just climbed out of was in any way different from any of hundreds of such gullies that fringed the steeper edges of the plateau.

The horses grazed nearby, wary of all sounds and shadows. All that forced Janna to mount Zebra was the memory of Ty's eyes pleading with her to be safe, and the gentle kisses that still burned on her fingertips, sealing her promise. Torn between fear and grief, rebellion and love, Janna mounted Zebra and waited, counting off the minutes.

Three minutes went by. Then five. Eight. Nine. Ten.

I'm safe enough here. It won't hurt to wait just a bit more. The mustangs will tell me if anyone else is near.

Twelve minutes. Fifteen. Seventeen.

Janna had reached eighteen when the mustangs lifted their heads and turned to watch the mouth of the gully with pricked ears and no nervousness whatsoever. Minutes later Ty came scrambling up out of the ravine.

"I told you—ten minutes," he said, breathing heavily.

"I don't know how to c-count," Janna said, trying to blink back tears and laughter at the same time.

Ty swung up on Lucifer, brought the stallion alongside Zebra and gave Janna a fierce kiss.

"Sweet liar."

Ty smacked Zebra hard on the rump, sending the mare into startled flight. Lucifer leaped to follow. Together the two mustangs settled into a ground-covering gallop. The plateau's rumpled surface flew beneath their hooves.

Twice Janna and Ty heard gunfire. Each time they veered more to the east, for the sounds were coming from the north and west. About every ten minutes Janna would slow the pace to a canter, allowing the horses to catch their breath. Despite the itching of his backbone, Ty never complained about the slower pace. He knew that the mustangs might be called upon to outrun Indians at any moment; the horses wouldn't have a prayer if they were already blown from miles of hard running.

During the third time of resting, the distant crackling of rifle fire drifted to Janna and Ty on the wind. This time the sound was coming from the east.

"Should we—" began Janna.

She was cut off by a curt gesture from Ty. He pulled Lucifer to a stop and sat motionlessly, listening.

"Hear it?" he asked finally.

"The rifles?"

"A bugle."

Janna listened intently. She was turning to tell Ty she couldn't hear anything when the wind picked up again and she heard a faint, distant cry rising and falling.

"I hear it. It must be coming from the flatlands."

"Where's the closest place we can get a good look over the edge?" Ty asked.

"The eastern trailhead is only a few miles from here."

Janna turned Zebra and urged the mare into a gallop once more, not stopping until she came to the crumbling edge of the plateau where the trail began. Lucifer crowded up next to Zebra and looked out over the land, breathing deeply and freely, appearing for all the world as though he had barely begun to tap his strength.

Ty examined the land through his spyglass, sweeping the area slowly, searching for signs of man. Suddenly he froze and leaned forward. Six miles north and east of his present position, a small column of cavalry was charging over the land, heading south, sweeping a handful of renegades before it. Well behind the first column of soldiers, a larger one advanced at a much more sedate pace.

Ty swung the spyglass to look to the south, closer in to the plateau's edge.

"Christ almighty," Ty swore. "Cascabel's got an ambush set up where the trail goes through a ravine. That first group of renegades is the bait. He's got enough warriors hidden to slaughter the first group of pony soldiers before the rear column can get there to help."

"Can we get down in time to warn them?"

Grimly Ty looked at the trail down the east face of the plateau. It was even more precipitous than he had remembered. It was also their only hope of getting to the soldiers before Cascabel did.

"Would it do any good to tell you to stay here?" Ty asked.

"No."

"You're a fool, Janna Wayland."

Ty jerked his hat down on his forehead, settled his weight into the rope stirrups, gave a hair-raising battle cry and simultaneously booted Lucifer hard in the ribs.

The stallion lunged over the rim and was launched onto the steep trail before he had a chance to object. Front legs stiff, all but sitting on his hocks, Lucifer plunged down the first quarter mile of the trail like a great black cat. In helping the stallion not to overrun his balance, Ty braced his feet in the rope stirrups and leaned so far back that his hat brushed the horse's hard-driving rump.

When Lucifer stumbled, Ty dragged the horse's head back up with a powerful yank on the hackamore reins, restoring the stallion's balance. Surrounded by flying grit and rolling, bouncing pebbles, horse and rider hurtled down the dangerous slope.

Zebra and Janna followed before the dust had time to settle. As had the stallion, Zebra sat on her hocks and skidded down the steepest parts, sending dirt and small stones flying in every direction. Janna's braids, already frayed by the wind, came completely unraveled. Her hair rippled and swayed with every movement of the mustang, lifting like a satin pennant behind her.

When Lucifer gained the surer footing on the lower part of the trail, Ty risked a single backward look. He saw Zebra hock-deep in a boiling cloud of dirt and pebbles, and Janna's hair flying behind. The mustang spun sharply sideways, barely avoiding a stone outcropping. Janna's body moved with the mare as though she were as much a part of the mustang as mane or tail or hooves.

Lucifer galloped on down the sloping trail, taking the most difficult parts with the surefootedness of a horse accustomed to running flat out over rough country. Ty did nothing to slow the stallion's pace, for each second of delay meant one second nearer to death for the unsuspecting soldiers in the first column. As soon as the trail became more level, Ty pointed Lucifer in the general direction of the advancing column, shifted his weight forward over the horse's powerful shoulders and urged him to a faster gallop.

When Zebra came down off the last stretch of the eastern trail, she was more than a hundred yards behind Lucifer. But Janna knew the country far better than Ty. She guided Zebra on a course that avoided the roughest gullies and rocky rises. Slowly the mare began to overtake Lucifer, until finally they were running side by side, noses outstretched, tails streaming in the wind. Their riders bent low, urging the mustangs on.

Rifle fire came like a staccato punctuation to the rhythmic thunder of galloping hooves. A lone rifle slug whined past Ty's head. He grabbed a quick look to the right and saw that the Indians apparently had abandoned the idea of leading the soldiers into a trap. Instead, the renegades had turned aside to run down the great black stallion and the spirit woman whose hair was like a shadow of fire. Even Cascabel had joined the chase. Dust boiled up from the ambush site as warriors whipped their mounts to a gallop and began racing to cut off Janna and Ty from the soldiers.

Ignoring the wind raking over his eyes, Ty turned forward to stare between Lucifer's black ears, trying to gauge his distance from the column of soldiers. Much slower to respond than the renegades, the cavalry was only now beginning to change direction, pursuing their renegade quarry along the new course.

It took Ty only a few moments to see that the soldiers were moving too slowly and were too far away to help Janna and himself, whose descent from the plateau had been so swift that they were much closer to Cascabel than to the soldiers they had wanted to warn of the coming ambush. What made it worse was that the renegades who had waited in ambush were riding fresh horses, while Zebra and Lucifer had already been running hard for miles even before the hair-raising race down the eastern trail. Now the mustangs were running flat out over the rugged land, leaping ditches and small gullies, whipping through brush, urged on by their riders and by the whine of bullets.

Ty knew that even Lucifer's great heart and strength couldn't tip the balance. The soldiers were simply too far away, the renegades were too close, and even spirit horses couldn't outrun bullets. Yet all that was needed was two minutes, perhaps even just one. With one minute's edge, Janna's fleet mustang might be able to reach the soldiers' protection.

Just one minute.

Ty unslung his rifle and snapped off a few shots, knowing it was futile. Lucifer was running too hard and the country was too rough for Ty to be accurate. He hauled on the hackamore, trying to slow the stallion's headlong pace so that he could put himself between the renegades and Janna. Gradually Zebra began pulling away, but not quickly enough to suit Ty. He tried a few more shots, but each time he turned to fire he had to release the hackamore's knotted reins, which meant that Lucifer immediately leaped back into full stride.

Dammit, horse, I don't want to have to throw you to make you stop. At this speed you'd probably break your neck and I sure as hell wouldn't do much better. But we're dead meat for certain if the renegades get us.

And I'll be damned in hell before I let them get Janna.

Ty's shoulders bunched as he prepared to yank hard on one side of the hackamore, pulling Lucifer's head to the side, which would unbalance him and force him to fall.

Before Ty could jerk the rein, he heard rifle fire from ahead. He looked over Lucifer's ears and saw that a group of four horsemen had broken away from the column of soldiers. The men were firing steadily and with remarkable precision, for they had the platform of real stirrups and their horses had been trained for war. The repeating rifles the four men used made them as formidable as forty renegades armed only with single-shot weapons. The horses the four men rode were big, dark and ran like unleashed hell, leaving the cavalry behind as though the soldiers' mounts were nailed to the ground.

For the second time that day, Ty's chilling battle cry lifted above the thunder of rifles and hooves; but this was a cry of triumph rather than defiance. Those were MacKenzie horses and they were ridden by MacKenzie men and Blue Wolf.

Janna blinked wind tears from her eyes and saw the four horses running toward her, saw the smoke from rifles and knew that had caused Ty's triumphant cry: the speed of the four horses had tipped the balance. They were going to reach Ty and Janna before Cascabel did.

"We're going to make it, Zebra. We're going to make it!"

Janna's shout of joy turned to a scream as Zebra went down, somersaulting wildly, sending her rider hurtling to the ground.

Chapter Forty-Three

Before Janna hit the ground Ty was hauling back and to the right on the reins, forcing Lucifer into a hard turn. Despite the speed of Ty's reflexes, the stallion was galloping so fast that momentum alone swept them far past the place where Janna had fallen. Long before the stallion completed the turn, Zebra staggered to her feet to stand alone and trembling, favoring her left foreleg. Rifle fire erupted around her. She lunged to the side, seeking the cover of nearby piñons.

Ty saw the mare's three-legged motion and knew that she would be no help to Janna. A few yards from the mustang, Janna was struggling to her hands and knees, obviously dazed and disoriented by the force of her fall. A half mile beyond her, Cascabel and his renegades were bearing down in a cloud of dust and triumphant yells, certain that their prey was finally within their reach.

Measuring the distances involved, Ty quickly realized that Lucifer wasn't running fast enough to get Janna to safety before the Indians came within range. The stallion was straining, running with every bit of strength in his big body, but he was carrying more than three hundred pounds on his back.

Ty's knife flashed, severing the leather band that held the saddlebags full of gold on Lucifer's lathered body. The heavy pouches dropped away just as the mustang leaped a small gully. The gold vanished without a sign into the crease in the earth. Freed of the dead weight, Lucifer quickened his gallop.

"Janna!" Ty shouted. "Janna! Over here!"

Barely conscious, Janna turned toward the voice of the man she loved. She pushed hair from her eyes, forced herself to stand and saw Lucifer bearing down on her at a dead run. Ty was bent low over the horse's neck, giving the stallion all the help a rider could and at the same time calling for Lucifer's last ounce of speed.

Rifle slugs whined overhead and kicked up dirt around Janna. She noticed them only at a distance, as if through the wrong end of a spyglass, for she was concentrating on the wild stallion thundering down on her with Ty clinging like a cat to his black back.

A hundred yards behind Ty, four riders raced over the land like the horsemen of the Apocalypse, sowing destruction and death to any renegade within range of their rifles. The barrage of bullets slowed the charging Indians, who were unused to coming up against the rapid-fire rifles.

At the last possible instant, Ty twisted his right hand tightly into Lucifer's flying black mane and held his other hand out to Janna. He knew that he had to grab her and not let go— the momentum of the racing stallion would lift her quickly from the ground, allowing Ty to lever her up onto the horse's back.

"Get ready!" Ty shouted, hoping Janna could hear him.

His voice stitched between the war cries of the Indians behind Janna the erratic thunder of rifles and the drumroll of galloping hooves. She gathered herself and waited while Lucifer bore down on her like a runaway train. Despite the danger of being trampled, Janna didn't flinch or move aside, for she knew that her only hope of life lay in the man who was even now bending low over the stallion's driving body, holding his hand out to her.

Between one heartbeat and the next Janna was yanked from the ground and hurtled onto Lucifer's back just behind Ty. Automatically she scrambled for position, thrusting her arms around his waist and hanging on with all her strength while Ty hauled the mustang into a plunging, sliding turn that would take them away from the renegades. As the mustang straight-

ened out again, Ty let out another chilling battle cry. Lucifer
flattened his ears and his hooves dug out great clots of earth
as he gave his riders the last bit of strength in his big body,
running at a furious speed despite the additional weight he
was carrying.

Ty's battle cry came back to him doubled and redoubled as
the four horsemen bore down on him. They split evenly
around the lathered, hard-running stallion. Each man fired
steadily, making full use of the tactical superiority their repeating rifles gave. They were close enough now for accuracy,
even from the back of a running horse. The relentless rain of
bullets broke the first ranks of the charging renegades, which
slowed those who were immediately behind and confused
those who were on the sides.

A shout from the biggest MacKenzie sent all four horses
into a tight turn. Soon they were galloping hard in Lucifer's
wake, snapped at by sporadic rifle bullets from the disorga-
nized melee of renegades.

There were only a few warriors who gave chase, for
Cascabel had spotted the larger column of soldiers, which had
been galloping hard to catch the smaller group since the first
burst of rifle fire had come. Cascabel was far too shrewd to
fight the Army on its own terms. An ambush was one thing;
a pitched battle was another. The renegade leader turned his
horse and began shouting orders. In a short time the renegades
had reversed direction and were retreating at a dead run, pre-
serving their arms and ammunition for a better battleground.

The first group of soldiers swept by Ty and then the
MacKenzie brothers. Neither group broke pace. Not until the
brothers were within sight of the larger Army column did they
overtake Lucifer.

Knowing that it was finally safe, Ty slowed the stallion to
a walk, stroked the mustang's lathered neck and praised him
over and over. The biggest of the MacKenzie brothers reined
in alongside.

"That's one hell of a horse you're riding. Am I to presume
he's the fabled Lucifer?"

Ty's flashing grin was all the answer that was needed.

"Then that must be your famous silken lady riding postil-ion," the man said dryly.

Janna flinched and looked away from the tall rider's odd, golden-green eyes. She knew instantly that this man must be Ty's brother, for surely no two men could look so alike and be unrelated. Tall, powerful, dark haired—on first glance he was Ty's twin. A second glance showed the differences; a hardness of feature, a sardonic curl to the mouth, eyes that summarized what they saw with relentless pragmatism.

"Janna Wayland, meet Logan MacKenzie, my older brother," Ty said.

Janna's arms tightened around Ty's waist. She didn't speak or turn her face from its hiding place just below his shoulder blades.

"Sugar? You're all right, aren't you?"

"Yes," she said, her voice muffled. "Can we go back for Zebra?"

Logan's black eyebrows lifted at the husky, tantalizing, feminine voice issuing from such a disheveled creature.

"No. Cascabel won't keep running. He'll split his forces and double back to pick off scouts, stragglers or anything else he can get in his sights before the sun sets."

"But—"

"No," Ty said roughly, interrupting. Then, more gently, "I'm sorry, sugar. It's just too dangerous for you. Zebra will be all right. Mustangs are tough. They have to be. She was limping off to cover before you even got to your hands and knees."

"Zebra?" Logan asked mildly. "Were you keeping a zoo?"

When Janna didn't answer, Ty said, "Zebra is a mustang. Janna talked her into becoming a friend."

Logan gave Ty a slanting green glance. "'Talked' her into it?"

"That's right, big brother. Talked. No ropes. No saddle. Not even a bridle or stirrups. Just those soothing hands and that sweet, husky voice promising all kinds of things...and then delivering each and every one of them."

Logan's eyes narrowed at the seething mixture of emotions he heard in Ty's voice—affection, anger, bafflement, passion.

"Seems she caught herself more than a zebra mustang that way," Logan muttered.

If Ty heard the statement, he ignored it.

A renewed clash of rifle fire came from behind. The second column of soldiers had just come within range of the fleeing renegades. A bugle's wild song rose above the sound of shots.

"Hope whoever is leading those soldiers knows his business," Ty said. "Cascabel had an ambush laid that would have wiped out the first column before reinforcements could arrive."

"So that's why the two of you came down like your heels were on fire. Case heard something and put the glass on the cliff. He knew right away it was you."

"Surprised Blue didn't spot me first. He's got eyes that would put an eagle to shame."

"Blue was talking with the lieutenant at the time, trying to convince the damned fool that we might be galloping into an ambush."

"And?"

"Blue was told that when the lieutenant wanted a breed's advice, he'd ask for it."

Ty shook his head in silent disgust. "Well, at least he'll keep Cascabel busy long enough for Janna to get clear. Cascabel made some strong vows on the subject of her hair."

Logan looked from his brother to the auburn-haired girl who had refused to face the MacKenzies after that first brief look. Logan remembered the flash of pain he had seen in Janna's face before she turned away. He reined back slightly, leaned over and slid his hand beneath her chin. Gently, firmly, he turned her face toward himself.

"Easy, little one," Logan said soothingly. "No one's going to hurt you. I just want to be sure you're all right. That was one hell of a header you took."

Reluctantly Janna turned toward Ty's older brother. Long, surprisingly gentle fingers touched the bruised spot on her cheek and the abrasion along her jaw.

"Feeling dizzy?" he asked.

"I'm all right. No double vision. No nausea. I didn't land hard enough to get a concussion."

"She knows what she's talking about," Ty said. "Her daddy was a doctor."

Black eyebrows rose again, then Logan smiled, softening the harshness of his face. "You'll do, Janna Wayland. You'll do just fine." He turned toward the other three riders. "Listen up, boys. This lady is Janna Wayland. Janna, the big one is Blue Wolf."

"Big one?" Janna asked, looking at the men surrounding her. "Are you implying that one of you is small?"

One of the riders tipped back his head and laughed, reminding her of Ty.

"The laughing hyena is Duncan," Logan said. "The dark-eyed, mean-looking one on the chestnut horse is Blue Wolf."

"Pleased to meet you, Janna Wayland," Blue Wolf said in educated tones, and his smile refuted the very idea of "mean." He tipped his hat to her and went back to scanning the countryside for danger.

"The quiet one is Case. He's the baby of the family."

Case nodded slightly to Janna. A single look at his pale green eyes told her that Case might have been the youngest in years but not in harsh experience. There was a darkness in him that transcended words. A wave of overwhelming sadness and compassion whirled up in Janna as she looked at Ty's youngest brother.

"Hello, Case," she said softly, as though she were talking to an untamed mustang.

Ty heard the emotion in Janna's words, smiled rather grimly to himself and said in a voice too low to carry to Case, "Save your sweetness for something that appreciates it, sugar. Except for blood family, Case has all the feelings of a stone cliff."

"Why?"

"The war."

"You went to war, too."

Logan looked over at Janna. "All the MacKenzie men fought," he said. "Case is the only one who won't talk about it. Not one word. Ever. Not even with Duncan, who fought at his side most of the time. Duncan doesn't talk much, either, but it's different somehow. He still laughs. Case doesn't.'' Logan shook his head. ''Damned shame, too. Case used to have the most wonderful laugh. People would hear him and stop and stare and then smile, and pretty soon they'd be laughing, too. No one could resist Case. He had a smile like a fallen angel.''

The clear regret on Logan's face changed Janna's opinion of him once more; despite his hard exterior, Logan was a man who cared deeply for his family. Rather wistfully, Janna wondered what it would have been like to grow up with that kind of warmth surrounding her. Her father had loved her, but in a rather distracted way, never really stopping to discover his daughter's needs and yearnings, always pursuing his own dreams and never asking about hers.

''What a sad smile,'' Logan said. ''Is your family back there?''

''Where?''

''In Cascabel's territory.''

''Not unless you could call Mad Jack family,'' Janna said. ''Besides, he ran off rather than hang around and be dragged to the fort. He knew how mad we would be about the gold.''

''Gold?'' Logan asked, looking at Ty.

''More than a hundred pounds of it.''

Logan whistled. ''What happened?''

''He gave us half and we promised to take half to his kids.''

''Where did you leave it?''

''We didn't,'' Janna said. ''It's in those saddlebags in front of Ty.''

Ty and Logan exchanged a look.

''It was too much for Lucifer to carry,'' Ty said. ''I cut it loose.''

Janna stiffened. ''But that was how you were going to buy your silken la—''

''One more word, Janna Wayland,'' Ty interrupted savagely, ''and I'm going to hand you over to that scalp-hunting renegade myself!'' He took a deep breath and struggled to leash his volatile temper. "Anyway, the gold isn't lost. Soon as I'm sure that Lucifer didn't hurt himself on that run, I'm going back for the saddlebags."

Janna wasn't surprised that Ty would risk his life looking for the gold once more, but she yearned to be able to talk him out of it. Hopefully she looked over at Logan. His smile didn't comfort her—it fulfilled the sardonic promise she had first noticed in the line of his mouth.

"So Janna isn't your silken lady after all?" Logan asked Ty. "Damned white of you to save her hide anyway at the cost of all that gold."

The cold, needling edge to Logan's tone didn't escape Ty. Nor did the censure in Logan's eyes, for he had realized that Ty was Janna's lover the first time Ty had called her sugar in a soft, concerned voice.

"Drop it," Ty said flatly.

Logan's smile changed indefinably, becoming almost sympathetic as he realized Ty's dilemma. For years Ty had been pursued by the finest that southern and northern society had to offer; he had turned everyone down in his own pursuit of a dream of the perfect silken lady. Now he found himself hopelessly ensnarled with a wild, gray-eyed waif whose voice could set fire to stone.

Logan leaned over and cuffed Ty's shoulder with rough affection. "Forget the gold, little brother. I'll turn Silver loose on your uncurried mustang lady. In a few weeks you'll never know she wasn't paddock born and raised."

Janna turned her face away, trying to conceal the red tide that climbed up her face as she thought of the unbridgeable gap between silk purses and sows' ears. Eyes closed, she held on to Ty, saying goodbye to him in silence, for she knew with bittersweet certainty that he would go after the gold...and she would walk away from the MacKenzies and never look back, freeing Ty to pursue his dream.

"You planning on taking her to Wyoming?" Case asked. Like his eyes, his voice was cool, passionless. He had been watching Janna with measuring intelligence.

Ty turned and glared at Case. "Yes. You have any objections?"

"Not a one."

Ty waited.

"She doesn't want to go," Case added matter-of-factly.

"She'll go just the same."

"Is she carrying MacKenzie blood in her womb?"

If anyone else had asked that question, Ty would have beaten him into the ground. But Case wasn't anyone else. Because Case had destroyed or walled off all emotion within himself, he didn't concede its presence in anyone else.

"She could be carrying my child," Ty said tightly.

"Then she'll be in Wyoming when you get there."

With no warning Case bent over, plucked Janna from Lucifer's back and put her across his saddle.

"Ty!"

"It's all right. Case will take good care of you." Ty smiled oddly. "Don't try running from him, sugar. He's the best hunter of all of us."

Chapter Forty-Four

"They must have magic mirrors in Wyoming," Janna said, looking in disbelief at her own reflection. "That can't be me."

Silver MacKenzie smiled, touched up the dusting of rouge on Janna's cheeks and stepped back to view the results. "It's amazing what three weeks of regular food and sleep can do for a body, isn't it?"

"More like four," Janna said.

Silver's ice-blue eyes closed for an instant as she composed herself; the thought of losing Logan made her heart freeze.

"I'm sure the men are all right," Silver said firmly. "It must have been harder to find the gold than they thought, that's all. Perhaps Ty couldn't remember precisely where he cut the saddlebags loose. You left rather in a rush, from what Case said."

Janna smiled wanly. "You could say that. At least, Ty was in a rush to get away."

"Speaking of getting away..." Silver began, changing the subject eagerly.

A flush crawled up Janna's cheeks as she remembered the night after she had arrived in Wyoming. Case had dropped her rather unceremoniously at the doorstep, told Silver that Janna had come to be combed and curried like a paddock horse for Ty and that she might be carrying Ty's child. Silver had been sympathetic, Cassie had been angelic, and Janna had gone out the second-story window the first time everyone's back was turned.

The next morning a very tight-lipped Case had brought Janna back, set her on the doorstep and told her that she could give her word not to run until Ty came back or she could spend the time waiting for him trussed hand and foot like a chicken going to market.

"...now you know why men like their women dressed in yards of silk," Silver finished. She blew a wisp of moon-pale hair away from her lips as she bent and adjusted the voluminous skirt of Janna's cream silk ball gown.

"What?" asked Janna, distracted by her memories.

"We can't run worth a darn for all the hoops and flounces, that's why. The best we can manage is a serene face and a dignified, very slow exit."

Janna smiled just as Silver straightened. The older woman stared, arrested by the sight Janna made. Her dark auburn hair was piled high in deceptively simple coils, which had been threaded through with strings of pearls. Pearls circled her neck in a delicate choker whose centerpiece was a ruby that had been in Silver's family for three hundred years. Earrings of pearl and teardrop rubies hung from Janna's ears. The ball gown's off-the-shoulder style dipped to a modest point in the front. The hint of a shadow between Janna's breasts was as seductive as the lines of the ball gown were simple. A brooch of ruby and pearls was pinned at the base of the gentle décolletage. With each breath, each movement, ruby fire shimmered, echoing the secret fire of Janna's hair.

"Shadow of Flame," Silver murmured. "The renegades saw you very clearly, didn't they? You're really quite stunning. The dress looks far better on you than it ever did on me, as do the rubies."

"It's very kind of you to say so."

"The truth is rarely kind," Silver said grimly.

Janna saw the shadows of worry on Silver's face and knew that she was concerned about her husband.

"I'm sure Logan is all right," Janna said. "He's a smart, tough man."

''All the MacKenzies are smart and tough. Even the women. You'll fit in just fine.''

There was silence, then Janna said huskily, ''Ty wanted something different in his wife.''

''Ah, yes, Ty's famous silken lady.'' Silver saw Janna wince. ''Don't worry, he'll take one look at you and see the woman of his dreams. He may be MacKenzie stubborn but he's not stone-blind.''

Tears ached behind Janna's eyes at hearing her own secret dream spoken aloud. The hope of having Ty turn to her and see his silken lady was so overpowering that she was helpless against it. That, as much as Case's threat, had held her in Wyoming.

Silver's hand rested lightly on Janna's cheek. ''Does he know how much you love him?''

Janna nodded slowly and whispered, ''It wasn't enough. His dream…''

''It was the war, Janna. Each MacKenzie responded to it differently. Logan wanted revenge.'' Silver's mouth turned down in sad remembrance. ''He found it, but it wasn't what he thought it was. I think Ty will discover that silk isn't what he thought it was, either.''

A call came from the front of the house. Both women froze in wild hope before they realized that it was Case greeting guests rather than Case announcing the return of Blue Wolf and the MacKenzie brothers. But Janna had to be sure. She ran to the window and looked out. The first of the guests were indeed arriving.

''I still find it hard to believe that there are lords and ladies running loose about Wyoming,'' Janna said.

Silver smiled wryly. ''Unfortunately, it's true. What's worse, I'm related to most of them by blood or marriage.'' She looked out the window. ''Those specimens are Cousin Henry's guests. They don't actually live in Wyoming. They just came here to hunt.'' She sighed and shook out the folds of her skirt so that it fell properly. ''I'd better go meet them. Case has impeccable manners, but he tires of the game very quickly. I don't want Melissa to drive him away before the ball even begins. He's a marvelous dancer. Almost as good as Ty."

"I can't imagine a woman driving Case anywhere."

"It's my fault, really," Silver said as she hurried out the bedroom door, her ballgown billowing gracefully. "I made him promise not to hurt Melissa's feelings. Case takes promises very seriously. Come down as soon as you're ready, but don't be too long. Everyone is dying to meet you. Women are so rare in this place. Especially young and pretty women."

Janna looked in the mirror for a moment longer. A stranger looked back at her, a woman not unlike her mother in elegant appearance, but a stranger all the same. Janna wondered if she would ever become used to dresses and rustling folds of cloth. Even after nearly a month, she was still aware of the muffling yards of material swathing her legs and the contrasting snugness of bodice and waist. Even if the cloth had allowed her to run, the tight waist would have made deep breathing impossible. The shoes were the hardest to bear, however. They pinched.

She looked toward the armoire, where her father's hand-me-downs hung. She had washed and mended the clothes very carefully, for they were all that she could call her own. Her moccasins were patched as well, using doeskin she had traded a few of her precious herbs to obtain. Her canteen, medicine pouch and ragged blanket roll were set aside, waiting to be picked up on a moment's notice.

Maybe I won't need them. Maybe Ty will look at me and see a woman he could love. Maybe...

With hands whose creamy softness still surprised Janna from time to time, she reached into the medicine pouch and pulled out the sketch of her mother. Broodingly Janna looked from her reflection in the mirror to the sketch and then to her reflection again.

Will what he sees please him? Will he turn to me out of love rather than duty?

After a few minutes Janna set the sketch aside and went downstairs through the huge ranch house, which had been restored after a fire had all but razed it. She walked through rooms whose furniture had been shipped from England and France and whose rugs had come from China. She barely noticed the elegant furnishings. Nor did the sparkle of crystal reflecting candle flames catch her eye. In her mind she was once again in the secret valley, where Ty was holding out his arms to her with a smile on his face and love in his eyes.

Janna went through the ritual of introductions and polite words, moving with a natural grace that enhanced the seductive rustling of silk around her body. Men were drawn to her, both because of her restrained beauty and the natural thirst of men in a rough country for that which was soft and fragile. Janna was like the ruby between her breasts—clear yet enigmatic, sparkling yet self-contained, the color of fire yet cool to the touch. When the violins played she danced with men from neighboring ranches, men both titled and common, men who shared a common interest—Janna—and a common complaint—her lack of interest in them.

"May I have this dance?"

With a subdued start, Janna focused on the man who was standing between herself and the blaze of candlelight from the buffet table. For one heart-stopping instant she thought that Ty had come back; then she realized that the familiar, broad-shouldered silhouette belonged to Case.

"Yes, of course," Janna said, extending her hand to take his.

Moments later she was whirling and turning to the stately strains of a waltz played by Silver on the grand piano. The music was rich and civilized, a brocade of sound embroidered upon the wilderness night. Case danced with the casual perfection of a cat stalking prey.

"I've been watching you," he said.

Janna looked up at his pale green eyes. "That's not necessary. I gave you my word. I'll keep that word."

He nodded. "I wasn't worried about that. I was afraid that you'd get to believing all the polite nonsense Silver's cousins and guests are pouring into your ear."

With a smile that hovered on the brink of turning upside down, Janna shook her head. "I know what I am and what

I'm not,'' she said huskily. "I'm not the 'fairest flower ever to bloom on the western land,' among other things. Nor am I a fool. I know what men hope to gain by flattering a woman." She met Case's eyes and said evenly, "Your brother didn't lie to me in any way, even that one. He always stated quite clearly that my feminine attractions were…modest.''

Case looked at the proud, unhappy set of Janna's mouth. "That doesn't sound like Ty. He always had a line of flowery speech that was the envy of every man around."

"Flowers and silk go together."

"And you weren't silk, so he saved the flowers and got right down to business, is that it?"

Janna's eyelids flickered. It was the only sign of her pain, but Case saw it. As Ty had warned her, Case was the best hunter of all the MacKenzies. Nothing escaped his cool, dispassionate eyes.

"No, I wasn't silk," Janna agreed huskily.

"But you are now."

She smiled sadly and said nothing.

One of Cousin Henry's guests cut in. Janna tried to remember his name, but nothing came to her mind except the memory of the young man's intense, hungry eyes watching the ruby brooch shift and shimmer with her breaths. She prayed for the waltz to end, freeing her.

"Are all western women so charmingly quiet?"

Janna opened her mouth to answer. Nothing came out except a soft, startled sound when the waltz ended in an abrupt jangle of notes. She looked over at the piano in time to see Silver lifted into Logan's arms for a kiss that conceded nothing to silk or ritual politeness.

"They're back!" Janna said.

She looked around frantically but saw only one tall, roughly dressed man mingling with the guests—Blue Wolf, not Ty. Then she felt a tingling all the way to her fingertips. She turned and saw Ty standing at the doorway. He was leaning against the frame, his arms crossed over his chest and his eyes narrowed. Slowly he straightened and began walking toward her.

As he closed in on her, there was no welcoming smile on his bearded face. There was only anger.

"Willie," Ty said coldly, "your nanny is looking for you."

For a moment the young aristocrat holding Janna thought of taking the insult personally; then he shrugged and handed Janna over to Ty.

"Apparently this dance belongs to the rude frontiersman?"

When Janna didn't object, the man bowed and withdrew. Ty ignored him completely, having eyes only for the *bruja* who stood before him gowned in silk and shimmering with gems.

The waltz began again, played by four hands. Ty took Janna into his arms, holding her too close for propriety. He moved with the graceful, intricate, sweeping motions of an expert dancer. An equally expert partner could have followed him, but Janna was new to ball gowns and dips and whirls. Inevitably she stumbled. He took her weight, lifted her, spun her dizzyingly until she had to cling to his arms for support.

"Ty, stop, please."

"Why? Afraid those fancy Englishmen will see you holding on to me?" Ty's narrowed green eyes glittered coldly at Janna through his black eyelashes. His voice was equally icy. "Not one of those titled fops would touch you if they knew your past. When they see past the silk they'll be furious at the joke you've played on them."

"Men never look past the silk."

"I've looked, Janna Wayland. I know what's beneath all the finery—and it sure as hell isn't a fragile silken lady."

The words sank into Janna like knives, killing the last of her foolish hope. A feeling of emptiness stole through her as she realized that no matter how she dressed she would never be Ty's dream, for he would always look at her and see the ragged waif dressed in men's clothes.

Silk purse. Sow's ear. Never the twain shall meet.

Janna tried to turn away from Ty, but his fierce grip on her never wavered. She would have fought despite all the people around, but even if she had won free she would still have been trapped within swath after swath of silk. Silver had been right:

men preferred silk because it prevented women from running off.

Janna was in a silken prison. There was no escape, no place of concealment for her but deep within herself. Yet even then her tears gave away her hiding place.

Case tapped Ty firmly on the shoulder. "This dance is mine."

Ty turned on his younger brother with the quickness of a cat. "Stay out of it."

"Not this time," Case said matter-of-factly. "I brought her here, forced her to stay here until you came back, and now you're spoiling the Thanksgiving ball Cassie has looked forward to all year. Your family deserves better than that, don't you think?"

Ty looked beyond Case and saw Blue Wolf starting through the throng in Ty's direction. He knew that Blue was even more protective of Cassie than Case was. Then Ty spotted Duncan and Logan closing in on him with grim expressions.

Silver began playing a waltz again. Its slow, haunting melody recalled formal summer gardens and elegant dancers glittering with gems. Calmly, Case disengaged Janna from Ty's arms. As Case whirled Janna away, he said over his shoulder, "Go take a bath. You aren't fit company for anything but a horse."

Without a word Ty turned and stalked off the dance floor, shouldering aside his brothers.

Behind him Case and Janna danced slowly, gracefully, for Case matched his demands to his partner's skill. When the final strains of the waltz dissipated among the candle flames and rainbows trapped within crystal prisms, Case and Janna were standing at the doorway. He held her hand and looked at her for a long moment.

"Cassie told me you aren't pregnant," Case said finally. "I'm sorry. A child with your grit and grace and Ty's strength and fancy speech...well, that would have been something to see."

Janna tried to smile, couldn't, and said simply, "Thank you."

"There's a fiesty zebra dun in the corral. That fool brother of mine packed more than a hundred pounds of gold all over Utah Territory for three weeks looking for that zebra mare. Sixty pounds of that gold is now in a bank waiting for you to draw on it. The MacKenzies will honor Ty's promise to see that Mad Jack's half gets to his kids."

"Half of my gold is Ty's."

Case shook his head. "No."

Janna started to object again. Case watched her with the patience of a granite cliff. She could object all she wanted and nothing would change.

When Case saw that Janna understood, he bowed to her more deeply than custom required and released her hand.

"You're free, Janna. All promises kept."

Chapter Forty-Five

The oil lamps in Janna's room turned her tears to gold, but that was the only outward sign of her unhappiness. Cream leather shoes stood neatly next to the armoire. Pale silk pantalets were folded neatly on the chair. Hoops and petticoats were hung out of the way. Earrings and necklace and brooch rested in an open, velvet-lined box. All that stood between Janna and freedom was the maddening fastenings on her ball gown. The dress had been designed for ladies who had maids in attendance, not for a mustang girl who had nothing but her own ill-trained fingers and a burning need never to see or touch or be reminded of silk again.

"Allow me."

Janna spun so quickly toward the door that candle flames bowed and trembled.

Ty stood in the doorway watching her, but he was a different man. Gone was the rough frontiersman. Ty was clean shaven except for a black mustache. He smelled of soap and wore polished black boots, black slacks and a white linen shirt whose weave was so fine it shone like silk. He looked precisely like what he was: a powerful, uncommonly handsome man who had been born and raised to wealth and fine manners, a man who had every right to require that the mother of his children be of equal refinement.

Janna turned away and said carefully, "I can manage, thank you. Please close the door on your way out."

There was silence, then the sound of a door shutting behind Janna's back. She bit her lip against the pain ripping through her body.

"A gentleman never leaves a lady in distress."

Janna froze with her hands behind her back, still reaching for the elusive fastenings that held her confined within a silken prison.

"But I'm not a lady, so your fine manners are wasted. Nor am I pregnant, so you needn't feel dutiful."

The bleakness of Janna's voice made Ty's eyes narrow. He came and stood behind her, so close that he could sense her warmth.

"Case told me," Ty said.

His nostrils flared at the fragrance of crushed roses that emanated from her skin and hair. Memories blazed for an instant in his eyes. He brushed her hands away from the fastenings that went down the back of her dress.

"You're a satin butterfly," Ty said, unfastening the dress slowly, feeling a hunger to touch her that was deeper and more complex than a desire, a hunger that tightened his body as each tiny hook silently gave way, revealing a bit more of Janna's skin. "And I'm going to release you from your cocoon."

Ty's long index finger traced the graceful centerline of Janna's back. She made a stifled sound as the dress fell away, leaving her naked. Ty had never seen anything quite so beautiful as her elegant feminine curves. He traced her spine once more, following it to the shadow crease of her hips.

"During the war, Case kept his sanity by walling off his emotions," Ty said quietly. "I kept my sanity in a different way. I swore that I would never see such ugliness again. If I survived, I vowed to surround myself with fine and fragile things that had never known even the shadow of violence and death. Every time grapeshot ripped through living flesh, every time I saw young children with empty eyes, every time one of my men died…I renewed my vow."

Eyes closed, body trembling, Janna felt the lingering caress of Ty's fingertip tracing her spine; but it was the pain in his voice that broke her heart and her control. She had loved him recklessly, without regard for the future cost. Now the future had come to demand its reckoning.

"It's all right, Ty," she said huskily. "I understand. You've earned your silken lady. I won't—"

Janna's voice shattered as Ty's hands caressed the length of her back before smoothing up her torso until her breasts were cupped in his hands.

"Run away?" Ty offered, finishing Janna's sentence for her. The feel of her nipples hardening at his lightest touch made blood rush in a torrent through his body. "That's good, because touching you makes me so damn weak that I can hardly stand, much less run after you." With aching gentleness he caressed the breasts whose textures and responsiveness never ceased to arouse him. "So soft, so warm. No, hold still, love. It's all right. We're going to be married just as soon as I find the strength to leave this room and round up a preacher."

"Ty..." Janna's throat closed around all the tears she hadn't shed, all the dreams that couldn't come true. "You have to let me go."

"Why?" His long fingers shaped her, caressed her, made her tremble with a wild longing. "You want me as much as I want you. Have I told you how much I like that? No games, no coyness, just the sweet response of your body to my touch."

Janna bit off a telltale moan and asked desperately, "Did your parents love each other?"

Ty's hands stilled in surprise. "Yes. Why?"

"Think how you would have felt if they hadn't. Think how a child would feel growing up and knowing that his father felt a combination of desire and duty and disappointment toward his mother. Your child deserves better than that. So do you. And," Janna added softly, "so do I. Seeing you, having your body but not your heart... It will break me, Ty. Is that what you want?"

Gently Ty turned Janna around. She met his eyes without evasion despite the slow, helpless welling of her tears.

"Janna," he said softly, bending down to her, "I—"

She turned her head aside and spoke quickly, interrupting Ty, words tumbling out in a desperate effort to be heard. "No. Please listen to me. Please. I may not be fine or fragile, but even mustang ladies can be broken. You said once you owed me more than you could ever repay. You can repay me now. Let me go, Ty. *Let me go before I break.*"

Eyes closed, hands clenched into fists at her side so that she wouldn't reach for the man she loved too much ever to cage, Janna waited for Ty to leave. She heard him make a hoarse sound that could have been anger or pain, sensed currents of air moving as he moved, and she trembled with the violence of her emotions.

Tears touched the sensitive skin between her breasts, and she was shocked to know how hot her own tears were. Then she felt Ty's cheek against her body, saw him kneeling at her feet, felt his arms close tightly around her waist, and she realized that the scalding tears weren't her own.

Moved beyond words, Janna stroked Ty's hair with trembling hands, feeling as though she were being torn apart. She had thought she could leave him, but every instant she was with him told her how wretched life without him would be.

"I won't let you go," Ty said finally. "Don't ask me to. Don't beg me to. I can't do it, Janna. I need you too much."

"Ty, don't," she whispered achingly, trying to still the trembling of her body, failing. "I want so much for you to have your dream."

"I dreamed of you every minute I was away. You're my dream, Janna. I went back to get that gold for you, not for myself. I couldn't close my eyes without seeing you, couldn't lick my lips without tasting you, couldn't sleep for wanting you. Then I walked into that ballroom and saw the perfect silken lady of my dreams dancing with the perfect silken man. *And I wasn't that man.* I went—crazy. I wanted very much to kill that high-nosed son of a blue-blooded bitch for even looking at you."

"But you said—you said that you'd seen past the clothes, that I wasn't a fragile silken lady."

"Yes, I'd seen past the clothes, and I thank God for it."

Ty turned his head slowly, kissing the smooth breasts that smelled of roses.

"Listen to me, Janna. There's far more to being a lady than silks and bloodlines. A true lady is more concerned with the needs of the people around her than she is with the state of her wardrobe. A true lady gives succor to the sick, laughter to the lonely, respite to the weary. And to one very, very lucky man, a true lady gives herself...and asks nothing in return but that she be allowed to give the gift of her love."

Ty smoothed his cheek between Janna's breasts, absorbing the beauty of her living warmth. "That kind of gift is so rare that it takes a man by surprise."

He kissed the velvet tips of Janna's breasts, smiled to hear her breath break and tremble even as her body did. His mouth caressed the smooth skin of her stomach and the auburn cloud at the apex of her thighs.

"My sweet satin butterfly," he said in a low voice. "Let me love you again." His hand eased between her legs and he groaned to feel her heat once more. "Janna...please, let me."

Janna's knees gave way at the first gliding penetration of his caress. Ty's arm tightened, holding her still for a searing instant while he was still within her warmth. Her breath unraveled as he slowly released her, leaving her body shimmering and without the strength to stand.

With a dark yet oddly tender smile, Ty caught Janna and came to his feet, taking the warm weight of her in his arms once more. He walked the few steps to the bed, put her on the fur coverlet and kissed her lips gently before he stepped back and unhurriedly removed his own clothes, watching her with smoldering green eyes the whole time.

When he was as naked as she, he lay next to her on the bed, gathered her against his body and kissed her as tenderly as though she were a frightened maiden. The caresses he gave her were equally restrained, almost chaste, but his words were elemental fire.

"Your body is all satin, strong and hot and sleek. You're

perfect for a man who is more rawhide than silk. For me, Janna. Just for me. You are...perfect.''

Janna's breath caught, then broke when Ty's hand smoothed down her body. She didn't deny him the intimate warmth he so gently sought. She could no more have refused him than she could have told her heart to stop beating. Nor could she hold back the shimmering pulse of her pleasure, the heat that welled up and overflowed at his touch; and she cried out his name with each pulse.

The evidence of Janna's need for him was an exquisite shaft of pleasure so intense that it was also pain. Ty groaned and sought her secret warmth once again, and once again she didn't deny him. Eyes closed, he bent and kissed her lips, her breasts, the taut curve of her belly, trying to tell her things for which there were no words. And then her fingers threaded lovingly through his hair and the words came to him.

''Once,'' Ty whispered, ''I saw Lucifer go to you, put his head into your hands with such trust that I was reminded of the legend of the unicorn and the maiden. It made me... restless, baffled, angry. I felt sorry for the unicorn, trapped by his reckless love.

''And then the maiden opened her hands and let the unicorn go, for she loved the unicorn too much to hold it against its will.''

Janna's fingers stilled until Ty's head shifted against her palms, asking to be stroked once more, asking to be held by her touch even as the unicorn had been held.

''The unicorn ran off and congratulated himself on his clever escape, and then...'' Ty turned slowly, covering Janna's body with his own. He touched the hot center of her just once, slowly, drawing a long, broken moan from her. ''And then,'' Ty whispered, watching Janna's eyes, ''the unicorn realized what a fool he had been. There was nothing in the forest as exciting as the maiden's touch, no beauty to equal her companionship, no pleasure as deep as the ease she had given his soul. So he went running back and begged to be given the maiden's gift once more.''

When Ty neither spoke nor moved to join their bodies, Janna's heart hesitated, then beat with redoubled strength.

"What did the maiden say?" she whispered.

"I don't know. Tell me, Janna. What did the maiden say to the unicorn?"

Tears magnified Janna's eyes. "I love you," she said huskily. "I'll always love you."

She felt the emotion that shuddered through Ty's strong body as he bent and kissed her tears away.

"Yes," Ty said, watching Janna's eyes. "I want you to be my wife, my mate, my woman, the mother of my children, the keeper of my heart, the light of my soul. I love you, Janna. *I love you.*"

Janna reached for Ty even as he came to her. Their bodies merged, softness and strength shared equally, defining and discovering one another in the same elemental moment. Ecstasy blazed as they lost and then found themselves, man and woman forever joined in the reckless, incandescent union known as love.

* * * * *

Dark Stranger

by Heather Graham

Chapter One

Summer, 1862
The Kansas/Missouri border

The hoofbeats were the warning. The relentless, pounding hoofbeats. The sound of them sparked a sense of primal fear deep inside Kristin. Strangely, before she'd first felt the staccato rhythm through the ground, she hadn't contemplated such a danger. The day had been too ordinary, and perhaps she had been too naive. She had expected a storm, but not of the magnitude that was to come.

It began with the stillness in the air. As she came along the path through the orchards from the river, Kristin paused. The breeze had dropped. The day had gone dead still. The sudden calm gave her a strange feeling, and she searched the sky. Overhead, she saw blue, a beautiful blue. No clouds marred that endless blue.

It was the calm before the storm, she thought. Here, on the Missouri side of the Kansas-Missouri border, storms were frequent and vicious. Blue skies turned to smoke, and vicious twisters whirled out of nowhere.

Then she heard the hoofbeats.

She looked out across the plain that stretched away from the house. A tumbleweed caught by a sudden gust of wind blew across a patch of parched earth.

Bushwhackers.

The word came unbidden to her mind, and raw fear swept through her, fear and denial. Please, God, no...

Pa! Matthew, Shannon...

Kristin began to run. Her heart began to race, thundering along with the sound of the hoofbeats.

Pa was already dead, she reminded herself. They'd already come to kill him. They'd come, on a cloudless day, and they'd dragged him out in front of the house. He had drowned in a pool of his own blood while she had stood there screaming. There had been nothing, *nothing* she could do.

Matthew was safe. He'd gone off to join up with the Union Army near the Mississippi. He had said she would be safe. After all, they'd already killed Pa in his own front yard, killed him and left him bleeding.

Bleeding. They called it "bleeding Kansas," and though they were on the Missouri side of the border here, the blood ran thick and deep. The War Between the States had boiled down to a barbarian savagery here. Men did not just fall in battle here, they were cruelly, viciously executed—seized, judged and murdered. Kristin had few illusions; one side was almost as bad as the other. The dream of freedom, the dream of endless land and a life of dignity and bounty had drowned in rivers of blood. The dream was dead, and yet it seemed that was all she had left to fight for. Her father had died for it, and they thought she would flee, but she wouldn't. She couldn't. She had to fight. There was nothing else to do.

Shannon.

Cold dread caught in her throat. Shannon was up at the house. Young, frightened, vulnerable.

Her feet slapped against the dry earth as the hoofbeats came closer. How many of them were there? Maybe twenty, like the day they had come to kill Pa? Maybe not so many. Maybe they knew that Matthew had gone off to fight in the war and that no one remained behind but the girls, the foreman, a maid and a few young hands. She almost felt like laughing. They'd tried to take Samson and Delilah the last time they had come. They didn't understand that the two were free, able to make their decisions. Pa wasn't a fanatical abolitionist; he had just liked Samson, plain and simple, so he had freed them on the occasion of their marriage. Little Daniel had been born free, and they'd all come here together in search of the dream...

Kristin stumbled and fell, gasping for breath. The riders were just behind the trees to her left. She heard screams and shouts, and she knew they were slaughtering whatever cattle they could lay their hands on. This wasn't war.

This was carnage.

She staggered to her feet, smoothing back stray tendrils of hair still damp from her early-morning swim in the river.

They could hold the attackers off. She would be prepared this time. She wouldn't assume that some of these men would be old friends and acquaintants. She wouldn't assume that they were human, that they knew anything about morals or ethics or simple decency. She didn't think she would ever trust in such things again.

Suddenly, while Kristin was still several hundred yards from the house, the horsemen burst through the trees.

"Samson!" she screamed. "Samson! Get me Pa's six-shooter. Samson!"

Samson, a tall, dignified black man, burst through the front door. He glanced at Kristin, then at the horsemen racing through the corn, trampling the tender green stalks.

"Run, Miss Kristin, run!"

She could hardly breathe, could hardly speak. "Pa's Colt, get me the Colt! Tell Shannon to get to the cellar!"

"Samson, what is it?"

Samson turned to see Shannon standing behind him in the hallway.

"Bushwhackers," he said grimly. "Where's Delilah?"

"Out back, feeding the chickens."

She was in the barn. His wife was in the barn. God, he prayed silently, give her the good sense to stay there!

"Shannon," he told her, "you get yourself in the cellar."

She turned away, and Samson hurried back to the hallway, then paused. He thought he'd heard something around back.

When the sound wasn't repeated, he looked out the front door again. He could see the riders, and he could see Kristin running.

There were about twenty men, Samson reckoned. Just an offshoot of a bigger raiding party, probably. Some of Quantrill's raiders.

Quantrill himself was a damned butcher. He sanctioned the horror, and the death. Once upon a time he'd been friends with Gabriel McCahy, Kristin and Shannon's father, but one of his henchmen, a man named Zeke Moreau, had wanted Kristin. She hadn't wanted anything to do with him though. She was in love with Adam Smith. But Adam was dead now, too. Dead like her pa, dead like hundreds of men.

Now Zeke Moreau was coming back. He was coming for Kristin. Samson was sure of it.

"Samson!"

Her eyes met his, desperate, pleading.

Those might be God-fearing gentlemen out there, but if they captured a black man after he had leveled a Colt at them, even in his own defense, they would skin him alive.

It didn't matter. Gabriel McCahy had been the most decent man Samson had ever met. He would lose his skin over old Gabe's daughter if he had to.

He swung around, ready to rush into the house and get the guns. Then he paused, his eyes going wide and his throat closing up, hot and dry.

Zeke Moreau was already in the house. He was standing in the hallway, on the polished oak floor, and he had a double-barrelled shotgun leveled right at Samson.

A slight sound caught Samson's attention. He turned swiftly to see that another man was holding Delilah, one arm around her waist, a hand tight against her mouth.

"Watch it, Samson," Zeke said. "Be quiet now, or I'll hang you, boy. Hang you 'til you're dead. Then I'll see that your woman and your kid wind up on the auction block down Savannah way."

Zeke Moreau smiled slowly. He was dark-haired, with a dark, curling moustache, and Samson thought he would look more at home on a riverboat with a deck of cards than he did now, standing there in chaps and a vest, holding a shotgun. He was a good-looking man, except for his eyes. Cold, pale eyes, just like Kristin had always said.

Samson smiled back. "You murdered Gabriel, didn't you?"

Zeke rested his shotgun against his thigh. Samson was a big man, a good six-foot-six, and he was all muscle. But Zeke knew Samson wasn't going to move. Not while Delilah was being held.

"Now, Zeke, Gabe was my friend. He had some bad acquaintances, and he shot off his mouth too much, but I was mighty sorry to hear what happened to him. And it hurt me, hurt me bad, to hear about young Matthew running off to join up with them Yanks."

"Samson!"

He spun around at the sound of Kristin's voice. Just as she reached the steps, her voice rose in a sudden scream.

The horsemen had reached the steps, too and Kristin was trapped. She was choking in a cloud of dust as they circled her, chasing her back into the center of their trap every time she tried to elude them.

As Samson watched, she cried out and ran again. An Appaloosa ridden by a yellow-toothed scavenger in a railroad man's frock coat cut her off completely. She turned again, and the man rode closer, reaching down to sweep her up. She clawed at him, and Samson saw the blood run down the man's cheek. Kristin cursed and swore, fighting like a tigress. The Appaloosa reared and shrieked as its rider wrenched hard on the reins. The man struck out with a whip, and Kristin fell. As Samson watched, the Appaloosa reared again and again, its hooves just missing Kristin's face.

She didn't move, didn't flinch. She just stared up at the man, hatred in her eyes.

Samson charged toward the door, but Zeke stepped up behind him, slamming his head hard with the butt of his shotgun.

Kristin cried out as she saw him fall through the doorway, blood trickling down his forehead.

Then she saw Zeke. He stepped over Samson's body and

onto the porch. A man came from behind, holding Delilah. She screamed, and the man laughed, then threw her down on top of Samson. Sobbing, she held her husband.

The horses around Kristin went still, and the men fell silent.

Kristin got to her feet and stared at the man. She even managed a semblance of a smile.

"Why, Mr. Moreau, what a pleasure." Her voice dripped with sarcasm.

Zeke Moreau let out a long sigh. "Dear, dear Kristin. It just never seems to cross that little mind of yours that you're in deep trouble, girl."

"Trouble, Zeke? I'm not in any trouble. Trouble is something that's hard to handle. You're just a fly to be swatted away, nothing more."

"Look around, Kristin. You know, you've always been a real sassy piece of baggage. The boys and me, we think it's about time you paid for that. You *are* in trouble, honey. Deep trouble." He started walking toward her.

Kristin held her ground. She'd never known what it was like to hate before. Not the way she hated Zeke. Her hatred for him was fierce and intense and desperate. She stared at him and suddenly she knew why he had come, knew why he was moving slowly, why he was smiling. This was vengeance, and he meant to savor it.

She didn't give a damn. She wasn't even really frightened. She knew that she would scratch and claw and fight just as long as she was still breathing, as long as her heart was still beating. He couldn't understand that she had already won. She had won because she hated him so much that he *couldn't* really touch her.

Zeke kept walking toward her, his smile still in place. "Fight me, Kristin," he said softly. "I like it that way."

"You disgust me," she hissed. She didn't tell him that he would pay, didn't threaten revenge. There was no law to make him pay, and whatever revenge she dealt out would have to be now.

"You know, once upon a time, I wanted to marry you. Yeah, I wanted to head out to the wild, wild west and make you my wife. I wanted to hit the gold fields out in California, and then I wanted to build you a fine house on a hill and make you into a real lady.''

"I am a real lady, Zeke. But you're just dirt—and no amount of gold could make you anything but."

She raised her chin slightly. There was a hard core of fear inside her, she realized. This man didn't want her to die. He wanted her to pay. He wanted her to cry out in fear, wanted her to beg for mercy, and she was afraid that he could make her do it.

Zeke would never, never be prosecuted. No matter what he did to her.

He smiled and lunged toward her, and his men hooted and called from the backs of their mounts.

Kristin screamed. Then she grabbed a handful of the loose Missouri dirt, cast it into Zeke's eyes and turned to run.

The Appaloosa came at her again, with its dead-eyed rider. She tried to escape, but the animal reared, and she had to fall and roll to avoid its hoofs.

She heard Zeke swearing and turned to see that he was almost upon her again. The dirt clung to his face, clumps of it caught in his mustache.

She leaped up and spun toward him. The catcalls and whistles from the mounted men were growing louder and more raucous.

Escape was impossible. Zeke caught hold of her arms. She slammed her fists against his chest and managed to free herself. In a frenzy, she brought up her knee with a vengeance. Zeke let out a shrill cry of pain; his hold on her eased, and she broke free.

Someone laughed and before Kristin could gain her breath the back of Zeke's hand caught her. Her head swam, and she felt his hands on her again. Wildly, she scratched and kicked and screamed. Sounds rose all around her, laughter and catcalls and cheers. Her nails connected with flesh, and she clawed deeply. Zeke swore and slapped her again, so hard that she lost her balance and she fell.

He was quick. He straddled her while her head was still

spinning. The hoots and encouraging cheers were growing louder and louder.

She gathered her strength and twisted and fought anew. Zeke used his weight against her while he tried to pin her wrists to the ground. Gasping for breath, she saw that while she might be losing, Zeke's handsome face was white, except for the scratches she had left on his cheek. He was in a cold, lethal rage, and he deliberately released his hold on her to slap her again with a strength that sent her mind reeling.

She couldn't respond at first. She was only dimly aware that he had begun to tear at her clothing, that her bodice was ripped and that he was shoving up her skirt. Her mind cleared, and she screamed, then began to fight again.

Zeke looked at her grimly. Then he smiled again. "Bitch," he told her softly. He leaned against her, trying to pin her mouth in a savage kiss while his hands roamed over her.

Kristin twisted her head, tears stinging her eyes. She could probably live through the rape. What she couldn't bear was the thought that he was trying to kiss her.

She managed to bite his lower lip.

He exploded into a sound of pure rage and jerked away, a thin line of blood trickling down his chin.

"You want it violent, honey?" he snarled. "That's the way you're going to get it then. Got that, Miss High-and-Mighty?"

He hitched up her skirt and touched her bare thigh, and she braced herself for the brutality of his attack, her eyes shut tight.

Just then the world seemed to explode. Dirt spewed all around her; she tasted it on her tongue.

Her eyes flew open, and she saw that though Zeke was still posed above her he seemed as disoriented as she was.

Even the men on horseback were silent.

A hundred yards away, stood a single horseman.

He wore a railroad man's frock coat, and his hat sat low over his forehead, a plumed feather extending from it.

He carried a pair of six-shooters, holding them with seeming nonchalance. Yet one had apparently just been fired. It had caused the noise that had sounded like an explosion in the earth. Along with the six-shooters, there was a rifle shoved into his saddle pack.

His horse, a huge sleek black animal, began to move closer in a smooth walk. Finally he paused, only a few feet away. Stunned, Kristin stared at him. Beneath the railroad coat he wore jeans and a cotton shirt and he had a scarf around his throat. He wasn't wearing the uniform of either army; he looked like a cattleman, a rancher, nothing more.

Or a gunfighter, Kristin thought, bewildered.

His face was chiseled, strong. His hair was dark, lightly dusted with gray. His mustache and beard were also silvered, and his eyes, beneath jet-black brows, were silver-gray, the color of steel.

"Get away from her, boy," the stranger commanded Zeke. His voice was deep, rich. He spoke softly, but the sound carried. It was the voice of a man accustomed to being obeyed.

"Who's gonna make me?" Zeke snarled.

It was a valid question. After all, he was surrounded by his men, and the stranger was alone.

The man tipped his hat back from his forehead. "I'm telling you one more time, boy. Get off the lady. She doesn't seem to want the attention."

The sun slipped behind a cloud. The stranger suddenly seemed no more than a silhouette, an illusion of a man, atop a giant stallion.

Zeke made a sound like a growl, and Kristin realized that he was reaching for his Colt. She inhaled to scream.

She heard a sound of agony rend the air, but it wasn't hers. Blood suddenly streamed onto her chest. In amazement, she realized Zeke had cried out, and it was Zeke whose blood was dripping down on her. The stranger's bullet had struck him in the wrist.

"Fools!" Zeke shouted to his men. "Shoot the bastard."

Kristin did scream then. Twenty men reached for their weapons, but not one of them got off a shot.

The stranger moved quickly. Like double flashes of lightning, his six-shooters spat fire, and men fell.

When the shooting stopped, the stranger dismounted. His

guns were back in his gun belt, but he carried a revolver as he walked slowly toward her.

He tipped his hat to Zeke. "I don't like killing, and I do my damnedest not to shoot a man in cold blood. Now, I'm telling you again. Get away from the lady. She doesn't want the attention."

Zeke swore and got to his feet. The two men stared at one another.

"I know you from somewhere," Zeke said.

The stranger reached down and tossed Zeke his discarded Colt. "Maybe you do." He paused for just a moment, arching one dark brow. "I think you've outworn your welcome here, don't you agree?"

Zeke reached down for his hat and dusted it furiously against his thigh, staring at the stranger. "You'll get yours, friend," he promised softly.

The stranger shrugged in silence, but his eyes were eloquent.

Zeke smiled cruelly at Kristin. "You'll get yours, too, sweetheart."

"If I were you," the stranger said softly, "I'd ride out of here now, while I still could."

Furiously, Zeke slammed his hat back on his head, then headed for one of the now riderless horses. He mounted the animal and started to turn away.

"Take your refuse with you." The stranger indicated the dead and wounded bodies on the ground.

Zeke nodded to his men. A number of them tossed the dead, wounded and dying onto the skittish horses.

"You'll pay," Zeke warned the stranger again. Then his mount leaped forward and he was gone. The stranger watched as the horses galloped away. Then he turned to Kristin and she felt color flood her face as she swallowed and clutched her torn clothing. She stumbled to her feet.

"Thank you," she said simply.

He smiled, and she found herself trembling. He didn't look away gallantly. He stared at her, not disguising his bold assessment.

She moistened her lips, willing her heart to cease its erratic beating. She tried to meet his eyes.

But she couldn't, and she flushed again.

The day was still again. The sun was bright, the sky blue. Was this the calm before the storm?

Or had some strange new storm begun? Kristin could sense something in the air, an elusive crackling, as if lightning were sizzling between them. Something tense and potent, searing into her senses.

And then he touched her, slipping his knuckles beneath her chin.

"Think you might offer a drifter a meal, Miss—"

"McCahy. Kristin McCahy," she offered softly.

"Kristin," he murmured. Then he smiled again. "I could use something to eat."

"Of course."

She couldn't stop staring at him now, searching out his eyes. She hoped fervently that he couldn't feel the way she was trembling.

He smiled again and brushed her fingers with a kiss. Kristin flushed furiously, suddenly aware that her breast was almost bare beneath her torn chemise and gown. She swallowed fiercely and covered herself.

He lowered his eyes, hiding a crooked smile. Then he indicated Samson, who was just coming to in the doorway. "I think we should see to your friend first, Kristin," he said.

Delilah stood up, trying to help Samson. "You come in, mister," she said. "I'll make you the best meal this side of the Mississippi. Miss Kristin, you get in here quick now, too. We'll get you some hot water and wash off the filth of that man."

Kristin nodded, coloring again. "Shannon?" She whispered softly to Delilah.

"Your sister's in the cellar. Things seem to be all right. Oh, yes, bless the heavens, things seem to be all right."

The stranger started toward the steps, and Kristin followed, watching his broad shoulders. But then she paused and shivered suddenly.

He had come out of nowhere, out of the dirt and dust of the plain, and he had saved her from disaster and despair.

But Zeke Moreau had ridden away alive.

And Zeke Moreau would surely ride back, once the stranger had ridden on and she was alone again.

It wasn't over. Zeke had come for her once, and he would come again. He wasn't fighting for Missouri, for the South, for the code of chivalry. He was in this to loot, to murder, to rob—and to rape. He would come back for her. He sought out his enemies when they were weak, and he would know when she was weak again.

They would have to leave, she thought. This was her home, the only home she could remember. This land was a dream, a dream realized by a poor Irish immigrant.

But that immigrant lay dead. Gabriel McCahy lay with his Kathleen in the little cemetery out back. He lay there with young Joe Jenley, who had tried to defend him. The dream was as dead as Pa.

She couldn't just give it up. She had to fight the Zeke Moreaus of the world. She just couldn't let Pa's death be in vain.

But she had fought, and she had lost.

She hadn't lost, not this time. The stranger had come.

Kristin straightened, squared her shoulders and looked after the tall, dark man who was moving up her steps with grace and ease. The man with the set of six-shooters and the shotgun. The man who had aimed with startling, uncanny precision and speed.

Who was he?

And then she knew it didn't matter, she just didn't care. Her eyes narrowed pensively.

And she followed the curious dark stranger into her house.

Chapter Two

A fire burned warmly against the midmorning chill in the enormous kitchen. Even with her head back and her eyes closed, she could imagine everything Delilah was cooking from the aromas that surrounded her over the rose scent of her bath. Slab bacon sizzled in a frying pan along with hearty scrapple. There would be flapjacks, too, with melted butter and corn syrup. Delilah was also going to cook eggs in her special way, with chunks of ham and aged cheese. They were usually careful about food these days. If Quantrill's raiders didn't come looking to steal horses and cattle—or worse—the Union side would come around needing supplies. Kristin had long ago been stripped of all her illusions about the ethics of either side. There were men on both sides who claimed to be soldiers but were nothing but thieves and murderers. This wasn't a war; it was a melee, a bloody, desperate free-for-all.

It was amazing that the family still had enough to eat. There was the secret cellar, of course. That had saved them many a time. And today it didn't matter. Today, well, today they all deserved a feast.

The stranger deserved a feast.

The kitchen door was pushed open, and Kristin sank deeper into the bubbles that flourished in the elegant brass bathtub, an inheritance from Kristin's mother, who had dragged it all the way over from Bristol, in England.

She needn't have feared. It was only Delilah. "How you

doin' there, child?'' she demanded. She reached into the cabinet above the water pump and pulled out a bottle of Kristin's father's best Madeira. She set the bottle and a little tray of glasses on the counter and pulled the kettle off the kitchen fire to add more steaming water to Kristin's bath.

Kristin looked into Delilah's dark eyes. "I feel like I'm never going to get clean, Delilah. Never. Not if I wash from here to doomsday."

Delilah poured out the last of the water, warming Kristin's toes. Then she straightened and set the kettle down on the hearth. She walked over to the stove to check the bacon and the scrapple. "It could have been a lot worse," she said softly, staring out the window at the now deceptively peaceful day. "Thank the Lord for small miracles." She looked back at Kristin. "You hurry up there, huh, honey?"

Kristin nodded and even managed a small smile. "Do we have a name on him yet?"

The kitchen door burst open again. Kristin shrank back and Delilah swung around. It was Shannon, looking flushed, pretty and very excited.

"Kristin! You aren't out of there yet?"

Kristin looked at her sister, and she didn't know whether to be exasperated or relieved. She was still shaken by the events of the morning, but Shannon had put them all behind her. Of course, Shannon had been down in the cellar. And that was what Kristin had wanted. It seemed that everyone here had lost their innocence. The war didn't let you just stay neutral. Man or woman, a body had to choose a side, and you survived by becoming jaded and hardened. She didn't want that for Shannon. She wanted her sister to retain a certain belief in magic, in fantasy. Shannon had turned seventeen not long ago, and she deserved to be able to believe in innocence. She was so young, so soft, so pretty. Blue-eyed and golden blond, a vision of beauty and purity. Kristin didn't think she'd ever looked like that. When she looked at herself in the mirror she knew that the lines and planes and angles of her face were hard, and that her eyes had taken on an icy edge. She knew she looked much older than eighteen.

She had aged ten years in the last two. Desperation had taught her many lessons, and she knew they showed in her face.

"I'm coming out in just a minute, Shannon," Kristin assured her sister.

"Slater," Delilah said.

"Pardon?" Kristin asked her.

"Slater." Shannon came over to the bathtub, kneeling beside it and resting her elbows on the edge. "His name is Cole Slater."

"Oh," Kristin murmured. Cole Slater. She rolled the name around in her mind. Well, that had been easy enough. Why had she thought it would be so difficult to drag the man's name out of him?

Shannon jumped to her feet. "Kristin's never coming out of this old tub. Shall I get the Madeira, Delilah?"

"Sounds like someone's got an admirer," Kristin murmured.

"I'm trying to be polite," Shannon said indignantly. She arranged the little glasses on a silver serving tray. "Honest, Kristin, he's a right courteous fellow, and he told me I shouldn't rush you, says he understands you might feel you need a long, long wash. But I think you're just plain old rude and mean. And you know what else I think? I think you're afraid of him."

Kristin narrowed her eyes at her sister, tempted to jump from the tub and throttle her. But it was far more serious than that. "I'm not afraid of Zeke Moreau, or even Bill Quantrill and all his raiders, Shannon. I just have a healthy respect for their total lack of justice and morality. I'm not afraid of this drifter, either."

"But you *are* beholden to him," Delilah reminded her softly.

"I'm sorry," Shannon murmured.

When Kristin looked at her sister, she saw the pain that welled up in her eyes, and she was sorry herself. Shannon had lived through the same horrors she had. She just wasn't the eldest. She wasn't the one with the responsibility.

She smiled at Shannon. "Bring the Madeira on in, will you please? I'll be right out."

Shannon smiled, picked up the tray and went out of the kitchen. Kristin grinned at Delilah. "Pa's Madeira, huh? You must think highly of this drifter."

Delilah sniffed as she fluffed out the clean petticoat she'd brought down from Kristin's room. She sent Kristin a quick glare. "He ain't no ordinary drifter. We both know that. And you bet I think highly of him. Moreau might—just might—have left you alive, but he'd have hanged Samson. Slater kept my husband alive and he kept me from the block at the slave market. You bet I think highly of him."

Kristin grinned. From what she remembered of her lovely and aristocratic mother, she knew Kathleen McCahy would have been shocked by such blunt language. Not Pa, though. Pa had made himself a rancher and a farmer; he'd learned all the rough edges of the frontier. He'd have laughed at the plain truth of her statement. Then he'd have been grateful to have Delilah safe and sound, because she and Samson were part of the family, too.

"Want to hand me a towel, Delilah?" Kristin said, thinking again about the stranger who had arrived among them just in the nick of time. No, he wasn't any ordinary drifter, not judging by the way he handled a weapon. What was he, then? A gunslinger from down Texas way, maybe? Perhaps he'd come from farther west—from California, maybe. Somewhere he'd learned to make an art of the use of his Colts.

He made an art of the simple act of walking, too, she thought. She shivered suddenly, remembering the silence that had followed the sudden burst of gunfire. She remembered the way his eyes had looked as he'd ordered Zeke away from her. Slate-gray eyes, steel eyes, hard and merciless. She remembered the way his frock coat had fallen along the length of his tall body, remembered his broad shoulders, remembered the way he'd looked at her. A heat that didn't come from the water seemed to flutter to life deep inside her.

It hadn't been a romantic look, she reminded herself. She knew about romantic looks. She knew about falling in love.

It was easy and gentle. It was slow and beautiful. It was the way she had felt about Adam, and it was the way he had felt about her. When he had looked at her, he had looked into her eyes. He had held her hand, awkwardly at first. He had stuttered sometimes when he had spoken to her, and he had whispered tenderly to her. That was romance. That was love. She had never felt this shameful burning inside when she had been with Adam. She had been content to hold his hand. They had been content to sit and dream. She had never once imagined him...naked.

Appalled by her thoughts, she swallowed hard. She hadn't imagined any man naked, and certainly not this stranger. No, he had not given her any romantic looks. What he had given her was an assessment. It had been just as if he were studying a horse and liked what he saw, good bones and decent teeth. And then he had smiled, if not tenderly, at least with a certain gentility.

Still, the way he had looked at her...

And he had seen her nearly naked.

Color seemed to wash over her body. She rose to reach for her towel, then fell back into the water again, shamed by the way her breasts swelled and her nipples hardened. She prayed that Delilah hadn't noticed.

"You cold?" Delilah asked her.

Delilah had noticed.

Kristin quickly wrapped the big towel around herself. "A little," she lied.

"Get over by the fire. Dry off good and I'll help you get your clothes on."

Kristin nodded, rubbing her pink flesh dry. The fire warmed her, the flames nearly touching her. At least she would have an excuse for being red.

When she was finished she sank into the old rocker by the fire and Delilah brought over her corset, pantalets and stockings. Kristin quickly slid into the knit stockings and pantalets, and Delilah ordered her to hold her breath while she tied up the corset.

Kristin arched a tawny brow when she saw the dress Delilah

had brought down for her. It wasn't one of her usual cotton
day dresses. It was muslin, with soft blue flowers and double
rows of black-and-white lace edging along the puff sleeves,
the bodice and the hem. It was one of her best dresses.

"Delilah—"

"Put it on, child, put it on. We are celebrating here, remember?"

"Oh, yes." Kristin grinned, but then she started to shiver
again. She was afraid she was going to burst into tears. They
were never going to be done with it. They couldn't ignore it,
and they couldn't accept it. Pa had been murdered, and the
same—or worse—could have happened today. Today could
have been the end of everything.

They had been saved today, but it was only temporary. Zeke
would be back.

"Lordy, Lordy," Delilah said. She and Kristin hugged one
another, holding tight.

"What are we going to do?" Delilah said.

"We—we have to convince him to stay around a while,"
Kristin said softly.

"Think he needs a job, maybe?" Delilah said hopefully.

"Does he look like he needs a job?" Kristin said, smiling
shakily as she pulled away. She turned her back to Delilah.
"Hook me up, please."

Delilah started with the hooks, sweeping Kristin's bountiful
hair out of the way. When she was done she stepped back,
swirling Kristin around. She surveyed her broadly, then gave
her a big smile. "Miss Kristin, you're the prettiest little thing
I ever did see!"

Kristin flushed. She didn't feel pretty these days. She felt
tired and old and worn most of the time.

"Brush your hair now. Your little Chinese slippers are by
the door. Slip them on. And go out there and see what else
you can find out about that man beyond his name."

"Yes, yes," Kristin murmured. Delilah searched her pockets for a brush. Kristin stood on tiptoes to stare into the small
mirror on the kitchen door. She combed out her hair, leaving
it thick and free and a little wild. She looked too pale, she

thought. She pinched her cheeks and bit her lip. Then she thought about the man beyond the door again and all the color she could have wanted flooded into her face.

"Thanks," she said, handing the brush back to Delilah. Then she pushed the door open and hurried out.

She went through the family dining room first. Ma had always wanted a dining room, not just a table in the middle of everything else, as in so many ranch homes. Dining rooms were very proper, Ma had thought. And it was nice, Kristin decided now. The Chippendale table was covered with a lace cloth and with Ma's best silver, crystal and Royal Doulton plates. The table was set for three. The four young ranch hands they had remaining ate in the bunkhouse and she couldn't let a stranger know that she and Shannon usually just sat down with Samson and Delilah. Of course, they didn't use the silver or the crystal or the Royal Doulton every day, either.

After the dining room she came to the parlor. There was another big fireplace here, and a braided rug before it, over the hardwood floor. Large windows looked out on the sunshine. Ma had liked things bright, even though there were heavy velvet-and-lace curtains in crimson softened by white that could be closed at sunset to hold in the warmth. The furniture here was elegant, a small settee, a daybed and fine wood chairs, and a spinet that both girls had learned to play. It was a beautiful room, meant more for a lady than for a man. Kristin knew she would find the stranger and her sister in the next room, Pa's office and library. That was a far more comfortable room, with rows of books, a huge oak desk and a pair of deacon's benches that drew up to the double-sided fireplace.

Kristin was right. When she came through the parlor doorway, she saw that the stranger—no, Cole, his name was Cole Slater, and she had to stop thinking of him as the stranger—was indeed in this room. It was a great room. It smelled of pipe tobacco and fine leather, and it would always remind her of her father.

Cole Slater looked good here, as if he fit the place. He'd removed his plumed hat, his spurs and his railroad coat. Kristin paused, annoyed that she was trembling again just at the sight of him. He was a handsome man, she thought, though not in any usual way. He was far from pretty, but his steel-gray eyes were arresting, and what his face lacked in actual beauty it made up in strength. It was fine-boned yet powerful, sensual yet hard. And Kristin thought that she saw still more in his face. Cole Slater was another one who had lost all his illusions. She saw it when their eyes met. She studied him, and it was several long moments before she realized that he was studying her, too.

His knee was up, and his booted foot was resting against one of the footstools that seemed to have been cast haphazardly alongside the rows of books in the study. His boots were high, like cavalry-issue boots. His trousers hugged his long legs, betraying the lean muscles there, the trim line of his hips and the contours of his strong thighs and buttocks. His shoulders were broad, and he was tightly sinewed, and yet, he gave the appearance of being lean. A tuft of dark hair showed where his shirt lay open below his throat, and Kristin thought that his chest must be heavily matted with it.

Then she saw that his gaze was resting on her chest, too, and that just the hint of a smile was playing at the corners of his mouth. She almost lowered her lashes. Almost. She kept her eyes level with his and raised her chin a fraction. Then she inclined her head toward the glass of Pa's that he held—the little pony glass seemed ridiculously small contrasted with the size of his bronzed hand and the length of his fingers—and smiled graciously. "I see that Shannon has been taking good care of you."

He grinned at Shannon, who sat on one of the deacon's benches with a happy smile glued to her features. "Your sister is a most courteous and charming hostess."

Shannon colored with pleasure at the compliment. Then she laughed and jumped to her feet with the curious combination of grace and clumsiness that always reminded Kristin of a young colt. "I'm trying, anyway," she said. "And you two haven't been properly introduced. Miss Kristin McCahy, I give you Mr. Cole Slater. Mr. Slater, my sister, Miss Kristin McCahy."

Cole Slater stepped forward. He took Kristin's hand, and his eyes met hers just before his head lowered and his lips touched her hand. "I'm charmed, Miss McCahy. Quite charmed."

"Mr. Slater," she returned. She tried to place his accent, but she couldn't. He didn't sound as if he came from the deep South, and he didn't sound as if he came from any of the New England states. He wasn't a foreigner, but he didn't speak with the twang of the midwesterner, either.

He was still holding her hand. There was a feeling of warmth where his lips had touched her flesh, and the sensation seemed to seep into her, to enter into her bloodstream and head straight for the coil of liquid heat that churned indecently near the very apex of her thighs.

She pulled her hand away.

"We really don't know how to thank you, you know," she said, remaining still and seeking out his eyes again.

"I don't want to be thanked. I stumbled along at the right moment, that's all. And I'm damned hungry, and everything cooking smells damned good. A meal will make us even."

Kristin raised a brow. "You'll forgive me if I find my life, my friends, my sister, my sanity, my—"

"Chastity?" he offered bluntly.

"My person," she returned quietly, "are worth far more than a meal."

"Well, now..." He set his empty glass down, watching her thoughtfully. "I reckon that you are worth much, much more, Miss McCahy. Still, life isn't like a trip to the dry-goods store. I don't sell my services for any price. I was glad to be here when I was needed. If I helped you—"

"You know that you helped me. You saved all of us."

"All right. I helped you. It was my pleasure."

His voice matched his eyes. It wasn't quite a baritone, but it was still deep and full of the same hard, steely confidence. A drifter, a man who knew his guns. He had faced death out there today almost callously. Where did such a man come from?

Kristin stepped back. He was a tall man, more than six feet, and she was no more than five foot two. She felt more comfortable when there was a little distance between them.

And distance helped keep her heart from pounding, helped keep her blood from racing. Dismayed, she wondered what it was about him that made her feel this way. She never had before, not even with Adam.

Of course, not even Shannon could be completely innocent here. This was a working ranch, after all. Her father's prize bulls were the most valuable possessions he had left behind, and no matter how many of their cattle were stolen, Kristin knew they could start over with the bulls. But because of them and the other animals on the ranch, none of them could escape the details of the act of procreation.

Of course, watching the bulls made it all seem horribly crude. And nearly falling prey to the likes of Zeke Moreau made the bulls look like gentlemen of quality. She had never—never—imagined that a woman could actually wonder about what it would be like with a man, think about his hands touching her, think of his lips touching places other than her mouth.

She wanted to scream. She wondered suddenly if Cole could read her mind, for he was smiling again, and his smile seemed to reach into the heart and soul and heat of her. He knew.

She scowled and spun around, forgetting that he had saved her from a fate worse than death.

"I believe the meal that is worth so much to you is just about on the table, Mr. Slater. Shannon...let's all come along, shall we?"

Cole Slater followed his hostess through the parlor and into the formal dining room, suddenly and keenly aware of the soft scent of roses wafting from her flesh.

Then he noted that the fragrant flesh was as soft and smooth and tempting as cream silk. Her hair, loose around her shoulders, was like spun gold. And her eyes were level and filled with a surprising wisdom.

She was a very beautiful woman.

Outside, not so long ago, he had seen her differently. He had seen the Missouri dirt that had clung to her, and he had seen her spirit, but he had seen someone very young then. A girl, over-powered but fighting madly. Memory had clouded his vision, and he had seen the world through a brilliant red explosion.

He should have killed the bastard. No matter what his own past, no matter his codes when it came to dealing out death, that was one bastard he should have killed. Zeke Moreau. He had recognized Cole. Well, Cole had recognized Zeke, too. Zeke was one of the creatures that had been bred here in this den of blood, creatures that could shoot an unarmed man right between the eyes without blinking.

Zeke wanted this girl bad. No, this woman, he thought, correcting himself. She really wasn't a child. What was she? Twenty, perhaps? Older? Her eyes spoke of age, and so did the grace of her movements, and the confidence with which she spoke.

She was built like a woman.

Longing, hard and desperate, like a lightning bolt out of a clear blue sky, suddenly twisted and seared into him, straight into his groin, with a red-hot heat that was even painful.

He was glad he was walking behind her and Shannon. And he was glad his button-fly trousers were tight.

He clenched his teeth as another pain sizzled and burned in the area around his heart. This was a decent woman, this girl who had fought a strong man so desperately. Decent and still innocent, he imagined—thanks to his timely arrival.

This was the kind of girl men married.

Exhaling through clenched teeth, Cole wondered if there was a bordello anywhere nearby. He doubted it. There was probably a cold river somewhere, though. He would eat and then head out and hit that river.

Damn her, he thought suddenly, savagely. So she was innocent—maybe. The way she had looked at him had been too naked. He had seen too many things in her eyes. Too much that was sensual and tempting. He could have sworn she had been wondering about things that she shouldn't have been wondering about.

He would eat and then get out. And he would bear in mind

that his range of experience far surpassed hers. Did she think she could play cat and mouse with him? She might not know it, but she was the mouse.

Still, when she seated herself at the head of the table, he felt the lightning again. It filled the air when she spoke. It raced through him when she lightly brushed her fingers over his hand as she reached for the butter. It filled him when their knees brushed beneath the table.

"So…" She handed him a plate of flapjacks. "Where do you hail from, Mr. Slater?"

Kristin watched as the stranger helped himself to the flapjacks. He buttered them lavishly, then poured what seemed like a gallon of syrup over them. He shoveled a forkful into his mouth, chewed and swallowed, then answered her.

"Oh, here and there."

Here and there. Kristin sat back, dissatisfied.

Delilah came into the room, bringing more coffee. "Mr. Slater," she said, filling his cup again, "can I get you anything else?"

"Thank you, Delilah, no. This is one of the finest meals I've ever had."

Delilah smiled as if someone had just given her the crown jewels. Kristin sent her a glare over Cole's bowed head as he sipped his coffee.

Delilah nudged her firmly. Kristin sighed inwardly, and her eyes answered Delilah's unspoken question. She knew as well as Delilah that they needed Cole Slater.

"Where are you heading, Mr. Slater?" she asked.

He shrugged. "Just drifting at the moment, Miss McCahy."

"Well," Kristin toyed idly with her fork. "You certainly did drift into the right place for us this morning, sir."

He sat back, studying her in a leisurely fashion. "Well, ma'am, like I said, I'm right glad to be of service." She thought that was all he was going to say, but then he leaned forward, his elbows on the table, his steel-gray eyes on hers.

"How did you get on the wrong side of this Moreau man?" He paused again, just for a split second. "Isn't he one of Quantrill's boys?"

Kristin nodded.

Shannon explained, "She turned him down, that's what happened. Pa used to know Quantrill. The bastard—"

"Shannon!" Kristin protested.

Shannon ignored her. "They act like he's Jesus Christ come back to life, some places in the South—"

"Shannon! What would Pa say! You're supposed to be a lady!"

Shannon grimaced in exasperation and submitted reluctantly to Kristin's chastisement. "Oh, all right! But Mr. Slater, Quantrill is a bloody traitor, that's all!" She insisted. "He used to be a jayhawker out of Kansas, preying on the Southerners! Then he led a band of abolitionists down here, pretended he was spying out the terrain and turned on his own people! He got out of it by passing out a lie about his older brother being killed by jayhawkers. He didn't have an older brother, but those stupid fools fell for it!"

Kristin looked at her plate. "Quantrill is a murderer," she said softly. "But he usually leaves women alone. He won't let them be murdered."

"But Zeke would," Shannon said. "Zeke would kill anybody. He wants to kill Kristin now, just because she turned him down. She was in love with Adam, you see."

"Adam?"

"Shannon!"

"Adam, Adam Smith. Adam was like Pa. He had no stake in this war. He just wanted to be a rancher. But when the bushwhackers came and killed Pa, Adam went out with a group of jayhawkers to find Zeke's boys. Kristin didn't know about it, not until they sent her back his horse. They killed him down southwest somewhere, and we don't even know where they left his bones. At least Pa is buried out back."

Kristin felt his eyes on her again. She looked up, but that steel-hard gaze was unreadable.

"So this was no random raid here today," he said. It was a statement, not a question.

"No," Kristin admitted. She felt as if she were holding her

breath. He must realize that once he left they were all at the mercy of Zeke's bushwhackers again.

"You should get out," he told her.

"What?"

"You should get out. Pack your bags, get some kind of an escort and get the hell out."

It was a cold, callous statement. But what could she say in reply? He had stumbled upon them and he had saved her, but it had happened almost by accident. He didn't owe her a thing. She already owed him.

"I can't get out. My father died for this land. I owe it to him to keep it for him."

"To keep it for what? Your father is dead, and if you stay you'll probably wind up that way, too."

"That's all you can say?"

"What do you want me to say? I can't change this war, and I can't change the truth. Trust me. I would if I could."

For the first time she heard the bitterness in his voice. She wondered briefly about his past, but then she saw that he was rising, and panic filled her. He couldn't be about to ride away.

She stood. "You're not leaving?"

He shook his head. "I saw a few cigars in your father's study. Mind if I take one out back?"

Kristin shook her head, speechless. He wasn't leaving. Not yet.

She heard his footsteps as he walked through the dining room, heard them soften as he walked over the braided rug by the stairs. A moment later she heard the back door open and close.

"Kristin, are you all right?"

Kristin saw that Shannon was watching her, grave concern in her eyes.

"You're all pale," she said.

Kristin smiled, biting her lower lip and shaking her head. She squeezed Shannon's hand. "Help Delilah with the chores, won't you?"

Shannon nodded. Kristin turned around and followed the path the stranger had taken out of the house.

He was out back, puffing on one of her father's fine Havana cigars, leaning against the corral and watching as a yearling raced along beside its mother.

He heard Kristin and turned his fathomless gray gaze on her as she approached. He waited, his eyes hooded and curious.

Kristin wasn't at all sure how to say what she had to say. She folded her hands behind her back and walked over to him with what she hoped was an easy smile. Once she had thought she had the power to charm the male of the species. Once. She had been able to laugh and tease and flirt, and at any dance she had been breathless and busy, in unending demand.

Those days seemed so long ago now. Now she felt very young, and totally unsure of herself.

She had charmed boys, she realized. This was a man.

Still, she came over to him, leaning against the wooden gate of the corral.

"It's a good ranch," she told him.

He stared at her relentlessly, she thought. He didn't let a woman use her wiles. He didn't let her smile or flirt or tease.

"It's a good ranch," he agreed.

"Did I tell you just how much we appreciate your timely arrival here?"

"Yes, you did." He hiked himself up suddenly and sat on the gate, staring down at her. "Spit it out, Miss McCahy," he demanded, his eyes hard. "You've got something to say. Say it."

"My, my, you are a discerning man," she murmured.

"Cut the simpering belle act, Kristin. It isn't your style."

She flashed him an angry glance and started to turn away.

"Stop, turn around and tell me what you want!" he ordered her. He was a man accustomed to giving commands, she realized. And he was a man accustomed to his commands being obeyed.

Well, she wasn't going to obey him. She had paused, but she straightened her shoulders now and started to walk away.

She heard his boots strike the dirt softly, but she didn't realize he had pursued her until she felt his strong hands on her shoulders, whirling her around to face him. "What do you want, Miss McCahy?" he demanded.

She felt his hands, felt his presence. It was masculine and powerful. He smelled of leather and fine Madeira and her father's fine Havana cigar. He towered over her, and she wanted to turn away, and she wanted to touch the hard planes of his face and open his shirt and see the dark mat of hair that she knew must cover his chest.

"I want you to stay."

He stared at her, his eyes wary, guarded. "I'll stay until you can get some kind of an escort out of here."

"No." Her mouth had gone very dry. She couldn't speak. She wet her lips. She felt his eyes on her mouth. "I—I want you to stay on until—until I can do something about Zeke."

"Someone needs to kill Zeke."

"Exactly."

There was a long, long pause. He released her shoulders, looking her up and down. "I see," he said. "You want me to go after Zeke and kill him for you."

Kristin didn't say anything.

"I don't kill in cold blood," he told her.

She wanted to lower her eyes. She had to force herself to keep meeting his demanding gaze.

"I—I can't leave this ranch. I can give you a job—"

"I don't want a job."

"I—" She paused, then plunged on desperately. "I can make it worth your while."

He arched a brow. Something brought a smile to his lips, and suddenly his face was arrestingly handsome. He was younger than she had thought at first, too. But then he was talking again.

"You—you're going to make it worth my while."

She nodded, wishing she could hit him, wishing he would quit staring at her so, as if she were an unproved racehorse.

"Come here," he said.

"What?"

"Come here."

"I—I am here."

"Closer."

He touched her. His hands on her shoulders, he dragged her to him. She felt the steely hardness of his body, felt its heat and vibrancy. Through his pants and through all her clothing she felt the male part of him, vital and pulsing, against the juncture of her thighs. She still stared at him, wide-eyed, speechless, her breasts crushed hard against his chest as he held her.

He smiled crudely. Then his lips touched hers.

Curiously, the touch was very, very light. She thought she might pass out from the feel of it, so startling, so appealing. His lips were molded to hers....

Then hunger soared, and his tongue pressed between her teeth, delving deep, filling her mouth. She was engulfed as his mouth moved over hers, his lips taking hers, his tongue an instrument that explored her body boldly and intimately. Her breasts seemed to swell and she felt her nipples harden and peak almost painfully against his chest. He savaged her mouth, moving his tongue as indecently as he might have moved another part of his hard body...

Something inside her exploded deliciously. Heat coursed through her, filling her. She could not meet the power of his kiss, but she had no desire to fight it. It was shameful, maybe more shameful than what had happened to her this morning.

Because she wanted it.

She savored the stream of liquid sensations that thrilled throughout her body. Her knees shook, and the coil deep inside her abdomen that was so much a part of her womanhood seemed to spiral to a peak, higher and higher. She wanted to touch him. To bring her fingers against him, exploring. To touch him as his tongue so insinuatingly invaded all the wet crevices of her mouth...

Then he released her. He released her so suddenly that she nearly fell, and he had to hold her again to steady her.

He stared down at her. Her lips were wet and swollen, and her eyes were glazed. He was furiously angry with himself.

"Worthwhile?" he asked.

Kristin's mind was reeling. What did he mean?

"You don't even know how to kiss," he told her.

"What?" she whispered, too stunned to recognize the anger rising inside her.

"I'm sorry," he said. His voice was softer now.

"Damn you!" Kristin said. "I'll make a bargain with you! If you'll just stay—"

"Stop it!" he said harshly. "I'm sorry. I just don't have the time or the patience for a silly little virgin."

"What?" She stepped back, her hands on her hips, and stared at him. The insolence of him! She wanted to scream and she wanted to cry.

"I don't want a love affair, Miss McCahy. When I do want something, it's a woman, and it seldom matters who she is, just so long as she's experienced and good at what she does. Understand?"

"Oh yes, I understand. But I need help. I need you. Doesn't that mean anything?"

"I told you, I don't want a virgin—"

"Well then, excuse me for an hour, will you?" Kristin snapped, her eyes blazing. "I'll just run on out and screw the first cowhand—oh!"

She broke off in shock as he wrenched her hard against him. "Shut up! Where the hell did you come up with language like that?" he demanded heatedly.

"Let me go! It's none of your business! It's a rough world here, Slater!" she flailed desperately against him. He didn't feel her fists, and he didn't even realize that she was kicking him.

"Don't ever let me hear you say anything like that again!"

"Who do you think you are, my father?" Kristin demanded. She was very close to bursting into tears, and she was determined not to, not here, not now—not anywhere near this drifter. He had made her feel as young and naive and foolish and lost as Shannon. "Let me go!"

"No, I'm not your father. I'm a total stranger you're trying to drag into bed," he said.

"Forget it. Just release me and—"

"You just stop, Miss McCahy!" He gave her a firm, hard

shake, then another. At last Kristin stopped fighting. Her head fell back, her hair trailing like soft gold over his fingers, her eyes twin pools of blue fire as she stared into the iron-gray hardness of his.

"Give me some time," he said to her very softly, in a tone that caused her to tremble all over again. "I'll think about your proposition."

"What?" she whispered warily.

He released her carefully. "I said, Miss McCahy, that I would think about your proposition. I'll stay tonight. I'll take my blanket out to the bunkhouse, and I'll give you an answer in the morning." He inclined his head toward her, turned on his heel and started off toward the house.

Chapter Three

When she walked back into the house, Kristin was in a cold fury. She didn't see Cole Slater anywhere, and for the moment she was heartily glad.

He had humiliated her, plain and simple. She'd been willing to sell honor, her pride, her dignity—and he hadn't even been interested in what she'd had to sell. She wished fervently that she wasn't so desperate. She'd have given her eyeteeth to tell the man that he was a filthy gunslinger, no better than all the others.

Yet even as she thought of what she'd like to be able to say to him, she realized it would be a lie. He'd saved her from Zeke, from the man who had murdered her father. She owed him.

And she'd paid, she thought drily. With humiliation.

Shannon wasn't around when Kristin reached the dining room. Delilah was there, though, humming a spiritual as she carefully picked up the fine crystal and china on the table. She glanced Kristin's way curiously and kept humming.

"Where's Shannon?" Kristin asked.

"Out feeding the chickens," Delilah said.

Kristin decided to help clear away the remains of the meal, but when her fingers clenched too tightly around a plate, Delilah rescued it from her grip. "Sorry," Kristin muttered.

"Kristin, for the sake of your mama's fine things, you go do something else here this morning, hm?"

Kristin stepped away from the table, folding her hands behind her back.

"You didn't ask where Mr. Slater had gotten himself off to," Delilah said.

"I don't care where Mr. Slater has gotten himself off to," Kristin replied sweetly.

Delilah shot her a quick glance. "The man saved our lives," she said sharply.

Kristin strode furiously across the room to look out the window. "He saved our lives...and he really doesn't give a damn."

"He's riding out?"

Kristin exhaled slowly. She could see Shannon by the barn, tossing feed to the chickens. If she had any sense she would leave. Shannon was precious to her, just as Delilah and Samson were. She should do whatever was necessary to protect them.

But the dream was precious, too. The dream and the land. And where would she go if she did leave? She could never embrace the Southern cause—she had been treated too cruelly by the bushwhackers here for that—nor could she turn against Missouri and move into Yankee territory. She wanted desperately to fight, but she was helpless.

It didn't matter where she went, Richmond, Virginia or Washington, D.C. Nowhere was life as cruel and violent as it was here on the border of "bleeding Kansas." Nowhere else did men murder each other so callously.

"Kristin?" Delilah said.

"Slater..." Kristin murmured. Her pride was wounded, she realized. She had offered up her finest prize—herself—and he had informed her crudely that he wasn't interested.

"Kristin, if you're mad at that man for something, you remember the rest of us here. You understand me, missy?" Delilah came toward her, waving a fork. Kristin tried not to smile, because Delilah was deadly serious. "Quantrill's men get ahold of us and they'll think nothing of a hanging. You saw what they did to your pa. I got a baby boy, Kristin, and—"

"Oh, Delilah, stop! I'm doing my best!" Kristin protested. She tried to smile encouragingly. She couldn't quite admit to Delilah yet that she had offered her all and that it hadn't been enough. She hadn't even tempted the man.

She clenched her teeth together. She'd like to see him desperate, his tongue hanging out. She'd like to see him pining for her and be in the position to put her nose in the air, cast him a disdainful glance and sweep right on by. Better yet, she'd like to laugh in his face. If it hadn't been for this war, she could have done just that. She could have had any rich young rancher in the territory. She could have had—

Adam. She could have had Adam. A numbing chill took hold of her. Adam had loved her so much, and so gently. Tall and blond and beautiful, with green eyes that had followed her everywhere, and an easy, tender smile.

Adam was dead. The war had come, and Adam was dead, and she had few choices. Yes, Slater had humiliated her. But part of it was the fire. Part of it was the feeling that he had embedded in her, the hot, shameful longing for something she didn't know and didn't understand. She had loved Adam, but she had never felt this way when she had been near him. Never. Cole Slater *did* frighten her. She didn't like the feelings he evoked in her. They shattered her belief in her own strength.

"Cole Slater is staying tonight," she told Delilah.

"Well, glory be!"

"No, no," Kristin said. "He's bunking with the hands for the night. He'll, uh, he'll probably be gone by morning."

"By morning?" Delilah repeated blankly. "Kristin, I don't want to suggest anything that ain't proper, but chil', I'm just sure that if you tried being friendly to the man…"

"Delilah," Kristin murmured, her sense of humor returning at last, "I'm sure I don't remember what proper is anymore. I tried. Honest to God, I tried." She shrugged. "I'm not going to do you any good around here. I'll see you in a bit, huh?"

She hurried toward the stairs, giving Delilah a quick kiss on the cheek as she passed. She felt the older woman's worried gaze follow her, but by the time she reached the landing, she had forgotten about her.

The house felt so empty now.

Delilah and Samson and their baby had the rooms on the third floor. Kristin's and Shannon's were here on the second floor. But Matthew's room was empty now, as was the big master bedroom where her father and mothers had slept. The two guest rooms were empty, too. They hadn't entertained guests in a long, long time.

Kristin walked down the hallway, not toward her own room but toward the room that had been her parents'. She opened the door, stood there and smiled slowly. Her mother had been dead for years, but her father had been unable to part with the big Bavarian sleigh bed that his wife had so cherished. After her death he'd slept in it alone. And it was beautiful still. Delilah kept the mahogany polished and the bedding clean, as if she expected Pa to come back anytime.

Kristin walked into the room. There were giant armoires on either side of the window. One still held Pa's clothes, and the other still held her mother's.

We don't take to change easily here, Kristin thought. She smiled. It was the Irish blood, Pa had always told her. They were too sentimental. But that was good. It was good to hold on to the past. It helped keep the dream alive. Someday Pa's grandchildren would have this room. Matthew's children, probably.

If Matthew survived the war. It couldn't be easy for him, a Southern boy fighting in the Yankee army.

Kristin turned away. If Zeke Moreau had his way, none of them would survive the war. And when he was done torturing and killing, he would burn the house to the ground.

She started to close the door. Then she hesitated and turned back. She could suddenly see Cole Slater stretched out on that sleigh bed. It was a big bed, plenty big enough for his height and for the breadth of his shoulders. She could imagine him there, smiling lazily, negligently. Then suddenly, a whirlwind, a tempest of heat and fire…

She gritted her teeth, closed her eyes tightly and swore. She was sick of thinking about Cole Slater, and she was sick of remembering how grateful she had to be to a man who made her feel this way.

She slammed the door to her parents' room and hurried to her own. She threw her good dress on her bed and did likewise with her silk slippers and her corset. She slipped on a chemise, a cotton shirt, a pair of breeches and her high leather boots, and headed straight for the stables. She didn't bother with a saddle, but grabbed a bridle from a hook off the wall for Debutante and slipped into the stall to find her horse.

Debutante was an Arabian mare, a gift to Pa from one of the men he'd done business with in Chicago. She was a chestnut with white stockings, a deep dish in her nose and a tail that rode as high as the sun. Kristin loved her. She was amazed that the horse hadn't been stolen yet, but so far she had managed to have the horse out in the far pasture when the various raiding parties had swept through.

"Hello, you beautiful thing," Kristin whispered as she slipped the bit into the mare's mouth. Debutante nudged her. Kristin stroked the horse's velevety nose, then leaped on her back. Debutante nudged the stall door open, and Kristin gave her free rein as they left the stables behind.

It felt good to ride. It was good to feel the wind strike her cheeks, to feel the coolness of the air as it rushed by her. She was glad she had come bareback. She could feel the power of the animal beneath her, the rhythm of her smooth gallop, the great constriction and release of superbly toned muscle. Kristin leaned close to Debutante's neck. The horse's mane whipped back, stinging her cheeks, but she laughed with delight, glad simply to be alive.

Then Kristin realize she was being followed.

She wasn't sure how she knew she was being followed, except that there was an extra beat to the rhythm churning the earth, something that moved in discord.

She tried to look behind her. Her hair swept into her face, nearly blinding her.

There was a rider behind her. A lone figure, riding hard.

Panic seized her. She was already riding like the wind. How much harder could she drive the mare?

"Debutante! Please! We must become the wind!" She locked her knees more tightly against the animal's flanks. They were moving still faster now. The Arabian mare was swift and graceful, but the horse behind them seemed to be swifter. Either that, or Debutante's stamina was fading.

"Please!"

Kristin leaned closer to the mare's neck. She conjured up a mental image of the terrain. Adam had once owned this land. Ahead, just to the right, was a forest of tall oaks. She could elude her pursuer there.

The trees loomed before her. She raced the mare into the forest, then reined in when the trees became too dense for a gallop. She moved to the right and to the left, pushing deeper and deeper into the maze of foliage. Then she slid from the mare's back and led her onward.

Kristin's heart was pounding as she sought shelter.

If Zeke had come back, if he found her now...

She would pray for death.

But he was alone this time, she thought, praying for courage. She could fight him.

A twig snapped behind her. She spun around. She couldn't see anything, but she knew that her pursuer had dismounted, too, that he was still following her.

The branches closed above her like an arbor. The day was not bright and blue here, it was green and secretive, and the air was cold. She began to shiver.

She wasn't even armed, she realized ruefully. She was a fool. After all that had happened this morning she had ridden away from home without even a pocketknife with which to defend herself.

Kristin searched the ground and found a good solid branch.

Another twig snapped behind her. She dropped the mare's reins and crouched down against an oak. Someone was moving toward her.

Someone was behind her.

She spun around, the branch raised, determined to get in the first blow.

"Son of a bitch!" he swore.

She had gotten in the first blow—just barely. The man had raised his arm, and the branch struck it hard.

The impact sent her flying, her hair in her eyes. She landed in the dirt, and he was on top of her in an instant. She slammed her fist into his face, and heard a violent oath.

"Stop it! Kristin!"

He caught her wrists and straddled her.

She blinked and went still. It was Cole Slater.

"You!"

He rubbed his jaw. "You pack a hell of a punch."

"A hell of a punch?" she repeated. "You—you—" She was trembling with fear and with fury. She didn't mean to strike him again but she was nearly hysterical with relief, and she moved without thinking, slapping him across the face.

She knew instantly it was a mistake. His eyes narrowed, and everything about him hardened. Kristin gasped and looked around her for another weapon. Her fingers curled around a branch, and she raised it threateningly.

Cole wrenched the branch from her grasp and broke it over his knee, then pulled her roughly against his chest.

"What do you think you're doing?" he asked.

She had never seen him so furious, not even when he had gone up against Zeke and his gang of bushwhackers. Then he had seemed as cool as a spring stream. Now his eyes were the dark gray of a winter's sky, and his mouth was a white line of rage.

Kristin clenched her teeth hard, struggling to free herself from his grip. "What am I doing? You scared me to death."

He pulled her closer, and when he spoke again, his words were a mere whisper. "You're a fool, girl. After a morning like this you take off into the woods, without a word, without a care."

"I'm not a fool, and I'm not a girl, Mr. Slater, and I'd appreciate it, sir, if you would take your hands off of me."

"Oh, great. We have the grand Southern belle again."

Kristin gritted her teeth, wishing she could stem the rising tide of rage within her, rage and other emotions. He was too close. He was touching her, and she could feel the power of his anger, the strength of his body, and she was afraid of her own reactions.

"Let go of me. Just who the hell do you think you are?"

"The man who saved your life."

"I'm getting tired of eternal gratitude."

"Gratitude? A crack with a stick?"

"I didn't know it was you! Why didn't you say something? Why didn't you let me know—"

"You were running that mare a little fast for casual conversation."

"Why were you chasing me?"

"Because I was afraid you were going to get yourself in trouble."

"What were you afraid of? I thought you'd decided I wasn't worth the effort."

"I hadn't made any decisions yet. You are a girl, and you are a fool. You didn't give Moreau's men a chance to get far enough away. I didn't save you this morning for a gang rape this afternoon."

"Well, Mr. Slater, I wouldn't have been an annoying little virgin then, would I?"

Kristin was stunned when his palm connected with her cheek. Tears stung her eyes, though she wasn't really hurt. She hadn't expected his anger, and she hadn't imagined that she could humiliate herself this way again.

"Get off me!" she demanded.

"I don't want to hear it again, Kristin. Do you understand me?" He stood and reached down to help her up. She ignored his outstretched hand, determined to rise unaided, but he wouldn't even allow her to do that. He caught her arms and pulled her up. She hated him at that moment. She hated him because she needed him. And she hated him because this heat filled her at his touch, and this curious longing grew within her. She was fascinated by the scent of him, amazed by her desire to touch his face, to feel the softness of his beard....

To experience the sweeping wonder of his kiss once again.

She jerked free, and the leaves crackled under her feet as she whistled for Debutante. He followed behind her, dusting his hat off on the skirt of his coat.

"Kristin…"

She spun around. "You know, I've been wondering where you come from. You certainly aren't any Southern gentleman."

"No?" he queried. They stared at one another for a moment. Then his lips began to curl into a rueful smile. "I'm sincerely beginning to doubt that you're a Southern lady—or any kind of a lady, for that matter."

She smiled icily. She could manage it when he wasn't touching her. Then she turned away from him, squared her shoulders and walked toward her waiting mare.

"Sorry. I haven't had much time lately for the little niceties of life."

When she reached Debutante, he was there beside her. She didn't want his help, but he was determined to give it anyway. He lifted her onto the mare's back and grinned up at her.

"I may have to accept your generous offer."

"My generous offer?"

"Yes." His eyes suddenly seemed dazzling. Smoke and silver. His smile lent youth and humor to his features. He laughed. "I may have to bed you yet. To save you from yourself."

She wanted to say something. She wanted to say that her offer was no longer valid, that she would rather go to bed with Zeke and every single one of his raiders, than spend a single night with him, but the words wouldn't come. They weren't true. And it didn't matter, anyway, because he had already turned away. He picked up the reins of his big black horse and leaped upon the animal's back with the agility of long practice.

Kristin started out of the forest, heading for the house. She didn't look back. She rode ahead all the way. He rode behind her, in silence.

By the time they reached the house she was trembling again.

She didn't want to see him, she didn't want to talk to him. The whole thing had been a deadly mistake. He needed to get his night's sleep and head out in the morning.

She didn't even know who the man was! she reminded herself in dismay.

When they had dismounted she spoke at last, but without looking at him. "The hands eat out in the bunkhouse at about six. Sleep well, and again, thank you for rescuing us all. I really am eternally grateful."

"Kristin—"

She ignored him and walked Debutante toward the stables. Her heart began to pound, because she imagined that he would follow her. He did not.

She didn't rub Debutante down as she should have. She led the mare into the stall and removed her bit. In a worse turmoil than she had been in when she had left, she walked to the house.

Cole Slater was no longer in the yard. Kristin walked into the house. It was silent, and the drapes were drawn against the afternoon sun. Kristin bit her lip, wondering what to do. Depression suddenly weighed heavily upon her. It was all lost. She would have to leave, and she would have to be grateful that they were alive and accept the fact that nothing else of their life here could be salvaged.

She wasn't sure it mattered. They had already lost so much. Pa. Adam. Her world had been turned upside down. She would have done anything to save it. Anything. But anything just wouldn't be enough.

With a soft sigh, she started up the stairway. At the top of the stairs, she paused, her heart beating hard once again.

There was someone there, on the second floor with her.

There was someone in her parents' bedroom.

She tried to tell herself it was Delilah, or Shannon, but then she heard Delilah calling to Shannon below and heard Shannon's cheerful answer.

"Oh, God," she murmured, her hand traveling to her throat.

Something inside of her went a little berserk. She couldn't bear it if Zeke or one of his cronies had managed to enter that room. Her father's room, a place he had cherished, a place where all his dreams remained alive.

She ran toward the doorway. If Zeke had been in the room, she might have managed to kill him with her bare hands.

But it wasn't Zeke. It was Cole Slater. He had his blanket laid out on the comforter, and he was taking things from it. He looked up at her in surprise as she stared at him from the doorway. He frowned when he noticed the way her breasts heaved and noticed the pulse beating hard at the base of her throat. He strode to her quickly.

"Kristin, what happened?"

She shook her head, unable to speak at first.

"I—I didn't expect you. I mean, I didn't expect you to be here," she said.

He shrugged and walked back into the room, taking a shirt from the blanket and striding toward her father's armoire. "I didn't intend to be here. Delilah insisted there was plenty of room inside the house." He paused and turned back to her. "Is there something wrong with that? Do you want me out of here?"

She shook her head and had to swallow before she could speak again. "No...uh, no. It's fine." He was going to come toward her again. Quickly, before he could come close enough to touch her, Kristin turned and fled to the sanctuary of her own room.

She didn't know what seized her that afternoon. She didn't dare sit and think, and she certainly couldn't allow herself to analyze.

She went out in the early evening to speak with the hands. There was Jacob, who was nearly seventy, and his grandsons, Josh and Trin, who were even younger than she was. Their father had been killed at Manassas at the beginning of the war. And there was Pete, who was older than Jacob, though he wouldn't admit it. That was all she had left—two old men and two young boys. Yet they had survived so far. Somehow they had survived so far.

Cattle were missing again. Kristin just shrugged at the news.

Zeke's boys had been through. They had simply taken what they wanted.

Pete wagged a finger at her. "We heard what happened, missy. I think it's time you got out of here."

She ruffled his thin gray hair. "And what about you, Pete?"

"I've gotten along this far. I'll get along the rest of my days."

She smiled at him. "We'll see."

"Hear tell you've got a man named Slater up at the house."

Kristin frowned. "Yes. Why? You know him, Pete?"

Pete looked down at the wood he was whittling, shaking his head. "Can't say that I do."

She thought the old man was lying to her, and she couldn't understand it. He was as loyal as the day was long.

"You just said his name. Slater."

"Yeah, I heard it. From someone. Just like I heard tell that he managed to get rid of the whole lot of the thieving gutter rats." He looked up, wagging his knife at her. "You can't beat the likes of Zeke Moreau, Kristin. He doesn't have a breath of mercy or justice in him." He spat on the floor. "None of them do, not the jayhawkers, not the bushwhackers. It's time to get out."

"Well, maybe," Kristin said distractedly. She stood from the pile of hay she'd been sitting on. "Maybe."

"Your Pa's dead, Kristin. You're smart and you're tough. But not tough enough to take on Zeke on your own."

He looked at her expectantly. She felt like laughing. Everyone thought she could help. Everyone thought that all she had to do was bat her eyelashes at Cole Slater and he'd come straight to their rescue. If they only knew.

"We'll talk about it in the morning," she told him.

When she returned to the house, it was dinnertime.

Delilah had set out the good china and fine crystal again. She'd made a honeyed ham, candied yams, turnip greens and a blueberry pie.

Shannon and Cole Slater talked all through the meal. There might not have been a war on. There might not have been anything wrong with the world at all, the way the two of them talked. Shannon was beautiful and charming, and Cole was the perfect gentleman.

Kristin tried to smile, and she tried to answer direct questions. But all she could remember was that he had rejected her—and that she needed him desperately. She hated him, yet trembled if their hands so much as brushed when they reached for something at the same time.

She drank far too much Madeira with dinner.

When he went out back to smoke a cigar afterward, Kristin decided to take another bath. She hoped Delilah would think she hadn't been able to wash away the miserable stench of the morning.

Shannon was a sweetheart, tender and caring. Kristin realized when Shannon kissed her good-night that her sister was suffering more then she had realized. She was just taking it all stoically, trying to ease Kristin's pain with smiles and laughter.

Shannon went to bed.

Kristin dressed in her best nightgown. It had been part of her mother's trousseau. It was soft, sheer silk that hugged her breasts in a pattern of lace, then fell in gentle swirls around her legs.

She sat at the foot of her bed in the gown, and she waited. She was still, but fires raged inside her.

She had to make him stay, no matter what it took.

This was something that she had to do.

She heard his footsteps on the stairs at last. She heard him walk down the hallway, and then she heard the door to her parents' room open and close.

She waited, waited as long as she could, as long as she dared. Then she stood and drifted barefoot across the hardwood floor. She opened her door and started across the hall. She nearly panicked and fled, but something drew her onward. She wondered if she had gone mad, wondered if the world really had been turned upside down. Nothing could ever be the same again.

She hated him, she told herself. And he had already turned her down once.

One day she would best him.

She placed her hand on the doorknob and turned it slowly. Then she pushed open the door.

The room was dark. Only a streak of moonlight relieved the blackness. Kristin stood there for several seconds, blinking, trying to orient herself. It was foolish. She had waited too long. He was probably fast asleep.

He wasn't asleep. He was wide awake. He was sitting up in bed, his chest bare. He was watching her. Despite the darkness, she knew that he was watching her, that he had been waiting for her and that he was amused.

"Come on, Kristin," he said softly. He wasn't whispering like a man afraid of being caught at some dishonorable deed. He was speaking softly out of consideration for the others in the house, not out of fear. He wouldn't give a damn about convention, she thought. And yet he seemed to expect her to respect it.

Men.

"I, uh…just wanted to see if you needed anything."

"Sure." He smiled knowingly. "Well, I don't need anything. Thank you."

The bastard. He really meant to make it hard for her.

"That's a nice outfit to wear to check on your male guests, ma'am." He said the last word with a slow, calculated Southern drawl, and she felt her temper flare. Where the hell was he from?

"Glad you like it," she retorted.

"Oh, I do like it. Very much."

This was getting them nowhere. No, it was getting *her* nowhere.

"Well…"

"Come here, Kristin."

"You come here."

He grinned. "If you insist."

She should have known he would be lying there nude beneath the sheets.

Well, she had come to seduce him, after all.

She just hadn't imagined his body. The length of it. She

couldn't remember what she had imagined. Darkness, and tangle of sheets... She had known it involved a naked man, but she hadn't known just how a naked man could be.

She tried to keep her eyes on his, aware that a crimson tide was rushing to her face. She wished she had the nerve to shout, to run, to scream, but she didn't seem to be able to do anything at all.

Her eyes slipped despite her best efforts, slipped and then widened. She knew that he saw it, and she knew that he was amused. But she didn't move and she didn't speak, and when he stood before her at last, his hands on his hips, she managed to toss her head back and meet his gaze with a certain bravado.

He placed his hands against the wall on either side of her head. "Like what you see?" he inquired politely.

"Someone should really slap the living daylights out of you," she told him sweetly.

"You didn't do badly."

"Good." She was beginning to shake. Right now it was a mere tremor, but it was growing. He was so close that...that part of his body was nearly touching the swirling silk of her gown. She felt his breath against her cheek. She felt the heat radiating from him. She bit her lip, trying to keep it from quivering.

He pushed away from the wall. He touched her cheek with his palm, then stroked it softly with his knuckles. She stared at him, unable to move. She knew then that he could see that she was trembling. His eyes remained locked with hers. He moved his hand downward and cupped her breast.

The touch was so intimate, so bold, that she nearly cried out. He grazed her nipple with his thumb, and sensations shot through her with an almost painful intensity. She caught her breath, trying desperately to keep from crying out. And then she realized that he was watching her eyes carefully, gauging her reactions.

She knocked his hand away and tried to push by him, but he caught her shoulders and threw her against the wall.

"I hurt your feelings before. But then, I don't think that you were lacking in self-confidence. You must know that

you're beautiful. Your hair is so golden and you have the
bearing of a young Venus. Kristin, it isn't you. It's me. I
haven't got any emotion left. I haven't got what you need,
what you want. Damn it, don't you understand? I want you.
I'm made out of flesh and blood and whatever else it is that
God puts into men. I want you. Now. Hell, I could have
wanted you right after I ripped another man away from you.
I'm no better than he is, not really. Don't you understand?''

She drew herself up against the wall. She hated him, and
she hated herself. She had lost again.

''I only know that I need you. Emotion! I saw my father
murdered, and Adam...''

''Yes, and Adam.''

''And Adam is dead, too. So if you're worried about some
kind of emotional commitment, you're a fool. I want help
against Zeke Moreau.''

''You want me to kill him.''

''It's worth any price.''

''I told you...I don't murder men in cold blood.''

''Then I just want protection.''

''How badly?''

''Desperately. You know that.''

''Show me.''

She stepped toward him and placed her hands around his
neck. Suddenly she realized that she hadn't the least idea of
what to do. Instinct guided her, instinct and nothing more.

She stepped closer, pressing against him so that she could
feel the length of his naked body through the thin silk of her
gown. She wound her arms around his neck and came up on
tiptoe to press her lips against his, summoning up the memory
of the kiss he had given her. She felt him, felt the instrument
of his desire pulsing against her. She felt the muscles of his
chest and belly and thighs. Then she felt his arms, powerful
around her.

Then she plunged her tongue into his mouth and the world
began to spin. She had come to seduce him, and she was ready
to fall against him, longing for him to sweep her away.

To help her...

She felt the passion in him as he held her, and for a moment, victory was hers. She burned, she longed, with an astonishing hunger, and she could not know where it would lead. His lips held hers, his mouth devoured hers, and with each second that passed she entered deeper into a world that was pure sensation. Her pulse soared, and there was a pounding in her ears that was like the rush of the sea. His kiss was her life, his body was her support. She was afraid, and she was ecstatic.

And then he suddenly pushed her away.

His breathing was coming rough and ragged.

He watched her for a long, long moment. She felt his eyes on her, felt them as she would have felt an approaching storm. Then he shook his head.

"Go to bed, Kristin."

She inhaled sharply, furiously. "You let me make a complete fool of myself and then you— Damn you!"

Kristin slammed her fists against his shoulders, catching him off guard. He staggered, and she found the doorknob. Throwing the door open, she tore across the hall. She threw herself onto her own bed, tears hovering behind her lashes, fury rising in her throat.

The door crashed open behind her, and she spun around. He had followed her across the hall without even bothering to dress.

"Get out of here!" she snapped, enraged.

He ignored her and strode calmly toward the bed. Kristin shot up, determined to fight. It was all to no avail. His long stride quickly brought him to her. She came to her knees hastily, but he joined her on the bed, grabbing her hands and pressing her down.

"I should scream!" she told him. "Samson would come and—"

"Then scream."

She held her breath. He pressed her down on the bed and straddled her.

"Why won't you leave me alone?"

"You wanted to make a deal," he said harshly.

"What?"

"You said you wanted to make a deal. All right. Let's talk. I'm willing to negotiate."

Chapter Four

Kristin was glad the room was steeped in darkness. His features were shadowed, his body was shadowed, and she prayed that her own emotions were hidden by the night. She wanted to hate him. She could not. She wanted to think, to reason, and she could think of nothing but the hard male body so hot and intimate against her own.

He had come here, naked, to accept her proposition, it seemed. And yet he was angry again, angrier even than before. Hard and bitter and angry.

Moonlight cast a sudden soft glow over the room. She saw his features, and they were harsh, taut, almost cruel, as if he were fighting some inner pain.

"Negotiate?" she whispered.

"First, Miss Kristin, if you're going to play a game of chance, make sure you're playing with a full deck."

"I don't know what—"

"Exactly. That's why I'm going to explain things to you. I'll meet any man in a fair fight, but I won't go out and commit murder, not for you, not for myself, not for anyone. Do you understand?"

She nodded. She didn't understand him at all, but she was suddenly too afraid to do anything else. She had lost her mind. The war and the bloodshed had made her insane. She, Kristin McCahy, raised to live up to the highest standards of Southern womanhood, was lying on her bed with a naked stranger.

And she wasn't screaming.

"No involvement, Miss Kristin." The mock drawl was back in his voice, making her wonder again where he hailed from. She was filled with awareness of him. His muscled chest was plastered with crisp dark hair. She thought of how quickly he had drawn his Colts and his rifle, and she shivered. He carried with him an aura of danger that drew her to him despite her best intentions.

His sex pulsed against her belly, and she fought wildly to keep her eyes glued to his. It was all she could do to remember that she had intended to seduce him, to leave him gasping and longing and aching, his tongue hanging out for her.

He would never long for her that way, she realized now. Nor would he be denied. He had mocked her, but now he was determined to have her, and she felt sure he must despise her more with each passing second.

She steeled herself and whispered harshly, "No involvement. You needn't worry. I need a gunslinger. I could never love one."

A slight smile curved his lip. "This deal is made on my terms, lady. No involvement, no questions. And I won't murder Zeke. I'll go after him when I can. I'll do my damnedest to keep you and Shannon safe and your place together. But I've got other commitments, too, Kristin. And I can't forget them."

She didn't say anything. She didn't know what to say or do, didn't know where to go from here. This was so easy for him. He was so casual. He didn't even seem to know he was naked.

He touched her cheek, brushing it with his fingertips. "Why?" he said suddenly.

She shook her head, uncomprehending. "Why what?"

"This is all Zeke wanted."

"I hate Zeke. I hate him more than you could ever imagine. He killed my father. I'd rather bed a bison than that bastard."

"I see. And I'm a step above a bison?"

"A step below."

"I can still leave."

Panic filled her. She wanted to reach out and keep him from disappearing, but her pride wouldn't let her. Then she realized that he was smiling again, that he was amused. He leaned down low and spoke to her softly. His breath caressed her flesh, and the soft hair of his beard teased her chin. "There's one more point to this bargain, Miss McCahy."

Her heart was suddenly pounding mercilessly, her body aching, her nerves screaming.

"What's that, Slater?"

"I like my women hungry. No, ma'am, maybe that's not enough. I like them starving."

Words and whispers could do so much. As much as his slow, lazy, taunting smile. Fever ran through her, rife and rampant. She wanted to strike him because she felt so lost, and in spite of herself, she was afraid. She wasn't afraid he would hurt her. She might have gone insane, but she believed with all her heart that he would never hurt her. And she wondered, too, if this madness hadn't been spawned by the very way he made her feel, alive as she had never been before, haunted and shaken and...hungry, hungry for some sweet sensation that teased her mind and heart when he was near.

And yet she lay stiff and unyielding, numbed by the fear that swept through her, the fear that she would be unable to please him, the fear that she didn't have what it would take to hold him. Women... He had used the plural of the word. He liked his women hungry....

No, starving.

She didn't know him, and she didn't want involvement any more than he did, and yet this very intimacy was involvement. Even as she lay there, unable to move, she felt a painful stirring of jealousy. She had sacrificed so very much pride and dignity and morality for this man, and he was herding her together with every other female he had ever known.

He touched her chin. Then he brushed her lips with his, with the soft sweep of his mustache.

"Hungry, sweetheart." She sensed his smile, hovering above her in the dark. "This is as exciting as bedding a large chunk of ice."

She struck out at him blindly, but he caught her arms and lowered his weight onto her. She clenched her teeth as his laughing eyes drew near.

"Excuse me, Mr. Slater. My experience is limited. You wouldn't let me run out and screw a ranch hand, remember?"

"Kristin, damn you—"

"No, damn you!" she retorted, painfully close to tears. This couldn't be it. This couldn't be the night, the magic night she had wondered about in her dreams. No, it couldn't be, she thought bitterly. In her dreams this night had come after she had been married. And Adam had been in her dreams. And there had been nothing ugly or awkward about it. There hadn't even been any nude bodies, except beneath the sheets, and even then she had been cloaked all in white and he had whispered about how much he loved her and how beautiful she was and it had been wondrously pure and innocent....

She hadn't known these feelings then. And she hadn't known she could sell herself to a man who didn't even really want her.

"Please!" she cried suddenly, trying to escape his touch. Tears were beginning to sting her eyes, and she didn't want him to see them. She couldn't bear any more humiliation. "Just leave me alone. I—I can't be what you want, I can't—"

"Kristin!"

She went still when she heard the pained tenderness in his voice. He touched her cheek gently. Then he lay beside her and swept her into his arms.

She was stunned to realize that he was trembling, too, that his body was racked by heat and fever. He murmured her name again and again, and his lips brushed over her brow, as light as air. "Don't you see? I don't want to need you like this. I don't want to want you!"

There was passion in his voice, dark and disturbing. There was bitterness in it, too, pained and fervent, and as he continued to touch her, his emotions seemed to burn and sear her along with his touch. His hands were tender, then demanding, then gentle again.

"I don't want to want you," he murmured, "but God help me, I do."

Then he kissed her, and there was nothing left to worry about, for she was suddenly riding swiftly across the dark heavens and there was no time to think, no time for reason. She could only hold tight.

It all seemed to come together, everything she had felt since she had first set eyes on the man. Hungry...his mouth was hungry, and he was devouring her. His lips molded and shaped hers, and his tongue seemed to plunge to the very depths of her being, licking her deep, deep inside, taunting her, arousing her still more.

His hands roamed her body with abandon, abandon and a kind of recklessness. He caressed her tenderly, even delicately, then touched her with a force that told her that he wanted to brand her, wanted to leave his mark on her.

She never knew where the awe and the trembling and fear ceased and something entirely different began. She didn't even know when she lost the elegant nightgown brought west in her mother's trousseau, for his touch was so sweeping, so swift, so heady. She knew only that her breast was suddenly bare and his mouth was upon it. He cupped the soft mound of flesh with his hand, his lips hard around the nipple, drawing, suckling, raking the peak with his teeth as he demanded more and more.

She nearly screamed. She had never imagined such intimacy, and she never dreamed that there could be anything like the sensation that gripped her now with burning fingers, drawing a line of raw excitement down her spine and into her loins. She clutched his shoulders, barely aware that her nails were digging into him, that she was clutching him as if he were a lifeline in a storm-swept sea.

And still the tempest raged. His lips found her throat, and he raked his palm down the length of her, kneading her thigh and her buttocks. He moved swiftly, and she tried to follow, but she could not, for she was breathless, gasping in shock and amazement at each new sensation. He began anew. He touched her, held her, all over again. His lips trailed a line down the valley between her breasts to her navel, and the soft, bristling hair of his mustache and beard taunted her naked flesh mercilessly. She felt his knee force her thighs apart, and she knew that she was close to the point of no return, to being changed forever, and even then she could not keep pace with the winds that buffeted her.

And then he stopped. His palms on either side of her head, he caressed her with that curious tenderness he possessed and lowered his head to hers, whispering into her mouth.

"Hungry?"

She didn't want to face it. It was too new, too startling. She lowered her head and nodded, but it wasn't enough, not for him.

"Kristin?"

"Please..."

"Tell me."

"Oh, God!" she cried, trying to twist away from him. His palms held her fast, and her eyes were forced to meet his. Her lips were moist and her hair was a mass of gold between them, startlingly pale against the darkness of his chest.

He smiled at her, watching her as he drew his hand down to the pulse at her throat, then over her breast, down, down, to draw a circle on her abdomen and then plunge lower. He kept his eyes on her as he stroked her upper thigh. Then, suddenly, he swept his touch intimately inside her, moving with a sure, languorous rhythm.

She cried out again and tried to burrow against him, but he held her away from him. He watched her eyes, watched the rise and fall of her breasts, watched her gasp for air.

He caught her lips with his own, caught them and kissed them, and then he whispered against them again.

"Yes. You are...hungry."

Was this it? Was this the hunger he demanded, this burning sensation that filled her and engulfed her? She was grateful for the darkness, for the night, for with the moon behind a cloud, she could believe that all her sins were hidden, all that she had bartered, all that she had given so freely. She couldn't believe how she lay there with him, and yet she would not have changed it for the world. A soft cry escaped her, and she threw her arms around his neck, hiding against his chest at last. Something surged within her, and she gasped and murmured against his chest, barely aware that her hips were pulsing to his rhythm, that he hadn't ceased taunting her, that his strokes were growing more enticing.

Cole knew vaguely that he shouldn't be there. He should have told her that morning that nothing could make him stay, nothing could make him help her. She was the last thing in the world he needed. He had commitments of his own, and come heaven or hell or death itself, he meant to see them through.

And this innocence...

This, too, was the last thing he needed. She was hardened, and there were jagged edges to her. War did that. War and death and pain and blood. But the innocence was still there, too. He had thought he could make her run, and he had thought he could be strong enough himself not to touch her. He was used up. He knew that. He was used up, and she deserved more than that. He was still alive, though, still breathing, and she touched every raw cord of desire within him. Maybe he had known what was to come, and maybe he hadn't expected it at all, but now that it was happening, he couldn't even try to deny it. She spun a golden web of arousal and passion as soft and silky and luxuriant as the long strands of hair that tangled around them both, dampened by the glistening sheen of their bodies. She had beautiful features, exquisite features, fine, high cheekbones, a small, slim nose and eyes like an endless blue sky, darkly fringed with rich lashes and glazed now with blossoming passion. And her mouth...it was full and giving, sensual in laughter, sensual when her lips parted beneath his own. She was soft, she was velvet and she was created for desire, with high, firm breasts, a slim waist and flaring hips, and smooth, fascinating buttocks. He hadn't meant to stay. He hadn't meant to come here, and he hadn't meant to stay. He hadn't meant to touch her....

But he had.

And she moved. She moved with exquisite grace. She made

sweet, soft sounds that entered his loins and caused the blood
to pound in his head so that he could think no more. Only one
thought guided him, and that was that he had to have her, had
to have her or go mad. Her nipples pressed against his chest,
and she arched against his hand. Despite his best efforts, the
agony of the past was erased, the vengeance of the future
forgotten. Even the present meant nothing at all. All that mattered was this woman, and she was hot and wet and begging
for release.

He pulled her to him almost roughly. Her eyes widened,
and he commanded her to hold tight. He caught her lips in a
heady kiss and swept his hands beneath her. He fought hard
to remember her innocence. He kissed her with sweeping ardor, and then he entered her.

He was slow, achingly slow, and she was sleek and damp,
a hot sheath ready to encase him, and still he felt her shudder,
heard the sudden agonized cry that she muffled against his
chest.

He'd heard it before. On his wedding day.

The irony, the bitter, bitter irony touched him for a moment,
and for a moment he hated her and himself. For a moment he
was still. Then he felt her shudder again and thought she might
be crying, and then he was whispering things without thinking.

Yes…he'd been here before. Making love tenderly to a
woman for the very first time. Her very first time.

He held her, caressed her, promised to help her. And then
he moved again, slowly at first, carefully, tenderly.

And then she was moving beneath him, subtly at first. She
was taking him in, and the tears were gone, and the shock was
gone, and the desperate tension was growing again.

Care and consideration left him. A thirst that he was frantic
to slake ripped through him and into his loins. He couldn't
remember ever being so fevered, and still the sensations grew.
He touched her breasts, struck anew by their beauty. He inhaled the clean, sweet scent of her tangled hair and the fever
soared higher and higher. He wrapped her legs tightly around
him and cupped her buttocks, and rocking hard, filled her with
himself again and again. He threw back his head and rough

sound tore from him as the relief began to shake and convulse through his body. Again and again he spilled into her. She cried out, her voice ragged. He was aware that she had reached some sweet satisfaction, and he was pleased. She fell still, and the last of the fever raked through him. He thrust deep, deep inside her one last time. It was shattering, and he couldn't remember when he had known such a deeply satisfying climax.

He fell to her side, covered with sweat, breathing heavily.

She was silent. He touched her cheek and found tears there.

Suddenly he was furious with himself and with her. This should never have happened. She should have married some young buck and worn white, and she should have been loved, not just desired.

She twisted away from his touch, and he let her go. She turned her back on him, and he wondered if she was crying again. Maybe she had a right to, but it was damned insulting. He'd taken even greater care with her than he had with— Elizabeth. With Elizabeth.

There. He dared to think her name.

Though he gritted his teeth and wished it away, agony gripped him from head to toe. He wondered if the pain would ever leave him.

"You can...you can go back now," Kristin said suddenly.

"What?" His voice was sharp.

"Our deal." She spoke softly, her voice a mere whisper, as if tears hovered behind her words, tears and just a touch of anxiety. "It's—it's made now, isn't it?"

He hesitated before he answered her. "Yes, your bloody bargain is made, Miss McCahy."

"Then you could...you could go back. Across the hall."

He didn't know what demon seized him. He didn't care if he was heard by the others in the house, didn't care about anything at all. He sat up in a sudden fury and wrenched her around to face him. He spoke bitingly, trying to make every word sting like the stroke of a lash.

"Not on your life, my little prima donna. You invited me

in here. Now you've got me. That was the game, Kristin. You knew it was going to go by my rules—''

"My God!" she cried, jerking away from his touch. "Have you no consideration, no—"

"Compassion? Not a whit. This is what you wanted, and now you've got it."

She was beautiful still, he thought. The moonlight was playing over her breasts, and they were damp and shimmering and very, very fine, the nipples still enlarged and hard. He felt a quickening inside him all over again, and with it felt the return of the pain. The pain of betrayal. It was all right with whores, with tavern girls. It was something else with this innocent young beauty.

He scowled fiercely and turned his back on her. "Go to sleep, Kristin."

She didn't move. She didn't answer him. Not for endless seconds.

"Go to sleep?" she repeated incredulously.

"Damn it, yes, go to sleep." He swung around again and pressed her down on the bed. She started to fight him, and he wasn't in the mood to take it. Dark anger was in him, dark, brooding anger, and though he didn't mean to be cruel to her, he didn't seem to be able to help himself. He caught her shoulders and shook them. "Good night, Kristin. Go to sleep."

"Leave," she said stubbornly.

"I'll be damned if I will."

"Then I'll leave."

"And I'll be damned if you'll leave, either. Now go to sleep!"

He turned around, offering her his back once again. He didn't know why he had started this bout, but now that he had begun it, he wasn't about to lose.

He felt it when she started to rise, and he turned with frightening speed, sweeping his arm around her waist and holding her still. He felt her heart beating like that of a doe.

"Go to sleep!"

He heard her teeth grating, but she didn't move, not again.

He knew she was planning to wait until he fell asleep, then slip away.

He smiled. She had another think coming. He would feel her slightest movement. He would awaken.

When she did try to move, he kept his eyes closed and held her fast. He heard her swearing softly, and he heard the threat of sobs coming to her whispering voice.

But then it was she who fell into an exhausted sleep. And it was he who awoke first with the morning. He stood and stretched and padded naked to the window and looked out on a beautiful summer's day. It was a fine ranch, he thought. Then he sighed, and he knew that she would think she had sold herself dearly in the night.

He had sold himself dearly, too. He had sold his honor, and he would have to stay, and he would have to protect her.

He walked over to the bed. The evidence of their night together was painfully obvious in the twisted bedding.

Her face was covered by long, soft tendrils of hair that picked up gold from the sun. A hand seemed to tighten around his heart and squeeze. Cole stepped closer to the bed and covered Kristin with the top sheet and the comforter. Then he stepped to the door, glanced out and returned to the room across the hall to wash and dress.

Kristin knew it was late when she awoke. She opened her eyes and saw that the sun had risen high, then closed her eyes again and discovered that she was shaking.

She had almost believed that she had dreamed the entire episode.

But she hadn't. Cole Slater was gone, but he had definitely been there, and just thinking about everything that had happened made her shake again and burn crimson to the roots of her hair.

A knock sounded at her door. "Kristin?"

It was Shannon. Kristin sat bolt upright and looked at the bed. The comforter seemed to hide the sins of the night.

"Shannon, just a minute!" she cried out. Her gown was on the floor beside the bed. She made a dive for it, wincing at the soreness that plagued her thighs. Then she realized that the gown was torn and ragged, and she knew why it had seemed to melt away the night before. Bitterly she wound it into a ball, stuffed it into her dresser and dragged out an old flannel gown. Breathless, she told Shannon to come in.

Shannon came in with a pot of coffee and a cup and breakfast on a silver tray. Kristin stared at it blankly and arched a brow at her younger sister.

"Good morning, sleepyhead," Shannon told her.

"Breakfast? In bed?" The ranch was a place where they barely eked out their existence. Breakfast in bed was a luxury they never afforded themselves. "After I've slept all morning?"

"Delilah was going to wake you. Cole said that maybe things had been hard on you lately and that maybe you needed to sleep."

"Oh, Cole said that, did he?"

Shannon ignored the question. "I rode out to the north pasture with Cole and Pete, and everything's going fine for the day."

Kristin kissed her sister's cheek and plopped on the bed, wincing again. It even hurt a little to sit.

She felt her face flood with color again, and she lowered her head, trying to hide her blush behind her hair. She still didn't know if she hated him, or if her feeling had become something different, something softer.

A little flush of fever seemed to touch her. She was breathing too fast, and her heart was hammering. She couldn't forget the night. She couldn't forget how she had felt, and she didn't know whether to be amazed or grateful or awed—or ashamed. The future loomed before them. They had a deal. He had said he would stay. And he hadn't left her room, and she—

She couldn't help wondering what he intended for their personal future together. Did he mean to do it…again?

"My Lord, Kristin, but you're flushed!" Shannon said with alarm.

"I'm all right," Kristin said hastily. She sipped the coffee too quickly and burned her lip. She set the cup down. "This was really sweet. The breakfast."

"Oh," Shannon said nonchalantly, "this was Cole's idea, too. He seemed to think you might have a little trouble getting up this morning."

"Oh, he did, did he?" She bit so hard into a piece of bacon that her teeth snapped together. He was laughing at her again, it seemed, and he didn't even have the decency to do it to her face. She longed for the chance to give him a good hard slap just once.

She caught herself. He had warned her. They were playing by his rules. And there was only one thing she was gaining from it all. Safety. She had agreed to the rules. She had meant to seduce him, she had meant for it all to happen, she had wanted the deal. It was just that she wasn't at all sure who had seduced whom.

"Where is Cole now?" she asked Shannon. She was surprised to find that she had a ravenous appetite.

Shannon shrugged. "I'm not sure. But do you know what?" she asked excitedly.

"No. What?"

"He says he's going to stay around for a while. Isn't that wonderful, Kristin?"

Kristin swallowed and nodded. "Yes. It's wonderful."

"Samson says it's a miracle. He says God has looked down on us with mercy at long last."

"The Lord certainly does work in mysterious ways," Kristin murmured dryly.

Shannon, who had seated herself at the foot of the bed, leaped up and hugged Kristin. "We're going to make it," she whispered. "We're really going to make it."

She had underestimated Shannon, Kristin realized. She had felt their father's death every bit as keenly as Kristin had.

And because she felt it so strongly, she had learned to hate, just as Kristin had.

"I've got to get back downstairs. Delilah is baking bread and making preserves and I promised to help."

Kristin nodded. "I'll be right down, too."

When her sister had left, Kristin washed hastily. She couldn't help remembering every place he had touched her, everything he had done to her. And then, naturally, she started trembling again, thinking about the feeling that had come over her. In the midst of carnage, a brief, stolen moment of ecstasy.

Shameful ecstasy.

Ecstasy.

She wondered if it had ever really been, if it could ever come again.

She dressed, trying desperately to quit thinking. If she didn't, she would walk around all day as red as a beet.

She dressed for work. There was some fencing down on the north side, and she had told Pete she'd come out and look at it. The stash of gold hidden in the hayloft was dwindling, but they could afford to repair the fencing. And if she could just hang on to her stock a while longer, she could command fair prices from any number of buyers in the spring. She had to remember that she was fighting for the land. Nothing else mattered.

In breeches and boots, Kristin started for the doorway. Then she remembered her bedding, and the telltale sheets.

Delilah usually did the beds. She kept the house with Shannon's help. Samson kept it from falling apart. Pete and Kristin ran the ranch. That was just the way things had worked out.

But she didn't want Delilah doing her bed. Not today.

He liked his women hungry. *Women.* Plural.

Kristin let loose with a furious oath and ripped the sheets from the bed. She jumped up and down on them a few times for good measure, then realized how ridiculous she was being and scooped them up. She carried them down with her to the stables, stuffing them into the huge trash bin. She would burn them later, with some of the empty feed bags.

She headed for the stable, determined to saddle Debutante and ride out. She paused in the doorway, aware that Cole was there, brushing down his black thoroughbred stallion. It was a beautiful animal, Kristin thought.

Very like the man who owned him.

She wasn't ready to see Cole Slater yet. She almost turned

around, ready to change her plans for the day to avoid facing him. But he had sensed her there, and he turned, and there seemed to be nothing for her to do but stand there and meet his stare.

It was long, and it was pensive, and it gave no quarter. She would never accuse the man of being overly sensitive or overly polite. His gray eyes were sharp and curious, and she still thought he must be amused by her, because he was smiling slightly. There were times when she thought he hated her, but then he would stare at her in a way that warmed her and offered her a fleeting tenderness.

Very much like the way he made love…

She shouldn't have thought it. The color that had so alarmed her rose to fill her face, and she had to lower her eyes to still the blush. She prayed fervently that she could appear sophisticated for just this one encounter. But it was impossible to stand here now, fully clothed, and not remember what had gone on the night before. Things could never be the same again. She could never see life the same way again. She could never see him the same way again, for she knew the power of the form beneath the shirt and jeans, and he knew all that made up the woman she was.

"Sleep well?" he asked her after a moment.

There was something grating in the question, something mocking, and that helped. She squared her shoulders and tried to walk by him, heading for Debutante's stall. He caught her arm and swung her around. His eyes were serious now.

"Where do you think you're going?"

"Out to the north pasture. I have to see the fencing. I should have gone yesterday, but…" She paused, her voice fading away.

He shook his head impatiently. "I'll meet Pete."

"But it's my ranch!"

"And it's my life, Miss McCahy." He dropped her arm and put his hands, the currycomb in one, on his hips. "You're taking up my time. We made some ridiculous deal—"

"Ridiculous deal!" She was choked with rage. She was going to slap him this time. Right across the face.

She didn't make it. He caught her wrist. "I'm sorry, Kristin. I didn't mean it that way."

"I'm so terribly sorry if I disappointed you."

She'd thought his eyes would drop with shame. They didn't. Hers did. He was still smiling.

"You didn't disappoint me. You surpassed my wildest expectations. I'm sorry. I didn't mean to insult you. I meant that you really should be the hell out of here."

"You're not reneging?" she asked crisply.

He smiled slowly, tilted back his plumed hat and shook his head. "No, Kristin," he said softly. His low, grating voice sent tremors up her spine. "I never renege on a deal. But I'll be damned if I'm going to stick around so you can run off and be swept away beneath my very nose."

"But I—"

"Forget it, Kristin. I warned you. We play by my rules. And you're not riding out anywhere."

"But—"

"You ride out, I ride out."

"But...but you've already been...paid!" Kristin exploded.

His brows shot up, and his lips curled mockingly. "Paid?"

"You know what I mean."

He shook his head. "I sure as hell don't! That was it? One night in your arms and I'm supposed to gladly lay down my life and die?"

"You are no Southern gentleman."

"Did I say I was?"

"You are no gentleman at all!"

"I never claimed to be one, Kristin. In fact, I haven't made any claims to you at all. Remember that."

"I find it difficult to forget."

"Are you trying to renege?" he queried softly.

She drew herself up stiffly, determined to counter-attack. "So you're not from the South?"

"Does it matter where I'm from?"

"Maybe it does!"

He caught her hand and held it. They stared at one another. Behind them, the massive black stallion snorted. Cole stared at her seriously for a long moment and then said, "No, it doesn't, Kristin. Nothing about me matters at all. No questions. No involvement. Remember that."

She jerked her hand away. "I'll remember, Mr. Slater."

She started toward Debutante's stall. Maybe she couldn't go riding, but she had to get away. She would take a moment to stroke the mare's velvet nose, and then she would escape. She didn't know how she would be able to bear it, though. She would be like a caged animal with all the emotions that were playing havoc in her heart.

She patted Debutante's nose and promised the horse in a low whisper that she would come out and give her a good grooming as soon as *he* was out of the stable.

Then she turned around, determined to walk out of the stables with her head held high, determined to hang on to her few remaining shreds of dignity.

"By the way, Kristin…" he began.

She paused, her back to him. She straightened, stiffening her shoulders, and turned in a swift circle. He wasn't watching her. He was combing the stallion's shining flanks.

"Why don't you move your things into the larger bedroom? We'll have more space there."

"What?"

"You heard me."

"But—but everyone will know! And just how many times do you intend to…to…"

"Get paid?" he suggested politely. He didn't even seem to be paying attention to her. He stroked the stallion's ears, then stared directly at her. "You want blood, Kristin. That's an expensive commodity. And as far as everyone knowing is concerned, that's exactly what I want."

"But—"

"I make the rules, remember?"

"I can't! I can't go by this one—"

"Delilah will understand. So will Shannon and Sam and Pete and everyone else. And if Zeke Moreau hears anything about it, he'll get the message, too."

"But—"

"Do it, Kristin."

She spun around in a dead fury again. She didn't look back. She stormed into the house, wishing desperately that *she* were a man. She would run away and join the army in two seconds.

She wouldn't even give a damn whose army she joined. Just as long as it was someone who hated Quantrill and his animals.

"Kristin, that you?" Delilah came into the hallway, smiling. "Want to give us a hand with the wax? I could surely use some help stirring. I've got Shannon jarring and sealing while I've been kneading the bread."

"Er...of course," Kristin said. She'd much, much rather run away and join the army.

Shannon gave her a bright smile when she came into the kitchen. "Did you find Cole?"

"Yes. I found him."

Shannon nodded. It was obvious that she approved of it all. They were all mad, Kristin decided.

"He wants me to move into Pa's bedroom with him," she blurted out.

Shannon had been holding a jar of jam, sealing it with wax. The jar slipped from her fingers and shattered loudly on the floor.

Delilah sent the bread she was kneading into the air. It fell back on the block table.

Both of them stared at her. Then they glanced at one another. Neither of them said a word.

"Say something!" Kristin demanded. "Help me make some kind of a decision!"

"You can't!" Shannon gasped.

"Seems to me like you've already made your decision," Delilah said softly. "But it ain't right. It just ain't right. Still..."

"He's much, much better than Zeke Moreau," Shannon said. She stooped to pick up the broken glass and the jam that was seeping into the floorboards. "Yes, maybe you have to. And he *is* much better than Zeke."

"So that's why I'm sleeping with a stranger." Kristin sank

into a chair before the fire. "I cannot believe I'm doing this," she murmured.

"These are different times," Shannon murmured, staring at the floor. She looked up at her sister. "Kristin, we can't be blind to the facts! We need him. We need him, or else we just have to give up and pull out."

"Shannon!" Kristin exploded. "You're shocked, and you know it. Pa must be turning in his grave. We don't even know where Cole Slater comes from!"

Shannon's beautiful blue eyes widened. "But of course we do, Kristin."

"What?"

Shannon smiled broadly. "He's from Missouri. He was originally from Virginia, but his family bought a big spread out here. I think he comes from tobacco money, a lot of it. He went to West Point. He was in the same class as Jeb Stuart!"

Kristin stared at her sister, who appeared about to swoon. Shannon thought that the Confederate general Jeb Stuart was the handsomest, most gallant gentleman in the whole world. Shannon's reaction to Stuart's name didn't surprise her, but the fact that she seemed to know so much about Cole stunned her.

"What?" she repeated numbly.

Shannon sighed with supreme patience, as if she were the elder, explaining things to a sullen child.

"He's a Virginian, Kristin, moved to Missouri. He went to West Point. Once upon a time he was in the army in Kansas. He and Stuart served together."

"Wonderful," Kristin murmured.

So he *was* a Southerner. And he wasn't in uniform. He was one of them, one of the breed that ran with Quantrill....

She was a Southerner herself, she thought dully. Not all Southerners were like Zeke Moreau.

But Cole...

Cole had talked freely to Shannon. But the questions hadn't all been answered yet.

He had gone to West Point. He had served in the Union

Army before the war with the gallant Southern calvary officer, Jeb Stuart.

But he wasn't wearing a uniform now. Not the Union's, and not the Confederacy's. Why not?

Delilah stirred something over the fire. She wiped her hands on her apron. "Well, Kristin? What do we do? If you want, I'll go move your things."

Kristin swallowed. She wanted to protest. She wanted to refuse Cole Slater.

She looked at Delilah. Delilah wasn't making any judgments.

Kristin nodded. She could give up the place or she could hold tight to Cole Slater. She really had no choice. But she vowed to herself that she'd find out everything there was to know about the man.

Chapter Five

Kristin spent the day worrying about the night ahead. She prowled around upstairs, trying to keep busy. Though she hated it, she did what Cole had told her to, taking a few of her dresses and nightshirts and putting them in the armoire in her parents' bedroom.

Shannon came upstairs while she was at it. There was something about her knowing glance that made Kristin feel terribly ashamed. "Cole—Mr. Slater—thinks that Zeke ought to think there's something...um, that he and I, that..."

"I understand," Shannon said softly. Even her innocence was dead, Kristin thought. There was an awkward silence, but then Shannon came into the room and hugged her. "I like him," she told Kristin. "I like him a whole lot."

"Only because he knows Jeb Stuart."

Shannon made a face. "That helps." She sat down on the bed. "What happened here?" she queried softly.

"What do you mean?" Kristin asked her.

"So many men are so fine. General Lee is such a gentleman, by all accounts. And Jeb Stuart is so dashing! And then out here..."

"We get the bushwhackers and the jayhawkers," Kristin finished for her. She sat down beside Shannon and hugged her. "And don't forget," she reminded her, "we have a brother fighting in Mr. Lincoln's army."

"I never forget!" Shannon said.

They sat there in silence for a long time. Then suddenly, there was a volley of shots from outside. Kristin leaped to her feet and raced to the window.

Cole was out back with Samson. He'd set a few rows of old liquor and tonic bottles on the back fence to serve as makeshift targets. He'd already shot up the first set.

Kristin watched as he reloaded, then twirled his six-shooter in his hand and shoved it back in its holster. He paused. Then, in the wink of an eye, he cleared away another row. Then he spoke to Samson, and Kristin realized that it was a lesson.

Then it was Samson's turn with the guns. Kristin strained to hear Cole's words.

"Quantrill's boys usually carry four or five Colts, a shotgun or a rifle or maybe both. That's why they keep licking the pants off the Union troops. They're well armed, and the boys in blue are still trying to fire off muzzle-loading carbines. Zeke will always be well armed. So we've always got to be prepared to outshoot him in return. You understand, Sam?"

"Yes, Mr. Slater, that I do."

"Let's try it again. Hold your hand steady, and squeeze the trigger, don't jerk it."

Cole took off his plumed hat, ran his fingers through his hair and set the hat back on his head, low over his eyes. Then he said, "Go!" and Samson drew. He shattered a fair number of the bottles, then laughed. Cole slapped him on the back, congratulating him. Then the men's voices grew low, and Kristin couldn't hear any more.

Suddenly Cole looked up at the window. It was too late. She couldn't draw away.

He smiled and waved. She almost waved back, but then she realized that Shannon had come up beside her and that it was her sister he was waving to, because she was waving down to him.

"We're moving Kristin in!" Shannon called down.

Kristin was mortified. She felt his eyes on her, she saw his slow, lazy smile. She wanted to hit Shannon over the head. She backed away from the window instead.

"You coming up?" Shannon called.

''Shannon!'' Kristin hissed.

But Cole shook his head. He looked handsome then, as tall as Samson, and hard and lean in his long coat and his plumed hat. ''Tell your sister I'm on my way out to find Pete. Might be gone awhile. If I can take care of some things today, I will.''

Shannon turned to Kristin. ''Cole said—''

''I heard what Cole said.''

''Shannon!'' Cole said.

''Yes, Cole?''

''Tell your sister I may be back late. Tell her she doesn't have to wait up.''

Shannon turned to Kristin. ''Cole said—''

''I heard what Cole said!''

Kristin spun around and stormed out of the room. She returned to her own room and slammed the door. She sat down on her own bed and pressed her hands against her temples. She had a staggering headache, and her nerves were as shattered as the bottles Cole had shot up.

Well, he had shattered her world, too.

She needed to get this over with quickly. She needed him to be around. She wanted him. She hated him.

She wished to God she knew him. She wished to God she could get to know him. But she didn't think he would let anyone get close to him. Anyone at all.

No involvement...

She didn't want any involvement. And he couldn't possibly make her as nervous as Zeke Moreau made her hateful.

Or could he?

If he came back at all that night, Kristin never knew it. She lay on her parents' bed until the wee hours of the morning, and then exhaustion claimed her. When she awoke, it was almost noon. No one came for her. When she dressed and went downstairs, Delilah was busy with a big pot of lye and Shannon was putting their last two-year-old colt through his paces. Kristin longed to do something, to ride somewhere, but Samson found her in the stable and warned her that Cole had said she should stay close to home. She bit her lip but did as she was told, and Samson proudly showed her something of what he had learned.

Kristin was impressed with his newfound skill with a gun, and she told him so, but then she rested her chin on the fence and sighed. "Is it enough, Samson? Is it enough against Zeke?"

"Maybe not me alone, Miss Kristin, but Mr. Slater had all the boys out here this morning, and he can teach a whole lot about gun play, as well as practice it."

"You sound like you like him a lot, Samson."

"Yep. Yes, miss, I do. He complimented me on my language this morning, and when I told him how big your pa was on learning he said that he thought fine men came in both black and white, and that he was mighty proud to know me."

Kristin smiled. "That's nice, Samson. That's mighty nice."

They were both silent for a moment. Then Kristin began to grow uncomfortable, wondering what he really thought of what was going on with Cole Slater.

"The world just ain't the same anymore, Miss Kristin," Samson said at last. "The world just ain't the same." He chewed on a long blade of grass and stared out at the pastureland. "No, the world just ain't the same, and we can only pray that it'll right itself when this awful war is over."

Kristin nodded. Then she turned to him and gave him a big hug. She didn't know what she'd do without him and Delilah.

She didn't see Cole again all that day and night. He was still out with Pete and the boys at dinnertime, and later, much later, she heard laughter and the strains of Pete's fiddle coming from the bunkhouse. That night she slept alone again in the big sleigh bed in her parents' room.

In the morning she didn't know if he had ever come to bed or not. For some reason, she didn't think he had, and she wondered why he was taunting her this way when he seemed to have so little real interest in her. Her temper rose, but then she remembered that she should be grateful to have him here. And then she was afraid he would leave.

And then she hated him. He was supposed to want her. They

were supposed to have a deal. She was supposed to loathe him for taking advantage of her weakness. But she was the one left wondering and wanting. No, not wanting. Merely curious, she assured herself. But she couldn't deny that she had been in a fever ever since he had come. She simply couldn't deny her emotions.

Then he was there. He was there all day. He passed her in the hallway and tipped his hat to her, a smile of amusement tugging at his lips.

"Wait!" she cried. "Where are you going?"

"Rounding up strays."

"Let me come."

His smile faded. "No."

"But—"

"My rules, Kristin."

"But—"

"My rules."

She gritted her teeth and stiffened, watching him for a moment in simmering silence. He smiled again. "But I will be back for supper this evening. Steak and sweet potatoes and Delilah's black-eyed peas, and blueberry pie for dessert. And then…" He let his voice trail off. Then he lifted his hat again and turned and left.

And she didn't even know where he had spent the night.

It was another wretched day. She fed the chickens. She groomed her horse. She played with little Daniel, marveling in spite of herself at the way the child grew daily. She wandered around upstairs. Then she found herself sitting at the foot of the big sleigh bed.

His blanket lay on the floor next to the dresser. Kristin hesitated, staring at it for a long while. Then she got up and went over to it.

And then she unrolled it and went through his personal belongings.

There wasn't much. If he had a wallet, he had it with him. There was a shaving mug and a tin plate, a leather sack of tobacco, another sack of coffee and a roll of hard tack.

And there was a small silver Daguerreotype frame.

Kristin stared at it for a moment then found the little silver clasp and flicked it open.

There were two pictures in the double frame. The first was of a woman alone, a very beautiful woman, with enormous eyes and dark hair and a dazzling smile.

In the second picture the woman was with a man. Cole.

He was in a U.S. Cavalry uniform, so the picture must have been made before the war. The woman wore a beautiful, voluminous gown with majestic hoops, and a fine bonnet with a slew of feathers. They weren't looking at the camera. They were looking at one another.

There was such tenderness, such love in their eyes, that Kristin felt she was intruding on something sacred. She closed the frame with a firm snap and put it back inside the blanket, trying to put everything back together as if she hadn't touched it at all. It didn't make any difference, she told herself dully. He should expect people who didn't know a thing about him to check up on him. No, that didn't wash, not at all, not even with her.

The woman was dead, she thought.

She didn't know how she knew, but she knew. Cole Slater had loved her, and Kristin was certain that he wouldn't be here with her now if the woman in the picture were still alive.

There seemed to be an ominous silence all over the house as dinnertime approached. Delilah had been out to feed the hands, and the table was set for the family.

Set for three.

They weren't using the fine service that evening. Shannon had set out the pewter plates, and the atmosphere in the dining room seemed as muted and subdued as the dull color of the dishes.

Cole had stayed out all day. Kristin had done her best to be useful, but the day had been a waste. There was no way out of it. She couldn't forget Cole's promise that he would be there that night, and she couldn't forget the woman in the picture, and she couldn't forget the startling array of emotions that it had all raised within her.

Kristin had dressed for dinner.

She was a rancher, and this ranch on the border between Kansas and Missouri was a far cry from the fine parlors and plantations back east, but she was still a woman and she loved clothes.

It was a weakness with her, Pa had told her once, but he'd had a twinkle in his eyes when he'd said it. He'd always been determined that his daughters should be ladies. Capable women, but ladies for all that. He had always been pleased to indulge her whims, letting her study fabrics, and to pick up her *Lady Godoy's* the minute the fashion magazine reached the local mercantile. Her armoire was still filled with gowns, and her trunks and dressers held an endless assortment of petticoats and hoops, chemises and corsets, stockings and pantalets. They had all lent a certain grace to life once upon a time. Before the carnage had begun. By day they had worked for their dream, and the dust and the tumbleweed of the prairie had settled on them. At night they had washed away the dust and the dirt, and after dinner Pa had settled back in his chair with a cigar and she and Shannon had taken turns at the spinet. Her own voice was passable. Shannon's was like that of a nightingale.

And there had been nights when Adam had been there, too. Sometimes winter had raged beyond the windows, but they had been warm inside, warmed by the fire and by the love and laughter that had surrounded them.

That was what Zeke had hated so much, she thought. He had never understood that laughter and love could not be bought or stolen. He had called her a traitor to the Southern cause, but she had never betrayed the South. She had merely learned to despise him, and so she had lost her father, and then Adam, too.

Today she could remember Adam all too clearly. He had loved books. He had always looked so handsome, leaning against the fireplace, his features animated as he spoke about the works of Hawthorne and Sir Walter Scott.

No one had told her that Adam was riding out after Zeke. She'd never had the chance to try to stop him.

And now she wondered painfully if she had ever really

loved him. Oh, she had cared for him dearly. He had been a
fine man, good and decent and caring, and he had often made
her laugh.

But she had never, never thought of Adam in the way that
she had Cole Slater, had never even imagined doing with
Adam the things she had actually done with Cole Slater.

And she didn't love Cole Slater. She couldn't love him. No,
she couldn't love him, not even now. How could a woman
love a man who had treated her the way he had?

But how could she forget him? How could she forget all
she had felt since she'd first seen the man? How could she
forget all that had passed between them? Kristin realized that
it was difficult just to be in the same room with him now. Her
breath shortened instantly, and she couldn't keep her gaze
steady, and she wanted to run away every time he looked her
way. She couldn't look at him without remembering their
night together, and when she did she wanted to crawl into a
hole in the ground and hide. She was ashamed, not so much
because of what she had done but because she had been so
fascinated by it. Because she still felt the little trickles of excitement stir within her whenever he entered the room, whenever she felt his presence.

She knew instinctively when he came into the house for
dinner.

Fall was coming on, and the evening was cool. She had
dressed in a soft white velvet gown with black cord trim. The
bodice was low, and the half sleeves were trimmed in black
cord, too. The skirt was sweeping, and she had chosen to wear
a hoop and three petticoats.

She'd made Delilah tie her corset so tightly that she wasn't
sure she'd be able to breathe all evening.

Her appearance had suddenly become very, very important
to her. He hadn't been cruel to her, but he had been mocking,
and he'd warned her again and again that this terribly intimate
thing between them had nothing to do with involvement. Her
pride was badly bruised, and all she had to cling to was her
dream of leaving him panting in the dust. Someday. When she
didn't need him anymore.

She'd braided her hair and curled it high atop her head, except for one long lock that swept around the column of her neck and the curve of her shoulder to rest on the mound of her cleavage.

She never used rouge—Pa hadn't allowed it in the house—but she pinched her cheeks and bit her lips, to bring some color to her features. Still, when she gazed at her reflection in the mirror over the dresser—she had refused to dress in the other room—she was terribly pale, and she looked more like a nervous girl than a sophisticated woman in charge of her life, owner of her property, mistress of her own destiny.

She tried to sweep elegantly down the stairs, but her knees were weak, so she gave up and came down as quickly as she could. Shannon was setting cups on the table. She stared at Kristin with wide blue eyes, but she didn't say anything. Nor did Kristin have to question her about Cole.

"He's in Pa's office," Shannon mouthed. Kristin nodded. Nervously, she started through the house. She passed through the parlor and came around, pausing in the doorway.

He was sitting at her father's desk, reading the newspaper, and his brows were drawn into such a dark and brooding frown that she nearly turned away. Then he looked up. She was certain that he started for a moment, but he hid it quickly and stood politely. His gaze never left her.

"Bad news?" she asked him, looking at the paper.

He shrugged. "Not much of anything today," he said.

"No great Southern victory? No wonderful Union rout?"

"You sound bitter."

"I am."

"You got kin in the army?"

"My brother."

"North or South?"

"North. He's with an Illinois troop." Kristin hesitated. She didn't want him to feel that they were traitors to the Southern cause. "Matthew was here when Pa was killed. He learned a whole lot about hatred."

"I understand."

She nodded. Then curiously she asked him. "And have you got kin in the army, Mr. Slater?"

"Yes."

"North or South?"

He hesitated. "Both."

"You were in the Union Army."

"Yes." Again he paused. Then he spoke softly. "Yes. And every time I see a list of the dead—either side—it hurts like hell. You've seen the worst of it, Kristin. There are men on both sides of this thing who are fine and gallant, the very best we've ever bred, no matter what state they've hailed from."

It was a curious moment. Kristin felt warm, almost felt cherished. She sensed depths to him that went very far beyond her understanding, and she was glad that he was here for her.

However briefly.

But then he turned, and she saw his profile. She saw its strengths, and she saw the marks that time had left upon it, and she remembered the woman in the picture, and that he didn't really love her at all. And she felt awkward, her nerves on edge again.

"Supper's about on the table," she said.

He nodded.

"Can I...can I get you a drink? Or something?"

Or something. She saw the slow smile seep into his lips at her words, and she blushed, feeling like a fool despite herself. He nodded again.

"Madeira?"

"A shot of whiskey would be fine."

Kristin nodded, wondering what had prompted her to say such a thing. He was closer to the whiskey than she was, and he knew it, but he didn't make a move to get it. He kept staring at her, his smile mocking again.

She swept into the room and took the whiskey from the drawer. They were very close to one another. He hadn't changed. He was still wearing tight breeches and a cotton shirt and his riding boots. She knew he had ridden out to meet with Pete, and she knew, too, that he seemed to know something about ranching. Well, he was from somewhere around here, according to Shannon.

She poured him out a double shot of the amber liquid, feeling him watching her every second. She started to hand him the glass, but he didn't seem to notice. His eyes were on hers, grown dark, like the sky before a tornado.

He reached out and touched the golden lock of hair that curled over the rise of her breasts. He curled it around his finger, his thumb grazing her bare flesh. She couldn't move. A soft sound came from her throat, and suddenly it was as if all the fires of hell had risen up to sweep through her, robbing her of all strength. She stared up at him, but his eyes were on her hair, and on her flesh where he touched her. She felt heat radiating from the length and breadth of his body, and yet she shivered, remembering the strength of his shoulders, the hardness of his belly, the power of his thighs.

And she remembered the speed of his draw. He was a gunslinger, she thought, bred to violence.

No. He had been to West Point. He had served as a captain in the U.S. cavalry. That was what he had told Shannon, at least.

Did any of it matter? He was here, and as long as he was here she felt safe from the Zeke Moreaus of the world. And yet, she thought, their's must surely be a bargain made in hell, for when he looked at her, when he touched her even as lightly as he did now, she felt the slow fires of sure damnation seize her.

"Do you always dress so for dinner?" he asked her, and the timbre of his voice sent new shivers skating down her spine.

"Always," she managed to murmur.

His knuckles hovered over her breasts. Then his eyes met hers, and he slowly relinquished the golden curl he held. Expectation swirled around them, and Kristin was afraid that her knees would give, that she would fall against him. The whiskey in the glass she held threatened to spill over. He took the glass from her and set it on the desk. She felt heat where his fingers had brushed hers, and it seemed that the air, the very space between them, hummed with a palpable tension.

"You are a very beautiful woman, Miss McCahy," he told her softly, and she felt his male voice, male and sensual, wash over her.

"Then, you're not...you're not too disappointed in our deal?"

He smiled again, and his silver-gray eyes brightened wickedly. "Did we need a deal?"

"I don't know what you mean," she told him, though she knew exactly what he meant.

The light went out of his eyes. He picked up the whiskey and swallowed it quickly. "I'm still damned if I know what the hell I'm doing here," he muttered.

"I thought—" she began, and her face flamed.

He touched her cheek. "You thought the payoff went well, is that it?"

She shoved his hand away. She didn't want him to touch her, not then. "You do have a talent for making a woman feel just like river slime," she said, as sweetly as she could. He arched a brow, and she saw fleeting amusement light his features. She could hold her own in any fight, she thought, but only for so long. She needed to escape him now.

"I didn't mean to make you feel like...river slime."

"Don't worry. You already did so. Last night." With a sweetly mocking smile, Kristin turned to leave.

Then she paused and turned toward him again, biting her lip. She kept forgetting how much she needed him. Her eyes must have widened with the realization, for he was smiling cynically again and pouring himself another shot of whiskey.

"Don't worry," he told her smoothly. "I'm not walking out on you. Not yet."

Kristin moistened her lips. "Not yet?" she whispered.

"Why, Miss McCahy! I really couldn't leave a lady in such distress, could I?"

"What do you mean by that?"

He raised the glass. "Take it as you will, ma'am."

Kristin swore under her breath and strode over to him again. She snatched the glass from his hand and thought seriously of pouring the contents over his head. His eyes narrowed, and she quickly reconsidered.

She swallowed the whiskey down so quickly that her head spun in an instant and her throat burned with the fury of a brush fire. A double shot, straight. But she steeled herself, and she still managed to smile sweetly. "You don't owe me anything."

"No, darlin'. You owe me." He smiled, took the glass from her and poured another double. "And I'm real anxious for the next installment."

Kristin snatched the glass again and swallowed the liquid down. She didn't know if she was alive with anger or with desire.

She slammed the glass down and tried to spin around. He caught her arm, pulling her back. She tossed her head back, staring into his eyes.

"Isn't it what you want?" he asked her.

"I want revenge, nothing more," she told him.

"Nothing more?"

"I want you to—I want you to stay. I want to hold on to the ranch. I just want to hold on to what is mine."

"The precious ranch," he muttered darkly.

Fear fluttered briefly in her heart. "Cole...Mr. Slater, you really wouldn't...you wouldn't go back on your word, would you?"

"Not so long as you follow the rules."

Her head was really spinning now. He had poured so much whiskey, and she'd swallowed it down so fast. He was so warm, and so damn vibrant, and so shockingly male. And she'd already been in bed with him.

Her mother would be spinning in her grave, Kristin thought.

He was using her. He was using her because he had loved another woman and now he just didn't give a damn.

"Your rules! Just don't forget that the place belongs to me!"

She wrenched free of him, and this time she walked out.

She wasn't afraid of him leaving. He was having too fine a time torturing her to leave now.

When she reached the dining room, she was startled to discover that he was behind her. He had followed her, as silent as a wraith. It was disconcerting.

"Stop it!" she demanded.

Shannon came out of the kitchen. Delilah was behind her. Both women stopped, startled.

Cole ignored them both. "Stop what?" he demanded irritably.

"Sneaking up on me!"

"I wasn't sneaking up on you. You told me it was time for supper, so I followed you."

"Whoa!" Shannon murmured, looking at her sister. "Kristin, you've been drinking!"

"Yes!" she snapped, glaring at Cole. "And I'll probably do a whole lot more drinking before…before…"

"Oh, hell, will you just sit the hell down!" Cole growled. He caught her hand, pulled out a chair and directed her into it with little grace. Her wide skirts flew. He pressed them down and shoved her chair in.

Kristin wanted to be dignified. She wanted to be sophisticated and elegant, and most of all she wanted to be in control. "You arrogant scallywag!" she said quietly, her voice husky with emotion.

"Kristin, shut up."

That was it. She started to push herself away from the table, but his hand slammed down on hers, holding her fast. "Kristin, shut up."

"Bas—"

"Now, Kristin." He came closer to her, much closer, and spoke in a whisper. This was between the two of them. "Or else we can get up and settle this outside."

The whiskey seemed to hit her anew right then, hit her hard. She thought she was going to scream. She burst into laughter instead. "Outside? With pistols?"

"Hardly, but you can call it what you want, darlin'."

The buzz of the liquor was nice. If he stayed around too

long, Kristin thought, she'd find herself turning into a regular old drunk.

"Shall we eat?" Cole asked politely.

There was silence in the room. Shannon was staring at him.

"Sit!" he told her.

Shannon sat hastily, then lowered her head before looking surreptitiously over at Kristin, who hiccuped loudly.

Cole groaned, then he looked up at Delilah. "Don't you and Samson usually eat?"

"Oh, no, sir!" Delilah protested. "Why, you know it just wouldn't be right for black folks—"

"Delilah, cut the...er—" He broke off, looking from Samson to Kristin. Shannon was about to laugh.

"Manure," Kristin supplied.

Shannon did burst into laughter. Even Delilah grinned. Cole said, "Get your husband, woman, and sit down and eat. I once had the opportunity to discover that a black man could save my hide as good as a white one. Let's just have supper and get it over with, shall we?"

"Yessir, yessir," Delilah said, chuckling. "My, my, my," she muttered, moving off toward the kitchen.

Kristin sat primly, her hands folded in her lap. Her dress felt ridiculously heavy, now that she was sitting. She felt as if she was about to fall over. She realized that Cole was looking at her, but it didn't matter very much, and that was a nice feeling.

Delilah walked back in from the kitchen.

Cole gazed at her expectantly. "You've never washed her mouth out with soap, huh?" He indicated Kristin.

Kristin decided that she could sit straight. She told Cole that he reminded her of the stuff that people needed to wipe off their boots before they came in from the barn.

Shannon gasped, and then she began to giggle. Delilah stood stock-still. Samson, coming in behind his wife, turned an ashen color.

Cole was dead still. Explosively still. And then explosively in motion.

He was up, and Kristin sobered enough to know a moment's

panic as he came around behind her and purposely pulled her chair away from the table. He lifted her, and her petticoats and hoops and shirt went flying. Kristin swore at him and pounded on his back.

''Cole!'' Kristin gasped.

What manner of man had she let loose in her home, she wondered.

He started for the stairs.

''What are you doing?'' she shrieked.

''Putting you to bed.''

''I don't want to go!''

''My rules, Miss McCahy.''

They were all watching her, Shannon and Delilah and Samson, and they weren't doing a thing to save her. They were just staring. She raised her head and saw that Delilah was openly grinning and Samson was hiding a smile.

''You son of a bitch!'' she yelled.

''We are going to have to do something about that mouth of yours,'' Cole vowed grimly.

''This is my house!''

''My rules!''

She told him what he could do with his rules, but it was too late. They were already up the stairs. He booted open the door to the room he had decreed they would share, and before she knew it she had landed on the bed. She wanted to get back up, but she groaned instead and clutched her temples.

His leering face was above her.

''Why, what's the matter, Miss McCahy? Why, I would have thought you could drink any man west of the Mississippi under the table.''

''Madeira,'' she whispered. ''Not whiskey.''

He showed her no mercy. Suddenly his hand was on her leg and he was pulling off her shoe. She managed to pull herself up to a sitting position and pummel his back. ''What are you doing?''

''Taking your shoes off.'' But her shoes were off, and his hands were still on her, slipping along her calf, then her thigh.

When his fingers touched her thigh, she gasped and tried to stop him. ''Damn you Cole Slater—''

Her words ended in a gasp, for he turned quickly, pulling hard on her ankle so that she was lying flat on her back again. Her silk stockings came free in his hands, and he tossed them carelessly on the floor. She tried to rise, and he came down beside her on the bed, his weight on her.

''Where the hell are the damn ties to these things?'' he muttered, working on her hoop.

Kristin struggled to stop him, but he found the ties. She reached for his hands, but they had already moved, freeing her from her hoop and petticoats, and he pulled her up, working on the hooks of her gown. In seconds he had it free and she was down to her pantalets, chemise and corset.

''Come here!'' he demanded roughly. Kristin cried out, trying to elude him, but he pulled her back by the corset ties. He lossened the ties, and she gasped, amazed by the air that rushed into her lungs. But then she was naked except for her sheer chemise and pantalets, and his presence was overwhelming.

She began to protest. He caught her shoulders and slammed her down on the bed.

''Calm down and sleep it off!'' he commanded.

He was straddling her, and his eyes were like steel. She wanted to slap his superior face. She tried. She missed by a mile, and he caught her hand.

''My rules.''

She told him again what he could do with his rules.

''Stay here alone, or I'll stay here with you.''

She went still, trying to grasp the meaning of his words. The room was spinning madly.

Then she understood. He stared at her. Then he lowered his head toward her and kissed her, and somewhere, within her hazy mind and her bruised heart she knew that he did desire her. And she knew, too, that he didn't love her, not at all.

His kiss was hard and demanding and, in its way, punishing. But then it deepened, and it was rich, and it betrayed a growing passion and hunger. She felt her body respond. She felt his hands move over her, felt him grow warm and hard. She began to tremble and suddenly she wanted him, but she wanted him loving her, loving her tenderly, not just wanting her with the raw desire that had finally brought him to her.

His mouth opened and closed hungrily upon her flesh. His teeth grazed her throat, and the tip of his tongue teased the valley between her breasts. He was a flame setting on her, seeping into her, and she was stunned that he could so easily elicit this willingness...

This eagerness...

Within her. She stiffened, fighting the whiskey haze in her heart and in her mind. She had to stop him. He hadn't meant to do this, not now. He had stayed away from her on purpose, she was certain of it. He wanted no involvements.

And she could too easily fall in love with him.

She forced herself to feel nothing, to allow the bitterness of the last years to invade her, so that his searing warmth could not touch her. When he rose above her, she met his steely gaze and spoke to him in a quiet, toneless voice.

"Who was she? Your wife?"

She might have struck him. All the heat left him. It was as if he turned to ice. He stared at her, his jaw constricted, his features as harsh as a desert. He rolled away from her and sat on the side of the bed. His fingers threaded through his hair, and he pressed his hand against his temple as if he were trying to soothe some awful pain.

"Go to sleep," he told her. "And stay off the hard stuff from now on."

Kristin cast her arm over her eyes. "Your rules," she murmured.

"I don't like this kind of a fight, Kristin," he said dully, "but..."

"But?"

"You start it, and I'll end it. Every time."

She felt his weight lift from the bed, and she started to shiver. Suddenly she was warmed. He had laid a blanket over her, and he was close by her again.

"Go to sleep," he said softly, his voice almost tender again.

Almost.

He got up and walked away. She heard the door close quietly, and to her great dismay she closed her eyes and started to cry as she hadn't done since they had come to tell her that Adam was dead.

Chapter Six

It was the liquor, Kristin thought. Lying in the darkness, feeling miserable, she put her arm over her eyes and felt her head spin, and she wondered what had made her drink so much so fast. She was humiliated, but it was her own fault, and she was in no mood to do anything about it, except to suffer in silence.

And, in a way, she wasn't sorry. She could dimly hear the sounds of dinner, and she wondered if Samson and Delilah had sat down to eat. Cole Slater was an unusual man. A very unusual man.

The darkness closed in and whirled around her. She knew she ought to be sorry she had let the liquor ignite her temper, but instead she was glad of it. She didn't feel the awful pain for once. She didn't remember what it had been like to see Pa die, to see Matthew turn his back on his own people and ride away with the Union forces.

She didn't even quite remember what it was like to be with Cole Slater. To be so nervous that she lost all the wisdom her harsh life had taught her. To be afraid in a way, and yet to want something, some intangible thing, so badly.

Curiously—bless the liquor—she felt at peace.

She closed her eyes, and she must have dozed. Then she must have awakened, or else she was dreaming, because when she opened her eyes, the room was bathed in moonlight. Her mind was still spinning, and she still felt at peace.

He was in the room with her.

He had come in quietly, and the door had closed softly behind him. He stood just inside of it, his hands on his hips, and watched her where she lay upon the bed. The moonlight fell on his features, and they were both harsh and curiously beautiful. For the longest time he stood there. The wind seemed to rise, not to a moan, but to a whisper. She imagined that outside tumbleweeds were being caught and tossed in the strange, sweet dance of the West, buffeted as she was being buffeted. Her heart rose and fell like that tumbleweed, tossed around heedlessly.

No...

He was a marvelous creature, sleek as a cougar, sharp as an eagle. He was still standing there, his hands on his hips, his head at an angle, as if he were waiting, as if he were listening to the curiously tender whispering of the wind.

Then he moved. He unbuttoned his cuffs. He took off his boots and stripped off his socks. He came to her in silence, barefoot, and he dropped his gun belt beside the bed. Then he looked down at her, and saw that her eyes were open. "You're still awake."

She nodded gravely, and then she smiled. "I'm sorry. I was out of line this evening. And I...I don't want to fight."

Unbuttoning his shirt, he sat beside her on the bed. His eyes remained on hers. He reached over and touched her cheek. "I don't want to fight, either, Kristin. You've had a hard time of it, and you've done well. Someone else might have shattered a long, long time ago."

The gentle whisper of the wind was in his voice, and there was an evocative tenderness in his fingertips as they brushed her cheek. She didn't reply, but kept her eyes on his, and then the whisper of the wind seemed to sweep into her, to permeate her flesh and fill her veins. She was warm, and achingly aware of herself, and of the man. Surely, she was still asleep. Surely it was all a dream. It was a spell cast by the moonlight. It lived in the clouds of imagination.

But it was real. Very real. He leaned over then and caught her lips in a curious kiss. It was light at first. He tasted her lips, teasing them with the tip of his tongue. Then he plunged his tongue deep into her mouth, and she wrapped her arms around his neck and felt the rugged, steel-muscled frame of his chest against her. She felt his hands on her, rough and tender. Then his hands were in her hair, threading through the tendrils, and he was stroking her arm as he moved his lips over her throat and down to the place where her breasts spilled provocatively from her lace chemise. His mouth fastened over her nipple through the sheer fabric, and she cried out softly. He shifted swiftly, taking her mouth again, taking her cry into him.

He stood, dropping his shirt and stripping away his pants. The moonlight fell on him. He was tall and rugged, lean and sinewed, his skin shining almost copper in that light, his shoulders shimmering with it. She stared at him. If this was a dream, she was grateful for it. She wanted him. She wanted him with her heart and with her mind, she wanted him with every fiber of her being. She wanted him desperately.

She was not to be denied.

He came down beside her and took her in his arms, and she strained to meet his kiss again. He unlaced her chemise, and her breast spilled from it. He lowered his head again, touching her nipple with his tongue, fondling the weight of her breast with a touch so achingly soft.... She was barely aware that she arched to him, that she dug her fingers into his hair and cried incoherently for him to come to her. But it was not to be. His hands brushed her flesh, and where they had been she yearned for them again. His kisses ranged over the length of her, a mere breath, a mere whisper, and then were gone. She writhed. She tried to hold him, to pin him down. And she felt something move in her, like lava rising to the surface of the earth. She felt the earth teeming and bubbling with heat and steam, and still he pressed her. She moved her hands against him, felt the tension in his taut muscles, and touching him inflamed her, bringing her to still greater heights. She no longer knew herself. She had become some strange wanton. She felt his hands on her hips, and on her belly and she moved toward the feel of them, the promise of them. He made her touch him, and the pulsing heat and size of him gave her pause. Then a curious elation filled her, and for a moment she was afraid she might faint.

Her remaining clothes were gone now. Like him, she lay naked in the moonlight, her skin shimmering like copper beneath its glow.

Time had lost all meaning. She lay upon clouds of moonlight, and all that was real was the hardness of this man, the demand in his eyes. The wind had become the ragged cry of his breath, and the storm was the near-savage urgency that drove him. He did not tease. He sucked hard on her breast until she thought she would explode. He did not shyly caress her thighs, but stroked within, to the heart of her, and as he touched her, he caught her cries again with his lips. He knelt before her, caught her eyes again, then watched her, before he caught the supple length of her legs and brought them around him. He stared at her as he lowered his head, and she opened her mouth to stop him, but she could not.

He touched her intimately, with a searing demand, and she tossed her head, savagely biting her own lip so as not to scream. She could not bear it, and despite her efforts she did cry out. She lunged forward, she convulsed and she heard the soft tenor of his laughter. She longed to strike him, to hide from him. But he was above her, and he had her hands, and suddenly he was within her, igniting a fierce burning, and it was all happening again, all beginning again. His hands roughly cupped her buttocks, and again he led her into a shattering rhythm.

The clouds danced around them. She closed her eyes and buried her face against his chest, and she tasted the salt on his body. There was nothing gentle in him then. He moved in a frenzy, violent, urgent, and though she feared she would lose herself in him, she clung to him and fought to meet his every move. Ecstasy burst through again, even stronger than before, and she dug her fingers into his flesh, convulsing against him. He shuddered strongly against her, and she was filled with their mutual heat. Then he fell from her, smoothing the wild tangle of her hair.

They didn't say anything. Not anything at all.

The wind had died down again. It was a mere whisper. It caught the tumbleweeds down below and tossed them around.

Her heart was still beating savagely,. He must have felt it when he put his arm around her and pulled her against him. It was a wonderful way to sleep, her back to his chest, his fingers just below the full curve of her breast. She didn't think about the wind, or the night. The moonlight was still shining down on them. Perhaps it had all been a dream. She didn't want to know. She closed her eyes, and at long last the spinning in her head stopped. She slept.

He slept, too, and it was his turn to dream. The nightmare of the past, the nightmare that haunted him whether he was awake or asleep, came back to him now.

The dream unfolded slowly, so slowly. It always came to him first with sound…a soft, continual thunder, like the beating of drums. It was the sound of hooves driving across the earth, driving hard. Then he heard the shouts. They made no sense at first, they meant nothing, nothing at all. Then he realized that the hooves were churning beneath him. He was the rider. He was riding hard, riding desperately, and all he wanted to do was get home before…

Smoke. He inhaled sharply and it filled his nostrils and mouth with an acrid taste. There was something about that smell… He could feel a trail of ice streak along his spine. He recognized the awful odor of burning flesh.

Then he saw the horror up ahead. The house was burning; the barn was burning.

And he saw Elizabeth.

She was running, trying to reach him. He screamed her name, his voice ragged and harsh, and still he felt the movement beneath him, the endless thunder of the horse's hooves. He rode across the plain, across the scrub brush. And she kept coming. She was calling to him, but the sound of her voice could not reach him. She could not reach him.

She fell and disappeared from sight. He rode harder, and then he leaped from the horse, still shouting her name, over and over. He searched through the grass until he found her. Her hair, long and lustrous and ebony black, was spread over the earth in soft, silken waves.

"Elizabeth..."

He took her into his arms, and he looked down, and all that he saw was red. Red, spilling over him, filling his hands. Red, flowing in rivers, red...the color of blood.

He cast back his head, and he screamed, and the scream echoed and echoed across the plain....

He awoke with a start.

He was covered in sweat, and he was trembling. He shook his head, trying to clear it, and gazed at the woman beside him. He saw her golden hair, and the easy rise and fall of her chest with her breath.

She hadn't awakened.

He rose and went to the window, where he stared out at the moon. He hadn't woken her; it was going to be all right. Maybe he was getting better; at least he wasn't screaming out loud anymore.

He walked over to the bed and stared down at her; and she seemed incredibly young and pure, and very lovely. His fingers itched, and he wanted to shake her, to tell her that she didn't understand how deadly the game she was playing could be.

His fingers eased. Maybe she knew.

He went back to the window and stared at the moon again. Slowly, the tension left him, and he sighed. He went back to bed, but he couldn't bear to touch her, even though he knew that someday soon he would. He needed to touch her, just as he needed air to breathe.

He didn't sleep. In time, dawn came. He rose and dressed, then went outside. He gazed out over the plain, and in his mind he saw Elizabeth again, running toward him. He closed his eyes, and she was gone, but the pain was still with him, filling him, gnawing at his insides. He straightened his shoulders, and the pain slowly began to ebb, but it never fully left him. It clutched his heart with icy fingers, and he wondered what the hell he was doing here, then reminded himself that he had agreed to a "deal," and he might as well get on with it. He turned around and stared at her window. She was sleeping just beyond it. He marched back to the house.

She'd never expected to be awakened so rudely. One second she was so deep in blissful sleep, and the next she felt his hand against her rump. Her *bare* rump. He'd pulled the covers away from her.

Protesting, she grabbed the covers and sat with them pulled up to her chin, her eyes blazing with fury and indignation. He was up and dressed, standing at the foot of the bed and surveying her with cold eyes.

"I want you in the office. Now. If you want my help, you'd better show me the books."

"I'll come down to the office when I'm ready," she snapped. She couldn't understand the man. She couldn't understand his strange, distant behavior after the things they had shared in the night. It hurt.

"Get up."

She narrowed her eyes at this new battle.

"You get out and then I'll get up. When I'm ready."

He grabbed the sheets again. She lunged for them but she was too late, and he stripped them away. He eyed her dispassionately, his steely gaze sweeping over her form. She jumped out of bed, swearing once again, and leaped toward him, her temper soaring. He caught her arms, and his smile was curiously grim and somehow self-satisfied. It was as if he had been trying to pick a fight. She tried to wrench free of his touch. She didn't like the daylight on her naked flesh, and she didn't like the disadvantage of being undressed while he was clad from his scarf to his boots. He pulled her close against him. She felt the bite of his belt buckle and the texture of his shirt, but most of all she felt a hot tempest of emotions within him, no matter how calm, cold and in control he looked.

"I told you," he said sharply, "I call the shots. And you can't laze in bed all morning. You're a rancher. You should know that. Or do you just play at this thing? When you feel like riding with the boys, you do. And when you feel like playing the Southern belle, then you do that, too.''

She was furious, but she smiled to hide it. Tense and still against him and staring up into his eyes, she smiled. ''I don't play at anything, Mr. Slater. I am a rancher, and probably better at it than you ever were or could be. I just don't have to be as ugly as a mule's rump to do it. You call the shots? Well, that's just fine. When you want me up from now on, you knock. One knock, Mr. Slater, and I promise I'll be right out in less than five minutes. But don't you ever, ever touch me like that again!''

His brow arched slowly, and she saw his smile deepen. He released her and put his hands on his hips. She felt his gaze sweep over her again like fire. For a moment she thought he was going to sweep her up in his arms, right there, right then, in broad daylight. For a moment she was certain he was going to carry her over to the bed and take her there and then, with the morning sun shining on them.

She'd have to protest, she'd have to scream....

For the life of her she didn't know if she was afraid or if she wished he'd take a step forward and sweep her up in his arms....

He tipped his hat to her.

''I call all the shots, Kristin. All of them.''

He turned around then and left her. The door closed sharply behind him.

She washed and dressed, wondering again what kind of a monster she had brought into her home. She touched her cheeks, and it was as if they were on fire.

When she came down the stairs, he was just finishing his breakfast. He tossed his checkered napkin on the table and rose at the sight of her. Kristin went to her chair.

''Flapjacks, honey?'' Delilah asked her.

Cole was around the table before she had a chance to sit. He took her arm.

''Give her a cup of coffee, Delilah. Nothing else for the moment. We've got work to do.''

She could make a scene, as she had at dinner. Delilah was

staring at her, and Samson was staring at her, and so was Shannon. Her sister's eyes were very wide. They were all waiting.

Bastard! she thought. He was at fault! But she had been at fault the night before, and she knew she would look like a spoiled fool again if she created a problem.

"That's right. This is a busy, busy day, isn't it?" she said sweetly. "Coffee, Delilah." She accepted a cup and smiled her gratitude, gritting her teeth. She freed her arm from Cole's grasp. "Do come, Mr. Slater. The day is wearing on."

He followed her into the office, then swept past her, taking a seat behind her father's desk. He'd already been in there that morning, she was certain. He had the ledgers out, and before she could even seat herself he was firing out a barrage of questions. Where did she buy her feed, how much, how often? Had she considered moving any of the herd to avoid soldiers, Union and Confederate? Had she thought of leaving more pasture time, had she thought of introducing new strains? And on and on.

She didn't falter once. She was a rancher. She was bright, determined and well schooled, and she wanted him to know it. It occurred to her that he was just some drifter, that he had no rights here at all. But then she remembered that she had asked him to stay, that she had been desperate for him to stay.

That she had been willing to do anything at all to make him stay. And he had stayed, and she wasn't the same person anymore, not in any way. But whoever she was now, he wasn't going to treat her this way.

Suddenly he slammed the ledger he was examining shut and stood up. He stared across the desk at her, and for a moment she thought he must hate her.

He had saved her from Zeke, she reminded herself. He had ridden in, all honor and chivalry, and he had saved her from Zeke. Now he looked as if he wanted to flay her alive himself.

He looked as if he were about to say something. He shook his head impatiently. "I'm going out," he said. He jammed his hat low on his head, and came around the desk.

Kristin rose quickly and, she hoped, with dignity. "If you'd let me come with you—"

"No. I don't want you with me."

"I could show you—"

"God damn you, can't you hear? Or are you just incapable of listening? I'll see things myself. I'll see what I want to see. And you'll stay here by the house. Roam too far and come across Zeke and you'll wind up on your own this time. I swear it."

It might be better! she longed to shout. But she didn't do it, because it wasn't true. Zeke had killed her father. No matter how outrageously bad Cole's manners were turning out to be, he didn't compare with Zeke.

She crossed her arms over her chest and leaned back. "Don't let me keep you," she said sarcastically.

He walked past her.

She didn't know where he went. She was pretty sure he was never far away, but he didn't come by the house.

He had left a newspaper on the table, and she sat down and stared at the articles. War. It was all about war. About the Union troops holding Kansas, about the measures they intended to take against Quantrill and his raiders.

War and more war. The Union held New Orleans, and Grant was swearing he'd have Vicksburg soon. But whether the Union held sway or not, there was something that couldn't be changed. In the East, Lee was leading them all a merry chase. He had fewer men, he had less ammunition, he had less food. But he was brilliant, and not even the fact that the paper had been published in a town filled with Yankees could change the tenor of the articles. The South was strong. They could beat her and beat her, but she had the genius of Lee and Stonewall Jackson, and she had the daring of Jeb Stuart and Morgan Hunt and others like them.

Kristin laid her face against the cool wood of her father's desk. The news didn't make her happy or proud. It filled her heart with dread. It meant the war was going to go on and on. Nobody was going to go out and whomp the pants off anybody else. It was just going to keep going.

And Quantrill's outlaws would keep raiding and raiding....

After a while, Kristin lifted her head. There was a knock at the door. Delilah was there. She stuck her head in hesitantly.

"How about something to eat? Flapjacks and bacon?"

Her stomach was rumbling. She was starving. She hadn't had any supper, and she hadn't had any breakfast. She stood up and slid her hands into her back pockets.

"Flapjacks sound great."

"Fine. Come along."

"Delilah, wait."

Delilah hesitated there in the doorway. She met Kristin's eyes.

"Delilah, am I doing the right thing?"

"Honey, you're doing the only thing."

Kristin shook her head. "He made a fool out of me last night, Delilah."

"You let that happen."

"Yes, I did. But—"

"We need him," Delilah said bluntly. Then she smiled and gazed at Kristin, and Kristin was sure she was blushing beneath the gold and mahogany of her coloring. "We need him, and I like him. I like him just fine. You did well."

Kristin blushed herself. "I didn't marry him, Delilah. I'm...I'm his...mistress, Delilah."

"You did well," Delilah repeated. "I like him. I don't care what he seems to be, he's a right honorable fellow." She was silent for a moment. "You come along now and have something to eat."

Kristin did.

Then she set to the housework with a vengeance, cleaning and sweeping. Later she went out to the barn and spent some time grooming the horses that weren't out with the hands. She came back in and bathed, and while she sat in the tub she decided that although her feelings about him were entirely different from her feelings about Zeke, she still hated Cole Slater. She couldn't even take a bath in peace anymore. She kept thinking about him the entire time. She wanted to be clean, and she wanted to smell sweet, because she could just imagine him…

She promised herself she would be cool and aloof and dignified through dinner and all through the evening.

She promised herself she would be cool and aloof and wouldn't allow him to touch her.

But he didn't come back for dinner. He didn't come back at all. At midnight she gave up and went upstairs. She managed to stay awake for an hour, but then she fell asleep. She had taken care to dress in a high-necked nightgown, one with a multitude of delicate little buttons at the throat.

Cole stayed out for a long time that night, waiting for her to fall asleep. He smoked a cigar and sipped a brandy and wondered where Quantrill's boys might be.

Quantrill was no bargain, Cole thought, but he wasn't the worst of the lot. He rode with some frightening company. Bill Anderson was a blood-thirsty soul. Zeke was a horror. Cole had heard that some of the men liked to fight the way the Indians did, taking scalps from their victims.

Quantrill for the South…

And the likes of Lane and Jennison for the North. Killing anyone and anything that stood in their way. Making a jest out of a war that was being fought desperately on both sides for different sets of ideals.

Smoke rose high above him, and he shivered suddenly. He hadn't been able to get Elizabeth's face out of his mind all day. But now, curiously, when he closed his eyes, he saw Kristin. Saw her fighting for all she was worth. Saw her fallen in the dirt.

He stood up and dusted off his hands on his pants.

Kristin was alive, and Elizabeth wasn't. Elizabeth had died because of Doc Jennison and his jayhawkers; Kristin had been attacked by the bushwhackers.

He was angry with her for being alive, he realized. She was alive and Elizabeth wasn't. And he knew he couldn't explain that to her.

He threw his cigar down in the dirt and snuffed it out with the heel of his boot. Then he turned around. He couldn't back down on any of the demands he had made of her. Not ever. It was just part of his nature, he supposed. And it was important that Quantrill know that he was living with her—intimately.

He looked up at the house and swore, then entered it quietly. For a moment he paused in the darkness of the entry. It was a good house. It had been built sturdy and strong, and it had been made into a home. It had grace.

He paused and inhaled deeply. Then he started for the stairway and climbed the steps silently. He reached his room and opened the door, thinking that she must have returned to her own room.

She hadn't. She was curled up on the bed. Her hair spilled over on his pillow.

He cast aside his clothes impatiently and approached the bed, but before he could pull back the covers, his hand brushed a tendril of hair that lay on his pillow, and its soft scent rose up to greet him. Heat immediately snaked through him. He didn't want it this way. But all he had to do was touch her hair and see her innocent form and he was tied into harsh knots of desire.

He didn't have to give in to it, he reminded himself.

He stretched out and stared at the ceiling, drumming his fingers on his chest. She was sound asleep, and even if she were not she would surely not be particularly fond of him at the moment.

A minute later he was on his side, just watching her. He throbbed, he ached, his desire thundering, clamoring for release.

He touched her hair again and reminded himself that it should be black. He didn't love this girl.

He slipped his hand beneath her gown and slowly, lightly stroked her flesh, following the line of her calf, the length of her thigh, the curve of her hip. He rounded her buttocks with a feathery touch, then gently tugged her around and pressed his lips against hers.

She responded, warmly and sweetly and instinctively, to his touch. Her arms swept around him and her body pressed against his. Her lips parted and he plundered the honey-warm depths of her mouth with his tongue. His body pressed against hers intimately. He pulled her gown up further and wedged his hips between her bare thighs. Her eyes remained closed. She was barely awake.

Then she awoke fully. Her eyes widened, and she pressed furiously against his shoulders. He thought he saw tears sting her eyes as she pronounced him a son of a bitch.

"I know," he told her.

"If you know—"

"I'm sorry."

He tried to kiss her again, but she twisted her head, and his lips fell against her throat.

"You behave like a tyrant."

"I know. I'm sorry."

"You treat people like servants—"

"I know. I'm sorry."

"You behave—"

Her mouth was open, and he caught her lower lip between his teeth and bathed it with his tongue. Then he began to move against her. He caught her cheeks between his palms and stroked her hair, and when she stared up at him again, gasping for breath, he kissed her again quickly, speaking against her lips.

"I am sorry. So damned sorry, for so damned much."

She was silent then, staring at him in the darkness. She was very still, very aware of his sex throbbing against her, so close. If she fought him he would leave.

She didn't fight him. She continued to stare at him, and he met her eyes. Then he moved, thrusting deep inside her. She let out a garbled little sound, and her arms came around him and she buried her face against the hard dampness of his shoulder. Her long limbs came around him, and he sank deeper into her and then deeper still.

She was instinctively sensual, and she offered him greater solace than he could ever have imagined. When it was over he lay with her hair tangling over his naked chest and reminded himself again that it was blond and not ebony black.

They were strangers who had stumbled together. They had answered one another's needs, and that was all.

If he closed his eyes he would see her, Elizabeth, racing toward him. Running, running, running...

But it was not Elizabeth's face he saw in his dreams. Sweet blond hair flowed behind the woman who ran to him in his dreams. Kristin raced to him in the night, and he wanted to reach for her, but he was afraid to. He was afraid he might fail.

He was afraid he would take her in his arms and find her blood on his hands. He was afraid he would see Kristin's exquisite blue eyes on his and see her blood running red onto his hands.

Chapter Seven

When Kristin awoke, she could hear gunfire. Looking out the window, she saw that Samson and Delilah were practicing with Cole's six-shooters. She dressed quickly in a cotton shirt and pants and boots and hurried downstairs and out to the pasture. Delilah stumbled from the recoil every time she fired, but she had a set and determined expression on her face. Samson laughed at her, and she gave him a good hard shove. Cole actually grinned. Then he looked at Kristin and saw that she wasn't happy at all. Perched on a fence, he nodded to her and arched a brow, and she flushed. The nights they shared were real, she thought. But the nights were one thing, and the harsh light of day was another. She wasn't going to act like a child again, and she wasn't going to try to pretend that he hadn't touched her in a way she would never forget, that he hadn't awakened her to something incredible. What if it was wrong according to all moral and social standards? Murder was wrong, too. The world wasn't run according to moral standards anymore. She didn't mind getting close to Cole. He knew how to treat a woman, knew when to be tender, knew when to let the wild winds rage. Even now, as his eyes flickered over her, she felt the warmth of their intimacy, and it wasn't an unpleasant feeling, despite her current impatience. Cole just didn't seem to understand what he was doing to her. He didn't speak. He watched her. Waiting.

"Miz Kristin, I am going to get this down pat!" Delilah swore.

Kristin tried to smile. "Delilah, you can master anything you set your mind to. I've see you." She set her thumbs in the pockets of her pants and said to Cole, "May I speak with you a moment?"

"Speak," Cole said flatly. He had said he was sorry about lots of things, but his manner toward her didn't seem to be much better today than it had been before. And he didn't come down from the fence.

"Alone," she said.

He shrugged, and started to climb down.

"Don't you bother, Mr. Slater," Samson said behind her. Kristin whirled around in surprise. Samson looked at her, his expression almost sorrowful, and gave her a rueful grin. "Meaning no disrespect, Miz Kristin, and you know it. But you're gonna tell him that you don't want him teaching us any more about gunfire. 'Cause of us being free blacks. She thinks that if we don't shoot they'll just put us on a block and not think to shoot us or string us up. Delilah and me talked about it a long, long time. We're in this together. If there's more trouble, we got to stick together. Delilah's got to shoot just like everybody else. You see, Miz Kristin, I been a free man now a long time. And it's mighty sweet."

"Samson..." Kristin swallowed and closed her eyes. "Samson, if you're alive, you can get free again. If you're dead—"

"I believe in the good Lord, Miz Kristin. And one day there's going to be a meetin' 'cross that river. And I ain't going to that meetin' being no coward, or a man who didn't live up to what I believe in. We're in this together, Mis Kristin."

She stared furiously at Cole. He shrugged.

"You fool!" she snapped at him. "Samson is a black man."

"Samson is a man," he replied. "A free man. Your daddy made him so. The way I see it, he's made his choice."

They were all staring at her. No one said anything, and no

one moved. The sun streamed down on them all. Cole kept watching her. She couldn't begin to read the emotions in his eyes. I don't know this man, I don't know him at all, she thought in sudden panic. But did it matter? she asked herself. It couldn't matter. The die had been cast.

"I've got to get back to the house now," Delilah said. "I've got to get Daniel and let Shannon come on down here."

"Shannon?" Kristin whispered.

Cole hopped down from the fence at last. He took his gun from Delilah, and he slowly and deliberately reloaded it. His hat shaded his eyes from her when he spoke. "You want your little sister to be defenseless?" He looked straight at her.

Kristin smiled sweetly and took the gun from him. He had a row of bottles set up on the back fence. She took her time, aiming as slowly and deliberately as he had loaded. She remembered everything her father and Adam had ever taught her. Remember the recoil, and remember that it can be a hell of a lot for a small woman to handle. Squeeze the trigger gently. Don't jerk back on it....

She didn't miss once. Six shots, six bottles blown to bits, the glass tinkling and reflecting the sunlight as it scattered. With a very pleasant smile, she turned to Cole, daintily handing him the Colt.

He wasn't amazed; he didn't even seem surprised. He studied her. He slipped a second Colt from his gunbelt and handed it to her.

"What happens when the target moves?" he demanded.

"Try me."

Cole nodded to Samson. Samson grinned approvingly. He picked up a bottle and sent it flying high and fast into the air. Kristin caught the missile at its peak, just before it curved back downward to earth. Once again the sun shimmered on the exploding pieces, and they fell in a rainbow of color.

"Not bad," Cole murmured. He nudged back his hat and looked at her sharply. "And Shannon?"

Shannon was already on her way to the yard from the house. Delilah had gone inside. Shannon was dressed like a ranch hand today, too. She seemed all the more feminine for the way

her budding curves filled out her shirt and breeches. She
glanced slyly at Kristin, and Kristin knew that she was thinking of the fiasco at dinner the night before. She was tempted
to give her a sharp slap, but that would be wrong, and she
knew it. She decided to ignore her sister's amusement. "Shannon, Cole wants to see you shoot."

"I know." She smiled at Cole. Shannon liked him. A lot.
Kristin wanted to spin her around and shake her. He'll be gone
in a blink one day! she wanted to tell her sister. Don't care
too much!

Then she wondered if Shannon needed the warning, or if
Kristin did.

"Show him," Kristin suggested.

Shannon proceeded to do so. She was an even better shot
than Kristin, and Cole told her so. He didn't seem to give
anyone lavish praise, but he was always gentler with Shannon
than with anyone else.

"Good. Damned good," Cole told her.

Shannon flushed, delighted by the compliment.

Kristin turned on her heel and headed for the house. He
didn't want her riding away from the house, and he would
insist that she stay. If she didn't, he would leave her to the
mercy of the bushwhackers. She was going to be mature today,
mature and dignified, and she wasn't going to get into any
fights over the ranch.

"Kristin!" he called to her.

She turned to look at him.

"What are you doing?" His plumed hat was set at a cocky
angle, his hands were on his hips, and his frock coat hung
down the length of his back. There was something implacable
about him as he stood there, implacable, unfathomable and
hard. But that was why she had wanted him. He couldn't be
beaten. Not by Quantrill's gang. Not by her.

That last thought made her tremble slightly. She clamped
down hard on her jaw and wondered just how long the war
could last, and wondered if maybe she shouldn't run after all.

"Paperwork," she told him calmly. "I wouldn't dream of

going against your rules, Mr. Slater,'' she said, and walked away.

He rode out later. She knew when he rode out; she heard the sound of his horse's hooves as she sat in the office, trying hard to concentrate on numbers. She walked out front and watched him, and she was restless. This was hard. She had always been such an important part of things.

But they were playing for high stakes. Damned high stakes. She forced herself to sit down again. She weighed the prices she could receive for her beef against the distances she would have to take the herd to collect the money. Then her pencil stopped moving, and she paused and chewed the eraser, and she wondered what it would be like when he came home for dinner that night.

If he came home for dinner that night.

It didn't matter, she told herself. She was forgetting that this whole thing was business. She was certain Cole never forgot for a moment that it was a deal they had made and nothing more.

She had to learn to be aloof. Polite and courteous and mature, but aloof. She had to keep her distance from him. If she didn't, she would get hurt.

Maybe it was too late already. Maybe she had already come too close to the fire. Maybe no matter what happened she was doomed to be hurt. She wasn't so naive that she didn't know she pleased him, but neither was she so foolish as to imagine that it meant anything to him. There was a coldness about him that was like a deep winter frost. It wasn't that he didn't care at all—he did care. But not enough. And he never could care enough, she was certain.

She gave herself a mental shake and decided that she would have to remember herself that it was business—all business. But still she wondered what he would be like if he returned for dinner, and she swore to herself that her own behavior would be the very best the South had ever had to offer.

Cole did return.

And Kristin was charming. She dressed for dinner again, elegantly, in a soft blue brocade with underpanels and a massive, stylish skirt. She remembered her mother, and she was every bit as gracious as she had been. She was careful to refer to him as "Mr. Slater" all the way through the meal. He watched her and he replied in kind, perfectly courteous, as if he'd been trained for society in the finest drawing rooms back East.

When the meal was over, he disappeared outside. Kristin tried to stay up, but at last everyone else had gone to bed, and she walked up the stairs and to the window. She could see him out on the porch, smoking one of her father's fine cigars and drinking brandy from a snifter. He was leaning against one of the pillars and looking up at the night sky.

She wondered what he was thinking, where his heart really lay.

He turned and stared up at her, there in the window. Her face flamed, but he smiled at her.

"Evening," he said softly.

She couldn't reply to him. He watched her curiously for another moment, and his smile deepened, striking against his well-trimmed beard and mustache.

"I'll be right up."

Her heart hammered and slammed against her chest, and she nearly struck her head trying to bring it back in beneath the window frame. She clutched her heart and reminded herself that she had decided to be mature and dignified and not get as flustered as a schoolgirl.

But she was still trembling when he came up the steps. She heard his footsteps in the hallway, and then he opened the door and came into the room. She was still dressed in her blue brocade. He stared at her for a moment, watching the way her breasts rose and fell above the deep décolletage of her gown. He saw the pulse that vibrated against the long, smooth line of her throat. He smiled, and she sensed the curious tenderness that could come to his eyes. "Come here," he told her softly. He held out a hand to her, and she took it and found herself in this arms. And there was nothing awkward about it at all. He kissed her and touched her face, and then he turned her around, and the touch of his fingers against her bare back as he released her gown set her skin to glowing. Like her heart, her flesh seemed to pulse. It occurred to her that he disrobed her so expertly because he had done the same for many women, but it didn't really matter. All that mattered was that her clothing was strewn on the floor and that he was lifting her in his arms and that the soft glow of the moon was with them again. He carried her to the sleigh bed and set her down, and she saw the passion rise in his eyes and come into his touch. She wrapped her arms around him and sighed, savoring the exquisite feel of him against her, the masculine hardness of muscle and limb, the starkly demanding feel of his shaft against her. Somewhere the tumbleweeds tossed, and somewhere the wind blew harsh and wicked and cruel, but here a tempest rose sweet and exciting, wild and exhilarating.

Somewhere battles raged. Somewhere Northerner fought Southerner, and the nation ran with the blood shed by her youth. Blood washed over Kansas and Missouri as if some shared artery had been slashed, but for tonight, Kristin didn't care.

She was alive in his arms, feline and sensual. She was learning where to touch him, how to move with him and against him and how to leave the world behind when she was with him. No drug and no liquor could be so powerful as this elation, so sweet, so all-encompassing.

That night he slept. She stared at his features, and she longed to reach out and touch them, but she did not. She decided that even his nose was strong, long and straight, like a beak against his features. His cheekbones were high, his forehead was wide and his jaw was fine and square beneath the hair of his beard. She wondered at the fine scars that crisscrossed his shoulders and his chest, and then she remembered that he had been with the Union cavalry before the war, and she wondered what battles had done this to him. She longed to touch him so badly....

She reached out, then withdrew her hand. He was an enigma, and he was fascinating. He drew her like the warmth of a fire, and she was afraid. There was so much she didn't know about him. But her fear went deeper than that, for she sensed that though he cared he would never stay. He liked her well enough. He could even be patient with her temper and her uncertainties. He could be careful, and he could be tender, and he seemed as immersed in this startling passion as she was.

But she sensed that he would not stay, could not stay. Not for long. Worse, she sensed that he could never love her, and that she could fall in love with him all too easily. Already, she thought, other men seemed to pale beside him.

Other men...if any remained when the carnage was over.

She walked to the window and looked out at the night. The moon was high, and the paddocks and the outbuildings looked so peaceful there, rising against the flatland. She sighed. For the rest of the country the war had begun when the first shots had been fired at Ford Sumter back in April of '61, but Kansas seemed to have been bleeding forever, and Missouri along with it. The Army of Northern Virginia had defeated the Army of the Potomac at Manassas twice, while along the Mississippi the Union troops were faring a bit better. The North had won the Battle of Shiloh, and just last April New Orleans had fallen to Union troops under Farragut.

It should matter, she thought. It should matter to her who lost and who won. She should care. At Sharpsburg, Maryland, by Antietam Creek, both sides had suffered horribly. She had been in town when the list of the dead had arrived, and it had been devastating. The papers had all cried that the single bloodiest battle of the war had been fought there, and that men had slipped in the blood, and that bodies had fallen on top of other bodies. All she had seen was the tears of the mothers, the sweethearts, the lovers—the families of boys who had left to join the Union Army and the families who had sons fighting with the Confederacy. She had looked for Matthew's name, and she had not seen it, and she had thanked God. But then she had felt the tears around her, felt the agony of the parents, the sisters, the brothers. And yet sometimes it felt as if the real war were remote here. Here the war had been reduced to sheer terrorism. Men did not battle men; they set out to commit murder.

Here it had become a question of survival. All she wanted to do was survive.

She shivered suddenly and realized that she had come naked from the bed and that the night air was cold. She turned and saw that Cole was awake. His eyes were caught by the moonlight as he watched her. They glimmered curiously, and again she wondered at his secret thoughts. Then his gaze fell slowly over the length of her and she realized again that she was naked, and that his very eyes could touch her like a caress.

"Are you all right?" he asked her.

She felt as if she were going to cry, and she didn't know why.

"I was just thinking about the war," she said quietly.

Something covered his eyes, some careful shield. "It seems far away right now, doesn't it? Then again, I don't think we're even fighting the same war as the rest of the country here." There was a harsh bitterness in his tone, and she suddenly felt cold, as if she had turned him against her, or as if she had even made him forget she was there. But then his eyes focused on her again, and they were rueful and surprisingly tender. "Don't think about it," he told her. "Don't think about the war. You can't change it."

She wanted to say something, but she couldn't find her voice, and so she nodded.

"Come back to bed. It's late," he said. Even when he whispered, his voice was so deep. It entered into her and became the wind again.

She forgot about the war. She forgot about the rest of the world. His voice, his beckoning, had that power over her. Her stomach fluttered and her nipples hardened, and she felt she had to cover herself quickly. She had become so bold, so brash. She was standing here naked as a jaybird, and they were talking, and she should have the decency to reach out for something and cover her nudity.

But she did not. She straightened and tossed back her head, and her hair, golden fire in the moonlight, tumbled down the length of her back. She walked toward him. If nothing else, perhaps they could have honesty between them. She honestly wanted him. She wanted these nights. She wanted the way she felt in his arms, wanted this ecstasy that seemed sweeter than life itself.

She came, he thought, very slowly, very sinuously. She allowed a natural sway to come into her walk, and she moved with a feline grace and purpose that set his blood aflame. He was glad that covers lay over his body, for his response to her was instant and instinctive. He clenched his fists at his sides and waited for her. Waited until she stood above him. Then he reached out, pulled her down to him and held her in his arms. He savaged her lips, groaning with the sweet, aching pleasure of it.

He had never thought it could happen, but he had found an oasis with her. He had known she was beautiful, like a sunrise, like the corn that had grown endlessly in the fields before they had run with blood. He had known that he wanted her.

He had not known how badly, how completely, he would come to need her.

Her eyes were a distant sea that claimed him, and the golden skeins of her hair were webs that entrapped him and brought him softly into a dream of paradise. He could not love her, but he could want her, and he did. He hungered for her, as if he could not be filled. She sated him completely, but then she touched him again, or she moved, or she whispered, and he wanted her again. He had taken her from innocence and he had set the woman within her free, and though she came to him with sensual grace, she held on to something of innocence too, and he wondered at that gift. He had to touch her, had to run his fingers over the fine, delicate beauty of her face, had to press his palms against the lush curve of her breast. He had to breathe in her scent.

It had to end, he knew. But he groaned aloud as her nails stroked against his back, as her hips thrust forward. It had to end, he reminded himself....

But then he ceased to think and gave way to urgent need and fevered desire. He looked into her eyes, blue eyes that were soft, radiant and glazed with passion. He swept her beneath him, and he sank into her as he sank into the dream.

She eased the pain. She gave him moments of ecstasy. He could not remember ever having needed a woman so badly. He could not remember so insistent a beat, so desperate, so thunderous a rhythm.

This was like nothing he had ever known. Beautiful, sleek, sensual, she moved beneath him. He became as taut as wire, then shook and shuddered, and spasms continued to rack him.

Later she slept. He cast an elbow behind his head and stared bleakly at the ceiling, shadowed in the moonlight.

It was wrong, he thought. When vengeance lay upon his soul and his heart was barren, it was wrong.

But he could not, would not, make himself cease. She had come to him with the deal. He had not wrung it from her.

That didn't excuse him.

But he needed her....

That didn't excuse him, either. But it mattered. Somehow they had interwoven their lives, and that—as with so many other things—was simply the way it was.

That was simply the way it was.

But still he turned to her. He saw the beautiful curves of her body as she slept, and the tangle of her hair over her shoulders, falling to her flanks, wild and yet somehow virginal. He saw her features, her parted lips and the soft way she breathed. He saw her brow, and he touched it gently, trying to ease the frown line from it. She seemed so very young to have suffered so very much. But she was a fighter. No matter what they had done to her, she had come back up, kicking, fighting. Maybe that was why he couldn't leave her.

He had to leave her, he reminded himself. Soon.

This time it was he who rose. He walked to the window and looked out at the moon. He would have to leave soon, for a time, at least.

He watched the moon, and at last he shrugged. He'd get to the telegraph office tomorrow and hope he could get a message through. He didn't know how long he would have to be gone, but he didn't want her alone. Not now.

Just how long could he guard her?

And would he keep dreaming? He closed his eyes. Dreaming again and again, of one death, of another...

The question washed over his heart, cold as ice. He didn't know. No, he did know. Come hell or high water—or Yankees or Quantrill's raiders—he would find a way to guard her. He wasn't sure why. Maybe it was because this was a matter of honor, and there wasn't much honor left in his world.

And maybe it was because he wanted her so badly. Because she was the only antidote to pain. Because when he was with her he could almost forget...

He didn't want to forget.

Yes, he did. For those few moments.

Whatever the reason, he thought impatiently, he had struck a bargain. He would protect her. He would protect her if she grew hair all over her body and sprouted a full mustache, he swore to himself.

Then he smiled slowly. He was one hell of a liar, he thought, even to himself. She needed him, and he wanted her. That was the bargain.

No. He would protect her, damn it and he would do it so that he never had to hold her bleeding in his arms. He clenched his jaw to keep from crying out. He would protect her because he could not let it happen again.

He breathed slowly and tried to relax.

He would protect her. He had the power. They would help each other, and then he would ride away. The war had to end some day.

Please, God, he thought bleakly. It had to.

The days passed and things were very much the same. After a few days Cole let Kristin ride with him. It was necessary, because the men were busy with the cattle. Kristin showed Cole the length and breadth of her land. She showed him the water holes, and where the land was apt to flood when the rains came too heavily. They went out together searching for a calf that had strayed, and they went into town to buy a length of fencing for the north pasture.

But things felt strange even though they were together. They were polite workmates, cool, courteous acquaintances. Kristin and Shannon always dressed for dinner, because Kristin was determined to cling to what was left of civilization in her life, and the evening meal was her chance to do that. But the conversation there was stilted, too. Cole seldom had much to say to her that wasn't directly concerned with the ranch, with guns, with warnings about the future. She was never to wander around unarmed, and neither was Shannon. He didn't seem to need to warn Delilah or Samson.

He was always polite to Shannon. It seemed to Kristin that her little sister was growing up before her very eyes. Shannon would be eighteen soon, and she was beginning to look every inch the woman. Cole treated her like a child, not condescendingly but with a gentle patience that irritated Kristin. She would have liked some of that patience for herself. Sometimes she asked him very blunt questions, but he invariably ignored her or turned the tables on her. When she demanded to know why he insisted on being such a mystery to her, he merely replied that she had no right to know anything about his past or his future and that she shouldn't be asking.

It didn't matter if she walked away from him, and it didn't matter if she made a sharp reply. He just let her go, or he let her say whatever she wanted and then walked away himself.

But the nights were always the same.

There were times when she couldn't believe she was the same girl who had first met him, innocent, frightened, naive. Even when she felt her temper soar she longed for the night. And even if she turned away from him he stroked her back slowly, moving his fingers down her spine to her buttocks, so lightly that she thought she had imagined it. But his touch was lightning, and it always instilled the same seeds of desire within her. If she really tried to ignore him and he let her be, she sometimes resorted to a soft sigh, feigning sleep, and rolled against him...until he touched her again. Then she sensed his smile, and knew that he knew that she wasn't asleep at all, and that he didn't mind pretending that he needed her more than she needed him.

* * *

It went on....

It went on until she woke up one morning, cold and alone. That wasn't so unusual. He was able to get by on much less sleep than she. But somehow she didn't think he had awakened and gone downstairs. She felt a growing sense of dread.

He was gone.

She heard sounds. A rider. Wrenching a sheet from the bed, she raced to the window and stared down at the paddock area. A man had just come riding in on a big bay horse.

She put her hand to her mouth, biting down hard to keep from crying out. He was dressed in gray. She studied the uniform and gold trim.

Cavalry. The man was a Southern cavalry officer.

She turned around and dressed quickly, finding pants and a shirt and her boots. She told herself that she was a Southerner, that she had been born a Southerner and that only Quantrill had made her fear and hate her own people. She tried to smile, reminding herself that Shannon's great hero was Jeb Stuart, a Southern cavalry officer.

It didn't help. Fear raced through her, and she wondered if the officer had been sent by Zeke or his men.

Cole had told her never to walk around unarmed. She had proven she could use a Colt six-shooter and use it well. She slid her narrow gun belt over her hips and nervously checked to see that her weapons were loaded. Then she started down the stairs.

The house was silent. Where was Shannon? she wondered. She couldn't help it. She had awful visions of her beautiful sister caught in the stables with the men all out on the ranch, caught and thrown down in the hay and viciously raped.

She swallowed and tried to tell herself that she was panicking for nothing. But the house was silent, and she still sensed that Cole was gone. Not just off on the ranch somewhere— gone. She couldn't have explained how she knew. It was an emptiness. It festered inside her, and it held her in an awful anguish.

But this...

This was more urgent. "Delilah?"

No one answered her. Delilah was not in the kitchen, and neither was Samson. She didn't hear the baby crying, and she had no idea where Shannon was.

And the cavalry officer hadn't come to knock at her door.

She crept out the back door, careful to keep it from slamming behind her. Walking as quickly and silently as she could, she came around the corner of the house. The man was gone, and the horse was gone.

Her heart was beating much too quickly. She dropped low and raced over the dry sand to the barn. She followed the line of the buildings, coming closer and closer to the corner.

She paused and inhaled sharply. Her blood raced, and she tried desperately to still her erratic breathing.

She rounded the corner and she came face-to-face with an Enfield rifle.

Behind it stood the man in the Confederate cavalry officer's uniform. It was worn and faded, the gold epaulets frayed.

"Drop it!" he warned her. His eyes were teal, a beautiful color. They were also sharp as razors.

She realized that she was aiming the Colt at him.

"You drop it!" she barked.

He smiled. She realized that he was young and very, very good-looking. And familiar in some way she couldn't quite put her finger on.

"This Enfield can blow a hole right through you."

"It's not a totally dependable weapon."

"At this range? Impossible to miss."

"A Colt will scalp you faster than an Indian would dare dream."

He was tall, masculine and elegant in the worn uniform. He didn't intend to harm her, she was certain. But she didn't lower the barrel of the gun. She had learned not to take any chances.

"Kristin McCahy?"

"Yes."

He laughed and lowered the rifle. "Why in God's name were you sneaking up on me like that?"

She jammed the Colt into her holster, instinct assuring her that she was in no danger. She shook her head ruefully.

"I'm sorry. This is my property. And you are a total stranger, you know. Slinking around on it. My property, that is. I mean...who the hell are you?"

"Slinking?" he inquired indignantly, but there was a twinkle in his eyes. He swept his hat from his head and bowed deeply, an elegant and manly cavalier. "Miss McCahy, I assure you that Slaters do not slink."

"Slater?" she demanded with a quick frown.

"Captain Malachi Slater, ma'am. Cole's brother. On leave—and on new duty, or so it seems. You mean to tell me that Cole didn't say anything?"

She felt as if her knees were going to crumble. Cole was gone. And he hadn't even said goodbye.

"Cole—"

"He had a few things to attend to. I'll be with you for a while. If you don't mind."

She did mind. She minded terribly. Not that Malachi was here, but that Cole was gone. She forced herself to smile and to extend her hand. "Why, Mr. Slater, I'm thrilled and grateful for your appearance. Completely thrilled and entirely grateful."

"Thank you, Miss McCahy." He took her hand and raised it to his lips. Then his blue eyes met hers again and she was certain that he knew everything. And there was something in his gaze that suggested that he understood her feelings.

She withdrew her hand suddenly. "Oh, my God!"

"What?"

"You're a Confederate officer."

He stiffened, and his jaw took on a stubborn set that reminded her of his brother. "Miss, last I heard, Missourians were still considering themselves Southerners—for the most part, that is."

Kristin nodded vaguely. "Well, yes, Mr. Slater. But this is a border country. Half the land around here is occupied by Federal forces."

"Don't worry about me. I'll change into civilian clothing quickly, and I'll avoid the Federals."

She shook her head again. "It's just that, well, I have a brother who is a—"

"A Yankee?"

"Ah...yes, a Yankee."

He looked a lot like Cole. A whole lot. He was very tall and very broad-shouldered in his dress shirt and cape, and at the moment he looked very severe, as if he were about to explode.

But he didn't explode. He suddenly started laughing. "Well, it's one hell of a war, isn't it, Miss McCahy? One hell of a war."

Suddenly the wall behind them exploded. Wood chips went flying from the solid impact of a bullet.

"What the hell?" Malachi shouted. He dragged her to the ground, shielding her with his body. Once again there was the sound of gunfire, and another bullet tore into the walls, sending more wood chips cascading down on them.

"Damn it, what the hell!" Malachi repeated.

What the hell indeed? Kristin had no idea who was firing at them.

Chapter Eight

Kristin lay facedown on the ground, dirt in her mouth, with Malachi on top of her, protecting her. Finally the firing stopped and she heard soft footsteps.

"Get off her, Reb!" Kristin almost laughed out loud with relief. It was Shannon.

"Watch it with that thing, little girl," Malachi said slowly, easing himself away from Kristin. He had angry narrowed eyes leveled on her sister. Kristin sprang to her feet and stepped between them. Shannon's temper was flaring, and her eyes were sparkling dangerously.

"I'm not a little girl, Reb, and I swear I'm damned accurate with this Colt," Shannon replied.

"Why, you little—" Malachi began.

"Stop, stop!" Kristin begged, reaching for the gun. She couldn't imagine trying to explain to Cole Slater why they had murdered his brother. "Shannon—"

"He's a Reb, Kristin. He's probably one of Quantrill's—"

"Don't you know a regular cavalry uniform when you see one, girl?"

Kristin lost patience and swung around. "Mr. Slater, please, just for a minute, shut up. Shannon, this is Cole's brother."

"Brother?"

Her eyes wide, she looked at Malachi, then at Kristin again. "Are you sure? They don't look much alike!"

"We have identical big toes," Malachi snapped sarcastically. Shannon stiffened.

Then, suddenly, there was the sound of another explosion. The three of them stared at one another blankly. Wood chips flew as a second bullet struck the barn wall above their heads.

"Get down—" Malachi began.

"Drop that gun!" The order was spoken in a commanding, masculine tone.

Shannon wasn't about to obey. She spun around, aiming. Malachi swore and slammed his fist down on her wrists. The Colt fell to the ground, and Shannon turned on Malachi, swearing and flailing at him with her fists. Malachi swore in return, and Kristin wondered how the two of them could be going at one another this way when someone else was firing at all three of them. They were warning shots, she realized. She stared blankly across the yard and saw that another man had come out of the shadows of the porch. He was younger than Cole and Malachi and dressed like a rancher in high boots, a long railway frock coat and a slouch hat that sat low on his forehead. Malachi paid no attention to him. As he came forward, the stranger tipped his hat to Kristin.

"They've got a set of rotten tempers between them, huh?"

"Do they?" Kristin crossed her arms over her chest and stared at the young man who had been doing the shooting. Shannon was still shrieking, fighting the hold Malachi had on her. Kristin ignored them both and kept staring at the newcomer. "Why were you shooting at us?"

"I thought she meant to poke a hole right through old Malachi there," he said solemnly. He had cloudlike blue-gray eyes and tawny hair. He smiled again. It was an engaging smile, and Kristin almost smiled, too, in spite of herself.

"I take it you're another Slater? Or are you a friend of the family?"

He stuck out his hand. "Jamie, ma'am."

Malachi let out something that sounded like a growl. "Damned brat bit me!" he thundered.

"Shannon!" Kristin implored.

She might have bitten Malachi, but the bite didn't keep him

from maintaining his hold upon her, his arms around her waist. Her toes were barely touching the ground.

"Ah, Malachi." Jamie shook his head sorrowfully and said to Kristin, "He met Grant at Shiloh but he can't handle a little wisp of a girl."

"I'm not—" Shannon began.

"You are a foolish little brat!" Malachi said, releasing her at last and shoving her towards Kristin. She would have swung at him again, but Kristin caught her sister's arms. "Shannon, please!"

But Shannon was still staring at Malachi, seething. "I am not a brat, Reb. You attacked my sister—"

"And you attacked my brother," Jamie said pleasantly. "We're all even. And if Cole were here he'd say the entire lot of us were a pack of fools playing around with firearms. But then, Cole isn't here, and that's why Malachi and I are. Maybe we ought to try and start over."

"Cole sent you, too?" Kristin asked Jamie.

"Yes, ma'am, he did."

"I see," Kristin said stiffly.

Jamie grinned broadly. "No, ma'am, I doubt if you see at all. He had some business to attend to."

"I told her," Malachi said.

"My brother is a cavalry officer," Shannon snapped at Malachi, ignoring everything else. "And if he knew you were on his property he'd skewer you right through!"

He shook his head, looking as if he were about to explode. Then he exhaled in an exaggerated display of patience. "I thought I was supposed to be looking out for Quantrill, not a two-bit piece of baggage!" He shoved his hat down hard over his forehead and started walking toward the house. Kristin, amused, stared after him. Shannon, amazed, placed her hands on her hips.

"Where do you think you're going?" she called.

Malachi stopped and swung around. "In. For coffee and breakfast. And if you don't like it, little girl, that's just too damned bad. You take it up with Cole the next time you see him. He asked me to be here, and I'm here, and I won't be

leaving, not until he gets back. Until that time, you do us both
a favor. You stay clear of me. Way clear.'' He paused, then
swore softly again. ''Hell, I could still be out there with the
Yankees. It'd be a hell of a lot less nerve-racking than a morning here!'' Once again he turned. Kristin saw that Delilah was
on the steps, watching them. She was grinning broadly.

''You must be Mr. Malachi.''

Delilah's voice floated down to Kristin, and Kristin arched
a brow at her. She and Shannon hadn't known that Cole's
brothers were coming, but Delilah had. Cole had told Delilah
what he was up to, and he hadn't said a word to them.

She gritted her teeth, damning Cole a thousand times over.
What was this business he had to attend to? They had made
a deal. Zeke was still out there somewhere. She didn't need a
pair of baby-sitters. She needed to have Zeke taken care of.

And she needed to have Cole talk to her, to tell her about
his life, not just walk away from her when the sun came up.

''You come on in,'' Delilah was saying to Malachi. ''Breakfast's on the table, boys. Breakfast's on the table.''

Kristin felt Jamie watching her. She turned to him, and she
flushed, surprised by the knowing assessment she saw in his
eyes. He had been reading her mind, or else he had been wondering about her relationship with his brother. No, he seemed
to know what their relationship was already. She could read
that in the look he was giving her.

Then he smiled, as if he had already decided that he liked
her, and so she smiled, too. She liked Jamie. And she liked
Malachi. She even liked the war he was waging with Shannon.
She had felt like laughing as she'd watched them and she
hadn't felt like laughing in a long time.

''I'm awful hungry, too,'' Jamie said. He offered her his
arm. ''Shall we go in for breakfast?''

Kristin hesitated, then took his arm, and they started toward
the house. She paused, turning back to her sister. ''Shannon?''

''I'll skip breakfast,'' Shannon said heatedly, her bright blue
eyes still on Malachi's retreating back. ''I don't rightly feel
like sitting down with—'' She paused when she saw that Jamie was studying her intently. ''I'm not hungry.'' She spun

around and stomped off to the barn. Kristin looked at Jamie again.

"Just where is Cole? I don't need looking after like this, you know. Cole and I had a—an agreement."

She studied his eyes, trying hard not to flush.

"You talk to Cole about his whereabouts later," Jamie said flatly. Neither of the Slaters was going to say a thing about Cole's absence, she realized. "And we're here 'cause of your agreement. We know Quantrill and his boys. We're just here to see that you're safe. Do you really mind? Terribly?"

"No, I, uh…of course not. You're both very welcome," she said, forcing herself to smile. They were welcome, they really were. It was just that…

It was just that she wondered where the hell Cole had gone. She wondered if it had to do with another woman, and she wondered if she could bear it if it did.

Don't fall in love with him! she warned herself again. But he was gone, and she was aching, and it was too late. He wasn't involved and she was, and it was gnawing away at her. She forced her smile to remain in place. "Jamie, you are very welcome. Come on. Delilah makes an incredible breakfast."

He rode southeast the first day. The farther east he went in Missouri, the more closemouthed and careful people were about Quantrill and his gang.

It was natural, he supposed. It had all turned into such a hideous, ugly thing. The ugliness had taken hold way back in the 1850s when John Brown had come into Missouri with his followers and killed slaveholders. Cole didn't really know what to think of John Brown. He had seen the man at his trial, and he had thought then that old John Brown spoke like a fanatic. But he had also thought that he spoke from conviction, too, when he said that only a bloodbath could cleanse the country of the sin of slavery.

John Brown and his followers had gone on to raid the arsenal at Harper's Ferry. Robert E. Lee—then an officer of the United States Army—had been sent in to capture John Brown. Jeb Stuart had been with the forces sent to Harper's Ferry, too.

Cole had been with them himself, riding right alongside Jeb. They had captured John Brown and taken him to Charlestown to stand trial. There hadn't been any Confederacy then. And Cole hadn't known what was to come.

In the North they had quickly begun to sing, "John Brown's body lies a-molderin' in the grave," conveniently forgetting that even if the man had been a God-fearing murderer, he had still been a murderer.

And in Missouri men had learned to retaliate.

Quantrill and his raiders were worshipped by the people here, people who had known nothing but death and destruction from the Kansas jayhawkers. Cole had to be careful. When he stopped at a farmhouse, he quickly made his presence known. He asked for a sip of water from a well, then asked if anyone knew where he might find Quantrill or any of his boys. He was polite, and he smiled, and he used his best country accent, and he kept it filled with respect.

In return he was pointed more and more toward the south. Finally, in a small town almost fifty miles south of Osceola, he heard that Quantrill was at the local saloon.

No one was afraid there. Quantrill's boys were in charge. The South had a good grip on its own here. At a farmhouse outside the town, Cole was invited in for a meal, and the farmer assured him that he could find Quantrill at the saloon at about six that evening.

Cole rode in carefully. If he saw Quantrill first, or Anderson, he'd be all right, but he didn't want to run into Zeke, not now. In case he did, though, he rode in with his six-shooters and two shotguns loaded and ready.

Things were quiet enough as he rode into town. It was almost as if there were no war. Nicely dressed women with stylish hats stood outside the mercantile. As he rode slowly along the dusty main street, they stared at him, and he tipped his hat. They blushed and whispered to one another.

That was when Cole realized that the quiet little town was pulsing with an inner excitement and that things weren't really quiet at all. He could hear the sound of laughter and piano music up ahead and saw a sign that read Red Door Saloon. There were at least eight horses tethered out front.

Quantrill and company do reign here, he thought. He reined in his horse and dismounted, dropping the reins over the post in front of the saloon and dusting off his hands. Then he headed for the red door that had given the saloon its name.

He opened the door and stood there, blinking in the dim light. Then he swiftly cast his gaze over the Red Door's patrons.

Zeke wasn't there.

But William Clarke Quantrill was, playing cards at a round table, leaning back with a thin cigar in his mouth. He was a pale, ashen man with dark hair and a neat brown mustache. He saw Cole just as Cole saw him, and he smiled. He tossed his cards down and stood. He was of average height, about five foot nine. There was nothing about the man to label him the scourge of the West. Nothing except his eyes. They were pale blue and as cold as death.

"Cole. Cole Slater. Well, I'll be damned. To what do I owe this honor?"

Cole didn't answer him. He'd already looked around the room, and looked hard. Zeke wasn't there, but Cole was certain that Quantrill wasn't alone. He wasn't. Cole recognized the other four around the table as young recruits. The two James boys, Jesse and Frank, were there, along with Bill Anderson and little Archie Clements. Cole was sure, too, that Quantrill had more men in the saloon. It wasn't that he had anything to fear here. He was a hero in these parts. It didn't matter that he made out lists of men to be executed. It didn't matter that his men were rapists, murderers and thieves. All that mattered was that what had been done to the Missourians by the jayhawkers was being returned to the Kansans twice over by the bushwhackers.

Cole hadn't come here to do battle, anyway. He strode into the saloon, toward the poker table. The piano player had stopped playing. Everyone in the room was watching him.

He reached Quantrill. Quantrill had his hand extended. Cole took it. "Quantrill," he acknowledged quietly, nodding to the other men at the table. "Jesse. Frank. Archie. Bill. You all look fit. War seems to agree with you."

"Bushwhacking agrees with me," Archie Clements admitted freely. He was dark and had a mean streak a yard wide. "Hell, Cole, I couldn't make it in no ordinary unit. Besides, I'm fighting Yanks for Missouri, and that's it. 'Course, now, you aren't so much regular army, either, are you, Cole? What do they call you? A spy? A scout? Or are you still just a raider?"

"I'm a major, Archie, and that's what they call me," Cole said flatly.

Quantrill was watching the two of them. He turned to the piano player and said, "Hey, what's the problem there, Judah? Let's have something light and fancy here, shall we? Archie, you and Bill take the James boys over to the bar for a whiskey. Seems to me that Cole must have made this trip 'cause he's got something to say. I want to hear it."

Archie stood, but he looked at Cole suspiciously.

"You alone, Cole?"

"That's right, Archie. I'm alone."

Archie nodded at last. Young Jesse James kept staring at Cole. "It was good to see you again, Major Slater. We miss you when we ride. You were damned good."

Damned good with his guns, that was what the boy meant. What the hell was going to be in store for these men when the war was over? If they survived the war.

"You take care, Jesse. You, too, Frank," Cole said. He drew up a chair next to Quantrill. Quantrill started to deal out the cards. "You still a gambling man, Cole?"

"Always," Cole told him, picking up his cards. A buxom brunette with a headful of rich curls, black fishnet stockings and a blood-red dress came over. She nudged up against Quantrill's back but flashed Cole a deep, welcoming smile.

"Want some whiskey for your friend there, Willy?"

"Sure. Bring over the best. We've got a genuine Confederate scout in our midst. But he used to be one of mine, Jennifer. Yep, for a while there he was one of my best."

"He'd be one of anybody's best, I'm sure," Jennifer drawled, fluttering her dark lashes.

Cole flashed her an easy smile, surprised to discover that he felt nothing when he looked at her. She was a pretty thing, very sexual, but she didn't arouse him in the least. You're too satisfied, he warned himself. He found himself frowning and wondering if he shouldn't be interested. At least then he'd know he could be. He shrugged. He was committed—for the moment. And he'd be taking a long ride away soon enough. There'd be plenty of time to prove things to himself then if he had to. That bothered him, too. He shouldn't have to feel the need to prove things to himself.

He shouldn't feel any of these things. Not when his wife lay dead.

"Get the man a whiskey," Quantrill said sharply. Jennifer pouted, then spun around. "What's this all about?" he demanded of Cole.

"The McCahy girls," Cole said flatly.

Quantrill frowned. He didn't seem to recognize the name, and Cole felt sure he wasn't acting. "I don't know them."

Jennifer returned with a new bottle of good Irish whiskey and a pair of shot glasses. She was going to pour out the amber liquid, but Quantrill shooed her away and poured out the shots himself.

"Your man Zeke has been after them."

Quantrill met his frown. "Zeke? Zeke Moreau? I didn't even know the two of you had met. Zeke came in after you were gone."

"Not quite. We met. But I don't think he remembered me when we met again."

Comprehension dawned in Quantrill's cold eyes. "The farmhouse? Near the border? That was you, Cole?"

"Yeah, that was me." Cole leaned forward. He picked up his glass and swallowed down its contents. It was good. Smooth. The kind of stuff that was becoming rare in the South as the war went on and on. He poured himself another shot. He could feel Quantrill's eyes on him. He sensed that Quantrill wasn't angry. He seemed amused more than anything else.

"So you came back to beat my boys up, huh?"

Quantrill poured himself another glass of whiskey, then sat back, swirling the liquid, studying its amber color. Cole looked at him. "No, I just happened by your boys at work, and I'll admit I was kind of sick to my stomach at the war they were waging. They dragged out an old man and killed him. Then they came back after his daughter. Seems the lady had the bad luck to dislike Zeke."

Quantrill shrugged. His amusement was fading. "You don't like my methods?"

"You've become a cold-blooded killer, Quantrill."

"I didn't know anything about the McCahy place."

"I believe you," Cole said.

Quantrill watched him for a moment, a sly smile creeping onto his lips again. "Hell, Cole, you're starting to sound like some damned Yankee."

"I'm not a Yankee."

"Yankee lover, then."

"I don't want the girl touched, Quantrill."

"My, my…" Quantrill leaned back, idly running a finger around the rim of his glass. "Seems to me that you weren't so finicky back in February of '61, Mr. Slater. Who was heading up the jayhawkers back then? Was it Jim Lane, or was Doc Jennison calling the shots by then? Don't make no real matter, does it? They came riding down into Missouri like a twister." He came forward, resting his elbows on the table. "Yessir, just like a twister. They burned down your place, but that wasn't enough. They had to have their fun with Mrs. Slater. Course, she was a beauty, wasn't she, Cole?"

Cole felt his face constrict. He felt his pulse hammering against his throat. He longed to jump forward and throttle the life out of Quantrill, to close those pale, calculating eyes forever.

"Nope, you weren't so finicky about methods when I met you first, Cole Slater. You had revenge on your mind, and nothing more."

Cole forced his lips to curl into a humorless smile. "You're wrong, Quantrill. Yeah, I wanted vengeance. But I could never see murder done in cold blood. I could never draw up a list of men to be gunned down. I could never see dragging terrified, innocent women out of their beds to be raped and abused. Or shooting down children.''

"Hell, Cole. Children fight in this war."

"And that's the hell of it, Quantrill. That's the whole bloody hell of it. The war is hell enough. The savagery is too much.''

"We fight like we've been attacked, and that's the plain truth of it. You go see the likes of Lane or Jennison. Tell them about innocents. You can't change the war, Cole. Not you, and not anybody else. Not anybody.''

"I didn't come here today to end the war, Quantrill," Cole said calmly.

"You just want me to rein in on Zeke, is that it?"

"Well," Cole told him casually, "you can rein in on him or I can kill him.''

Quantrill grinned and shrugged. "You're overestimating my power, Slater. You want me to call Zeke in when this girl isn't anything to you. Not anything at all. She's not your sister and she's not your wife. Hell, from what I understand, Zeke saw her first. So what do you think I can do?''

"You can stop him."

Quantrill sat back again, perplexed. He lifted a hand idly, then let it fall to his lap. "What are you so worried about? You can outdraw Zeke. You can outdraw any ten men I know.''

"I don't perform executions, Quantrill."

"Ah…and you're not going to be around for the winter, huh? Well, neither are we. We'll be moving south soon enough—''

"I want a guarantee, Quantrill."

Quantrill was silent. He lifted his glass, tossed back his head and swallowed the whiskey down in a gulp, then wiped his mouth with his sleeve. His eyes remained on Cole. He set the glass down.

"Marry her."

"What?" Cole said sharply.

"You want me to give the girl a guarantee of safety. A girl Zeke saw first. A girl he wants—badly, I'd say. So you give me something. Give me a reason to keep him away from her. Let me be able to tell the men that she's your wife. That's why they have to stay clear. She'll be the wife of a good loyal Confederate. They'll understand that."

Cole shook his head. "I'm not marrying again, Quantrill. Not ever."

"Then what is this McCahy girl to you?"

What indeed, he wondered. "I just don't want her hurt anymore, that's all."

Quantrill shook his head slowly, and there was a flash of something that might have been compassion in his pale eyes. "There's nothing that I can do, Slater. Nothing. Not unless you can give me something to go on."

The damnedest thing about it, Cole thought, was that Quantrill seemed to want to help him. He wasn't trying to be difficult and he wasn't looking for a fight. He was just telling it the way it was.

"We will be gone pretty soon," Quantrill said. "Another month of raids, maybe. Then the winter will come crashing down. I intend to be farther south by then. Kansas winter ain't no time to be foraging and fighting. Maybe she'll be safe. From us, at least. The jayhawkers might come down on the ranch, but Quantrill and company will be seeking some warmth."

"Another month," Cole muttered.

Quantrill shrugged.

The two men sat staring at one another for several moments. Then Quantrill poured more whiskey.

He couldn't marry her. She couldn't be his wife. He'd had a wife. His wife was dead.

He picked up the whiskey and drank it down in one swallow. It burned. It tore a path of fire straight down his throat and into his gut.

"You going east?" Quantrill asked.

Cole nodded. Maybe he shouldn't have, but Quantrill knew

he would have to get to Richmond sooner or later, and probably sooner.

Cole let out a snarl and slammed his glass down on the table. The piano player stopped playing again. Silence filled the saloon, like something living and breathing. All eyes turned toward Cole and Quantrill.

Cole stood. "I'm going to marry her," he told Quantrill. Then he looked around at the sea of faces. "I'm going to marry Kristin McCahy, and I don't want her touched. Not her, and not her sister. The McCahy ranch is going to be my ranch, and I'm promising a slow, painful death to any man who thinks about molesting any of my property."

Quantrill stood slowly and looked around at his men. "Hell, Cole, we're all on the same side here, aren't we, boys?"

There was silence, and then a murmur of assent. Quantrill lifted the whiskey bottle. "Let's drink! Let's drink to Cole Slater's bride, Miss McCahy! Why, Slater, not a man jack here would think to molest your property, or your woman. She's under our protection. You've got my word on it."

Quantrill spoke loudly, in a clear voice. He meant what he said. Kristin would be safe.

Quantrill offered Cole his hand, and Cole took it. They held fast for a moment, their eyes locked. Quantrill smiled. Cole stepped back, looked around the room and turned to leave. He had his back to the room, but he had probably never been safer in his life. Quantrill had guaranteed his safety.

He walked through the red door, his shoulders squared. Outside, he felt the sun on his face, but the breeze was cool. Fall was fading, and winter was on its way.

He had just said he would marry her.

Hell.

The sun was bright, the air was cool, and the sky was cloudless and blue. He stared at the sun, and he felt cold. He felt a coldness that seeped right into him, that swept right around his heart. It was a bitter cold, so deep that it hurt.

He found his horse's reins and pushed the huge animal back from the others almost savagely so that he could mount. Then he turned and started at a trot down the street.

It couldn't be helped. He had said he would do it, and he had to carry it through.

He had to marry her.

It wouldn't be real, though. It wouldn't mean anything at all. It would just be the way it had to be, and that would be that.

The cold seeped into him again. It encompassed and encircled his heart, and he felt the numbness there again, and then the pain.

He couldn't do it. He couldn't marry another woman. He couldn't call her his wife.

He would marry her. But he never would call her his wife.

Malachi was the more serious of Cole's two brothers, Kristin quickly discovered. Like Cole, he had gone to West Point. He had studied warfare, from the campaigns of Alexander the Great to the American Revolution to Napoleon's grand attempts to take over Europe and Russia. He understood the South's situation in the present struggle for independence, and perhaps that understanding was the cause of gravity. He was on leave for no more than three weeks, so he would have to be returning soon to his unit. Kristin wondered if that meant Cole would return soon. Malachi was courteous to her. He seemed to be the last of the great Southern gentleman, perhaps the last cavalier. Shannon retained her hostility toward him, though. Since Malachi's arrival, she had become a Unionist. She loved to warn both Malachi and Jamie that her brother would come back and make them into nothing more than dust in the wind. Jamie was amused by Shannon. Malachi considered her a dangerous annoyance. Since Kristin had her own problems with Cole, she decided that Shannon was on her own.

Kristin didn't think Matthew would make it home. The last letter she had received from him had stated that his company had been sent East and that he was fighting with the Army of the Potomac.

Malachi didn't wear his cavalry butternut and gray while he was with them at the ranch. He fit into Matthew's breeches fine, and since Federal patrols had been known to wander over the border, it seemed best for him to dress in civilian clothing. Two weeks after his arrival, Kristin heard hoofbeats outside and hurried to the porch. To her vast astonishment, Jamie sat whittling on the steps while Malachi held Shannon in a deep engrossing embrace, kissing her as hotly as a newlywed. Stunned, Kristin stared at Jamie. Jamie pointed to two men in Union blue who were riding away.

"She started to mention that things might not be all they seemed," Jamie drawled. "Malachi didn't take kindly to the notion of spending the rest of the war in a Yankee prison camp."

There was a sharp crack. Kristin spun around to see that Shannon had just slapped Malachi.

Her sister's language was colorful, to say the least. She compared Malachi Slater to a milk rat, a rattlesnake and a Texas scorpion. Malachi, her fingerprints staining his face, didn't appreciate her words. Kristin gasped when he dragged her onto his lap and prepared to bruise her derriere.

Shannon screamed. Jamie shrugged. Kristin decided she had to step in at last. Kristin pleaded with him, but he ignored her at first. She hadn't the strength to come to physical blows with him, so all she could do was appeal to his valor. "Malachi, I'm sure she didn't mean—"

"She damned well did mean!" Malachi shouted. "And I may fall to a Yankee bullet, but I'll be damned if I'll rot in a hellhole because this little piece of baggage has a vicious heart!"

His palm cracked just once against Shannon's flesh.

"Rodent!" Shannon screeched.

"Please—" Kristin began.

Malachi shifted Shannon into his arms, ready to lecture here.

Then Jamie suddenly stood up, dropped his knife and the wood he'd been whittling and reached for his Colt.

"Horses!" he hissed.

A sudden silence settled over them. Malachi didn't release

Shannon, but she froze, too, neither sniffling in indignation nor screaming out her hatred.

Kristin glanced at Jamie. She could tell he was afraid that the Union patrol was on its way back. That Malachi's act just hadn't been good enough. That Shannon had exposed them all to danger.

They all saw the riders. Two of them.

Kristin saw Jamie's tension ease, and then Malachi, too, seemed to relax. Even his desire for vengeance against Shannon seemed to have ebbed. He suddenly set her down on the wooden step, not brutally but absently. Still, Shannon gasped out, startled. Malachi ignored her. Even Kristin ignored her. Kristin still couldn't see the riders clearly, but apparently Malachi and Jamie knew something.

Then she realized it was Cole's horse. It was Cole, returning.

Instantly she felt hot and then cold. Her heart seemed to flutter in her breast. Then butterfly wings seemed to soar within her, and she was hot and then cold all over again.

Cole...

No matter what she wanted to think or believe, she had thought of nothing but him since he had gone away. Waking or sleeping, he had filled her heart and her mind. She had touched the bedding where he had lain and remembered how he had stood, naked, by the window. She had remembered him with the length of her, remembered the feel of his fingers on her flesh, the staggering heat of his body against hers, the tempest of his movement. She had burned with the thoughts and she had railed against herself for them, but they had remained. And in her dreams she had seen him naked and agile and silent and sleek and coming to her again. And he would take her so tenderly into his arms...

And in her dreams it would be more than the fire. He would smile, and he would smile with an encompassing tenderness that meant everything. He would whisper to her, and the whispers would never be clear, but she would know what they meant.

He loved her....

He did not love her.

He rode closer, a plump, middle-aged man at his side. She barely noticed the other man. Her eyes were for Cole, and his rested upon her.

And her heart ran cold then, for he was staring at her with a startling dark hatred.

Her fingers went to her throat, and she backed away slightly, wondering what had happened, why he should look at her so.

"Cole's back," Jamie said unnecessarily.

"Cole!"

It was Shannon who called out his name, Shannon who went running out to him as if he were a long-lost hero. Kristin couldn't move.

Cole's horse came to a prancing halt, and Shannon stood there, staring up at him in adoration, reaching for him. To his credit, Kristin admitted bitterly, he was good to Shannon. His eyes gentled when they fell upon her, and if there was a certain impatience about him, he hid it from her well. He dismounted from his horse in front of the house. Both Jamie and Malachi stood there watching him in silence, waiting for him to speak. He stepped forward and greeted both of his brothers.

"Malachi, Jamie."

He grasped both their hands, and Jamie smiled crookedly while Malachi continued to observe him gravely. Then Cole's eyes came to her again, and she would have backed up again if she hadn't already been flush against the door. His gaze came over her, as cold as the wind of a twister, and perhaps, for just a second, with the same blinding torment. Then the emotion was gone, and all that remained was the staggering chill.

Her mouth was dry, her throat was dry, and she couldn't speak. She was grateful then for Shannon, who told Cole how glad she was to see him, how grateful she was that he was back.

Then she was suddenly still, and Kristin realized that the pudgy middle-aged man was still sitting atop his horse, looking at them all. She was the hostess here. She should be asking him in and offering him something cool to his throat from the dust and dirt of his ride. She should be doing something for Cole, too. If she could only move. Cole should be doing something, too, she thought, not leaving the little man just sitting there.

She forced her eyes away from Cole's to meet those of the man. She even made her lips curl into a semblance of a welcoming smile. "Hello, sir. Won't you come in?"

Jamie smiled. "Welcome, stranger. Cole, you're forgetting your manners. Who is this man?"

Cole turned to the man on the horse. "Sorry, Reverend. Please, come down."

"Much obliged," the man said, dismounting from his horse. Jamie stepped forward to tether the horses. The wind picked up and blew a handful of dirt around.

"This is the Reverend Samuel Cotter," Cole said. "Reverend, my brothers, Malachi and Jamie. And Miss Kristin McCahy in the doorway there, and Miss Shannon McCahy here by my side."

The reverend tipped his hat. "A pleasure, ladies. Gentlemen."

Then they were all just standing there again. The reverend turned his hat awkwardly in his hands. He had a nice face, Kristin thought. Heavy-jowled, with a nice, full smile and bright little eyes. She wished she could be more neighborly, but she was still having difficulty moving.

"Maybe we should all move into the house," Jamie suggested.

"Perhaps the reverend would like a sherry," Shannon murmured.

"The reverend would just love a whiskey!" the little man said, his eyes lighting up.

Malachi laughed. Cole came forward, his hands on his hips. He stood right in front of Kristin, and his eyes were just like the steel of Malachi's cavalry sword. His hands fell on her shoulders, and she almost screamed.

"You're blocking the door, Kristin," he said.

"Oh!" She moved quickly, jumping away from his touch. Her face flushed with color. She looked at the little man. "For-

give me my lack of manners, sir. Please, please, do come in.''
She paused, looking at Cole's hard, dispassionate features,
then back at the reverend. "Um...just what are you doing
here, sir?''

The little man's brows shot up. "Why, I've come to marry
you, miss.''

"Marry me?''

"Why, not myself!'' He laughed hard, enjoying his own
joke. "I've come to marry you to Mr. Slater here.''

"What!'' Kristin gasped. She turned to stare at Cole again.
She saw the ice, and the hatred in his eyes, and she thought
it must be some horrible joke.

"Oh, no! I can't marry Mr. Slater.'' She said it flatly and
with grim determination.

His hands were on her shoulders once again. His eyes bored
into hers, ruthless, demanding. His fingers bit into her flesh,
brutal and challenging.

"You will marry me, Kristin. Now. While we have the nice
reverend here. It took me four days to find him, and I don't
intend to have trouble now.''

She gritted her teeth against the pain of his touch, against
the force of his will. She wanted to cry, but she couldn't do
that, and she couldn't explain that she couldn't possibly marry
him, not when the mere idea made him look at her with such
hatred.

"I will not—''

"You will!''

He turned around and shoved her through the door to the
house. His touch stayed upon her, the warmth and strength of
his body radiated along her spine, and his whisper touched her
ear like the wind.

"Damn it, Kristin, stop it! You will do this!''

Suddenly tears glistened in her eyes. She'd dreamed about
just such an occasion, but it hadn't been like this. He hadn't
looked at her this way.

"Why?'' she managed to whisper.

"We have to.''

"But..." She had to salvage some pride. "I don't love you."

"I don't love you."

"Then—"

"Kristin, you've got your choices."

"I see. This is another threat. If I don't go through with this, you'll ride away."

"I have to ride away, Kristin. No matter what. And this is the only safeguard I could find for you."

"I can't do it—"

"Then plan on entertaining Zeke Moreau, Kristin. And if you can't think about yourself, think about Shannon."

"This is a travesty!"

His eyes burned with silver emotion for a moment. He was a stranger again as he stood there, touching her yet somehow distant from her.

"War is a travesty, Kristin. Cheer up. If it ever ends, you can divorce me. I'm sure you'll have plenty of cause. But for the moment, Miss McCahy, get into the parlor, stand sweetly and smile for the nice reverend, please."

Chapter Nine

It was not what she had expected her wedding day to be like, and it was certainly not what she had dreamed it would be like.

Cole and the reverend were still covered with dust from their ride. She wore a simple cotton day dress with a single petticoat, since Cole had sworn impatiently when she had murmured something about changing. Shannon was wearing a shirt and trousers. The only concession to the fact that it was a wedding was the little bouquet she held, hurriedly put together by Delilah from ferns and late-blooming daisies.

They stood stiffly in the parlor. Cole was brusque, and the reverend tried to be kind. Malachi stood up for Cole, and Shannon acted as bridesmaid. Jamie, Delilah and Samson looked on. The reverend kept clearing his throat. He wanted to say more, wanted to speak about the sanctity of marriage and the commitment made thereby between a man and a woman. Cole kept shifting his weight from foot to foot. Then he snapped at the man, ''Get on with it!''

Hastily the reverend went on.

Kristin listened to the droning voice and found herself looking around her mother's beautiful parlor and wondering what it had been like for her parents. Not like this. They had loved one another, she knew. She could remember her father's eyes, and the way they had misted over when her mother's name had been spoken. They had built their lives on a dream, and the dream had been a good one.

But they weren't living in a world of dreams, and Cole didn't love her. He didn't even pretend to love her.

"Kristin?"

"What?"

Startled, she looked up at him. She realized that they were standing side by side, she in simple cotton, he in denim and Missouri dust. His hand was around hers, and his flesh felt dry and hot. He squeezed her hand, and she gasped at the pressure, her eyes widening.

"Kristin!" His eyes were sizzling silver and dangerous. "The reverend just asked you a question."

She looked at the reverend. He was flushed and obviously uncomfortable, but he tried to smile again.

"Kristin…do you take this man for your lawful wedded husband, to have and to hold, from this day forward, to love, to cherish and to obey in all the things of this earth?"

She stared at him blankly. It wasn't right. He didn't love her. And she was falling in love with him.

"I, er…"

"Kristin!" The pressure of his fingers around hers was becoming painful.

"Cole…" She turned to him, trying to free her hand from his grasp. "Cole, this is marvelously noble of you, honestly. But I'm sorry, I don't think—"

"Kristin!" Shannon gasped.

"Kristin…" Cole began, and there was a definite threat in his tone, like a low rumble of thunder. What could he do to her, here, with all these people, she wondered recklessly.

He caught her shoulders and jerked her against him. The revered was sucking air in and out out of his cheeks very quickly. "Mr. Slater, if the young lady isn't prepared to take this step, if she isn't completely enamored of you—"

"She's enamored, she's enamored!" Cole snapped. He wound his fingers into Kristin's hair and kissed her hotly. He kissed her with such conviction and passion that she felt herself color from the roots of her hair to her toes. His lips molded around hers, and his tongue plunged deep into her mouth. She couldn't breathe, and she could barely stand, and her knees were beginning to shake.

"Really, now—" the reverend protested.

"They really *are* in love!" Jamie assured him cheerfully.

"Cole—" Malachi tapped his brother on the shoulder, "I—er…think you've made your point."

Cole lifted his lips from Kristin's by just a whisper. His eyes burned into hers. "Say 'I do,' Kristin. Say it."

She inhaled. Her ribs felt as if they had been crushed. She tried to shake her head, but it wouldn't move. "Say 'I do,'" he insisted.

She felt as if the trembling in her heart were an earthquake beneath her feet. She parted her lips, and they felt damp and swollen.

"For God's sake, do it!" Shannon whispered. "We need him. Don't be so naive!"

She nodded, but she couldn't speak. Cole caught her fingers and brought their hands together and squeezed. "'I do,' Kristin! Say it!"

She formed the words at last. I do.

"Go on!" Cole roared at the reverend.

The reverend asked Cole the same question he'd asked Kristin.

He almost spat out the answer. "I do!" His lips twisted bitterly, as if, having forced her to do what he wanted, he had found a new contempt for her. She tried to wrench her hand away from him, but he held her firm and slipped a ring on her finger. It was a wide gold band, and it was too big for her.

She heard Delilah saying that if they twined some string around it it would fit fine.

Then the reverend announced that they were man and wife, and Cole released her. No one said anything, not a single word. The silence went on and on, but Delilah finally broke it.

"This calls for some of that fine white wine in the cellar, I think. Samson, you go fetch it up here, please."

"Yessir, a wedding sure calls for wine," Samson agreed.

The room seemed very still, and Kristin was still unable to move. She was hot and cold by turns. She had never felt more alone in her life. Cole had moved away from her, far away, as if he couldn't bear to touch her now that the words had been spoken. He thanked the reverend and paid him. Then he seemed to notice Kristin again. She had to sign the marriage certificate.

She balked again. He grabbed her hand and guided it to the paper, and she managed to scratch our her name. Nothing seemed real. Delilah said she would set out a cold supper, and Shannon promised to help. Somehow Kristin wound up in one of the big plush wing chairs in the parlor. Jamie stood beside her, resting a hand on her shoulder.

"He's really not as bad as he seems, you know," he whispered.

She clenched her teeth together to keep them from chattering. "No, he's worse." Jamie laughed, but there was an edge to his laughter. He sat down on the sofa across from her and took her hands in his. His eyes were serious. "Kristin, you have to try to understand Cole."

"He doesn't want to be understood," she replied softly.

"You're not afraid of him, are you?" he asked.

She thought for a moment, then shook her head, smiling ruefully. "Afraid of Cole? Never. He saved my life. No, Jamie, I'm not afraid of him. I just wish that—"

"That what?" Jamie murmured.

They could both see Cole. He was rubbing the back of his neck as he talked to Malachi. He looked tired, Kristin thought. She bit her lower lip, and wished for a moment that the marriage was real. She wanted to tiptoe up behind him and touch his shoulders with soothing fingers. She wanted to press her face against the coolness of his back and pretend there was no war, no Zeke, no chaos.

"I wish I understood him," she said at last, staring straight at Jamie. "Want to help?"

He straightened and released her hands. "I'm sorry, Kristin. I can't." He stood and smiled down at her. "Look at that, will you? Delilah is a gem. A cold supper, indeed. She's got biscuits and gravy, turnip greens and a shank of ham over there. Come on!'' He took her hands in his again and pulled her to her feet. Suddenly, impulsively, he gave her a kiss on the cheek. ''Hey, welcome, sister,'' he whispered.

Some instinct caused her to look behind him. Cole was watching them. He scowled darkly and turned his attention to Malachi again.

''I'm not very hungry, Jamie,'' Kristin said. It was true. She wasn't hungry at all. She smiled at him, though and whispered, ''Thank you, Jamie!'' She felt like crying again, and she shook herself impatiently. It was absurd. She had stood tall in the face of tragedy. Now there was only confusion, but it was tearing her apart.

Cole didn't seem to be very hungry, either. He waited with barely concealed impatience for his brothers to finish their meal. When they had, he started toward the door with long strides, and they followed. He paused in the doorway and said to Kristin, ''We're going to ride out and take a look at things. I want to tell the ranch hands.''

He was going to announce their wedding the way he might have spread the news of a battle. She nodded, wondering again at the fever that touched his eyes. He couldn't wait to be away from her, she thought. Then why, she thought angrily, had he done it at all? Surely his obligation to her wasn't as great as that.

She didn't say anything. He looked at the reverend, thanking him again for making the trip and urging him to make himself at home. Then he paused again. Malachi and Jamie shifted uncomfortably, exchanging worried glances.

''Write to your brother,'' Cole told Kristin. ''Write to him immediately. There's a good possibility I may stop a Yankee bullet before this is all over, but I don't intend it to be because of a stupid mistake.''

Then the three of them were gone. Kristin stood up, watching as the door closed, listening as their booted feet fell against the floorboards of the front porch.

Then, ridiculously, she felt her knees wobbling. She heard

a humming in the air, and it was as if wind were rising again, bringing with it a dark mist.

"Kristin!"

She heard Shannon calling her name, and then she heard nothing. She sank to the floor in a dead faint.

Several hours later the Slater brothers rode back from their inspection of the ranch. They'd told all the ranch hands about the marriage. Old Pete had spit on the ground and told Cole he was damned glad. He seemed to understand that with Cole and Kristin married, they were all safer from Zeke Moreau. He didn't seem to care much whether the marriage was real. He seemed to think it was none of his business.

The brothers had gone on to ride around the perimeters of the McCahy ranch. It was a quiet day. By the time they headed back for the house, night was coming and coming fast. Still, when they were within sight of the place, Cole suddenly decided he wanted to stop and set up camp.

Jamie built a fire, and Malachi unsaddled the horses. Cole produced a bottle of whiskey and the dried beef and hard tack. By then the stars had risen, bright against the endless black velvet of the night sky.

Malachi watched Cole, and he noticed the nervous tension that refused to ease from his features. There was a hardness about him today. Malachi understood it. He just didn't know how to ease it.

Let it rest! Malachi thought. Let it go. Kristin McCahy— no, Slater now—was young, beautiful and intelligent, and if he wasn't mistaken, she was in love with Cole. Cole was too caught up in his memories of tragedy to see it. Even if he did see it, it might not change anything. Malachi knew his brother had acted out of a sense of chivalry. He also knew Kristin would have preferred he hadn't. Malachi sighed. Their personal lives were none of his business. He had to leave. He was a regular soldier in a regular army, and his leave was about up.

"This is kind of dumb, ain't it?" Jamie demanded, swallowing some of the whiskey.

"Dumb?" Cole asked.

"Hell, yes. You've got yourself a gorgeous bride, young and shapely—"

"And what the hell do you know about her shape?" Cole demanded heatedly.

"Come on, you can't miss it," Malachi protested dryly. He was determined to have a peaceful evening. He sent Jamie a warning scowl. They both knew what was bothering Cole. "Jamie...stop it."

"Why? Does Cole think he's the only one who's been hurt by this war?"

"Damned brat—" Cole began angrily.

"But the damned brat came running when you asked, Cole, so sit back. Hell, come on, both of you stop it."

"I just think he should appreciate the woman, that's all. And if he didn't mean to, damn it, he shouldn't have tied her up in chains like that."

Cole, exasperated, stared at Malachi. "Will you shut him up, or should I?"

"There's a war on, boys!" Malachi reminded them both.

"He should be decent to her—" Jamie began.

"Damn it, I am decent to her!" Cole roared.

"Leaving her alone on her wedding night—"

"Leaving her alone was the most decent damned thing I could do!" Cole said. He wrenched the whiskey bottle from his brother's hands. "You're too young for this stuff."

"Hell, I'm too old," Jamie said softly. He grinned ruefully at his brother, and all the tension between them seemed to dissipate. "I'm twenty, Cole. By some standards, that's real old. Seventeen-year-old boys are dying all over the place."

"Quantrill is running a bunch of boys," Cole said. He lifted his hand in a vague gesture. "The James boys. The Youngers. And that butcher Bill Anderson. He's just a kid."

He swallowed the liquor, then swallowed again. He felt like being drunk. Really drunk.

Malachi reached for the bottle. The firelight played over his hair, and he arched his golden brows at Cole. "You think that

Quantrill can really control his men? That marrying Kristin
can keep her safe?''

Cole looked out at the Missouri plain before him, gnawing
on a blade of grass. He spit out the grass and looked over at
his brothers, who were both looking at him anxiously. If he
hadn't been knotted up inside he might have smiled. They
were both concerned. There was something about the McCahy
place that got to a man. He could understand how even the
great struggle between North and South had ceased to matter
here, had ceased to matter to Kristin. The brutality here was
too much. It left the mind numbed.

"I know Quantrill is about to head south for the winter. He
doesn't like the cold. He'll make one more raid, I'm certain.
Then he'll head on somewhere south—maybe Arkansas,
maybe Texas. I'll stick around until he moves on. Then I'll
go on over to Richmond. If I can just find some train tracks
that are still holding together, I should make it in time.''

"If Jefferson Davis is still in the Cabinet,'' Jamie said
glumly.

Cole looked at him sharply. "Why? What have you heard?''

"Nothing. It's just that the battle of Sharpsburg left a lot of
dead men. A whole lot of dead men.''

"Watch your step around here,'' Malachi warned Cole.
"There's Federal patrols wandering all around the McCahy
place.''

"Yeah, I know.''

"That little witch just about got me hauled in today.''

"Witch?'' Cole asked.

"Shannon,'' Jamie supplied.

Malachi grunted. "I envy you your wife, Cole, but not your
in-laws.''

"And he doesn't mean the Yankee brother.'' Jamie laughed.
"It's a good thing Malachi has to ride out soon. I don't think
she's too fond of him, either.''

Malachi looked as if he wanted to kill somebody, Jamie
thought, but at least Cole laughed, and Cole needed it the
most. "What have I missed?'' Cole asked.

"The antics of a child,'' Malachi replied, waving a dismissing hand in the air. He reached for the liquor bottle. It was going down quickly.

"Some child!" Jamie said. "Why, she's coming along just as nicely as that wife of yours, Cole."

Malachi and Cole looked at one another. "We could end this war if we just sent this boy to Washington to heckle the Union commanders," Malachi said.

Cole grunted his agreement. Jamie grinned and lay back against his saddle, staring up at the stars. "You know, Cole," he said suddenly, "I am sorry about the past. I sure am."

There was a long silence. The fire snapped and crackled. Malachi held his breath and held his peace.

"But if I were you," Jamie went on, "I wouldn't be out here with my brothers. Not when I had a woman like that waiting. A woman with beautiful blond hair and eyes like sapphires. And the way she walks, her hips swinging and all... Why, I can just imagine what it'd be like—"

"Son of a bitch!" Cole roared suddenly. He stood up, slamming the nearly empty whiskey bottle into the fire. The liquor hissed and sizzled. Jamie leaped to his feet, startled by the deadly dark danger in his brother's eyes. Malachi, too, leaped to his feet. He couldn't believe that Cole would really go for Jamie, but then he had never seen Cole in a torment like this. Nor had he ever seen Jamie so determined to irk him.

"Cole—" Malachi reached for his brother's arm, and they stared at one another in the golden firelight.

"No!" Jamie told Malachi, his eyes on Cole. "If he wants to beat me up, let him. If he thinks he can strike out at me and feel better, fine. Let him hurt me instead of that poor girl waiting for him at the house. At least I understand why he strikes out. Hell, she doesn't even know why he's so damned hateful."

"What the hell difference does it make?" Cole thundered. "All she wanted from me was protection!"

"She deserves some damned decency from you!"

"I told you—"

"Yeah, yeah, you came up with some puny excuse. You are a bastard."

"You don't know—"

"I know that it wasn't my wife killed by the jayhawkers, but we loved her, too, Cole. And she loved you, and she wouldn't want you making your whole life nothing but ugly vengeance."

"Why, I ought to—"

"Cole!" Malachi shouted. Between the three of them, they'd consumed almost an entire bottle of liquor. This wasn't a good time for Jamie to be goading Cole, but Jamie didn't seem to care. And now Cole was losing control. He shook off Malachi's arm and lunged at Jamie with a sudden fury. Then the two of them were rolling in the dust.

"Jesus in heaven!" Malachi breathed. "Will the two of you—"

"You don't know! You don't know anything!" Cole raged at Jamie. "You didn't find her, you didn't feel the blood pouring out all over you! You didn't see her eyes close, you didn't see the love as it died. You didn't watch her eyes close and feel her flesh grow cold!"

"Cole!"

His hands were around Jamie's neck, and Jamie wasn't doing anything at all. He was letting Cole throttle him. Malachi tried to pull him off, and Cole suddenly realized what he was doing. Horrified, he released his brother. Then he stood and walked away, his back to his brothers.

"I need to stay away from Kristin," he said softly.

Jamie looked at Malachi and rubbed his throat. Malachi spoke to Cole.

"No. You don't need to stay away from her. You need to go to her."

Cole turned around. He came over to Jamie and planted his hands on his brother's shoulders. "You all right?"

Jamie nodded and grinned. "I'm all right."

Cole walked over to his horse. He untied the reins which were tethered to a tree, and walked the horse into the open. Then he leaped up on the animal's back without bothering to saddle it.

"You going back?" Malachi asked.

"Just for another bottle of whiskey."

Malachi and Jamie nodded. They watched as Cole started back toward the house, the horse's hooves suddenly taking flight in the darkness.

"He's just going back for another whiskey bottle," Jamie said.

Malachi laughed. "We betting on when he's going to make it back?"

Jamie grinned. "You get to bring his saddle in the morning." He lay down again and stretched out, feeling his throat. "Too bad I wasn't blessed with sisters!" He groaned.

Malachi grunted, pulled his hat low over his face and closed his eyes. The fire crackled and burned low, and at last the two of them slept.

Cole heard one of Pete's hounds barking as he approached the house. Then Pete himself, shirtless, the top of his long johns showing above his hastily donned trousers, came out to challenge him.

"Just me, Pete," Cole assured him.

"Evening, boss," Pete said agreeably, and headed back to the bunkhouse.

Cole dismounted from his horse, sliding from the animal's back without his accustomed grace. He gave his head a shake to clear it. The whiskey had gotten to him more than he would have cared to admit, but not enough to really knock him out the way he wanted, not enough to take away the last of his pain. He was determined to be quiet, but it seemed to him that his boots made an ungodly noise on the floorboards of the porch.

The house was dark. He stumbled through the hall and the parlor and into what had been Gabriel McCahy's office. He fumbled around for a match and lit the oil lamp on the desk, then came around and sat in the chair, putting his feet up on the desk and digging in the lower right hand drawer for a bottle of liquor—any kind of liquor.

Then he heard a click, and the hair on the back of his neck

stood straight up. His whiskey-dulled reflexes came to life, and he slammed his feet to the floor, reaching for his revolver.

He pointed it at the doorway—and right at Kristin, who stood there with a double-barreled shotgun aimed at his head. He swore irritably, returning his gun to his holster and sinking back into his chair.

"What the hell are you doing?" he growled.

"What am I doing? You son of a bitch—" She lowered the shotgun and moved into the room. She stopped in front of the desk, caught in the soft glow of the lamplight. Her hair was loose, a soft storm of sunshine falling over her shoulders. She was dressed chastely enough, in a nightgown that buttoned to her throat, but the lamplight went through the fabric and caressed her body. He could see all too clearly the sway of her hips, which Jamie had so admired. He could see the curve of her breasts, the flow and shape of her limbs, and suddenly the sight of her hurt him. It was as if some mighty hand reached down and took hold of him, squeezing the life from him. He felt his heart pounding, felt his shuddering pulse enter his groin and take root there. His fingers itched to reach out to her, to touch her. She was staring at him, her blue eyes a raging sea of fury, and not even that deterred him. It only made the pulse within him beat all the harder.

He didn't love her. To love her would be disloyal. But he had married her. What the hell else could she want?

"What are you doing in here?" she snapped.

"Kristin, put the gun down. Go to bed."

"You scared me to death! And *you* taught *me* not to go wandering around unarmed!"

"Kristin, put the gun down." He hesitated. Then he smiled suddenly. "Come on. We'll go to bed. Together."

Her eyes widened. "You're out of your mind, Cole Slater."

"Am I?" He came around the desk, slowly, lazily, yet purposefully. Kristin raised the shotgun again.

"Yes! You are out of your mind."

"You're my wife."

"And you walked out of here this afternoon and didn't come back until three in the morning—after treating me with

he manners of a rabid squirrel. I promise you, Mr. Slater, if
you think you're going to touch me, you're out of your mind.''

He *was* out of his mind, and he knew it. He swallowed
raggedly. He had forgotten so much. He had tried to forget.
He had forgotten that she could hold her head with such incredible pride. He had forgotten her eyes could snap this way,
and he had forgotten that her mouth was wide and generous
and beautifully shaped. He had forgotten that she was beautiful
and sensuous, and that her touch was more potent than whiskey or wine or the finest brandy. He had forgotten so much....

But now he remembered. The revealing lamplight glowed
on the lush curves of her body, and the thunder inside him
became almost unbearable. He took a step forward, and she
cocked the shotgun. His smile deepened.

''Fire it, Kristin.''

''I will, damn you!''

He laughed triumphantly, stepped toward her again and took
the shotgun from her hands. He pulled her hard against him,
and he lowered his head and seized her lips in a kiss. It was
not at all brutal, but it was filled with a shocking need and a
shocking thirst. For an instant she thought to twist from him,
but his kiss filled her with a searing, liquid heat, and she felt
as if she were bursting with the desire to touch him, to be
touched by him.

He broke away from her, and his eyes sought hers. ''No!''
she told him angrily, but he smiled and swept her up into his
arms. Her eyes were still angry but she locked her arms around
his neck. He carried her effortlessly through the darkened parlor, up the stairs and into the bedroom. He closed the door
with his foot and set her down by the window. The moonlight
found her there, dancing over her fine, delicate features and
her rich, feminine curves.

''You're horrid,'' she told him.

He smiled tenderly. ''You're beautiful.''

''You're filthy.''

He kissed her forehead, and he kissed her cheeks, and he
rimmed her lips with the tip of his tongue, teasing them, dampening them. His fingers went to the tiny buttons of her gown,

and he tried to undo them but they wouldn't give, and he finally ripped the gown open impatiently. The moonlight fell on her naked flesh. He groaned and kissed her shoulder and her throat, feeling the urgent quickening of her heart.

"Does it matter so terribly much?" he whispered.

She didn't answer. He stroked her breast. Then he lowered his head and touched his lips to the nipple. He teased it with his teeth, then sucked it hard into his mouth and finally gentled it with his tongue. Rivers of pleasure streaked through her, and she threaded her fingers roughly into his hair, and he savored the little tug of pain. He lowered himself slowly to his knees, holding her hips, then her buttocks.

"Does it matter so terribly much?" he repeated, looking up into her dazed eyes. He teased her navel with the tip of his tongue.

"Yes!" she whispered. He started to move away from her, but she wouldn't let him. He bathed her belly with kisses, cupping her buttocks hard and pressing close to her, sliding his tongue along the apex of her thighs and into the golden triangle there. She shuddered and cried out, but he held her firmly, and when it seemed she was about to fall he lowered her carefully to the floor. He touched her gently and tenderly, and then he brought his mouth over hers again. "Does it really matter so terribly much?" he demanded.

She closed her eyes and wrapped her arms around his neck. "No," she whispered, and she released him to tug at his buttons and then at his belt buckle. She groaned in frustration, and he helped her, stripping quickly. She was so very beautiful, there in the full flood of the moonlight. All of him quickened, and desire spread through him like a raging wind, and he cried out in a ragged voice. She was there, there to take him, there to close around him, a sweet and secret haven. Nothing on earth was like this.

He sank into her, swept into her, again and again. She rose to meet his every thrust, and the pulse raged between them. She was liquid fire when she moved. She was made to have him, made to love him, made to take him. The culmination burst upon them swiftly. She gasped and shuddered, and he thrust heatedly, again and felt his climax spew from him. He held her tight. He felt the sweat, slick between them. He felt the rise and fall of her breath and the clamor of her heart, slowing at last.

He stroked her hair, and he marveled at the ecstasy of it.

Then he remembered that he had made her his wife, and suddenly he hated himself again.

He should have said something. He should have whispered something to her. Anything. Anything that was tender, anything that was kind.

He couldn't bring himself to do it.

Instead, he rose, his skin glistening in the moonlight. Then he bent down and took her naked form in his arms. She was silent, her eyes lowered, her hair a tangle around them.

He laid her down upon the bed. Her eyes met his at last, and he saw in them a torment that seemed to match that within his heart. She was so very beautiful. Naked, she was a goddess, her breasts firm and full and perfect, her limbs shapely and slim, her belly a fascinating plane between her hips. He pulled the covers over her. Her sapphire eyes still studied him.

"I'm...I'm sorry," he muttered at last.

She let out a strangled oath and turned away from him.

He hesitated, then slipped in beside her. He crossed his arms behind his head and stared up at the ceiling, wishing he were drunker, wishing fervently he could go to sleep.

But he lay awake a long, long time. And he knew she didn't sleep, either.

At dawn he rose and left.

And at dawn Kristin finally slept. She had the right to stay in bed all day, she told herself bitterly. She was a bride, and this was the morning after her wedding day.

Cole wasn't in the house when she finally did get up. Shannon told her he had gone out with Malachi.

Jamie was there, though. He told her that they were low on salt and that they needed a couple of blocks for the cattle to lick through the winter. Cole had said that she and Pete were to go into town and buy them.

The Union had control of most of the border area—despite Quantrill's sporadic raids—and the town had managed to remain quieter than the McCahy ranch. Kristin was glad to take the buckboard and ride into town with Pete. She was glad to be away from the house.

It was a three-hour ride. The town of Little Ford was small, but it did have two saloons, one reputable hotel, two doctors old enough to be exempted from military service and three mercantile stores. In Jaffe's Mercantile she saw Tommy Norley, a newspaperman and and old friend of Adam's from over the Kansas border.

"Kristin!"

He was limping when he came over to her. He tipped his hat quickly, then took both her hands in his. "Kristin, how are you doing out there? Is everything all right? You and Shannon should have moved on, I think. Or maybe into town. Or maybe out to California!"

She smiled. He was a slim man, pale-faced, with a pencil-thin mustache and dark, soulful eyes.

"I'm doing well, Tommy, thank you." She searched his eyes. She had last seen him when they had buried her father. He had written a scathing article about guerrilla attacks.

"You should move, Kristin."

She chose to ignore his words. "Tommy, you're limping."

He smiled grimly. "I just got caught by Quantrill."

Her heart skipped a beat. "What do you mean? What happened?"

"The bastard attacked Shawneetown last week. I was with the Federal supply train he and his maniacs caught up with on their way in." He paused and looked at her, wondering how much he should say to a lady.

"Tommy, tell me! What happened?"

He took a deep breath. "Kristin, it was awful. Quantrill and his men came after us like a pack of Indians, howling, shouting. They gunned down fifteen men, drivers and escorts. I rolled off the side of the road, into the foliage. I took a bullet in the calf, but I lived to tell the tale. Kristin, they went on

into town and murdered ten more men there. Then they burned
the village to the ground.''

''Oh, God! How horrible!'' Kristin gasped.

''Kristin, come to Kansas. I'm opening an office in
Lawrence, and I'm sure you'll be safe.''

She smiled. ''Tommy, my home is in Missouri.''

''But you're in danger.''

''I can't leave the ranch, Tommy.'' She wondered if she
should tell him that she had married to save her ranch and that
she would probably be in real danger from her new husband
if she deserted him and ran off to Kansas.

''You should have seen them,'' Tommy murmured. ''Kristin, they were savages. You should have seen them.''

She held on to the counter in the mercantile, suddenly feeling ill. He kept talking, and she answered him as politely as
she could. She cared about Tommy. He had been a good friend
to Adam. It was just that Adam had begun to fade from her
life. It was not that she hadn't loved him. She had. But Cole
was a stronger force in her life.

Kristin hesitated, then asked him if he thought he could get
a message to Matthew for her. He promised to try, and she
bought some stationery from Mr. Jaffe and quickly wrote a
letter to Matthew. It wasn't easy to explain her marriage. She
did it as carefully and as cheerfully as she could, then turned
the letter over to Tommy, hoping she had done well.

She kissed Tommy and left him. Pete had gotten the salt
licks, and he had stacked the remaining space in the buckboard
with alfalfa to help get them through the coming winter.

She told him about Shawneetown, then fell silent. The news
bothered her all the way home.

When they arrived at the ranch, she still felt ill. She went
out back and stood over her parents' graves. Cold and chilled,
she tried to pray, but no thoughts came to her mind.

A while later she felt a presence behind her, and she knew
that it was Cole. She was angry, and she didn't know why,
unless it was because she knew he didn't love her, and because
she knew she was falling in love with him. He was attracted

to her, certainly. Maybe he even needed her. But he didn't love her.

She spun around, ready to do battle.

"Quantrill and his animals attacked Shawneetown last week. They killed the men escorting a supply train, and then they went into the village and killed some more, and then they burned the whole place down."

His eyes narrowed, and he stared at her warily, but he didn't say anything. She walked up to him and slammed her fists against his chest. "He's a captain! The Confederates made him a captain!"

He grabbed her wrists hard. "I don't condone Quantrill, and you know it. The Missouri governor considers him and his raiders like an elephant won at a raffle."

"Let go of me!" she hissed furiously.

"No. You listen to me for a minute, lady. Quantrill has no monopoly on brutality! Quantrill came *after* the likes of Lane and Jennison. Unionists, Kristin! Jayhawkers! You want to know some of the things they've done? They've ridden up to farmhouses and dragged men out and killed them—men *and* women! They've murdered and they've raped and they've tortured, exactly the same way Quantrill has! You remember that, Kristin! You bear that in mind real well!"

He pushed her away from him and turned, his long, angry strides taking him toward the house. The rear door opened and then slammed shut, and he disappeared inside.

She waited a moment, and then she followed him. She didn't know if she wanted to continue the fight or try to make up with him somehow.

It didn't matter. He wasn't in the house anymore.

And that night he didn't come back at all.

Chapter Ten

Cole might have slept somewhere else during the night, but he appeared at the breakfast table in the morning. Kristin was angry and wondered what everyone must think. He came and went like the breeze, with no regard for her feelings. Kristin was sharp when he spoke to her. When he asked her to pass him the milk, she seriously considered splashing it in his face or pouring it in his lap. He caught her hand and the pitcher before she could do either. He stared at her hard, and she looked away.

She didn't like Cole's ability to stay away from her. She wanted to fight with him. She wanted to do anything just to bring him close to her again. It was an effort to turn away from him, to find some trivial thing to discuss with Jamie and Shannon.

Cole remained in a foul temper all day. With winter coming on, there was a lot to do. Cole was anxious to have it all done before he left for the East and before Malachi and Jamie had to leave to rejoin their units. They spent the day gathering up as much of the herd as they could for Pete to drive to market. Kristin had been surprised that Cole was willing to let her sell the beef on the Union side of the line, but he had reminded her that the ranch belonged to her brother, Matthew, and that Matthew was fighting for the Union. Cole couldn't go north himself, but Pete could handle the cattle drive, and Malachi and Jamie would be around until he got back at the end of the week.

By dinnertime, Cole seemed to be in a somewhat better mood, and Kristin maintained a polite distance from him. Cole, Jamie and Malachi all sat down to dinner with Kristin and Shannon that night. Delilah refused to sit and made a big fuss over everyone. Jamie made the meal a pleasant affair. He told the two girls about a pair of hammers his mother had bought for Cole and Malachi when they were boys and about how the two of them had used their hammers on one another. Even Shannon laughed and refrained from engaging in verbal warfare with Malachi. Cole listened to the story with a smile on his face, and at one point his eyes met Kristin's and he gave her an entrancing grin and a sheepish shrug.

After dinner, Kristin played the spinet and Shannon sang. She sang a few light tunes, then gave a haunting rendition of "Lorena", a ballad about a soldier who returns from the wars to find that his love is gone. When it was over, they were all silent. Then Cole stood up and told Shannon in a strangled voice that her singing was very beautiful. He excused himself and left them.

Kristin bit her lip as she watched him leave the room. Jamie gave her an encouraging pat on the knee, and Malachi practically shoved Shannon out of the way and began a rousing chorus of "Dixie."

When he had finished, Shannon regained her place and sang "John Brown's Body."

"Shannon McCahy, you are a brat," Malachi told her.

"And you're a rodent," Shannon replied sweetly.

"Children, children!" Jamie protested with a sigh.

But Shannon said something, and though Kristin could see that Malachi was striving for patience, he replied sharply, and the battle was on once again.

Kristin rose and left them bickering. She went upstairs and was surprised to find that Cole was already in bed. She thought he was asleep, but when she crawled in beside him, trying not to disturb him, he turned over and took her in his arms. She tried to study his eyes in the darkness, but she could see only

their silver glow. She tried to speak, but he silenced her with
a kiss. Tenderly at first, and then with a growing passion, he
made love to her. When it was over, he held her close, his
bearded chin resting against the top of her head. He didn't
speak, and neither did she. She knew he lay there awake for
a long time, and she wished she could reach out to him, wished
she knew what to say to him. She could not apologize, for she
had done nothing wrong. She kept silent.

Eventually Kristin fell asleep.

Sometime later, something woke her. She didn't know what
it was at first. She heard something, some hoarse, whispered
words that she didn't understand. Struggling to free herself
from the web of sleep, she opened her eyes, just as Cole's
arm came flying out and slammed against her shoulder.

She sat up in bed, calling out his name. He didn't answer
her, and she fumbled for a match to light the oil lamp on the
bedside table. The glow filled the room and fell on Cole.

The bare flesh of his shoulders and chest was gleaming with
sweat. The muscles there were tense and rigid and knotted.
His fingers plucked at the sheet that lay over him.

His features contorted, his head tossing from side to side,
he screamed, "No!" His entire body was stiff and hard.

"Cole!" Kristin pleaded, shaking him. "Cole—"

"No!" he screamed again.

She straddled him, took him by the shoulders and shook
him hard, determined to wake him.

His eyes flew open, but he didn't see her. He called out
again, and then he struck out at her, and the force sent her
flying to the floor. He jerked upright as she fell. Stunned,
Kristin sat on the hard floor, rubbing her bruised behind.

"Kristin?"

He whispered her name slowly, fearfully. There was something in his voice that she had never heard before, a frightened
tone, and it touched her deeply.

"I'm here," she whispered ruefully.

He looked over the side of the bed and swore. He leaped
swiftly from the bed, and took her in his arms. She felt the

pounding of his heart, felt the tremors that still racked him as he laid her down on the bed again.

"I hurt you. I'm so sorry."

His voice was deep, husky. She felt her own throat constrict, and she shook her head, burrowing more deeply against his naked chest. "No. You didn't hurt me. I'm all right, really."

He didn't say anything. He didn't even move. He just held her.

She wanted to stay there, where she was, forever. She had never felt so cherished before. Desired, admired, even needed. But never so cherished.

"You had a nightmare," she told him tentatively.

"Yes," he said.

"I wish you would tell me—"

"No."

It wasn't that he spoke so harshly, but that he spoke with absolute finality. Kristin stiffened, and she knew he felt it. He set her from him and rose. She watched as he walked over to the window, and as he stood there in the moonlight a dark web of pain seemed to encircle her heart. He walked with a pride that was uniquely his. He stood there for a long time, naked and sinewed and gleaming in the moonlight, and stared out at the night. Kristin watched as his muscles slowly, slowly eased, losing some of their awful rigor.

"Cole—" she whispered.

He turned back to her at last. He walked across the room, and she was glad when he lifted the covers and lay beside her again, drawing his arm around her and bringing her head to his chest. He stroked her hair.

"Cole, please—"

"Kristin, please. Don't."

She fell silent. His touch remained gentle.

"I have to leave tomorrow," he said at last.

"Where are you going?"

"East."

"Why?"

He hesitated for a long time. "Kristin, there are things that you probably don't want to hear, and there's no good reason for me to tell you.''

"No questions, no involvement," she murmured. He didn't answer her, but she felt him tighten beneath her.

"It's late," he said at last. "You should—"

She rose up and touched his lips with her own, cutting off his words. She wondered if she should be angry, or at least cool and distant. Nothing had changed. He had married her, but he still didn't want any involvement.

That didn't matter to her. Not at that moment. She only knew that he was leaving, and that in these times any man's future was uncertain at best. She ceased the flow of his words with the soft play of her tongue and leaned the length of her body over his, undulating her hips against his groin and the hardened peaks of her breasts against his chest. She savored the sharp intake of his breath and the quick, heady pressure of his hands upon her back and her buttocks.

Now it was her turn to inflame him. She nuzzled her face against his beard, and she teased his throat and the hard contours of his shoulders and chest. She tempted him with her tongue and with her fingertips and with the entire length of her body. She moved against him, crying out again and again at the sweet feel of their flesh touching. She teased him with her teeth, moving lower and lower against him. He tore his fingers into her hair and hoarsely gasped out her name. She barely knew herself. She was at once serene and excited, and she was certain of her power. She took all of him without hesitation. She loved him until he dragged her back to him and kissed her feverishly on the lips, then drew her beneath him. There was a new tension etched into his features, and a new blaze in his eyes. Taut as wire, he hovered above her. Then he came to her, fierce and savage and yet uniquely tender.

She thought she died just a little when it was over. The world was radiant, painted with shocking strips of sunlight and starlight, and then it was black and she was drifting again.

He held her still. He didn't speak, but his fingers stroked her hair, and for the moment it was enough. His hand lay over her abdomen. Tentatively she placed her fingers over his. He laced them through his own, and they slept.

But in the morning when she awoke, he was gone.

Three days later, Kristin was pumping water into the trough when she looked up to see a lone rider on the horizon, coming toward the house. For a moment her heart fluttered and she wondered if it might be Cole returning. Then she realized it couldn't be him. It wasn't his horse, and the rider wasn't sitting the horse the way he did.

"Malachi!" she called. He and Jamie would be with her for another few days. She frowned and bit her lip as she watched the approaching rider. It wasn't Zeke, she knew. Zeke never rode alone. Besides, there was no reason for her to be afraid of Quantrill's boys. Cole had gone through with the wedding to protect her, and anyway, Quantrill was supposed to be moving south for the winter. There was no reason to be afraid.

She was afraid anyway.

"Malachi—" she began again.

"Kristin?" He appeared at the door to the barn, his thumbs hooked in his belt, his golden brows knit into a furrow. He hurried over to her and watched the rider come. His eyes narrowed.

"Anderson," he murmured.

"Who?"

"It's a boy named Bill Anderson. He's...he's one of Quantrill's. One of his young recruits."

"What does he want? He is alone, isn't he?" Kristin asked anxiously.

"Yes, he's alone," Malachi assured her.

Jamie appeared then, coming out of the barn, his sleeves rolled up, his jacket off. He looked at Malachi. "I thought Quantrill was already on his way south. That's Bill Anderson."

Malachi nodded. "He seems to be alone."

The rider came closer and closer. He was young, very young, with a broad smile. He had dark, curly hair and a dark mustache and beard, but he still had an absurdly innocent face. Kristin shivered, thinking that he was far too young to be going around committing murder.

He drew his horse up in front of them. He was well armed, Kristin saw, with Colts at his waist and a rifle on either side of his saddle.

"Howdy, Malachi, Jamie."

"Bill," Malachi said amiably enough. Jamie nodded an acknowledgment.

"Cole's headed east, huh?" Anderson asked. He smiled at Kristin, waiting for an introduction. "You his new wife, ma'am? It's a pleasure to meet you."

He stuck out his hand. Kristin thought about all the blood that was probably on that hand, but she took it anyway and forced herself to smile.

"I'm his new wife," Kristin said. She couldn't bring herself to say that it was a pleasure to meet him, too. She could barely stand there.

"Kristin Slater, this is Bill Anderson. Bill, what the hell are you doing here? There's a lot of Union soldiers around these parts, you know," Malachi said.

"Yep," Jamie agreed cheerfully. "Lots and lots of Federals in these parts. And you know what they've been saying about you boys? No mercy. If they get their hands on you they intend to hang you high and dry."

"Yeah. I've heard what the Union has to say. But you've been safe enough here, huh, Malachi? And you, too, Jamie."

"Hell, we're regular army," Jamie said.

Anderson shrugged. "They have to catch us before they can hang us. And I'm not staying. I just had...well, I had some business hereabouts. I've got to join Quantrill in Arkansas. I just thought maybe I could come by here for a nice home-cooked meal."

Malachi answered before Kristin could. "Sure, Bill. Jamie, why don't you go on in and ask Delilah to cook up something special. Tell her we've got one of Quantrill's boys here."

Jamie turned around and hurried to the house. Delilah was already standing in the doorway. As Kristin watched, Shannon's blond head appeared. There was a squeal of outrage, and then the door slammed. Jamie came hurrying back to them.

"Malachi, Delilah says she needs you. There's a bit of a problem to be dealt with."

Malachi lifted an eyebrow, then hurried to the house. Kristin stood there staring foolishly at Bill Anderson with a grin plastered to her face. She wanted to shriek, and rip his baby face to shreds. Didn't he understand? Didn't he know she didn't want him here?

Men using Quantrill's name had come here and murdered her father. Men just like this one. She wanted to spit in his face.

But he had evidently come for a reason, and Malachi seemed to think it was necessary that he be convinced that Kristin was Cole's wife and that this was Cole's place now.

Kristin heard an outraged scream from the house. She bit her lip. Shannon obviously realized that one of Quantrill's men was here, and she didn't intend to keep quiet. She certainly didn't intend to sit down to a meal with him.

Anderson looked toward the house, hiking a brow.

"My sister," Kristin said sweetly.

"Her baby sister," Jamie said. He smiled at Kristin, but there was a warning in his eyes. They had to make Bill Anderson think Shannon was just a little girl.

And they had to keep her away from him.

Apparently that was what Malachi was doing, because the screams became muffled, and then they were silenced.

Malachi—the marks of Shannon's fingernails on his cheek—reappeared on the front porch. "Come on in, Bill. We'll have a brandy, and then Delilah will have lunch all set."

Bill looked from Malachi to Kristin and grinned. "That came from your, uh...baby sister, Mrs. Slater?"

"She can be wild when she wants," Kristin said sweetly. She stared hard at Malachi. He touched his cheek and shrugged. Kristin walked by him. "Too bad they can't send her up to take on the Army of the Potomac. We'd win this war in a matter of hours. Old Abe Lincoln himself would think

that secession was a fine thing just as long as Shannon
McCahy went with the Confederacy.''

"Malachi!" Kristin whispered harshly. "You're talking
about my sister!"

"I ought to turn her over to Bill Anderson!" he muttered.

"Malachi!"

Anderson turned around, looking at them curiously.
"Where is your sister?" he asked.

"The baby is tucked in for her nap," Malachi said with a
grin. "We don't let her dine with adults when we have company in the house. She spits her peas out sometimes. You
know how young 'uns are."

Kristin gazed at him, and he looked innocently back at her.
She swept by him. "Mr. Anderson, can we get you a drink?
A shot of whiskey?"

"Yes, ma'am, you can."

Kristin took him into her father's study and poured him a
drink. As he looked around the room, admiring the furnishings, Malachi came in and whispered in her ear.

"Shannon's in the cellar."

"And she's just staying there?" Kristin asked, her eyes
wide.

"Sure she's just staying there," Malachi said.

Soon they sat down to eat. Sizzling steaks from the ranch's
own fresh beef, fried potatoes, fall squash and apple pie. Bill
Anderson did have one big appetite. Kristin reminded herself
dryly that he was a growing boy.

He was polite, every inch the Southern cavalier, all through
the meal. Only when coffee was served with the pie did he sit
back and give them an indication of why he had come.

"Saw your husband the other day, ma'am."

Kristin paused just a second in scooping him out a second
slice of pie. "Did you?" she said sweetly.

"Sure, when he came to see Quantrill. He was mighty worried about you. It was a touching scene."

She set the pie down. "Was it?" She glanced at Malachi.
His eyes were narrowed, and he was very still.

"He used to be one of us, you know."

"What?"

Despite herself, Kristin sat. She sank right into her chair. "What?" she repeated.

Jamie cleared his throat. Malachi still hadn't moved.

Bill Anderson wiped his face with his napkin and smiled pleasantly. "Cole is one of the finest marksmen I ever did see. Hell, he's a one-man army, he's so damned good. It was nice when he was riding with us."

Kristin didn't say anything. She knew all the blood had fled from her face.

Bill Anderson forked up a piece of pie. "Yep, Cole Slater was just the same as Zeke Moreau. Just the same."

Malachi was on his feet in a second, his knife at Anderson's throat. "My brother was never anything like Zeke Moreau!"

Jamie jumped up behind him. He was so tense that Jamie couldn't pull him away. Kristin rushed around and tugged at his arm. "Malachi!"

He backed away. Bill Anderson stood and straightened his jacket. He gazed at Malachi, murder in his eyes. "You'll die for that, Slater."

"Maybe I'll die, but not for that, Anderson!" Malachi said.

"Gentlemen, gentlemen!" Kristin breathed, using her softest voice. "Please, aren't we forgetting ourselves here?"

It worked. Like most young men in the South, they had both been taught to be courteous to females, that a lack of manners was a horrible fault. They stepped away from each other, but their tempers were still hot.

"You came here just to do that, didn't you?" Malachi said quietly. "Just to upset my sister-in-law. I'm willing to bet Zeke Moreau asked you to do it."

"Maybe, and maybe not," Anderson said. He reached over to the sideboard for his hat. "Maybe she's just got the right to know that Cole Slater was a bushwhacker. You want to deny that, Malachi?"

Kristin looked at Malachi. His face was white, but he said nothing.

Anderson slammed his hat on his head. He turned to Kristin. "Mighty obliged for the meal, ma'am. Mighty obliged. Cap'n

Quantrill wants you to know that you should feel safe, and
he's sorry about any harm that's been done to you or yours.
If he had understood that your loyalties lay with the Confederacy, none of it would have come about.''

It was a lie, a bald-faced lie, but Kristin didn't say anything.
Anderson turned around, and she heard the door slam shut as
he left the house.

Delilah came in from the kitchen. The old grandfather clock
in the parlor struck the hour. They all stood there, just stood
there, dead still, until they heard Bill Anderson mount his
horse, until they heard the hoofbeats disappear across the Missouri dust.

Then Kristin spun around, gripping the back of a chair and
staring hard at Malachi. ''Is it true?''

''Kristin—'' he began unhappily.

''Is it true?'' she screeched. ''Is Cole one of them?''

''No!'' Jamie protested, stepping forward. ''He isn't one of
them, not now.''

She whirled around again, looking at Jamie. ''But he was!
That's the truth, isn't it?''

''Yes, damn it, all right, he was. But there was a damned
good reason for it.''

''Jamie!'' Malachi snapped.

''Oh, God!'' Kristin breathed. She came around and fell into
the chair. Malachi tried to take her hand. She wrenched it away
and jumped to her feet. ''Don't, please don't! Can't you understand? They are murderers! They dragged my father out
and they killed him!''

''There are a lot of murderers in this war, Kristin,'' Malachi
said. ''Quantrill isn't the only one.''

''It was Quantrill's men who killed my father,'' she said
dully. ''It was Quantrill's men who came after me.''

Malachi didn't come near her again. He stood at the end of
the table, his face pinched. ''Kristin, Cole's business is Cole's
business, and when he chooses, maybe he'll explain things to
you. He's asked us to mind our own concerns. Maybe he knew
you'd react just like this if you heard something. I don't know.
But you remember this while you're busy hating him. He

stumbled into this situation. He didn't come here to hurt you.'' He turned and walked to the door.

"He rode with Quantrill!" she whispered desperately.

"He's done the best he knows how for you," Malachi said quietly. He paused and looked back at her. "You might want to let your sister go when you get the chance. I tied her up downstairs so she wouldn't take a trip up here to meet Bill Anderson. He might not have liked what she had to say very much...and he might have liked the way that she looked too much.''

He went out. The clock suddenly seemed to be ticking very loudly. Kristin looked miserably at Jamie.

He tried to smile, but the attempt fell flat. "I guess I can't tell you too much of anything, Kristin. But I love my brother, and I think he's a fine man. There are things that maybe you can't understand just yet, and they are his business to discuss.'' He paused, watching her awkwardly. Then he shrugged and he, too, left her.

It wasn't a good day. She sat there for a long time. She even forgot about Shannon, and it was almost an hour before she went downstairs to release her. When she did, it was as if she had let loose a wounded tigress. Shannon cursed and ranted and raved and swore that someday, somehow if the war didn't kill Malachi, she would see to it that he was laid out herself.

She would probably have gone out and torn Malachi to shreds right then and there, but fortunately he had ridden out to take a look at some fencing.

Shannon was even furious with Kristin. "How could you? How could you? You let that man into our house, into Pa's house! After everything that has been done—''

"I did it so that Quantrill would leave us alone from now on! Maybe you've forgotten Zeke. I haven't!''

"Wait until Matthew comes back!" Shannon cried. "He'll take care of the Quantrill murderers and Malachi and—''

"Shannon," Kristin said wearily, "I thought you were going to take care of Malachi yourself?" She was hurt, and she was tired, and she couldn't keep the anger from her voice. "If you want to kill one of the Slater brothers, why don't you go after the right one?''

"What do you mean?" Shannon demanded.

"Cole," Kristin said softly. She stared ruefully at her sister. "Cole Slater. The man I married. He rode with Quantrill, Shannon. He was one of them."

"Cole?" Shannon's beautiful eyes were fierce. "I don't believe you!"

"It's the truth. That's why Bill Anderson came here. He wanted me to know that I had married a man every bit as bad as Zeke Moreau."

"He's lying."

"He wasn't lying. Malachi admitted it."

"Then Malachi was lying."

"No, Shannon. You two have your differences, but Malachi wouldn't lie to me."

Shannon was silent for several seconds. Then she turned on Kristin. "They are Missourians, Kristin. They can't help being Confederates. We were Confederates, I guess, until...until they came for Pa. Until Matthew joined up with the Union. And if Cole did ride with Quantrill, well, I'm sure he had his reasons. Cole is nothing like Zeke. You know that, and I know that."

Kristin smiled. Shannon was right, and so was Malachi. Cole was nothing like Zeke, and she knew it. But she was still hurt, and she was still angry. She was angry because she was frightened.

And because she loved him.

"Maybe you're right, Shannon," she said softly.

"Cole would never do anything dishonorable! He wouldn't!" Shannon said savagely. "And—"

"And what?"

"He's your husband, Kristin. You have to remember that. You married him. He's your husband now."

"I'll give him a chance to explain," was all that Kristin said. She would give him a chance. But when? He was gone, and winter was coming, and she didn't know when she would see him again.

* * *

Two days later Pete and the hands returned from the cattle drive, and Jamie and Malachi prepared to ride back to the war. Kristin was sorry she had argued with Malachi, and she hugged him tightly, promising to pray for him. She kissed Jamie, and he assured her that since his unit was stationed not far away he would be back now and then to see how she and Shannon were doing.

Shannon kissed Jamie—and then Malachi, too. He held her for a moment, smiling ruefully.

Then the two of them rode away.

Kristin stood with Shannon at her side, and they watched until they could no longer see the horses. A cool breeze came up, lifting Kristin's hair from her shoulders and swirling around her skirts. Winter was on its way. She was very cold, she realized. She was very cold, and she was very much alone.

Chapter Eleven

Winter was long, hard and bitterly cold. In December Shannon turned eighteen and in January Kristin quietly celebrated her nineteenth birthday. They awaited news from the front, but there was none. The winter was not only cold, it was also quiet, ominously quiet.

Late in February, a Union company came by and took Kristin's plow mules. The young captain leading the company compensated her in Yankee dollars which, she reflected, would help her little when she went out to buy seed for the spring planting. The captain did, however, bring her a letter from Matthew, a letter that had passed from soldier to soldier until it had come to her.

Matthew had apparently not received the letter she had written him. He made no mention of her marriage in his letter to her. Nor did he seem to know anything about Zeke Moreau's attack on the ranch after their father's murder.

It was a sad letter to read. Matthew first wrote that he prayed she and Shannon were well. Then he went into a long missive on the rigors of war—up at five in the morning, sleeping in tents, drilling endlessly, in the rain and even in the snow. Then there was an account of the first major battle in which he had been involved—the dread of waiting, the roar of the cannons, the blast of the guns, the screams of the dying. Nightfall was often the worst of all, when the picket's were close enough to call out to one another. He wrote:

We warn them, Kristin. ''Reb! You're in the moonlight!''
we call out, lest our sharpshooters take an unwary lad.
We were camped on the river last month; fought by day,
traded by night. We were low on tobacco, well supplied
with coffee, and the Mississippi boys were heavy on tobacco, low on coffee, so we remedied that situation. By
the end of it all we skirmished. I came face-to-face with
Henry, with whom I had been trading. I could not pull
the trigger of my rifle, nor lift my cavalry sword. Henry
was shot from behind, and he toppled over my horse, and
he looked up at me before he died and said please, would
I get rid of his tobacco, his ma didn't know that he was
smoking. But what if you fall? he asks me next, and I
try to laugh, and I tell him that my Ma is dead, and my
Pa is dead, and that my sisters are very understanding, so
it is all right if I die with tobacco and cards and all. He
tried to smile. He closed his eyes then, and he died, and
my dear sisters, I tell you that I was shaken. Sometimes
they egg me on both sides—what is a Missouri boy doing
in blue? I can only tell them that they do not understand.
The worst of it is this—war is pure horror, but it is better
than being at home. It is better than Quantrill and Jim
lane and Doc Jennison. We kill people here, but we do
not murder in cold blood. We do not rob, and we do not
steal, nor engage in any raping or slaughter. Sometimes
it is hard to remember that I was once a border rancher
and that I did not want war at all, nor did I have sympathy
for either side. Only Jake Armstrong from Kansas understands. If the jayhawkers robbed and stole and murdered against you, then you find yourself a Confederate.
If the bushwhackers burnt down your place, then you ride
for the Union, and the place of your birth doesn't mean
a whit.

Well, sisters, I do not mean to depress you. Again, I
pray that my letter finds you well. Kristin, again I urge
you to take Shannon and leave if you should feel the
slightest threat of danger again. They have murdered Pa,
and that is what they wanted, but I still worry for you

both, and I pray that I will get leave to come and see you soon. I assure you that I am well, as of this writing, which nears Christmas, 1862. I send you all my love. Your brother, Matthew.

He had also sent her his Union pay. Kristin fingered the money, then went out to the barn and dug up the strongbox where she kept the gold from the cattle sales and the Yankee dollars from the captain. She added the money from Matthew. She had been feeling dark and depressed and worried, but now, despite the contents of Matthew's letter, she felt her strength renewed. She had to keep fighting. One day Matthew would come home. One day the war would be over and her brother would return. Until then she would maintain his ranch.

By April she still hadn't been able to buy any mules, so she and Samson and Shannon went out to till the fields. It was hard, backbreaking labor, but she knew that food was growing scarcer and scarcer, and that it was imperative that they grow their own vegetables. Shannon and she took turns behind the plow while Samson used his great bulk to pull it forward. The herd was small, though there would be new calves soon enough. By morning Kristin planned the day with Pete, by day she worked near the house, and supper did not come until the last of the daylight was gone. Kristin went to bed each night so exhausted that she thought very little about the war.

She didn't let herself think about Cole, though sometimes he stole into her dreams uninvited. Sometimes, no matter how exhausted she was when she went to bed, she imagined that he was with her. She forgot then that he had been one of Quantrill's raiders. She remembered only that he was the man who had touched her, the man who had awakened her. She lay in the moonlight and remembered him, remembered his sleek-muscled form walking silent and naked to her by night, remembered the way the moonlight had played over them both...

Sometimes she would awaken and she would be shaking, and she would remind herself that he had ridden with Quantrill, just like Zeke Moreau. She might be married to him now, but she could never, never lie with him again as she had before. He was another of Quantrill's killers, just like Zeke. Riding, burning, pillaging, murdering—raping, perhaps. She didn't know. He had come to her like a savior, but Quantrill's men had never obeyed laws of morality or decency. She wanted him to come back to her because she could not imagine him dead. She wanted him to come back to her and deny it all.

But he could not deny it, because it was the truth. Malachi had said so. Malachi had known how the truth would hurt, but hadn't been able to lie. There was no way for Cole to come and deny it. There was just no way at all.

Spring wore on. In May, while she was out in the south field with Samson, Pete suddenly came riding in from the north pasture. He ignored the newly sown field, riding over it to stop in front of Kristin.

"He's back, Miz Slater, he's back. They say that Quantrill is back, and that Quantrill and company do reign here again!"

The house was still a long way off when Cole reined in his horse and looked across the plain at it. Things looked peaceful, mighty peaceful. Daisies were growing by the porch, and someone—Kristin? Shannon?—had hung little flowerpots from the handsome gingerbread on the front of the house.

It looked peaceful, mighty peaceful.

His heart hammered uncomfortably, and Cole realized that it had taken him a long time to come back. He didn't know quite why, but it had taken him longer than necessary. He hadn't been worried at all, at least not until he had heard that Quantrill was back. He didn't understand it. All through the winter, all through the early spring, he'd had dreams about her. He had wanted her. Wanted her with a longing that burned and ached and kept him staring at the ceiling or the night sky. Sometimes it had been as if he could reach out and touch her. And then everything had come back to him. The silky feel of her flesh and the velvety feel of her hair falling over his shoulders. The startling blue of her eyes, the sun gold of her hair, the fullness of her breasts in his hands...

Then, if he was sound asleep, he would remember the smell of smoke, and he would hear the sound of the shot, and he would see his wife, his first wife, his real wife.... Running, running... And the smoke would be acrid on the air, and the hair that spilled over him would be a sable brown, and it would be blood that filled his hands.

It hurt to stay away. He needed her. He wanted her, wanted her with a raw, blinding, burning hunger. But the nightmares would never stay away. Never. Not while his wife's killer lived. Not while the war raged on.

He picked up the reins again and nudged his mount and started the slow trek toward the house. His breath had quickened. His blood had quickened. It coursed through him, raced through him, and it made him hot, and it made him nervous. Suddenly it seemed a long, long time since he had seen her last. It had been a long time. Almost half a year.

But she was his wife.

He swallowed harshly and wondered what his homecoming would be like. He remembered the night before he had left, and his groin went tight as wire and the excitement seemed to sweep like fire into his limbs, into his fingertips, into his heart and into his lungs.

They hadn't done so badly, he thought. Folks had surely done worse under the best of circumstances.

When the war ended...

Cole paused again, wondering if the war would ever end. Those in Kansas and Missouri had been living with the skirmishing since 1855, and hell, the first shots at Fort Sumter had only been fired in April of '61. Back then, Cole thought grimly, the rebels had thought they could whomp the Yankees in two weeks, and the Yankees had thought, before the first battle at Manassas, it would be easy to whip the Confederacy. But the North had been more determined than the South had ever imagined, and the South had been more resolute than the North had ever believed possible. And the war had dragged on and on. It had been more than two years now, and there was no end in sight.

So many battles. An Eastern front, a Western front. A Union navy, a Confederate navy, a battle of ironclads. New Orleans fallen, and now Vicksburg under seige. And men were still talking about the battle at Antietam Creek, where the bodies had piled high and the corn had been mown down by bullets and the stream had run red with blood.

He lifted his hands and looked at his threadbare gloves. He was wearing his full dress uniform, but his gold gloves were threadbare. His gray wool tunic and coat carried the gold epaulets of the cavalry, for though he was officially classified a scout he'd been assigned to the cavalry and was therefore no longer considered a spy. It was a fine distinction, Cole thought. And it was damned peculiar that as a scout he should spend so much of his time spying on both sides of the Missouri-Kansas border. He wondered bleakly what it was all worth. In January he'd appeared before the Confederate Cabinet, and he'd reported honestly, as honestly as he could, on the jay-hawkers' activities. Jim Lane and Doc Jennison, who had led the jayhawkers—the red-legs as they were sometimes known because of their uniforms—were animals. Jim Lane might be a U.S. senator, but he was still a fanatic and a murderer, every bit as bad as Quantrill. But the Union had gotten control of most of the jayhawkers. Most of them had been conscripted into the Union army and sent far away from the border. As the Seventh Kansas, a number of jayhawkers had still been able to carry out raids on the Missouri side of the border, plundering and burning town after town, but then Major General Henry Halleck had ordered the company so far into the center of Kansas that it had been virtually impossible for the boys to jayhawk.

As long as he lived, Cole would hate the jayhawkers. As long as he lived, he would seek revenge. But his hatred had cooled enough that he could see that there was a real war being fought, a war in which men in blue and men in gray fought with a certain decency, a certain humanity. There were powerful Union politicians and military men who knew their own jayhawkers for the savages they were, and there were men like Halleck who were learning to control them.

No one had control of Quantrill.

By that spring, General Robert E. Lee had been given command of the entire Confederate Army. When he had met with that tall, dignified, soft-spoken man, Cole had felt as if the place he had left behind could not be real. War was ugly, blood and death were ugly, and screaming soldiers maimed and dying on torn-up earth were ugly, too. But nothing was so ugly as the total disregard for humanity that reigned on the border between Kansas and Missouri. Lee had listened to Cole, and Jefferson Davis, the Confederate president, had listened long and carefully to him, too. Judah P. Benjamin, secretary of war, had taken his advice and when Quantrill had demanded a promotion and recognition, his request had been denied.

Cole wondered briefly if the violence would ever stop. He wondered if he would ever be able to cleanse his own heart of hatred.

Suddenly he forgot the war, forgot everything.

He could see the well to the left of the house, near the trough, and he could see Kristin standing there. She had just pulled up a pail of water.

Her hair was in braids, but a few golden strands had escaped from her hairpins and curled over her shoulders. She was dressed in simple gingham—no petticoats today—and she had opened the top buttons of her blouse. She dipped a handkerchief into the bucket and doused herself with the cool water, her face, her throat, her collarbone, then flesh bared by the open flaps of her blouse. Hot and dusty, she lifted the dipper from the pail and drank from it. Then she leaned back slightly and allowed the cool water to spill over her face and throat.

Cole's stomach tightened, and he felt his heartbeat in his throat, and he wondered what it was about the way she was standing, savoring the water, that was so provocative, so beguiling, so sensual. He nudged his horse again, eager to greet her.

He came in at a gallop. She spun around, startled. The water spilled over her blouse, and the wet fabric outlined her young breasts. Her eyes widened at the sight of him, first with panic, he thought, then with startled recognition. He drew up in front of her and dismounted in a leap. Her blouse was soaked, and her face was damp. Her lips were parted, and her face was streaked with dust. She was beautiful.

"Cole..." she murmured.

He pulled her hard against him. He found her lips, and he kissed her deeply, and she tasted even sweeter than he remembered. She was vibrant and feminine. He choked out something and touched her breast, feeling her nipple hard as a pebble beneath his palm. She melted against him. She gasped, and she trembled beneath his touch. Her lips parted more fully, and his tongue swept into the hot dampness of her mouth.

Then, suddenly, she twisted away from him with another choking sound. Startled, he released her. She shoved hard against his chest, backing away from him, wiping her mouth with her hands as if she had taken poison. Her eyes remained very wide and very blue. "Bastard!" she hissed at him. She looked him up and down. "Stupid bastard! In a Confederate uniform, no less! Don't you know this whole area is crawling with Yankees?"

"I'll take my clothes right off," he offered dryly.

She shook her head stubbornly. She was still trembling, he saw. Her fingers worked into the fabric of her skirt, released it, then clenched the material again. Her breasts were still outlined by her wet blouse, the nipples clearly delineated. He took a step toward her. "For God's sake, Kristin, what the hell is the matter with you? You're my wife, remember—"

"Don't touch me!"

"Why the hell not?"

"You're a bushwhacker!" she spat out. "You're his—you belong to Quantrill, just like Zeke."

That stopped him dead in his tracks. He wondered how she had found out. A haze fell over his eyes, a cool haze of distance. It didn't really matter. He'd had his reasons. And though he wasn't with Quantrill anymore, if he'd found the right man when he had been with him, he would have been as savage as any of them.

"A friend of yours stopped by here right after you left in the fall," Kristin informed him. "Bill Anderson. You remember him? He remembered you!"

"Kristin, I'm not with Quantrill any longer."

"Oh, I can see that. You got yourself a real Reb uniform. It's a nice one, Cole. You wear it well. But it doesn't cover what you really are! Who did you steal it from? Some poor dead boy?"

His hand slashed out and he almost struck her. He stopped himself just in time.

"The uniform is mine, Kristin," he said through clenched teeth. "Just as you're my wife."

He didn't touch her. Her face was white, and she was as stiff as a board. He started to walk past her, heading straight for the house. Then he spun around. She cringed, but he reached for her shoulders anyway.

"Kristin—" he began. But he was interrupted by a man's voice.

"You leave her alone, Johnny Reb!"

Cole spun around, reaching for his Colt. He was fast, but not fast enough.

"No!" he heard Kristin scream. "Matthew, no, you can't! Cole, no—" She threw herself against his hand, and he lost his chance to fire. She tore her eyes from his and looked over at the tall man in the Union blue coming toward them with a sharpshooter's rifle raised. Kristin screamed again and threw herself against Cole. He staggered and fell, and he was falling when the bullet hit him. It grazed the side of his head. He felt the impact, felt the spurt of blood. He felt a sheet of blackness descend over him, and wondered if he was dying. As he railed against himself in black silence for being so involved with Kristin that he never heard or saw the danger, Cole heard the next words spoken as the man who had called to him, the man who had shot him, came forward.

"Oh, no! Oh, my God—"

"Kristin! What's the matter with you? I'm trying to save you from this jackal—"

"Matthew, this jackal is my husband!"

* * *

As he slowly regained consciousness, Cole realized he wasn't dead. He wasn't dead, but he'd probably lost a lot of blood, and it seemed as if he had been out for hours, for it was no longer daylight. Night had fallen. An oil lamp glowed softly at his side.

He was in the bedroom they had shared, the bedroom with the sleigh bed. Everything was blurred. He blinked, and the room began to come into focus. He could see the windows and a trickle of moonlight. He touched his head and discovered that it had been bandaged. He drew his fingers away. At least he couldn't feel any blood. Someone had stripped off his uniform and bathed the dust of the road from him and tucked him between cool, clean sheets.

Someone. His wife. No, not his wife. Kristin. Yes, his wife. He had married her. She was his wife now.

She had stopped him from killing the man.

But she had stopped the man from killing him, too.

A sudden pain streaked through him. He was going to have one terrible headache, he realized. But he was alive, and he was certain that the bullet wasn't embedded in his skull. It had just grazed him.

He heard footsteps on the stairs, and then on the floor outside his door. He closed his eyes quickly as someone came into the room. It was Delilah. She spoke in a whisper. "Dat boy is still out cold." She touched his throat, then his chest. "But he's living, all right. He's still living, and he don't seem to have no fever."

"Thank God!" came in a whisper. Kristin. Cole could smell the faint scent of her subtle perfume. He felt her fingers, cool and gentle, against his face. Then he heard the man's voice again. Matthew. She had called him Matthew. Of course. The brother. The one he had told her to write to just so that this wouldn't happen.

"A Reb, Kristin? After everything that happened—"

"Yes, damn you! After everything that happened!" Kristin whispered harshly. "Matthew, don't you dare preach to me!

You left, you got to go off and join up with the army! Shannon and I didn't have that luxury. And Zeke came back—''

''Moreau came back?'' Matthew roared.

''Shut up, will you, Matthew?'' Kristin said wearily. She sounded so tired. So worn, so weary. Cole wanted to open his eyes, wanted to take her into his arms, wanted to soothe away all the terrible things that the war had done to her. He could not, and he knew it.

She probably didn't want him to, anyway. She would probably never forgive him for his time with Quantrill. Well, he didn't owe anyone any apologies for it, and he'd be damned if he'd explain himself to her. And yet…

''Kristin,'' Matthew was saying huskily, ''what happened?''

''Nothing happened, Matthew. Oh, it almost did. Zeke was going to rape me, and let every man with him rape me, and then he was probably going to shoot me. He was going to sell Samson and Delilah. But nothing happened because of this man. He's a better shot than Shannon or me. He's even a better shot than you. He happened by and it was all over for Zeke.''

''Zeke is dead?''

''No. Zeke rode away.'' A curious note came into her voice. ''You see, Matthew, he won't murder a man in cold blood. I wanted him to, but he wouldn't. And after that, well, it's a long story. But since he's married me, none of them will harm me, or this place. They're—they're afraid of him.''

''Damn, Kristin—'' He broke off. Cole heard a strangled sound, and then he knew that brother and sister were in one another's arms. Kristin was crying softly, and Matthew was comforting her. Cole gritted his teeth, for the sound of her weeping was more painful to him than his wound. I will never be able to touch her like that, he thought. He opened his eyes a fraction and took a good look at Matthew McCahy. He was a tall man with tawny hair and blue eyes like his sisters. He was lean, too, and probably very strong, Cole thought. He was probably a young man to be reckoned with.

He shifted and opened his eyes wider. Sister and brother broke apart. Kristin bent down by him and touched his forehead. Her hair was loose, and it teased the bare flesh of his chest. "Cole?"

He didn't speak. He nodded, and he saw that her brow was furrowed with worry, and he was glad of that. She hated him for his past, but at least she didn't want him dead.

"Cole, this is Matthew. My brother. I wrote him, but the letter never reached him. He didn't know that—he didn't know that we were married."

Cole nodded again and looked over at Matthew. He was still in full-dress uniform—navy-blue full-dress uniform. As his gaze swept over Matthew, Cole couldn't help noticing that Matthew McCahy's uniform was in far better shape than his own, and in much better condition than that of the majority of the uniforms worn by the men of the South. The blockade was tightening. The South was running short of everything—medicine, clothing, ammunition, food. Everything. He smiled bitterly. The South had brilliance. Lee was brilliant, Jackson was brilliant, Stuart was brilliant. But when a Southerner fell in battle, he could not be replaced. Men were the most precious commodity in war, and the Confederacy did not have nearly enough.

The Union, however, seemed to have an inexhaustible supply of soldiers, volunteers and mercenaries.

Cole knew a sudden, bleak flash of insight. The South could not win the war.

"Reb—Sorry, your name is Cole, right? Cole Slater." Matthew came around and sat at the foot of the bed. He swallowed uncomfortably. "You saved my sisters' lives, and I'm grateful to you. I wouldn't have shot you if I'd known. It was the uniform. I'm with the North." He said it defensively. It was not easy for a Missourian to fight for the North.

"You had just cause," Cole said. His voice was raspy, his throat dry. His mouth tasted of blood.

Matthew nodded. "Yes. I had just cause." He hesitated. "Well, I'm home on leave, and I guess that you are, too."

"Something like that," Cole said. Kristin made a little sound of distress, but she quickly swallowed it down. Cole didn't glance her way. He smiled at Matthew and reached for her hand. She was playing the loving wife for her brother, he knew, and he wondered how far she would go. She let him take her hand, let him pull her down beside him.

"We'll have to manage while we're both here," Matthew said. He stretched out a hand to Cole, and Cole released Kristin's long enough to take it. "Does that sound fair to you, Reb?"

"It sounds fine to me, Yankee."

Matthew flushed suddenly. "Well, maybe I'd best leave the two of you alone." He rose quickly.

Kristin was on her feet instantly. "No! I'm coming with you!"

Matthew's brow furrowed suspiciously. "Kristin—"

"Sweetheart…" Cole murmured plaintively.

"Darling!" Kristin replied sweetly, syrup dripping from her tone, "I wouldn't dream of disturbing you now. You must rest!"

She gave him a peck on the forehead, and then she was gone, practically running out of the room.

Matthew smiled at Cole. "Too bad there's a war on, ain't it?"

"Yeah. It's too damn bad," Cole agreed.

"She's stubborn," Matthew said.

"Yeah. I've noticed."

"Just like a mule."

"Well, I guess I agree with you there, Yankee."

Matthew laughed, then left and closed the door behind him.

Three days later, Cole was feeling damned good, and damned frustrated. Kristin had managed to elude him ever since his return, sweetly pleading his weakened condition. She had spent her nights in her own room, leaving him to lie there alone. But as night fell on his third day back, Cole jerked awake from a doze to realize that Kristin had come into the room.

He heard her breathing in the darkness, each breath coming in a little pant. Her back was against the door, and she seemed to be listening. She thought he was sleeping, he realized.

Cole rose silently and moved toward her in the dark. He clamped a hand over her mouth and pulled her against the length of his naked body. She gave a muffled gasp and stiffened then began to struggle to free herself.

"Shush!" he warned her.

She bit his hand, and he swore softly.

"Let me go!" she whispered.

"Not on your life, Mrs. Slater."

"Bushwhacker!"

His mouth tightened grimly. "You're still my wife, Kristin."

"Try to rape me and I'll scream. Matthew will kill you. You don't even have a gun up here!"

"If I touch you, Kristin, it wouldn't be rape," Cole assured her.

"Let go—"

He did not let go. He kissed her, plunging his tongue deep into her mouth, holding her so firmly that she could not deny him. He caught her wrists and held them fast behind her back, pressing his naked body still closer to hers. She wore a thin white cotton nightgown buttoned to the throat. It was so thin that he could feel all the sweet secrets her body had to offer.

He raised his lips from hers at last, and she gasped for breath. He pressed his lips to her breast and took the nipple into his mouth through the fabric, savoring it with his tongue.

"I'll scream!" she whispered.

"Scream, then," he told her. He lifted her into his arms and carried her to the bed, searching feverishly for the hem of the gown. He found it and pulled it up, and then they were together, bare flesh touching bare flesh. He seared the length of her with his lips, and she raged against him with husky words and whispers. But then she rose against him. She wrapped her arms around him and pulled his head down to hers and kissed him again. And then she told him he was a bastard, but she gasped when he caressed her thighs, and she buried her face against him when his touch grew intimate and demanding.

"Scream," he whispered to her. "Scream, if you feel you must…"

He thrust deep into her. She cried out, but his mouth muffled the cry, and then his tongue filled her mouth.

It had been so very long, and she had dreamed of him so many times.

He stroked and caressed her insides until she was in a frenzy. Then he drove into her with all the force he possessed, and she felt the familiar sweetness invade her once, and then again and again. Then, suddenly, he was gone from her. She was cold, and she was lost, but then he was kissing her again, her forehead, her cheeks, her breasts, her thighs.... He turned her over gently, and his lips trailed a path of fire down her spine. Then she was on her back again, and his silver-gray eyes were upon her and she swallowed back a shriek of pleasure as he came to her again....

The night was swept away.

Later, as she lay awake in the ravaged bed, Kristin berated herself furiously for her lack of principles. She reminded herself again that he had been with Quantrill, and she fought back tears of fury.

She slept with her back to him, and he did not try to touch her again. In the morning, she avoided him. At dinner she was polite, though she wanted to scream. She was disturbed to see that her brother and Cole talked about the cattle and the ranch easily, like two old friends. Shannon had talked to Matthew, and Shannon thought Cole was a hero, no matter what.

He's a bushwhacker! she wanted to shriek to her brother, but of course she could not. Matthew would want to kill Cole, if he knew. And Kristin had never seen anyone as talented with a gun as Cole. No one. If Matthew tried to kill him, Matthew would be the one who died.

Later that evening, when it was time for bed, Matthew walked upstairs with them, and Kristin had no choice but to follow Cole into her parents' bedroom. When the door closed behind them, Kristin stared at it. Cole was behind her, so close that she could feel his warm breath on the back of her neck.

"I hate you," she told him.

He was silent for a long time. She longed to turn around, but she did not.

"I don't think you do, Kristin," he said at last. "But have it however you want it."

He stripped off his clothes and let them lay where they fell, and he crawled into bed. She stayed where she was for a long time. She heard him move to blow out the lamp, and still she stood by the door. Then, finally, she stripped down to her chemise and climbed gingerly into the bed. She knew he was still awake, but he did not try to touch her. She lay awake for hours, and then she drifted off to sleep. While she slept, she rolled against him, and cast her leg over his. Their arms became entwined, and her hair fell over him like a soft blanket.

They awoke that way. Her chemise was up to her waist, her shoulders were bare, and her breast was peeking out. She gazed over at Cole and saw that he was awake and that he was watching her. Then she felt him, felt him like a pulsing rod against her flesh. He moved toward her, very, very slowly, giving her every chance to escape. She couldn't move. Her flesh was alive, her every nerve awake to shimmering sensation, and when he came inside her she shuddered at the pleasure of it, of having him with her, of touching him again, of savoring the subtle movement of his muscles, of feeling the hardness of him as he moved inside her.

And yet, when it was over, she could still find nothing to say to him. She rose quickly and dressed, aware all the while of his brooding eyes upon her.

"Where have you been?" she demanded at last.

"In Richmond."

"Not with—"

"You know I wasn't with Quantrill. You saw my uniform."

Kristin shrugged. "Some of them wear Confederate uniforms."

"I wasn't with Quantrill."

Kristin hesitated, struggling with her buttons. Cole rose and came up behind her, and she swallowed down a protest as he took over the task. "How long are you staying?"

"I've got another week."

"The same as Matthew," she murmured.

"The same as Matthew."

"And where are you going now?"

"Malachi's unit."

She hesitated. Liar! she longed to shout. Tears stung her eyes. She didn't know if he was lying or not.

He swung her around to face him. "I'm a special attaché to General Lee, Kristin. Officially, I'm cavalry. A major, but the only man I have to answer to is the grand old man himself. I do my best to tell him what's going on back here."

Kristin lifted her chin. "And what do you tell him?"

"The truth."

"The truth?"

"The truth as I see it, Kristin."

They stared at one another for a moment, enemies again. Hostility glistened in her eyes and narrowed his sharply.

"I'm sorry, Cole," Kristin said at last. "I can't forgive you."

"Damn you, Kristin, when did I ever ask you to forgive me?" he replied. He turned around. He had dismissed her, she realized. Biting her lip, she fled the room.

She avoided him all that day. She was tense at dinner as she listened to the conversation that flowed around her. Matthew, puzzled by her silence, asked if she was unwell, and she told him she was just tired. She went up to bed early.

She went to bed naked, and she lay awake, and she waited.

When Cole came to bed, she rolled into his arms, and he thought she made love more sweetly than ever before, more sweetly and with a greater desperation.

It went on that way, day after day, night after night, until the time came for Matthew to ride away again.

And for Cole to ride away again.

And then they were standing in front of the house, ready to mount up, one man she loved dressed in blue, one man she loved dressed in gray. Both handsome, both young, both carrying her heart with them, though she could not admit that to the man in gray.

Kristin was silent. Shannon cried and hugged them both again and again.

Kristin kissed and hugged her brother, and then, because there was an audience, she had to kiss Cole.

Then, suddenly, the audience didn't matter. May was over. They had heard that Vicksburg had fallen, and Kristin thought of all the men who would die in the days to come, and she didn't want to let either of them go.

She didn't want to let Cole go. She couldn't explain anything to him, couldn't tell him that she didn't hate him, that she loved him, but she didn't want to let him go.

She hugged him fiercely, and she kissed him passionately, until they were both breathless and they both had to step away. His eyes searched hers, and then he mounted up.

Shannon and Kristin stood together and watched as the two men clasped hands.

Then one rode west, the other east. Cole to Kansas, Matthew deeper into Missouri.

Shannon let out a long, gasping sob.

"They're gone again!" she said, and pulled her sister closer to her. "Come on. We'll weed out the garden. It's hot, and it'll be a miserable task, and we won't think about the men at all."

"We'll think about them," Shannon said. She was close to tears again, Kristin thought. Shannon, who was always so fierce, so feisty. And Kristin knew that if Shannon cried again, she would sob all day, too.

"Let's get to work."

They had barely set to work when they heard the sounds of hooves again. Kristin spun around hopefully, thinking that either her brother or her husband had returned.

Shannon called out a warning.

It was Zeke, Kristin thought instantly.

But it was not. It was a company of Union soldiers. At its head was a captain. His uniform was just like Matthew's. They stopped in front of the house, but they did not dismount.

"Kristin Slater!" the captain called out.

He was about Matthew's age, too, Kristin thought.

"Yes?" she said, stepping forward.

He swallowed uncomfortably. "You're under arrest."

"What?" she said, astonished.

His Adam's apple bobbed. "Yes, ma'am. I'm sorry. You and your sister are under arrest, by order of General Halleck. I'm right sorry, but we're rounding up all the womenfolk giving aid and succor to Quantrill and his boys."

"Aid and succor!" Kristin shrieked.

She might have been all right if she hadn't begun to laugh. But she did begin to laugh, and before she knew it, she was hysterical.

"Take her, boys."

"Now, you just wait!" Delilah cried from the porch.

The captain shook his head. "Take Mrs. Slater, and the young one, too."

One of the soldiers got down from his horse and tugged at Kristin's arm. She tore it fiercely from his grasp.

The young man ruefully addressed his captain. "Sir..."

"My brother is in the Union army!" Kristin raged. "My father was killed by bushwhackers, and now you're arresting me...for helping Quantrill? No!"

The soldier reached for her again, and she hit him in the stomach. Shannon started to scream, and Delilah came running down the steps with her rolling pin.

"God help us, if the Rebs ain't enough, Halleck has to pit us against the womenfolk!" the young captain complained. He dismounted and walked over to Kristin. "Hold her, men."

Two of them caught her arms. She stared at him.

"Sorry, ma'am," he said sincerely.

Then he struck her hard across the chin, and she fell meekly into his arms.

Chapter Twelve

"Y'all have just the blondest hair! And I do mean the blondest!" Josephine Anderson said as she pulled Shannon's locks into a set of high curls on top of her head. She was a pretty young woman herself, with plump cheeks and a flashing smile and a tendency to blush easily. She never smiled when their Yankee captors were around, though. Josephine was a hard-core Confederate. She and her sister Mary had been brought in a week after Kristin and Shannon, and they all shared a corner of a big room on the second floor of a building in Kansas City. Josephine and Mary were both very sweet, and Kristin liked them well enough, despite their fanaticism. They had both wanted her and Shannon to meet their brother Billy—who turned out to be none other than Bill Anderson, the Bill Anderson who had stopped by the house to make sure that Kristin knew about Cole's position with Quantrill's raiders.

That was all right. At the very beginning, Kristin had sweetly told the girls that she did know their Billy. She also told them what had happened to her father—and that she wished that she were anything other than what she was: a citizen of a country whose people tore one another to shreds.

Josephine and Mary had turned away from her in amazement, but then the next day they had been friendly. They respected her right to have a passionate stand—even if it was a strange one.

And when Cole's name was mentioned, Mary acted just the way Shannon did. "Ooh! You're really married to him?" she gushed.

It seemed that Cole had been to dinner once at their house with Bill when he had first started out with Quantrill. But they didn't know very much about him, only that there was some deep secret in his past.

"He can be real quiet like, you know!" Mary said.

"But, oh, those eyes!" Josephine rolled her own.

"It's such a pity he left Quantrill!" Mary told her fiercely. "Why, he'd have cleaned out half of Kansas by now; I just know it."

Kristin assured them that Cole was still with the Confederate Army—in the cavalry, like his brothers. Then Shannon went on to tell them about their brother Matthew and how he had gone off to join up with the Union Army after their father's death.

Mary and Josephine thought that was a terrible tragedy, but they understood that, too. "I'm surprised he didn't become a jayhawker, because that's how it goes, you know! They say that old John Brown was attacked way back in '55, that one of his sons was killed. So he killed some Missourians, and some Missourians went up and killed some more Kansans. But you two—why, I feel right sorry for you! Missourians, with a brother in blue and your husband in gray. It's a shame, a damned shame, that's all."

It was a good thing they were able to come to an understanding. All summer long, General Ewing, the local Union commander, had women picked up so that their men couldn't come to them for food or supplies. There were a great many of them living at very close quarters. The authorities holding them weren't cruel, and the women weren't hurt in any way. A number of the young officers were remarkably patient, in fact, for the women could be extraordinarily abusive when they spoke to their captors. But though the men behaved decently toward their prisoners, the living conditions were horrid. The building itself was in terrible shape, with weak and rotting timbers, the food was barely adequate, and the bedding was full of insects.

Kristin wanted desperately to go home. At first she had been angry. She had fought and argued endlessly with various commanders, and they had all apologized and looked uncomfortable and shuffled their feet, but none of them had been willing to let her go. And finally she had become resigned.

She grew more and more wretched. She had often been sick in the first weeks of her captivity and she had thought it must be the food. She was still queasy much of the time, but, though she hadn't told anyone, she knew why now. She was pregnant. Sometime in February of the following year she was going to have Cole's baby. She had been stunned at first, but then she had taunted herself endlessly. Why should she be surprised, after all. Children were the result of a man being with a woman.

She wasn't sure how she felt. Sometimes she lay there and railed against a God that could let her have a baby in a world where its blood relations were destined to be its mortal enemies, in a world where murder and bloodshed were the order of the day.

Then there were nights when she touched her still-flat belly and dreamed, and wondered what the baby would look like. And then, even if she was furious with Cole, even if she had convinced herself that he was as evil as Zeke, she knew she loved him. And she did want his child. A little boy with his shimmering silver eyes. Or a girl. Or maybe the child would be light, with her hair and eyes. Whoever the child took after, it was destined to be beautiful, she was certain. Cole's baby. She longed to hold it in her arms. She dreamed about seeing him again, about telling him.

And then there were times when she sank into depression. Cole probably wouldn't be the least bit pleased. He probably intended to divorce her as soon as the war was over, she thought bitterly. She was imprisoned for being the wife of a man who intended to divorce her.

Then not even that mattered. She wanted the baby. She wanted the baby to hold and to love, and she wanted it to be born to peace. The war could not go on forever. She didn't care who won. She just wanted it to be over. She wanted her baby to be able to run laughing through the cornfields, to look up at the sun and feel its warmth. She wanted peace for her child.

And most of all, she wanted it to be born at home. She did not want to bear her baby here, in this awful, crowded place of degradation.

Kristin looked up from the letter she was writing to her brother asking if there was anything he could do to get the authorities to free Shannon and herself. The three other women in the room looked as if they were preparing for a ball.

Josephine stepped back. "Oh, Shannon, that just looks lovely, really lovely."

"Why, thank you, ma'am," Shannon said sweetly. Then she sighed. "I wish I could see it better."

Mary dug under her pillow and found her little hand mirror. "Here, Shannon."

Suddenly the room fell silent. One of the young Federal officers, a Captain Ellsworth, had come in. The women looked at him suspiciously.

His dark brown eyes fell on Kristin. "Mrs. Slater, would you come with me, please?"

She quickly set aside her paper and pen and rose, nervously folding her fingers in front of her and winding them tightly together.

A middle-aged woman called out to the captain, "Don't walk too hard on this here floor, sonny! Those Yankee boots will make you come right through it!"

He nodded sadly to the woman. "Sorry, Mrs. Todd. The place is awful, I know. I'm working on it."

"Don't work on it!" Mary Anderson called out gaily. "You tell them to let us go home. You tell them that my brother will come after them, and that he'll kill them all."

"Yes, miss," Captain Ellsworth said, staring straight at her. "That's the problem, Miss Anderson. Your brother already does come to murder us all." He bowed to her politely. Then he took Kristin's elbow and led her out of the room. He preceded her down the groaning staircase to the doorway of the office below. Kristin looked at him nervously.

"It's all right, Mrs. Slater. Major Emery is in there. He wants to talk to you."

He opened the door for her, and Kristin walked in. She had never seen Major Emery before. He was a tall, heavyset man, with thick, wavy, iron-gray hair and great drooping mustache to match. His eyebrows were wild and of the same gray, and beneath them his eyes were a soft flower blue. He seemed a kind man, Kristin thought instantly, a gentleman.

"Mrs. Slater, sit, please." Kristin silently did so. The major dismissed Captain Ellsworth, then smiled at Kristin. "Can I get you some tea, Mrs. Slater?"

"No, thank you." She sat very straight, reminding herself that, no matter how kindly he looked, he was still her captor. He smiled again and leaned back in his chair.

"Mrs. Slater, I'm trying very hard to get an order to have you and your sister released."

A gasp of surprise escaped Kristin. Major Emery's smile deepened, and he leaned forward again. "It will take a few days, I'm afraid."

Kristin and Shannon had been here almost three months. A few more days meant nothing.

"Because of my brother?" Kristin said. "Did Matthew find out that we were here? I didn't want to tell him at first because I didn't want him going into battle worrying, but I was just writing to him—"

"No, no, Mrs. Slater. I haven't heard anything from your brother at all."

"Oh, I see," Kristin murmured bitterly. "You've finally decided that a woman who had her father killed by some of Quantrill's men is not likely to give aid and comfort to the enemy, is that it?"

Major Emery shook his head. "No. Because of your husband," he said quietly.

"What?" Kristin demanded suspiciously. "Major, I'm in here because I'm married to Cole Slater. No one seems to believe me when I say that he isn't with Quantrill anymore."

Major Emery stood and looked out the window. Then he turned back to Kristin. "Do you believe it yourself, young lady?"

"What?" She was certain she was blushing, certain her face had turned a flaming red.

"Do you believe in him yourself, Mrs. Slater?"

"Why...of course!" she said, though she was not at all sure she did.

Emery took his seat again and smiled. "I'm not sure, Mrs. Slater, I'm not sure. But that doesn't really matter. You see, I do have faith in your husband. Complete faith."

Kristin stared at him blankly. She lifted a hand in the air. "Do go on, major. Please, do go on."

"I'm wiling to bet I know your husband better than you do, Mrs. Slater. In certain ways, at least."

She tightened her jaw against his mischievous grin. He was a nice man, she decided, a gentle, fatherly type, but he seemed to be having a good time at her expense at the moment.

"Major..."

His smile faded. He looked a little sad. "He was a military man, you know. He went to West Point. He was in the same class as Jeb Stuart. Did you know that?"

Yes, he had said something to Shannon about it. To Shannon. Not to her.

"I know that he was in the military, yes."

Major Emery nodded. "Cole Slater was one of the most promising young cavalrymen I ever knew. He fought in Mexico, and he was with me in the West. He's good with the Indians—fighting them and, more importantly, talking with them, making truces. Keeping truces. Then the war came."

"And he resigned," Kristin murmured.

"No, not right away. He didn't resign until they burned down his house and killed his wife."

"Killed? His wife?" She didn't realize that she had gotten to her feet until Major Emery came around the desk and gently pushed her back into her chair. Then he leaned against the desk and crossed his arms over his chest, smiling down at her kindly. "I reckoned you might not know everything. Cole is a closemouthed man. Tight-lipped, yes sirree. He was an officer in the Union Army when South Carolina seceded from the Union. That didn't matter none to the jayhawkers. He was a Missourian. And Jim Lane had sent out an order that anybody who was disloyal to the Union was to be killed. The boys got pretty carried away. They rode to his place and they set it on fire. Cole was out riding the range. I imagine he was giving his position some pretty grave thought. Anyway, Jim Lane's jayhawkers rode in and set fire to his place. His wife was a pretty thing, real pretty. Sweet, gentle girl from New Orleans. She came running out, and the boys grabbed hold of her. Seems she learned something about gunfire from Cole, though. She shot up a few of them when they tried to get their hands on her. Cole came riding in, and by then she was running to him. Only some fool had already put a bullet in her back, and when Cole reached her, she was dying. She was expecting their first child right then, too. She was about five months along, so they tell me. Of course, after killing his pregnant wife, none of the men was willing to let him live, either. Someone shot Cole, too, and left him for dead. But he's a tough customer. He lived.''

''And he joined up with Quantrill,'' Kristin whispered. She swallowed. She could almost see the fire, could almost smell the smoke, could almost hear the screams. She suddenly felt ill. As if she were going to throw up.

''Oh, my God!'' she whispered, jumping to her feet. Major Emery, too was on his feet in an instant, yelling for a pail and some water.

To her horror, she *was* sick. Major Emery was a perfect gentleman, cooling her forehead with a damp cloth and then insisting that she have tea with lots of milk to settle her stomach. When it was over and they were alone again, he said to her, ''You are expecting a child, Mrs. Slater?''

She nodded bleakly.

''Well, my point exactly. I just don't think you should be here anymore. And I don't think Cole is still with Quantrill, because it just isn't his style. Ma'am, I want you to know that I find our jayhawkers every bit as loathsome as the bushwhackers. They're all murderers, pure and simple. Cole isn't a murderer. I think he went with Quantrill to try to get the man who led the attack on his ranch, and only for that reason. Only he wasn't easy to find, because he retired along with Lane. Hell, Lane is a U.S. senator! But the man who attacked Cole's place is back in the center of Kansas, and like Lane, he owns a lot of things, and a lot of people. Cole knew he couldn't get to him, not with Quantrill. And he knew that what Quantrill was up to was murder. He's regular army now, all right.''

Kristin swallowed some of her tea and nodded painfully. She hurt all over, inside and out. She had despised Cole, despite everything that he had done for her, just because Bill Anderson had told her that Cole had ridden with Quantrill. She desperately wanted to see him again. She wanted to hold him. She wanted to make him forget, if only for a moment, what had been done to him.

It made men hard, this war did. It had made her hard, she knew, and it had made him harder. She realized anew that he did not love her, and now, she thought, he never would. He had loved his first wife.

"Mrs. Slater?"

Kristin looked at the major. "Yes...yes I think that he's in the regular army. That's—that's what he said.''

The major frowned suddenly, his hands flat on his desk. He looked up at the ceiling.

Then Kristin felt it. There was a trembling in the floor beneath her, in the very air around her.

"Hellfire and damnation!'' Major Emery shouted. He leaped to his feet, hopped over his desk and pulled her out of her chair. He dragged her over to the door and kicked it open, then huddled with her beneath the frame, shielding her with his bulk.

Suddenly floorboards and nails were flying everywhere and great clouds of dust filled the room. Dirt flew into Kristin's mouth and into her eyes, and she heard screams, terrible screams, agonized screams.

The whole building was caving in. The awful place had

been faulty structurally and decaying and now it was actually caving in.

"Shannon!" Kristin screamed. "Shannon!" She tried to pull away from the major, but she couldn't. He was holding her too tightly. The rumbling continued, and inside was chaos. Boards were falling and breaking and clattering on the floor. A woman's body fell right next to Kristin, who was able to pull away from the major at last to kneel down by the girl.

It was Josephine Anderson, and Kristin knew instantly that she was dead. Her eyes were wide open, glazed as only death could glaze them. "Jo!" she cried out, falling to her knees. She touched the still-warm body and closed the pathetic, staring eyes. Then she looked up from the body to the gaping hole above her. "Shannon!" she screamed. She twisted around to look at what had been the hallway and the stairs. Only the bannister was left. Everywhere, the floor had crumbled. Tears and screams filled the air. "Shannon!"

"Mrs. Slater! You must remember your child!" the major urged her, grabbing her arm.

"Please!" She shook herself free and stumbled through the wreckage that littered the floor. She found Mary, her body grotesquely twisted beneath a pile of boards. "Mary!" After clawing away the debris, Kristin knelt and felt for the other woman's pulse. Mary was alive. She opened her eyes. "Jo?"

"It's Kristin, Mary. Everything...everything is going to be all right." She squeezed the girl's hand and turned around, searching for someone, anyone. "Get help here!" Kristin shouted, suddenly choking back tears. Where was Shannon? The girls had all been together.

Several young medics rushed in. Kristin moved away as they knelt over Mary. There were clanging bells sounding from outside, and the sound of horses' hooves was loud as a fire hose was brought around.

"Mrs. Slater!"

The major was still trying to get her out.

"Shannon!"

An arm was protruding from a pile of lumber. Kristin began

to tear away the planks. This was the worst of it. The woman beneath was dead. Kristin inhaled on a sob and turned away.

"Kristin!"

She looked up. Shannon, deathly pale, was clinging to a board that looked as if it were just about to give way.

"Shannon! Hold on! Just hold on a little longer—"

There was a cracking sound. The board began to break. Shannon's toes dangled ten feet over Kristin's head. "Hold on!"

"No, Miss McCahy, let go now! I'm here. I'll catch you!"

It was Captain Ellsworth. He stepped in front of Kristin and reached out his arms to Shannon. Shannon still clung to the board. "Come down, now! Please, before it breaks!"

Kristin saw the problem. If the board broke, Shannon could fall on a splinter in one of the beams that had been exposed, and she would be skewered alive.

"Shannon! Where the hell is your courage? Jump!" Kristin called out. She watched as Shannon's eyes fell on the splintered beams below her. But then Shannon looked down at her and she grinned. "What the hell! We can't all live forever, now, can we? Thumbs up, Kristin. Say a prayer."

Shannon released her hold on the board. She fell, her skirts billowing out around her, and suddenly, Captain Ellsworth was falling, too. He had caught her and the impact had brought him down with her.

"Get them both out of here!" Major Emery shouted. He picked Kristin up bodily and carried her outside. Captain Ellsworth swept Shannon up and followed. When they were finally out in the street, Kristin and Shannon hugged each other, sobbing.

"Jo—"

"Jo is dead," Kristin said softly. Then they stared at one another as they realized how lucky they were to be alive. And they just hugged one another again and sobbed, and listened to the chaos as more women were carried from the building, some alive, some injured...and some dead.

* * *

A week later, Kristin and Shannon were in the home of Captain Ellsworth's sister, Betty.

Four women besides Josephine Anderson had been killed. Rumor had it that Bill Anderson had gone berserk, foaming at the mouth, when he had heard that one of his sisters had been killed and the other had been seriously injured. Many Confederates were saying that General Ewing had purposely ordered that the women be incarcerated in the ramshackle building so that just such a tragedy might occur. There would be repercussions. To make matters worse, General Ewing had issued his General Order Number Ten, ordering all wives and children of known bushwhackers to move out of the state of Missouri.

That night, Major Emery rode out to the small house on the outskirts of the city with Captain Ellsworth beside him. It was quite apparent that an attachment was forming between Shannon and the captain, and Kristin didn't mind at all. After all, the young captain had come valiantly to her rescue. Kristin liked him herself. He was quiet and well read and unfailingly polite. And Shannon was eighteen, a young woman who already knew her own mind.

But though both the captain and the major were charming in Betty's parlor, Kristin knew that something was very wrong. The major called her onto the porch.

He looked at the moon, twirling his hat in his hand. ''Quantrill attacked Lawrence, Kansas, yesterday.''

''Oh, God!'' Kristin murmured.

''It was a massacre,'' Major Ellsworth said grimly. ''Almost the entire town was razed to the ground. At least one hundred men were killed...one twelve-year-old boy was shot down for being dressed up in an old Union uniform. And Quantrill only lost one of his boys. A former Baptist preacher named Larkin Skaggs. He was too drunk to ride away with Quantrill. An Indian found him and shot him dead, and then the survivors ripped him to shreds.'' Major Emery was silent for a moment. ''What is it coming to? None of us, not one of us, it seems, is any better than a bloody savage.''

Kristin wanted to say something to comfort him. A lot of

good men were experiencing the same despair, she knew. But she could think of nothing to say.

He turned around and tipped his hat to her. "You're free, young lady. I'm going to see to it that an escort takes you and your sister home.

"But how—"

A grin tugged at his lower lip. "Someone got through to your brother, and he raised all kinds of hell with the higher-ups. And then..."

"And then?"

He shrugged. His eyes twinkled. "Well, you see, Kristin, I know Cole. And a lot of other cavalry boys know Cole, so we know damned well that he isn't any outlaw. But people who don't know him, well, they're still convinced that he's a bad 'un. At the moment, that's all right, because there's a rumor out that he's heard about you and Shannon being held up here and that he's steaming. After everything that's happened, well...we can't have troops everywhere. Some folks are afraid he might ride in here and destroy the town just to get to you. I decided not to dispute that with any of them. I thought you deserved the right to go home if that was what you wanted."

Kristin stared at him a long time. Then she kissed him on the cheek. "Thank you."

"You see Cole, you tell him I sent my regards. You tell him I miss him. I never did meet another man who could ride or shoot like him."

She nodded. "Thank you. Thank you so much. For everything."

"Be there for him. He probably needs you."

Kristin smiled ruefully. "He doesn't love me, you know. You see, he only married me because he felt he had to. To protect me."

"Love comes in a lot of ways, young lady. You give him a little time. Maybe this war will end one day."

He tipped his hat to her again, and then he was gone.

In retaliation for the attack on Lawrence, General Ewing issued General Order Number Eleven, which forced almost everyone in Missouri to leave. People were given fifteen days to leave their property. The exodus was a terrible thing to watch, one of the worst things Kristin had seen in all the years since the fighting had begun. Poor farmers were forced to leave behind what little they possessed, and others were shot down where they stood because they refused to leave. Because the McCahy ranch belonged to Matthew, a soldier serving in the Union army, Major Emery was able to keep his promise and send Kristin and Shannon home, however.

The young lieutenant who escorted them was appalled by what he saw of the evacuation. Once he even told her that it was one of the cruellest measures he had ever seen taken. "This war will never end," he said glumly. "We will not let it end, it seems. The people who do not fight are ordered to leave, and the bushwhackers will come through here when they're gone, stealing whatever they leave behind!"

It was true, Kristin discovered. Even when they were home, when it seemed that they had returned to something like a normal life, Peter often came to her at night to tell her that he had seen another house burning somewhere, or that he had found cattle slaughtered, a sure sign that guerrillas had been in the area, living off the land.

In the middle of September they had a letter from Matthew. He was trying to get leave to come and see them, but so far he hadn't been able to manage it. He explained:

But the Rebels are in worse shape than we are. I think that perhaps by Christmas I will be able to come home. There was a battle fought in a little town in Pennsylvania called Gettysburg. Kristin, they say it was the most awful yet, but General Lee was stopped, and he was forced to retreat back to the South. Since then, there has been new hope that the war may end. Some of these fellows say that they will force the South to her knees. They do not know Southerners. I cannot imagine your husband on his knees, nor do I ever quite forget that I am a Missourian myself. But I pray for it to end. I watched another friend die yesterday of the dysentery, and it seems that we do not even have to catch bullets to drop off like flies. John Maple, who was injured in our last skirmish, had to have his leg amputated. Kristin, if I am caught at all by shot, I hope that the ball passes straight to my heart, for those operations are fearful things to witness. There was no morphine, but we did have some whiskey, and still, John screamed so horribly. Now we must all pray that the rot does not set in, else he will die anyway.

Kristin, forgive me, I wander again into subjects that do not fit a lady's ears, but you are my sister. I am still so grateful that you and Shannon are home. Every man who heard of the incident in Kansas City was appalled, and none was proud. That you might have been killed there chilled me to the bone, and I waited very anxiously for the news that you were safe.

As I said before, the Rebs are hurting badly. They have good generals, and good men, but those that die cannot be replaced. I am telling you this, aware that you must be worried for your husband. If you do not see him, you must not instantly fear the worst. They have probably refused to give him leave. They are desperate now to hold on to Virginia, and perhaps they are keeping him in the East.

Kristin set her brother's letter down and stared out the window. She wondered if Cole would come if she thought hard enough about him. Then she wondered, not for the first time, if he had been at the battle of Gettysburg. They talked of it constantly in Kansas City. It seemed that the death toll had been terrible there, but she had read the lists endlessly, looking for his name, and she had not found it. She had thought, too, that he might have been with John Hunt Morgan, along with Malachi, but she had read that Morgan had been captured in July, though what had become of his men was unknown. She had checked the lists of the dead again and again. Once her heart had nearly ceased to beat when she had read that a Slater had been killed, but it had been Samuel Slater from South Carolina, no relation, she hoped, to Cole.

Looking out the window would not bring Cole back to her. Wishing for him to appear would not help, either.

Every night she left a light burning in the window, hoping he would return. Even if he were to try, it would be hard for him to do so, she knew. The Union was getting a firm grip on the area. There were almost always patrols somewhere in the vicinity.

Every night she stood on the steps before going up to bed, and she lifted her chin, and she felt the breeze, and she waited. But it was all to no avail.

All to no avail…

Until one night in late September.

There had been no breeze all day, but there was the slightest whisper of one now. The night had been still, but now a tumbleweed lifted from the ground. Fall was coming, and in the pale glow of the moon the world was dark brown and pale gold and rich orange.

She thought she had imagined the sound at first. The sound of hoofbeats. But she had learned how to listen, and she closed her eyes, and she felt the wood beneath her feet shiver.

She stumbled out onto the porch and down onto the bare earth. She felt the hoofbeats more clearly. A rider was approaching, a single rider.

She needed to run into the house. She needed to grab one of the Colt six-shooters, or her rifle. The breeze was cool, and she was standing there barefoot on the cold ground, dressed only in a white cotton nightgown. The wind swept the gown around her and molded it to her breasts and hips and thighs. The breeze picked up the tendrils of her hair and sent them cascading behind her.

Then she saw the horse, and saw the rider, and she was exhilarated and incredulous and jubilant.

"Cole!"

"Kristin!" He reined in his horse, cast his leg over the animal's haunches and slid quickly to the ground. He frowned at the sight of her there, but she ran to him, laughing, and threw herself into his arms.

They closed around her.

Cole felt her, felt her soft and fresh and fragrant and clean, the way he had dreamed her, the way he had imagined her, the way he had feared he would never feel her again. The road home was always long and hard and dangerous. He had been riding for days, trying to avoid the Union patrols that were all over the place.

But now she was in his arms. There were no questions, no answers. She was in his arms, whispering his name. He began to shake. Her hair spilled over his hands like raw silk. She pressed against him, and she was so feminine and sweet that he nearly lost his breath. He breathed deeply, and her scent filled him, and it made his heart pound and his loins quicken.

"Kristin—"

She caught his face in her hands and kissed him. She kissed him as if she had starved for him, she kissed him deeply, passionately, like a woman. She kissed him with the fullness of her mouth and with the fullness of her body. Her tongue was wickedly sensual, touching all of him, plunging deep into his mouth. When his tongue invaded her mouth in turn, she moaned and fell against him, suddenly weak. After a long time he lifted his head to stare down into her eyes, eyes as blue as sapphires beneath the moon.

"What are you doing out here?"

"Waiting."

"You couldn't have known I was coming."

"I'm always waiting," she told him, and she smiled. It was just the slightest curve of her mouth, a rueful admission that left him feeling as if the earth trembled beneath his feet. He swept her hard against him again, heedless of whether she felt the emotion that racked him.

"I heard about Kansas City. I tried to come for you. Malachi and Jamie knocked me flat. Then I heard about the building, and I heard they let you go at the same time—"

"Hush!" She pressed a finger to his lips. She smiled again, and it was a dazzling smile. She was so soft, all of her. Her arms wound around him. Her thighs molded to his, naked beneath the gown. Her breasts pressed against his chest, against the gray wool of his uniform. "It's all right. We're home. Shannon and I are home, and you've come home now, too."

It wasn't his home. He could have told her that. But he didn't want to. Not tonight. She might not understand.

He wove his fingers into her hair, savoring the feel of her. Then he swept her up into his arms and stumbled up the steps, somehow keeping eyes locked with hers.

It seemed to take forever to reach their room, and it was not until much later that he wondered if his poor horse had managed to wander to the trough and into the barn. If not, the animal had known much worse nights upon the road.

For the moment, all that he knew was the woman in his arms and the sweetness of his homecoming.

When they were alone in their room he set her down. With trembling fingers, he undid the buttons of her nightgown and let it float to the floor. He stared at her. He wanted this moment to be etched in his memory forever, and he wanted the memory to be as incredible as the reality. Her eyes luminous. Her smile welcoming. Her breasts full and round and firm, more entrancing even than he had remembered. Her legs long and beautifully shaped.

Then he touched her.

And he wanted, too, to remember the feel of her skin against his fingertips, and so he touched her again and again, marvelling at the softness of her. And he kissed her, for he had to remember the taste of her. He kissed her lips, and he kissed her forehead, and he found the pulse at the base of her throat. He kissed her breasts, and the desire inside him grew. He savored the taste of her shoulders, of the little hollows there. He turned her around and kissed her back, trailing his fingers down the beautiful line of her spine and over the curve of her buttocks. He had to touch and taste and feel all of her. He went on and on, drinking deeply of her, until the whole of his body shook and trembled, until she cried out his name with such anguish and passion that he came to his feet, crushed her in his arms and lifted her again, bearing her to the bed.

Whispering to him, telling him how much she wanted him, how she needed him, how she desired him, she feverishly helped him out of his clothes, desperate to touch him as he had touched her. Soft as a feather, gentle as a breeze, sensual as the earth, she touched and petted and loved him. Then, at last, they came together, a man and a woman meeting in a breathless fusion.

All that night she felt she was riding the wind, an endless, sweet, wild wind that swept away the horrors of the world and left her drifting on the clouds of heaven. Anticipation had sown its seeds, and their first time together was erratic and wild and thunderous for them both. Barely had they climaxed before he touched her again, and again the clamor of need rose quickly in them. They were slower this time, easier, for the first desperate hunger had been appeased.

And still the night lay ahead of them.

She never knew just how many times they loved that night, never knew when she slept and dreamed, never knew when she awakened to find that he was holding her again. She only knew that it was heaven, and that however long she lived, however old she grew, she would never, never forget it, or the crystalline beauty of the desire that surged between them.

It was morning before they spoke.

Dazed and still delighted, Kristin lay in his arms, wondering lazily how to tell him about the child. She wondered if he could tell by the subtle changes in her body. He hadn't said anything. She smiled. His need for her had been too great for him to have noticed anything. She thought to speak then, but he was speaking already. He was talking about the war, and his tone was cold.

"Stonewall Jackson was the greatest loss. Lee might have taken Gettysburg if he hadn't lost Stonewall. It was the first battle he had to go into without Jackson. God, how I shall miss that man!"

"Sh..." she murmured. She drew a finger across the planes of his face, and she felt the tightness there, and the pain. It was a strong face, she thought, a striking face. And it was so hard now.

"And Morgan...God help Morgan. He has to escape." He shook his head. Then he turned to her and took her in his arms, whispering, "How can I say these things to you? You've been through so much already, you've witnessed so much. That horror in Kansas City..."

"The deaths were terrible," Kristin admitted. She drew away, smiling at him. "But Major Emery was very kind."

Suddenly Cole was stiff as steel, and every bit as cold. "Emery?"

She didn't understand the abrupt change in him. "Yes. He said that you had been with him, before the war. He—"

He sat up and ran his fingers through his hair. "He what?" She didn't answer, and he turned, setting his hands firmly on her shoulders. "He what?"

"Stop it! You're hurting me!" Kristin pulled away from him. "He told me about—he told me about your wife."

Cole smiled suddenly. It was a bitter smile. "I see," he said softly.

"What do you see?" she demanded.

"Nothing, Kristin, nothing at all." He tossed the covers aside and stood and wandered around the room, picking up his clothes.

"Cole!"

He stepped into his gray trousers and pulled on his shirt. Still ignoring her, he sat and pulled on his boots. She frowned when she realized that he was putting his uniform back on—something he wouldn't be doing if he was staying.

"Cole, you can't be leaving already?"

He stood up, buckling on his scabbard. He nodded gravely. Then he walked to her and stroked her chin. "I only had five days. It took me three to find my way through the Federal troops. I have to pray I can make it back more quickly." He bent down and touched her lips lightly with his own. "You are so very beautiful, Kristin," he murmured to her. But he was still distant from her. Very distant.

"Cole—" She choked on his name. Her heart was aching. There were so many things that needed to be said, and none of them mattered. She had said or done something to offend him and she didn't even know what it was. "Cole, I don't understand—"

"Kristin, I don't want your pity."

"What?"

"Pity, Kristin. I don't want it. It's worthless stuff, and it isn't good for anyone. I wondered what last night was all about. You were barely civil to me when I left in May. Hate me, Kristin. Hate me all you want. But for God's sake, Kristin, don't pity me!"

Incredulous, she stiffened, staring at him, fighting the tears that stung her eyes.

"I've thought about having you and Shannon move to London until this thing is over with. I had a little power with Quantrill, but I'm afraid my influence with the Yankees is at a low ebb. This is a dangerous place—"

"Go!" Kristin said.

"Kristin—"

"Go back to your bleeding Confederacy!" Kristin said heatedly. "I've already met with the Yankees, thanks, and they were damned civil."

"Kristin—"

"I'm all right here! I swear it. We are fine."

He hesitated, then swept his frock coat over his shoulders and picked up his plumed hat.

"Kristin—"

"Cole, damn you, get out of here! You don't want my pity, you want my hatred! Well, then, you've got it! Go!"

"Damn you, Kristin!"

He came back to the bed and took her in his arms. The covers fell away, and she pressed against the wool of his uniform, felt the hot, determined yearning of his kiss. She wanted to fight him. She wanted to tell him that she really did hate him. But he was going away again, going away to the war. And she was afraid of the war. The war killed people.

And so she kissed him back. She wound her arms around him and kissed him back every bit as passionately as he did her. And she felt his fingers move over her breast, and she savored every sensation.

Then he lifted his lips from hers, and their eyes met, and he very slowly and carefully let her fall back to the bed.

They didn't speak again. He kissed her forehead lightly, and then he left her.

Chapter Thirteen

June, 1864

He never should have come to Kansas.

Cole knew he should never have come to Kansas. A scouting mission in Kentucky was one thing. He could slip into Virginia or even Maryland easily enough. Even in Ohio he might be all right. In the East they were slower to hang a man as a spy. In the East they didn't shoot a man down where he stood, not often, not that Cole had heard about anyway.

He should never have come to Kansas.

But the war effort was going badly, very badly. First General Lee had lost Stonewall Jackson. Then Jeb Stuart had been shot, and they had carried him back to Richmond, and he had died there. Countless men had died, some of them brilliant men, some of them men who were perhaps not so brilliant but who were blessed with an endless supply of courage and a fine bravado, even in the face of death.

Jeb was the greatest loss, though. Cole could remember their days at West Point, and he could remember the pranks they had pulled when they had been assigned out west together. The only comfort in Jeb's death was the fact that his little daughter had died just weeks before. They said that when he lay dying he had talked of holding her again in heaven. They had buried him in Hollywood Cemetery. Cole had been with

Kristin when they had buried him, but he had visited the grave when he'd come to Richmond, and he still found it impossible to believe that James Ewell Brown Stuart, his friend, the dashing cavalier, could be dead. He had visited Flora, Jeb's wife, and they'd laughed about some of their days back in Kansas, but then Flora had begun to cry, and he had thought it best to leave. Flora had just lost her husband, a Confederate general. Her father, a Union general, was still fighting.

The war had never been fair.

Cole had to head out again, this time to the Indian Nation, to confer with the Cherokees and Choctaws who had been persuaded to fight for the Confederacy. The Union armies were closing in on Richmond, and Lee was hard pressed to protect the capital without Jackson to harass the Federals as they made their way through the Shenandoah Valley.

When he had left Virginia Cole had gone to Tennessee, and from Tennessee he had been ordered to rejoin his brother's unit. The noose was closing tighter and tighter around the neck of the Confederacy. John Hunt Morgan had managed to escape his captors, and he needed information about the Union troops being sent into Kentucky and Tennessee from Kansas City. Cole had taken the assignment in the little town outside the big city for only one reason—he would be close to Kristin. He had to see her. It had been so long, and they had parted so bitterly. He'd received a few letters from her, terse, quick notes telling him that they were all fine, telling him that the Union was in firm control of the part of Missouri where the ranch sat, that he was better off away and that he should take care.

Jamie and Malachi had received warmer letters. Much warmer letters. But still, even to his brothers, Kristin had said very little. Every letter was the same. She related some silly little anecdote that was sure to make them laugh, and then she closed, telling them she was praying for them all. She thought there might be a wedding as soon as the war was over or maybe even before. Shannon was corresponding regularly with a Captain Ellsworth, and Kristin said she, too, thought he was a charming gentleman. He was a Yankee, but she was sure the family would forget that once the war was over. They would all have to, she added forcefully, if there was to be a future.

Cole wasn't sure there could be. There was that one part of his past that he couldn't forget, and he never would be able to forget it, not unless he could finish it off, bury it completely. Not until the redlegs who had razed his place and killed his wife were dead could he ever really rest. No matter how sweet the temptation.

Sitting at a corner table in the saloon, his feet propped and his hat pulled low, he sipped a whiskey and listened to the conversation at the bar. He learned quickly that Lieutenant Billingsley would be transferring eight hundred troops from Kansas to Tupelo and then on to Kentucky by the following week. The saloon was crowded with Union soldiers, green recruits by the looks of them—he didn't think many of the boys even had to shave as yet—but they had one or two older soldiers with them. No one had paid Cole much heed. He was dressed in denim and cotton, with a cattleman's chaps and silver spurs in place and a cowhide vest. He didn't look much like a man who gave a damn about the war one way or the other. One man had asked him what he was doing out of uniform, and he'd quickly invented a story about being sent home, full of shrapnel, after the battle of Shiloh. After that, someone had sent over a bottle of whiskey and he'd set his hat low over his forehead and he'd listened. Now that he had his information, it was time to go. He wanted to reach his wife.

His wife.

He could even say it out loud now. And only once in a while did the bitterness assail him. His wife… His wife had been slain, but he had married a little spitfire of a blonde, and she was his woman now. His wife.

He tensed, remembering that she knew, knew everything about him, about his past. Damn Emery! He'd had no right to spill out the past like that for her. Now he would never know…

Know what? he asked himself.

What her feelings were, what her feelings really were. Hell, it was a damnable time for a marriage. He could still count on his fingers the times he had seen her....Kristin. He'd been impatient with her, and he'd been furious with her, but he'd always admired her courage, no matter what, and from the beginning he'd been determined to protect her.

Then he'd discovered that he needed her.

Like air. Like water. Like the very earth. He needed her. When he'd been away from her he'd still had the nightmares, but time had slowly taken them away. When visions of a woman came to haunt him while he slept, it was Kristin's delicate features he saw, her soft, slow smile, her wide, luminous eyes.

He'd never denied that he cared for her.

He just hadn't wanted to admit how much.

He didn't want a wife feeling sorry for him. He didn't want her holding on, afraid to hurt a traumatized soldier. The whole thing made him seethe inside. He'd swear that he'd be quit of her as soon as the war was over, and then he'd panic, and he'd pray that everything was all right, and he would wish with all his heart that he could just get back to that little patch of Missouri on the border where he could reach out and just touch her face, her hand....

And if he did, he wondered glumly, what good could it do him? He could never stop. Not until one of them lay dead. Him or Fitz. Maybe Fitz hadn't fired the shot that had killed his wife, but he had ordered the raid on Cole's place, and he had led it. In the few months that he had ridden with Quantrill, Cole had managed to meet up with a number of the men who had been in on the raid.

But he'd never found Henry Fitz.

His thoughts suddenly shifted. He didn't know what it was that told him he was in danger, but suddenly he knew that he was. Maybe it was in the thud of a new pair of shiny Union boots on the floor, maybe it was something in the air. And maybe he had lived with the danger for so damned long that he could smell it.

He should never have come to Kansas.

It wasn't that he wasn't armed. He was. And the poor green

boys in the saloon were carrying muzzle-loading rifles. He could probably kill the dozen or so of them in the room before they could even load their weapons.

He didn't want to kill them. He'd always hated that kind of warfare. Hell, that was why Quantrill had been able to run circles around the Federals for years. Quantrill's men were so well armed that they could gun down an entire company before they could get off a single shot.

He prepared to leave, praying that the newcomer wasn't someone he knew. But when he saw the man's face beneath the brim of his hat, his heart sank.

The man was his own age, and he wore a lieutenant's insignia. He had dark hair and a long, dark beard, and the lines that furrowed his face said that he should have been older than thirty-two.

It's been a long hard war for all of us, Cole thought bleakly.

The Union officer's name was Kurt Taylor, and he had ridden escort and trails out in the Indian country with Cole when he had been with Stuart. Another West Pointer. They'd fought the Sioux side by side many times.

But now they were on opposite sides.

When Cole stood, Taylor saw him. The men stared straight at one another.

Cole hesitated. He wasn't going to fire, not unless he had to. He didn't cotton to killing children, and that was about what it would be. He looked at the boys standing at the bar. Hell, most of them wouldn't even have started school when the trouble had started in Kansas.

Do something, Taylor, Cole thought. *Say something.* But the man didn't move. The two of them just stood there staring at one another, and it was as if the world stood still.

Then, miraculously, Taylor lifted his hat.

"Howdy," he said, and walked on by.

Taylor had recognized him. Cole knew it. He had seen the flash of recognition in his eyes. But Taylor wasn't going to turn him in.

Taylor walked up to the bar. The soldiers saluted him, and he told them to be at ease. They returned to their conversations, but they were no longer as relaxed as they had been. They were in the presence of a commissioned officer now.

But Kurt Taylor ignored the men, just as he was ignoring Cole. He ordered himself a brandy, swallowed it down quickly and ordered himself another. Then he turned around, leaned his elbows on the bar and looked out over the room.

"You know, boys," he said, "war itself, soldiering, never did bother me. Joining the army seemed to be a right noble position in life. We had to defend American settlers from the Indians. We had to keep an eye on Mexico, and then suddenly we had our folks moving into Texas. Next thing you know, our great nation is divided, and we're at war with our Southern cousins. And even that's all right, 'cause we all know a man's gotta do what a man's gotta do." He paused and drained his second brandy. He didn't look at Cole, but Cole knew damned well that Taylor was talking straight to him.

"Bushwhackers!" Kurt Taylor spit on the floor. Then he added, "And bloody murdering jayhawkers. I tell you, one is just as bad as the next, and if he claims to wear my colors, well, he's a liar. Those jayhawkers we've got up here, hell, they turned half of Kansas and Missouri against the Union. Folks that didn't own no slaves, that didn't care one way or another about the war, we lost them to the Confederacy because they so abhorred the murder that was being done. Quantrill's boys started up after Lane and Jennison began their goddamn raiding."

"Pardon me—" one young man began.

"No, sir! I do not pardon you!" Kurt Taylor snapped. "Murder is murder. And I hear tell that one of the worst of our Kansas murderers is right here, right here in this town. His name is Henry Fitz. He thought he could make himself a political career out of killing Missourians. He forgot there were decent folk in Kansas who would never condone the killing of women and children, whether it was done by bushwhackers or jayhawkers." He stared straight at Cole, and then he turned his back on him.

He knew Cole wouldn't shoot him.

He knew Cole wouldn't shoot a man in the back.

Cole was trembling, and his fingers were itching. He didn't even want to draw his gun. He wanted to find Fitz and wrap his fingers around the bastard's throat and choke the life out of him.

"Give me another brandy there, barkeep. Boys, you watch your step while Fitz is around. He's down Main Street at the McKinley barn with his troops. I'd say there's about a dozen of those marauders. Yep, I think you ought to steer clear of the area."

He tossed back another brandy, and then he turned and looked at Cole again.

And then he walked out of the saloon.

Cole left a few minutes after Taylor did. He wondered if his old comrade in arms had put on the performance he had so that Cole would get out of town or so that he would stay in it.

He came out on the steps and looked up at the noonday sun, and he smiled. He came out to the hitching post and mounted his horse, a bay he had borrowed from Malachi because he had been afraid his own stallion was too well known here.

Taylor had even told him where to find Fitz. Straight down Main Street.

Cole started the bay at a walk. Within seconds he had urged the horse to a trot, and then to a canter, and then to a gallop. The barbershop whizzed by him, then the savings bank, the newspaper office and Ed Foley's Mercantile. He passed rows of neat houses with white picket fences and summer gardens, and then he was on the stretch of road leading to the farms beyond the town limits.

He must have headed out in the right direction, because suddenly there was a line of troops coming toward him. Redlegs, so called for the color of their leggings. Raiders. Murderers. Jim Lane had led them once. Now Senator Jim Lane was in Washington, and even Doc Jennison, who had taken command of them after Lane, had gone on to new pursuits. But Henry Fitz was still leading his band, and still striking terror into the hearts of innocent men, women and children.

Cole slowed the bay to a walk as the men approached. Henry Fitz sat atop a piebald, dead center. He had narrowed his dark little eyes, and he was staring down the road at Cole.

Cole kept moving. He had to do this. He had to kill Fitz. And if he died, too...

Would Kristin care? he found himself wondering. He had never doubted her gratitude, but he wondered now what she would feel if she heard that he had been gunned down on a Kansas road. Would she shed any tears for him? Would she miss him? Would she revile him for dying a senseless death, for leaving her alone?

He closed his eyes for a moment. He had to do this. If they were to have any kind of a future together, he had to do this. Now.

For a moment he remembered the flames, remembered them clearly. He remembered the crackling of the fire and he remembered the acrid smell of the smoke. And he remembered her, running, running to him. He remembered reaching out and touching her, and he remembered the way she had looked into his eyes and smiled and died. And he remembered the blood that had stained his hands...

I loved you! his heart cried out. I loved you, Elizabeth! With all my heart and with all my soul.

And in that moment he knew at last that he loved Kristin, too. He had to bury the past, because he longed for a future with her. He had been afraid to love again. He had not wanted to destroy Elizabeth's memory by loving again. Yet he knew now that if Elizabeth could speak to him she would tell him to love Kristin, to love her deeply and well, in memory of all they had once shared.

He brought the bay to a halt and watched the road. The redlegs were trotting along easily, none of them expecting trouble from a lone man atop a single bay horse. But in the center of the group, the frown upon Henry Fitz's face was deepening. Another five feet—ten—and he would recognize Cole.

"Howdy, there," Fitz began, drawing in on his reins. The rest of the party stopped along with him. His hat was tilted low over his thickly bearded face, and his eyes seemed to disappear into folds of flesh. "I'll be damned!" he said suddenly. Then he laughed. "Come all the way to Kansas to die, boy?"

And he reached for his revolver.

Cole had been fast before the war. He had been fast in the West. He was faster now.

Fitz had been the inspiration that had taught him how to draw faster than sound, faster than light. He had always known that someday, somehow, he would meet up with this man.

And he did now, guns blazing. Holding the reins in his teeth, he tightened his thighs around the bay and rode into the group.

He watched Fitz fall. He saw the blood stain his shirt crimson, and he watched him fall. The rest of it was a blur. He heard men and horses screaming as he galloped through their midst. A bullet struck his saddle, and then the bay went down beneath him. Cole tasted the dust roused by the multitude of horses. He jumped away from the fallen bay, grabbed his rifles and fired again. The gunfire seemed to go on forever.

Then there was silence. He spun around, a cocked rifle in either hand.

Three men remained alive. They stared at him and raised their hands. Their faces meant nothing to him.

He hurried away from his fallen horse and leaped into the saddle of a large, powerful-looking buckskin. Warily eyeing the three men, he nudged the horse forward. The buckskin had been a good choice. It surged forward, and Cole could feel the animal's strength and sense its speed. He raced forward, his heart pounding, adrenaline pumping furiously through his system.

He was alive.

But as he raced toward the town he saw the soldiers. Rows of blue uniforms. Navy blue. On both sides of the road. He slowed his horse to a walk. There was nowhere to go. It was over. They would build a gallows in the middle of town, and they would hang him as a bushwhacker.

Suddenly Kurt Taylor was riding toward Cole. "Hear

there's been some shooting up at the end of town, stranger. You might want to hurry along and let the army do the picking up.''

Cole couldn't breathe. Taylor lifted a brow and grinned at him. Cole looked down at his hands where they rested on the pommel. They were shaking.

He saluted Taylor.

Taylor saluted back. ''Someone ought to tell Cole Slater that the man who killed his wife is dead. And someone also ought to warn him that he's an outlaw in these parts. Someone ought to warn him that he'd best spend his time way, way deep in Dixie. I know that the man isn't any criminal, but there aren't many who served with him like I did. The rest think he ought to wear a rope around his neck.''

''Thank you kindly, sir,'' Cole said at last. ''If I meet up with him, I'll tell him.''

He rode on, straight through the ranks of blue uniforms. He kept riding. He didn't look back, not even when he heard a cheer and realized that the Union soldiers were saluting him, that Kurt Taylor had won him a few friends.

His thigh was bleeding, he realized. He had been shot after all, and he hadn't even known it. It didn't matter much. He had to keep riding. He wanted to get home. Night was falling. It was a good time to ride.

A little farther down the road he became aware that he was being followed. He quickly left the road and dismounted, whispering to the buckskin, encouraging it to follow him into the brush.

He was being followed by a single horseman. He hid behind an oak tree and listened to the hoofbeats. He waited until the rider was right by his side. Then he sprang up and knocked the man to the ground.

''Damn you, Cole Slater! Get off me.''

''Taylor!''

Cole stood and dragged Taylor to his feet.

''You son of a bitch!'' Taylor laughed, and then he clapped Cole hard on the shoulders. ''You damned son of a bitch!

Hasn't anybody told you that the South is going to lose the war?''

"It wouldn't matter what they told me," Cole said. "I can't much help what I am." He paused a moment, and then he grinned, because Kurt really had been one damned good friend. "Thank you. Thank you for what you did back there. I've seen so many men tearing one another to shreds. The truth meant more to you than the color of a uniform. I won't forget that, Kurt. Ever."

"I didn't do anything that God wouldn't call right," Kurt said. "You got him, Cole. You got that mangy bastard. 'Course, you do know they'll shoot you on sight now and ask questions later."

"Yes, I know that."

"You're heading south, I hope?"

"East, and then south."

"Don't stay around the border too long," Taylor warned him. "Even to see your boy. Major Emery said that if I ever came across you I was to warn you—"

"What?" Cole snapped, his hands on Taylor's shoulders.

"I'm trying to tell you. Major Emery said—"

"The hell with Emery! What boy?"

Taylor cocked his head, frowning. "Why, yours, of course. Born last February. A fine boy, I understand. Captain Ellsworth gets out there now and again, and he reported to the major that both mother and child were doing fine. Don't rightly recall what they named him, but Ellsworth says he's big and healthy and has a head of hair to put many a fine lass to shame. Cole, let go, you're about to snap my damned shoulder blade. Oh, hell! You mean you didn't know? Listen to me now. Don't you go running off half-cocked after everything that happened here today. You move slow, and you move careful, you hear me, Slater? Most of the Union boys would shoot me if they knew I let you slip through my fingers. Cole?''

"I'll move careful," Cole said.

Yes, he'd move careful. He'd move damned careful. Just to make sure he lived long enough to tan Kristin's sweet hide.

Why in God's name hadn't she told him?

It was hot and humid on the Fourth of July, 1864. Scarcely a breeze had stirred all day.

It had been a difficult day for Kristin. She had learned long ago to keep her mind off her worries, to try not to think too much, to concentrate on her tasks. Anything was better than worrying. If she worried all the time she would drive herself mad.

But the fourth was a particularly difficult day.

There were celebrations going on everywhere. Union soldiers letting off volleys of rifle fire, ranchers setting off fireworks. Every gunshot reminded Kristin that her husband could meet her brother on the field of battle at any time, that they were still at war, that the nation celebrating its birthday was still bitterly divided.

There was smoke in the air, and the noise was making the baby restless. She'd had him with her down in the parlor, and Delilah's Daniel, almost three years old now, had been laughing and entertaining the baby with silly faces. But then Cole Gabriel Slater had decided enough was enough, and he had jammed one of his pudgy little fists into his mouth and started to cry.

"Oh, I've had it with the entire day anyway!" Kristin declared to everyone in the room and to no one in particular. She picked up the baby and started up the stairs. Delilah, sewing, stared after her. Shannon, running her fingers idly over the spinet, paused. Samson rolled his eyes. "Hot days, yes, Lordy, hot days," he mumbled. He stood up. "The hands will be back in soon enough. I'll carry that stew on out to the bunkhouse."

Upstairs, Kristin lay down with her fretful baby and opened her blouse so that he could nurse. She started, then smiled, as he latched on to her nipple with a surprising power. Then, as always, an incredibly sweet feeling swept through her, and she pulled his little body still closer to her. His eyes met hers. In the last month they had turned a silver gray, just like Cole's. His hair was hers, though, a thatch of it, blond, almost white.

He was a beautiful baby, incredibly beautiful. He had been born on the tenth of February. Stroking his soft cheek, she felt her smile deepen as she remembered the day. It had been snowing, and it had been bitterly cold, and she had been dragging hay down for the horses when she had felt the first pain and panicked. It would have been impossible for Dr. Cavanaugh to come out from town, and it would have been impossible for her to reach town. Pete had been terribly upset, and that had calmed her somehow, and Delilah had assured her that it would be hours before the baby actually came.

Hours!

It had been awful, and it had been agony, and she had decided that it was extremely unfair that men should be the ones to go off to war to get shot at when women were the ones stuck with having babies. She had ranted and raved, and she had assured both Delilah and Shannon in no uncertain terms that she despised Cole Slater—and every other living soul who wore britches, as a matter of fact—and that if she lived she would never do this again.

Delilah smirked and assured her that she was going to live and that she would probably have half a dozen more children. Shannon waltzed around in a daydream, saying that she wouldn't be complaining one whit if she were the one about to have the baby—if the baby belonged to Captain Ellsworth.

The pain subsided for a moment, and Kristin had smiled up at her sister, who was pushing back her soaked hair. It was "colder than a witch's teat," as Pete had said, but she was drenched with sweat.

"You really love him, don't you, your Captain Ellsworth?"

Shannon nodded, her eyes on fire. "Oh, Kristin! He saved my life. He caught me when I fell. He was such a wonderful hero. Oh, Kristin! Don't you feel that about Cole?"

She hesitated, and she remembered how happy she had been to see him. And she remembered how they had made love, how tender he had been with her, how passionate. With a certain awe she remembered the way his eyes had fallen upon her, how cherished that look had made her feel. And she remembered the ecstasy…

But then she remembered his anger and his impatience, and how he had grown cold and distant when she had mentioned his past. He was in love with another woman, and though that woman lay dead, she was a rival Kristin could not best.

"Cole was a hero!" Shannon whispered. "Kristin, how can you forget that? He rode in here and he saved our lives! And if you think you're having a difficult labor, well, then…that is God's way of telling you you had no right to keep the information about this baby from your husband!"

I meant to tell him…. Kristin almost said it. But if she did she would have to explain how he had acted when she had mentioned his past, and she would have to think about the fact that he didn't love her, right in the middle of having his child. She shrugged instead. "What can he do? There is a war on."

A vicious pain seized her again, and she assured Shannon that Cole was a rodent, and Shannon laughed. And then, miraculously—for it had been hours and hours, and it was nearly dawn—Delilah told Kristin that the baby's head was showing and that it was time for her to push.

When he lay in her arms, red and squalling, Kristin knew that she had never imagined such a love as swelled within her.

And she prayed with all her heart that her son's father was alive, that he would come home to them all. She vowed that she would ask no questions he could not answer, that she would not ask for anything he could not give.

Lying with the baby, nursing him as she did now, was the greatest pleasure of her life. Kristin forgot the world outside, and she forgot the war, and she even forgot that his father probably did not know he existed. She loved his grave little eyes, and she loved the way his mouth tugged on her breast. She counted his fingers endlessly, and his toes, and she thought that he was gaining weight wonderfully and that he was very long—even Delilah said he would grow to be very tall—and that his face was adorable. He had a little dimple in his chin, and Kristin wondered if Cole had a dimple like it. She had seen all of his body, but she had never seen his naked chin. He had always had a beard.

Delilah had warned her to let Gabe, as they called him,

nurse only so long at one breast. If she did he would ignore the other, and she would experience grave discomfort. Consequently she gently loosened his grasp on her left breast, laughing at his howl of outrage.

"Heavens! You're more demanding than that father of yours!" she told her baby, cradling him against her shoulder and patting his back. Then, suddenly, she realized that she was not alone. She had been so engrossed with her son that the door had opened and closed without her noticing it.

A peculiar sensation made its way up her spine, and suddenly she was breathless. She dared to look at the door, and found him standing there.

Her hero.

He was in full dress uniform, tattered gray and gold, his sword hanging dangerously from its scabbard. He was leaner than she remembered him, and his face was ashen, and his eyes...his eyes burned through her, seared into her.

"Cole!" she whispered. She wondered how long he had been standing there, and suddenly she was blushing, and it didn't matter that he was the child's father, she felt awkward and vulnerable and exposed.

He pushed away from the door and strode toward her, and despite herself she shrank away from him. He reached for the baby, and she clung to her child. Then she heard him speak, his voice low and hoarse.

"My God, Kristin, give him to me."

"Cole—"

She had to release the baby for Cole meant to take him. She nervously pulled her dress together but he had no eyes for her. He was looking at the baby. She wanted to shriek his name, wanted to run to him. It had been so long since she had seen him last, and even that had seemed like a dream. But she couldn't run to him, couldn't throw her arms around him. He was cold and forbidding. He was a stranger to her now.

He ignored her completely, setting the squalling child down on his back at the foot of the bed, freeing him from all his swaddling so that he could look at the whole of him. Kristin could have told him that Gabe was perfect in every way, but she kept silent. She knew he had to discover it for himself. Suddenly she was more than a little afraid of her husband. Should she have written to him? What good would it have done? Cole shouldn't be here even now. There were far too many Union troops around. Was that the real reason? she wondered. She had hesitated once because he had made her angry, because she had realized that he did not love her. But she hadn't written, she knew, because she had been afraid that he would be determined to come home, and that that determination would make him careless.

For a moment Gabe quieted and stared up at his father. He studied Cole's face as gravely and as purposefully as Cole studied him. His little body was perfectly still.

Then he had had enough of his father. His mother was the one he wanted. He lifted up his chubby little legs and screwed up his face and kicked out and howled in outrage all at once. The cry brought a surge to Kristin's breasts that soaked the bodice of the gown he held so tightly against her. Cole covered his son again, then picked him up and set him against his chest. Kristin reached out her arms.

"Please, Cole, give him back to me. He's...he's hungry."

Cole hesitated, staring at her hard. Then he handed the baby to her. Kristin lowered her head and wished he would go away, but then she remembered that he had just come, and that if he went away again he might be killed this time. Color spilled over her cheeks, and she remembered just how they had gotten the baby, and she touched the baby's cheek with her finger and let her bodice fall open and led his little mouth to her breast. He latched on with an awful, pigletlike sound, and she found that she couldn't look up at all, even though she knew that Cole was still in the room and that his eyes were still on her.

The room was silent except for the baby's slurping. Then even that stopped, and Kristin realized he had fallen asleep. She lifted him to her shoulder and tried to get him to burp, but he was sleeping too soundly. Biting her lip, she rose and set him in the cradle that Samson had brought down from the attic. All the while she felt Cole's eyes on her.

Still, he didn't touch her, and he didn't speak to her. He stood by the cradle and stared down at the child. He was going to touch him again. Kristin bit her lips to keep from protesting. She watched in silence as Cole's long fingers tenderly touched the tiny cheek. She tried to button her bodice, then realized that she was drenched and that it was a foolish gesture. Flushing, she hurried to change her gown, but it didn't matter. Cole didn't seem to have noticed. She wondered if she should tiptoe away and leave him alone, but the moment she started for the door he was on his feet, and she realized that he had noted her every movement.

"Where do you think you're going?"

His voice was low, but there was real anger in it, and real menace.

"I thought you might be hungry."

He was silent. His gaze fell over her. Then he took a step toward her, and she almost screamed when his fingers gripped her arms and he shook her. "Damn you, Kristin! Damn you a thousand times over! You knew! You knew—and you didn't tell me! What right did you have to keep him from me?"

She tried to free herself, but she could not. She looked in his eyes, and she hated what she saw there, the uncompromising hardness.

"What rights have you got!" she choked out. "You ride in whenever you choose.... You may feel you have obligations, but that is all you have! I—"

"I ride in when I can get here!" he snapped, shaking her again. Her head fell back, and her eyes, glazed suddenly with tears, stared into his. "Lady, there is a war being fought out there! You know that. Of all women, you know that. I have done everything that is humanly possible, I have given you everything—"

"No! No, you have not given me everything! You have never given me the least little part of your—"

"I could have been killed. I don't know how many times I could have been killed on some stinking battlefield, and I wouldn't even have known I had a son!"

"Let me go!"

"No!"

"Please!" He was so close to her, and he felt so good. He was so warm, and she could feel the hardness of his body, and the touch of his hands. She wanted to touch his face and soothe away the lines around his eyes, and she wanted to fill the emptiness in his heart. She wanted to see his eyes alight with passion again. As she thought of the passion they had known together, her breasts seemed to fill again, but it was not for her child this time, it was for him. She needed to be held, to be touched.

To be loved.

"Please!" she repeated softly. She was so glad to see him, and their time together should be a precious respite against the war that raged on around them.

"Cole, I wanted to tell you when you were here, but all of a sudden we were fighting, because Major Emery had committed the horrible sin of telling me that you had been hurt. Mr. Cole Slater had been hurt, cut open and left bleeding, and he just couldn't bear that! Well, you are human, Cole, and you're supposed to bleed! And I should hurt for you, too, because damn it, what happened was awful!"

"Kristin, stop—"

"No! No, I will not stop! What have you got now? One week, one day? One lousy hour? Not long, I'll warrant. There are too many Federals around. So you stop, and you listen to me! I am grateful to you, Cole, eternally grateful. And I've been glad of this bargain of ours, heartily glad. You have fulfilled every promise you ever made me. But don't you dare yell at me now! I didn't write because I didn't want you getting killed, because I was afraid of your temper."

"My temper! I would never—"

"Yes, you would! You would have taken foolish chances to get here. You would have been afraid because of what happened to you with—"

She broke off, remembering that Emery had said that his wife had been pregnant when she had been killed.

"Oh, God, Cole, I'm sorry. I just realized that you would probably rather that she…that I…"

''What the hell are you saying?'' he asked hoarsely.

Kristin shook her head miserably. ''Your wife, your first wife... You were expecting a child. I'm sorry, you must be thinking of her, that you would prefer—''

''That she had lived? That you had died? My God, Kristin, don't you ever say such a thing, don't you even think it, do you hear me?'' He caught her against him. He threaded his fingers roughly through her hair, and suddenly he lowered his head and buried his face in the fragrant strands. ''Don't you ever, ever think that!'' he repeated. Then he looked at her again, and he smiled. It was a weary smile, and she saw how much the past few years had aged him, and her heart ached.

''He is a beautiful boy. He is the most wonderful child I've ever seen. And he is mine. Thank you. Thank you so very much.''

''Oh, Cole!'' she whispered. She was dangerously close to tears. He saw it and his tone changed.

''I'd still like to tan your hide for keeping the truth from me!''

''Cole, I really didn't mean to. I was afraid. I'm always afraid, it seems.''

''I know, I know.'' He held her against him.

''Cole, you must be starved. Let me go down and have Delilah—''

''No, not now.''

''Cole, you must need—''

He stepped away from her.

''I need my wife,'' he said. ''I very, very badly need my wife.''

He bent his head and kissed her, and then he lifted her into his arms and they fell upon the bed together.

''We have a son, Kristin,'' he said, and she laughed. ''We have a son, and he's beautiful, and...and so are you.''

It was a long, long time before either of them thought of any other kind of sustenance.

Chapter Fourteen

The days that followed were glorious for Kristin. It wasn't that anything had been settled between them. It was just that for a time they seemed to have achieved a private peace, and it was wonderful.

They did not stray far from the house. Cole explained how hard it had been to elude the patrols to reach her. But Kristin knew her own land, and she knew where they could safely travel. They picnicked on the banks of the river with the baby, and while he slept they splashed in the deliciously cool water. Kristin was first shocked and then ridiculously excited to dare to strip away her clothes in the broad daylight and make love in the water.

In the evening they sat beneath the moon and felt the cool breezes play over them. Kristin listened while Cole and Samson talked about what was left of the herd, and it seemed that everything that was said began with the words "When the war is over..."

At night, lying curled against her husband's body, Kristin asked him if he thought the war would ever end. He hesitated a long time, stroking her hair.

"It's ending now, Kristin. We're being broken down bit by bit, like a beautiful animal chewed to bits by fleas. We never had the power. We never had the industry. We never had the men. It's going to end. If the Confederacy holds out another year I'll be surprised. Well, we went a long way on courage and tactics. But that Lincoln is a stubborn cuss. Tenacious. He's held on to his Union, so it seems.''

He sounded tired, but not bitter. Kristin stroked his chest. "Can't you just stay here now? If you know you're losing..."

"I can't stay, Kristin. You know that."

"I don't know anything of the kind! You've done your best for the Confederacy! You can't—"

"Kristin, Kristin!" He caught her hands. "I'm an outlaw as long as the war is on. If I stay here, I'll be in terrible danger. If some glory-seeking commander hears about it, he might just waltz in and string me up. If I'm going to die, I'd rather it be fighting than dangling from the end of a rope!"

"Cole, stop it—"

"And it isn't over, Kristin. I'm in the game and I have to stay with it. If I don't go back, Malachi will come here and shoot me for a traitor."

"He would not!"

"Well, someone would," he said.

"Cole—"

"Kristin, I have to go back."

"Cole—"

He rolled over and swept her into his arms and kissed her and then looked into her eyes. "When I ride now, I will think of my son. Thank you for Gabe, Kristin. Thank you." He nuzzled her lips and kissed her forehead and her throat and the valley between her breasts. She tried to keep talking, to keep arguing, but he nuzzled his way down the length of her torso, and she grew breathless and couldn't speak. When he had finished she couldn't remember what she had wanted to say, only that it was terribly important that she hold him as long as she could.

The next day Kristin was overjoyed when Matthew arrived unexpectedly. He quickly warned her that both he and Cole could be shot if they were caught together. Still, for a few hours, it was a wonderful homecoming. Matthew admired his nephew, and Shannon clung to her brother, and Delilah managed a fine feast. Then Cole and Matthew shut themselves up in the library together. Kristin finally had to force her way in.

"You're discussing me, I know it, and I will know what is going on!" she insisted.

"Cole has to leave," Matthew told her. "Right away. To-night."

"Why?"

Matthew looked unhappily at Cole. Cole shrugged and gave her the explanation. "Matthew is putting the ranch under the protection of a Federal troop."

"But—"

"I can't be here, Kristin. And Quantrill's group has split up."

"What?"

"During the spring," Matthew explained, "Quantrill and his men got into some heavy feuding in Texas. Bill Anderson has some men under him, and George Todd has a group, too. Quantrill still has his followers. Bill attacked some Federals during the summer, and Archie Clements scalped the men he murdered. The situation is frightening, and no one knows where Zeke Moreau is, or who he's with. So you see, Kristin, Cole has to get out of here. And you have to be protected."

Tears stung her eyes, and she gritted her teeth to keep from spilling them. She turned away from the men.

"I fixed the tear in your frock coat, Cole. And Delilah has been washing everything. The two of you, sometimes your clothes smell as if you'd been sleeping with skunks for a year. I'll see that you're packed up and have Shannon wrap up a supply of jerky."

She stumbled into the hallway. Cole found her there and swept her into his arms and took her upstairs to their room. She cried the whole time they made love, her tears spilling over his shoulders and his chest and dampening his cheeks.

Then he kissed her and held the baby tightly. She insisted on coming down with him, and when he was mounted he leaned down to kiss her again. Holding their child close to her breast, Kristin waved as he left.

That night some Union soldiers moved into the bunkhouse. Kristin supposed it was necessary. But it was still hard.

The bushwhacker situation grew much worse. On the thirtieth of September Kristin was surprised when she came out on the porch to see that Major Emery was riding toward her. She stood and smiled, ready to greet him, but her smile died when she saw his face. She went pale herself, and the world spun, and she was afraid that she was going to faint.

"Oh, my God, it's Cole—"

"No, no, Mrs. Slater," he assured her hastily, taking Gabe from her. "He's a fine boy, ma'am. A fine boy." He looked around uncomfortably. "I don't think your sister should know the whole of this, ma'am, but...Captain Ellsworth is dead."

"Oh, no!"

"That damned Bill Anderson! Since his sister died they say he froths at the mouth every time he fights. Fights—bah!" He spat into the dirt. "He tore up Centralia. He made twenty-five unarmed soldiers strip, and then he shot twenty-three of them dead. The troops that went out after him fared worse. It was a massacre. At least a hundred killed. Stripped, scalped, dismembered, their bodies mutilated as they died—"

"Oh, God! Oh, God!"

They both heard the scream. Kristin turned around to see that Shannon was standing in the doorway. She had heard every word. She knew.

"Oh, God! No!" she shrieked. Major Emery took a step toward her, barely managing to catch her as she pitched forward in a dead faint.

"Could you take her to her room for me, please?" Kristin whispered.

Major Emery nodded and carried Shannon upstairs. "We've a company surgeon out in your bunkhouse. I'll send him over and see that he gives her something."

The doctor didn't come soon enough. Shannon awoke, and she started to cry. She cried so hard that Kristin was afraid she would hurt herself. Then she was silent, and the silence was even worse. Kristin stayed with her, holding her hand, but she knew that she hadn't reached her sister, and she wondered if anyone ever would again.

* * *

Fall came, and with it more tragedy for the South. General Sherman was marching to the sea through Georgia and the Carolinas, and the reports of his scorched earth policy were chilling. In the west, the Union bottleneck was almost complete.

On the twenty-first of October George Todd died when a sniper caught him in the neck. Five days later Bill Anderson was killed in the northwestern corner of Missouri.

Kristin was alarmed to see how eagerly Shannon received the news of their deaths.

Thanksgiving came and went. It was a very quiet affair. Kristin was Matthew McCahy's sister, but she was also Cole Slater's wife, and so it didn't seem right to invite any of the Union men in for a fancy supper.

Matthew made it back for Christmas Day, and Kristin was delighted to see him. She asked if he had heard anything, and he told her that the last he had heard, Cole Slater was still at large. John Hunt Morgan, the dashing cavalry commander, had been killed late in the year, and Matthew hadn't heard anything about where Cole or Malachi or Jamie had been assigned.

She cried that night, cried because no news was good news. It seemed so long since she had lost her father, and she could hardly remember Adam's face. She didn't want to lose anyone else. She could hardly stand to see Shannon's pale face anymore. She hadn't seen her sister smile since Captain Ellsworth had been killed. Not once.

After Christmas dinner, Kristin sat before the fire in the parlor with her brother and her sister. She began to play a Christmas carol on the spinet, but Shannon broke down and ran upstairs to her room. Kristin sat staring silently at her hands for a long time.

Finally Matthew spoke.

"Kristin, nothing's going to get better, not for a long, long time, you know."

"They say it's almost over. They say the war is almost over."

"The war, but not the hatred. I doubt they'll fix that for a hundred years, Kristin. It isn't going to be easy. The healing will be slow and hard.''

"I know,'' Kristin whispered.

"You just make sure, Kristin, that if Cole comes around you get him out of here fast. He isn't going to be safe anywhere near this place, not until some kind of a peace is made, and then only if amnesty is given.''

Kristin's fingers trembled. She nodded. "He won't come back. Not until...not until it's over.''

Matthew kissed her and went upstairs. Kristin stared at the fire until it had burned very low in the grate.

In February Gabriel had his first birthday. The news that month was good for the Union, grim for the Confederacy. Sherman had devastated the South. Robert E. Lee was struggling in Virginia, and Jefferson Davis and the Confederate cabinet had abandoned Richmond half a dozen times.

By March, everyone was talking about the campaign for Petersburg. Grant had been pounding away at the Virginia city since the previous summer, and the fighting had been fierce. The Union had tried to dig a tunnel under the Confederate lines. Mines had exploded, and many Confederates had been killed, but then they had rallied and shot down the Union soldiers who had filled in the crater. The soldiers shuddered when they spoke of it.

Kristin had become accustomed to the men who had made their headquarters on her land. They were mostly farmers and ranchers, and more and more she heard them speak wistfully of the time when the war would be over, when they could go home. The Confederate general Kirby-Smith was still raising hell in the West, and the Southern forces were still fighting valiantly in the East, but the death throes had already set in for a nation that had never had a chance to truly breathe the air of independence. Major Emery came one day and sat with them on the porch while the first warmth of spring touched them. Morosely he told Kristin that the death estimates for the country were nearing the half-million mark. "Bullet, sword and disease!" He shook his head. "So many mothers' sons!"

When he left her that afternoon, Kristin had no idea that she would never see him again alive.

April came. General Lee's forces were gathering around Richmond for a desperate defense of the capital. Gabe was learning to walk, and Kristin had agreed with Samson and Pete that he might be allowed to try sitting on top of a horse.

Kristin came outside one April afternoon, and she knew instantly that something was wrong. There was a peculiar stillness in the air.

There should have been noise. There should have been laughter. The dozen or so Union troops billeted on the ranch should have been out and about, grooming their horses, hurrying here and there in their smart blue uniforms with their correspondence and their missives.

Pete was nowhere in sight, and neither was Samson.

"Samson?" Kristin called out.

Then she heard the barn door creak as if the breeze had moved it, but there wasn't any breeze. She looked toward it, and she saw a hand. Its fingers were curled and crumpled, and it was attached to a bloodstained blue-clad arm. Kristin felt a scream rising in her throat, but she didn't dare release it. She wrenched Gabe into her arms and ran for the house as fast as she could.

"Shannon!" she screamed. In the hall she found a gun belt with the two Colt six-shooters Cole had insisted she keep loaded and ready. With trembling fingers she wound the belt around her waist and reached for the Spencer repeating rifle Matthew had brought at Christmas.

"Shannon!" she called again.

Her sister came running down the steps, her eyes wide, her face pale.

"Something is wrong. Take Gabe—"

"No! Give me the rifle!"

"Shannon, please—"

"I'm a better shot than you are, damn it!"

"Maybe, yes! But I'm not as desperate and reckless as you are!" Kristin snapped. "Shannon, for God's sake, you are the

best shot! So for the love of God take Gabriel and get upstairs
and try to pick them off if they come for me.''

''Who?''

She didn't know how she could be certain, but she was.

''Zeke is back. He's out there somewhere. Shannon, please,
don't let them get my baby!''

With that she pushed Gabriel into her sister's arms and
started out the door again. Shannon watched her. Gabriel began to cry, and she pulled him close and hurried up the stairs.

''Holy Mary!'' Private Watson muttered. ''Will you look at
that? Fool Yankee, he's all alone and coming right at us!''

Cole looked up from where he sat polishing the butt of his
rifle. His eyes narrowed as he watched the trotting horse. Judging by the way the man riding it sat, he was injured, and
injured pretty badly.

''Should we shoot him?'' someone murmured uncertainly.

''Somebody already done shot him,'' came the wry answer.

''Leave him be, boys,'' Cole said, rising curiously. Cole
had been promoted to Colonel, which made him the highest-
ranking officer in the group. Malachi was now a major and
Jamie a captain. The three of them were with a small company
of men simply because small companies were all that was left
in their sector of the West. They had decided to find Kirby-
Smith, wherever he was, and join forces with him, but for the
last month they had kept a field headquarters in this abandoned
farmhouse deep inside an overgrown orchard.

''I know that man,'' Cole muttered suddenly. He hurried
forward, his brothers and his ragged troops at his heels.

He reached the horse, and the Yankee fell right into his
arms. Cole eased him down to the ground, wresting his own
scarf from around his neck to soak up the blood pouring from
the wound beneath the man's shoulder blade.

''Matthew McCahy, what the hell happened to you, boy?''
he said gruffly. He looked at Captain Roger Turnbill, the company surgeon, and then he looked down at Matthew and wondered how the hell his brother-in-law had found him. Then he
decided it didn't matter, not until Matthew was looked after.

"Let's get inside the house," Captain Turnbill said.

The men started to lift him. Matthew opened his eyes, huge blue eyes that reminded Cole painfully of his wife, so very close by, so endlessly far away. Matthew reached up and clutched the lapel of Cole's frock coat.

"Cole, listen to me—"

"You know this blue belly well, colonel?" Captain Turnbill asked.

"He's my wife's brother. I know him well enough."

"Then let's get him inside. He's bleeding like a stuck pig."

"Matthew—" Cole gripped the hand that clutched him so tightly. "Matthew, the captain is going to help you. I swear it." Cole wondered if Matthew was delirious, or if he was merely wary of the Confederate surgeon. Doctors on both sides had been known to boast that they had killed more of the enemy than all the artillery shells in the service.

"Cole! For God's sake, listen to me!" Matthew rasped out. His fingers held Cole's like a vise. "It's Zeke—"

"What?"

Matthew swallowed painfully. "We met up with him southeast of here, in a little two-bit place called James Fork. We were a small detachment, thirty of us, heading over to Tennessee. I went down, I was knocked out and they took me for dead. I heard him talking over me. Said he couldn't wait to get to the McCahy place and tell Kristin McCahy that he'd managed to murder her brother now, too. They spent the night at James Fork. I waited till they were drunk and I found a horse, and here I am—"

Cole was ashen and tense. He didn't realize how hard he was gripping Matthew's shoulders until Captain Turnbill said softly, "Ease off, colonel."

"How did you find us?" Jamie asked carefully. He was the only one who seemed to be capable of rational thought at the moment.

Matthew smiled. "Your location isn't exactly a secret, gentlemen. Kurt Taylor was out here with a scouting party a few weeks ago. Some of the higher-ups know where you are.... They're just hoping the war will be over before they have to come in and clean you out.'' His smile faded, and he choked and coughed and then groaned in pain.

"Get him up and in the house!" Turnbill ordered. A half-dozen men quickly obeyed him, Jamie Slater tensely and carefully taking Matthew's head and his wounded shoulder.

"Slater! You've got to get there. You and your men, you've got a chance. Riding straight west—''

Cole followed after him. "There's a dozen Yankees on the ranch,'' he said tensely. "I know it.''

"So does Zeke Moreau,'' Matthew gasped out.

Then he was suddenly silent.

"Is he dead?'' Malachi asked tonelessly.

Turnbill shook his head. "Passed out from loss of blood. It's amazing that he made it here.''

Cole didn't follow any farther. He paused in the yard in front of the farmhouse and looked around at the men who remained with him. Besides his brothers and the doctor, he had one sergeant, two corporals and twenty-two privates. They had survived a hell of a lot. How could he ask them to die at this point?

"I've got to leave you, boys,'' he said. The soldiers who hadn't helped carry Matthew into the house ranged silently around him. "This is a private battle, and some of you might say it's being waged against one of your own—''

"Hell, Quantrill and his kind were never one of my own,'' Bo Jenkins, a shopkeeper in peacetime, said. "My kind of Southerner ain't never shot down a man in cold blood.''

"Glad to hear it, private,'' Cole said quietly. "But still, I can't rightly ask you to come along and get killed—''

"Hell, colonel, how's this any different from all the other times?'' Jenkins said.

His brother John stepped up beside him. "Seems like we've been following you a long time, sir. We'll keep on doing that. I mean, what the hell, colonel? You think we all want to live forever?''

Cole felt a smile tug at his lips. "Then let's get ready. We've got to ride fast. We've got to ride like the wind.''

* * *

Armed and ready, Kristin came out of the house and moved quickly toward the barn, toward the bloody hand lying in the spring sunshine.

She paused at the gaping doorway and flattened herself against the wall. Then she kicked open the door and stepped inside, both her Colts cocked and ready to fire.

She heard nothing, saw nothing. She blinked in the dim light, then she saw that at least five men in Yankee blue lay on the ground and in the hay. Their killer or killers had interrupted them in the middle of a poker game. The cards were still sitting on a bale of hay in the center of the barn.

Someone had been holding a full house.

Kristin swallowed painfully.

"Drop 'em," came a sneering voice from behind her. It was one of Zeke's men. She didn't know his name, but she recognized the voice from its jeering tone. She had heard the man's raucous laughter when her father had died.

She froze, aware that she hadn't a chance in hell of turning quickly enough to kill the man. She wondered whether she shouldn't turn anyway and die quickly. Zeke surely no longer desired her. All he wanted was revenge.

Suddenly there was an explosion right over her shoulder. She screamed, stunned, wondering if she'd been hit. She hadn't. She stared toward the center of the barn, and there lay one of the Yankee soldiers she had thought were all dead. Blood was pouring from his temple, but he was smiling at her, and his pistol was smoking. She whirled around. The man behind her lay dead, very dead. There was a black hole burned right into his chest.

She slammed the Colts back into the gun belt and ran over to the Yankee who had saved her life, falling down on her knees beside him. "Bless you! What can I—"

"Lady, you can save yourself!" the man whispered, and he winced. "If all goes well, then you come back for me. Damn it to hell, but I can't help you no more now. My leg is all busted up. You go careful. He's in the house."

Chills swept up her spine. "He's...where?"

"Moreau, their leader. He's up in the house."

He was in the house, with her sister and her child. Kristin raced for the doorway. She found Samson and Pete slumped against the far wall of the barn. Pete was dead, his eyes wide open and staring. Samson was still breathing, a thin stream of blood trickled from his forehead.

She paused for a split second to tear apart her skirt and dab at the wound. She lowered him to the ground and pressed the hastily made bandage against his forehead. Then she raced into the yard, across the paddock and toward the house, easing the Colts from the belt once again.

Suddenly there was a shot. She stopped where she stood, feeling the dust rise around her feet where a bullet had bitten into the earth. She looked up, way up, to her bedroom window.

Zeke was standing there, a handful of Shannon's hair caught in his filthy fingers.

"Drop the guns, Mrs. Slater," Zeke drawled. "Drop 'em right now, else I'll let this pretty gold stuff in my fingers run red with McCahy blood."

Kristin stared up at him in despair. She heard a shuffling around her, and she knew that his men were emerging from the bunkhouse, from the far side of the house, from behind the watering trough. She looked around, and the faces spun before her. How many of them were there? Twenty? Thirty? It was hard to tell.

"Drop 'em in the dust, Kristin, slow and careful!" Zeke laughed then, fingering Shannon's hair. "She sure did come along nicely, Kristin. Why, I think she's even prettier than you are. Hard to tell, though. You're both nasty as rattlers."

Shannon cursed and bit Zeke's hand savagely. Zeke swore in turn and cuffed her hard. Suddenly Gabe began to cry. Kristin cried out involuntarily and bit her lip.

Shannon screamed as Zeke tore at her hair. Zeke, shouting insanely, addressed Kristin again.

"Drop the guns or else I'll kill the kid first. Slow. I'll blow off his legs one by one, and then his arms and then, if he's still alive, I'll cut off his ears!"

Kristin set the Colts on the ground. She heard Zeke's wild laughter, and then he and Shannon disappeared from the window. The shuffling around her began again. She closed her eyes and tried to ignore the soft jeers and the horrible smell as the men moved closer and closer.

The door to the house burst open, and Zeke appeared, shoving Shannon before him. Shannon was white, but Kristin was, perhaps ridiculously, glad to see that her sister's hatred seemed to outweigh her fear. There would be plenty of time for fear.

Zeke, keeping his punishing grip on Shannon's hair, forced her into the center of the circle. He came close to Kristin, and he smiled. "I'm going to tell you about the afternoon, Kristin. Just so you can anticipate it all. Every sweet moment. See Harry over there? The guy with the peg leg and the rotten teeth? He's had a real hankering for you, so he gets to go first. I'm going for little sister here. Fresh meat. Then, well…hell, we've learned to share and share alike. We are going to make sure you stay alive, though. At least until we've had a chance to fire the house and the barn. You should get to hear the horses scream. That's a real fine sound. Then—maybe—Harry will scalp you. He learned the art real well from little Archie Clements himself. But we'll see how the afternoon goes. We may not have time for everything. There's lots of Yankees in these parts. Did you know that, Mrs. Slater? Sure you did. Your brother's a turncoat Yankee, ain't he? But don't worry about him none. I killed him last night."

Kristin's knees sagged, and she fell into the dirt. Matthew! It couldn't be. No!

Zeke started to laugh.

Something inside her snapped. She catapulted from the ground, flying at him in a fury. Shannon screamed but quickly rallied, and together they fell on him, biting him, tearing at him with their nails. Zeke screamed but none of his men moved to help him at first. And they couldn't shoot. They might kill him.

Then they heard it. The unmistakable sound of hoofbeats pounding the Missouri earth, pounding like thunder, coming closer and closer.

"Take cover!" one of the bushwhackers shouted.

Zeke let out a terrible growl and threw Shannon down hard

in the dirt. He slammed the back of his hand against Kristin's cheek, and when she reeled, stunned by the blow, he caught her by the hair and dragged her up the steps to the porch and behind the oak rocker.

The hoofbeats came closer, thundering like a thousand drums. "Bastard!" Zeke muttered. "How could they know…"

It was only then, as Zeke aimed his gun through the slits in the back of the rocker, that Kristin got her first glimpse of the riders.

They were dressed in gray, and they might have been a sorry sight had they not ridden with such grace and style. A rebel yell suddenly rose up in the air, and the horses tore around the front of the house. Dust flew everywhere. Gunfire erupted, and Kristin bit back a scream.

Cole was leading them, whirling his horse around, his head held high. Malachi was there, too, and Jamie.

The Union army had failed endlessly against the bushwhackers because the bushwhackers were so well armed and so fast. But now they were fighting a man who knew their ways. A man who was faster. A man with a company of soldiers who were every bit as well armed as they were, a company of soldiers who were determined to salvage something of honor and chivalry from a war they were destined to lose. They fought their own kind, for their own kind had defied the very code of the South that so many had fought to preserve.

Kristin couldn't see for the clouds of dust the horses and the gunfire had churned up. All she knew was that Zeke was dragging her viciously along the porch.

She fought him. He swore he would turn around and shoot her, but she didn't really care. He had murdered Matthew, and he had murdered her father, and he was probably going to murder her. All she dared hope for was that Delilah had hidden somewhere, and that she had found Gabe. She wanted her son to live. She wanted something good to rise from the dust and ashes of this war. She wanted her child, Cole's child, to live, to remember, to start over.

"Damn you!" Zeke screamed. He twisted her arm cruelly

behind her back, and she cried out in pain. He pushed her to the front door and then into the house. He pushed her toward the stairs, and the pain in her arm was so piercing that she had to stumble up the steps.

"Maybe we do have a little time. Maybe they'll all stay real busy out there for a long, long time. I wouldn't mind having you on Cole Slater's bed while he chokes on his own blood down below."

Suddenly the front door flew open and Cole was standing in the doorway. Zeke whirled, and Kristin stumbled and almost fell, but Zeke caught her and held her in front of him.

Framed by the doorway, the sunlight behind him, Cole was frightening and yet strangely beautiful. In his left hand he held his cavalry saber, and with his right he aimed his Colt.

"Put it down nice and easy, Slater, nice and easy," Zeke said. He pulled Kristin close against him, so close that she could breathe in the reek of his breath and feel the sweat of his body.

"You get your filthy hands off my wife, Zeke."

"You know, Slater, I started in with Quantrill late. That's why I didn't remember you the first time we met here. But now I remember you real well. And I've thought about this moment. I've dreamed about it. So you put the gun down. See how I've got this beautiful silver barrel aimed right at her throat? Think about how her blood will pour out where the artery's cut...."

Suddenly they heard a cry. It was Gabriel, crying in fear and rage. Delilah must have him in a closet close by, Kristin thought.

Her stomach twisted, and she saw that Cole had gone white. She sensed that Zeke was smiling. Now Cole was forced to think not only about her but about his son.

"That's a real fine boy you got there, Slater," Zeke drawled. He moved the barrel of the gun against Kristin's cheek. "A real fine wife, a real fine boy. You want to see them live, you'll set that gun down, slow and easy. No fast moves."

"No fast moves," Cole echoed tonelessly.

Gabe was still crying. Kristin bit into her lip. As soon as Cole set the gun down, Zeke would shoot him, and there was so much she had to tell him. Gabe was walking now, could say so many words. She had taught him to say papa. He had the most wonderful laugh in the whole world, and his eyes were so very much like his father's....

"Cole, no!" she cried out.

He smiled at her. "I have to do this, Kristin."

Zeke laughed. "Yeah, he has to."

Cole was looking at her. A curious smile touched his lips. "I never got a chance to tell you that I loved you, Kristin. I do, you know. With all my heart."

"Oh, God, Cole!"

"I love you. I love you. Duck, Kristin."

"What?" she gasped,

He didn't drop his Colt. He aimed it right over her head. She screamed, and the world exploded.

Chapter Fifteen

Kristin fell, and it was as if the earth had opened up beneath her feet. All she knew was that Cole had fired.

And that Zeke had not.

Zeke's body was tumbling down the stairs after hers. Kristin came to a halt at the landing, and something fell hard on top of her. She stared up at Zeke, at his wide, staring eyes, at his forehead, where flesh and bone had been ripped away. She pushed away from him, desperate to get him away from her.

"Kristin, Kristin!"

Strong arms were around her, pulling her up from beneath him. She couldn't tear her eyes away from him. His face was still frozen in a sneer, even in death.

"Kristin!"

Cole turned her into his arms. "Kristin!" She looked up and saw his face, his eyes. Concern furrowed his brow as he eased his knuckles over her cheek. "Are you hurt?" he asked anxiously.

She shook her head. She couldn't speak. She stared at him blankly, and then she shrieked out his name and threw herself against him and started to cry. He stroked her hair and murmured comfortingly to her. Then he held her away from him and studied her anxiously. She struggled desperately for control.

"Oh, Cole! How did you know to come? They slaughtered all the Yankees.... Oh, no, a few of them might still be alive.

You have to help them. Him. One of them saved me." Tears flooded her eyes. No matter how hard she tried, she couldn't keep from crying. "Cole! He killed Matthew! He found my brother and he killed him."

"Hush, Kristin, hush," Cole murmured. He pulled her against his body again and smoothed back her hair. Then he tilted her chin and sought her eyes. He had to make sure she understood. "Kristin, Matthew is fine. Well, I'm sorry, I suppose he's not fine. He's injured, but he's alive, Kristin. I would never have known—" He was suddenly unable to speak. It was all over, and now he was suddenly paralyzed by the fear. His hands trembled as he held her. "Kristin, Matthew's company was attacked. Zeke left him for dead, but he wasn't dead, and he got away in the night. Thank God, the Yanks knew where I had my men all along, and Matthew knew the area so well that he came straight to me."

Her eyes were wide with hope, with a joy she dared not feel. "Oh, Cole! Please, don't tell me that unless—"

"It's the truth, Kristin, I swear it."

"But they didn't come after you? The Yankees, they let you be?"

"I have a few friends in the right places," Cole said with a wry smile. "It gives me hope. Maybe, when this thing is over, some of the hatreds will be patched up. Some of them won't be. But, oh, God, I want it to end. I want it to be over!"

He pulled her against him again and she felt the beating of his heart. The rough wool of his frock coat tickled her cheek, and she had never been so glad of anything in her life. She wanted to look at him again. She wanted to study his features, and she wanted to see him smile, because he was young again when he smiled. She wanted to see the silver light in his eyes when he held her, and most of all she wanted to hear him speak again. She wanted to hear him say he loved her.

Of course, this wasn't really the right time. There was a dead man at her feet, and though the guns had gone silent outside the house, dead men littered the earth there, too, and— please God—a few living men, too. She had to go back to the barn for the young Yankee who had saved her life, and she had to find her son.

"Kristin—" Cole began, but he was interrupted by an outraged cry.

"Miz Kristin! Mister Cole! Why, thank the Lord," Delilah called. She was at the top of the stairs with Gabe, who was struggling fiercely to free himself from her grasp. Cole stared at his son with the awe of a parent who has not seen his child in a long, long time. Gabe might have been a grown man the way Cole was staring at him.

Kristin's eyes twinkled. "He walks now. And he talks. I taught him how to say papa."

Delilah hurried down the stairs. She saw Zeke's body, but she didn't pause. She spat on it and stepped over it, and then she set Gabriel down. He tottered for a moment. Kristin watched Cole as he went down on his knees and reached out for the boy. Gabe waddled carefully over to inspect the stranger.

"Say papa!" Kristin urged him.

Gabriel wasn't interested in saying anything. He turned away from the stranger who was his father and buried his face in his mother's skirts. He reached out his arms, and Kristin laughed and picked him up. Then, suddenly, she crushed him against her, so hard that he cried out in protest. "Oh, Gabriel!" she murmured, holding him tight.

Cole came to his feet and rescued his screaming son. He lifted Gabriel very high and silver eyes gazed into silver eyes. "I'm your papa, little man!" He laughed. "And you'd best get used to the idea."

Gabriel couldn't possibly have understood what Cole had said to him, of course, but he smiled anyway, as if he had decided to accept the stranger in gold and gray. Cole lowered him at last and set him on his hip, smiling at Kristin.

Suddenly there was an awful commotion at the door.

"Put me down, you piece of trash!" Shannon shrieked.

Malachi—Shannon thrown over his shoulder—came through the doorway, his face dark and thunderous. "I don't mind bushwhackers, and I don't mind the damn Yankees, but Cole, I will be damned if I'll be responsible for this brat!''

"Put me down!" Shannon screamed.

He did. He dumped her in front of Cole, and she was thrashing and flailing, trying to get her balance. She rolled over and came face-to-face with Zeke Moreau's body.

"Oh!" she gasped, and fell silent at last.

Kristin looked at Malachi and arched a brow.

He sighed with great patience. "Kristin, I didn't know what the hell was happening in here. I didn't want her barging in to get shot, or to cause you or Cole to get shot. Mainly. It would be her own damn fault if she did get shot, but since she is your sister, I thought I'd try to save her sweet, darling, precious little life!"

For once Shannon didn't reply. She was still staring at Zeke's face. She began to tremble uncontrollably, and then she burst into tears.

Kristin started toward her sister, but Cole pulled her back. Malachi was kneeling beside Shannon, and he pulled her up and away from the body.

"It's over! It's all over!" he told her roughly. "Don't go falling apart now."

Shannon stiffened momentarily, and then she hiccuped. Malachi gave her his handkerchief, and she dried her face, nodding an acknowledgement. Then she jammed it back into his hand.

"I never fell apart, you backwoods bastard!"

''Well, good. Get your derriere out there and start helping!''

"Helping?"

"There are injured men out there. Unless you're too damned prissy to help the men who were willing to die to save your miserable life."

"Miserable?"

"Go!"

"I am going, Malachi Slater! I'm going because those are fine men out there—even the rebels! I'm going for them, and I'm going because I choose to go, and I'll never, never do anything because you tell me to, do you understand?"

With an elegant toss of her golden curls, she swept past him. It was a splendid exit except for one thing. Malachi smacked her rump soundly as she went past. She yelped in outrage and slapped him hard across the face. He caught her by the elbow and turned her toward him, his face dark with rage.

"Malachi! Please! She is my sister," Kristin reminded him sweetly.

Slowly, his eyes narrowed, he released Shannon. "Why, thank you, kind sir!" she said. Then she kicked him hard in the shin and raced out the door.

Kristin began to smirk, and then Cole laughed, and the baby giggled. Delilah laughed along with them, but then her laughter faded, and she gasped, "Samson! My man! Oh, Mister Slater—"

"The barn," Kristin said quickly, her eyes on Cole. "He was breathing—"

Cole ran out the door, Delilah hard on his heels. Kristin followed but when she stepped out on the porch she stood there stunned, her son in her arms, staring at the scene of destruction.

There were bodies everywhere. Men in gray were collecting them, dragging them away. A weary-looking young man nodded to her in grim acknowledgment as he passed her. She swallowed and caught his arm. "Thank you. Thank you for coming here."

He smiled and tipped his hat. "I'd go anywhere Colonel Slater invited me, ma'am. I'm right glad we got here in time."

He had work to do, and he went back to it. Dazed, Kristin stepped down into the yard.

Then someone called out, asking for water. She hurried over to the trough and found one of Cole's boys behind it, clutching his shoulder and trying to stand.

"Here, here!" she whispered, ladling up some water. Gabe gurgled. He seemed to think they were playing.

"Thank you, ma'am," the soldier said. Then he winced, and she saw that he had a ball lodged in his flesh.

"Help me over here!" she called. Another soldier lifted the

wounded man, and within minutes she had him in the house and on the couch and she had Cole's men scurrying around, boiling water, ripping up sheets for bandages, setting up the parlor as a temporary infirmary.

Gabriel refused to sleep, so she set up a little playpen in the parlor and busied herself with the injured. Shannon was at her side and Delilah, too, now that she knew that Samson was all right. He had been knocked cold, and he had a blinding headache, but otherwise he was none the worse for wear.

Samson was out on burial detail now. Zeke Moreau's body had been removed from the house.

There had been a scene when that had happened. Shannon had followed them out. She had stood on the porch and begged the men, "Please…please! Don't bury that man's body anywhere on this property!"

"Miss McCahy—"

"Please! Let the vultures eat him, let the wolves finish him, but I beg you, don't bury him near here!"

And so some of the men had set out with a wagon, and they were taking Zeke and the bodies of the other bushwhackers far, far away. Pete was dead, and he was family, and three of Cole's men had fallen, and there were the Yankees that the bushwhackers had killed. They were being laid to rest with infinite tenderness in the family plot, beside Kristin's mother and father.

By nightfall, most of the traces of the gun battle had been cleared away. Delilah managed to produce a hearty stew in abundance to feed everyone.

At ten they heard the sound of a wagon creaking along. Cole had just finished eating, and he was sipping a brandy on the porch. Gabriel was in bed, and Kristin was sitting at Cole's feet, listening to a sad tune being played on a harmonica somewhere nearby.

She felt Cole stiffen. Then she realized that he had sentries posted, for there was something like a Rebel yell in the darkness, and then the wagon came through.

"Cole?" Kristin murmured.

"It's a surprise," he said, squeezing her shoulder. She followed him down the steps and out to the yard. There was something lumpy in the back of the wagon, something cried out plaintively, "Kristin, Shannon?"

"Matthew!" She screamed her brother's name and flew to the wagon. She kissed him, and she held him so tightly that he muttered, "Kristin, I survived being shot, you're going to kill me here in my home at last with kindness!"

"Oh, Matthew!"

Then Shannon was flying down the steps. The three Mc-Cahy's greeted one another, and the men looked on, and then the harmonica player started up again, with "Lorena" this time bringing tears to eyes that had nearly run dry in all the years of bloodshed.

Matthew was brought in and put to bed in his own room. Once he was tucked in, he caught his sister's hand, and Kristin smiled and kissed him on the forehead again and told him to rest.

"Kristin!" He pulled her back. "Kristin, there'll be a bunch of Yankees here soon. They'll find out that Major Emery and his men were slaughtered, and they'll know that Cole and his men came in for the cleanup, and they'll be damned glad. But there's still a war on. They'll have to take them prisoner, or else they'll have to fight, and a lot of men will die needlessly. They're true heroes—to both sides, probably—but that won't make any difference. Kristin, are you understanding me?"

No, she wasn't. Or perhaps she was and she wanted to deny it. She couldn't have her husband taken away from her so soon.

"Kristin, Cole is considered an outlaw. Worse than ever before."

"Why? What do you mean?"

"He'll have to explain that to you himself. But be prepared. They need to sneak away now, tonight."

She felt weak, as if she had been drowning and she had reached and reached for a rope and it had been viciously wrenched away.

"Thank you, Matthew," she told her brother.

She blew out the lamp and left him. She hesitated, leaning against the door.

When she came back downstairs, she quickly discovered that everything that Matthew had said was true. The Confederate surgeon who had so carefully tended to her brother was checking the men she had sutured and bandaged—and preparing them for travel. He smiled at her when he saw her.

"Your brother is going to be just fine. Keep the wound clean. Never use the same sponge twice when you're cleaning out a wound. I'm becoming more and more convinced that rot travels that way. Seems we have been doing better with sanitation than the blue bellies." He paused, and she thought that he, too, looked weary. "He's a fine young man, your brother. You take care of him."

"Thank you, Captain Turnbill," said Kristin. He was about to turn away, but she stopped him with a hand set lightly upon his arm. "Captain, are you sure these men are fit to travel?"

"The worst wounded are the Yankees we found in the bunkhouse and the barn, and they don't have to travel anywhere. My men have one broken arm, a broken leg, some shot in the shoulder and two concussions. They'll be all right." He paused, looking at her unhappily. "Mrs. Slater, they'll be a lot better off traveling now than they would be in a Yankee prison camp. I'm not a man to say that all Yanks are butchers, but there's not much good to be said about prison camps, whether they're Yankee camps or Confederate camps."

The able-bodied men were walking past her, making ready to leave. Kristin couldn't see her husband anywhere.

Malachi came around behind her and squeezed her shoulders. He turned her around. "Hope Cole won't mind," he said, and he hugged her and gave her a kiss on the cheek. "Hell, I don't care if Cole does mind!" he said, and he kissed her again. She didn't know there was a tear on her cheek until he wiped it away.

"Oh, Malachi…"

"It's all right. We won't be far away."

"Not far away at all."

It was Jamie who spoke. He was right behind Malachi, and

he took her from his brother and kissed her cheek, too. "You take care of yourself, little sister, you hear? Take good care of that nephew of mine, too."

She nodded, unable to speak for a few seconds.

"Cole—"

"Cole is right here," her husband said. Tears blurred her vision. He took her in his arms. "Hey!" he whispered, his lips nuzzling her throat. "Stop that! You can't send my brothers away with tears in your eyes."

"Your brothers…"

She whirled around in his arms. Cole looked over her head. Malachi tipped his hat and grinned, and Cole grinned back. The two of them went out, and the house slowly fell silent. "I'm not leaving tonight, Kristin."

"What?" she whispered.

There was a bit of a commotion outside. Shannon was saying goodbye nicely to Jamie, and not so nicely to Malachi. Cole grinned, and Kristin grinned back, her eyes searching his. Then the door slammed, and Shannon whispered. "Oh, excuse me!"

Neither of them turned around. They heard Shannon tiptoe into the parlor to stay with the Union injured.

He was beautiful, Kristin thought. He was the most beautiful man she had ever seen. He was leaner than he had been that first day she had seen him. Strands of gray were creeping into his hair and into his beard, but somehow they were beautiful, too. They went well with the silver light in his eyes, with the handsome, dignified planes of his face.

"Oh!" she whispered heatedly. "You have to leave! Matthew says they consider you an outlaw—"

"They won't know I'm here, Kristin. My men are gone. They've taken my horse. They've learned how to disappear with the night. And for now I'm staying with my wife."

"Oh!"

"If she'll have me."

"Oh!" She touched his cheek, tenderly moving her fingertips over the coarse beard there. "Oh, she will have you!" she breathed.

He caught her hand and kissed her fingertips. Silently he led her up the stairs and through the doorway to their bedroom. Then he leaned against the door, and she smiled as she watched him.

"I never thought I would be here with you now!" he whispered.

"But you are," she said.

"Yes, I am."

Kristin walked over to him. She lifted off his hat and tossed it on the floor, and she unbuckled his scabbard and his gun belt and cast his weapons aside. Studiously, she unbuttoned his frock coat and his uniform shirt, and when his shoulders and chest were bare she felt the sweet thrill of anticipation invade her. Her fingers grew awkward, and she found that she was trembling. She whispered his name, and she pressed her lips to his chest and to the pulse at the base of his throat. He caught her lips and kissed her hungrily, tasting and tasting her mouth, trembling with ever-greater ardor. She was breathless when he released her and turned her around to work at the tiny buttons of her dress. He was shaking as badly as she, but was more practiced, and more determined, and she was startled when the dress fell quickly away from her, and then her chemise, and then her petticoats. He lifted her up with her stockings and shoes still on and carried her quickly to the bed, pausing with a rueful laugh to check on Gabriel, who was sleeping sweetly in the little bed in the corner.

Then he tossed her on the bed and fell upon her, and she threaded her fingers joyously through his hair. He groaned and kissed her again, and then he kissed her breasts, staring at them, savoring them, easing his tongue over each nipple, then his teeth, then the fullness of his mouth.

"Oh, Cole!" Her head tossed from side to side, and lightning swept through her, embedding a sweet, swirling heat at the apex of her thighs, a dizzying need for him. He filled it, touching her with a light and tender stroke and then with a demanding one, watching her eyes, watching her body, feeling the thunder of the desire that grew and grew within him.

He kissed her belly, and he stroked her thighs, and he

played his touch over the golden triangle at their juncture, and then he delved within it. He made an incredibly sensual act of taking off her shoes, peeling away her garters and hose. Then he rose boldly above her. He drew a steady pattern with the searing tip of his tongue from her throat down the valley between her breasts to her navel and into the very heart of her fire. And she cried out for him, and he came to her.

Then he hovered, just above her, and she opened her eyes wide, waiting, pleading, wondering why he denied her. A great sound of agony escaped him, and he buried his head against her breasts.

"I do love you, Kristin. I do love you."

"Oh, Cole!" she said, clinging to him. "Please..."

He pushed away from her, and stared at her. "Well?"

And then it dawned on her what he wanted, and she pressed hard against him, arching to meet his need. "Cole, I have loved you for ages! I love you so very much. I could never admit it, I was so afraid, I knew you didn't love me."

"I just didn't dare admit it," he said softly.

"Say it again!" she demanded.

"I love you. I love you, Kristin McCahy Slater, and I swear that I will do so until the end of time."

"Oh, Cole!" She buried her face against his chest. It was hot and sleek and damp with perspiration. And he chose that moment to plunge deep, deep within her, and even as he did he was whispering again, the sweet words over and over again.

He loved her.

Later that night—much later, for making love took on a sweet new dimension when the words were spoken, and they were tempted to explore that dimension again and again—Cole held her in his arms and told her everything. First he told her about the day the jayhawkers had come, and how they had burned down his home and killed his wife. She heard the agony in his voice, but she didn't stop him, because it was important that he say everything, that he lay his soul bare for her, as she had hers. He needed to trust her in that way, and, Kristin thought, he needed the healing power of words. His heart needed the cleansing.

She listened, and she was not afraid of the past, merely saddened. Then she listened as he told her what had happened in Kansas, how his old friend Kurt Taylor had been there and how he had purposely alerted Cole to the fact that Henry Fitz was in town with his jayhawkers.

"I killed him, Kristin. I knew what I was doing. I knew exactly what danger I was riding into, but I had to face him." His arms tightened around her. "If we were to have a future, I just had to do it. Can you understand that?"

She didn't really have to answer him. She planted little kisses over his chest, and he groaned, and his hands rode roughly over her hair, and then they were in one another's arms once again. They were still so desperate, so hungry, so determined to have all that they could of one another, to cherish, to hold, to keep always for their dreams.

It was near dawn before they dozed off. Kristin was startled when she awoke almost before she had slept. Day was breaking, bright and fresh as a rainbow. Pink light fell upon her.

She heard the sounds of hoofbeats below.

With a soft gasp, she rose and raced to the window.

Down by the well she saw a single Union officer. She glanced at Cole, and he seemed to be asleep. He seemed at peace, the lines of strain erased from his features at last.

Kristin struggled into her gown and left the room without stockings or shoes, closing the door behind her. She padded silently down the stairs and hurried out to the well.

She couldn't imagine how she looked to the man, her face pale, her blue eyes wide, her hair in complete and lovely disarray around her fine-boned, very worried face.

He smiled at her and looked her up and down. He suddenly envied Cole Slater very much.

"Good morning, ma'am. This the McCahy ranch?"

"It is. My brother, a Union officer, is inside, recovering from wounds."

And your husband, a Southern officer, is inside, too, I'd wager, he thought, but he was silent.

"This is sweet, clear water. Thank you."

"You're very welcome to it."

"Zeke Moreau came here and gunned down most of the men?"

Kristin swallowed and nodded.

"There's a detachment of medics coming for the injured later today."

"That's fine. We're doing our best."

"I'm sure you are."

"Would you like to come in?"

He shook his head. "No thanks. I'm not here officially." He spoke softly. "I came here to tell you that the war is over. Well, all but the shouting. I'm sure it will take a while for all the troops to surrender. Kirby-Smith is a tenacious soul. Proud man, fine fighter, but—"

"The...the war is over?" Kristin breathed.

"Yes, ma'am, like I said, all but the shouting. Two mornings ago, on April twelfth, General Robert E. Lee surrendered the Army of Northern Virginia to General Ulysses S. Grant at a little place called Appomattox Courthouse. Word has it that President Lincoln is determined that this great nation must unite in peace and brotherhood as quickly as possible, and he seems determined that there be brotherhood between North and South again."

She was shaking. She had to sit down. He saw her lips and her limbs tremble, and he came around to her and helped her over to the porch. He gave her a sip of water, and she nodded her thanks.

"The war...is really over?"

"Really over." He smiled. "I hear tell that Colonel Slater and his men came in here yesterday. Yep, I hear tell they cut down Zeke Moreau and his bloody bushwhackers. That must have been a fine piece of work, yes, ma'am. I'd have liked to have been here. No doubt the Union commanders—and the law—will hear about it." He smiled at her again. "'Course, Slater's men are gone, I take it?"

Kristin nodded. "Yes...they're gone."

"You his wife?"

"I'm his wife."

"Someone ought to tell him that the war is over. 'Course,

they should warn him that he needs to take care. Some people still don't take kindly to a few of his exploits. Once with Quantrill, you know, and then there was Kansas..." He shrugged. "If you should happen to see him, Mrs. Slater, you might warn him to lie low for a while. Ride on to Texas, maybe. Fitz had a brother, and he's sure to make an outcry. But tell him that he has to remember—the war is over. It will all come right. You hear? Tell him Kurt Taylor said so."

Kristin nodded.

"Thanks for the water. That's mighty good water."

"You're welcome, sir. Mighty welcome."

Kristin stood and waited. She waited until the Union officer in his blue uniform had disappeared on the dusty Missouri horizon.

Then she turned and screamed, "Cole! Cole!"

She tore up the stairs. He was up. He had been watching her and the officer from the window. Kristin threw herself at him, sending him flying across the room.

"It's over, it's over! The war is over! Lee has surrendered! Oh, there are still troops that haven't surrendered yet, but they're saying it's over! Oh, Cole!" She caught his face between her hands, and she kissed him. She kissed his throat and his shoulders, and she was so alive and vibrant that even though he had been worried and wary he had to laugh.

"Kristin, Kristin, it can't be that easy—"

"No, it isn't that easy," she said solemnly, and she told him what the man had said. "His name was Kurt Taylor, and he said you should head for Texas."

"I will," Cole said.

Kristin corrected him. "We will."

"We will?" he asked her, arching a brow. "I do seem to recall that there was once a woman who would not leave this ranch. She sold her honor to a disreputable rebel in order to stay right here on this property."

Kristin smiled at him. She had never felt so deliciously alive and sensual and vibrant and aware of all the world around her. It was spring—and the war was over. Over.

"It isn't my ranch. I was just holding on to it for Matthew, and Matthew is here now. You see, it's time to move on, anyway. And I consider that my honor was sold for a fair price. It was rather useless, you see, while my son—he's just magnificent. And—''

"And?"

"Well, there is this other minor thing. I fell desperately in love with that disreputable rebel. Even when I wanted to hang him myself, I was very much in love."

"Very much?"

"Incredibly, inestimably, most desperately in love."

"Really?" He laced his fingers through hers and bent his head and kissed her. She felt a shudder rake through him, and she sought his eyes.

"Cole?"

"We really have a future."

"Yes!"

"We can watch Gabriel grow, and we can have more children. And I can hold them when they are little tiny infants—"

"And you can change their little bottoms, too," Kristin informed him sweetly.

He smiled, and he kissed her again, and she let out a sweet, shuddering sigh. "Cole?"

"My love?"

She smiled, slowly, lazily, sensuously. "If you go to Texas, I will follow you wherever you may lead. But for the moment…"

"Yes?"

"We've never made love in peacetime before. Never," she told him with very wide eyes. "We've never made love in peacetime, whispering that we love one another!"

He threw back his head and laughed, and his eyes sizzled, silver and mercury, into hers, and she thought that he would always be her cavalier, the tall, dark stranger with the plumed hat who had stepped into her life like a hero, taking her from darkness into light. They weren't clear of the darkness yet. There would be pain. There would be time to mourn Pete, who had always been her friend, always at her side. There would be time to mourn Major Emery, who had been their friend, too, noble and caring, until the very end.

For now, though, they had one another.

Cole grinned wickedly. "Then," he said, "we must make love at peace, and whisper that we love one another. Kristin!"

"Yes?"

He came close against her lips, his mouth a breath away from hers.

"I love you!" he whispered fervently. "I love you, I love you, I love you!"

And though they were at peace they soared into the sweetest tempest, and through it all they never ceased to whisper the words.

The sun entered their room, and a new day had truly dawned.

Cole stroked his wife's beautiful hair, luxuriating in the sweet satisfaction she brought him. He stared at the ceiling, at the new light of day.

It would take the country a long time to heal, he knew. A long, long time. A long time to unite.

But she had brought healing to him, and his heart was united with hers now. "A new age," he murmured.

"What?"

"I said I love you!" Cole lied, and he turned to her again.

The war wouldn't end as easily as Kristin thought. Life was never as easy as that. But they did have a future.

And Texas could wait just a little while longer.

Author's Note

The war did not end easily, and especially not in the West, on the Kansas-Missouri border where it had really begun, long before shots rang out at Fort Sumter.

General Kirby-Smith was determined, and he held out with his troops until the twenty-sixth of May, holding the last Southern command to stand in the field.

William C. Quantrill died on June 6, 1865, fatally wounded by Union troops while conducting a raid on Louisville, Kentucky. On his deathbed he swore that if he had captured Jim Lane, leader of the jayhawkers before Doc Jennison, he would have burned him at the stake.

Jim Lane himself fired his last shot on July 1, 1865—with his revolver in his own mouth.

Frank and Jesse James and the Younger brothers—Quantrill's men—went on to find a separate infamy.

For Cole and Kristin, all those things were in the future. Cole was to have his own problems.

But those are really part of Malachi and Shannon's story, and must be told by them.

Columbine

by Miranda Jarrett

For Kempy
who gave me nightmares long ago
with tales of Hannah Dustin

Chapter One

London, 1704

Twenty paces to the end of the red Turkey carpet, twelve more across its width, then twenty paces back to the fireplace....

Over and over Kit Sparhawk counted his steps as he tried to control his impatience. It was nearly nine o'clock now, the pale winter moon framed high in the arched windows of Sir Henry Ashe's drawing room. Only Kit's promise to Jonathan kept him there, and his jaw tightened at the last memory of his brother, delirious with pain and fever. In Jonathan's place, he had travelled eight weeks and six thousand miles. Another four hours in a baronet's mansion should make little difference. He owed Jonathan that much. Yet it still rankled Kit to wait at all for Sir Henry. Gentry or not, the man was a rogue, fat and florid and too cunning by half for a partner in trade. A sly, cheating son of a—

Eighteen, nineteen, twenty steps, turn...

Once again Kit forced himself to swallow his irritation, counting the footprints his boots left in the deep plush. The bank drafts were there on the desk, waiting for the signature that Sir Henry never quite found time to give. Tonight Kit wouldn't leave until he did. He'd had enough of the baronet's excuses to last a lifetime. He struck one fist into the palm of his other hand, remembering how Sir Henry had tried every trick he could to avoid paying what he owed. God knew the colonies weren't free of scoundrels—Kit's own past was hardly spotless—but in the three months he had been in London, Kit had not met one man he'd trust beyond an empty handshake.

He dropped into one of the silk-covered armchairs and stared moodily into the fire. Praise Heaven he would be sailing again in less than a fortnight, and leaving London well behind. His thoughts rolled ahead, as they always did, to home—to his sisters and Jonathan and Plumstead.

A woman's scream, high and shrill with fear, pierced the house's silence. Without thinking Kit was on his feet and through the door. All was still in the front hall, the flame in the blue night lantern casting eerie shadows across the portraits that ringed the walls. Kit hesitated by the staircase, listening. He had no idea from where the scream had come or where to turn next, and he cursed the vastness of the mansion.

Suddenly one of the panelled doors opposite flew open and a small figure in white hurtled through it and into Kit. Automatically he caught the woman and steadied her. In that split second his senses registered the slipperiness of silk over soft flesh, round breasts crushed against his chest, a tangled cloud of dark hair redolent of lavender.

"Stay now, lass, and let me help," he said gently. Her face was white with the terror that filled her eyes, and her breath came in ragged shudders. Her feet bare, wearing only a night shift, she scarcely came to his shoulder.

"I've killed him," she whispered hoarsely. "I left him there, still as death itself. Oh, Mother of God, what will become of me now?"

"Hush, sweet, there's not enough of you to kill a butterfly, let alone a man," said Kit as he stroked the hair back from her forehead. Despite the fear that marked her face, he saw she was very pretty and young, perhaps twenty. Who could she be, he wondered. Sir Henry had no daughters, and this was decidedly not Lady Frances. Nor could she be a servant:

there was a delicacy to her that spoke of ease and wealth, and her speech was that of a lady.

"But I swear by all that's holy that he *is* dead, and by my hand!" With a little sob she buried her face in Kit's shirt, and protectively he slipped his arms around her shaking shoulders. He knew he should go find the man she claimed to have killed, but he was reluctant to leave her just yet. She seemed so small and vulnerable in his arms, as fragile as a wounded sparrow.

Suddenly the girl broke free and stared up at him with wild eyes. "Who are you?"

"Christopher Sparhawk, lass, though most call me Kit." In the uneven light, he now saw how her shift was torn, the costly lace at the neckline ripped across the twin curves of her breasts. She was aware of his scrutiny and, shamed, she tried to clutch the torn edges together. Red marks that would darken to bruises stained her throat and shoulders, and Kit felt a surge of anger at the man who had done this to her. Some cut-throat intruder, a thief perhaps, that she'd unwittingly surprised: who else would treat a lady so? Instinctively Kit felt beneath his coat for the long knife he always carried, even now in London.

Slowly, so as not to startle her further, he extended his other hand to her. There was no mistaking the desperation in her eyes, and he felt sure she wanted to trust him. "Please, let me help you. Tell me what has happened, and then we'll go to Sir Henry."

"You're one of his friends, aren't you?" She backed further from him, her chin tucked low with wariness like a hunted animal. "No, stay where you are! I should have known he'd not come alone. I've heard what's said about him, how he likes to watch others before he can take his own pleasure. A guinea he gave to a footman last month, as if he could buy that silly knave's silence for what had passed on Lady Frances's dining table! Perhaps he's paid you, too, then, to be a party to his debauchery?"

Her gaze swept over him, noting the expensive cut of Kit's calamanco coat and the linen ruffles at his throat. "But, no, you're a gentleman. You came for the sport alone, didn't you?"

"Nay, I came to talk matters of trade, nothing more," said Kit uneasily. God, she meant Sir Henry. It couldn't be anyone else.

Her laughter was choked with bitterness, and tears glistened in her lashes. "Trade, was it? Where did he promise you could have me, then? At his counting house, on his desk, with all the clerks to gawk and cheer at my shame?"

The tears spilled over, streaming freely down her cheeks. "Oh, how I wish I were the one who was dead!"

"Nay, lass, never wish that," said Kit as he stepped toward her again. But before he reached her, his eye caught a movement in the shadows. Quickly he wheeled around, and the girl followed.

"Sparhawk! By all that's holy, I'm glad you're here!" exclaimed Sir Henry Ashe, leaning heavily against the doorframe for support. "Mark all that you see, man, and be ready to swear to it!"

The girl's hand fluttered to her mouth. "You're—you're not dead!"

"Aye, and no thanks to you, you murdering slut!" growled the baronet. His wig was gone and across his shaven head was a gash that bled profusely across his face, and his shirt and coat were soaked red. "Strike me with a candlestick and leave me to die like a dog!"

"You frightened me. You would not listen—"

"Ungrateful baggage, after all I've done for you!"

"Oh, such fine things you've done for me, Sir Henry!" the girl cried bitterly. "You took my trust and respect and my innocence, too, and treated them as if they were worth no more than a handful of dust!"

"Enough of your lies, you little chit!" His mouth twisted with rage, Sir Henry raised his blood-streaked fist to strike her. The girl squeezed her eyes shut and braced herself for the blow.

But the blow never fell. Instead Kit grabbed Sir Henry's wrist, holding it so tightly over the man's head that the baronet yelped with pain and frustration.

"The devil take you, Sparhawk, let me go! How dare you interfere in my personal affairs!"

Disgusted, Kit released Sir Henry and watched him retreat, rubbing his wrist. Kit could feel the girl hovering close behind him, her hands resting lightly on the back of his coat. She needed him to protect her, and he would not let her down. "If you call beating this young lady part of your personal affairs—"

"Lady!" Sir Henry spat out the word contemptuously. "This jade's no more a lady than I! She's a wicked, cunning little creature, and don't let her tell you otherwise."

"Hold your tongue, Ashe." Kit struggled hard to control his anger. He was a large man and a strong one, and Sir Henry was neither. If he gave in to the impulse to strike the baronet's fat, choleric face, he'd likely finish the task the girl had begun with a single blow. "From what I can see, you've precious little right to call yourself a gentleman."

"Take care what you say, sir, or I'll demand my satisfaction!"

"Don't tempt me, Sir Henry," snapped Kit. "Pistols or swords make no difference to me."

Furiously Sir Henry blotted at the cut with his folded handkerchief, peering up at Kit with his other eye. "You would defend her, Sparhawk? Be her gallant? God's blood, are you her lover, too?"

"No, blast you! I don't even know her name!"

"Then permit me to introduce you to the little strumpet you've staked your honor on." Slowly he circled around Kit until he faced the girl. To Kit's surprise, she did not flinch when Sir Henry took her hand and drew her forward. "Lady Dianna Grey, meet Christopher Sparhawk. He's from the American colonies, and more accustomed to red savages than London ladies like yourself, sweetheart. He can't see beyond your pretty face to the black, rotten heart you keep inside."

The girl twisted back to look beseechingly over her shoulder at Kit. "Go now, Master Sparhawk," she said hurriedly. "You need hear none of this. Sir Henry was right. This is not your affair. Aye, you've been kind, but there is no place for kindness here. Go, please, I beg you!''

Before Kit could answer, Sir Henry jerked her sharply by the arm. ''Oh, he's not going yet, Dianna. I'll wager he won't leave you. What did you say to make him your champion? Did you tell him I'd seduced you? Did you play the poor, piteous orphan, the wounded dove?''

Bewildered, Kit watched the emotion drain from the girl's face until her expression was wooden as a doll's. He told himself he should take her in his arms and away from this house at once, but her reaction made him pause, uncertain, as Sir Henry continued.

''The dove it was, then. A pretty tale, that, and so much easier to tell him than the truth.'' Sir Henry lightly stroked the bruise on the girl's jaw, and she quivered beneath his fingertips. ''But then, you can't help yourself, can you, Dianna? You like to meld your pleasure with pain, same as I do, don't you?''

Sickened, Kit did not want to hear any more. He had known of men who claimed enjoyment in hurting their partners, but never a woman who enjoyed it, too, nor had he seen the results of such practices on a woman's body. He'd been so eager to rescue her that he'd read her all wrong, seen only what he wanted to see. And she had let him hold her, so fragile and tempting, torn silk, skin like velvet, and her hair tousled, as though she'd just stumbled from her bed....

God, he'd been such a trusting fool, a naive idiot come stumbling from the Massachusetts forest, just as Sir Henry had said. So why did he feel so damned disappointed?

''*You* are your father's legacy to me,'' continued Sir Henry smugly. ''The best he had to leave, too, considering how the money lenders chased him. Poor Jack Grey! It was perhaps for the best that he broke his neck.''

The girl winced as if she'd been struck again. ''Don't slander my father! He was a good man and loved me well!''

''Of course, he did, just as I love you, niece. But tonight you went too far.'' The baronet's hand tightened around her jaw, and his voice grew harsh. "You would have killed me, you little chit, and I cannot forgive you that."

The landing above them echoed with clattering footsteps and shadows danced from a dozen candles. Lady Frances swept down the staircase, her purple wrapper flapping loosely. Behind her followed two hastily dressed footmen carrying candelabra, one still shoving his shirt into his breeches. Lady Frances peered crossly first at Kit, and then the candlelight found her husband, covered with blood. She shrieked and ran toward him, arms outstretched. "Oh, Henry, what has happened to you?"

"It is a long story, Fanny, of no matter to you at present." While his wife hung around his neck, Sir Henry's gaze never left the girl.

"But you are injured, Henry, you are bleeding!" cried Lady Frances, and frantically she gestured to one of the servants. "Wilson, quickly now! Summon a physician for Sir Henry!"

Sir Henry shook off her embrace. "My dear, first we shall need a magistrate," he said, his voice icy calm. "Our niece has tried to murder me."

Chapter Two

Dianna sat curled on the edge of the rough, wooden bench, her feet tucked beneath her petticoats and her fur-lined cloak pulled tightly around her. She was a lady, she reminded herself fiercely, a gentlewoman of breeding who could trace her family back to kings and queens. Nothing anyone did or said could change that. No one could take that from her. And here in the chill of Bridewell Prison, it was all she had left.

In the center of the cell was a small, smoky brazier, but Dianna hung back, uncertain what her reception would be from the other women who clustered close to its meager warmth. They were debtors and drunkards, prostitutes and thieves, but she was the only gentlewoman. And the only one of them charged with murder.

Dianna sighed softly. She'd been here scarcely a week, and already the desolation of the place seemed to seep into her bones with the cold. But what lay ahead would be worse. From listening to the other women, she had come to understand what a sentence of transportation meant. In the spring, they would all be chained together and herded through the London streets to a convict ship bound for the southern colonies. She would be auctioned off like some heathen African slave, sold to a planter to work in his fields until she dropped from exhaustion. And the judge who sentenced her had pompously claimed to be merciful by not sending her to the gallows!

It shouldn't have come to this. Her lawyer had assured her

that Sir Henry's case was not a strong one, his wound not severe enough, and that the matter would likely be dismissed as a family quarrel. But that was before Master Christopher Sparhawk had testified. He'd sworn she'd tried to murder her uncle, and the judge had listened. Inwardly she winced when she remembered how, that awful night, she had trusted him, how he had seemed like a fairy-tale hero come to save her. Taller than any man she'd known, he was a handsome, golden giant with kindness in his eyes and touch. Yet once he learned her name, she had watched the kindness vanish and his expression harden. There was no point denying her uncle's lies, for no one ever believed her. She had seen it happen before with other people, and though the stranger's rejection hurt her, she was not surprised by it. She had been foolish and weak to believe he was any different from the rest. But oh, how easily he had stood before the judge to damn her with those few careless words!

She pressed her cheek against the cold stone wall and squeezed her eyes shut. Like everything else, it all came back to her handsome, charming father. Dianna's whole life had been the Honorable John Grey, and she had loved him without question. The fifth son of the Marquis of Haddonfield, her father had always lived as if he had all the prospects of the eldest heir instead of the youngest. He was witty and amusing, with a gift for music that he'd passed on to Dianna, and because he was such good company, he and Dianna had been welcome at court and in every noble house in England. But then came the September morning when his bay gelding had balked at a stream. Dianna's father was dead the moment his forehead struck the ground. The bankrupt estate of the Honorable John Grey left Dianna nothing except gambling debts and mortgaged properties and the condolences of fashionable friends who disappeared as soon as the will was read.

Of all her grand relatives, only her uncle, Sir Henry Ashe, had offered her a home, and he had expected considerably more than gratitude from his impoverished niece. By the time Dianna realized the truth, the rest of the world had already guessed, and no one believed she'd gone to Sir Henry quite as innocently as she claimed. After all, she was twenty-two, whispered the gossips, too old and too poor to make a fashionable match. What better could she hope for than the protection of a wealthy gentleman like Sir Henry?

Against Dianna's will returned the memory of his squeezing hands upon her breasts, his mouth wet upon her throat, her own cries of terror as he struck her again and again in frustration at her refusal, and then her fingers blindly grasping the cool metal behind her, the polished whorls of the heavy silver that caught the firelight as she swung it through the air—

With a noisy creak, the barred door to the cell swung open and the turnkey peered inside. The other prisoners shuffled to their feet and stared at him belligerently.

"Ah, Master Will, 'ave ye come for yer sweet Jenny again?" taunted one woman as she swung her hips lasciviously and hiked her dirty petticoats up her leg. "Ye 'ad a taste o' what I can give ye, pretty fellow, and there be more a-waitin' if yer game!"

The other women hooted and whistled at the proposition, but the man ignored it. "Dianna Grey be wanted below. She be here, ain't she?"

With every eye on her, Dianna slipped off the bench and stepped forward, and the others shuffled out of her path. The turnkey squinted at her and automatically touched his forehead and ducked as if she were still a grand lady instead of one of his prisoners. "Ye come wit' me, my lady. Master Potter, the keeper, wants words wit' ye."

"La, so it's words old Potter be wantin' with our gentry!" jeered Jenny. She caught Dianna's sleeve. "I fancy 'e'll be puttin' his tongue to other uses. Garnish, m'lady, garnish be what 'e expects from his guests 'ere, an' you'll be no different. On yer back on th' floor, you'll be no different from th' rest o' us!"

Her cheeks flaming, Dianna tried to ignore the woman's warning as she followed the turnkey, leaving the jeering laughter behind. The warder's quarters were scarcely better than the prisoners' cells, but at least he had a fireplace and a fire. Potter himself rocked back on two legs of a mouldy armchair, his feet propped up on the table that served as his desk. In one hand was a tankard of ale, in the other some sort of formal document at which he was scowling, his lips silently forming each word as he read it. For several long minutes, Dianna and the turnkey waited, until finally the turnkey noisily cleared his throat and Potter looked up.

"So this be the Grey wench, then, Allyn?"

Dianna drew herself up with what she hoped was dignity. "I am not the 'Grey wench'. I am Lady Dianna—"

Potter slammed the tankard down on the table, sloshing foam across the other papers. "Shut yer trap, hussy, or I'll toss ye down amongst th' men. They'd make short work o' a little mouse like yerself, they would. Or maybe me an' Allyn'll jes' take turns with ye ourselves. Ye be a bit scrawny for my tastes, but I ain't never had a *lady* before." He gestured impatiently. "On with it now, wench. Up with th' petticoats."

Her mouth suddenly dry, Dianna could only shake her head in mute refusal.

"Please yerself. It's naught to Allyn if he must do th' task hisself." Potter reached into the basket beside his chair and pulled out two iron rings connected by a heavy chain and tossed them to the turnkey.

Swiftly Allyn bent and grabbed one of Dianna's ankles. She jerked free and kicked his arm as hard as she could. The turnkey growled and swore under his breath, but deftly caught her leg again. This time he shoved her onto the floor and straddled her flailing legs as he clamped the irons around her ankles. Rubbing his arm, he let her go, moving quickly out of the range of her feet.

Panting from both fear and exertion, Dianna sat up and stared at her feet. Around each slender ankle was a dark band of iron. She struggled to rise and tripped on the short chain that held her legs together, pitching forward onto her hands and knees. While Potter and Allyn laughed, she awkwardly tried again, finally managing to stand.

Angry humiliation made her temper flare. "How dare you treat me this way! You're insolent rogues, the pair of you! My father never even chained his dog!"

"Aye, but th' dog was likely better bred, eh, Allyn?" Potter guffawed. "Eh, let her be. She's no matter t' us anymore anyways." He leaned over Dianna and waved the letter he'd been reading in her face. "You be leavin' us tonight, my lady. That fine gen'leman ye tried t' murder wants ye gone at once, and off ye shall go with th' tide."

"But why would Sir Henry want me gone so soon?" Dianna's voice rose with panic. "What harm could I bring him where I am now?"

"Mebbe his lady wife caused a row and wanted ye gone. Mebbe he can hear yer yappin' all the way to 'is country house. How should I know why he done it? Ye should be thankful he didn't jes' 'ave you throttled. Fer the coin he offered, he might 'ave, y' know."

"But tonight! I'm not ready to leave, not so soon—"

"Awh, yer fondness touches me, m'lady," said Potter, smirking. "But ye wouldn't 'ave suited me in the end. Guards!"

Dianna stared at him, unwilling to believe his words. As long as she remained in England, even though in prison, there was still a chance that she would be freed, that all this would turn out to be some awful mistake. "You're lying, I know it! There are no ships to the colonies until spring, until April!"

From behind, two soldiers hauled her roughly to her feet. She twisted and turned, but even in her frenzy to break free, her strength was soon exhausted and the soldiers dragged her stumbling down the stone steps and into the courtyard. After a week in Bridewell, the sky overhead seemed impossibly blue, the sun blindingly bright, and, squinting, Dianna tried to shield her eyes.

"Come on now, up wit' ye!" One of the soldiers prodded her with the butt of his rifle. She whirled around and tried to strike him, but instead he deftly caught her around the knees. Hoisting her effortlessly across his shoulders like a sack of meal, he tossed her into the back of a closed sided wagon. With a *thump* that knocked the breath from her lungs, Dianna landed on the rough-planked wagon bed, her nose jammed into a pile of ancient straw reeking of chickens.

''Don't be thinkin' of tryin' to escape, ye little baggage. Th' driver's got a pistol bigger'n you, an' he ain't 'fraid to use it. Never lost a pris'ner yet, and he won't be beginnin' wit' ye.'' The soldier slammed the gate shut and turned the key in the padlock with a clank. At once the wagon lurched forward and jostled unevenly across the rutted courtyard.

Unsteadily Dianna sat up and leaned against the wagon's rocking sides. From what she could glimpse through the slats, the wagon was travelling through streets she'd never seen before, narrow, crowded streets lined with ginshops and dilapidated taverns. Dianna shivered, and not from the cold alone. She'd fare better in China than in this part of London. Not that she had any hope of escaping. Even if she could somehow elude the guard and shed the iron shackles, she had no friends or family to turn to, no money, not even any clothes beyond those she wore.

With a sigh she reached down to rub her ankles. The heavy cuffs had shredded the silk of her stockings and left the skin beneath raw and bruised. The lace on her petticoats had been caught and torn by the chain and now, stained with mud, it trailed forlornly beneath her skirts. She had worn the same gown since her trial, and the white lace cuffs and kerchief around her neck were also creased with soil. At least the black mourning she wore for her father hid the worst of the dirt.

Finally the wagon slowed, then stopped. Dianna could hear the mewing of gulls overhead, and the air was heavy with the pungent scent of the river. She peered through the slats and saw the forest of masts and spars that marked the ships at the quays. So Potter had been right after all, and she would soon be carried away from England. Her heart pounding, she struggled to control her panic.

The driver opened the wagon's gate, and clumsily Dianna climbed out. The man said nothing as he took her arm, but the long-barreled pistols he wore belted across his chest were warning enough, and the curious crowd along the waterfront melted away in a path before them. In a way, Dianna was grateful for the guard's strong grasp, for she wasn't sure she could walk without his help. With each step the irons dug farther into her ankles, and she pressed her lips tightly together to keep from crying out from the pain. Slowly the guard led her up the gangplank of a ship bustling with final preparations for sailing, and down the narrow companionway to the captain's cabin.

Captain Abraham Welles stood leaning over his desk, reviewing orders with his first mate. He frowned at the interruption, and his scowl deepened as the guard explained his errand.

"Damn it, man, they told me you'd come tonight, not here with the sun bright as brass!" he exclaimed impatiently. "I've no time to deal with the wench now."

"I'd my orders, sir," replied the guard. "I'll not take 'er back."

"I didn't ask you to, did I? She's here and there's no changing that." Welles sniffed, then motioned irritably to the mate. "Harper, take her below with the others. And find her a bucket of water, too. She stinks like a ruddy henhouse."

"Aye, aye, Cap'n Welles." The young seaman came forward and nodded respectfully to Dianna, but the guard still clung to her arm.

"She's a bad 'un, Cap'n," he explained doggedly. "Taken for murder, she was. Best I stow her below for ye."

Dianna caught the startled glance Harper shot to Welles, and the way the older man's bushy eyebrows came sharply together. "I never murdered anyone," she began. "It was not my—"

"Silence, woman!" roared Captain Welles. He stalked around the desk, and to Dianna's embarrassment, jerked up her skirts to her knees. "Good God, so they've got you in chains, have they? What do they take me for, a blasted slaver? Free her, you black dog, then off my ship before I have you thrown into the Thames with the rest of the offal!"

Muttering to himself, the guard unlocked the shackles and stomped from the cabin. The mate followed, carefully closing the door behind him, and Dianna was left alone with the sandy-haired captain. His arms crossed, Welles leaned against the front of his desk, still scowling as he studied her.

Dianna waited, watching him warily in return. In Bridewell, she'd heard plenty of stories about shipmasters who treated the female convicts in their care as their own private harems. True, he'd had the shackles removed, but Captain Welles was still a man, and thanks to her uncle, she knew too well the folly of trusting men.

"You haven't the look of gallows-bait, I'll grant you that," said Welles at last. "No, nor slattern, neither, and God knows a mariner sees his share of those."

Dianna bristled and drew herself up proudly. "I'm no slattern, sir, but a lady. Lady Dianna Grey."

The captain's laugh was harsh. "Oh, no, my girl, you've lost your claim to that nicety. English law says you've tried to murder a man, and it's only through the mercy of the Crown that you'll not be strung up by that pretty neck of yours. On my ship there's no place for lords and ladies and other such trumped-up gentry."

"I'm none of your trumped-up gentry, any more than I'm a rascally Yankee sailor like you!" cried Dianna. "My family is older than Queen Anne's, and more noble, too, and—"

"Hold your tongue! You should have thought of that noble family before you started behaving so common. I'm your master as long as you're on this vessel, and I'll hear no more lady this-and-that, or I'll dangle you from the yard-arm myself. Do you understand me, woman?"

He glowered at her from beneath his brows until, reluctantly, Dianna nodded.

"Good." Welles cleared his throat, drumming his fingers on his crossed arms as a slow, knowing smile crept across his face. "Now, pretty lady, as to what I'm intending."

Chapter Three

Dianna braced herself for the demand that she felt sure would come.

"You don't deserve it, not for a moment," continued Welles, "but on my ship you'll have one last chance to set your life to rights. I'll put you among honest people who know nothing of you or your sins, and you'll be like any other poor lass out to make her way through indentures, though, to be sure, you'll work off your passage when I sell your papers in Saybrook."

"And what..." asked Dianna slowly, "...what will you expect in return?"

"Only that you behave like a decent woman on my ship and keep yourself clear of my men."

Even to Dianna, the proposal seemed odd, and she peered at him closely, waiting for the catch. It was very much to her advantage, and none to Captain Welles's, and yet she had the distinct feeling he was trying to coax her into agreement.

He laughed again, this time with a false heartiness, and nervously drew his hand across his upper lip. "I warrant I'm just soft-hearted and loath to see a little mite like you suffer. You'd likely not last through the crossing on one of the ships bound for the plantations in the spring. Worse than slavers for disease and dying, they are. But *Prosperity* here, she's true to her name."

There were little beads of sweat on his upper lip as he once again wiped his hand above his mouth. He's lying, Dianna realized with surprise, lying and afraid he'll get caught.

Welles glanced past Dianna to the cabin's door. "Look here, girl, I haven't all day. Truth is, *Prosperity*'s owner is a God-fearing man and wouldn't take well to a convict wench on board. You swear to act proper, and I'll see you're treated well enough."

The truth perhaps, decided Dianna, but only part of it. "It's my uncle, isn't it," she said softly. "Sir Henry Ashe. He has paid you very well to take me away, hasn't he?"

Beneath his weather-worn skin, Welles flushed and Dianna had her answer, just as she knew it didn't matter. Her life here in England was over, and had been, if she were honest, since her father's death. If she were honest, too, she would admit that the opportunity Captain Welles was offering her was not so very bad. She would be done with prison and beyond the groping reach of Sir Henry Ashe. Besides Captain Welles, no one would ever know she had been a convict.

She lifted her head high and bravely met Welles's eyes. He had accepted money from her uncle, but he had neither abused nor robbed her nor, as Potter had suggested, had he simply claimed the money and tossed her overboard.

"Please, would you tell me, Captain Welles," she said. "Is it hard work, this planting and harvesting of tobacco?"

"Tobacco! Nay, girl, I told you before. *Prosperity*'s no convict ship, and she doesn't traffic with the southern colonies. She's a Yankee ship to the heart of her timbers, and you should thank your maker she is. You won't break your back pulling tobacco leaves where we're headed! We're bound for New England, the prettiest, finest country under heaven."

"To New England, then," said Dianna defiantly. "And may I never see the old one again!"

"Cap'n's respects, sir," said the boy, "but we're passing the last landfall, if you've a mind to see it."

"Very well, Isaac, tell the captain I'll be topside directly." Carefully Kit sanded and blotted the ledger before closing it. He had worked without stopping since before dawn, striving to settle the last loose bits of his London business while the details were still fresh in his mind. The sun was high overhead now, and a break would do him good. "The last of England," some sentimental fool would feel bound to say to him, and though Kit shared no such attachments, the dark strip on the horizon would be the last land he would see for weeks, maybe months, and he'd do well to look his fill while he could.

He plucked his hat from the narrow bunk while and, with a sigh, glanced around his tiny quarters. The bunk, a folding, triangular table, a mended chair and his trunk were all the cabin's meager furnishings, yet Kit still had the sensation of squeezing his outsized frame into a child's playhouse. He thought again, longingly, of the captain's cabin and the seven-foot-long bunk tailored to fit his brother. By rights, Kit could have claimed it in Jonathan's place—he was, after all, the vessel's owner, if not the captain—but in a moment of rash generosity, he'd chosen the first mate's cabin instead, and it was too late to switch now. Besides, after the mess he'd made of this voyage, he didn't deserve any rewards.

It wasn't that he'd failed to turn a profit, for the ledgers showed he was every bit as sharp a trader as Jonathan. But in the process he'd managed to destroy the carefully built relationship with one of London's most powerful merchants and abruptly ended their best market for Sparhawk timber.

Even now he wasn't exactly certain how he'd become so embroiled in the personal affairs of Sir Henry Ashe. It had been bad enough to stumble into the quarrel between the man and his mistress, and worse still to have to testify against the girl in that circus of a courtroom. Although Kit had told only the truth, no more, no less, the lawyers had twisted his words to serve Sir Henry's case. No wonder the dark-haired girl had blamed him for her own misfortune. She had listened in silence to his testimony, denying nothing, but the look that flashed from her silvery eyes might have scalded him with hatred and reproach.

No, not a girl, but a lady, and an elegant one, too. Lady Dianna Nerissa de Vere Grey. With her face and throat ivory pale above the black silk bombazine of her gown, she had stood as proud as a queen in the defendant's box, and as the lawyers had accused her of every sort of debauchery, Kit had found it almost impossible to reconcile this self-possessed noblewoman with the frightened girl who had wept in his arms. A practiced performance, that was all it had been, and now Kit felt thoroughly disgusted with her—and with himself, which was worse—for believing it.

The disgust hadn't lessened when Sir Henry congratulated Kit on his useful testimony and gleefully expressed his hope to see his niece on the gallows. But when the man offered to show his appreciation by completing the Sparhawks' return cargo without charge, Kit's temper had boiled over. He had first wished Sir Henry to the devil, and then, while the baronet had sputtered indignantly, Kit had struck the man's fleshy jaw so hard that Sir Henry might still be lying glassy-eyed in the muddy street. No, thought Kit sourly, there would be no further business between the Sparhawk brothers and Sir Henry Ashe.

On deck, an icy wind whipped off the Channel. With his hands in his coat pockets, Kit watched with satisfaction as the ship raced across the dark green water, dancing neatly through the whitecaps. At this rate, they'd be home in no time. He pulled his hat down lower on his head and hunched his shoulders as he made his way into the wind, back to where Abraham Welles stood by the wheel.

"A fair morning and a stout breeze at our tails," said the older man cheerfully. "What more could a man want? I'll have you back among your blessed trees before you know it."

Kit grinned. After the stuffy little cabin, the wind felt good on his face and in his lungs. "I'd wager by now my brother's just as eager to back on *his* blessed ocean. He hasn't been this landlocked since he hopped off our mother's lap and toddled off to sea."

"Aye, he's part fish, that lad. Though we likely could 'ave made a shipmaster out of you, too, if you'd a mind to try." Welles shifted his clay pipe from one side of his mouth to the other, and his expression grew serious. "Have you heard more of him, Kit?"

"Nay, just that first letter from Dr. Manning, and that was only a fortnight after we'd sailed. Too soon to know anything for certain. Months ago, now." Kit frowned, his green eyes clouding as his thoughts turned to his brother. Two days before the *Prosperity* had left Portsmouth, a snapped cable had sent his brother tumbling twenty feet to the deck. His right leg had borne the brunt of the fall, an ugly, jagged fracture splintering bone and tearing into muscle. It was the kind of injury that could easily turn putrid and cost a man first his leg, then his life. That fear had haunted Kit in the months since he'd left. Again and again he'd prayed for his brother. Please, God, not Jonathan, too!

Welles touched Kit lightly on the shoulder. "Your brother's a strong man and too full of spark and rum to let a little fall best him. You'll find him hobbled, mayhap, but well enough."

Kit forced himself to smile. "Thank you, Abraham, for both of us. Jonathan couldn't have sailed the *Prosperity* better himself."

"'Twas nothing I wouldn't do again for you boys, for your father's sake, and I 'spect you know it." Embarrassed, Welles cleared his throat gruffly and squinted up at the sails. Kit, too, looked away, to the bow. For the first time he noticed a small group of people clustered along the rail, three men, and women and children, too.

"Ah, Kit, those are the passengers I told you of," said Welles, noting Kit's interest. "Likely having second thoughts about leaving home, from the looks of them."

The little group huddled against the wind as they stared back at the last glimpse of their homeland, and Kit felt a surge of sympathy for them. "Immigrants, are they?"

"Aye, and so desperate for passage they offered me double the fare. One of the women's with child, and they want to be settled before her time. When Sir Henry pulled out his cargo that way—"

Kit's tone turned chilly as the wind. "That could not be helped, Abraham."

"I'm not saying it could, Kit, am I? Nay, it just seemed

wiser to take a few passengers 'tween decks than leave the space empty.''

"I told you before that the decision was a good one, Abraham. You don't have to justify it to me again.''

"They won't be any bother to you, Kit, none at all. They'll keep to themselves. They're only on deck now to say farewell, then they'll go back down. Why, you'll scarcely know they're on board!''

Kit listened curiously. This was at least the fourth time Welles had explained about the passengers, and Kit wondered if perhaps his father's old friend had accepted that offer of a double fare and kept the difference himself. Not that Kit particularly cared—Welles had done him an enormous favor by replacing Jonathan as captain on such short notice—but Kit hoped that he wouldn't have to hear about these miserable immigrants for the entire voyage home.

"More women than men, I see," said Kit, hoping at least for a different perspective on the same wearisome topic. "Any comely daughters to ease my journey?"

"Two girls of an interesting age, but you keep those thoughts to yourself, Christopher Sparhawk! I swore to their father that this was an honest, Christian ship and his daughters' virtue would be safe enough. So you leave them be, mind, and the wives, too.''

Kit laughed. "Lord, Abraham, you make me out to be a threat to all womankind!''

Welles studied him narrowly, working the pipestem in his teeth. "You know what I mean. You're too handsome for your own good, you and Jonathan both. The pair of you have the mamas lined up from Falmouth to New Haven, hoping to get a good shot at landing one or the other!''

"It's not the mothers I fancy, Abraham.''

"Young or old, you leave them all a-sighing and swooning.'' Welles shook his head. "Now I've heard Sam Lindsey's youngest girl has set her cap for you.''

"Constance? Oh, aye, I suppose she has, like her sisters before her.'' Kit tried to remember the girl: yellow hair, or maybe it was red. He'd done no more than dance with her twice at a party last summer, and now the gossip already had them linked. "A pretty enough little poppet. I'm bringing her the ribands she begged from London, but if it's a husband she's after, she'd best look elsewhere."

"Pray her father thinks the same."

"Save your warnings, Abraham. I'm always careful with the maids, no matter how they tempt me. I'll be thirty-three years a bachelor come next spring, and I know well how to keep my neck from that particular noose."

"Truth is, Kit, you're married already, to Plumstead and the mills and trading posts and warehouses and whatever else you've built. That's well and good, I warrant, excepting I don't know how a sawmill's going to keep you warm on a January night the way a wife can."

Kit shrugged. "The farm and the rest give me back double what I give to them, which can't be said of most wives. Hester keeps my house and sets the best table in the colony, and the nieces and nephews my sisters seem so fond of producing are children enough for me." He couldn't resist grinning wickedly at the older man. "As for warming my bed, the world's full of loving, lonely widows."

Welles snorted. "You're bad as your father was before your mother caught him, sneaking around kitchen doors like some old rogue tomcat!"

But Kit only half heard him. Now that England had slipped below the horizon, the little group of passengers was beginning to abandon the post by the rail, and the men and women were carefully feeling their way across the rolling deck to the companionway. Finally only one woman remained. Although her face was hidden by the hood of her black cloak, Kit knew at once she was different from the others. She alone looked westward, her gaze intent not on what she was leaving, but on what lay ahead. Her small figure stood braced against the wind as her cloak and skirts swirled about her legs, and there was something oddly touching about how bravely she turned to meet the unknown. One of the daughters, he guessed. No matter what Abraham had promised, she might be worth seeking out. He liked spirited women, and this one, Kit felt sure from her posture alone, would have spirit to spare.

She turned her face upward, to the sky, and the wind caught her hood and whipped it back. Now Kit could see her clearly, her cheeks rosy from the wind and her lips slightly parted, and the way her dark hair, shining with copper streaks in the bright sunlight, swirled around her shoulders. He stared at her there at the rail and swore, violently, under his breath. So this was the reason why Abraham had been so anxious to keep him away from the immigrants.

Immigrants, hell. The woman was a convict.

Chapter Four

Dianna remained at the rail long after the others had left. She had spent the first three days of the voyage either retching into a bucket or curled miserably on an ancient, wool-stuffed mattress. But this morning, she had finally begun to become accustomed to the ship's motion, and the wind and spindrift on her face made her feel almost like herself again. She had never been on the open sea before, and she found the wildness of the ocean and sky exhilarating and limitless. For the first time in her life she felt truly free—free of the past and the present, and free of the responsibilities of being Lady Dianna Grey. Lost in her thoughts, she was oblivious to the curious interest of the seamen working around her, and oblivious, too, to the heated words between the captain and the *Prosperity*'s owner near the wheel. Not until her fingers and nose were numb from the cold did Dianna reluctantly turn away from the ocean and head back down the companionway.

The space she shared with the other passengers was nothing more than the orlop deck usually reserved for cargo. By hanging quilts and lashing their trunks to the bulkheads, the women had managed to divide the area for the three families travelling together.

"Ah, there now, I told ye th' wind would bring th' color back to your cheeks!" declared Mary Penhallow as Dianna slowly made her way through the clutter toward the older woman. From the first day, Mary had adopted Dianna into her

own large family. She had been the one who held Dianna
when she'd been seasick, and dosed her with peppermint oil
to ease the quaking in her stomach. Plump and pink-cheeked
and always slightly out of breath, Mary reminded Dianna of
the nurse she'd had as a baby, and she couldn't help but warm
to her.

But although Dianna's mattress was now a part of the Penhallows' circle, she still felt shy around them. She had no
experience with the boisterous give and take of a large family,
and she could not quite sort out the six younger children. But
the eldest daughter offered no such problems. Eunice Penhallow had latched on to her with the instant devotion of a shy,
dreamy fourteen-year-old, who found Dianna just old enough
to be fascinating, but not so old as to be lumped among her
mother's friends.

Even now the girl rushed forward eagerly to greet Dianna.
"I'd have stayed with ye, Dianna, but Mam said it weren't
proper to be so long before th' sailors."

"Nay, child, ye put th' words crossways," scolded her
mother. "I said 'twasn't proper for ye to be ogling th' sailor-
men, not t'other way 'round. Come sit by me, ye silly goose,
and leave Dianna to settle herself."

Eunice tossed her head smugly. "Nay, Mam, 'tweren't no
common sailor caught my eye, but Master Sparhawk, what
owns this very ship. Isaac says that where we're bound he
owns farms an' a great manor house an' acres an' acres o'
land that jus' sits fallow, he's so much of it!"

Dianna whipped around. "What is the man's name?"

"Christopher Sparhawk." Eunice's eyes grew dreamy.
"An' a more comely gentleman never lived! His smile alone
would fetch you, Dianna, an' th' span o' his shoulders, oh,
lud!"

"Christopher Sparhawk!" Dianna wailed. "By all that is
holy, how could I land on the same wretched ship with that—
that rogue!"

"Ye know the gentleman then, miss?" asked Mary curiously. "There could be more than one man by th' name."

"A great, blond, green-eyed ox who begs you to trust him

even as he lies? The worst kind of colonial oaf, so long among the savages that he can hardly speak the Queen's English?''

''Aye, Master Sparhawk is a large gentleman, and very fair,'' answered Mary cautiously. ''But for lying and th' rest, I cannot say. Captain Welles spoke most winningly of Master Sparhawk as a Christian gentleman.''

''What else could he say when he owes the man his livelihood? A scoundrel of the first order, that's your fine Master Sparhawk!'' Just in time, Dianna stopped, in her frustration nearly forgetting that the Penhallows knew nothing of her trial. Angrily she pounded her fists across her knee. Once again she'd been the foolish, trusting innocent. How Sir Henry and Christopher Sparhawk, and likely Captain Welles, too, must have laughed at her naïveté!

The boy, Isaac, came clattering down the companionway. ''Dianna Grey, yer wanted for'ard!''

Dianna stood, her hands on her hips. ''Oh, I am, am I? Dare I ask by whom?''

''Master Sparhawk himself, that's *whom*,'' said the boy scornfully, ''an' you'd best move yer tail, for he be in a righteous temper!''

Mary laid her hand gently on Dianna's arm. ''Go with th' lad, miss. Whatever th' quarrel, yer pride's not worth the sorrow ye could bring t' us all if ye cross Master Sparhawk.''

''Oh, yes, I'll go to lordly Master Sparhawk,'' Dianna said as she gathered up her skirts to climb the narrow steps, ''though when I'm done, he might well wish I hadn't.''

Muttering crossly to herself, Dianna followed the boy aft to where the *Prosperity*'s few cabins were. Without thinking she ran her palms across her hair to smooth it before she caught herself in the gesture and pulled her hands away. What did she care how she looked before a man like Christopher Sparhawk? She tipped her head forward and with angry fingers tousled and ruffled her hair and then tossed it back, satisfied that now he wouldn't think she'd primped for him.

They stopped before a narrow louvered door. Isaac knocked twice, shoved the door open for Dianna and then abandoned her at the doorway. Tentatively she peeked inside. The cabin was much smaller than she expected, low and cramped, and when Christopher Sparhawk rose from the single chair, he seemed to fill it.

Lord, how had she forgotten the man's size, his height and the breadth of his shoulders? Yet it was more than that that made the tiny space seem smaller: there was an air about him of strength and confidence that would have filled a ballroom. Although he was dressed like a gentleman, his skin was burnished dark as a common laborer's, and his hands were worn like workman's hands, the long, tapered fingers scarred and callused. Instead of a wig, he wore his own hair, dark near his jaw, but streaked to pale gold near the crown. Around his eyes and mouth the sun had etched fine, pale lines that would, she suspected, crinkle with amusement when he laughed.

But there was no laughter in his eyes now. "So it is you," he said coldly, with no further greeting. "Come in, then, and close the door. I don't want what's said between us becoming gossip for the seamen's supper."

Dianna drew herself up sharply, refusing to be intimidated by his rudeness. "Why do you wish to see me? So you can laugh or gloat at my change of fortune? Was that part of the bargain you struck with my uncle? You are a merchant, I'm told, so perhaps such transactions are common to you." She couldn't resist letting her gaze sweep past him, around the cabin. "A merchant, yes, but not a very successful one, if these are the accommodations you can buy yourself."

For a long moment Kit stared at her in silence. She stood as straight and tall as such a diminutive creature could, her whole person radiating the same pride and defiance as she had during her trial. But she was much changed from the elegant lady in the defendant's box. Her silk bombazine gown was crushed and salt-stained. Gone were the cuffs and collar of Alençon lace, and gone, too, were the dangling earbobs of pearls and onyx, and the jeweled rings that had decorated half her fingers. The wind off the Channel had brought a rosy color to her cheeks, and her hair was wild and loose, tumbling down over her shoulders and breasts as though she'd just risen from her bed. It was easy now for Kit to recall her as she had been that first night, and the memory of how neatly she'd played him for a fool returned as well.

"Oh, your tongue's tart enough now, isn't it, when there's nothing to be gained by honeyed words," he said softly. "The only transaction that's brought you here is between you and your dear uncle."

"Why should I believe you? I know Sir Henry paid Captain Welles to take me on board. Why should you be any different?"

"Because I *am* different." He remembered how Welles had sputtered and squirmed when confronted about this one special passenger. "Likely more different than any man you've ever known."

His arrogance infuriated her, all the more since he was right: she hadn't ever known a man like him. His features were hard and lean, his nose and cheekbones prominent, and there was none of the indolence about him that Dianna remembered from her father's friends. "Do you think I would have willingly come aboard this ship if I'd know you were here, too?"

"Perhaps the shackles and a Bridewell guard colored your choice." Welles had told him how she'd come stumbling into the cabin, her face white with pain and her ankles torn and bleeding from the irons. Kit caught himself wondering if the wounds had healed yet, and what the curve of her ankles must be like. "Either one of us is lying, or else Sir Henry Ashe has played us both for fools."

"You lied readily enough under oath!"

"I don't lie, my girl, not under oath, and not for the likes of you." Kit wanted to grab her by the shoulders, to shake some sense into her foolish, overbred head, but he remembered too well how soft her body was and how it had addled his judgment before. He wouldn't let it happen again, and he clasped his hands behind his back to be sure. "I told the court exactly what you told me, that you had killed your uncle."

"I struck my uncle in my own defense, not to kill him. And I am not your girl." Dianna forgot her promise to Captain Welles. "I'm Lady Dianna—"

But Kit cut her off. "You are Dianna Grey, spinster, no

more. I understand Welles made that quite clear. Or do you prefer Dianna Grey, wanton? Dianna Grey, murderess? Dianna Grey, actress? There, I think that's the one I like best.''

Dianna winced. His words hurt her so effortlessly. *Spinster, wanton, murderess, actress...* Dianna thought of the Penhallows, of Mary and Eunice and the children. She would lose their friendship in an instant if they found out about Sir Henry and the trial. ''Captain Welles promised that no one else would know.''

Kit shrugged. ''Why do you care? You've broken your part of the agreement by insisting on your title.''

''But I haven't, not with anyone else, anyway.'' Her dream of a new beginning was crumbling before it had even begun, and all because of one selfish man. She could sense him watching her with those green eyes, cat's eyes, waiting for her reaction. What does it matter to him, she wondered desperately. Why should he care? ''I swear the other passengers know nothing of who I am, and I'd—I'd rather they didn't.''

She raised her chin a little higher, and for the first time Kit noticed the cleft that divided it neatly in two. Her face was not conventionally pretty. Her aristocratic nose was a shade too long, her mouth too full to be the fashionable rosebud. But there was a sensuality to her features that attracted him more strongly than he wanted to admit. In spite of his intentions, his irritation with finding her on board was quickly changing to something a good deal more enjoyable.

''No matter how far you run, my girl,'' he said softly, ''you won't leave the past behind.''

''Then what will you do with me?'' she asked bitterly. ''Pitch me over the side? Aren't you afraid I'll defile the whole ocean as well as your sainted ship?''

He cocked one eyebrow in surprise at the bleakness of her tone. ''Nay, there must be some better use for you than that, isn't there?''

He had meant it as teasing, a way to coax the bitterness from her. But Dianna heard only the bare words. Her uncle had said the same things to her, and she knew what they had meant, just as now, she understood why she had been brought to Christopher Sparhawk's ship. The man wanted her—no, expected her to be his whore for the voyage. She felt her cheeks burn with shame, and automatically she glanced at the bunk behind him. Lord, a man of his size could kill her! Her mouth went dry, and she bit her lower lip to fight back the tears as she looked down, unable to meet his gaze.

Kit in turn could not take his eyes from her. The way she'd blushed so prettily as she'd looked at the bunk, her little white teeth nibbling on her lip as she'd glanced up at him through her lashes—God's blood, she'd have to have her invitation engraved to spell it out any clearer!

"Dianna, lass," he murmured, low and dark, as he reached out gently to stroke her hair. But when he touched her, she gasped and turned her face full toward him. It was not the tears in her eyes that stopped him. It was the fear. She was so clearly terrified of him that his hand drew back at once as if it had been burned. Awkwardly he jammed both hands in his coat pockets, wondering what the devil had gone wrong.

Dianna saw how he pulled away and relief washed over her. But mixed with the relief was a kind of chagrin, too. She had saved herself by crying, and though she hadn't done it intentionally, she felt no better than some blubbering milk-maid cornered by the master. Weak and cowardly, that's how she'd acted. What had happened to her pride?

She squared her shoulders and sniffed back the tears, fumbling for her handkerchief. "I'll have you know," she said with as much dignity as she could muster, "that I don't usually do this."

He narrowed his eyes at her suspiciously. "Don't do what?"

"Why, cry, of course." She sniffled again, loudly, and without comment he handed his own handkerchief, an enormous square of bleached homespun. "Thank you. I'm sure I don't know what happened to my own, but I'm quite short of linen for a journey of this sort."

"Indeed," he said dryly. "Not what you're accustomed to?"

"Faith, no! When Father and I travelled to Paris last spring, we had four trunks between us, and that didn't count what we bought there. You should have seen the long faces on the porters when they saw all the baggage on top of the coach!'' She began to laugh at the memory, until she realized Kit wasn't laughing with her.

He wasn't even smiling. For an instant she dared to meet his gaze and the intensity of those half-closed cat's eyes. Their expression baffled her. She saw none of the hostility that her uncle had shown when she'd refused his advances, no threats, but the question she found instead was one for which she had no answer. Quickly she looked away, lower, to the front of his shirt. His neckcloth was loose, his waistcoat partly unbuttoned, and his shirt hung open at the throat in a deep V.

She had never stood so near to a man other than her father, and curiosity unwittingly made her bold. Intrigued, she stared at the tanned triangle and the pattern of the dark curls upon it. Her eyes wandered farther, following the horsetail braid down the front of his waistcoat, across a belly that was flat and lean. Lower still, his hips seemed surprisingly narrow for the breadth of his shoulders, while his breeches were cut so snugly that Dianna looked hastily away. The breeches were tucked into tall leather boots, the leather worn and comfortable from long use, and his feet, like the rest of him, seemed enormous. She raised her gaze, stopping short again of his chin. At the base of his throat she could see the measured beat of his pulse, and wondered if it matched the quickening rate of her own.

She was no longer frightened, though even in her innocence she knew she had more reason to be now than before. Still, she stood before him and could not bring herself to meet his eyes. Instead her own gaze shifted sideways, past the row of polished coat buttons, across the expanse of his chest and shoulders. With a little shiver, she remembered how his arms had felt around her that night at her uncle's house, how he'd held her gently, like a fragile piece of porcelain, yet how aware she'd been of his strength.

For Kit, her eyes roamed over him with the intensity and the intimacy of a caress, and he wondered how she'd react if once again she looked lower and discovered the effect she'd had on him already. My God, what would happen when she actually touched him? He wanted to catch her and take her now, fiercely, while the desire ran hot in his blood. A woman this brazen would not expect to be wooed, nor deserve to be, either.

"What shall we do with you, eh, Dianna?" His question came from deep in his chest, almost a growl.

She swallowed, "That, Master Sparhawk, is—"

"Kit. Call me Kit, Dianna."

"That's—that's a decision you'll make, not I," she answered in an odd, throaty voice that refused to sound like her own. What is wrong with me, she thought uneasily. She felt giddy, almost light-headed. "Whether I like it or not, you own this ship, and I am only an unwilling passenger."

He didn't answer, and her voice slipped even lower, to scarcely more than a whisper. "That is the way of it, isn't it...Kit?"

He heard the promise in her voice, and almost groaned aloud at the eager way her lips were parted, beckoning to him. The sound of his name on her tongue was heady magic. He couldn't remember the last time he'd wanted a woman this badly.

But the tears that still glistened like tiny diamonds in her lashes stopped him. She kept changing like quicksilver, by turns coyly shy, then seductive. She was playing with him, reeling him in as neatly as a fat, open-mouthed trout. Well, he'd be damned if he took her bait. If he could get his wits out of his breeches and back into his head, he'd realize there were too many things about the girl that promised trouble. She was a convicted felon for one. She was also the niece of one of the most debauched noblemen in England, and she'd already made a fair start on a similar reputation herself. She might even try to kill him, too, the way she had her uncle; maybe Sir Henry himself had put her up to it. At the very least he might end up with a case of the French pox.

Kit frowned and shook his head, almost as if he were arguing with himself, and for the first time since she had entered the cabin, he looked away from her. Slowly Dianna felt her heart begin to quiet, and the breath return to her lungs. Strangely, too, she felt an odd sense of regret that she couldn't put into words.

"Because Welles is the *Prosperity*'s master, I'll honor your agreement with him," Kit said carefully, looking somewhere over her head. "You behave yourself, and you'll be treated as decently as any woman on board. God knows you don't deserve it, and I don't like it, but I'll honor it just the same."

With a sigh, he dropped heavily into the cabin's one chair. He stretched his legs out before him, and, with his elbows on the chair's arms, touched his fingertips together and pressed them lightly to his lips.

"You might," he said at last, "thank me."

"For what, offering to treat me decently?" She knew that was not what he meant, not really, but she gambled that he wouldn't correct her. "No, I don't think I shall thank you for that. May I return to my quarters, Master Sparhawk?"

So he was once again Master Sparhawk. Kit scowled and bent his head deeper against the arch of his fingers. "Aye, go." Damn her nose-in-the-air politeness! She made him feel as if he'd been the one dismissed, not the other way around. "No, one moment, stay."

She faced him again, waiting, and without any real reason to call her back, he asked the first question that came to his mind. "In the court, they said you wore mourning only as a sham to sway the judge to pity. Yet still you dress yourself in black. Why?"

She hadn't heard that before, and she stiffened at the implication. "My father was killed while hunting four months ago. It is for his memory alone I wear mourning."

"And your mother?"

"She died birthing me. May I go now?"

He should have said something to her then, for he knew too well the pain of parents lost. Instead he merely nodded and watched her go.

But at the door she paused, her hands balled in tight fists at her sides. "Whatever else my uncle told you about me, about my—my being his mistress, I would have you know he lied. He lied!''

She saw the disbelief on Kit's face and fled before he could see the disappointment show on her own. He despised her, that was clear, and he had accepted every foul word Sir Henry had said against her. And what was that to her? He was a liar, a rogue, the over-sized colonial ox responsible for her conviction. Why, she'd almost fainted from being shut in the same cabin with him! So why, then, did it matter so much that he believe her?

She slammed the door after her, and Kit heard her heels echo on the deck as she ran toward the forward companionway. Why the devil did she have to say that about her uncle? The more the chit denied her past, the worse he decided it likely was. He swore to himself and kicked the bulkhead. He had no choice but to avoid her for the rest of the voyage. Two months, at most three. Not so very long.

He remembered how her silvery eyes had roamed so freely over his body, and he swore again. He knew he had to leave her alone. And he knew, just as surely, that he probably wouldn't.

Chapter Five

Carefully, Dianna opened her hand and stared down at the hard half-biscuit that would be her supper and her dinner, as well. For the past four weeks, since the end of the fresh food, ship's biscuit had been all any of them between decks were given to eat, and even that had dwindled from three biscuits a day to one. The slow starving worsened each day, gnawing mercilessly at both strength and will.

Sitting on the deck beside Dianna, Mary Penhallow cradled her youngest son in her lap. The dry rattle of the boy's breathing shook his wasted little body, and he was too weak now to resist the fever that unnaturally brightened his cheeks. The arc of light from the swinging lantern overhead caught the dread in Mary's face, and Dianna looked away.

The sailor who brought the biscuits and water each morning growled that they should expect no better on a winter crossing, but Dianna didn't believe him, not with his jowls and fat belly. But the Penhallows and the others did not agree with her. The *Prosperity* was a Christian vessel, they argued doggedly, the captain a good man, a gentleman who had promised to treat them well, and to question him would only cause trouble.

The sick boy cried out fretfully. As Mary tried to comfort him, something inside of Dianna at last rebelled. Abruptly she shoved the dry biscuit back into her pocket and rose, steadying herself against the ship's rocking, and hurried toward the companionway. She could no longer sit and do nothing. Somewhere in the ship there was still plenty to eat, and she meant to find it.

Kit pushed his chair back from the captain's table and let his head drop back on his shoulders. He was past exhaustion, but even the hot stew and Abraham's rum could not make the tension in his body fade. To fight his boredom and restlessness, he'd chosen to work the same watches as the crew, and it was hard work, made harder by the winter storms that haunted the North Atlantic. Kit would not soon forget this last one, a blizzard that had shrouded the deck in white and treacherously coated every line with ice. For fourteen hours they had struggled to keep the *Prosperity* from destroying herself in the shrieking wind and snow.

Despite his inexperience, Kit was strong and agile, and that was what had mattered most. Another man on the foremast had not been so lucky. One moment Caleb Tucker had been beside Kit, reefing the sternsheets, and then the next he was gone. Kit wished he could forget the memory of Caleb's startled face as he'd lost his footing. And Caleb still scarce a bridegroom when they'd left New London, his pretty wife—widow, now—Patience, newly with child. Although he'd make sure Patience never wanted for anything, the old fear ate at Kit again. Why had Caleb died, and why had he, Kit, been spared?

"By my reckoning, Kit, we'll make New London in less than a week," said Abraham with satisfaction as he lit his pipe with a wisp from the candle. "Your *Prosperity*'s a sweet sailer, no mistake."

"She's Jonathan's, not mine," said Kit automatically. It bothered Kit that Abraham had made this assumption about his brother before, just as it bothered him that the captain seemed so unaffected by Caleb's death. But then Kit had learned more than he wished about his father's old friend on this voyage. Abraham was a superb mariner, but as a companion, he was far less satisfactory. "I may be the *Prosperity*'s owner on paper, but she's all Jonathan's in every other way."

Abraham sucked on his pipestem. "About Jonathan, Kit.

I'm not wishing ill to the lad, but if he's still not well-mended, I'd be willing to take on as captain for you again.''

"There'll be no need," said Kit quickly. "I'm certain Jonathan's fine." If Kit said it often enough, maybe he'd come to believe it, too.

"There now, Kit, I told you you'd be taking it wrong." Suddenly Abraham scowled and laid down his pipe. The rapping on the cabin door was sharp and insistent. "In with you, then, if you be in such an infernal hurry!"

It was the heady fragrance of the stew that struck Dianna first, the sweet smell of onions and, oh, could that really be chicken? She inhaled convulsively, gulping at the air as if it alone could end her hunger.

"Don't stand there a-gapin', girl," said Abraham irritably. "If you've something to say, then say it and be gone. You don't have no place here anyways."

With a little shake, Dianna drew her attention away from the table and boldly confronted the captain. "You don't give your passengers the food they've paid for."

Abraham snorted. "No French pasties and kickshaws, y'mean! What would a spoiled female like yourself know about seagoing fare?"

"I know that you're letting them starve so you can fill your purse with the difference! There's half of them sick already, some close to death, and the children—oh, the children..." She faltered, thinking of little Benjamin Penhallow.

Abraham struck his palm sharply on the table. "If things be so bad, why don't one of the menfolk come to me, eh? Why did they send a little baggage like you t'do their begging?"

"They don't know I'm here. They don't believe you'd try to cheat them or that there's more in your stores than one mealy biscuit apiece each day!"

"One biscuit apiece?" asked Kit incredulously. There should still be plenty for the passengers to eat. "One biscuit a day?"

Dianna tried to answer him evenly. Why hadn't she noticed

him there before, sprawled in the chair at the end of the table?
"Aye, one a day, and that often as not ripe with weevils."

"She's daft, Kit, a troublemaker," said Abraham quickly.
"You've told me that yourself."

But Kit wasn't listening. "Leave us, Abraham," he ordered.
"Now."

Crumbling, Abraham shrugged on his coat and left the
cabin. If the captain cared at all for his reputation, thought Kit
grimly, he'd be off to find those missing provisions, and fast.

With a sigh, Kit turned his attention to Dianna. He had
intended to ask her more about the conditions between decks,
but now that he really looked at her, he knew she had not
exaggerated. Hunger had hollowed her cheeks, and her black
gown hung loosely from her shoulders. He'd been so intent
on avoiding her that he'd forgotten the other nineteen passengers in his ship. God only knew what else that avaricious
bastard Welles had done to them, and it was Kit's fault for
letting it happen. The girl had mentioned children, sick children. Wasn't his conscience burdened enough already? Angrily he swore beneath his breath.

Dianna watched him warily in return. Kit looked well-fed,
true, but his eyes were red-rimmed, and beneath a ragged
growth of dark beard, the lines around his mouth were drawn
deeper than before. She was no longer afraid of him—if the
man had left her alone this past eight weeks, she doubted he'd
be interested in her now.

Curiously, she was almost sorry. Throughout the long misery of the crossing, she had clung to an image of Kit Sparhawk
that likely didn't exist. Instead of his scorn and betrayal, she
remembered his kindness when he'd come to her defense and
how gently he'd held her. And more. She remembered the
strange warmth she'd felt when he'd told her—or dared her?—
to call him by his given name; how his voice alone had made
her tremble. It was all pure foolishness, she reminded herself
sternly. Yet, once again in his presence, she felt agitated and
unsure, and she wished Captain Welles had stayed.

"I hope you enjoyed your meal," she said pointedly, glancing at the empty dishes. "I trust Captain Welles has gone to share your bounty with the others."

"He'll damned well do what I tell him to!" thundered Kit with a fierceness Dianna hadn't expected, and her own anger flared in response.

"So it's you who decides who goes hungry, is it?" She stepped closer to stand defiantly before his chair, her hands on her hips. "But then, Captain Welles would have nothing to gain from letting others suffer, while you could claim the profit."

Kit did not bother to correct her. Though she could not be more wrong about Welles, Kit doubted she'd listen to the truth from him.

"Why didn't you come to me sooner?" he demanded instead.

In confusion, Dianna's thoughts flew back to the last time they'd been together, in the little cabin, and how he'd rejected her. "I did not seem to find your favor, Master Sparhawk," she answered stiffly.

"God's blood, I meant come if you'd found fault with your quarters!"

Dianna's cheeks flamed with embarrassment and shame. Of course, he hadn't meant *her*. There was no graceful way to recover, so instead she rushed on. "I came to Captain Welles because I believed he could help. I did not know you would be here, or I would not have knocked. I am, you see, not accustomed to dealing with men who are not gentlemen."

His green eyes narrowed, and his response was washed with sarcasm. "Then tell me, my lady, how a gentleman would address these particular circumstances. A fine fellow of breeding and fashion. Your uncle, say."

Dianna's dark eyebrows drew sharply together. "I do not see—"

"Oh, aye, I think you do," he said softly, watching the quickening beat of her pulse at her throat. He was intentionally baiting her, challenging her, though he wasn't sure why. In a week he would be back in New London, and there would be any number of women, beautiful, uncomplicated women, to welcome him home. But, strangely, he didn't care. Dianna Grey was arrogant and corrupt, and currently quite filthy, yet he couldn't deny the excitement he'd felt when he'd seen her in the doorway. She'd plagued his thoughts, awake and asleep, ever since they'd cleared London, and he didn't like it.

She didn't flinch beneath his scrutiny, and that irritated him, too. She was too proud by half, this one. She looked close to fainting from hunger, yet not once had she asked for food for herself. Although her gown was scarcely more than rags now, she still acted the grand lady, dismissing him as if he wasn't worth her notice. Maybe that was why he was goading her now, trying to make her as angry with him as he was with her. Slowly he rose from the chair, using his full height to compel her to look up at him.

"Now tell me true, my lady," he continued with deceptive calm. "A gentleman like Sir Henry wouldn't give a crooked farthing for that sorry bunch of pilgrims between decks, and I'm surprised, my lady, that you've become their champion. Mayhap you've a favorite among the good farmers? I recall now your uncle wasn't too particular in his pleasures either, was he?"

Dianna gasped. "You have no right to speak to me like that—no right at all! The Penhallows and the others welcomed me and accepted me with kindness and without question. Not like you! You can't forget the tattle and the slander, and then you dare to stand in judgment of me for sins I've never committed! Why can't you and all the others understand! I am *not* like my uncle!"

The hint of a smile seemed to play around the corners of his mouth. "There is, my lady, one way to tell if you are, isn't there?"

Before she realized what was happening, he caught her by her arms and lowered his face swiftly to meet hers. She pushed against his chest, struggling to free herself, but his lips were already on hers and he was kissing her. The more she fought, the more insistent he became, his mouth slashing boldly across hers. She felt the rough stubble of beard across her cheek and the surprising softness of his lips as they pressed against hers.

She tried to twist away and began to protest, but he captured her open mouth. The only other man who had kissed her had been her uncle, and this was nothing like that awful experience.

This was different, very different. Dianna was unprepared for the masculine taste of him and for the sinuous dance of his tongue against hers as he coaxed a response from her that she had not known was hers to give. A curious languor swept through her body. Tentatively her hands circled around his neck for support, her fingers tangling in the thick mane of his hair. His arms tightened around her and he lifted her upward and closer against him until her feet were off the deck. She was floating weightless on a sea of new sensations, and she had no idea where it would end.

The reality of kissing Dianna was unlike anything Kit had imagined. She was smaller than he remembered, a tiny bit of a thing who'd had little enough flesh to spare before the voyage's hardships and now seemed swallowed up in his embrace. But there was nothing slight about her ardor. From the first moment their lips met, he realized she was different. There was fire there, to be sure, and a promise of more. Yet there was an unexpected wistfulness, almost an uncertainty to her response, as well, that captivated him. He tried to remind himself that this guilessness was only part of her acting, but still the kiss he'd begun in anger deepened into something else.

Or maybe it hadn't been anger at all. Maybe it was just because Caleb Tucker was dead and Dianna Grey was alive, wonderfully, gloriously alive, and able to make Kit feel that way, too. His lips traced along her jaw to the special soft place beneath her ear, and she rewarded him with a little gasp of startled pleasure.

It was that same little gasp that finally roused Dianna's numbed conscience. Why was she letting him do this to her? She heard the ragged catch in her own breathing as he whispered her name, and she closed her eyes tight against the miserable truth. He had kissed her and held her, and she had scarcely fought him at all. Rather, she had enjoyed it, and worse yet, she had freely kissed him back. Kit was right. She *was* as wanton as Sir Henry had always claimed. She tried to remember why she'd come here at all. *Remember Mary Penhallow and Benjamin and mealy biscuit with weevils.*

She twisted in his arms, trying to pull free. "You will give them food now, won't you?" she asked unsteadily.

"Hush, sweeting, now's not the time or place for chatter." Gently his lips feathered down her throat and she shivered in spite of her intentions.

"Nay, mind me." Resolutely she placed her palms against his shoulders and shoved as she tried to make her voice stern. "I want you to swear, Master Sparhawk, that you will grant your passengers the food they're owed."

"'Master Sparhawk', is it again? You kiss me like the devil's in your blood, and then it's Master Sparhawk?" Unceremoniously Kit released her, and she slipped clumsily down his body. She backed away slowly, rubbing her arms where he'd held her. The unconscious gesture jabbed at Kit's pride almost as much as her words. He felt perversely disappointed, even as he realized once again she'd bettered him. His own desire had been all too genuine. He clenched his hands behind his back and stared coldly down at her. "Pray, tell me, Dianna, are you bargaining with me?"

Dianna swallowed. There was no sign of affection in that handsome, stone-hard face. Part of her wished that he hadn't been willing to set her aside quite so easily, but his callousness also served to steady her nerve. "You are a merchant, a trader," she said disdainfully, managing a small, careless shrug. "If such terms are those you understand, then aye, we shall bargain."

Kit wondered if she would have given herself to Welles if the man had been here alone. Maybe, on another night, she already had. "A simple transaction, then, between us alone?"

Dianna nodded, though her thoughts were full of uncertainty. She had nothing to trade beyond what she wore, and he knew it. What she had asked was not complicated. Why was he bent on making it so?

His jaw tightened, his green eyes as cold as the winter sea around them. "Where I am from, my lady," he said contemptuously, "there is a word for women who would sell themselves for favors. And it's a great deal worse than being called 'merchant'."

Dianna gasped. "You're a vile, hateful rogue, a despicable snake, a—a— Oh, damn you!" She slapped him as hard as she could, so hard that her wrist stung. "I hate you and wish I'd never, ever met you!"

"And I'd say the same about you, madam!" The mark of her hand burned red on Kit's cheek, and it was all he could do to control his temper. He was tired of her everlasting games, and he refused to play them any longer. He stalked to the cabin door and jerked it open. "There, go! We have no more than a week before we reach land. If you don't wish me to throttle you before then, you will keep to your quarters and out of my sight!"

Dianna was too angry to reply, and with a little roar of frustration, she stamped her foot. She had failed miserably, and she hated to return to the others empty-handed, with no promise of relief to come. Then her gaze caught the tureen that was still half-filled with stew. She grabbed it with both hands and, cradling it to her chest, she raced past Kit and down the companionway.

Dumbstruck, Kit watched her scurry away with her prize. He slammed the door and walked back to the table, staring down at the damp, steamed circle left on the wood by the tureen and considering the maddening contradictions of Dianna Grey.

The morning the *Prosperity* finally reached Saybrook was cold and clear, the sky whipped to a brilliant blue by an icy March wind. As the word spread that their journey was almost over, the passengers rushed to the deck, eager for this first sight of their new homeland. But while everyone around her at the rail chattered excitedly, Dianna's spirits plummeted as the ship rounded Lynde Point and the town itself came into view.

No, she decided, *town* was too grand a word for the forlorn assortment of buildings strung along the waterfront. Houses and businesses alike had a raw, unfinished look, their un-painted clapboard or shingled sides weathered to a silvery gray, their proportions squat and mean. No trees softened their harshness, only mud and dirty snow and wisps of smoke that the wind tore from the chimneys.

Dianna twisted her hands in the worn remains of her cloak and tried to picture herself in such a setting. As a lady, she was both educated and accomplished. She could read and write and cipher, play on the spinet and sing, speak French and a little Italian. But none of that would matter unless the buyer of her indenture was genteel as well, and Saybrook, to her eyes, did not have the look of a genteel place.

She glanced back to where Captain Welles stood by the wheel, and at once felt reassured. He was a good man, if plain-spoken, one she could trust. He had treated her civilly since the moment he'd had the shackles removed, and he had risked the displeasure of his employer to bring the passengers food. He had promised to find her a decent place, and she was confident he would, and she thanked God once again that her future did not depend on a man as unpredictable as Kit Sparhawk.

News of the *Prosperity*'s safe return had raced through Saybrook, and already a crowd was gathering—wives and mothers with new babies, children hopping with excitement, friends and neighbors calling greetings across the water, their words frozen into clouds in the cold air. As soon as the ship bumped alongside the uneven cob dock, the welcomers swarmed on board, the joyful reunions began in earnest. The happiness was infectious, and Dianna couldn't help grinning herself. She had come this far without harm. What worse could lie ahead?

Across the heads of the jostling crowd, she spotted Kit, hatless, his long hair blowing wildly in the wind. Against her will something inside her gave a little lurch. He was laughing, his flashing smile brilliant with the pleasure of homecoming. But his eyes seemed joyless as he scanned the faces around him, and curiously Dianna wondered whose he sought. Then abruptly his grin vanished and his expression grew solemn. Effortlessly he dropped over the side and hurried to meet a young woman with auburn hair who blushed shyly as Kit took both her hands in his. She was pretty, noted Dianna miserably, very pretty, indeed and even the heavy cloak she wore was unable to disguise her obvious pregnancy. Seven months the *Prosperity* had been away, but time enough.

"Ah, so he's found Patience Tucker already," said a sailor softly to his wife. "Poor lass! 'Tis well she'll have Master Sparhawk to watch after her now."

"Not before the young ones, mind," murmured his wife, cocking her head toward the two boys who tugged excitedly at their father's coat. "They'll learn such things soon enough."

The chill that passed through Dianna had nothing to do with the wind. Too well she remembered the scandal when one of her friends had let herself be seduced by a handsome favorite of the Queen's, an earl he was. He'd gotten the girl with child, killed the girl's brother in a duel, and then Dianna's friend had drowned herself. The earl, along with the rest of London society, had merely shrugged it all away as unfortunate unpleasantness and been back again at court the next week as if nothing had happened.

So Kit Sparhawk was kinder than that, but still there seemed no likelihood of him wedding the girl. Perhaps he, too, was already married to another. Dianna watched the pair walk slowly away, her arm in his for support.

Dianna shivered, all pleasure in the morning now gone. What would have become of her if she, too, carried Kit's child? She'd come so close, so dangerously close, to lying with him, Lord help her! She had been weak and Kit had been strong, and his kiss and touch had brought a fire to her blood that she hadn't known existed. She had been willing. He had been the one to stop. Again she heard her uncle's taunting voice and his bitter accusations. New England or old, some things would never change.

For the next week, Dianna continued to live on the *Prosperity,* waiting while Captain Welles sought a buyer for her indenture. From the way he avoided her, she suspected this had not proved as easy as he'd hoped, and she hated not knowing what would come next. But steadfastly she ordered herself not to worry and tried to fight back the insecurity that gnawed at her. She still had the company of the Penhallows, who also remained on board. Soon they would begin their journey westward, by wagon, to their new land.

It was late one afternoon when Dianna and Eunice stood together on the deck, idly tossing biscuit crumbs to make the gulls wheel and dive. Dianna had been careful to choose the larboard side, away from the dock, and away from Kit, who was supervising the men unloading the hold. Every so often she could hear his laughter over Eunice's chatter, and her back would stiffen with irritation. What cause did he have to be so merry? If he was the fine gentleman he pretended to be, he wouldn't be here carousing with common sailors. Why didn't he just go away, so she could forget she'd ever seen him? Crossly she bounced a bread crust off a gull's head, wishing it were Kit's instead.

Suddenly a great clattering on the dock scattered all the gulls into noisy flight, and every man raced across to the starboard side, cheering and waving. Excitedly Eunice hurried to join them, and with an impatient sigh, Dianna followed.

"Oh, lud, ye know who it must be, don't ye, Dianna?" exclaimed Eunice, her eyes round with wonder. "It must be Cap'n Jonathan Sparhawk hisself, what everyone feared were dead!"

Dianna stared down at the man on the back of the black stallion, calling out to the crewmen as he swung his three-cornered hat over his head. He wore a scarlet coat laced with gold, the polished buttons winking in the late afternoon light, and his neckcloth fluttered over his shoulder as he expertly brought the horse to a halt at the water's edge. His clumsiness as he dismounted surprised Dianna, until she saw how he favored his right leg as it touched the ground, and the brass-headed cane he untied from his saddle.

And even if Kit had not leaped at him at once, nearly knocking him sideways with the fierceness of his greeting, Dianna would have known they were brothers. They were too much

alike not to be, both pounding each other delightedly on the
back, grinning and howling like madmen. Jonathan stood a
shade shorter and his hair was black as the stallion's coat, but
he had the same green eyes as Kit, the same powerful build
and easy physical confidence. And, decided Dianna instantly,
he had the same damnable charm.

"What a sight they be," Eunice said with a sigh, "each
one handsomer than th' other! To think there be two such,
oh!"

"And twice the trouble to bedevil womankind," said
Dianna tartly. Yet her eyes still lingered on the brothers, just
as Jonathan, over the first flush of reunion with Kit, had instinctively turned to find the two young women watching from
the rail.

"By all that's holy, Kit, you've women in my sweet *Prosperity!*" he exclaimed with relish. "Delectable ones, too, from
the look of them. And here I pitied you old Abraham's company!"

Kit scowled and made a disgusted noise deep in his throat.
"The one's a silly little maid with her whole clacking family
behind her, but the other's worse trouble by far." Briefly he
recounted Dianna's past, carefully omitting himself.

"A rogue gentlewoman!" Jonathan's eyebrows rose sug-
gestively. "She's still a plump enough little chick with that
cloud of golden hair."

"Nay, Jon," said Kit too quickly. "It's the beauty, the dark-
haired one."

Jonathan scratched his jaw, considering. He had spent
enough nights wenching side by side with his brother to know
the scrawny little creature with the thatch of eyebrows was not
to Kit's usual taste, nor had his explanation rung quite true.
"So Abraham expects to get ten guineas for her. She doesn't
look worth half that to me, but I'll buy her for you if you
wish." He grinned wolfishly. "For those cold nights at Plumstead."

"Toss your gold in the river before you spend it on her!"
exclaimed Kit, appalled at the idea. "I'd not have the little
baggage within twenty miles of Plumstead!"

Kit saw the gleam in his brother's eye and realized he'd tipped his hand. Blast the girl for showing her face to Jonathan! Tonight, in some tavern, he'd likely spill the whole sorry tale, and Jonathan, the cocksure little whelp, would just as likely gloat and taunt him for being an old, worn-out fool.

But then he recalled how close he'd come to losing Jonathan's taunts forever. For the first time, Kit noticed how heavily his brother leaned on his cane, the strain on the edge of his smile, and he realized just how much pain Jonathan's bravura entrance on horseback had cost him. He swung his arm around Jonathan's shoulder, offering support, and was both surprised and concerned by how readily his brother leaned into him.

"Come along, Jon," he said gruffly. "We've much to say, you and I, and there's far warmer places to say it."

But first Jonathan looked back to the ship, and, with a grand flourish, doffed his hat to the two girls. "Ten guineas," he said slyly to Kit, "and she's all yours. Call her my gift to you."

Eunice giggled into her hand at the attention, but Dianna wished it had been Kit, not his brother, who had turned back. With Jonathan Sparhawk now here to oversee the *Prosperity,* there would be no need for Kit to remain. This, then, could be the last she ever saw of him....

"Dianna Grey!" Captain Welles's voice was sharp, and Dianna guiltily wondered how many times he'd called her before she noticed. "Come, girl, I haven't all day."

There was a stranger beside the captain, and the frank appraisal the man gave Dianna made her blush. He wore a large-brimmed hat with a beaded band, a long black coat like a parson's and greasy leather leggings. He was not tall, but stocky, his legs bowed outward, and although his hair was wispy and white, Dianna could not guess his age. The bones of his face seemed to almost jut through his leathery skin, and Dianna feared the man himself would be equally sharp, with no softness or gentleness, no humor in him anywhere.

"Stop gawking like a lackwit, girl," growled Captain Welles impatiently. "You won't favor yourself keeping your new master a-waiting."

Chapter Six

Dianna sat on the deck of the sloop *Tiger,* her back braced against the hatch cover and sheltered from the wind. She had been there since they had left Saybrook that morning, preferring the open air to the small, stuffy cabin below and the seemingly endless dice game' her new master had begun with the two other passengers. Every so often she heard Asa Wing's voice rise above the others, and she wondered if he had won or lost.

The only thing she now knew of the man was that he liked gaming; he had volunteered nothing else about himself or their destination. She didn't even know why he had bought her indenture in the first place. He was clearly not accustomed to servants, nor did he seem interested in her in the lustful way her uncle had been. In fact, he really didn't seem interested in her at all.

She rested her head on her arms. She hated the feeling of helplessness, the way a total stranger now controlled her life for the next seven years. *Seven years!* She would be thirty then, an ancient crone, too old by far for any husband. When her father had lived, he had been family enough, but after two months with the Penhallows, she imagined herself more and more with a home of her own and babies and a husband that, to her dismay, always looked like Kit Sparhawk.

She sighed and brushed her hair back from her face. She had never been in love, but she realized how close she'd come to it with Kit. She tried hard to forget his unpredictable kindness and his smile and the way his kiss had left her breathless and eager, and tried to remember instead how he always believed the worst of her, how he'd played along with her uncle, and how he'd tried to starve them all on the *Prosperity*. And, too, she couldn't forget the auburn-haired girl who'd met him at Saybrook.

No, it was better like this, better to never see Kit again. There were other men as handsome in the world, and others who might come to love and cherish her in a way Kit Sparhawk never would.

She stared out over the water. The river had grown narrower, and shallower, too. The rippled surface had changed from green to silver, and the tang of the ocean faded as salt water gave way to fresh. The landscape was changing as well. First the town had been replaced by neat farms, barns and houses centered in snow-dappled fields. Then had come the wild meadows, where big trees had long ago been cut for timber and firewood and where new saplings grew brave and leggy among the stumps. But now, as the sun dropped low, there seemed nothing but old snow and rocks and trees, endless trees, their dark boughs hanging over the river and brushing against the sloop's mast.

"Here, girl, you'd best eat." Startled, Dianna looked up as Asa squatted beside her and handed her a chunk of the coarse bread he was eating. He wore soft-soled shoes, sewn of leather, that had made his footsteps silent, and the ease with which he could appear without warning unsettled her.

Chewing, he flipped up one corner of her cloak and fingered the fur lining. "What d'ye Londoners pay for a cloak like this?"

"I don't recall exactly," said Dianna. "Seven, perhaps eight guineas. My father bought it for me."

Asa grunted with disbelief. "Mighty dear for rabbit."

"Nay, it's beaver. Madame du Paigne would not have sold rabbit in her shop."

"Nay, girl, 'tis rabbit," he countered amiably, unimpressed by Madame du Paigne or her shop. "Oh, it's been dyed an' clipped to look fair, but them pelts grew up by hoppin', not swimmin'.''

He uncorked a small earthenware jug and tipped it back. When he was finished drinking, he sighed contentedly, wiped the jug's neck with his thumb and offered the jug to Dianna. She shook her head, but decided instead to take advantage of his good humor. He must, she thought, have been the winner in the game below.

''Where are we bound?'' she asked.

''Wickhamton.''

He might have said the moon for all that meant to her. ''Is that where you live?''

''Near enough. Though the house be Mercy's now.''

''Is Mercy your wife?''

''Nay. *That* needle-tongued article left so long past I disremember her face. But I miss our lad,'' he said sadly. ''Aye, Tom I miss.''

He recorked the jug and pointed ahead to where the river curved. High on the spit of land stood a square log building. ''We'll sleep at Brockton's ordinary this night.''

There was no dock, and Dianna wondered if she'd be expected to wade ashore through the icy water, or worse yet, be carried. As the sloop hove too close to the bank, one of the crewmen swung a long, thin board from the sloop's side to the riverbank to serve as a gangplank. Asa went first, and quickly Dianna followed—too quickly. To her surprise, the plank still bounced up and down from the weight of his footsteps, tossing her upward. Instinctively she outstretched her arms for balance like a ropewalker and kept her eyes straight ahead. When she reached the shore, the sailors laughed raucously behind her, and she knew then they'd expected her to tumble off. So much for *their* fun, she thought crossly, and trotted after Asa.

She had not realized how cold she'd become until she stepped inside the ordinary and felt the welcoming warmth from the hearth. There was only the one room, the walls unpeeled logs and the floor packed earth. Five men, dressed piecemeal much like Asa, sprawled on benches around a trestle table, eating and drinking with their hats still on. Before the hearth, a haughty black woman with notched earlobes stirred her kettles, and a man leaned against the wall, smoking a Dutch clay pipe. Every last one of them turned to stare at Dianna.

"Ye be a mite old to start up with a trollop, Wing," said the man with the pipe, speaking what the others were all thinking. "How'd you coax her t'come with yer sorry old carcass?"

Asa rested his hand on Dianna's shoulder. "Keep yer foul thoughts to yerself, Brockton. This be a lady, not a trollop, and she's come to help me wit' Mercy. Stay close to me, Annie," he said stoutly, "and these rogues will show ye no mischief."

It was the first time anyone had shortened Dianna's name to Annie and the first time Asa had called her anything more than "girl." Dianna stared up at him in wonder. He was defending her honor. There was no other way of looking at it. He believed her a lady, and even here in this rough inn in the wilderness, he was insisting on her being treated like one. The questions of what her tasks would be or who Mercy was, seemed suddenly insignificant. She would have her new start after all. Asa's unexpected gesture warmed her more than the fire, and she couldn't help smiling shyly as she slid onto the bench beside him for supper.

They ate beans steeped in molasses and laced with salt pork, and drank cider that was thick and sweet. When at last the wooden trenchers were cleared away and the table and benches pushed back, each man wrapped himself in his blanket or coat and lay down on the dirt floor. Reluctantly Dianna joined them, doubting she'd sleep at all among the snoring and wheezing bodies.

But almost at once the black woman was shaking her awake, and Dianna gulped down her breakfast as she hurried to meet Asa. She found him by the river, loading his bundled belongings into a long, bark canoe. With him was a wiry young man with waist-length hair like cornsilk and pale eyes that were oddly blank.

"We'll make our own course from here," explained Asa.

''I've stops to make along the way, but we should reach Wickhamton in three days' time. This 'ere be Jeremiah, and he'll paddle stern.''

The pale young man stared at Dianna, but did not return her smile, and inwardly she shivered at the emptiness of his expression.

''Y'must not mind Jeremiah,'' said Asa. ''He's not full right with his thoughts. When he was a lad, the Abenakis took him captive. Six years he lived with 'em, until his people finally paid the ransom. More red than white he was by then, an' kind of daft in th' head. But he's good with a paddle an' don't talk overmuch.''

''How terrible,'' murmured Dianna, but she still found Jeremiah's staring eyes disturbing. ''Thank God the Indians are gone now.''

Asa snorted. ''That's what ye Londoners may believe, but here, we know otherwise. Oh, Indians don't go in fer showin' their faces unless they've a reason, an' these days, they've kept to themselves, mostly, 'cepting for all that trouble at Deerfield, of course. Sorry sad business, that. But there be good Indians an' bad, same as white folk, an' if I knew for certain what riled 'em, I'd be sittin' in Boston with the other peri-wig-lords.''

''Are there Indians at Wickhamton?''

Asa shrugged nonchalantly. ''Nay, not t'bring ye any grief. I'd worry on other things afore Indians, like bears an' snakes an' wildcats an' such.'' He fastened the last bundle in place with rawhide straps. ''Now get ye in, Mistress Annie, else we stand here a-jawin' 'til midsummer.''

Not at all reassured, Dianna climbed into the center of the canoe. Of course, she'd read about Indians—Asa was right about Londoners loving every thrilling story about dangerous savages in the wilderness, especially those vanquished by true-hearted Englishmen—but she hadn't dreamed they'd be part of her new home, any more than she'd considered the string of wild animals he'd named. Now behind every tree or rock, she was convinced she saw an Indian lurking, or a bear at the very least, and she was relieved when Jeremiah shoved the canoe into the water and they floated gently into the river.

As Asa promised, they reached their destination after three days of travelling. At nightfall, they pulled the canoe onto the bank as they had the two previous nights, but this time Asa and Dianna left Jeremiah behind and headed off into the woods. After months of inactivity, Dianna was in no condition to keep pace with Asa, and even though he willingly paused for her to rest, she was out of breath and the stitch in her side refused to go away. Although it was April, snow still covered most of the ground and ice soon packed into Dianna's shoes until her feet were numb from the cold. She had no idea how long or how far they trudged through the moonlit forest, and it seemed as if they had crisscrossed the same piece of ground over and over. She was close to weeping from cold and weariness when Asa stopped and pointed to a clearing ahead.

"We're here at last, Annie," he said happily. "You'll take to little Mercy, I know it. Ye both be cut from th' same cloth."

Yet even by moonlight, the house in the clearing was not what Dianna had expected. It was small, very small, with a peaked roof that slanted lower over the back. The clapboarding was unpainted and worn dark, and the windows were tiny casements of oiled paper, not glass. There were no shutters or trimmings, no decoration at all beyond a crude border of nailheads hammered into the massive plank door.

Eagerly Asa hurried to the house, and pulled open the rope latch. "Mercy, child, come and give yer old grandfer a kiss!" he called. "I'm happy ye not be abed yet, for I've someone for ye to meet, someone t'help ye wit' the house."

"But I don't need any help, Grandfer!" cried a small, anguished voice. The only light in the room came from the last embers of the hearth fire, and by it Dianna could finally make out Mercy herself. She had plump cheeks and a turned-up nose and dark hair that straggled from beneath her linen cap. A knitted woolen tippet was tied over her shoulders and around her narrow waist, and her hands, in fingerless mitts, twisted nervously in her apron. She looked to be six, perhaps seven, and Dianna was shocked that a child so young had been left alone. No wonder she seemed frightened! "If you'd only let me stay at Plumstead—"

"Nay, Mercy, an' that's an end to it!" said Asa sharply, and his granddaughter's shoulders sagged unhappily. Huddled in the half-light, she looked as lonely and forlorn as Dianna had often felt herself, and her heart went out to the waifish child.

"Mercy, my name is Dianna, Dianna Grey," she said softly, holding her hand out in greeting. "I hope we might be friends, you and I—"

But Mercy cut her off, shaking her head fiercely. "Nay, I want none of ye, mind?" Her words strangled on the sob in her throat. "None of ye at all!" With her head down, she bolted past them and out the door.

Dianna called her name and began to follow, but Asa held her back and gently closed the door instead. "She'll be back in her own time. She'll be off to weep among th' beasts in th' barn, an' she'll come to no harm." Sighing, he prodded fresh life into the dying fire and sat heavily on the three-legged stool Mercy had fled.

"But where are her parents? Surely a girl her age—"

"Dead, the pair o' them, not twelve months past, of a putrid quinsey," said Asa. "My lad, Tom, an' his wife, Lucy. Poor Mercy! She cannot accept it as God's will that she be spared an' her parents taken, an' she grieves more than is right for a young one. Y'see now why she needs ye."

No wonder she had felt a bond to the girl, thought Dianna sadly. "And this place she spoke of, Plumstead…?"

"Ah, that be the colonel's great fine house." Asa's voice hardened. "Like a lord he be in these parts, that man, an' because my Tom called him friend, he strives to take Mercy from me. Claims he could do better by the girl. Well, that may be, but Mercy's all th' blood kin I've left in this world, an' kin should stay wit' kin, t'my mind."

Dianna rubbed her arms and stared at the closed door. "Are you sure we shouldn't go after her? It's a cold night."

Asa shook his head. "Nay, it's best to let her sort it out

herself. She'll come in when she be ready.'' He rose stiffly from the stool. ''Now I'll show ye where you're t'sleep, up here in the loft.''

But tired as she was, Dianna did not sleep until she heard Mercy come inside. Quietly the girl refastened the latch and, creeping past her snoring grandfather, joined Dianna in the overhead loft. From her breathing, Dianna was certain the girl did not sleep, either, but she respected her silence and the privacy of her grief. Cut from the same cloth they most definitely were.

Chapter Seven

Dianna intended to rise early the next morning and have breakfast waiting on the table for Asa and Mercy. But the sun was well up by the time she awoke, and ruefully she realized the other two were already gone from the house. After three months of sleeping on floors or decks, one night in a bed, albeit one with rope springs and a mattress stuffed with rustling corn husks, had reduced her to a lazy sluggard.

She washed quickly in a bucket of water by the ladder, hoping that Asa hadn't brought it especially from the well for her, and neatly braided her hair the way Eunice had taught her on the *Prosperity*. Then came the question of what to wear. With her London gown little more than rags, Asa had told her to take what she needed from the chest of clothing in the loft. First came a bleached linen shift, the soft, clean fabric almost unbelievably luxurious against her skin. Over that she put a dark red kersey skirt and a bodice of blue linsey-woolsey. She fumbled awkwardly to thread and tie the laces behind her back and cursed the lifetime of pampering lady's maids that had made her embarrassingly clumsy at dressing herself. Finally she tied on an apron and backed down the loft's ladder to the one large room below that served as kitchen, keeping room and parlor.

Hands on her hips, she surveyed her new domain and considered where to begin with breakfast. That she had absolutely no experience cooking did not faze her; it could not be so very difficult, given some of the thick-witted cooks she'd met in her father's houses. She decided to try eggs. All men liked eggs for breakfast, and there was a large basket of them on the table. But first she must build up the fire, and she went outdoors in search of firewood.

The woodpile was not far from the house, and for good measure she chose the largest log from the top, staggering with it in her arms as she returned to the house. At the doorway she spotted Mercy, trudging from the barn with a bucket of milk.

"Good morning!" called Dianna cheerfully. "It's a fine day, isn't it?"

Stunned, Mercy's face went white as she studied Dianna from head to foot. "You're not my mother," she said as she backed away, the milk sloshing from the bucket over her clogs. "Ye may take her place and her clothes, but you're not her and ye never will be!"

"Mercy, wait, please!" But Mercy had already retreated to the cowshed, leaving a trail of spilt milk on the bare ground. Of course, the girl would be upset to see her dressed like her mother; Dianna blamed herself for not being more considerate. After breakfast she would go and set things right with Mercy. With a sigh, she dropped the snow-covered log onto the banked embers of last night's fire, prodded the ashes for a spark and turned her attention to the eggs.

With both hands she lifted a heavy iron skillet onto the table and cracked an egg on the side. The eggshell burst with the impact, and its contents splattered down Dianna's clean apron and onto the floor, white and yolk slipping between the floorboards. The next egg made it into the skillet, but so did its broken shell, and the next three fared no better. As carefully as Dianna tried to pick out the bits of shell, the pieces only slid farther from her fingers into the slippery mess in the skillet. She frowned, concentrating, and not until her eyes stung and she was coughing did she realize the house was filled with smoke. The fire, something was wrong with the fire, and she turned toward where she thought it was. But there was only more smoke, thick and acrid and blinding her, choking her.

Panicking, she tripped and stumbled to her knees and groped across the floor.

Then suddenly she felt an arm circling her waist and pulling her from the smoke, a masculine arm that, even as she coughed, she knew was too strong and muscled to belong to Asa. The man was carrying her now, out the door and to the fresh air, murmuring odd bits of nonsense to comfort her. He propped her up against the well as she struggled to get her breath.

Then Kit Sparhawk sat back on his heels and swore, long and colorfully, at the woman he thought he'd never see again. She was garbed simply now, like any decent Yankee good-wife, though covered with soot and her eyes red-rimmed from the smoke. But even before he'd seen her face he had recognized her at once from the way her small body had filled his arms, and the dismay he'd felt had been tempered by a fierce joy at finding her again—a joy that angered him for being both unreasonable and irrational.

Coughing, Dianna could only stare at him in return with equal dismay. She had believed him left behind with the *Prosperity* in Saybrook, yet here he was, every bit as handsome as she remembered, and every bit as angry with her, too. He was, she decided, dressed quite outlandishly. Gone was his English gentleman's suit. In its place was a coarse linen hunting shirt, the yoke and collar elaborately fringed to emphasize the width of his shoulders, and a bright woven sash knotted around his waist. He wore deerskin leggings, not breeches, the soft leather straining across the muscles in his thighs as he knelt, and on his bare feet were moccasins. A curved powder horn with pewter tips swung from his neck, along with a fringed leather bag for rifle balls, and tucked into his sash was a long knife with a stag-horn hilt. Yet it all suited him, and with his long, sun-streaked hair and his cat's green eyes, he looked like a savage himself.

"Dianna Grey," he said at last. "What in God's holy name are you doing here?"

Dianna's lungs were still too choked to reply, but Mercy, standing close to Kit, was quick to answer for her. "Grandfer says she's to watch o'er me, but I ask ye, who's to watch o'er her? She don't even know wet wood from dry, nor split from a blessed log. Faith, she near smoked us like a very ham in our own house!''

Humiliated, Dianna saw the wretched log still smoking beside the door where Kit had tossed it, and she prayed he hadn't seen the mess she'd made of the eggs, as well.

Kit stood, wiping the soot from his hands with a red handkerchief. ''You'd best come back with me. I can't leave you here, not until your house has a chance to air. Asa will guess where you are.'' He smoothed his hair back from his brow, and settling a broad-brimmed beaver hat on his head, he gazed contemptuously at Dianna. ''Are you well enough to ride?''

Dianna nodded. She should thank him for rescuing her, but the words stuck stubbornly in her throat. If he'd known it was she in the house, he probably wouldn't have bothered. ''How should I know the log would smoke?''

''Because any child in these parts should, and would, or risk killing himself with stupidity like you very nearly did.'' He clicked his tongue, and a black stallion like the one Dianna had seen his brother ride into Saybrook came to him and nuzzled his shoulder affectionately. He had been hunting; his rifle and three dead partridges hung from the saddle. ''Though ladies, I suppose, do not dirty their hands with such tasks.''

''Lady!'' exclaimed Mercy, her turned-up nose turned even higher. ''She looks like no lady I've ever seen!''

''Oh, aye, Mercy Wing, and you've seen so many to judge,'' said Kit dryly. ''Don't be fooled by how she looks now. She's more things than you've ever dreamed.''

Mercy frowned and sucked in her lower lip, considering. ''How d'ye know her, Kit?''

''I know Master Sparhawk from London,'' answered Dianna, tired of being discussed as if she wasn't there. ''And don't be impertinent, Mercy. He's your elder, and you call him Master Sparhawk.''

Mercy's frown deepened. ''Kit's my friend,'' she said stubbornly, ''and I'll call him Kit.''

''Dianna's right, Mercy,'' said Kit, laughing. He caught the little girl's hands and lifted her, giggling, high into the air. With each word he pretended to drop her, and she shrieked with delighted excitement. "You're the most impertinent little baggage in this entire colony, and you'll never be a lady yourself until you learn some manners! Now up with you!"

Lightly, he boosted the girl up onto the horse and turned expectantly to Dianna.

"Where will you ride?" she demanded crossly. The silly play between the two had made her feel even more like an outsider.

"Why, on Thunder, of course. He'll scarce notice a mite like you in front of me." Slowly he smiled, smug and superior. "Unless you're afraid."

Exasperated, Dianna stepped closer to him, her hands on her hips. "By now, Master Sparhawk, you should well know I am not afraid of you or anything to do with you. But I don't see what good will come of traipsing off with you God knows where just because you wish it."

Kit toyed with the reins in his hands, and ever so slightly, his smile widened. "Mercy wants to come with me. She's had no breakfast and knows she'll eat well at my house. You are, nominally at least, her caretaker. You can come with her and with me, or you can remain here and answer to Asa as to why you abandoned your charge."

Dianna hated to admit that Kit was right, though, of course, damn him, he was. She had already turned the house into a smoky disaster. What would Asa think if she let his granddaughter run off without her, as well? In frustration she stamped her foot. "Well, then, let's be off. I've no— *Oh!*"

With his hands on her waist, Kit picked her up as easily as a doll and sat her on the horse behind Mercy. In another moment he had swung himself into the saddle, and with his arms circling around them both, he urged the big horse forward. Dianna fell back against Kit's chest; there was no way to avoid it. Despite the layers of clothing between them, she was aware of the warmth of his body touching hers, the strength of his thighs beneath her own as he guided the horse. Sternly she reminded herself that Mercy was her responsibility, and she clasped her arms around the little girl's waist for safekeeping. Better to think of Mercy than of how her own body seemed determined to slide against Kit's. Lord help her, how far *was* his house?

But for Kit, who knew the distance was short, the ride seemed interminable. He was all too aware of the soft curve of her hip and bottom pressed against him, and her wriggling as she tried to ease away from him only made matters worse. He recalled how sweet her mouth had been to kiss and how passionately she had responded to him, and he almost groaned aloud at the memory. Beneath his nose her hair smelled smoky, plaited into a thick, tight braid. How he'd like to set it free and bury his face in the silkiness as he kissed her lips, her throat, her breasts—

"There be Plumstead now!" cried Mercy excitedly.

Sitting high on the crest of a hill, the house itself was old-fashioned by English standards, a bit rough-hewn in its lines, with sharply peaked gables and diamond-paned windows. The second story overhung the first, and elaborately carved pendants hung at the corners like giant water drops. From the center of the shingled roof rose a massive chimney, shaped and angled like a castle's tower, the pink brick in contrast to the dark, weathered clapboarding below. But in this setting, on land so recently claimed from the forest, the house seemed exactly right. Dianna could imagine it in the summer, when the hill that rolled down to the small river would be green and the two huge beech trees would shade the twin benches by the front doorway. Plumstead: Kit Sparhawk's home, and the home of the man who wished to steal Mercy away from her grandfather.

"Follow the child," Kit said to Dianna as Mercy scrambled off the horse and raced for the back door. "She knows today's baking day, and she'll lead you straight to Hester and the sweetbuns."

Self-consciously Dianna untangled herself from Kit and slid off the horse before he could help her. She began toward the house, then paused. "Why do you wish to take Mercy from

Asa?'' she asked curiously. ''That you are fond of the girl is
clear, but he is her grandfather and he loves her.''

She was startled by how quickly Kit's expression grew hard
as flint. ''You have been among us but one day,'' he said
sharply. ''Don't be so quick to judge matters you can't understand.'' He jerked the horse's head toward the barn and left
her alone and puzzled.

''Welcome to Plumstead, mistress!'' called a merry female
voice, and in the kitchen doorway stood a tall, angular woman
wiping her hands in her apron, squinting into the sun as she
smiled at Dianna. ''I'm Hester, Hester Holcomb, an' y'must
be Asa's new servant, Dianna! Mercy's already told me ye
had a smidge o' trouble with th' hearth. No matter, I say.
Ever'one's different. Ye best come get yerself tidied, now, an'
have some tea an' cookies.''

Shyly, Dianna followed Hester into the house. The Plumstead kitchen was huge, running almost the entire length of
the house, and the plaster above the wainscotting was painted
golden yellow. Iron skillets and kettles, marsh-willow baskets
and bundles of dried herbs hung from the rafters overhead.
Three dozen loaves of new bread were laid out to cool on the
long table, and the sweet fragrance of baking filled the room.
There was no sign of Mercy, and in a way, Dianna was glad.
Responsibility or no, she'd had quite enough of the girl this
morning.

She watched as Hester deftly used a long-handled peel to
shove a pan of cookies into the oven behind the hearth. ''Are
you Master Sparhawk's cook?''

''His cook, his housekeeper, his laundress, his chambermaid
an' whatever else he needs.'' Hester swung the iron door of
the oven shut. ''With only Kit, Plumstead don't need more'n
me. Not like th' days when there were six Sparhawk children,
all runnin' wild an' underfoot.''

''Is that why he likes having Mercy here?''

''I warrant so, aye.'' The woman looked away, and her
answer had a forced heartiness that made Dianna wonder what
she hid.

"Will Kit—I mean, Master Sparhawk—eat all this himself?"

Hester laughed. "Nay, 'tis just for th' dinners for th' farm workers. Kit believes a man gives better work when his belly's full. He be a good master that way, better'n most. But tell me of London! It's been forty years since I left, an' neither Jonathan nor Kit be much for recalling how th' ladies be dressin' their hair."

Dianna perched on the edge of a tall stool and scrubbed at her face with a towel. "Of course, I can tell you such things, if you wish, Hester, but this morning I'd rather speak of useful things—all the things I can't do and you can."

Now that she'd begun, the words tumbled out, and she balled the towel up in her fist. "I can't cook or bake or make a fire or *anything!* I don't even know how to get water from the well! Mercy's right. She'd be better off looking after me, for all the good I can do her!"

"Ah, now, 'tis only because you've never had t'make do, not because y'can't." Hester patted her shoulder, leaving a floury white handprint on Dianna's sooty bodice. "Ye be clever enough. I can see that. Y'only need someone t'show ye how."

"Then, please, please, I beg you, Hester, teach me how!" cried Dianna eagerly. "Teach me now, this morning, how to cook and keep a house and—"

Hester laughed again, deep in her chest. "Oh, lass, I'll be needing more'n a morning to learn you all that! I'll send ye home today with enough t'keep Mercy an' Asa from complaining. Tomorrow's the Sabbath, an' no work's done, but ye come back with Mercy on Monday, an' I'll begin your schooling proper. We'll make a huswife from ye yet!"

But Dianna's enthusiasm faded. "I'm sorry, Hester, but I don't believe your master would want me back in his home. He—he doesn't care for me."

Hester rolled her eyes. "I'd like t'see the time when Kit Sparhawk turns a pretty young lass like ye out o' Plumstead!"

"Nay, truly, he hates me. I sailed from England on the *Prosperity*—"

"On the *Prosperity!* Don't mark a single word Kit said on *that* ill-starred venture!" exclaimed Hester warmly. "Why, ye be lucky ye weren't starved down t'your bones by that old skinflint Welles, th' devil claim his greedy soul! Fancy him trying t'blame it on Kit, too, as if the Sparhawks haven't always been known for their charity t'others! Keeping back food from children—why, that near broke Kit's heart, he's so besotted with th' little creatures."

Dianna listened in confused silence. It had been Captain Welles, not Kit, who had brought the food to the passengers, yet Hester would know the two men far better than she. Loud voices outside interrupted her thoughts, and both she and Hester hurried to the window.

"I'll see t'my own granddaughter, Sparhawk!" Asa was shouting angrily. He had jerked off his hat and was shaking it for emphasis. "She don't belong to ye, mind? Ye can't make Mercy take th' place o' the one that be lost!"

On his way from the stables when he'd met Asa, Kit held his long-barreled rifle in one hand and the string of bloody partridges in the other, and even from the window Dianna could see the anger in his green eyes. "You're a trapper and a trader, Wing. You've no place in your life for a child. You can't go off with Jeremiah and leave Mercy behind in that house alone!"

"But I'm telling ye, she won't be alone!" insisted Asa. "That's why I brought Annie back from Saybrook!"

"Worse than alone, then! Did Welles tell you why she's here? What kind of woman she is?" Dianna felt her face grow warm. Better he should have left her to die in the smoke than to have to suffer through this!

"I'll not hear you speakin' ill of Annie! She seems a good lass t'me, an' if she's made mistakes, she's a right t'leave them behind."

Kit slammed the stock of his rifle down on the ground. "But to leave a sweet child like Mercy in the care of an ignorant hussy like Dianna Grey—"

It was too much for Dianna. She charged past Hester and out the door, and with both hands shoved into Kit's chest as hard as she could. "I am neither ignorant nor a hussy, you great mindless bully, and—"

But before she could finish, Asa's open palm caught her square on the jaw. Off balance, she tumbled backward onto the ground. She rolled over quickly, ready to fly at Asa now, but the shocked look on his face stopped her.

"Don't ever shame me like that again, Annie," he said, his voice shaking, almost pleading. "Master Sparhawk be a selectman an' colonel of the militia an' the magistrate, too, an' yet in your temper, ye struck him. Annie, he could have ye whipped in Wickhamton for less!"

He glanced briefly at Kit, then down at the ground. "The lass meant no harm, Master Sparhawk, an' I'll see she'll not do it again," he said contritely. "Now fetch Mercy, Annie, an' we'd best go home."

It was all Kit could do not to pick Dianna up out of the dirt himself. He had never hit a woman, nor would he ever order one whipped, despite what that old fool Wing had said. She looked so small and pitiful, rubbing the dirt from her hands as she slowly rose to her feet, that he instantly regretted what he'd said about her. No, not what he'd said, for that was the truth. But regretted that she'd overheard him. He wished he could let her leave her mistakes behind and begin all over with her, as he would with any other woman he might meet. But that meant wishing away the past, and not even the Sparhawks had the power to do that.

Drawn by the noise, Mercy came behind him, her small hand clutching the hem of his shirt. For one bittersweet moment, Kit let himself imagine it was his sister Tamsin there instead, giggling, counting on him to rescue her again from whatever mischief she'd started. But he hadn't rescued her when she'd needed him most, and she'd been only seven then, Mercy's age.

With measured carefulness, Dianna smoothed back her hair and brushed the new dirt from the fall off her sooty apron. Only then did she dare to meet Kit's eyes. But instead of the smug satisfaction she'd dreaded to find on his handsome face, there was nothing. His thoughts were clearly a thousand miles away, and she felt his disinterest more sharply than the contempt she'd been prepared for. It hurt her feelings, but more than that, it hurt the one thing she still clung to most: her pride.

She would adapt, and she would learn what they knew. She would survive. She would prove to them all that Lady Dianna Grey could be as clever, as resourceful, as any Yankee woman.

And she would make certain that Kit Sparhawk could never again call her an ignorant hussy.

Chapter Eight

"**Y**ou will pay for this, little brother," said Kit in exasperation as he climbed down from Thunder's back, "and I'll make certain that you'll pay in blood."

But Jonathan only laughed. "After that debacle with little lost Lady Grey, I thought you'd welcome the chance to restore your confidence with the fair sex. Consider this my last gift to you before I sail. Though you're not being particularly grateful."

"I'm feeling ambushed, that's why," said Kit glumly, wishing he'd told his brother last night that Dianna Grey was now anything but lost. He tied their two horses to one of the rings fastened to the oak tree on the green, then resettled his hat, the dark red plume fluttering in the breeze. "To bring Constance here to Wickhamton, to the meetinghouse on the Sabbath, for God's sake!"

Jonathan shrugged and brushed a nonexistent speck of dust from his coat. "I merely served as the lady's escort from New London so that she might visit her aunt."

"So she might visit herself on me like a plague is more the truth," grumbled Kit. "Well, let's get on with it, or she'll talk the ears off Dr. Manning."

They walked slowly toward the meeting house, Kit measuring his steps to match his brother's limp and in no hurry to reach the young woman waving madly from the porch. She was dressed more for a ball than Sabbath services, her purple, quilted cloak turned back to show a yellow satin gown cut far too low to be appropriate, and the way she was shrieking his name set his teeth on edge. Oh, she was pretty enough with her golden curls and pert little nose, but to have her here, in his own town, where he couldn't avoid her chattering and her husband-hunting tactics, was almost enough to make him join Jonathan on the *Prosperity*.

Inside the meeting house, Dianna sat alone on one of the back benches reserved for servants. Neither she nor her father had been much for church-going, but Asa had been adamant about her bringing Mercy to Sabbath services, though, Dianna noticed, he showed no interest in going himself. Still, the morning had dawned sunny and with the first warm promise of spring, and Dianna was eager to see Wickhamton, at three miles away the nearest town. Even Mercy had seemed less hostile, though she had been quick enough to abandon Dianna to her place with the servants while she joined another family closer to the front.

Dianna watched as the congregation gradually straggled in, hoping Hester would come and join her. Asa had made the service sound like a grim, serious affair, but at least before-hand people were whispering and smiling among themselves, and Dianna wished Hester were here to identify everyone and perhaps introduce her. So far she had received only nods and curious stares in response to her shy smiles, and when, at last, another young woman came to sit beside her, she eagerly made room.

The newcomer introduced herself as Ruth and made a great show of arranging her skirts neatly on the bench on either side of her. ''I don't know how my mistress thinks she'd fare in a forsaken place like this,'' she sniffed. ''She'd perish, she would! Our meeting house in New London's ten times finer than this, with silver candlesticks an' carving on th' pulpit!''

True, the Wickhamton meeting house was plain, the walls simply whitewashed and the benches pegged together from pine. There were no statues and no stained glass, none of the rich cushions for kneeling or embroidered hangings that Dianna remembered from the churches in London. But she

doubted the New London meeting house was so much grander
that Ruth had reason to complain, and, besides, Dianna liked
the building's simplicity, much as she liked Plumstead's and
much, too, as she already disliked Ruth. "You are visiting?"

"My mistress be here by th' especial invitation of a certain
gentleman," said Ruth archly. "Though, of course, as is
proper, she stays wit' her aunt, Madame Bass."

Before Dianna could ask the man's name, Ruth leaned forward excitedly. "Oh, there they be now! Did ye ever see a
more handsome couple?"

Dianna looked, and her heart sank. Walking proudly to the
first bench was Kit, his dark green velvet coat the ideal color
for his eyes, the white linen of his shirt in striking contrast to
his sun-browned face. No other man there could even come
close to him, decided Dianna sadly, except perhaps Jonathan,
though Dianna found his darker coloring less appealing than
Kit's gold.

But while under one arm Kit carried a wide-brimmed beaver
hat with a plume, tucked beneath the other was the hand of a
young woman every bit as fair as himself. She was elegantly
tall, her movements fashionably languid. Her blond hair was
artfully dressed in a tumble of curls, crowned by a tiny lace
cap, and her skin was pale and perfect. As Kit stepped to one
side to let her pass, she smiled brilliantly at him and boldly
brushed her skirts across his legs as she moved by him.

"That be my mistress, Constance Lindsey," whispered
Ruth importantly. "Don't that gown become her? It's in the
latest fashion at court."

"Nay, it's not," Dianna whispered back. It was small of
her, she knew, but she couldn't help herself. "No one's worn
turned-back petticoats for at least three seasons. I'm new arrived from London myself," she added hastily as Ruth eyed
her with suspicion.

"Well, no matter, it does become her," said Ruth firmly.
"And when she marries Master Sparhawk, then he can take
her to London an' she can see for herself. Master Sparhawk
be rich enough t'give her whatever she fancies."

Dianna tried to keep her whispered voice level. "They are betrothed?"

Ruth tossed her head. "Well, nay, not yet, but they will be before she goes back to New London." Behind them an older woman shushed Ruth loudly, and Dianna realized that, while they'd been whispering, the service had begun. She bowed her head with the others, glad no one could see the unhappiness she knew clouded her face.

Miserably she pictured herself as she must look in Lucy Wing's worn grey linsey-woolsey, her hair braided beneath a plain white cap. Her hands were red and rough from the cold, and when she'd caught sight of her reflection this morning in a polished pewter bowl, she had been shocked by how pale and thin her face had become. She had never been a beauty like Constance Lindsey, but, oh, how she wished Kit had seen her, just once, before her father's death, when she had been plump and merry and beautifully dressed!

Trapped. That was how Kit felt. Trapped, with Constance pressing into him as she pretended to study her prayer book. At least she held it right side up; he doubted she was smart enough to know the difference. He glanced down at her half-naked breasts, and she simpered slyly back at him. He liked female flesh as much as any man—more, perhaps—but so much of Constance on display on a Sunday morning was vulgar, not seductive, and again, he doubted she knew the difference. If he had anything to say about it, she would be on her way back to New London in the morning.

"Of course, my mistress will send th' little chit packing," Ruth was whispering crossly. "Look at her, sitting plain as day between Master Christopher an' Cap'n Jonathan!"

Dianna saw Mercy's small head barely showing above the bench, her little white cap flanked by the two broad-shouldered Sparhawk men. As she watched, Mercy tugged on Kit's sleeve, and he bent down to listen. Dianna smiled. She didn't know how Mercy had managed it, but Dianna was delighted for once to see her claiming her share of Kit's attention.

"My poor mistress!" sputtered Ruth indignantly. "To be forced t'bear such shame! That he would bring his little bastard wit' him into meeting! He might not care about th' gossip, but, oh, poor Mistress Constance!''

Her thoughts spinning, Dianna once again bowed her head. There was nothing beyond this woman's gossip that said Mercy was Kit's daughter, no resemblance between them. Yet it could explain so much. What had Asa said—that Mercy could not replace the other Kit had lost. Was the other Lucy Wing, the wife of a man he called his friend? First the woman in Saybrook, and now this. Troubled and confused, Dianna found herself praying for the strength to keep away from Kit Sparhawk.

Kit knew Dianna was there. He had found her the moment he'd entered the door, and her presence only made Constance all the more unbearable. He felt badly about what had happened yesterday. Servant or no, Asa should not have struck her, and he should not have let it happen. That Hester had railed at him about the girl while she slammed pots and kettles about in the kitchen hadn't helped, either. He was surprised that Dianna wanted to learn from Hester. He hadn't expected that from her, any more than he'd expected her to fly at him for merely calling her a hussy. He still thought her a strumpet, though Jonathan had scoffed and called him a righteous prig and said the girl could not be blamed for the gossip of others.

Almost unconsciously Kit's eyes strayed back to the servant's bench, where the morning light streamed over Dianna's small figure. He liked her in the pale, simple clothing, a foil to her aristocratic features and dramatic coloring. The sunlight caught her in profile, outlining her nose with the little bump on the bridge, her full lower lip, her dimpled chin. Kit could not believe that Jonathan had dismissed her as a little wren: there was more grace in the line of Dianna Grey's throat than in Constance's entire body. If she were a little wren, then Constance was an over-bright, squawking parrot and Jonathan was welcome to her.

Somehow Dianna sensed he was studying her and she turned her face toward him, her lips slightly parted with surprise. For a moment, across the rows of bowed heads, their eyes met. A soft flush colored her cheeks and she quickly looked down.

Reluctantly Kit tried to return his attention to Dr. Manning's sermon. This was his first Sunday home after a long and difficult journey and he had much to be thankful for: Jonathan's recovery, a profitable voyage with the loss of only one man, a good harvest at Plumstead while he'd been away. And yet all his best intentions toward prayer were pushed aside by the thought of Dianna behind him.

When the break in the services came in early afternoon, Kit was the first to his feet, impatiently searching for Dianna. He wanted to find her, talk to her, not to apologize exactly, but to say he understood how difficult Asa could be. But with Constance hanging on his arm and a crowd of neighbors welcoming him home, he was one of the last to leave the meetinghouse. Outside, the congregation dawdled in the churchyard in the warm spring sunshine, chatting among themselves as the baskets with cold suppers were unpacked from wagons and horses. Kit spotted Dianna at once. She was hard to miss, with Jonathan in his scarlet coat dawdling beside her, giving her the full benefit of his considerable charm. Kit almost swore, remembering in time that it was the Sabbath. But it was so like Jonathan to saddle him with Constance and then go after Dianna himself.

"I swear you've not heard a word I've told you, Christopher," Constance was saying petulantly. "You'd sooner see me starve than fetch me my supper!"

But before Kit answered, a man on horseback cantered up to the meetinghouse, sending children and a neighbor's chickens scurrying for safety. The rider laughed and cruelly jerked the horse's head around, scattering flecks of spittle and blood from its mouth. He was a heavy-set man and strong, easily controlling the horse with one gloved hand. His round, florid face was framed by a black, curling beard streaked with white, and his hair was carelessly tied back with a limp riband. A single pearl on a gold loop dangled from one ear. His clothes were expensive, velvet and broadcloth, though stained with neglect, and his tall boots, too, were scuffed and mud-stained, the silver spurs glinting in the sun.

"Sparhawk!" the man called to Kit, challenging. "*Sacré sang,* the savages for once did not lie, and your filthy English soul is back among us!"

"Haul your black carcass out of the sight of decent folk, Robillard," answered Kit evenly, but the threat in his voice was clear. The crowd around him had melted away, leaving an open path between him and the rider, and even Constance had vanished.

Defiantly, the man dismounted and sauntered toward Kit. "You have no power over me, Sparhawk. Your *Anglais* laws mean nothing, just as your *Anglais* borders and your *Anglais* treaties mean nothing, either. You are the interlopers, the intruders, here merely by the whim of *Nouveau France,* and when she wishes to be rid of you, she will."

Every muscle in Kit's body tensed. He hated Robillard, hated him with a passion that had been handed down from his father. "This land belongs to us, and to England, Robillard, and there's an end to it."

Robillard laughed, his velvet-covered belly shaking. "You talk bold, but you know the truth. Someday I will own your land, Sparhawk. I have offered you a fair price for it, and like your father, you were too *stupide* to agree. So I will try other ways, eh? I will take it for *la belle France,* and see you mewling *Anglais* at last gone from my woods."

The Frenchman was close enough that Kit could smell the burgundy on his breath, but he was not so foolish as to judge the man drunk. "I don't discuss business on the Sabbath, Robillard, with you or any man. If you have anything to say to me other than your customary empty threats, you may call on me tomorrow at Plumstead. But now, you will leave Wickhamton." Kit's eyes narrowed. "Now, Robillard. I want you gone *now.*"

As he spoke, Jonathan had come to stand beside Kit, and Dianna wondered how the Frenchman could dare to face both Sparhawk brothers. The tension in the air was palpable; the rest of the congregation stood frozen, watching. She knew that neither Kit nor Jonathan was armed; she had seen the long rifles they always carried left in the back of the church. Robillard, too, had left his gun on his saddle. But she still had a sick feeling that something very bad was about to happen.

She wasn't wrong.

"Fah, Sparhawk, you insult me!" Robillard spat in the dirt before Kit. "Which should frighten me more, eh? Your *imbécile* warnings or your crippled brother?" With both hands he began to scratch his belly, or so it seemed to Dianna. But in that instant Kit was on him, knocking the Frenchman onto his back and pinning him with the length of his own body. The blade of Robillard's knife glittered as it slid harmlessly from his open hand across the packed dirt. A murmur of exclamations swept around the others as Jonathan bent to collect it.

It was the other knife that held Dianna's attention, the one Kit held poised across the Frenchman's throat. The blade was long, the hilt carved from horn, and the ease and swiftness with which Kit handled it shocked her. His eyes were hard, his mouth a grim slash, and Dianna realized how ruthless a man had to be to survive in this land. If he'd had to, Kit would have slit Robillard's throat. And what was worse was knowing that the Frenchman would have done the same.

Slowly Dianna let her fingers uncurl and release the apron she'd clutched into a knot, and she followed the others back into the church as Jonathan and Kit shoved Robillard toward his horse. In England, gentlemen did not scuffle in the dirt. Disputes were not settled with knives. But everything was different here. Civility was a luxury, hesitation a weakness that invited death.

Oh, Lord, how was she going to survive in such a place?

"I would've gone if I'd known there was going t'be a fight," said Asa sadly as Dianna cleaned the plates from their supper. Mercy was already in bed in the loft, asleep, worn out after the day's excitement. "Kit's a rare man with a knife, an' Robillard's cunning enough t'make it a good match. I'm sorry t'miss it."

"Even if you'd been there, you might have missed it all if you'd blinked an eye. It was over that fast. I don't understand why they had to fight at all."

Asa snorted. "Ye don't waste words with a scoundrel like Robillard. Frenchies like him, don't understand 'em, Annie. He's been a thorn in th' side of th' Sparhawks for twenty years, always a-yammerin' about English land belongin' to th' priests an' the King o' France instead. Kit treated him no worse'n he deserved."

"Perhaps. But he might have picked a better place and time to do it." Dianna was still unsettled by the fight and didn't wish to discuss it again. She gave the table one last pass with the towel, and then sat across from Asa, her hands clasped before her.

"Asa, I don't know what Captain Welles told you about me," she began. "You needed someone to watch over Mercy and chose me, and I'm grateful. But I'm not exactly what you wanted. For one, I can't cook."

Sucking on his pipe with his head angled back, Asa studied her through half-closed eyes. "Supper tonight was fine. More'n fine."

"I didn't make it. Hester Holcomb did." Dianna smiled ruefully. "Hester has offered to teach me cooking and such, things I need to know to be useful to you and Mercy. But I'll have to go to Plumstead, and I'll have to take Mercy with me."

Asa merely listened, watching her through the tobacco haze.

"I know you don't like Kit Sparhawk, but I'll be there to watch Mercy," Dianna plunged onward, from his silence expecting him to say no. "And it will only be until I can make do on my own."

Still considering, Asa nodded slowly before answering. "Hester be a good woman. She'll learn ye well. The pair o' ye will keep th' lass safe enough." He pushed back the chair, stretching his arms over his head with a cracking in his joints. "An' truth be, Jeremiah an' I be headin' upriver for a fortnight in th' morning. Knowin' Mercy an' ye be wit' Hester will keep me from worryin'. But ye bring her back here at night, mind? This be her home, an' I don't want Kit puttin' other ideas in her head."

Dianna nodded. "Asa, there is one other thing."

"I'm not a-worryin' you'll burn down th' house, if that be it," he said mildly.

"Nay, not that." Dianna blushed, and looked down at her hands. "I want to know about Kit and Mercy. I heard what you told him about replacing the one that was lost. Mercy is wary of me and she doesn't believe that I want to be her friend. If you know something about her that might help me—"

Asa rose abruptly. "There's nothin' ye need to know, girl," he said sharply. "Don't ask questions about th' dead that can only hurt them that still live, mind. There's things that happened long past that be better forgotten."

A little gust of cold night air blew down the chimney, and for a moment the fire flared more brightly. Slowly Dianna lowered her head to her hands and stared into the flames. Like it or not, she had her answer.

During her first week working beside Hester at Plumstead, Dianna found it easy enough to keep Mercy away from Kit, for not once did they see him. He was always gone before they arrived: meeting with the grist miller about the grind for the winter wheat or with the saw miller about the pine planking he was shipping to Barbados; overseeing the plowing of the outer fields or the grafting in the orchards; or conferring with the other officers of the Wickhamton trainband about defenses for the outermost farms. After seven months away from home, explained Hester, there was much that demanded Kit's attention. And, she added with a wink, much to keep him out of the path of Constance Lindsey.

But on Friday, Constance intercepted him at last by the river warehouse, and reluctantly he had given over the day to riding with her. It was late afternoon before the pair returned to Plumstead. Constance's trilling laughter caught Dianna's ear as she peeled turnips in the kitchen, and she paused to watch them walking through the yard, Constance's arm looped familiarly through Kit's as they led their horses to the trough.

Hester followed Dianna's glance and harrumphed. "She may think she's caught him, but there's nary a chance Kit will be pulled along like th' horse."

"She's very beautiful," said Dianna wistfully. Constance wore a lavender riding habit closely tailored to display her figure, and a matching tricorn hat tipped artfully over one eye.

"An' very stupid, t'come chasing after Kit this way." For emphasis Hester gave an extra whack with her cleaver. "Don't know why Kit didn't send her back downriver with Jonathan on Tuesday."

"Jonathan's gone?" Dianna asked with surprise. She had assumed he was still at Plumstead, merely making himself as scarce as his brother.

"Only th' chance t'bedevil poor Kit with that woman brought him back. He's been landlocked too long with that bad leg to stay away from the *Prosperity* more'n he must. So he's the brother you fancy, eh? Nay, don't be shy about it. Every lass in the valley takes to one or t'other of 'em. Though I'd warrant that jade out there cares more for the fortune than the man, more fool she!"

"Are the Sparhawks wealthy?" asked Dianna, glad to divert Hester's attention from her own feelings and the fact that she'd guessed quite wrongly about the brothers.

"Aye, they own enough of th' land in these parts t'start their own country, if they'd a mind. An' with Jonathan's trading an' th' mills an' shops that Kit's begun, along with th' tenants, why, they'd make their grandfather, th' one that come over with Gov'ner Winthrop, prouder'n daylight if he'd lived t'see it."

It was hard for Dianna to comprehend that the Sparhawks could be so prosperous and yet still wish to work so hard. In England no gentlemen ever worked if he could help it. Even her uncle, with his shipping firm, spent more time at the gaming table than in his counting house. And there was her own poor, dear father, for whom making money was as much a mystery as alchemy. But then she looked down to the turnip in her hands and smiled wryly to herself. In England no lady would do such scullery work herself, either.

"But if one o'them don't take a wife soon," continued Hester, shaking her head, "an' get a son or two, then th'whole thing will get carved among th'sisters. Oh, not that they aren't good girls, Bess an' Grace an' Amy, but th'land would pass to their husbands an' away from th' Sparhawks. I don't want t'see that day, nay, I don't."

Dianna thought of Mercy, and wondered if Kit would acknowledge her openly if she'd been a boy. Surely Hester, who treated the Sparhawks like the family she didn't have, must know the truth. Yet it seemed odd to Dianna that she could speak so freely of Kit and children if she did.

Hester poured water over the vegetables already in the kettle, then handed the empty bucket to Dianna. "Here, lass, be a lamb, an' fetch this full for me."

Even empty, the oak bucket was heavy and Dianna carried it, swinging before her, with both hands. The well was around the front of the house, but as she came 'round the corner, she stopped at the sound of Constance's voice. She and Kit were sitting on the benches before the front door, and Dianna was reluctant to interrupt. She was trying to think of an excuse that Hester would accept if she retreated without the water when Constance began to sing.

Or at least Dianna guessed that was what the other woman's yowling was intended to be. She barely recognized the song, an old ballad with a new setting that had been quite popular at court two years ago. As Constance's off-key rendition wandered farther and farther away from the melody, Dianna's smile grew wider. She didn't have blue eyes like Constance or a lavender riding habit, but her singing voice was pure gold. She waited until Constance had come to the sorry end of the song, and then began it herself as she nonchalantly rounded the corner of the house and walked toward the well, ignoring the two on the bench.

Lowering the well's bucket on the sweep, she let her voice expand with the bittersweet minor notes, the tale of a shepherdess's lost love. As the notes floated into the warm spring air, she forgot her task and her intended audience, too, and lost herself in the pleasure of the music. When the song was done she smiled contentedly to herself until Kit's applause startled her back to the present. With a little gasp of surprise she spun around and immediately locked eyes with the furious Constance.

"Where might a wench like you have learned that song?" she demanded angrily. "Indeed, the music was just brought to me personally on the *Prosperity*."

From the corner of her eye Dianna saw that Kit was trying not to laugh, one hand over his mouth, and she did not dare look directly at him for fear of giggling herself.

"Aye, madam, the music might have been brought on the *Prosperity* by Master Sparhawk," Dianna said, her silvery eyes glinting mischievously, "but then, I was, too."

"But that air is in the very latest fashion at court!" Constance sputtered.

Dianna shrugged. "Two seasons ago, at the very least. I was in attendance when it was introduced at Lord Rathburn's Twelfth Night masque."

Constance looked down her nose scornfully. "Of all the impudence! Truly, Kit, you must have the baggage whipped for such lies! However could a common Wickhamton serving girl like you be at Lord Rathburn's entertainments?"

"The twists of fortune," explained Kit, "fortune both good and bad, and nothing more. Would you say otherwise, Dianna?"

At last, over Constance's shoulder, he caught Dianna's eye and winked wickedly. His grin was wide and easy, warm with the pleasure of a shared moment. His smile reached his eyes, too, which crinkled in the corners, and for the first time Dianna felt the full force of his masculine charm. But there was more. For the first time, too, she saw admiration in his eyes and respect for her. Could one song have done so much, she wondered breathlessly?

"So it's *Dianna*, is it?" Constance demanded suspiciously, narrowing her eyes at Kit. "I won't linger here any longer, Christopher, now that I see how things truly are, nor will I remain to be treated so insolently by this—this *creature* whom you refuse to discipline.'' She gathered her skirts with both hands to leave, though hesitating as if she expected him to beg her to stay.

But Kit only smiled past her to Dianna. ''You can't deny she sings a great deal better than you do, Constance.'' There was an unspoken invitation in his grin, something that made Dianna's heart race and her blood turn sweet and slow as honey. Foolishly she smiled back, oblivious to everything but the pull of those green cat's eyes.

He had rescued her from rape and from fire, yet she had kept her heart safe from him. He had called her names, assumed the worst about her past, while she had learned things about his that had shocked her and she had tried not to care. He had kissed her and caressed her, and she had held her emotions at bay. But now, with only a shared smile over a silly, showy prank, he could claim her heart, and she knew she had lost it forever.

Chapter Nine

"How did ye know that ye could rid us o'that old Constance Lindsey so easy?" asked Mercy the next morning as she and Dianna walked to Plumstead. "I tried an' tried t'make her leave Kit be, an' she only called me names an' wouldn't go."

Dianna tried to hide her surprise. This was the most the girl had ever said to her, and she was almost afraid to reply for fear that Mercy would withdraw again. "I didn't think she would be so angry as that, but I couldn't bear to hear what she did to that lovely song."

Mercy laughed gleefully. "Ye shamed her right, ye did, an' before Kit, too, with him sayin' how beautiful ye sing an' how ugly she did it!"

"I don't remember him saying it quite like that," Dianna replied, but she was laughing, too.

"He be right, though, ye do sing beautiful." The girl looked shyly up at Dianna. "I've never heard anything like it. Like angels, it was."

"Thank you," said Dianna softly, moved, and when this time she reached to take Mercy's hand, the little girl did not pull it away. "My father loved music, and he saw to it that I had the best teachers. We sang often together."

Mercy's wooden clogs kicked along through the dead leaves. "He be dead, your father. Kit told me I should be kind to ye, on account o' ye bein' an orphan, too, like me."

That surprised Dianna, too. "Sometimes I still cannot believe my father is dead. You must miss your parents very much, too."

"Aye, I do." Mercy sighed. "But having Kit helps. He an' Father were closer'n brothers. He'd keep me at Plumstead if it weren't for Grandfer." She lowered her voice confidentially. "Kit wept at Father's funeral sermon. He didn't think I saw him, but he did."

"Kit is very fond of you, Mercy," said Dianna carefully, wishing the girl's new confidences involved something other than her father, whoever he was. "But your grandfather loves you, too, even—"

She stopped suddenly, and listened. They were on the low side of a small hill crowned by a rocky outcropping, and though the new leaves of the trees and scrub brush around them hid little, Dianna was certain she'd heard something from beyond the hill. She stood perfectly still, straining to hear the noise again.

Mercy continued shuffling through the leaves. "Oh, Dianna, 'tis only a rabbit or squirrel—"

But Dianna caught her and pulled her back, her hand across her lips as she shook her head fiercely. There was the sound again: footsteps, a pair of footsteps, just beyond their sight. She had no idea whether the stranger was friendly or not, and her imagination pictured a man like Robillard or one of the rough traders she'd seen with Asa and Jeremiah. All she knew for sure was that she was a small, vulnerable woman, alone and unarmed, with a child. Quickly she led Mercy to the rocky hilltop, cursing the noise that her own feet made. She pressed close to the flat, grey stones and, her heart pounding, inched up until she could just peek over the top. She gasped and froze, unable to move from fear.

The man below was watching her calmly. He was tall and lean, his prominent cheekbones peppered with smallpox scars, and his skin was a rich coppery brown. He wore a blanket wrapped over his shoulders like a cloak, a breech cloth, patched elkskin leggings and little else beyond a collection of beaded necklaces. More beads were woven into his blue-black hair, and tied around his shoulders and waist were several lumpy packages and bundles. In his raised hand, ready to throw, was a tomahawk.

Dianna's nails dug into the rock. *Oh, dear God, it's an Indian, a red savage....*

Mercy crawled up the rock beside her and looked over the edge. Too late Dianna grabbed for her as the girl bounded over the rocks, slipping and hopping down the hill toward the Indian. Horrified, Dianna stumbled after her, dreading the awful moment when the tomahawk would strike the child.

But instead, a wide grin split the Indian's face, and, lowering his tomahawk, he tucked it back into the sash at his waist. "Tom Wing's daughter, yes?" he said amiably in English. "You've grown, little one."

Mercy was nearly dancing with excitement. "Kit's back, Attawan!"

"Mercy!" Dianna caught the child by her shoulders and pulled her protectively close. Although the man had put away his weapon, she was still frightened by his wild, half-naked appearance, and she remembered every story she'd ever heard about what Indians did to hapless settlers.

"This is Attawan, Dianna," explained Mercy. "He's a Pocumtuck, and he's a friend of Kit's."

"It seems the whole colony is a friend of Kit's." Dianna ducked her head quickly, unsure how one responded to an Indian. She began backing away, pulling Mercy with her, and rattled on nervously. "In truth, he's likely waiting for us now, Mercy, wondering where we are, mayhap even coming to look for us. Farewell, umm, Master Attawan."

But Attawan only nodded solemnly as he tugged his blanket into place. "He is a good friend to have, mistress," he called after them. "A very good friend."

As the miller droned on with his list of grievances, Kit hoped his own expression showed the proper mixture of sternness and concern. He only heard every tenth word of the man's endless litany, and even that took more concentration than he wanted to spare. It seemed that every moment since he'd returned, he'd been listening to some complaint or another, and he'd often wondered how Plumstead and his other concerns had managed to run at all in the months he'd been away. That things might have slipped while Jonathan had been in charge was understandable; he had, after all, been recuperating, and he didn't share Kit's interests under the best of circumstances. But what stunned Kit was that, since he'd returned, he himself rankled under the responsibilities. He had no patience with his tenants or their problems, little interest in the profits of his mills and less in Wickhamton affairs.

It had taken him less than a week to discover why: Dianna Grey. Somehow he'd become bewitched by the woman, and in a way that was beyond his experience. He wished he could take Jonathan's advice to just bed her and be done with it. But he couldn't. She was the servant of one of his tenants, and by extension, one of his own, as well, until her indenture ran out. She wasn't some tavern wench he could leave behind with a handful of coins. And, of course, there still remained all the reasons he hadn't taken her during their voyage.

But even those objections seemed to fade each time he saw her. She never played the coquette with him, and unlike every other woman he knew, she seemed little enough impressed by his position. He could have bought and sold her blasted blue-blood father ten times over, and she herself now belonged to a rootless old trapper, yet she still found him beneath her notice. And the worst part of it was that he *wanted* her to notice him. He liked to be around her because she always surprised him. He smiled when he thought of how effortlessly she had been able to send Constance scurrying back to New London. Lord, and her voice—he'd never heard a voice that breathtakingly beautiful before, and he wondered what it would take to make her sing again, and for him alone this time.

"Nay, Master Sparhawk, I don't see th' mirth in millstones worn almost flat," said the miller, sounding a bit wounded. "If ye can't bring the stone dresser up from Saybrook, well then, I can't answer for th' spring wheat."

"You'll have your stone dresser, Morgan, and within the fortnight," said Kit quickly. If he wasn't careful, he'd have the gossips whispering how he'd lost his wits in London. "You were right to bring it to my attention, and I know you'll be ready when that spring wheat comes in."

Kit left the man preening happily, and soon was on Thunder's back and heading toward Plumstead. It was still early afternoon. Today he would be sure to reach home before Dianna and Mercy left.

"I'm not certain we should be here, Mercy," said Dianna uneasily as the girl led her into Plumstead's parlor chamber. The room was seldom used, the door kept shut, and like most of the house, Dianna had never seen it. The lavishness of the furnishings surprised her: although the furniture was in the old style of King Charles, dark walnut and oak with heavy turnings and carving and cane seats on the chairs, it had all obviously come from first-rate cabinetmakers in London. The window hangings were dark green velvet, as were the chair cushions, and a bright-patterned Turkey carpet lay across the polished pine floorboards. A tall chest, lacquered in red and black chinoiserie, dominated one wall, and along the mantelpiece sat a row of polished silver chargers. But it was to a small table near one of the diamond-paned windows that Mercy drew Dianna to as she pointed to a long, flat box elaborately inlaid with wood and pearl veneers.

"Jonathan said this be for music-making," she told Dianna, resting one hand reverently on the top. "Mayhap ye know how t'make it sing."

Dianna pulled the tasseled stool from beneath the table, sat and carefully opened the hinged top of the box. "It's a virginal, Mercy," she explained as the girl crowded over her arm to peer at the black and white keys. Carefully Dianna fingered a chord, and Mercy gasped at the ringing sounds of the plucked strings. The instrument was sadly out of tune, but after months of no music at all, the little instrument brought an unexpected joy to Dianna. With growing confidence, her fingers danced lightly over the keyboard, and she began to sing softly as she accompanied herself. This time she sang not to outdo another but to please only herself, and the song she chose was "Greensleeves," the old ballad somehow suiting the melancholy sound of the virginal. Spellbound, Mercy settled on the floor beside her, her knees tucked up and her mouth open with rapt admiration. Both were so lost in the music's magic that neither heard Kit's boots in the hall, nor did they notice him standing in the doorway to listen, too.

The music brought back a hundred images fresh to Kit, memories of his childhood, of his brother and sisters tumbled around on the floor before the fire while their mother played and the winter wind howled outside. He saw again the look on his father's face as he turned the pages of his mother's music and the way he would kiss her on the forehead when she was done.

"No one has touched that since my lady mother's death," he said when Dianna was finished. Still half-lost in his own memories, his voice was oddly uneven with emotion.

Startled, Dianna hurriedly shut the instrument and shoved back the stool to rise. "Forgive me, I did not know."

"Nay, do not stop, I pray! It's not for sentiment that the thing's been stilled, but for the lack of a player." He smiled, a sad smile that struck deep into Dianna's grief for her own lost parents. "My sisters had neither the gift nor the patience, and so it has sat idle. Waiting, I dare to say, for you."

Dianna's cheeks brightened at the unexpected compliment. She was a servant, he was a wealthy man, and it was not right for him to say pretty nonsense to her. But to see him there, smiling like that, she could forgive him anything, and once again she felt the power of his undeniable attraction to her. He was dressed simply, a coarse worsted vest unbuttoned over a linen shirt, open at the throat and the sleeves rolled up, and she caught herself staring, fascinated, at the curling dark hairs on his bare forearms and chest. He came closer, mindless of the dust his boots left on the carpet, and Dianna sank back onto the stool, not to play again, but from fear her legs would not hold her.

"You won't play more?" he asked with a surprising wistfulness, and Dianna shook her head, doubting now that she could fumble through the simplest piece.

"Then you force me to talk, Lady Dianna, to fill the space between us." He leaned against one of the arm chairs, his long legs crossed before him, and wondered why, for the first time, he had called her by her title without sarcasm. "At least Constance would wish me to speak to you."

Guilt made Dianna's words rush over one another. "Oh, Kit, I don't know what the devil made me act so! She meant to please you, that was all, and I had no right to shame her for that, especially if she is your betrothed."

Kit snorted, and Dianna then noticed the teasing spark in his green eyes, the same one that had been there when she'd bettered Constance. "She has no more claim to that title than the spotted sow in the sty, and, now that I consider it, her singing belongs in the barnyard, as well."

"Aye, Dianna made th' ninny turn tail an' run, didn't she, Kit?" piped up Mercy, and the way that Kit cocked one eyebrow told Dianna that he, like she herself, had entirely forgotten the little girl's presence. She waited, expecting him to decide whether Mercy would remain as an unwitting chaperone or be sent from the room. But that eyebrow cocked a fraction higher, and she realized he was leaving the decision to her instead. That eyebrow, and all it implied, irritated Dianna. A man's comely face was no reason for letting herself be intimidated. She could quite easily stay in the room alone with him, and, her composure returning, she would prove it to him, too.

"Mercy, please go to Hester. Kit and I must talk alone for a few moments, and then you and I shall go home for dinner." The girl began to protest, but one stern look from Kit was enough to send her reluctantly away.

With a swiftness that startled Dianna, Kit shifted from the armchair to her own bench. Self-consciously she tugged her skirts away from him and he chuckled. The bench was small enough that she could not escape his thigh pressing against hers, but she refused to amuse him more by moving again. "I would speak to you, too, Kit," she began, planning to tell him of meeting Attawan, "and it's better said without Mercy."

"Stay, it cannot be more important than what I must say to

you.'' His voice dropped lower, his green eyes watched her closely beneath half-closed lids. ''Why do you plague me so, Dianna? In North Boston, they'd try you for witchcraft for what you've done to me.''

Her back very straight, Dianna stared down at her hands clasped in her lap. ''I don't know what you mean.''

''Aye, sweeting, I think you do.'' Gently he took her hand in his, her slender fingers swallowed in his broad, rough palm. He meant merely to talk, not seduce her. There would be no harm in that. ''Would your hand be shaking like this, your palm damp, if you did not know?''

But already her nearness was testing his intentions. In the heat of the kitchen, she had loosened the neckerchief she wore modestly tucked around her throat, leaving the soft curves of her breasts exposed. As she self-consciously pulled the neck-erchief back in place, the simple gesture of her graceful fingers twisting in the linen was more seductive than Kit could have dreamed possible. What was it about this woman that had that effect on him? He turned her hand over in his own, coaxing the clasped fingers open by tracing along the pale veins in her wrist, and he felt a shiver run the length of her arm. Slowly he lifted her hand to his lips, and let them retrace the same path.

Dianna could have held firm if he had been demanding with her again, as he had on the *Prosperity*. She was prepared for that. But this gentleness caught her unawares. One by one she felt her defenses flutter and fall before these feather-light, teasing caresses. Through her clothes, she could feel the heat from his body where their legs touched on the bench, and his own special masculine scent almost overwhelmed her senses. Too vividly she recalled how he had kissed her before, and while her conscience weakly tried to rebel, she felt her heart beating faster in anticipation, her lips parting expectantly.

He raised his hand to touch her jaw, turning her face toward his. His eyes held hers fascinated, and for the first time Dianna noticed how their green depths were flecked with tiny sparks of gold.

Lightly he touched a forefinger to the cleft in her chin. "I like this," he said simply.

She closed her eyes to try to break the spell, but his voice, his touch remained. With one final effort her conscience struggled for something, anything, to save herself.

"Today an Indian tried to kill Mercy and me," she blurted out, her eyes still tightly shut. "Down beyond the west field, not two miles from here."

Kit froze, all desire instantly gone. "What the devil are you saying?"

"There was an Indian in the woods, and he drew his tomahawk and threatened us and was most fierce."

"Dianna, by all that's holy, if you seek to mock me…"

Again he saw the place where the path curved to follow the bend in the river, the terrible, unexpected stillness of the late afternoon, the twisted body of his father's yellow dog lying half in the water, her long tail floating gently with the current….

"There are no hostile Indians near Wickhamton," he said hoarsely. "No Englishman has died here by a savage's hand for ten years. The militia, the trainband patrols, have made certain. There are no more hostile Indians."

"But he said he knew you," said Dianna defensively. Why didn't he believe her? "He said his name was Attawan, and he called you friend."

"Attawan. Aye, he has a right to call me that." Kit knew he should be relieved, but the tight coil of pain within his chest refused to unwind. It was more than just hearing his mother's virginal again, though God knows that would be enough. No, it was Dianna herself and the old danger of caring too much.

He let her fingers slip from his own, and Dianna's heart sank when she saw how cold and withdrawn his expression had become. Did she really mean so little to him that her fear was only a disagreeable interruption?

"It matters not if he knew you, Kit. He didn't know *me*," she persisted. She must have imagined the sympathy between them, for there was none of it now in those cold green eyes.

"If I'm to live in this wilderness, I don't ever want to feel that helpless again."

He rose and turned away so she could not see the anguish he was certain was on his face. How could he tell her that the helplessness never ended, that he faced it every day? "You are a woman, Dianna," he finally said, "and gently bred at that."

"And that should be my excuse?" she asked incredulously. "Nay, Kit, I can't accept that. I want you to teach me to shoot a gun like yours."

"You don't know what you ask, sweeting." His laugh was harsh, and the endearment this time was so tinged with bitter mockery that Dianna winced. "A musket is nigh as long as you're tall. If by some rare bit of luck you could hoist the butt to your shoulder, I doubt you've the strength to hold it steady enough to aim and fire. And if the recoil doesn't knock you flat, then what? It's half a minute for a grown man to reload. For you, twice that. In that time your enemy would have his leisure to dispose of you, and I'd be left with the blame. Nay, Dianna, I won't do it."

"You'd rather I stand meekly and meet my fate, and Mercy hers with me, than teach me to defend myself?" She was standing now, too, her hands defiantly on her hips. She hated his contempt, and in that moment she hated him, as well. "Then forgive me for insulting your curious sense of honor. I'll ask Hester instead."

"An' I'll be happy t'teach ye, too," answered the older woman tartly from the doorway, "if th' grand fine Colonel Sparhawk can't bring himself t'do it." Dianna saw Kit's shoulders tense, and knew Hester's barb had struck home, just before the woman turned on her next.

"Mercy's eager for home," Hester said bluntly, the dismissal clear. "Ye be done here this day. Best t'leave."

Dianna paused uncertainly, hoping Kit would turn and look at her one more time. So they had come back to this once again, back to the distrust and the sharp words, and all the wishing in the world wasn't going to change it. Angry tears stung her eyes, and with her head down, she hurried from the room.

Kit heard her leave. "Mind your tongue, Hester," he said sharply. "You forget yourself, and your place."

"Devil take your place, Kit Sparhawk," snapped Hester. "I thrashed your hindquarters when you were a lad, and I'll do it again if I must. I'll warrant ye been using that self-same tender part o' your person for thinkin' rather than sittin' anyways, least where that girl's concerned. I heard your ravin' clear in th' kitchen. Dianna Grey's no part o' your demons, Kit. Unless ye let her be told or tell her yourself—"

"*Nay.*" Through the diamond-paned window, Kit saw Dianna and Mercy walking hand in hand across the west field.

"Nay," he said wearily. "It's past. I would not have her know."

That night Asa returned home with Jeremiah, and after Mercy had gone to sleep, Dianna told him about meeting Attawan in the woods. Unlike Kit, Asa did not scoff at her story.

"It's not the Indians that a-worry me," he said, frowning. "But with that rogue Robillard kickin' up dust again, it don't be safe for th' pair o' ye walkin' clear t'Plumstead alone. I'll send Jeremiah t'tell them that ye won't be comin' back t'morrow."

Dismayed, Dianna realized that that was not at all what she wanted. "You have two muskets, Asa. If you left one here for me—"

"Nay, it be my place to keep ye safe," said Asa firmly. "Ye best stay here wit' me, and we'll see what Hester's learned ye since I left."

For the next weeks, until early June, Dianna and Mercy stayed within sight of the Wing house and yard, but with Hester's advice still fresh, Dianna found there was plenty to do. Cooking took more time than she'd ever dreamed, though thanks to Hester, she had become an adept, if simple, cook, and she was pleased when even Jeremiah began appearing at the house at mealtimes. Tom Wing had been a miller by trade, not a farmer, and he had bought or bartered for most of his family's food. But his wife had kept a kitchen garden, now run to seed and overgrown, and it was this that Dianna sought first to reclaim. Next came the house itself, and after scouring and sweeping and scrubbing nearly a year's dirt away, Dianna could finally see the little saltbox as a decent place to live. But best of all was the change in Mercy. Each day the girl seemed to giggle more, her cheeks growing rosier and her eyes brighter, and her periods of solitary grief became fewer and less severe as she followed Dianna around like a puppy.

In these early days of summer, Dianna worked harder and longer than she ever had before. Yet she would have been happier, too, than she'd been since her father's death, were it not for the emptiness left by Kit Sparhawk.

It had taken nearly a fortnight for her to be able to think of him with anything short of outright hostility, and when her anger had faded, she was left with only a dull sadness that was infinitely harder to bear. Her heart loved him and ached to be loved in return, and her body desired him with an intensity that almost frightened her, while her mind and conscience remained painfully aware of how foolish and futile all her hopes were. She saw him each Sunday, of course, sitting there on the first bench in the meetinghouse with his pride and position for company, but when she noted how careful he was to avoid meeting her eyes, she kept her distance. She, too, had pride to protect.

"I wish Grandfer'd let us go back. I'll wager Kit misses us up t'Plumstead," confided Mercy sadly. "I'll wager he be lonely without us."

Dianna had only shrugged and continued her weeding. She could not answer for Kit, but she herself had learned volumes about loneliness.

It was Hester who finally invited them back. "It's been too long since we've seen ye," she said warmly to Dianna after services. "There be new kittens in the barn, an' I can use another pair o' hands with th' strawberries."

Recognizing Dianna's hesitation, Hester patted her hand and lowered her voice confidentially. "Kit won't be there, if that's a-worryin' ye. I know how you two be always at odds. He be headin' to the upper river sawmill at daybreak.''

With reluctant permission from Asa and a promise to return well before nightfall, Mercy and Dianna headed to Plumstead the next afternoon. The day held the first true summer's heat, and the green canopy of the forest offered a welcoming coolness after the brilliance of the sun. The paths that they had crossed with ease in the early spring were now crowded with ferns and other undergrowth, the buzzing of insects mingling with the birdcalls overhead. Indians and Frenchmen seemed improbably remote on a day like this. Wildflowers nestled among the tree roots, and Dianna wove the blossoms Mercy picked into wreaths for their hair. After twenty-two summers of being encased in sweltering layers of stays and petticoats, Dianna felt gloriously free with her feet bare on the moss and pine needles, her single skirt looped ankle-high over her shift. Impulsively she unbraided her hair, and laughing, shook the dark waves free over her shoulders.

"It be well Dr. Manning don't be here t'see ye," said Hester drily when they appeared in her kitchen. "A proper pair o' heathen strumpets ye look t'be."

"Oh, Hester, 'tis almost midsummer's night," teased Dianna as she plucked one of the deep-red strawberries from the baskets on the table and popped it into her mouth. "Soon the Queen of the Faeries will come to dance from those very forests."

Hester frowned sternly. "I'll hear none o' that nonsense. Faeries! Next you'll be beggin' for Maypoles! Wickhamton may not be so strict as them t'the east, but we still be good Christian folk, with no use for such flummery."

Wide-eyed with her chin in her hand, Mercy stared up at Hester. "Dianna's told me of th' faeries, but what be Maypoles?"

"There now, Dianna, I hope ye be happy!" The glance Hester shot her was sharp as a blade, and with both hands on Mercy's shoulders she steered the girl toward the door. "Maypoles be wickedness from Old England, Mercy, with no place in the New. Now come set your hands t'useful tasks an' help me with th' berryin'.''

Contritely Dianna gathered up an empty basket to follow, but Hester waved her back. "I'll thank ye t'take those shirts o' Kit's up t'his chamber for me first. My knees have had enough o' the stairs for this day.''

"But which chamber?"

"Faith, lass, where be your wits?" called Hester over her shoulder. "His be th' only one that's open!"

Three newly laundered shirts were draped across the back of a chair. Dianna picked one up gingerly and held it outstretched by the shoulders. Lord, he was a giant of a man, she marveled, with more admiration than she'd intended. Where were her wits, indeed? Hastily she collected the other shirts and ran up the front stairs.

Kit's bedchamber was square and spacious, filling the house's southwest corner. Unlike the parlor, the furniture here was plain, hewn from local oak and maple: a clothespress, a table and leather-covered armchair, the chest she remembered from the *Prosperity,* a poster bed. Easily Dianna pictured Kit here, his long legs sprawled under the table that served as his desk, pausing at his work to gaze out the windows to the river. The table was strewn with papers, bills and letters mostly, but what caught Dianna's eye was a page of ink sketches of Thunder. In a few bold pen strokes, Kit had captured the horse's spirit, and the confidence of the drawings surprised Dianna. Unexpected, too, was the well-worn copy of Aristotle. How did a man who wrestled with knives in the dust come to sketch and read Greek?

With the shirts folded and placed on the chest, Dianna had no reason to linger, yet hungrily she continued to gaze around the room. The uniform coat hanging from a peg, the engraving of Jamaica pinned to the wall, the boyish collection of pinecones arranged by size along the mantel—all were clues to Kit. Slowly she pushed back the dark green curtains to the bed, the horn rings overhead squeaking as they slid along the rod. The pillows were neatly laid against the bolster, the coverlet smoothed in place, but Dianna could still make out the deep impression his broad frame had left in the feather mattress, and his scent still clung to the linens. Lightly she ran her hand across the coverlet and closed her eyes, imagining him lying there.

"Dianna?"

At first she thought she imagined Kit's voice, too, but when he repeated her name, her eyes flew open with horror. He'd caught her trespassing, pure and simple. But her apology died on her lips as she confronted the vivid reality of the man before her.

Hot and dirty from a day's riding, Kit had stripped off his shirt and boots outside and dumped bucket after bucket of icy well water over his head. His hair was still swept sleekly back from his forehead and his bare torso held the sheen of the water, the sun slanting through the windows highlighting the muscles in his arms and shoulders. Stray droplets glistened in the dark curls of his hair across his chest and down lower, across his abdomen to the top of his breeches. There the water had made the wet fabric cling shamelessly to his all-too-male body. How long she stood there, and how long she stared, Dianna could not begin to guess.

Oh, God in Heaven, what must he think of me!

Chapter Ten

W hat Kit thought was that Dianna was the most enchanting woman he'd ever seen.

He had met Hester in the yard, grumbling about Dianna and faeries, but he'd had no idea that Dianna herself would be waiting in his chamber like some wild woodland queen. Her hair streamed gloriously around her like a cape with wildflowers strewn through the chestnut waves. Gone was the pallor of the long voyage. Her skin was burnished to a rosy gold, her face and body once again pleasingly rounded. As she bent over his bed, her shift had slipped low off her shoulders above her laced sleeveless bodice, offering him a tantalizing view of her breasts. Her lips were half-open with surprise, her pale eyes wide with—with what? Invitation? He had been mistaken about her before, but to find her here this way, with no one else in the house…no, there could be no other explanation than that she wanted him as much as he did her.

And Kit had never desired a woman more. He had spent these past weeks alternately blessing and damning Asa for keeping her from Plumstead, but most often he had cursed himself for driving her away. He tried to be a good man, a kind master and generous neighbor, and yet with her he always seemed to become an overbearing boor. He couldn't blame her if she loathed him. She was as mercurial as the silver color of her eyes, and each time he had tried to hold her, she had slipped from his grasp. Would this, then, be his last chance with her to prove he was different?

"So you've come back at last," he said softly, unwilling to risk frightening her again.

"For the kittens," answered Dianna hastily, and then winced at how foolish she sounded. How could she think at all with him watching her like a great golden lion? She stepped away from the bed and folded her arms across her chest. Where was the apology that she needed to make before she could escape? "And Mercy wished to see you again."

"Aye, and I've missed her, too." The beginnings of a smile played around the corners of his mouth. "But I've missed you more."

"Missed me!" cried Dianna scornfully, all the frustration of these past weeks rising up. "How can you miss me when you scarcely know me?"

"In some way I feel I've always known you. From that night at Sir Henry's—"

"The night you betrayed me!" said Dianna bitterly.

"Ah, you wrong me now, just as I wronged you then," he said with genuine sadness. With her hair loose, it was too easy to remember how she looked that night and the things that had gone so poorly between them since then. He no longer cared that she had been Sir Henry's mistress, nor did he believe that she had tried to kill the man, but he was at a loss to admit it without angering her, and justly. "I would give much to begin again with you, Dianna."

"Master Christopher Sparhawk would care what became of a convict, a ten-guinea bondswoman?" She had intended to be sarcastic, but instead her words came out as a poignant little plea. She wanted so very much to believe him!

"Master Sparhawk cares very much," he said, his voice deep and seductive. Slowly he circled around the bed to come stand before her. Even barefoot, he towered over her. "And you don't need me to tell you your worth, Dianna."

With a lazy smile, he plucked one of the flowers from her hair and brushed the star-shaped petals along her cheek. "Columbine, isn't it?"

Dianna nodded, her own words scarcely more than a whisper. "The roots when boiled are a good poultice for burns and scalds."

He chuckled. "All from this pretty little flower? Hester has taught you well." He let the flower fall, and his hand alone traced along the curve of her cheek. Gently his callused fingertips cradled her chin, and he marveled at her delicacy as he turned her face upward toward his. "And here I always favored columbine for its beauty alone."

She closed her eyes as his mouth swept down. All her senses were focused on his lips upon hers, coaxing her, wooing her with a tenderness she hadn't expected. Without thinking, she uncrossed her arms and rested her hands on his chest, her fingers uncertainly exploring the damp, curling hair over smooth skin. In response his hands found and spanned her waist and drew her closer. Her breasts crushed against his chest, the water that still clung to him dampening her shift above the bodice. She felt the heat of his body against hers, and the coolness of the water, and an unfamiliar warmth began to build inside her.

Gradually her lips parted, and she welcomed his deepening kiss. He pulled her closer, molding her body against his, and she felt oddly soft and pliant against the hardness of his muscles and sinews. Her hands climbed up the wide expanse of his chest, across his shoulders and twined around his neck. Hungrily she stretched herself along his body as his tongue explored the velvety depths of her mouth.

It was all she remembered from kissing him before, and more, for this time, strangely, she was not frightened. She was a virgin, true, but she was not innocent of what passed between men and women. Four years at court had taken care of that. She realized that she would not flee from Kit this afternoon. Right or wrong, she wanted him, all of him, too much to fight him or herself any longer.

Kit felt the hot pulse of his desire throbbing through his veins, and as she moved her lithe form seductively against him, his low moan of pleasure sounded deep where their mouths were joined. It had been too long since he'd had a

woman, but, God's blood, Dianna would be worth the wait.
Her mouth was unbelievably sweet, and the fire he remembered was there again, searing him with the heat of her unfulfilled passion. He broke free long enough to bury his face
in the silky ripples of her hair, relishing the fragrance of her
skin mingled with the wildflowers. His lips brushed down her
throat, and she stretched her head back with a little shiver,
shaking her hair down over his hands.

With unsteady fingers, he untied the ribbons of her skirt and
eased it down over her hips, then unlaced her bodice and
pulled it off as well. Only her shift remained to cover her, the
thin linen clinging damp and translucent to her body where
she had pressed against him. He groaned at the sight, and his
kisses now held no gentleness, only the fierce demand of his
rising passion. His large hands slid down her body and grasped
her hips, kneading the soft flesh as he lifted her up against
him.

Dianna let herself be drawn into the irresistible spell of his
touch. She was light-headed with desire, her breath shortened
to brief gasps, and she scarcely noticed when he tipped her
back onto the billowy softness of the mattress. His lips left
hers to find first the little hollow at the base of her throat, and
then moved lower, to the top curves of her breasts above her
shift. With both hands he cupped them, nuzzling the valley
between as he tugged her shift's neckline lower over the dark
peaks. His callused fingers circled and teased her, his skin
rough against hers, until she moaned and arched up against
him. Her nipples tightened beneath his touch and then beneath
his tongue as his mouth repeated the sweet torture. She tangled
her fingers in his hair, pulling him closer. Deep in her belly
she felt the tension building, the unbelievable yearning that
made her heart pound, and she twisted as he tried to free her
breasts from the shift. Frustrated, he grasped the linen and tore
it to the hem, baring her pale body to his gaze. She was even
more beautiful, more perfect, than he had imagined.

Driven by his desire, his caresses grew bolder, more possessive. He would make her forget every other lover but him,
and he would make her his. Kneeling between her legs, he

traced a teasing trail of kisses along the insides of her thighs
until she quivered beneath him, and he caught her knees over
his arms and lifted her to his mouth.

Stunned, Dianna gasped first with surprise and then with
pleasure. Her whole being seemed concentrated on coiling
tighter and tighter around the secret place he'd found, and her
back arched uncontrollably as she clutched handfuls of the
coverlet. Her knees drew higher, shaking, her body begging
for release.

She cried out his name when he came to her at last, and her
arms clutched convulsively around him to pull him closer.
Instinctively she opened herself to him, and when his fingers
slipped between their bodies to ease his way, her hips jerked
upward to meet him, and he was deep inside her.

Wild-eyed from the unexpected pain, she stared up at him
in confusion. Kit's expression was rigid with the effort of control; he wanted to prolong the pleasure as far as he could, but,
sweet Lord, she was so hot and tight. He began to move as
slowly as he could, and with each stroke, Dianna felt the sting
fading and the pleasure once again building. He filled her so
completely, this huge man, and she could not swear to where
he began and she ended, he was so much a part of her. He
pulled back and plunged deeply into her, and then again, and
tentatively she began to follow his rhythm, her own hips rising
to meet his thrusts until finally it was too much, and she could
only cross her ankles over his flanks and trust him to bring
her through with him. And he did, carrying her with him to
an exquisite level of rapture that neither had dreamed possible.

Her heart still pounding, Dianna lay exhausted beneath him,
her mind and body both dazed by what she'd experienced.
Surely he must love her, she reasoned joyfully, else how could
his lovemaking have been so passionate and wondrous? She
smiled shyly to herself and lightly brushed her lips across his
chest above her. He made a low growl of contentment, so deep
that she felt the vibrations within her own body where they
still lay joined.

Slowly he lifted himself up on his elbows to look down at
her. With her flower-strewn hair fanned around her face, her

lips still swollen from his kisses and her silver eyes liquid with
fulfillment, she was unbelievably beautiful. He had never
made love to a woman in this bed before, preferring to keep
his involvements safely away from Plumstead, but Dianna
seemed somehow to belong in this chamber. Already he was
planning, quite pleasantly, how to bring her here again. The
gossips in Wickhamton would run riot if they ever learned of
it, but Dianna was a worldly woman who could be counted
on to be discreet. And he hadn't had a doubt he'd pleased her
well in return: he'd never seen a woman look so blissfully
sated. Much, he thought wryly, as he probably looked in return.

Tenderly he brushed a dark lock of hair back from her forehead. "Ah, Dianna, sweeting, my goddess of the moon and
stars," he said lazily. "Though it will be with the summer
sun that I'll always see you in my mind's eyes. You're a lovely
woman, my Lady Grey. A lovely, tempting woman."

Dianna heard that "always," and her heart jumped. She'd
never dreamed she'd be loved by a man so handsome, so perfect, as Kit Sparhawk. Seductively he moved his hips against
hers, and with a little catch in her breath, Dianna immediately
echoed his motion and arched into him.

Kit groaned with the pleasure she gave him. God, he wanted
her again, right now, with a fierceness he found hard to believe
possible. "Little vixen," he growled, kissing her throat. "No
woman's ever done this to me."

"I've never known another man, Kit," she whispered
breathlessly.

"Another man like me," he finished for her. "Aye, sweeting, I've told you that before, and at last you've come to believe me."

A shadow fell across Dianna's happiness. Didn't he understand? He was the first, the only, man, she'd lain with. How
could he not have sensed the prize she'd so willingly surrendered to him? His mouth trailed lower, capturing one rosy
nipple in his lips, and her doubts fled, forgotten with the desire
he fanned within her again. As in a faraway dream, she heard

horses, then men calling Kit's name. She pulled him closer, certain these sounds had nothing to do with them, not now.

But Kit raised his head, listening, his face dark with anger. God in heaven, would he never have a moment to himself? With one final kiss, reluctantly he rolled away from her and crossed the floor to the open window.

Two tenants from an outlying farm were carefully lifting another man, wrapped in a blanket, from the back of a horse. He seemed unconscious, injured somehow, for his arms and legs flopped awkwardly against the horse. The Plumstead workers were clustered around them, and there was Hester, too. If it was her aid with physicking the injured man that brought them here, then why did they need him, too? People were forever falling from lofts or clumsily cutting themselves on scythes. Of course, he cared what happened to them, but why this afternoon, of all days?

Then the others moved apart enough for Kit to clearly see the injured man. He was pale as death, perhaps dead already, and the impromptu bandages that swathed his head were soaked through. Kit gripped the windowsill. He'd seen before what a rough-honed scalping knife could do to a man, swiftly, before he'd realized the Indians were upon him. And what it could do to a woman, a child.

He grabbed for his breeches, hastily jerking them up over his legs, and saw the blood on himself. He frowned, uncomprehending, then his glance flew back to Dianna. She lay curled on her side, propped up on one elbow as she watched him, but there was no mistaking the stains on her pale thighs. His conscience screamed that it was not possible, that he could not have done this to her. Virgins fought and wept; they did not wrap their thighs around a man's waist and writhe with pleasure. And what of her uncle and the other men who'd claimed to have known her?

I've never known another man. She had been willing, but he had led her. She'd been so deliciously tight around him, and now he realized why. Her eyes burned into him, uncertain and vulnerable, waiting for him to explain. Oh, God, what had he done?

He heard the voices in the kitchen below, his name called again. Soon they would come upstairs to find him. Hastily he tied the drawstring of his breeches. He longed to kiss her again, but there was no time. "Dianna, I promise we will talk," he said hurriedly, "I swear to it, sweeting, but now I must go."

Stunned, Dianna watched the door slam shut. She had given him her heart and her innocence, and he had sworn to talk. *To talk!* She pressed her palm across her mouth to hold back the tears. Oh, God, what had she done?

With old memories pressing on him like granite, Kit stared down at the man stretched out on the broad trestle table and wondered if he would live. Scalping didn't automatically mean death; it was usually exposure or the fever that came with the wound that killed. This man had been found soon after the attack, and he was young and strong enough that he might survive. Kit prayed he would, if only for the sake of all the families in Wickhamton and the surrounding farms.

If this was to be the end of the peace the valley had enjoyed for nearly nine years, then Kit, as militia captain, needed to know what tribe had attacked the man, how many braves had been involved. There was always the chance that this had been personal, reparation for some dishonor or crime that the man had committed. Kit sighed, knowing he couldn't risk doing nothing. Already he'd sent riders to the farthest settlers to bring the families to the safety of Plumstead, and he himself would lead the first patrol within the hour.

Kit watched while Hester cleaned and dressed the man's wound. He was a stranger, likely French, and a trapper from his clothes. Odd that the Indians hadn't bothered to strip him. His moccasins were almost new, and the glinting saint's medallion he wore on a thong about his neck should have been a great prize. Perhaps the Davies brothers had inadvertently frightened off the attackers when they found the man near their cornfield.

"There's all I can do for him now, Kit," said Hester grimly as she lifted the pail of dark-stained water from the table. "Put him in th' little chamber off th' kitchen an' I'll watch him best I can.''

Kit nodded to John and Samuel Davies, and together they began to gingerly lift the man from the table. But as they did, he groaned and his eyes fluttered open. *''Mon Dieu, qui est vous? Je n'ai pas d'argent!''*

''French,'' said Samuel with disgust. ''Wouldn't ye know we'd save a bloody Papist.''

Kit silenced him with a frown. ''You're among Englishmen, my friend,'' he said carefully to the wounded man. ''We wish to help you. Can you tell us who hurt you?''

But the man only stared up at him, his expression confused. *''Je ne comprends pas. Anglais? Anglais! Mere de Dieu, preservez moi!''*

''We won't hurt you,'' began Kit again, but the man's eyes were becoming more and more panicked, and Kit feared he would injure himself further. ''Pray, be calm.''

''Non, non, vous êtes Anglais—''

''Se taire,'' said Dianna as she entered the room and gently took the man's hand. She leaned over him so he could see her clearly. *''Vous êtes entre des amis.''*

''Oui?'' the man whispered desperately. *''Des amis, mademoiselle?''*

Dianna nodded. *''Oui, nous sommes amis. Maintenant, reposez vous.''* She was relieved when he closed his eyes again and his breathing became regular with either sleep or unconsciousness. She wondered what had happened to him and why he feared them so. As his face relaxed, she could see how young he was, perhaps only nineteen or twenty. His frame still had the rawboned look of adolescence, and his beard and moustache were pathetically sparse.

''Ask him who he be,'' demanded Samuel impatiently. ''Ask him—''

''Nay, Samuel, ye let him be for now,'' said Hester sharply. ''Best to put him t'bed, else he'll never answer yer questions in this life.''

As the unconscious Frenchman was slowly lifted from the table, Kit at last caught Dianna's eye. Her hair was once again neatly braided, the flowers gone, and he winced inwardly when he noticed how she'd folded her shift into the top of her bodice so the torn edges wouldn't show. "Thank you," he said quietly. "I did not know you spoke French."

Her chin shot up bravely, her eyes flashing. "There are many things you don't know about me, Master Sparhawk," she answered. "Now if you're done, I promised Asa that Mercy and I would be home before nightfall."

"You're not going anywhere." Fear for her made his tone sharp. "You will stay here."

"You are not my master!" How dare he treat her so coldly after what had just passed between them?

"You will stay, Dianna," he said curtly as he pulled on the hunting shirt that Hester handed him, and took his rifle from the pegs on the wall. "You're the only one who speaks this man's language, and you must be here when he wakes."

"But I—"

"That's an end to it," he growled. Already men were gathering outside the barn, talking excitedly among themselves as they checked their muskets and rifles, and the first wagon full of frightened women and crying children had drawn into the yard. He slung his powder horn over his shoulder and left to join the others.

His manner cut Dianna to the quick. *You're a silly, trusting fool, Dianna Grey,* she told herself miserably, *to dream of love with a man who never cared!*

"You'd do better to send Kit off with a smile, lass," said Hester so pointedly that Dianna blushed, wondering how much the older woman had guessed. "Else we may all end like that poor lad in there."

Dianna's expression was so confused that Hester rolled her eyes and clucked her tongue. "Where be your wits, girl? D'ye think that Frenchman cut himself shaving? 'Twas Indians, Dianna, Indians that took his scalp, and they'll take yours as well if they catch ye out a-walkin'. A head o'hair like yours would look mighty pleasing danglin' from some brave's waist."

Dianna's gaze flew past Hester to the departing men, and

in vain she searched for Kit's gold-streaked hair among them. If what Hester said were true, she might never see him alive again.

"Ah, but I disremember, you're fresh from London," said Hester more sympathetically, misreading Dianna's concern. "We'll be safe enough here at Plumstead. Built stouter than most forts, this house. An' Kit an' the rest o' them will come to no harm, neither. Indians be too clever t'attack a force o' armed men. It be the families livin' all alone that th' sneaking savages prey on. That's why we'll be havin' a houseful until Kit sorts this out."

At that moment a woman Dianna recognized from meeting appeared at the door, one child in her arms and four more following, each with hastily packed bundles of belongings. The youngest girl was weeping, and automatically Dianna went to comfort her. From then until long past nightfall, she was constantly busy, from peeling carrots for Hester to melting lead for musket balls over the fireplace coals to rescuing a kitten from an over-ardent child. There were thirty-four people at supper, and while the men took turns standing guard from the upper-floor windows, the women and children had to be settled in the five chambers upstairs, the lucky ones in the beds, but most rolled in blankets on the floor. It was a tense, somber gathering, with no one certain what the darkness would bring.

As Dianna scrubbed out the last kettle with a handful of sand, her whole body felt on edge from listening and waiting and trying to be cheerful. She watched Hester go for one more bucket of water, a man covering her with his musket from the doorway as she walked to the well and back. "We've one more task this night, lass," said Hester wearily as she leaned away from the full bucket in her right hand. "Ye must watch me wit' the Frenchman now an' learn, an' then th' care of him falls to ye."

The small room where the Frenchman lay was stifling. One wall backed on the kitchen chimney, and the two narrow windows were shut against the harm of the night air. As Hester lit the lantern over the bed and began to unwrap the bandages on the man's head, Dianna gasped with horror. The top of his head was completely gone, his bare skull white where his hair and scalp had been. At the sight, Dianna felt the room begin to spin around her and the blood pound in her ears.

"Don't faint on me now, lass," warned Hester as she quickly reached out to steady Dianna. "I can't take on two o' ye at once."

At the sound of her voice, the Frenchman stirred. *"Solange, c'est tu?"*

Hester nodded at Dianna. "There now, speak to th' lad," she prompted. "He needs t'hear his own tongue."

Dianna hesitated, unsure of how to reply, and the Frenchman struggled weakly to rise from the narrow bed. *"Solange? Ou est tu?"*

"Soyez calme, s'il vous plaît," murmured Dianna, gently pushing him back, and to her surprise he grasped her wrist with unexpected strength. "I am here."

"That's good, lass, hold him steady while I finish." Deftly Hester rinsed the wound and began to tie fresh linen strips around his head. "Mind me, now, for you'll do the same come morning. Call me if the wound turns putrid or a fever takes him." She finished at last and looked at Dianna curiously. "What's he been saying, anyways?"

"He thinks I'm a woman named Solange," said Dianna softly. "I thought it best to agree."

"Aye, let him be at ease. We'll not get much sense out o' him for a day or two at least. Mayhap never, if his wits went with his hair." Hester gathered up the soiled bandages and the bucket. "Ye stay with him tonight in case he wakes. Ye shall find more comfort in that chair than some of them upstairs. I'll be in the kitchen if ye need me."

Dianna nodded and looked down at the slow rise and fall of the man's narrow chest beneath his coarse shirt. He had once again fallen asleep, and gently she eased her hand free from his, wondering if she would ever learn who Solange was.

With a sigh, Dianna tried to make herself comfortable, curling her legs up in the rush-bottom chair and resting her head across her folded arms. From the kitchen, she could hear Hester chatting softly with the men on watch, and beyond that, outdoors, the whirring of cicadas in the trees. She was too exhausted to stay awake long. Although she wished it were otherwise, her last thoughts before sleep claimed her were of Kit and how sweet it had been to lie in his arms on an afternoon in June.

Chapter Eleven

It wanted still two hours until dawn and Kit hated to wake Dianna. The single candle's light from the tin lantern washed her figure in shadowy gold as she slept, her face pillowed in her crossed arms, her lips slightly parted. It seemed the one peaceful moment in Kit's world right now, a world gone horribly awry. He longed to find solace in her arms and in her embrace, forget the memories of old tragedies and the fresh, raw images of what he and the others had found beyond Plumstead. But he had no right to her comfort, not after the way he had treated her this afternoon. No, it had been yesterday, he reminded himself wearily. Only yesterday. It might have been a lifetime, given the way he felt now.

The Davies brothers had been lucky. Their house and barn had been burned to charred, smoking timbers, but their horses and cattle at pasture left unharmed. If the brothers had not brought the Frenchman to Plumstead, they would likely have met the same fate as their neighbors, the Barnards.

John Barnard and his three sons had been shot dead in their cornfield, their attackers boldly using the tall, new corn for cover. From the moccasin footprints between the rows, Kit doubted the Barnards had seen the Indians until it was too late. Their house, too, had been burned, and there was no sign of Dorothy Barnard or the two daughters. Women made useful captives, for ransom or to sell as servants to the French, and, grimly, Kit knew it unlikely that he'd ever see them again.

Kit and the others had pushed on to the rest of the surrounding homesteads, continuing to travel long after nightfall. They had found no more destruction, but Kit had warned the other settlers and urged them to come to Plumstead for safety. That most stubbornly refused did not surprise him. Many years had passed since the country surrounding Wickhamton had been attacked, and despite the attack on Deerfield to the north in February, newcomers in particular naively scoffed at the danger. But then few carried with them the memory that had haunted Kit every hour, every day, since the year of his twenty-second birthday.

It had been early autumn, still warm in the afternoons, though the leaves had begun to change and the first, weak frosts marked the ground at dawn. Kit's mother, Amity, had spent the night with a friend in Wickhamton, easing her through a difficult birth; with six children of her own surviving infancy, Amity's comfort was much in demand. It was Kit's task to bring his mother home, but at the last moment, for a reason he never could remember, his father had gone instead and taken his youngest daughter, Tamsin, with him. When they did not return by supper, Kit had ridden out to meet them, certain his mother had, as usual, dawdled to gossip with friends and that his father would welcome his elder son's company.

Instead what Kit had found were the slaughtered bodies of his parents and sister scattered across the Wickhamton road like mangled dolls.

If he'd only gone instead of his father…

If he'd left to meet them even a quarter-hour earlier!

No one held him to blame except himself. If Kit had been there, too, his friends had argued, then he would have perished as well. Even the minister had told him he'd been spared by God's infinite mercy. But Kit did not believe them then, and he did not believe them now. Some part of him had died that afternoon along with his parents and sister. Methodically he had tracked the four Mohegans responsible for the killing, and as he watched them hanged, he had realized the empty satisfaction of his revenge. He had thrown himself into running

Plumstead and governing the land around it as his father had done, building the mills to lure more settlers, and expanding into trade with Jonathan and other captains. But nothing had helped. Nothing had eased the anguish or given back to him what he'd lost.

How could he ever explain it to Dianna? He let himself watch her sleep a little longer, knowing he was wasting the short time he could spare to be alone with her. Even if he found the words, how could she possibly understand?

Even before she woke, Dianna sensed Kit was there. Her eyes opened and met his warily, uncertain what to expect. He stood on the other side of the injured Frenchman, his unshaven face streaked with dirt and sweat, and bits of leaves and brambles stuck in his hair. His eyes were red-rimmed from lack of sleep, his mouth a hard line that would offer no sweetheart's promises, and she steeled herself to be equally cold and unyielding.

"We need to talk, Dianna."

Dianna shook her head fiercely. "There is nothing to say."

So this was how it would be, thought Kit wearily. A "nothing" like that from her meant he could talk from now until Christmas and she wouldn't hear a word of it. But he had to try. "Dianna, dearling, I regret—"

"I want none of your regrets and none of you!" she answered hotly. "I'm sorrier than you will ever be about—about what passed between us yesterday, and I will thank you never to mention it again."

"Dianna—"

"Nay, I'll not hear more!" She scrambled out of the chair and grabbed a handful of the fresh bandages that she and Hester had torn last night. "This man needs to be tended, Master Sparhawk, and I'll ask you to let me go about my work."

Kit sighed and rubbed his forehead. How could he set things right with a half-dead Frenchman lying between them? If he weren't so tired and discouraged, he might have laughed. "Has the man said anything of use?"

"Nay," Dianna swallowed hard, concentrating on both

cleaning the wound as Hester had shown her and not fainting before Kit.

Kit hadn't imagined her as a nurse and was surprised by how gently she tended to the Frenchman. The man stirred and groaned restlessly beneath her touch, and Dianna murmured to him softly in French. The unknown words in her low voice struck Kit's ear as impossibly seductive, and as the man relaxed, Kit felt the first twinge of unexpected jealousy. "What are you saying to him?" he demanded impatiently.

Her eyes narrowed at the unmistakable suspicion. "You don't know how to trust, do you?" she said tersely. "I've said nothing to him that I wouldn't say to Mercy."

"Damn it, Dianna, there are four men dead, a woman and two girls missing, and yet you expect me to—"

"Colonel Sparhawk!" The man pounded unceremoniously on the chamber door. "The messenger's ready t'ride to th' garrison at Northfield."

His expression black with anger, Kit threw open the door and stalked into the kitchen filled with the men from the train-band. They all believed he'd been questioning the Frenchman, and Kit felt like a fool for concocting an excuse merely to talk to a woman who refused to listen. "Where's Eleazer? I'll need another copy of this letter to send to Lord Bellomar, and two more for Albany and New Haven. If it is the Sagomutucks again, then other Englishmen should be warned."

"Eleazer's gone t'warn 'em at Deerfield, Colonel," said John Davies uneasily. "Ye sent him there yerself."

Kit swore and dropped heavily into the chair at the end of the table. "Why the devil did I do that?" he demanded of no one in particular. From the corner of his eye, he caught Dianna's small figure slipping among the men, the bucket held before her. "Eleazer's the only man I trust to write a decent hand. Ah, well, there's no help for it but I must write the letter again myself." He reached for his pen and another sheet of paper.

"I can copy it for you," said Dianna quietly. Every man turned to stare at her, but she stood with her head high and her hands folded before her. "It takes no great manly strength to wield a pen, you know."

Kit looked up at her from under drawn brows, weighing her offer for only a moment before shoving the paper and pen toward her. "I need three copies for my signing by the time I return tonight, one to Lord Bellomar in Boston, and one each to the governors of Connecticut and New York. And mark that they're neat and true, for I want their lordships to read every word."

As all around him the other men rumbled and nodded in agreement, Kit finished the tall flacon of cider Hester had brought him. He should, he knew, eat something as well, for he intended to visit the farthest points of his settled land today, a good day's hard riding at best. But he was still too concerned about what he might find to linger at Plumstead any longer, and restlessly he rose to leave. Only at the doorway did he let himself pause to look back at Dianna, bending over the table to study the letters she was to copy. Let her read them, he decided as he left. Then perhaps she would understand.

Dianna stared down at the letter before her, the words blurring before her eyes. She wanted to take Mercy and go home, never to see Kit Sparhawk again. She needed time alone to think. She felt trapped in his house, trapped as much by his overwhelming presence as by the danger waiting in the forest. He hadn't bothered to thank her for copying his infernal letters, let alone bid her farewell. Because she had rebuffed his attentions, she knew she could expect no better. But, oh, how it hurt!

She forced herself to read the letter before her. Kit's handwriting was irritatingly like him, bold and confident and masculine. But the events his words described made her soon forget her own concerns. In short, blunt sentences, Kit described the massacre of the Barnard men and the kidnapping of the women, the scalping of the Frenchman and the destruction of barns and houses. And this, he concluded, might only be the beginning of a long, bloody conflict in the river valley.

"Is this true, Hester?" Dianna asked hoarsely, her face drawn with horror.

"If Kit's written it, then true it be," replied Hester. "Poor Dorothy Barnard! She be a timid soul anyways, and then t'lose her men an' her home on th' self-same day must be too much for her to bear. God preserve her an' restore her an' the lasses back to us!"

"But surely when the governor sends us the soldiers Kit has asked for—surely then they will be rescued!"

Hester shook her head sadly. "There's no certainty in this world, lass. This be a big land, and th' governor has many calls for his troops. One poor Wickhamton family don't account for much wit' those fine folks in New Haven. An' even if the soldiers come, why, th' trail will be so cold by then that Goodwife Barnard's sure to be lost t'English eyes forever."

"Can't Kit and the trainband men go after them?"

"Don't believe he hasn't thought on it!" exclaimed Hester ruefully. "But those roguish savages could lead them clear t'Montreal, an' who'd be left here? Trainband men have farms an' families t'tend, an' Kit—faith, there's hardly a soul 'round here that don't depend on him for something."

"What will the Indians do to the women?" asked Dianna. She thought of the day when she and Mercy had met the Indian in the woods. What if he hadn't been friendly?

"If they didn't kill them outright, they'll likely sell them in Montreal, where th'priests will try t'beguile them into turning Papist," said Hester with true Protestant contempt. "Else they'll keep th' women for themselves an' turn them into heathen squaws. Me, I never could decide which fate'd be th' worst."

Dianna had heard enough. With a sigh, she carefully began to copy Kit's letter as Hester, a broad wooden spoon in her hand, bent over Dianna's shoulder to watch.

"Then it be true? Ye can read an' write like a gentleman? I never learned beyond makin' my mark," she marveled. "With your French an' writin' an' all, ye can do more good for Kit than th' rest o' us women-folk combined."

But when Dianna remembered the cold expression on Kit's face, she knew he'd only one use for her, a use that would bring no good to any of them.

* * *

For the next two weeks, Dianna was never far from Kit's thoughts. Again and again, as he rode across open meadows and through uncleared forests, he could think of little beyond her—her smile, her laugh and, most of all, how she'd looked wearing nothing more than wildflowers—and again and again he cursed himself for being so besotted. It was dangerous, for one thing. He could be mooning away after Dianna and not see the glint of a musket or knife in the tree overhead until it was too late. Too many people were counting on him for him to risk his life and theirs by acting like a lovelorn schoolboy.

It was all Dianna's fault, of course. He'd tried to apologize, and God knows he'd never had to do that to a woman before, but she'd just stuck her haughty little nose in the air and dismissed him, there, in his own house. In front of Hester, she had shrugged off his thanks for copying the letters with a brusqueness that bordered on being rude, and had given him no opening to admit to the misspellings she'd corrected, an admission he'd felt sure would have melted her resistance. With Plumstead full of women, she was the only one who didn't look to him for reassurance, or smile at his jests when he sought to cheer them. She kept her distance, but her small, slender figure was always there, taunting him with her proximity alone until he thought he'd go mad from wanting to touch her. How could she have given herself so freely to him that one perfect afternoon and now not even deign to meet his eye?

Perhaps if he'd had more success in the forest, he could have borne her rejection more gracefully. Each day he and the others rode out on ever-varied patrols, checking on the farms and houses that had been so hastily closed and searching for any signs of the Indians that had killed the Barnards. But at dusk they returned to Plumstead with no news, and it ate at him that he still didn't even know which tribe was responsible. They had struck and then vanished, their identity and motives mysteries, and Kit had little patience with mysteries weighted against the lives of English women and children.

Kit's last hope for a clue lay with the Frenchman, and even

that was fading as fast as the trapper's life. He had never regained consciousness to be questioned about his assailants, and when the fever had settled into his weakened body, Hester and Kit each knew without speaking that the man would not survive. Only Dianna tenaciously believed he would recover and spent long hours talking to him in French and bathing his body with cool, damp cloths. Her attentions irritated Kit, not only because they struck him as so misplaced—before the attack, the man had probably been as coarse and wolfish as any other French trapper, certainly company Dianna would have taken pains to avoid—but also because it was at Kit's own order that she had begun tending the injured man in the first place. To be jealous of a dying man was ludicrous, yet Kit was, and knowing it didn't make it any easier to bear. Being jealous meant he cared about her in the way that he'd been doing his damnedest to deny.

Late one evening Kit sat at the kitchen table, moodily swirling the beer in his tankard as he watched Dianna with the trapper through the open door. The candle in the lantern brought out the mahogany streaks in her hair, like a soft red halo around her face. As she changed his bandages she sang, crooning almost, the seductive sound of her voice wrapping around the soft French words.

It was too much for Kit. In three long strides he was in the little room. Dianna's startled face upturned before him as he caught her by the arm.

"What do you want? You've no reason to hold me thus!" Her pale eyes flashed her anger.

"You wanted to learn how to fire a musket," he replied, "and by God, I'm ready to teach you."

"But you refused before—"

"Things are different now." He pulled her along after him, pausing in the kitchen only to grab a musket, bullets and powder, before he led her out the door and away from the house. Dianna struggled to break free, twisting and jerking back, but his grasp was too strong to break, and she followed stumbling after him.

"You said we all had to stay near the house!" she yelled at him. "Your orders, *Colonel* Sparhawk!"

He ignored her, intent on reaching the small copse of beech trees. The moon was just past full, the meadow they crossed almost as brightly lit as by day. He stopped before the trees, releasing her so suddenly that she reeled to one side.

"You're mad, you are," she said as she flung her loosened hair back out of her face. She was breathless from fighting him, and breathless, too, from being alone with him. For a fortnight she had been able to keep her true feelings about him buried behind a careful mask of indifference, but she did not trust herself without the safety of others around her. "To fire guns after dark with all the country fearful, we'll likely be shot ourselves! I'm going back to the house now—"

"You'll stay," he said as he unshouldered the musket, "and you'll learn." Before she could protest, he had caught her again and yanked her back hard against his chest. Holding her within the circle of his arms, he began to load the gun, shaking a little powder into the priming pan and snapping it shut with two fingers.

"This is the firelock. Make certain it's at half-cock before you begin, and only a smidge of the powder here." Deftly he then sloped the musket down, steadying it with one hand while with the other he shook more powder down the barrel. Next went the wadding and the ball. Then, after drawing the ramrod from the barrel's loops, he gave it three quick strokes to shove the ball in place. In spite of herself, Dianna watched him, fascinated by the practiced ease with which he loaded the musket. The confidence with which his long-fingered hands moved was almost graceful, and she remembered too well how those same hands had moved across her body.

Loading a musket was a task Kit could probably do while drunk, asleep or both, and considering the effect Dianna was having on him, it was just as well. Small as she was, she fit so neatly against him, her soft curves especially designed, it seemed, to complement the harder planes and hollows of his own body. Beneath his nose her hair smelled clean, like meadow grass, and he longed to bury his face in it. He handed her the musket, holding it steady while she found her aim, noticing how smooth and silky pale the skin of her shoulder looked beside the darkened maple of the musket's butt.

Dianna tried to concentrate on the tree branch that Kit had chosen as her target. Once her father had let her fire one of his small hunting guns, and, to his great amusement, the recoil had landed her on her backside. This musket was heavier and longer, and she dreaded giving Kit one more reason to scorn her. Feeling his warm breath just below her ear did nothing to help her concentration, nor did the way he guided her aim with one hand gently at her wrist. She took a deep breath, braced her legs apart and fired.

The gunshot exploded in her ear, the impact throwing her back against Kit. He stood firm, unmoving as she quickly scrambled away from him to peer out into the moonlight. The bark on the bottom of the branch had cracked and splintered, the leaves around it bouncing wildly from the impact. Elated, she spun around to grin at him, clutching the musket like a prize with both hands.

"Why did you not tell me you were a maid?" he asked softly, his eyes hidden in shadow.

Dianna stiffened, her excitement gone in an instant. "Would it have made any difference to you?" she demanded, her head high. "Maid or not, what could I ever hope to be to you beyond one more of your harlots? Another pitiful lass fallen under the spell of the irresistible Kit Sparhawk?"

"Merciful God in Heaven," murmured Kit to himself in disbelief. This was not what he'd expected, not at all, but when had Dianna ever been predictable?

"Is it because I'm but a woman, a lowly, base creature, you won't bother to defend yourself?" Her laugh was brittle, the strain of the last weeks catching her at last. "What of Patience Tucker then, and the babe she's likely borne you by now? Would you defend *her?*"

"If you were a man," said Kit quietly, "I'd call you out for speaking such nonsense."

Why doesn't he deny it? thought Dianna wildly. *Please, please, tell me I'm wrong!* She felt the tears welling up behind her eyes and roughly dashed them away. "And what about Mercy? She's your daughter, too, isn't she?"

Dianna was sobbing now, lost in her misery and disillusionment, and blindly she turned toward the house. But Kit caught her by the shoulders first, holding her straight before him. Having grown up with four sisters, he was generally unaffected by weeping women, but the desolation in Dianna's crying shocked him. Had he really hurt her that much?

"Listen to me, Dianna," he said urgently. "Listen to me!"

She shook her head and looked down at the grass, letting her tears fall unchecked, as the musket dropped to the ground. His hands slid along her shoulders and up her neck to turn her face up toward his. "Patience Tucker's husband was second mate on the *Prosperity*. When he was lost in the last gale, it fell to me as owner to tell her. I've never laid eyes, let alone anything else, on the lass before or since. As for Lucy Wing— sweet Jesus, Dianna, her husband was one of my closest friends! I know you're from a different world where such things may not matter, but I would never have done that to Tom if Lucy had tossed herself before me naked as Eve!"

"But Asa says—"

"Then Asa lies," said Kit firmly. "He never took to Lucy, or to me, either, for the time his son spent with us instead of him, and now he feels the same with Mercy. I love the little minx, aye, but where's the harm in that?"

Gently he stroked her cheeks with his thumbs, striving to reassure her with his touch as well as words. "I've never claimed to be a saint, sweeting, and there are women enough who can spin pretty tales of Jonathan and me both. But not Lucy, not Patience, and no bastards. I'm not nearly so free with my seed as you believe."

She blushed at his frankness, though she knew it was no less than she deserved. Through the tears she searched his face, hoping, praying that she could trust him.

He saw the doubt in her eyes and sighed. "Believe what you will, Dianna, but I swear by all that's holy and dear to me that that's the truth." His voice was deep and low. "Now why did you not tell me you were a maid?"

"I did not think I had to," she whispered hoarsely. "I thought you were different. I thought you would believe me instead of my uncle. But I was wrong, wasn't I? I was wrong...."

She spoke without malice, yet her words cut straight to his conscience and to his heart, too. "Nay, dearling, not wrong, but wronged," he said sadly. "I've no right to ever hope for your forgiveness."

She listened, incredulous, and tentatively touched her fingers to his rough cheek. "Ah, Kit," she breathed, her smile fragile and tremulous. "We are neither of us, I think, quite so good nor quite so bad as we each might fear."

He caught her hand in his and brushed his lips across her open palm. "I love you, Dianna Grey," he said simply, and he realized he had never meant anything more in his life than those words. "How much I love you!"

"No more than I love you, Kit Sparhawk, my perfect, precious love!" And now, at last, she believed him, and knew, in her heart, she always had.

This time when their lips met, their kiss was at once heated, urgent and wild. Dianna seized at the passion he offered and arched herself into him, opening her mouth fully to his demands. She forgot everything but him as she twined her limbs around his, and swiftly Kit scooped his arms under her knees and carried her into the purple shadows of the beech trees. Collapsing into the rustling leaves, she showered him with kisses, wet and soft, on his face and throat and chest, and tangled her fingers in the lion-like mass of his hair. She lay atop him, her breasts crushed against his chest, her legs slipping apart over his hips, and through their clothes she could feel the heat of him, hard and ready against her belly.

Kit's hands swept along her length, caressing and stroking her as he drew her even tighter against him. He kissed her hard, his tongue filling her mouth as he longed to fill her body. She tasted so impossibly sweet that he was sure he could kiss her forever and never tire of her. Hungrily he reached between their bodies and tugged her bodice open, the silky fullness of her breasts spilled over the lacings and into his palms. He cupped them gently, marveling at the softness of her skin as his fingers played across the crests, her nipples swelling and tightening. She moaned into his mouth, wanting more, needing more, and he jerked the rough wool skirt over her hips. He reached to stroke the backs of her thighs, the curves of her hips and buttocks, the little dimples at the base of her spine, and she arched back, gasping, as he caught one rosy nipple between his lips. Convulsively her fingers worked in the muscles of his shoulders, her head thrown back and her hair streaming over her shoulders.

Kit was almost shaking with the force of his desire. With a groan he separated from her only long enough to unfasten his breeches. He rose to his knees, and she threw her arms around his neck, climbing him, her movements frantic with need. His breathing harsh, Kit shoved her skirts up and found her wet and ready. As his fingers touched her, Dianna gasped raggedly, and then his hands were grasping her thighs and lifting her, her legs wrapping tight around his waist as he slid deep into her. With his hands spread to cradle her, he moved her powerfully against him, and she cried out in wonder. He was a part of her and she a part of him, joined in heart and spirit as surely as they now were joined in flesh, and as together they soared higher and higher, it seemed that their love, like their passion, would be ever boundless.

Afterward they lay together, coupled still, listening to the whirring of the cicadas and the muted calls of night birds as the pounding of their own hearts grew gradually quieter. Dianna wondered if she'd ever move again, so contented was she, and mindless of the wanton way she lay sprawled across Kit with her skirts rucked up and her bodice unlaced. His shirt beneath her cheek was damp with sweat, and she snuggled closer as his fingers twined randomly in her hair.

"I love you, sweeting," he murmured into the top of her hair. He could not remember feeling so contented, so at peace, as he did now with Dianna. "I would keep you here with me all night and let the white-faced cows find us come dawn."

Dianna giggled at the image and propped herself up on her elbows to study him. His face looked so relaxed, the dark lashes sooty shadows on his cheeks, that she wondered if he were asleep, and she spoke softly in case he was so he would not wake. "I love you too, Kit, and not even white-faced cattle can change that."

With his eyes still closed, Kit snorted. "At least my cows would keep their own counsel, which is a sight more than our good neighbors will be able to manage. I'll talk to Asa on the morrow and buy you out of that ridiculous indenture, and then—"

But Dianna silenced him with her fingers across his lips. "Hush, love. I want no promises, no plans from you tonight." No plans, no promises that could be broken along with her heart. "Knowing you love me is enough."

His arms tightened around her, praying she was right. How could love survive when life itself seemed so fragile? One by one, he kissed her fingertips and she shivered with delight.

"But cows or no, we cannot truly stay all night, can we?" she asked wistfully, though she knew the answer.

"Nay, there's no help for it, my love." He opened his eyes and smiled, his teeth blue-white in the moonlight, and Dianna thought she'd never seen such a beautiful man. Carefully he plucked a leaf from her hair. "Come, I'll play your lady's maid and help set you to rights."

They dressed slowly, pausing often to kiss and caress each other, and by the time they headed toward Plumstead, the only light left in the house came from the little lantern in the sickroom. As they walked through the tall meadow grass, already heavy with dew, Kit laughed ruefully and stopped to pick up the musket they'd left behind.

"Here's proof enough how I can think of nothing beyond you," he said, shaking his head. "The whole country in alarm, and here I leave musket, powder and balls for any savage to find."

Although he tried to make light of it, the gun was a sharp reminder of all they'd been able to forget in each other's arms. Irretrievably, the mood was gone, and each felt the loss sorely. Mindful of the two men on watch at the house, they walked self-consciously, as close as they could without actually touching. As they drew closer, one of the guards ran toward them, waving.

Kit frowned, fearing the worst. "What in blazes—"

"Colonel Sparhawk, sir," the man said quickly, tugging on his hatbrim before he impatiently turned to Dianna. "Where ye been hiding yerself, lass? Mistress Holcomb's been raisin' the devil tryin' to find ye! That ruddy Frenchman o'yours is dyin'!"

Chapter Twelve

Kneeling at the Frenchman's cot, Dianna noticed the change at once. She had never seen anyone die before, but there was no mistaking the man's condition now. He'd seemed to shrink into himself somehow, his breathing slow and labored, and beneath the white bandage his skin was waxy and oddly translucent. Already he looked more like a corpse than a man.

"He'll not see another dawn, lass," said Hester as she rested her hand on Dianna's shoulder. "Ye've done all ye can for him, but it be th'Lord decides these things, not us."

"How can he die?" said Dianna unevenly. "I never even learned his name."

From the doorway, Kit heard the catch in her voice, and he yearned to comfort her. He felt no jealousy for the Frenchman now, only a terrible sense of waste. He'd seen it so often, too often, Kit thought wearily, one more man's life cut short before its time.

But at the sound of her voice, the Frenchman moaned and strained upward toward her, and with obvious effort his eyes half opened. "Ah, Solange, you are here."

"*Dormez, mon ami,*" said Dianna as she touched her hand to the dying man's cheek, his skin hot and brittle.

"Tell François I saw him, Solange," he rasped in French. "He tried to hide, the swine, but I marked his face, and I tell you now!"

Dianna drew closer, aware of the significance of the man's

words, and aware, too, that his time was short. *"Ou est François, mon ami?"* Where was he?

"He waited in the trees...but I saw him. I saw Robillard, damn him, the coward!"

At Robillard's name, Kit leaped forward. "What did he say, Dianna?" he demanded urgently. "God in Heaven, if Robillard's filthy hand is in this—"

Dianna's eyes never left the Frenchman's wasted face. "He said he saw Robillard hiding in the trees when the others attacked him."

Kit leaned over her shoulder. "Ask him who the others were!"

But as Kit spoke the Frenchman slipped back, and Dianna watched the last bit of life drain from his face. *"Au revoir, mon ami pauvre,"* she said as Hester closed the man's eyes for the final time. *"Au revoir!"*

They buried the Frenchman the next morning; with the summer's heat, there was no reason to delay. Dianna and Kit were his only mourners. Some, like Hester, stayed away because the man had been French and a Papist, but most were simply too busy leaving Plumstead to bother with a stranger's burial. At dawn Kit had told the families in his keeping that they could return to their homes, that as much as he could guess, the danger was past for now. Still, he sent soldiers from the Northfield garrison along with each wagon and warned the men to keep watch for trouble. Now that Kit knew the attacks had come from Robillard, not Indians alone, he knew it was up to him to make some sort of move.

And Kit still wasn't certain what that move should be. To call in more soldiers to lead an attack in retaliation on French settlements to the north seemed pointless to Kit, though the governor's men, safe in Boston, would probably counsel it. All that would bring would be more French soldiers or French-sponsored Indians and more suffering to the English families in his protection. And yet to ignore Robillard's attack was cowardly and just as likely to bring more slayings and more kidnappings.

It was Sparhawk land that Robillard wanted, plain and simple. Kit believed that the man had only intended to cause enough damage to frighten away the English settlers on Kit's holdings and weaken his claim, although, thought Kit grimly, Robillard had shown typical French disregard for English tenacity where good, rich land was concerned. The poor French trapper must have had the misfortune to wander through the Davies' fields at the wrong time. Likely he'd been one of Robillard's own trappers to know him by name. Kit wondered if the other men had been French, as well, or Indians, Mohegans or Abenakis, in Robillard's hire. Not that it really mattered. Murder was the same in any tongue, and Kit wanted no more of it in his valley.

The two gravediggers tossed the last loose soil onto the new grave, hoisted their shovels over their shoulders and began the long walk back to Wickhamton. Dianna bent to lay a circle of wildflowers on the new grave, murmuring softly in French that, this time, Kit did not ask her to translate. Her eyes were dry, but her face was pale and solemn. The Frenchman's death had shaken her more than she wanted to admit, and Kit longed to be able to spare her from such sorrow. He'd grant that her spirit was as strong as any woman's, and her temper, too, but he could not forget that she'd been gently bred, and today her eyes were shadowed and her shoulders bent from sleeplessness and fatigue.

As they walked home in silence, Kit let his hand rest comfortably about her waist. Beside him she seemed so small, almost fragile. Yet there was no denying the strength of the passion that burned in that delicate frame, and at the memory of last night, his fingers slid down from her waist, fanning to caress the soft curve of her hip and buttocks. He heard her breath catch as she glanced up at him through her lashes, her eyebrows arched expectantly as her cheeks flushed.

"You tempt me sorely, lass," he growled as he bent to kiss her neck behind her ear. "I should toss you here, in plain sight of the house, to show you how dangerous your game can be."

Dianna smiled shyly. Why was it with one touch he could make her forget everything else except him? "Tonight, then, by the beeches,'' she whispered, feeling daringly bold. ''I swear I won't keep your cattle waiting.''

It was all Kit could do to steady himself. With all her chattering about illegitimate children, she'd never mentioned herself. Even now his child could be growing in her belly, and for the first time the idea of fatherhood warmed him with pleasure. Pleasure, but responsibility, too, and he knew then what he would do about Robillard.

''Nay, lass, not tonight. I'll say farewell to you now,'' he said, too abruptly even to his own ears. ''There won't be time alone when we're back among the others before I leave.''

She stared up at him, uncomprehending.

''I'm going to find Robillard myself,'' he explained hurriedly. Merciful heaven, why did those beautiful eyes have to be so full of questions? ''It's me he wants, and it's me he'll have, and perhaps then he'll listen to reason. My land's English, not French, and there's no law or treaty that says otherwise. I'll haul him clear to Quebec to prove it, if I must.''

''You'll take soldiers with you?''

''Nay, I don't want to give him any reason to send his men out to greet me with less than kind hospitality.'' The miserable jest fell flat, and he plunged on. ''I'll go with Attawan, if I can find him on my way, but that's all.''

Dianna stopped and yanked her arm away from his. ''Of all the braggartly, half-witted schemes—''

''Dianna, I've lived all my life on this land and know it as well as my own parlor.''

''That's not the point, is it?'' she asked incredulously. ''You're going to dance right into the arms of a man who'd like nothing more than to see you dead, a man who's killed your own tenants to get at you. And just so you can have the honor of playing hero!''

She waved wildly at the fresh grave behind them. ''Look what he did to one of his own countrymen! Why do you think he'll be willing to change just because you asked him genteelly?''

''Is that really what you believe? That it's only selfishness that makes me want to save the lives of my people? Aye, and your life, too, for I'm doing this as much for you as for any-one.'' The depth of his feelings for her was still so new that he felt clumsy trying to put it into words. "I do care what happens to you, Dianna.''

"Precious odd way you have of showing it, Master Spar-hawk!''

"Dianna, listen to me—''

"Nay, you listen to me! It's your ludicrous man's pride that makes you want to toss away your own life. Empty, vain, puffed-up pride that's not worth a tinker's dam!'' Kit tried to take her hand, but she shoved him away so hard, she herself stumbled backward. "Don't you understand that every mo-ment I spent with that poor man, I thought of how I'd feel if it were you lying there instead, with your life's blood slipping away?''

Her voice caught on a sob, her words rising in an anguished wail. "I hate this country! I hate how it turns every man into a murdering savage, and I hate the blood-letting and the re-venge, and I hate—oh, damn it, I hate how I'm crying, too, as if I truly cared what happened to your prideful, selfish hide!''

Once again Kit reached for her, and this time caught her wrist, but again she jerked away, her eyes bright with tears. "That's how you are with everything, Kit. Take it and force it to bend to your will, just because your name's Sparhawk. But it won't work with François Robillard. And it won't work with me.''

Dianna turned and fled, her bare feet flying beneath her skirts as she left Kit standing alone on the rutted dirt road. Her heart felt near to bursting, not from running, but from all that she'd heard and said. She needed desperately to be alone, and she headed for the barn, hoping that at midday, all the workers and animals would be in the fields. The wide doors were thrown open to catch any breeze, and she paused in the doorway, her breath coming in great shuddering sobs, while her eyes grew accustomed to the shadowy barn.

"Dianna!'' Mercy stepped from one of the empty stalls and grinned. Cradled in her arms was a white kitten patched with black, sleeping blissfully against the girl's chest. Automatically Dianna reached out to straighten Mercy's linen cap and pluck bits of straw from her apron.

"I'm glad you've come at last t'meet my Lily," said the girl proudly. "Lily, this be Dianna. She'll be nice to ye, Lily, an' she won't shoo ye away like Hester."

The girl held the little cat's paw out to Dianna to shake. "She be a fine catkin, my Lily," Mercy said fondly, stroking the sleeping kitten. Suddenly she noticed Dianna's tear-streaked face.

"Ye be mournin' that Frenchman, don't ye, Dianna?" she said with surprising empathy. "Well, ye grieve howsomuch ye want out here, an' I'll not tell Hester."

Not trusting her voice, Dianna knelt down and took Mercy in her arms, holding her tight until the kitten between them yowled in protest. With a shaky smile, Dianna sat back on her heels. She'd had little time to spend with Mercy these past weeks, and she'd missed the girl's company. "We'll make a special bed for Lily when we go home tonight, up in the loft with us. That way you can talk to her if she gets frightened in the night."

Mercy's grin widened, and with a pang Dianna noticed she'd lost another baby tooth. "I want you and Lily to say goodbye to Kit and thank him for having us as guests at Plumstead. Hurry now, I think he's likely at the house."

"Nay, Mercy, he's right here," said Kit, and Dianna's head whipped around. He stood with his legs widespread, a dark silhouette in the doorway against the bright afternoon. Though unable to see his face, Dianna could hear the anger barely contained in his voice, and she rose slowly as Mercy ran to meet him, poor Lily jiggling in her embrace.

Kit swept the little girl up into his arms. "Mind you take good care of Lily," he warned. "I don't give Tiger's kittens to just anyone."

Mercy giggled happily. "Nay, 'cause ye keep them all t'yerself! Hester says th'barn be so overrun with cats Jonathan'll have t'bring in rats from th' shipyards t'keep 'em busy."

"Aye, and right she may be. It's well you're taking Mistress Lily with you." He kissed the top of her head before setting her back on her feet. "Now off with you, poppet. I've things to say to our friend here."

There was an ominous sound to that which Dianna did not like, and she squared her hands on her hips, ready for a battle. He loomed before her, the sunlight behind him turning his tousled hair golden like a halo. *Halo, ha! More like the flames of hell, come to claim their own!*

He didn't waste any time. "I may be prideful and selfish, but I don't run away at the first sign of a fight. It makes me madder than a hornet in a bottle the way you keep flying off like that, and I won't have you doing it again!"

Dianna's chin jerked higher. "I believed, sir, our conversation was at an end."

"Not by half, it wasn't. Only a coward would say otherwise. And you, my lady, are no coward."

In an instant his hands were around her waist, drawing her closer. This time her pride kept her from rebuffing him, from confirming the accusation he'd just made. Defiantly she tried to raise her eyes to meet his, but somehow the path was slower than she intended, from the triangle of curling hair at the open throat of his untied shirt, along the stubborn strength of his jaw, already stubbled, to a mouth that, even set with sternness, could make her remember the sensual promise of kisses given and shared. She was certain she'd be betrayed by the pounding of her heart. Whether it raced from anger or desire she curiously couldn't decide, and for the first time she realized how closely twined the two passions could be.

He tried to remember all the things he'd decided as he followed her here, but his mind was empty except for the vibrant reality of her before him, her pulse thrumming there in the softest place on her throat. Swiftly he plucked Dianna up as easily as he had Mercy, and perched her on the edge of a tackbox so that their faces were now level.

"You're no coward, Dianna," he repeated as his thumb found the little cleft in her chin and he tilted her face toward his. "You're brave and beautiful and unlike any other woman in this world, and I'm so in love with you that to leave you today will be the hardest thing I've ever done.''

He caught her around the waist and slid her against him as his lips crushed hers. There was no coaxing or beguiling this time, no gentle seductions, only a raw urgency, a primal intensity that left both of them panting as their mouths met and moved hungrily against each other.

Then suddenly he pulled away, his breathing harsh. He closed his eyes and shook his head with the effort of stopping, and let his head tip forward until their foreheads touched. ''Dianna, sweetheart, this is how I'll take my leave, with both of us half mad from wanting,'' he said. ''Now you'll believe me when I tell you nothing will keep me from coming back. Nothing could keep me from loving you, and I swear to you on my heart and honor that nothing will!''

And believe him she did.

Kit set off soon afterward. He decided to travel by canoe instead of horseback, knowing that in high summer the rivers would be both easier and swifter than making his way through the heavy brush. With his provisions and gunpowder bundled in a moosehide to keep dry, he followed the Wickham River southwest, to where it joined the far larger Connecticut, and then headed north, toward Springfield and Deerfield, and Canada beyond. Even by water he guessed the journey would take him ten days, perhaps a week if the fair weather held, and then he planned to make certain all was well with his upriver sawmills. Only once before had he travelled to Robillard's holdings, and that was long ago, with his father. But though Kit's recollection of the route was hazy, he trusted his pathfinding instincts enough to be sure he'd find it again.

The sun was hot on his shoulders, and he welcomed the physical exertion of paddling against the current and the solitude and the beauty of the land and river around him. Overhead wild ducks flew against the brilliant blue of the summer sky, and through the trees he caught glimpses of curious deer and moose watching him. This was what he'd missed most when he had gone to England for Jonathan, this sense of boundless freedom. He began humming to the rhythm of his strokes, a tune he later realized to his amusement was the one Dianna had sung so much better than Constance.

At twilight he paused only long enough to stretch his legs and eat the cold ham and cornbread that Hester had packed, and then he was off again. He was too restless to need sleep, too unsettled. He continued through the night by the same full moon's light that had washed over him and Dianna the night before, and he marveled at how long ago that already seemed.

On the second night, he stopped at a small island, pulling the canoe well up beyond the sharp rocks of the riverbed and hiding it in the scrub pines. As boys, he and Jonathan had often come here, pretending the island was some Caribbean pirate stronghold. Strange to think that they could come all this way and still be on Sparhawk land, or so at least the parchment from his grandfather's time called it. Kit remembered his grandfather well, a fierce old Puritan with cropped white hair. He had been a soldier with Cromwell at Marston Moor, rewarded with a grant in land too wild for lesser men to tame. His grandfather had taught Kit much about combat and swordplay and leading other men to fight, lessons that had saved his life more times than he cared to count.

Foregoing the small luxury of a fire, Kit contented himself again with cold food and water, and rolled his tired body in a blanket to sleep, his rifle and knife beside him. Then, with the sound of the river running soft in his ears, he let his thoughts turn to Dianna: the way she smiled, the husky way she called him her love, the way her lips parted so eagerly to welcome his.

She might not wish to think of the future, but he couldn't help it. When he returned home, he meant to marry her. He frowned and quickly amended his thoughts. He would *ask* her to marry him and pray she agreed. For all his land and position in the colonies and for all she swore she loved him, he still remembered her grand family and how his in England had been minor west-county gentry at best. People like the Greys didn't wed for love, and he could only hope she was different. She had to be.

By the time Kit saw the other man's arm, bright in the moonlight over him, it was almost too late. He threw himself sideways, the knife already in his hand as he tossed off the blanket and clambered to his feet.

Attawan rested the butt of his musket on the ground and leaned nonchalantly on the barrel, his face all angles and planes in the moonlight. "You grow careless, Sparhawk," he said, shaking his head. "I could have killed you ten times in your sleep."

"And I might have slit you in two before I opened my eyes, Attawan," Kit replied with a grin. He and Attawan had been friends since boyhood, when Kit's parents had taken Attawan's mother in after she had been wounded by an English scouting party. "You've been a stranger to my home since I've returned, my friend."

Attawan shrugged. "This spring your English have been too quick with their muskets, Sparhawk." As always he ignored the clipped Yankee pronunciation of Kit's name, emphasizing the "hawk" instead.

Kit's smile vanished as he dropped down onto the ground with a sigh. "I can't fault them, not after Deerfield, and now Wickhamton, as well."

"Abenakis and Mohegans," sniffed Attawan scornfully. "Not Pocumtucks."

"A woman and two girls are gone, four men dead, and on my land," said Kit with sharp impatience. "I can't fault quick fingers after that."

Attawan squatted down beside Kit, spreading his blanket out to dry after wading to the island. "So you go by yourself to avenge this?" he asked. "One man against ten times ten in Quebec?"

"I don't think the men who attacked my people are the same ones who sacked Deerfield," said Kit slowly. "I think it was someone who'd like me to believe that. I think it was Robillard."

Skeptically Attawan raised his eyebrows, waiting for Kit to explain.

"The trapper they scalped lived long enough to tell me Robillard was with the party. I'm guessing he hopes we'll all flee, like they did at Deerfield, and leave everything to him. I plan to tell him how very wrong he is.''

Attawan stroked the barbs of the turkey feather in his hair, considering Kit's words. ''You're a man with more courage than wisdom to go alone,'' he said at last.

Kit's smile was tight-lipped. ''You're not the first to tell me that,'' he said softly, remembering the tears in Dianna's eyes. ''But Robillard is a coward. He only fights when he's sure others will stop him. He'll bluff and bluster, but he won't risk doing me any real harm. He's made his feelings about me too well known, and he'll have all New England on his tail if I don't return. Same way I don't want all of New France on mine.''

''This man Robillard keeps many worthless Abenakis in brandy,'' said Attawan. ''You've grown so soft, you'll need someone to make sure the thieving curs don't find your back.''

Kit reached out to grasp the Indian's shoulder. ''I was hoping, my friend, that you would feel that way.''

For a man who fancied himself a gentleman, François Robillard's home was an unkempt shambles. Wary as Kit was as he and Attawan paddled up beside the makeshift dock, he couldn't overlook the meanness of the place. The gossip said Robillard was French born, a wily veteran of the Turkish wars. But one glance at his house confirmed what Kit had always suspected, that Robillard was no more than a back-country trapper, a coureur de bois who'd made enough money from lucky trading to become a first-rate bully.

Sitting at the crest of a rocky hill overlooking the river, the large house was more of a stockade built of rough-hewn logs and chinked with dingy lime plaster. Oiled skins filled the narrow windows instead of glass, and the yard was bare, dry dirt. To the back was a lean-to used for storage, and a small stable. Two mongrel dogs wrangled over a goose carcass before the house's open doorway, while three Abenakis and a French soldier in haphazard uniform wagered on the outcome. When Kit and Attawan pulled their canoe onto the bank, the four men at once forgot the dogs, and their expressions turned hostile as they reached for their muskets. The French soldier barked an order to one of the Indians, who scurried into the house as the others trained their guns on the newcomers.

But Kit ignored them, nonchalantly taking his time as he took his own rifle from the canoe and swung it casually across his shoulders. Beside him Attawan had not taken his eyes from the men at the house. Kit could sense his friend's tension and disapproval. When Kit began to whistle the little tune of Dianna's, Attawan spoke so sharply in his own tongue that Kit smiled to himself, certain he was being soundly cursed. So far, everything was just as he had hoped.

Kit loped up the hillside, his boots crunching on the shale. He didn't like those muskets aimed at him any more than Attawan did, but he'd be damned if he'd let Robillard know it. He was within twenty paces of the house before the soldier called to him.

"Faire halte!" he demanded. When Kit shrugged his incomprehension, the man switched to garbled English. "What go there?"

"Christopher Sparhawk. Your master will know the name." The soldier scowled and did not move, and Kit sighed impatiently. "I'd be obliged if you'd tell him I'm here."

From the corner of his eye Kit caught the movement in the doorway, the sun glinting off the pistol's long barrel. *"Bonjour, Sparhawk,"* said Robillard. He laughed, but the gun in his hand remained steady. With a muted click he drew back the hammer. "Or is it *au revoir,* eh?"

Chapter Thirteen

For one sickening moment, Kit wondered if he'd miscalculated. There were five of them, five guns, odds a coward like Robillard would favor. At point blank like this, he and Attawan wouldn't have a breath of a chance.

But even as Kit was considering this, Robillard laughed again, his big belly shaking. He uncocked the pistol and tipped it back against his shoulder. "Even I would not kill you like this, Sparhawk," he said scornfully. "You are a *fou gros* to come here, eh? Did not your other *Anglais* tell you I would shoot you, bang, bang?"

He waved the pistol at Kit, laughing again at his own wit. Kit wanted nothing more than to knock the foolish wind out of the man, but he knew how precarious his position remained; the others still had not lowered their guns. "Aye, they warned me," he said, swallowing his temper, "but I believed you would wish to talk first."

Intrigued, Robillard scratched his jaw with the pistol's barrel. "Come, then, I would hear you talk."

"Nay, Robillard, not here. Inside. And alone. What I have to say needs reach no other ears than your own." Confident that the Frenchman would agree, Kit began walking toward him. "I'll leave my own man here, as well."

Robillard shrugged. "Eh, if you wish it. Your life is in my fist anyway."

Kit waited until the Abenakis and the soldier laid down their guns and reluctantly slumped back down beside the wall. He ignored Attawan's scowl of disapproval as his friend chose to sit far from the others, his musket still cradled in his arms. Only then did Kit follow Robillard into his house, ducking his head beneath the low doorway.

The front room was probably the finest in the house. The tall-backed chairs had cushions of padded leather, and a bright Turkey carpet was draped over the massive walnut table. A costly crucifix, carved and painted, hung between the windows. But the pewter candlesticks were dull with dirt, and the prints of saints' martyrdoms that were tacked to the log walls were fly-specked and yellowed.

Imperiously Robillard waved Kit toward a chair and dropped into an armchair that groaned beneath his weight. Kit ignored the seat the Frenchman had offered, choosing instead one that put his back to the wall and gave him a clear view of both the door and windows. Much like Attawan, he kept his rifle in his arms, although, he decided idly, indoors he'd likely do better with the knife.

"So you come to visit me in my home like a *gentilhomme*, Sparhawk?" asked Robillard jovially. "It's a fine holding, *oui?*"

Glad his visit had fed the man's pride, Kit was nonetheless thankful Robillard had never visited Plumstead. "Aye, a fine holding," he agreed. "A gentleman's house. But the deeds I've come to discuss are not gentleman's deeds, nor—"

He broke off as a young Abenaki woman entered the room with two leather tankards of brandy. As she set them on the table, Robillard reached out to caress her bottom, and the woman smiled and moved wantonly against his hand. He pulled her, giggling, back into his lap, her legs splayed over his knees and her deerskin dress riding high over her thighs.

"You do not like squaws, do you, *Anglais?*" asked Robillard as he freely fondled the woman. Kit shook his head, disgusted. Reluctantly Robillard pushed the girl to her feet, smacking her hip as she scurried away. "It is a pity you do not. She has a sister, that one, another plump beauty."

A sudden grin split the Frenchman's face. "But then I forget you will soon take a wife! *Félicitations!*"

Kit frowned. Surely he could not mean Dianna. No one knew that, not even her. "You must be mistaken, Robillard."

"Ah, but I have heard of this Lindsey girl, your *fiancée, non?*"

"Nay, she is not." God's blood, had Constance's aspirations really spread this far? "There is no betrothal between Mistress Lindsey and myself."

"Then you shall have my chit's sister. I swear it, she will do anything you wish with her mouth—"

"Enough!" said Kit abruptly, striking the table with his fist hard enough to bounce the tankards. "You've killed four of my men and carried off three of my women. I want the women back, unharmed. I'll even pay their ransom, if I'm certain the gold goes to the Indians and not you. And I want you to swear you'll never venture anywhere near my land again."

Robillard's face grew shuttered, and he tucked his jaw low against his chest. "I know nothing of this. What you say is the work of Indians. We all have such troubles with *sauvages.*"

"Nay, you forget, Robillard," said Kit, his voice rumbling with quiet menace. "Your men struck one of your own, as well, lifted his scalp and left him to die. But he did not die at once, not before he told me you were there, too."

"Do you not believe that Indians kill *Français,* as well?" Robillard blustered, but from the furtive panic in his eyes, Kit knew for certain he was bluffing, lying again. "Like all men, I have my enemies. This dead man must be one. Why would I have gone along to that *Anglais* farmer's house, to his corn field, eh?"

"Why you went matters not. But that you did, I don't doubt for a moment." Kit's eyes narrowed. "I didn't tell you the man was a farmer or that he was murdered in a corn field. It seems, Robillard, that your memory is improving."

Kit rose to his feet, towering over the other man. "I don't want war, Robillard, any more than you do. At present this is between us alone. Do as I say, and I'll leave you in peace.

But cross me again, and so help me, I'll be back with an army to burn your precious gentleman's house and see you hang for murder.''

Kit's voice had dropped to scarcely more than a whisper. ''Mark well what I say, Robillard. The three English women back and you off my land.''

He turned on his heel without waiting for the Frenchman to reply, and walked out the door and down the hill to the canoe. He heard Attawan hurry to join him, but he didn't turn, unwilling to give Robillard anything more satisfying then the sight of his back. While a small part of him wondered how many French bullets might find their way into that same back, the larger part was confident not one would dare.

Finally Robillard roused himself, stalking to the doorway as Kit and Attawan pushed off into the current. Swearing under his breath, he watched them go, all too conscious of the man who had come to stand behind him in the doorway. ''I told you Sparhawk was a *fou*, a *très gros fou*,'' he blustered. ''I should have shot his head from his shoulders when I had the chance!''

''You are the only fool here, Robillard,'' snapped Lieutenant Hertel de Rouville. Irritably he rapped his knuckles on the doorframe, his sword in its scabbard swinging back and forth from his hip. That he, the man who had destroyed that pitiful English village of Deerfield; he, Jean-Baptiste Hertel de Rouville, the special agent and friend of the Marquis de Vaudreuil, the governor of all Canada—that he should be reduced to dealing with a fat peasant like this Robillard, was almost beyond bearing. ''You couldn't have shot that man had he held the pistol for you.''

His pride wounded, Robillard's head jerked up and he sniffed loudly. ''Sparhawk is not worthy of my scorn, not him, nor his father, nor his father before him.''

''He is worth ten of you,'' said Hertel de Rouville with disgust. ''If you'd harmed him today, the forests would have been alive with English soldiers in a fortnight. He wouldn't have come here unless his governors knew of it. You cannot kill men like Sparhawk without consequences.''

"But you promised me his holdings if I helped you," said Robillard peevishly.

"My mission is to drive these English from French land, not to make you rich," declared Hertel de Rouville impatiently as he flipped back the lace-trimmed cuff on his shirt to scratch his wrist. There had been fleas in his bed last night, and God only knew what kind of vermin on the Indian woman who'd been waiting naked beneath the coverlet for him. The sooner he could return to the civilities of Quebec, the better. "Sparhawk must die, that is so. But it must be arranged so that no blame can fall to us. We must draw him to us of his own will, away from the others."

"If only he had a wife we could take as bait, eh? He is a *galant,* that one. He would follow."

"No wife, perhaps, but there is some lady he holds dear. Didn't you mark how he started when you asked of the Lindsey woman?" Hertel de Rouville chuckled, quite pleased with himself. "You will go to his home, Robillard, and you will learn the name of his *amourette.*"

Robillard shook his head. "I do not think that a good plan, *mon ami,*" he said doubtfully. He was reluctant to question a fine gentleman like Hertel de Rouville, but his own neck was the one at stake. "You heard Sparhawk. He'll kill me if I go to Plumstead."

"Not if you come with news of, say, those three English women. You may even claim the ransom for aught I care."

"You will give them to me to take back?" asked Robillard incredulously.

The lieutenant shrugged carelessly. "Not possible, I fear. The oldest one could not keep pace and perished. The two girls will find a new life of grace with the good sisters in Quebec."

De Rouville laughed to himself as he gripped Robillard's shoulder, his fingers tightening into the older man's flesh. "You tell Sparhawk whatever he wishes to hear, *oui?* And you do not return here until you know the woman's name and where she dwells. Then, *mon ami,* it will be high time for our Abenaki *compatriotes* to pay her our compliments."

* * *

"If we return tonight," suggested Attawan hopefully, "we ᵒuld kill him while he sleeps."

"And be killed ourselves in the bargain," said Kit matter-ᵒf-factly as he tossed a stone into the water. They sat on a ᵒcky outcropping high above the river, Kit watching the sun ᵢp behind the Green Mountains to the west while Attawan ᵢeaned the two bullheads he'd caught for their dinner. Earlier, ₐ the afternoon's heat, Kit had stripped off his shirt, and now, ᵣhile the stone beneath him still held the warmth, the evening ᵣeeze felt pleasantly cool on his bare back.

"There were four men that we saw," Kit continued, "and ᵒubtless others who chose not to show themselves. Besides, ₐd warrant Robillard expects us to be the same sort of skulk-ᵢg cowards he himself is and will double his watch tonight ᵢst in case."

Attawan struck his thigh with his fist. "I am not afraid, ᵢparhawk."

"So who is more brave than wise now?" asked Kit, grin-ᵢing. He leaned back on his elbows, his legs outstretched com-ᵣtably before him. "Nay, much as I'd like to throttle that ᵢan's fat neck, 'tis better this way. Once Robillard returns the ₐrnard women, I'll be free to hunt down the Abenakis re-ᵣonsible and bring them to Wickhamton for trial."

Attawan snorted, shaking silvery fish scales from his fin-ᵣers. "*If* he returns your captives. I don't believe he has the ᵒwer to find them."

"If he can, he will. He no more wants English soldiers in ᵢs fields than I want French ones in mine."

"Even if they're already there?"

Kit frowned, sitting upright, waiting for Attawan to con-ᵢnue.

"The Abenakis and Mohawks who destroyed your Deer-ᵢeld were led by French soldiers. Two hundred soldiers on ᵢowshoes, it is said."

Kit stared at him, stunned. "Would you swear to this?"

Attawan didn't answer, wounded to have his word ques-ᵢoned, but Kit was too disturbed to soothe his friend's feel-

ings. "Why didn't you tell me of this earlier?" he demanded.
"One hundred and forty-two English were lost that day, an
all has been blamed on the Indians alone!"

"These French are not foolish," said Attawan reasonably.
Having misdeeds blamed on Indians was nothing new to him
and though he called Kit friend, he didn't share his horror fo
the killed or kidnapped English and judged the fighting be
tween French and English no different than the skirmishe
among the Seven Nations. "They let the Abenakis attack first
and when the killing is done, they followed. It was the sam
at your English village of Pascommuck, too, though not s
many of your people were taken."

"Nearly two score," said Kit grimly, tugging on his boots
"We're heading for Deerfield this night and talk to Captai
Ferris. They must be warned. I knew the French had league
with the Indians to the east, but I didn't think they dared t
come here. I've been away too long, Attawan. I should hav
known this was happening. If I hadn't gone to England in m
brother's stead—"

The second boot caught on his foot, and in his frustratio
Kit yanked it off and sent it sailing into the brush. Calml
Attawan went to retrieve it.

"Your scars run deep, my friend," he said gently as h
dropped the boot into Kit's lap. "These are your people, aye
but they're not your family again. You cannot change the pas
and you must not let it blind you to the future."

Kit wished he could. He wanted no more killing, no mor
families torn apart, no more nightmares of Tamsin's screams
All he longed for was peace and a life with Dianna at Plum
stead. God in Heaven, was that so very much to ask?

The musket fired, and as the gunsmoke drifted clear, Diann
could see the rock she'd set on the fence post as a target wa
gone, shot clean away without touching the wooden post.

"Aye, ye be a finer shot than most o' th' men now," sai
Hester with considerable satisfaction. "I don't care what tha
old fool Asa says. It be a good thing ye know how t'handl
a gun, with ye an' Mercy all by yerselves in that house."

Carefully Dianna cleaned out the gun's barrel, remembering l that Hester had warned her about fouled firearms. "We'll e safe enough, Hester. We're too close to Wickhamton and umstead to be attacked. Besides, Asa and Jeremiah are never one for more than three nights running now. Asa promised."

"Well, ye keep that musket o'yours primed an' ready like told ye. Just because we haven't been plagued by any more the savages don't mean they're not waitin' and plannin' strike again. Mind, 'twas four months 'twixt Deerfield an' e Barnards," warned Hester. She shaded her eyes with her and, gauging the time by the sun's height in the sky. "Come, is time I turned th' joint, an' time, too, ye an' Mercy headed ack. Kit would have my head if I let ye tarry after dusk."

Dianna busied herself with collecting her powder horn and ullets, her face lowered so Hester wouldn't notice how she ushed at the mention of Kit's name. She always did. Having m gone more than four weeks hadn't changed that, nor had e stopped missing him every hour, every minute of each of ose thirty-one days. It was a part of being in love that she adn't expected, this constant caring laced with fear. She was ertain he'd be back, but she worried about all the dangers at might threaten him. What were his assurances against arws and hatchets?

For distraction she threw herself into a hundred tasks, from athering herbs to dry for physicking, to learning how to shoot musket, to teaching Mercy how to read from the one book at Asa owned, an Old Testament. But no matter how busy e kept her hands, Kit remained to haunt her thoughts by day d her dreams by night.

Yet it was Hester now who spoke, seemingly reading ianna's thoughts. "I wish th'lad would get himself back here oon," she said uneasily. "He's been gone too long t'suit e."

Swiftly Dianna stood upright. It was bad enough to worry one, but infinitely worse if Hester, who had lived here nearly l her life, was concerned as well. "You don't believe some has befallen him, do you?"

Hester sighed deeply, shaking her head. "Nay, I've no real

reason. He's young an' strong an' a good man in a fight, an
he knows th' woods better'n any other Englishman. An' he b
clever, too. If he reckons talkin' with that lout Robillard'
going t'set things to rights, then we must trust him t'do wh
be best. But I don't have to like it.'' Her voice rose indig
nantly. ''Nay, not a bit o'it! The Sparhawks be too unluck
with th'Indians for Kit t'be off testing fate like this.''

''Unlucky?'' echoed Dianna faintly. ''How so?''

At once Hester realized her indiscretion. ''So he hasn't tol
ye?'' she said uncomfortably, looking past Dianna to avoi
her eyes. ''Well, it don't be my tale to tell.''

''I know his father led the militia before him,'' Dianna per
sisted, determined not to be put off. ''Was he killed by th
Indians? Was that it?''

''Aye, lass, poor Master Samuel was, indeed,'' Heste
agreed eagerly, seizing on that much of the truth. ''Shot an
scalped wit' nary a chance t'defend himself. 'Twas Kit wh
found him.''

''Oh, poor Kit!'' breathed Dianna. She knew the pain o
losing a father suddenly, but she could not imagine the shoc
of finding his mutilated body as well. Now she understoo
why Kit had reacted so violently when the wounded Frenc
trapper had been brought to Plumstead. She'd been so swep
up in her own concerns that she hadn't realized Kit's anguis
or been able to recognize it for what it was. Oh, how sh
wished he'd told her himself!

''Aye, ye can see why I worry over him,'' said Hester ve
hemently, her eyes snapping. ''An' him off with one of th
blood-thirsty savages, too! Oh, I know Kit says that Attawa
be different, that red men must be judged a-piece, same a
Englishmen, but I ask ye, was it Englishmen that burned Dee
field? Master Samuel and Mistress Amity an' all their childre
were both thick as family wit' Indians, an' no good ever com
of it, t'my mind. Th' sooner they all be driven away or kille
for good, the better for us Christian folk!''

Then, to Dianna's surprise, the righteous anger vanishe
from Hester's face and her mouth seemed to crumple as he
eyes grew shiny with tears. ''I've no kin o'my own, you see,

she explained hoarsely. "No younglings t'worry over. But those two Sparhawk lads, aye, an' their sisters, too, they've been more'n enough t'love. An' if any harm comes to Kit, why I'd feel it as if he were my own flesh."

Near to tears herself, Dianna threw her arms around Hester and hugged her tightly. "He'll come back, I know it," she said fiercely, as much to convince herself as to reassure Hester. "He swore he would, and you know Kit Sparhawk would never break his word!"

"That be true enough, lass." Embarrassed by her emotions, Hester stepped back and wiped her eyes with the corner of her apron, sniffing loudly. "An' enough of this foolish old woman's fancies, too, ye be thinkin'. There'll be naught worth eating tonight if we don't go back."

They hurried back to the house and self-consciously, neither of them mentioned Kit again. "Now ye take that cheese wit' ve, like ye promised," said Hester as they entered the kitchen. "There be a nice piece for yer supper that surely will go wan-in' here otherwise."

Leaving Hester to poke at the roast on the spit, Dianna stepped into the cool shadows of the little buttery off the kitchen to search for the cheese. She paused, listening, when she heard the heavy footsteps in the kitchen, and a man's voice she didn't recognize. None of the field workers should be back at the house this early anyway, she thought, frowning. Then came the sound of shattering crockery, and Hester's voice raised in angry protest. Dianna peeked through the half-opened door just as the heavy-set man pinned Hester's arms behind her back.

Dianna pulled back quickly into the shadows, praying the man hadn't seen her. She recognized him as the one who'd challenged Kit outside the meetinghouse, Robillard himself, and she remembered, too, how quick he'd been with a knife. Now she would have to be even faster if she wanted to help Hester. *Why was he here? Where was Kit?* She shoved the doubts away. She could see her musket where she'd left it, leaning against a chair. Three steps and she would reach it.

She took a deep breath to steady her nerves and lunged fo
the gun.

Before Robillard even noticed her, she had grabbed th
musket and trained it on his startled face. "You let Mistres
Holcomb go free," she ordered, her heart pounding with
adrenaline, but her voice surprisingly calm. "Then off with
you! You've no business in this house."

Dianna watched the man's expression change, the surpris
changing to disbelief and then to bemused contempt. "Eh,
should be frightened by a *petite fille* like you?"

That contempt angered Dianna and steadied her, as well
"Better a little girl than a *cochon énorme!*" she answered
tartly, squinting down the barrel as she cocked the trigger. A
this range she'd no doubt she'd hit the Frenchman. The chal
lenge would be missing Hester.

Robillard frowned, the older woman he held forgotten. Thi
wild girl with the pale eyes puzzled him. She was dressed a
commonly as any English settler's wife, but she held hersel
proud like the grand ladies he'd seen in Quebec, and she wa
good at orders, too. Such a girl should not be trusted with
musket, and he swore in French.

"Don't sully my ears with your filth!" replied Dianna i
French. "Now let Mistress Holcomb go free, and pack your
self off before I help you on your way."

Sacré bleu, could the chit be French? Robillard stared a
her, his confusion growing. "What are you doing here, eh, *m*
petite?" he demanded, wondering if this could possibly be th
woman he sought. He'd always thought Sparhawk a pious
self-righteous prig, like all Englishmen, and never dreamed
he'd keep a mistress right here in his blessed Plumstead.

"Don't go a-tryin' her patience, Robillard," warned Hester
"Her temper's short as th' rest o'her."

"Fah, and what of my patience, eh?" With a flourish Rob
illard released Hester and shoved her away. Rubbing he
wrists, Hester quickly ran to safety behind Dianna, and Rob
illard snorted with disgust. "You do not care that I bring t
you a message for your master?"

"Master Sparhawk's not here," said Dianna sharply.

"And did I not know that already, *ma petite?*" he said, sneering. "My message is both for him and from him."

Hastily Dianna lowered the gun. "A message from him?" she asked eagerly. "You have seen him then, and he is well?"

Slowly Robillard smiled. So she *was* the woman, after all. She was not as beautiful as he'd expected, but beneath the coarse clothing, she was pleasingly rounded, and her lips were full enough to welcome a man's kisses. And she was at least part French: that alone would make her more desirable than the other English spinsters he'd seen. In fact, the more he studied her, the more he understood why Sparhawk had refused the squaw. *Mon Dieu,* why shouldn't he, with such a little delight waiting at home?

His smile widened to a leer, and he ran his tongue along his lower lip. "When Sparhawk was at my house, he was well enough. But that was long ago, maybe a fortnight. I thought he would be home by now, eh?"

He watched the fear flutter across Dianna's face and his last doubt about her disappeared. How he wished he could see Sparhawk's face when he learned the Indians had taken his mistress! "When he comes, tell him I have found the warriors who hold the English women, and they will be returned as soon as he pays the ransom."

He stepped forward, meaning to take the gun from her, but Dianna snapped it back to her shoulder, flushing at her own carelessness. Where were her wits to let this man toy with her? Likely everything he said was lies anyway. "Why should he pay any ransom to you?"

Robillard's smile twisted to a sneer. "You give him my message, *ma chère,* and that will be enough. He doesn't need a woman to make his decisions for him, eh?"

"If you've nothing more to say, then get out now," said Dianna irritably. "Though I've almost *decided* to shoot you now and save Kit the trouble."

"I'm going, *mademoiselle,* I'm going." Slowly Robillard retrieved his hat from the floor where it had fallen and inched his way toward the door. "You be a good girl and give my message to Sparhawk. If he wishes to see the women alive he pays me the ransom.''

Dianna followed his movements with the gun as he left the house and climbed onto the horse he'd tied near the well out front, not lowering the weapon until he had ridden from sight. Only then did she realize how tense she'd been and how her arms ached from holding the heavy musket. Sighing, she let her shoulders sag and rubbed her wrists.

''I don't believe he knows anything at all about the Barnards, do you, Hester?'' she asked wearily. For a long moment Hester didn't answer, standing in thoughtful silence beside Dianna with her arms crossed over her chest as she stared after Robillard.

''You an' Kit,'' she said at last, and clicked her tongue. ''Why didn't I see it coming?''

Chapter Fourteen

"An' where d'ye be headin' this day, eh, Annie?" Asa asked Dianna as she and Mercy swept out two large baskets they'd found in the barn. "Ye know I don't want ye two rangin' far."

"No farther than the apple orchard at Plumstead," said Dianna, frowning at Mercy behind Asa's back. If the girl didn't stop her nervous giggling, Asa was sure to suspect something unusual was planned, and harmless as Dianna judged a picnic to be, she wasn't sure Asa wouldn't forbid them to go. "We're going to gather the early windfalls so I can make my pies for tomorrow."

"Pies for tomorrow? What pies be those?"

"For the supper after training day," explained Dianna for what seemed like the hundredth time. "You promised you'd take us."

Asa sighed. "Aye, I warrant I did. Though training day's likely far more serious this year than you might be expectin'. If th' lads have any conscience, they'll spend more time learnin' their drills an' less chasin' maids. I warrant that Captain Tyler will see they're worked proper, better'n when Colonel Sparhawk be here. He be too gentle by half wit' th' men, that one. Too eager t'get to th' women an' spirits hisself."

Asa lit his pipe, puffing as the spark took, and looked closely at Dianna. "There not be some lad ye favor in the village, eh? Mind ye be bound t'me for seven years, an' I'll not have ye spoken for 'til your time be done. Ten guineas be too dear a sum t'toss away for naught.''

"Nay, there's no one in Wickhamton," said Dianna with carefully chosen words. How could any other man compete with Kit? "I wish to go for Mercy's sake. She sees too little of children her own age.''

"Aye, there be no harm t'that," Asa agreed, reaching for his hat. "I've business o'my own in Wickhamton this day, but I'll take ye back on the morn, as ye asked. Are ye certain ye will be safe enough without me here today?''

"Oh, Grandfer, you go on your business, an' Dianna an' I will go on ours," said Mercy airily. Asa harrumphed, but kissed the girl indulgently before leaving.

Dianna finished packing a third basket with food and cider for their supper. She liked planning little surprises and outings like this one for Mercy, just as her own father had done for her long ago. Lord knows it seemed to Dianna that Mercy had done precious few things for the pleasure of them alone. Even now the girl was dancing with excitement by the door, the little cat, Lily, jostling in her arms.

Dianna slung the basket with the food over one arm, handed the empty ones to Mercy and then pulled her musket out from its hiding place behind the cupboard. She often wondered which would upset Asa more: that she had the gun at all, or that it had come from the Sparhawks' collection. But after this summer, nothing Asa could say would dissuade her from keeping it now, and she never left the house without it.

There was a crispness to the day that hinted at autumn, and already the topmost leaves of the maples and oaks were beginning to change color. The apple trees were heavy with fruit, the branches bowed beneath the weight, and the fragrance of apples was sweet in the air. While Lily chased and pounced on every whirling leaf and imaginary mouse, Dianna and Mercy soon filled their baskets. They would come back again next week to help the field men and women harvest the bulk of the crop, and in return, Dianna would receive a share of the apples to press for cider or dry for winter cooking.

"May we eat now, Dianna?" begged Mercy. "I think this be the perfect spot, and Lily is near to starving."

Dianna glanced down doubtfully at the little cat, already grown plump from all the milk and scraps Mercy managed to send her pet's way. "'Tis early, but if Lily deems it time to dine, then I shall not be the one to deny her."

"So this be truly what lords an' ladies do in London?" asked Mercy excitedly as Dianna spread a homespun cloth on the grass and began to unpack the food. "They'd rather take their meals under a tree than in a fine dining hall?"

"Even the finest dining hall can grow tiresome," replied Dianna with mock seriousness. "Of course, we should have let the footmen bring the hampers, and have the dishes arranged before we arrived. The musicians would be waiting, too, to play for us while we ate, and then, after perhaps only a half-dozen dishes—for we are being quite informal—we might sing ourselves and dance on the grass with our beaux."

The more she had told Mercy about her past, the less real it had become, the people and places she'd grown up knowing reduced to a kind of fairy tale. And what was most curious, when she thought about it, was that she was far more content in her tiny shingled house, making do for herself, than she ever would have been in a grand home in London with a score of servants. If only Kit would come back, she thought longingly, then quickly amended her thoughts. *When* Kit comes back...

"What kind o' shoes do ladies wear for dancing?" prompted Mercy eagerly.

"Slippers made of calf-skin so fine that one night of dancing will wear them to pieces," said Dianna grandly. "All over embroidered with silk-thread flowers and tiny silver stars, and perhaps they'll fasten with buckles set with paste brilliants that sparkle like diamonds when you kick your feet high in the air!"

As she listened, Mercy's eyes sparkled like the paste brilliants, and Dianna thought with pleasure of how much the girl had changed these past months. Then suddenly Mercy's face twisted into a stern grimace.

"Grandfer says dancing's wicked," she said, sounding un-cannily like Asa. "He says it be wicked sport, born o' idle-ness."

Dianna hesitated. She did not like to scoff at what Mercy had been taught by Asa, but faith, what harm could possibly come of music and dancing? "When the day's tasks are done," she said cautiously, "then I don't see the wickedness in dancing."

Mercy pressed her cheek against Lily's fur and glanced imp-ishly up at Dianna. "Then if you teach me how, 'twill just be another secret best kept from Grandfer."

Dianna gasped, then laughed. With both hands she caught the girl by the waist and twirled her around and around, their skirts and aprons flying in a giddy circle around their bare legs. "Oh, Mercy, you shouldn't say such things! 'Tis disre-spectful and—"

It was the flicker of movement that caught Dianna's eye, the tall figure easing among the shadows in the trees. Swiftly she shoved Mercy behind her and grabbed for the musket be-side the basket. She shook her head to clear it as she raised the gun, cursing the silly spinning game that had left her dizzy, the trees before her eyes still careening wildly. Blast, she knew the man had to be there somewhere!

"I'm not afraid of you!" she called out defiantly, her heart pounding.

Dianna felt Mercy's fingers tightening in her skirts behind her, and she hoped the girl could not sense her own very real fear. The musket held but a single bullet. She had only seen the one man and prayed he was alone. She would have just one shot to kill him if she had to.

"Come out and show yourself or I'll shoot, see if I don't!" she called again, and this time she heard the desperation in her voice.

At last the trees had stopped spinning. She could make out a fringed hunting shirt, the glint of a rifle barrel as the man moved. He was very tall, broad-shouldered, and he was walk-ing toward them, daring her, it seemed, to shoot. She swal-lowed hard and cocked the dog-latch.

"Isn't this a fine welcome home!" exclaimed Kit as he stepped into the sunlight. "I didn't dream I'd find the womenfolk here as mad with blood-lust as any Abenaki brave!"

Simultaneously Dianna and Mercy cried his name, but it was Dianna who reached him first, flinging her arms around him as if she'd never let go. "Oh, Kit, praise God you're back! I feared so that you were gone, lost—"

"And so you hoped to finish the task when I returned?" he teased. So many elegant speeches he'd rehearsed for this moment, and here he was, instead, taunting her as though she were one of his sisters. But it still seemed impossibly right to have her in his arms again. At once he forgot how tired he was, forgot the desolation he'd seen and the sorrow he'd heard and how many miles he'd travelled to be here with her again.

Dianna drew back indignantly. "I might have killed you!"

"Not the way you were weaving, likely to trip over your own feet. I'd swear you'd brought hard cider in that jug, my lady, and had your share of it, too."

"Nay, Kit, it's not like that," said Mercy seriously. Self-consciously Dianna and Kit separated, though Kit kept hold of her hand. He had to reassure himself that this was real and not another dream. "Dianna and I are having a—" She stumbled over the foreign words "—having a 'fate sham-pader.'"

"A *what?*" asked Kit.

"A *fête champêtre*," answered Dianna, delighting in the incredulous look on Kit's face. Despite the dark beard that hid half his face, she thought he had grown even more handsome, his hair streaked with pale gold and his skin tanned as dark as Attawan's. She guessed that, wherever he had gone, he must have met with success to be looking so happy. "A country feast, a picnic. Not everything French is evil, you know."

"Aye, Kit, it be something that all the lords and ladies do in *Paris*," explained Mercy, pleased to prove her new knowledge to Kit. "They eat outside instead o' in."

"Then you mean to say Attawan and I have spent the last six weeks having these *fêtes*, and we didn't even know it?" He twined his fingers around Dianna's marveling both at the delicacy of her hand and at the new calluses that marked her palm.

Mercy frowned and folded her arms across her narrow chest. "Nay, Kit, you're jesting now. A *fête* needs dancing an' music an' gentlemen t'be our beaux." She sighed dramatically. "But since you're here now, I warrant you must be our beau, else you'll have naught of our food."

"I warrant I must, since it's your food I'm after." Kit's eyes met Dianna's over the girl's head. He grinned, and Dianna felt herself melt. "Among other things. And besides," he said to Dianna, "by my reckoning, you owe me for a certain stewed chicken. Most savory it was, as I recall, before you seized it from my own table and carried it off."

"'Twas not for myself, as well you know," she answered staunchly, but unable to keep the smile from her lips. "I took it for others who were a great deal more hungry than you were."

"A claim you'd be hard pressed to make this day." He sat cross-legged on the grass and began exploring the contents of the supper basket. Gingerly he lifted out the meat pie, sniffing the fluted crust with such a look of intense expectation that Dianna laughed out loud. In the short time since she'd known Kit, there had been precious little time for laughter, and it was good to feel the tension and worry slip away.

"The pie's squirrel," she explained, her voice still merry, "and there are pickled onions in the little jug; and a carrot sallet and cornbread wrapped in the cloth, and the little bundle, there, has a slip of honeycomb."

"You are a marvel, Dianna, an angel to a starving man," proclaimed Kit as he stuck his knife deep into the pie. "I did not tarry at the house when Hester said I might find you here, but she should have told me, too, that she'd provisioned you, as well."

"She didn't, Kit," said Dianna proudly, sitting back on her heels with her hands at her waist. "Like it or not, 'tis all of my own making."

He cocked one eyebrow doubtfully, balancing a slice of the pie on the blade of his knife as the sauce dripped and the pastry began to flake before he slid the entire piece into his mouth at once. He groaned with contentment that was not entirely due to the pie. Not a quarter of an hour had he been with her, and already he felt happier than the entire time he'd been away.

"I'll take that as well meant," Dianna said as he cut himself another piece. That there would be little, if any, left for her or Mercy mattered not. She would have given him anything he desired, anything at all.

"*I* made the cornbread!" declared Mercy jealously. She pushed herself closer to Kit, practically sitting in his lap to get the attention she felt she was missing.

"Then I must try that next," said Kit with his mouth full. With a great flourish, he cut into the yellow cake while Mercy waited expectantly, her hands clasped, for his verdict.

"Wait, you'll want honey." Carefully Dianna unwrapped the comb and trickled the honey onto the cornbread he held before him. Some trickled onto her fingers, and before she could wipe them in the cloth, Kit lifted her hand to his lips and licked them clean himself, sensuously tracing the length of each of her fingers. The touch of his tongue, soft and wet, on her fingers made Dianna shiver, and her thoughts flew back to how she and Kit had parted in the barn, each breathless with unfulfilled longing. She felt herself being drawn back to that moment, her gaze locked by the power of Kit's eyes and her own desire, and she leaned closer toward him, her lips parted.

"Oh, fah, Kit, how can you do *that?*" exclaimed Mercy, her turned-up nose wrinkled with disgust. "To lick another's fingers!"

Embarrassed that she'd so forgotten Mercy, Dianna tried to pull her hand away, but Kit held it fast. "Mercy, sweeting," he said, his eyes not straying from Dianna's. "Where's Mistress Lily? I can't believe you'd let that fine little catkin stray."

With a stricken look, Mercy's head whipped around, searching for the cat. She bounded to her feet, calling the cat's name, and scurried off to search for her pet.

Kit's smile was slow and lazy as he lifted Dianna's hand to kiss the pulse of her wrist. "I missed you."

"And I you," said Dianna softly, reaching forward to stroke his cheek. "To have you back is like the spring after winter's cold."

"You would turn poetess on me?"

"Poetess or fool, more like." Dianna's cheeks pinked. "Mayhap I am too much alone, with only Mercy and the beauty of the land for my companions."

"Nay, my love, never a fool," he said, chuckling, as his hands slid down around her waist to pull her closer. "But last you swore you hated this land, and all of us in it."

Dianna winced, hoping this was only more of his teasing. "Words I did not mean," she said quickly, "spoken in passion."

Their faces were nearly touching now, his voice so low that only she could hear. His easy, jesting manner had vanished, and to her surprise, she saw his eyes grow guarded.

Kit tried to swallow his rising doubt. Was she perhaps speaking in riddles to save his feelings? He knew well that often women, and men, too, mistook passion for love and used the words interchangeably. Could it be that the first time he truly cared about a woman, she did not care about him in return?

"Tell me true, Dianna," he asked quietly. "Were there other words you did not mean, too, words spoken in passion?"

"Other words?" she repeated slowly, searching his face for some clue as to what he asked.

"Damn it, Dianna, do you love me?" he demanded. "Because I love you, and if you don't love me back——" He broke off abruptly and looked away, unwilling to let her see the raw emotion her hesitancy raised.

"Oh, Kit," she murmured, her smile tremulous. She took his jaw in both her hands, cradling his face as her fingers sank into the rough bristles of his new beard. "I loved you before and I love you now, and I believe in my heart that I always will."

She kissed him lightly at first, her lips barely brushing their sweetness across his until, with a possessive growl, his mouth came down hard on hers, wild and rough with passion. Fearlessly she surrendered to him and the rising desires within herself as her fingers tightened on the hard muscles of his shoulders.

"Dianna, love, how you tempt me," he said roughly, his breathing harsh. "But not here, not now." Yet even as he protested, he was pushing her back against the grass, tugging the linen cap from her hair to tangle his fingers in the rich, dark strands. "Mercy will be back—"

"Mercy!" Awkwardly Dianna pushed Kit back and struggled to sit upright. She had once again, to her chagrin, completely forgotten the little girl. With fingers clumsy from interrupted desire, she tried to comb her hair back to neatness beneath her cap. "To find us thus would hurt the child to no end, and I'll not have her lose her trust in me because of you!"

Sprawled on his back, Kit watched and listened before the laughter erupted from deep inside him. Dianna had switched so completely from a woman abandoning herself to lovemaking to a prim, concerned goodwife that he couldn't help it. Yet he loved her all the more for putting the little girl's feelings first. Perhaps now, if he were wed to Dianna, Asa would at last let him adopt Mercy. Happily he realized he might have both a wife and daughter with him at Plumstead before the first snowfall.

"Dianna," he said softly, reaching out to rest his hand on her thigh. "I have so many things I wish to say to you. Tomorrow is training day in Wickhamton—"

"I know, and Asa is taking Mercy and me to the supper afterward."

"Then meet me at dusk on the rise behind the burying ground. I would have you alone, with no others to spy or listen."

Behind him Dianna saw Mercy skipping toward them, the cat swinging from her arms. Quickly Dianna touched her fingers to Kit's lips.

"Tomorrow, then," she whispered. "And I swear I'll listen to every pretty word you wish to tell me."

* * *

"You're sure she is Sparhawk's woman?" demanded Hertel de Rouville skeptically. "A serving wench?"

"Je le tiens pour certain," replied Robillard confidently. "Though it is strange. In the village, they say he brought her with him from London, and yet she lives in a wretched house with an old man and a child."

Hertel de Rouville shrugged. "It sounds to me that this woman is merely a convenience for Sparhawk. Otherwise why would he bother with a creature so low-bred?"

"Ah, but Lieutenant, one look at her and you would see that she is not common." Eagerly Robillard leaned across the table. "She is a little goddess, *mon ami,* a beauty with the manner and the temper of a noble lady."

"So you would have her for yourself, is that it?" Hertel de Rouville asked with a weary sigh.

Robillard's dark eyes glittered in the candlelight. It had been long since he'd had a white woman, even longer for one so young who spoke his language. And how he would doubly enjoy her knowing he had robbed the Englishman! "She would be a small prize to share if you capture Sparhawk."

The lieutenant downed the last of his brandy and tapped his fingers on the empty glass. "If, as you promise, she is the right bait to draw Sparhawk to us and if we succeed in capturing him, *and* if the woman herself survives, then, Robillard, then you may consider her a gift." His smile was cold as a frozen river. "But if you have promised wrong and she is of no more use to us than any other *Anglaise* drab, then you shall watch the Abenakis kill her. Slowly, painfully, however they choose to amuse themselves. And you, *mon ami,* will be next."

Chapter Fifteen

'Five, six, seven, eight—*ouch!*'' Dianna jerked her hand out of the brick-lined oven, shaking her fingers to cool them. At last she judged the oven hot enough to bake the six pies waiting on the table. She'd begun the fire before dawn, raking out the coals twice until she was satisfied that the heat was right to crisp and brown the pastry. The other women in Wickhamton would be harsh critics, and Dianna's pride wouldn't permit her first offerings to them to have soggy crusts or underbaked apples. And then there was the special pie they'd never see, the one fancifully trimmed with pastry hearts, that was reserved for Kit alone.

She smiled happily to herself. He was home and he was safe, and he loved her. *He loved her!* He might tell her times beyond counting and still she'd never tire of hearing it. All night she'd stayed awake, anticipating today. As leader of the militia, he would be much in demand on training day, and for him to arrange to see her alone showed how much he, too, longed to be alone. She chuckled, remembering how he'd sent Mercy scurrying away yesterday in the orchard. Perhaps he'd be as eager to kiss sweet apple from her lips as honey from her fingertips.

Quickly she shook off her daydreaming and with care, slid the first two pies off the long wooden peel and into the oven. Her pies would be done, but unless she wanted to greet Kit with a face shiny from the kitchen's heat and clothes blotched with flour, she'd have to hurry to be ready when Asa came to take them to the village.

Together she and Mercy bathed in the stream down the hill from their house, shrieking as the icy, spring-fed water puckered their bare skin with goose bumps. Dianna rinsed her hair first with vinegar for shine, then crushed lavender for fragrance, and sat in the sun before the house to comb it dry.

At Mercy's request, Dianna braided the girl's hair in sevens and bound the thick tail with red yarn. Her own hair Dianna left unplaited and drawn back loosely from her face so the dark chestnut waves tumbled freely down her back. Today, too, she refused to hide it beneath a cap or kerchief. Oh, there'd be talk enough among the older people about her immodesty, but she remembered how Kit liked to tangle his fingers in her hair when it was loose, the way it had been the first time they'd made love, and she was determined to wear it like that again today, for him.

Likely, too, there'd be gossip about how she was dressed. What Dianna lacked in skill as a seamstress she had more than made up for with ingenuity. She'd stood through enough fittings for gowns to absorb the tricks even quality dressmakers used by turning a facing here, adding a cuff there. Beginning with a plain grey bodice of Lucy's, Dianna had lowered the neckline and narrowed the waist to flatter her own smaller figure. The tattered remains of her black silk gown had been ruthlessly torn into narrow strips that Dianna had braided and appliqued along the seams and neckline. Finally, she'd found an old pair of Tom Wing's breeches, faded from maroon to pink, and from these she had fashioned the rosettes that crowned her shoulders and were scattered across her skirt. The final effect was not half as stylish as what she'd worn in London, but still considerably more frivolous than any other woman in Wickhamton would choose, certainly any other servant. But as she dressed, Dianna worried that perhaps she'd gone too far. Nervously she tugged at her neckline, wishing she had a mirror to see just how much of her breasts showed. She'd sewn every stitch with Kit in mind, and if he hadn't returned in time, she would have worn something else. But what if Asa found her dress too worldly and made her change before Kit had had the chance to see her?

"Oh, Dianna, but ye do look grand!" said Mercy proudly, hugging her knees as she sat on the bed. "Like the Queen o' Faeries again."

Dianna plucked at one of the rosettes on her skirt. "You don't think your grandfather will judge me too bold?"

"Aye, he will," agreed Mercy amiably. "But he'll be too 'shamed t'tell ye so."

Dianna chewed on her lower lip, considering. "Perhaps I should tuck a kerchief in the front."

"Nay, don't change it!" declared Mercy. "This way you'll make Kit blind t'all th'other lasses, see if ye don't!"

Dianna looked quickly at the girl, wondering how much she'd guessed about her relationship with Kit. She considered telling her the truth, at least as much of it as she herself knew, but Mercy's face was full of admiration and nothing else, and Dianna relaxed. "He'll be so busy with training and telling everyone about his journey that he'll have little time to spare for any of us lasses."

Unconvinced, Mercy reached across the coverlet to pull Lily into her lap. "Kit always has time for his friends. Ye know that. Else he wouldn't have come t'see us yesterday."

Friends or not, Dianna decided it was time to change the subject. "I'm afraid you'll have to leave Lily here. She'd be lost among all the people, and the guns might frighten her."

Mercy sighed heavily and let the cat climb from her lap back up the bed to the pillow. The front of the girl's dark blue skirt was covered with white cat fur, but Dianna kept her reproof to herself. "Say farewell to her now, Mercy, and then join me below," she said instead as she climbed down the ladder. "Your grandfather should be back soon, and we don't want to keep him waiting."

Taking care to keep her clothes clean, Dianna slid the last pie from the oven and balanced it on the open windowsill to cool. The long-handled peel was still in her hand when she heard the door swing open behind her.

"We're ready to leave whenever you wish, Asa," she called gaily. "I'd like to see the shooting if we—"

But as she turned, the words dissolved into a stunned gasp. In the doorway stood two Indians armed with muskets and tomahawks, their bare chests painted red and their faces striped fiercely with black and white.

There was no time for Dianna to think or plan, only react as the first Indian came toward her. As the man reached for her, she swung the peel as hard as she could. The wide paddle caught him flat across the face with a smack, and though he stumbled backward from the impact, he was still able to yank the peel from her hands. Desperately Dianna longed for her rifle, tucked beyond reach behind the cupboard across the room. But the paring knife still lay on the table, and she lunged for it just as the Indian grabbed her around the waist.

As he shoved her back across the table, she turned and twisted in his grasp to face him. His long black hair flicked across her cheek, and she could smell the bear grease that glistened on his skin. She raised her feet and kicked him hard in the stomach, glad today that she wore shoes. But though she felt her hard leather heels strike against his muscled flesh, the Indian only grunted and tightened his fingers on her waist as he arched her back against the table. She clutched the little knife convulsively at her side, breathing a prayer of thanks that he hadn't noticed it in her hand. She must kill this man if she could. She had to. She jerked the knife upward, aiming for his chest.

But the Indian sensed her movement before he saw it and deftly rolled away from her. The knife slashed instead across his upper arm as he caught Dianna's wrist and squeezed it until she cried out from the pain. Her fingers sprung open and the knife dropped harmlessly to the floor.

For an endless moment he held her hand forced overhead, her body pinned beneath his as the warm blood dripped from the cut in his arm onto her bare shoulder. Panting, Dianna struggled to control her fear and panic. Desperately she reminded herself that she was still Lady Dianna Grey, and Greys were never cowards. She swallowed hard, and forced herself to meet his gaze. The Indian's eyes were dark, almost black, and so bright with undisguised hatred that Dianna shuddered.

Roughly he pulled her to her feet. She winced as he twisted her arms behind her back and held her wrists together with one hand, his fingers as tight as an iron band.

"Dianna!" shrieked Mercy pitifully, her face white with terror as she clung to the ladder, Lily struggling in her arms. The cat broke free and scrambled back up to the loft just as the second Indian reached up and plucked the girl from the ladder. Mercy wailed with anguish, tears streaming down her cheeks as she stretched out her arms toward the lost pet.

"Lily will be fine, sweetheart," said Dianna unsteadily, trying to keep the tremor from her voice. "God gave cats nine lives, and Lily hasn't squandered one of them yet. She'll be fine."

Far better than we will, thought Dianna miserably. Through the open door she saw they'd set fire to the barn, the flames ate greedily at the dry thatched roof, while squawking chickens ran foolishly back and forth across the yard. The second Indian shoved Mercy at Dianna, and as the girl buried her sobs in Dianna's skirts, he retrieved the peel from the floor. He tore the linen curtain from the window, wrapped it around the peel's blade, and thrust it into the hearth fire. Immediately the gauzy linen ignited. Holding the improvised torch before him, the Indian methodically set fire to the remaining curtains, baskets and the rush-filled mattress of Asa's bed.

"Nay, stop!" cried Dianna, her voice wild with emotion as she watched the flames begin to curl and lick at the house's wooden beams. "You heartless rogues! You have *us!* Why must you destroy our home as well?"

For answer they shoved her and Mercy through the door and away from the burning house. They paused by the fence while the Indian with the brand returned to light the roof shingles, dry from the summer's heat and quick to burn. The other man contemptuously let go of Dianna's hands, confident now that she would not flee. She sank to her knees and wrapped her arms protectively around Mercy. The Indian took the tomahawk from his waist, pantomimed striking with it and nodded meaningfully as he slipped it back into his belt. The simple gesture chilled Dianna's blood more than any words of warning. God in heaven, what had they done to deserve this?

Dianna held Mercy more tightly as she watched the orange flames twist through the door of the house. *Her* house. In these past months, in a thousand little ways, she had made it her own. She thought of the herbs she'd hung to dry from the rafters, the musket Hester had given her, the pumpkins and Indian corn and turnips she'd grown herself for the coming winter, all lost forever by the hand of one vengeful savage.

She fought back the tears that stung her eyes, blaming them on the grey, acrid smoke. If only Asa had returned an hour before, she thought bitterly, then they would have been safe with the others in Wickhamton. How long would it be now before Asa came to find them gone, and how long before he could gather men to follow after them? By then she and Mercy would be on their way to Quebec and irretrievably lost from the English world. She pictured Kit waiting for her at dusk by the burying ground, wondering impatiently why she didn't appear.

Oh, Kit, my dearest, I may never see you, kiss you, love you again!

The second Indian rejoined them, and together the two men motioned for them to leave. Dianna kissed Mercy on the forehead, and with the girl's fingers clutched tightly in her own she followed their captors. Her last glimpse of her happily ordered life was distorted by the waves of heat from the fire, an apple pie on a windowsill silhouetted against orange flames.

For Kit, the best part of the training day came last with the shooting competition. Even though as colonel he'd long ago had to disqualify himself, he enjoyed watching the other men vie for the ten-pound prize and the praise of the young women so willing to be impressed. Greybeards from the east grumbled to Kit that more time should be given to proper exercise with pikes and musket volleys, but Kit disagreed. Against an enemy that could vanish at will among the trees, battles would be won by a single man's marksmanship, not a synchronized volley by a line of musketeers.

Kit grimaced as one over-eager apprentice's shot went wildly awry to the jeers and whoops of his friends, and he wondered if the hard cider, ale and rum that traditionally ended militia day had already begun to appear. He wished the men would take the practice more seriously. Most were too young or too new from England to have seen action in King Philip's War, and in the absence of obvious danger, crops and harvests still claimed their first attention. Perhaps what he'd told them today about the raw desolation he'd seen at Deerfield and the dozens of missing women and children would make them practice a bit harder.

Kit shook his head as another woeful shot missed the target. From what Hester had told him, Dianna could outshoot them all. It surprised him how much he liked the idea of her small, straight figure there at the line, aiming and firing better than the men. Once again he impatiently scanned the crowd of spectators, searching for her familiar face.

Damnation, she and Mercy should be here by now! He should have insisted on bringing them himself instead of relying on Asa. For all Asa's pious cant about family duties, the old fool had no sense of time or responsibility, and an unseasonable fondness for the bad French brandy he got from trading. Likely that was where he was now, sleeping it off somewhere, Kit fumed, but his irritation at Asa was only a part of the growing uneasiness he couldn't shake off.

He left the competition and went striding off to where the older women were preparing the evening meal. He recalled Dianna was baking pies. Perhaps she'd come here first. Again his gaze swept over the women, seeking the one that wasn't there. That morning, for Dianna, he'd taken special care with his red uniform coat, polishing the gold buttons and retying the silk sash across his chest a dozen times before he'd been satisfied, yet now he was oblivious to how even grandmothers turned to gawk with open admiration at him in his sword and plumed hat.

"She don't be here, lad," said Hester before he could ask,

"and it don't be like Dianna t'be late. Ye didn't have words yesterday, did ye?"

The way Kit's face changed at once into a blank, emotionless mask was answer enough for Hester. "Then like as not, it be Asa that's kept her," she said hurriedly, "an' they'll be here directly."

"I'm going back for them."

Hester's forehead furrowed with concern. "Take some o' the others with ye, then. It's likely nothing, but then ye can't be sure...." Her voice trailed off, with what was left unspoken still painfully clear between them.

"It will be quicker if I go alone." He knew she was afraid of what he would find and what it would do to him, and he hated her concern, for it mirrored his own.

"Kit, ye can't go alone, not again," pleaded Hester anxiously. "Ye leave now, an' the whole town'll be talking, they will!"

"Let them," he called back as he headed for the horses. "I'll be back with Dianna and Mercy, and God help Asa Wing when I find his shiftless old hide!"

Kit let Thunder have his head on the Wickhamton road, and they soon were near to the Wing house. Kit drew the horse in as they cut through the woods, but even though the last light of day filtered through the trees, the stallion was unusually skittish, his pointed ears swivelling to hear Kit's reassurances. But at the clearing near the stream, Thunder suddenly snorted and balked, then reared back as a score of crows rose like a noisy black curtain from the tall rushes before him. While the crows danced and chattered in the branches overhead, Kit fought to calm the horse, and then, reluctantly, dismounted to investigate.

A dead deer, he told himself automatically as he stepped through the swaying rushes. Animals often came to die at the same places they drank, but the carcass should be moved before it fouled the water. With the long barrel of his gun, he parted the rushes and found Asa's body.

The dead man lay face down in the marsh, felled by the bullet wound in his upper back, and though his wispy grey hair still fluttered in the breeze untouched, his murderer had looted and stripped his body before abandoning it to the crows.

Kit reeled back, his knees suddenly weak. He had seen worse things, far worse, and yet now when his eyes squeezed shut, it was not poor Asa that he saw in his mind's eye but his parents and his sister, and Dianna and Mercy.

"Nay, not Dianna!" he rasped out loud. He steadied himself against a tree, the blood still pounding in his ears, and cursed his own weakness. Not Dianna, not Mercy. He had no proof they weren't still waiting on the other side of the hill. Quickly he swung himself up onto Thunder and urged the horse across the stream. But as soon as they crested the hill, Kit smelled the smoke and his last fragile hope shattered.

The Barnard farm had looked much the same as the scene now spread before him. The fire had burned itself out, leaving the charred outline of the house, the thick, blackened beams still upright around the chimney. Of the less substantial barn, nothing remained but smoking rubble.

Kit drew closer and called Mercy's and Dianna's names on the slim chance that they might have escaped and be hiding nearby. He tied Thunder to the fence and forced himself to search the ruins for bodies. To his grim satisfaction, he found none, but near the doorway he did find footprints, two sets of moccasins and two smaller, heeled shoes. His spirits rose to know that they had been taken from here alive. In their arrogance, the Indians hadn't bothered to sweep away the tracks, and the footsteps across the dusty yard were a trail a blind man could follow. Until, of course, they had reached the forest. Then Kit knew it would take every bit of tracking skill he possessed to follow them.

And he *would* follow them. There was no question of staying back this time. From the warmth of the timbers, he guessed they had at most six hours lead on him. He'd lose another hour returning to Plumstead to change his clothes and gather provisions and leave word where he'd gone. Two Indians were manageable odds, odds he could accept. A dozen militiamen might panic the Indians, and Dianna and Mercy would be the ones to suffer. Besides, by now there wouldn't be a single man in Wickhamton sober enough to be worth the delay. No, Kit would go alone. He owed it to Dianna, and he owed it to the two men who dared take her from him.

As he turned to go, something round and half-blackened caught his eye in the rubble, and he knelt to look closer. The pie had cracked when it had slid to the ground, but the two pastry hearts were still intact. Lightly he traced their outline and crossed the filling that trickled from the crack. On his fingertips the cooked apples were sweet and spicy to taste, and still warm, and the sense of loss and desolation that swept over him was almost unbearable.

Something brushed against his leg, and he started and jerked his rifle to his shoulder. Lily mewed forlornly, her white fur singed and marked with soot she hadn't been able to lick away. With one hand Kit scooped her up against his chest.

"We've lost them, haven't we, catkin," he whispered hoarsely into Lily's fur as the cat rubbed her head against his thumb. "But I'll bring them back safe, I swear it. This time will be different. I swear to God, this time I won't fail them."

Chapter Sixteen

For ten days Dianna and Mercy travelled with the Indians. The men were careful to avoid other houses and farms, keeping to hidden trails through the forest. With the afternoon sun always over her left shoulder, all Dianna knew for sure was that they were heading north. She could not tell how many miles they had already walked or how many more lay ahead. She was thankful that both she and Mercy were accustomed to walking, for the pace the Indians set was rapid and their breaks for sleep only a few hours long each night. Dianna often remembered the evening she'd first arrived with Asa and how after months of inactivity on the *Prosperity,* even that short journey from the river to the house had left her aching and breathless. Her captors now did not have Asa's patience.

Each long day she stared at the back of the man ahead, the one who always walked first. It had not taken long for Dianna to see the differences between the two Indians. The one she had wounded was clearly the leader, both in his imperious posture and in the way the other deferred to him. His name was Mattasoit—though Dianna did not understand their language, she had figured out that much from the context of their conversations—and he was tall and lean and strong, his movements as spare and lithe as a panther's. Like Kit, she'd caught herself thinking more than once; before this she hadn't realized how unlike most Englishmen Kit was or rather, how much

more like an Indian. She found the idea unsettling and concentrated, instead, on noting the differences.

For one, there was Mattasoit's hair, shaved clean on either
side of his head, with the top crest left long and flowing. Two
turkey feathers were tied into his hair, along with several
strands of beads made from purple shells. Beneath his paint
he was tattooed, dark dots across his cheekbones and the mark
of a deer on one arm. On his other arm was the cut Dianna
had given him. From the way he ignored the wound, purposefully leaving it uncovered, Dianna sensed her action had
caused far greater injury to his pride, and secretly she rejoiced.
There on his arm was the proof that she had not always been
so helpless!

Though in appearance the second man looked much the
same, there seemed to be a hesitancy about him that lessened
the fierceness of his painted face. While he was quick enough
to prod Dianna with his musket if she slowed, he was more
patient with Mercy, helping the girl if she stumbled and offering her berries and parched corn from his pack. But Dianna
remained wary of his kindnesses, remembering that this man
had torched their house. Mattasoit called him Quabaug.

Both men were bare-chested, with trading blankets looped
over their shoulders in place of shirts or jackets. Dianna envied
them their leather leggings and the ease with which they glided
through the brush as again and again her own skirts caught on
branches and twigs. The invisible paths they followed were
not meant for English petticoats. Impatiently Quabaug would
yank the fabric off, tearing it rather than working it free. At
first Dianna thought with dismay of all her careful handiwork
shredded so ignominiously, but then she noticed how the
scraps of torn fabric were left behind. They would, she realized, be an easy trail to follow. As often as she dared, she
began to catch her skirts on purpose, and prayed that their
rescuers would spot the scraps.

If, that is, there were any rescuers. Desperately Dianna
wanted to believe that she and Mercy would be saved, but too
well she recalled all the reasons why the militia hadn't gone
after Goodwife Barnard, and she knew this was no different.

How could she reasonably expect them to come after a servant and a child?

Because Kit loves you, her heart answered fiercely. What had he thought when she hadn't joined him on training day? Had he been angry when she didn't come, or worse yet, had he despaired, believing she had changed her mind? She remembered how surprisingly insecure he had been about her loving him, betraying a desperation that she didn't understand. It was strange to think of a man like Kit so vulnerable, and she never wanted to hurt him, not even this way, when she couldn't help it. But surely Asa would have explained, once he'd seen the burning house and gone to Wickhamton for help. Asa was unpredictable, but he did love Mercy.

And Kit—Kit loved *her.* Even before he'd known her name he had rescued her from the nightmare in her uncle's house, and so much had changed between them since then. He would come for her and for Mercy. He would. Over and over Dianna repeated the words to herself as they went deeper into the wilderness.

She was worried most about Mercy. Once they had left sight of their home, the girl had stopped her weeping and instead had seemed to draw into herself, her face empty as she let Dianna draw her along by the hand. She did not seem to hear Dianna, nor did she speak in return, and when they stopped to rest, she would curl herself into a tight little ball with her eyes squeezed shut. To lose her parents, her home and her pet, too, was more than any child should have to bear, and the unfairness of their capture tore at Dianna. Nor could she tell how much longer Mercy could bear the strain. Each dawn she was harder to rouse, and her slender body was growing visibly weaker from the hardships.

The night they crossed the river brought reality to Dianna's fears. The Indians had not stopped at dusk as usual, but continued on, and in the darkness unseen branches lashed at Dianna's arms and face and roots and rocks seemed to rise from nowhere to trip her feet. The night was cold, too, with the chill of winter in the autumn air, and Dianna shivered in her tattered dress without a shawl or cape. Mercy's little hand was icy, and the child was almost weaving from exhaustion.

"We must keep up, Mercy," Dianna urged, as much to encourage herself as the child. "We're warmer walking than if we stop."

Dianna heard the rushing water ahead as they came through the trees. The river was narrow here, scarcely more than a wide stream as it raced over and around a cluster of large rocks. Mattasoit easily stepped from the bank to the first rock and then jumped across to the next in line. When he was half way across, he turned and beckoned sharply for Dianna and Mercy to follow.

"Nay, Dianna, I can't!" wailed Mercy, shaking her head as she backed away from the water. "I'll fall an' drown, an' they—they won't care!"

"*I* care, lamb, and I have no intention of letting you drown. See, the water's scarce a foot deep here, just like the stream at home." Gently Dianna tried to draw Mercy toward the water. She could feel the impatience radiating from Mattasoit. She didn't want to frighten Mercy, but this was definitely not the time to dawdle. Kit said that the trail between Deerfield and Quebec had been littered with the corpses of English women who had faltered. "At home you'd be hopping over these stones like a leap-frog. I'll hold your hand, I swear, and I won't let go. But we must go now, Mercy. Now!"

Whimpering, Mercy let Dianna pull her to the water's edge. "I'll count, Mercy, and we'll go together. One, two, three, jump!"

The rock was wet and more slippery than Dianna had expected, and their shoes skidded across the surface before Dianna could steady herself enough to stop. She took a deep breath as she looked at the next rock, the black water foaming and churning around her feet. She didn't like this any more than Mercy did, but there stood Mattasoit ahead of them, one hand on the tomahawk at his belt. Lord, how she hated the threat the gesture implied, and how much she hated the man who made it!

"Again, Mercy." They had come this far, and she wouldn't falter now. "One, two, three, *jump!*"

Fourteen rocks they crossed until only the last step remained to the bank. "Almost there, Mercy," coaxed Dianna, "and you've done it, just like I knew you could."

Mercy smiled tremulously up at Dianna, and for the first time dared to let go of her hand. "'Twas not so very hard," she said and took the last hop on her own. But she hadn't counted on the marsh grass that lined the bank, and though she scrambled frantically for a foothold, she tumbled back into the water with a shriek. The water here was not deep, and Dianna at once dragged her, weeping, to the river bank.

"Hush, Mercy, you're safe enough," murmured Dianna as the little girl clung to her neck. The water coursed from Mercy's skirts and petticoats into puddles around her sodden shoes and stockings, and the cold, wet wool clung to her legs. Already Dianna could feel her shivering.

Yet Dianna felt Mattasoit's hand on her shoulder as well. She did not need to understand his words to know that he was angry with the delay and demanding that they continue. Slowly she disengaged herself from Mercy's embrace and rose to face the Indian.

"We cannot go on, not tonight," she told him firmly, forgetting that the man knew no English. "The child needs to dry her clothes and to lose the chill with the warmth of a fire."

Mattasoit's eyes narrowed, and he pointed once again to the trail into the woods.

"Nay, I will not go," said Dianna angrily, her silver eyes flashing. "I refuse to risk the child's health so that you might continue to drive us like animals!"

Furiously the Indian raised his hand and struck Dianna across her jaw. She stumbled back from him, but kept her footing. Instead of subduing her, his blow only fanned her temper more, and all the indignities and fears she'd borne in the past few days came rising up.

"You have no right to treat me thus!" she said defiantly. "I'm not one of your heathen squaws, but an English gentle-woman, a lady, and nothing you can do or say to me can change that! You think you are such a brave warrior to bully and torment a woman and child! Mercy and I are ten times braver than you. Nay, a hundred times! You are a coward, and so I'll tell everyone in Quebec! *Vous êtes un très gros poltron!*''

Mattasoit's whole body tensed with fury as he answered her in flawless, unaccented French. ''If you were not worth so much to me unharmed, I would cut your tongue from your mouth so I would hear no more of your lies. You will call me master and you will obey me.''

Stunned, much of Dianna's anger evaporated with the knowledge that they could now communicate. ''Then you must understand—''

Swiftly his hand sliced the air before her face. ''I must do nothing you ask!'' he said sharply. ''Through your English cunning you have concealed from me that you speak the Frenchman's tongue, and as your master, I am displeased. I have sworn to deliver you unharmed, but not so your child. Perhaps she shall suffer in your stead.''

''Nay, you can't!'' protested Dianna wildly. Her gaze flew back to Mercy, huddled miserably on the river bank with Quabaug crouched beside her. ''Do whatever you wish to me, but leave her alone! She is innocent, she has done nothing!''

Mattasoit smiled triumphantly, his lips curling back over even white teeth. ''So, you give me the secret to your obedience.''

Another master, another man who demanded she obey. But for Mercy's sake, Dianna abandoned her pride and softened her voice with supplication. His belief that she was Mercy's mother could only add weight to her requests. ''My child is weary, and she will sicken if you refuse her the comfort of a fire's warmth. If she becomes ill, she'll only delay you longer.''

Mattasoit shook his head, the beads in his long hair clicking softly against one another. ''It matters not. If she cannot keep up, she will die.'' His smile widened. ''Monsieur le Lieutenant Hertel de Rouville will give me four gold pieces for an English child's scalp.''

"Nay, you could not!" gasped Dianna, horrified.

"Your words continue to be harsh to my ears, *Anglaise,* and unfit for your master. I care nothing for your child. It is Quabaug who wanted her, not I." He waved dismissively toward the other Indian. "He wishes to make a gift of her to his sister, to replace another claimed by death. I believe yours is likewise sullen and sickly, an unworthy gift, and I have told him so. But he will not listen and fancies her all the more."

While Mercy had been frozen by fear and cold, Quabaug had gently pulled off her wet socks and chafed her icy feet until the blood had returned. Modestly she had quickly tugged her skirts back down over her toes as soon as he was done, but she had not run away to Dianna's side, watching instead as he emptied his leather pack. At last he drew out a pair of child's moccasins, embroidered across the toes with porcupine quills. He held them up to Mercy's feet and frowned. He stuffed the toes of the moccasins with dry leaves until, satisfied that now they would fit, he held them shyly out to Mercy. The girl hesitated only a moment before accepting his gift. While Quabaug beamed and nodded, she slipped them on with a tentative smile and pointed her feet toward Dianna for approval.

But Dianna's eyes were on the contents of Quabaug's pack, piled neatly on the grass beside him. On the top was a white linen shirt, an Englishman's shirt, worn and crisscrossed with mending and covered with the stiff, dark blotches of dried blood. Dianna noted how the old shirt's collar had been turned and resewn to lengthen its wear; she had done the work herself not a fortnight before. Slowly, as if in a dream, she forced herself to see Quabaug's musket, still cradled protectively in his lap. Why hadn't she noticed before the two wedge-shaped notches in the stock, the notches that were Asa's special mark?

She wrapped her arms tightly around herself and dug her nails into her own skin, fighting back the impossible urge to laugh. No one was coming for them because no one knew they were gone. In her elegant courtier's French, she was left to barter for her life with a half-naked savage who painted his face like a skunk's back.

* * *

By the time they finally halted for the night, several hours before daybreak, Mercy's eyes were unnaturally bright and her cheeks were flushed with fever.

"I'm so c-cold, Dianna," she said, stammering with the chills that shook her weakened body as she sank to the ground.

One hand across the child's forehead told Dianna all she needed to know, and quickly she turned to Mattasoit. "Please, I beg you, my daughter needs hot food to eat. If you or Quabaug can bring me anything, a squirrel or a rabbit, I can make us all a stew."

"You would have us fire muskets, would you?" Mattasoit snorted with scorn. "So that every Englishmen will know we are here? I am no fool, *Anglaise*."

"A fire, then, just a small one," pleaded Dianna, "so that she might warm herself and her clothes."

"A fire and musket-shots? Why don't I let you go to the highest hill, and shout so that all might hear you?"

"But there is no one!" Dianna's voice cracked with the admission. "Please—"

"Do not test me, *Anglaise,* for you know my answer," he snapped. "We leave at sunrise."

Numbly Dianna watched as the two Indians rolled themselves in their blankets and were, it seemed, instantly asleep. Curled on the ground, Mercy, too, slept, but restlessly, her arms and legs thrashing as she muttered in her dreams. Taking care not to wake the girl, Dianna lay beside her and wrapped her own body around the sick child's to share what warmth she could. Mercy's breathing was harsh in her chest, a wheezing rasp that meant the chill had settled in her lungs. Dianna hugged her closer, trying not to think of tomorrow. She had truly come to love Mercy as her own, yet there was nothing she could do to save her or even give her comfort. Hot tears of fear and frustration slid down her cheek and angrily she wiped them away with her fingers. Weeping would serve no purpose to either of them.

Gradually the first light of the false dawn began to filter through the yellow leaves of the tall oaks overhead. A low mist drifted over the ground, enveloping the dark tree roots like an eerie shroud, and muffling all sound, for the woods were strangely silent in these last moments before the true dawn. Dianna remembered the elves and faeries and other woodland creatures that her father had used to amuse her as a child, but here their world seemed strangely real, and Dianna's heartbeat began to quicken at what she felt but could not see.

Mercy shifted uneasily in her arms, her eyelids fluttering open. "Dianna?" she asked hoarsely, each breath an effort.

"Hush, lamb, 'tis not time to rise yet." Dianna stroked the child's hair. Oh, Lord, she was so very hot to touch.

"But it hurts t'breathe!"

"Then here, sit upright in my lap, and perhaps that shall be better." Mercy climbed across Dianna's legs and rested her head against Dianna's chest. With each breath came the wheezing that meant congestion in her lungs, and Dianna's heart sank when she remembered the long day before them. She could not let them leave the child behind. Better to let them kill her, too, than abandon Mercy, and she curled her arms protectively around the girl's limp body.

"Would ye sing t'me, Dianna?" rasped Mercy. "The pretty song wit' th'queen's lament?"

Dianna hesitated, unwilling to disturb the sleeping Indians, but Mercy persisted. "Please, Dianna, th' queen's song be my favorite."

How could she refuse what might be the last favor the girl asked of her? "Oh, aye, if that's your favorite," she said, trying unsuccessfully to tease the way they always had before. Mercy's favorite was from an old-fashioned opera by Lully, and though Dianna was hazy as to which queen was doing the lamenting, the aria had always been one of her best pieces. She began softly, her own voice rough-edged from the chill, but soon the old beauty of the music filled her throat, and, closing her eyes, she let the notes rise and soar into the early morning mists.

When she was done, she kept her eyes closed just a moment longer to savor the vanishing pleasure of the music. When she opened them, Mattasoit loomed before them, and instinctively Dianna clutched at Mercy.

"You are *Me'toulin, Anglaise?*" he asked with a tentativeness that surprised Dianna. "They did not tell me that when I said I'd take you."

"*Me'toulin?*" repeated Dianna uncertainly. He was hanging back from her, unwilling to come too close, and Quabaug remained farther still, his dark eyes round with fear in the half-light.

"*Me'toulin, me'toulin.*" Mattasoit fanned his fingers, searching for the comparable word in French. "You have the gift to speak to the spirits, yes? You can make magic for them?"

Slowly his meaning dawned on Dianna. Her singing, that was it. Perhaps the Sun King's opera would sound like magic to ears that had never heard it. "Aye, I speak to them," she answered boldly, her chin high, "and they listen to me, too."

Mattasoit drew himself up confidently, but Dianna saw the fear come into his eyes now, too. "What did you tell them, your spirits, your gods?"

"I told them about you." Dianna paused for emphasis. "And I told them the truth."

Mattasoit flicked his hand, and Quabaug scurried forward. "We are within two days' journey of a village, *Anglaise,*" he said with an unwarrior-like nervousness. "There your daughter will be well tended. And she shall not walk further. Quabaug will carry her, and she shall have his blanket to warm herself. You will tell all this to the gods, *Anglaise?* You tell them so they will listen of Mattasoit and Quabaug?"

Dianna nodded. "They will listen," she said softly, and somehow, she thought they already had.

Chapter Seventeen

"**Y**ou are right, Sparhawk," said Attawan as he rejoined Kit. "The woman and the child are within the village."

Kit swore and slammed his hand down hard on the ground in frustration. They had been so close, not more than half a day behind. "Did you see them? Are they well, unhurt?"

Attawan dropped the bag of cornmeal he'd traded for a Dutch knife, his excuse for visiting the village, and sat on the log beside Kit. "The woman is well, but the girl has been ill with lung fever. They carried her here."

Kit shook his head, remembered the time they'd wasted. When Mercy's footprints had changed first to moccasins and then disappeared completely, he had insisted they search the surrounding woods in case she had been abandoned. He owed that much and more to Tom Wing and to Asa, too. *And to Tamsin...*

And instead the Indians had carried Mercy. A simple explanation, really, for only one of a hundred small missteps. The fleeing Indians had not gone north toward Quebec as Kit had expected, but northwest, farther into the wilderness claimed by the French than he'd ever ventured before. The falling leaves had obscured the trail more effectively than snow, leaving only a bent branch here, an overturned stone there, to mark that any had passed before them. The first little flag of Dianna's torn skirt had seemed like a miracle, and when Kit had found enough to realize she'd done it intentionally, his admiration for her rose even higher. He'd saved each scrap like a talisman, a tattered reassurance that she still lived. And now she was just ahead, beyond one more hill and one more stream.

"How many guards are there?" he demanded impatiently. "Are they kept in a house or out of doors? Is there—"

"I didn't judge it wise to be too inquisitive, Sparhawk."

"Damn it, Attawan, I didn't let you come along so you could pass judgment!"

"You did not 'let' me. I chose to come. If I weren't here, you would now be bound and waiting for the village women to torture you." Attawan slipped a finger inside his moccasin and scratched his heel, considering whether to take offense or not, and decided once again to let Kit's outburst pass. It was the ghosts that spoke, not his friend, and it was a good thing that he, Attawan, was here to protect Sparhawk from letting those ghosts steal the Englishman's wits completely. "You forget the Pennacooks have no love for things English, and that includes big bull-heads like you."

Kit sighed heavily and rested his hand on the Indian's shoulder. "Aye, bull-headed I am," he admitted, "and I couldn't have come this far without you. But I want them back, Attawan. Tonight I will come with you, and together we'll find them."

Attawan nodded, satisfied by the words. He reached into his bag for his pipe and a flint, for despite Kit's impatience, they would not be going anywhere until nightfall at the earliest. "They are prisoners of a brave named Mattasoit, an Abenaki, not of this tribe. They don't like having him here, but they fear him and let him stay. What is strange, Sparhawk, is how he treats this woman as a great prize, yet in your English village, she is only a slave."

"A servant, Attawan, not a slave," said Kit automatically. "But you're right, it makes no sense."

Attawan shrugged. "I heard Mattasoit believes her to be a *me'toulin,* that she can speak with the gods."

Kit stared in disbelief. "What about Dianna Grey would

make him think that? She is a Christian lady, not some kind of Abenaki witch!''

Attawan's expression grew serious. ''Then hope Mattasoit doesn't learn this Christian lady has lied to him. He would be dishonored, and he would beat her, maybe kill her, if others laugh at him. She would not be much good as a servant after that, Sparhawk.''

The smoke from Attawan's pipe filled Kit's nose, the tobacco's familiar scent pungent and oddly comforting. It was time Attawan knew the truth. ''She won't be a servant when she returns to Plumstead,'' he said softly, trying to blot out the image of Dianna's being tortured by Mattasoit, and remember instead the way she laughed, her little cleft chin tipped back. ''If she'll have me, Dianna Grey will be my wife.''

Attawan showed no surprise, and only nodded thoughtfully behind the haze of smoke. ''Then tonight we shall find your woman.''

Dianna and Mercy were given a small wigwam to themselves near the center of the village. Although Dianna realized that they had displaced the wigwam's regular occupants only that they might be more carefully guarded, she still welcomed the privacy of the little house's windowless walls of woven mats. Their only visitor was a stout, wary woman who never raised her eyes from the water and food she left on the floor before retreating backward out the deerskin flap that served as a door. And, of course, Mattasoit and Quabaug, who did not leave their post outside the doorway.

With a small fire in the center of the packed dirt floor, the house was pleasingly warm, and Dianna was relieved that Mercy's breathing had eased and her sleep had grown more peaceful. Gently Dianna stroked the child's hair if she stirred, and settled the blanket higher over her shoulders. Whenever Mercy woke, Dianna urged her to eat—fried cornmeal cakes, baked beans and small strips of roast moose. The villagers had obviously offered them their best, but even their hospitality made Dianna uneasy. At Plumstead she'd heard many stories of Indian captivity, and not one of them had included English-women as pampered guests in a village. But then none of the other captive women had been called a *me'toulin,* either.

In the afternoon of the second day, she waited until Mercy had fallen asleep again, and then drew back the deerskin to speak with Mattasoit. She had not realized how dim the house was until she stepped into the bright autumn sunlight and squinted, shading her eyes with her hand.

"Take yourself back inside, *Anglaise,*" ordered Mattasoit with a touch of his old arrogance. He had freshly painted his face, and there were more beads and feathers woven into his hair. "It's not fit that you show yourself."

Dianna raised her chin imperiously, remembering the haughtiest of the dowager duchesses at court as good inspiration for an aspiring *me'toulin.* "Clearly these people are not yours and this is not your village," she said, declaring what was obvious even to her. These villagers bore little resemblance to Mattasoit, and were obviously intimidated by him. "Why do we remain here with them when they are such lesser warriors?"

She could have sworn he preened at the compliment. "We wait here for the men who seek you."

"What men are these?" she asked quickly, unable to keep the excitement from her voice. Maybe he meant the men who made and carried the ransom for captives. This would be as far as she and Mercy would have to travel before they could go home.

"The Frenchmen will come first," he said, and Dianna's hopes plummeted. "Forty gold pieces the fat one offered me to take you. He wants you badly, that one."

"What is the man's name?" Somehow her voice remained calm, almost offhanded. She had been chosen, kidnapped by design. The fat Frenchman must be Robillard; no other knew of her. She remembered the coarse hunger in his face when he'd looked at her at Plumstead, and she knew Mattasoit was right. Robillard did want her, and the certainty sickened her.

Mattasoit looked at her shrewdly. "The spirits haven't told you?"

Dianna returned his gaze levelly. "I can only hear what they tell me, and they don't bother to speak of fat Frenchmen."

Mattasoit shrugged carelessly, and with his thumb wiped a smudge from the barrel of his musket. "A Frenchman. I know not his name, and it matters little to me if he brings his gold pieces. He'll have you, and Quabaug shall have your daughter. Then shall come the Englishman." He smiled, his teeth startling against the black warpaint. "You are like a fawn, set out to tempt the big wolf to come before the hunters."

Suddenly, horribly, she understood. She was the bait to trap Kit. "He's not coming," she said too rapidly, fighting against the tightness in her chest. "If he had followed us, he would have found us already. Don't you hear me? He's not coming!"

"He will come, and he will die. You will go to the Frenchman, and your daughter will go to Quabaug's sister." Mattasoit's smile faded, and he tapped three fingers together lightly on his lower lip. "Listen to your spirits, *me'toulin,* and you will hear that all this is true."

Dianna jerked back the deerskin and stumbled back into the little house, the world swimming before her. Now that she knew Kit must not come for her, she was certain that he had. Somewhere, not far away, he was waiting to try to steal her and Mercy back. He would die trying, and it would be her fault. She needed no spirits to explain it. She balled her fingers into a fist and pressed it silently to her lips as if she could take back all the words she'd spoken to bring her to this place.

"What is it, Dianna?" asked Mercy, her face by the firelight still puffy with sleep. "What has happened?"

Dianna took a deep breath, the effort sharp as a blade in her lungs. "It's nothing, lamb, nothing at all."

But outside they heard the jingle of horses' bridles and more voices in French, angry, agitated voices. Dianna seized Mercy and drew her to her breast.

The man who thrust himself into the house was ruddy-faced above his neatly clipped beard and moustache, his chest as round and solid as a hogshead barrel and his legs bowed as if from the weight of his body. But what Dianna noticed first was the silver cross around his neck and the neat white collar

above his dark cloak that marked the man for what he was: a
minister, or more likely, since he seemed a Frenchman, a
priest. Surely a man of God would help her escape!

"So this is the Englishwoman who claims to have gifts from
God," he said coldly. "It is no more than Protestant trickery.
With such blasphemy she dishonors you, Mattasoit, and damns
her own soul."

Behind him stood Mattasoit. "Beware, *mon père,* she
speaks your tongue."

"Aye, sir, and I'll not be shamed by anything I've done,"
said Dianna vehemently as she rose to her feet, her arms still
tight around Mercy's shoulders. "If I have spoken less than
the truth, I've done so to save my child."

The priest ignored Dianna and glanced instead over his
shoulder at Mattasoit. "You did not tell me there was a child
with her. The lieutenant has no use for innocents."

"The child is my prisoner along with the woman," said
Mattasoit stubbornly. "She will have a home among my people."

"Where she will become another soul lost to the true faith."
The priest slid the polished cross between his fingers thoughtfully. "I have decided. Come to me, child. Your mother has
chosen the path to damnation, but there is still time for your
redemption. The holy sisters will nurture you and teach you
the ways of goodness that come from Our Lord's Blessed
Mother."

The French words were meaningless to Mercy, but she understood well enough the beckoning hand of the man in black
and clung more tightly to Dianna.

"You can't take her from me!" cried Dianna. "Roman or
not, you are still a Christian, and no true Christian would separate a child from her mother!"

"If you truly love her, *madame,* you should thank me for
saving her immortal soul," said the priest coldly. "She will
be well cared for, much better than you yourself seem presently capable of."

Angrily Mattasoit gripped the man's arm. "I tell you, they
are both mine!"

The priest stared pointedly at Mattasoit's hand, and suddenly on some unseen cue, two French soldiers appeared at the narrow doorway, only their boots and the muzzles of their guns visible, but enough to make Mattasoit release his grip with a furious shove.

"You expect compensation for your efforts," said the priest calmly, and tossed the Indian a handful of coins. Scornfully, Mattasoit did not catch them but let the coins fall to the dirt floor. The priest's lips curled beneath his neat moustache. "As you wish, so shall it be."

With unexpected swiftness, he grabbed Mercy around the waist and jerked her from Dianna's arms. The child screamed as Dianna lunged after her, but as soon as the priest was safely through the door, the soldiers barred Dianna's way with their muskets. Dianna shoved against the cold metal, struggling to reach Mercy as the priest tossed the thrashing child onto his saddle and climbed behind her. One soldier shoved Dianna back into the doorway, and then the soldiers, too, mounted their horses. Dianna's final glimpse of Mercy was her skinny bare legs in the new moccasins, kicking vainly against the horse's side.

Dianna stared after the three horses, not caring that she wept before the silent crowd of curious Pennacooks. Her father, her name, her home and now Mercy and Kit: there was nothing left for her to lose.

It was Mattasoit who at last grabbed her shoulder and shook her roughly to break the spell of her own misery. "Come, we are leaving."

Uncomprehending, Dianna looked at him through the haze of her tears. "We're going after them?"

"Why? I've told you before that the child means nothing to me." The Indian's face was rigid with fury. "English and French, you have all lied, and betrayed me, and I will suffer it no longer. These white men will come for you, but you will be gone, and I will be the one to laugh at them as fools!"

His fingers tightened on her shoulder, his nails leaving crescent-shaped marks in her skin even through the wool of her bodice. "If you were true *me'toulin*, you wouldn't have shamed me before the priest. But you are false, like all your kind. And by the time we reach my village, you will beg me to have sold you to the French.''

Kit and Attawan waited through most of the night, until the last hour before dawn when sleep is deepest, before they crept together into the village. Clouds hid the moon in their favor, but still Kit tied his light-colored hair beneath his hat and shaded his face with soot. Although Attawan had assured Kit that the villagers had no interest in Mercy or Dianna, and would likely not fight to keep them, Kit refused to rely on their goodwill. Instead he planned to kill the two Abenakis, steal their captives and melt back into the night without waking anyone. They'd use knives, not guns. Knives were silent and quick and did not need to be reloaded. He had never come to enjoy killing, hunting other men, white or red, for sport the way some did, but neither did he shy from it. And he wanted this man Mattasoit. God's blood, if he had given even one moment's pain to Dianna or Mercy...

As he and Attawan slipped from the shadow of one house to another, their moccasined footsteps silent in the dust, Kit forced himself to put Dianna from his thoughts and concentrate instead on the long blade of the knife in his hand. But something was wrong. He sensed it with his body before his thoughts agreed, before he saw Attawan stiffen and scowl and gesture toward the rounded wigwam before them.

Neither of the Abenakis were standing guard, as Attawan said they had been earlier. Immediately Kit's gaze swept around the rest of the village, looking to see if they'd moved Mercy and Dianna to another house. But there was no sign of Mattasoit or Quabaug, no movement at all beyond one lame dog drowsily scratching his head. Impatiently Attawan ducked into the house, barking a warning that Kit didn't understand. A woman shrieked and was quickly muffled, and then came a babble of excited voices. Kit followed, his eyes straining to make sense of the mounded figures in the dark house. One, an old woman, waved her arms defiantly in Attawan's face as her shrill words rapidly rose and fell.

"For God's sake, Attawan, what is she saying?" demanded Kit. He could not stand upright against the low, curved ceiling, and bent over he felt awkward and vulnerable. "Where's Dianna?"

Disgusted, Attawan thrust his knife back into the sheath at his waist. "They left before sundown. A French priest and two soldiers took Tom Wing's daughter, and the Abenakis took your woman."

Kit fought against disappointment so sharp he felt it like a blow. "Strange they would be separated," he heard himself saying as he and Attawan stepped outside. *He had come too late. He'd failed again.* "Any notion of where they've gone?"

Attawan shook his head. "They force us to separate, too. I'll follow the priest." He laid his hand on Kit's arm and looked at him seriously, reading his doubts. "The Abenakis are yours by rights. You will find them, and you will show them that you are worth ten of their worthless braves, that they should not take what is yours. The courage is in your heart, Sparhawk."

He smiled and shoved Kit playfully. "Go now, or you shall feel the sharpness of Dianna Grey's tongue for making her wait."

The basket Mattasoit had tied to Dianna's back was heavy, and the hickory splints dug into her shoulders. She tried not to feel it, tried not to think beyond placing one foot after the other. That was difficult enough, burdened beneath the basket's lopsided weight. But if she stumbled, Mattasoit would hit her and curse her clumsiness. Her lip was swollen from the last time, when she'd tripped across the root, and the coppery taste of her own blood was still in her mouth. He'd been so disgusted that he'd gone on ahead by himself, leaving her with Quabaug's musket—Asa's musket—to prod the backs of her legs. *One step at a time, only one step, then one step more....*

She saw the flash in the fir trees from the corner of her eye, heard first the dry echo of the gunpowder and then the surprised little grunt that Quabaug made as he flopped forward on top of her. Beneath his weight she toppled face first into the dry maple leaves, her breath knocked from her lungs. Gasping, she looked around wildly for the shot's source and tried to pull herself free from beneath Quabaug's sprawling, still body.

Then Kit was there, truly there and not just another dream, the sun bright in his hair and the rifle in his hand as he jumped and ran down the hill through the brambles toward her. And above him, behind the broken oak tree, with one eye squinted as he peered down his musket's barrel, was Mattasoit.

Chapter Eighteen

Until Kit had seen Dianna there with the Indian, he had not realized how part of him already believed she was dead. By surrendering hope, he had tried to defend himself from the pain of losing her yet again. But it hadn't worked: he knew that the moment he saw her again. Without her, his life wasn't worth living, and all the pretending in the world couldn't change that.

From the trees he saw the discolored lump of the bruise on her jaw, the tattered, filthy clothing and the way she bowed beneath the basket she was forced to bear, while that Abenaki bastard ambled behind carrying nothing more than old Asa's musket. Kit's bullet found the Indian's breast in an instant, clean and neat, and too easy a death by half for what he'd done to Dianna. But none of that mattered now, he thought joyfully as he plunged through the underbrush toward her. She was alive, and he meant to take her in his arms and beg her to forgive him and swear to never let her suffer again.

Yet her expression was all wrong. Her mouth was twisted open in terror, her eyes rounded and staring away from him, past him.

Instinct made him dodge and drop to the ground, and the musket bullet rang instead into an alder's trunk, the bark splintering with a crack. Above him he heard Mattasoit's unearthly cry for battle, and Kit had only time to roll to his back as the Indian threw himself down from the hill, tomahawk in hand.

With both hands Kit held his rifle crossways, catching Mattasoit's wrist back against his chest. The Indian's face contorted as he strained to break Kit's hold. He twisted his leg beneath Kit's and threw his weight sideways, rocking Kit over with him. Kit slammed the rifle toward the man's throat and grabbed for his knife. In that half-second the Indian shoved the rifle away and swung the tomahawk upward. Swiftly Kit ducked, but not before a handful of severed gold-streaked curls drifted past his shoulder. He grabbed the Indian's wrist just as Mattasoit's fingers tightened around his own.

Helplessly Dianna watched as the two men tumbled over and over across the ground like wild dogs. They were well-matched in skill and size, each strengthened with blood-lust and anger. It would be a fight that ended only when one man was dead. She hated watching and looked away. There in the grass, not far, lay Asa's musket where Quabaug had dropped it. Her fingers clawed vainly at the loamy ground and leaves as she tried to reach it, her breath coming in short pants of frustration as she stretched toward the gun.

But it was too late. She heard the ragged cry, the last sound of a dying man. Dropping her head onto her arm, she squeezed her eyes shut, afraid to look. *Merciful God,* she prayed, *let Kit be alive! Let him be alive, and I shall never ask for anything else again!*

And then Kit was pulling her free from Quabaug's body and from the crushed carrying basket. The cry she heard now was her own, and tears of relief tracked down her grimy cheeks as she threw her arms around Kit's neck.

"Oh, Kit, I thought I'd never see you again," Dianna murmured hoarsely against his chest. "My own love, my only love!"

Yet strangely he did not embrace her in return, but held her too lightly with his hands on her shoulders. Puzzled, Dianna drew back, and he seemed to follow, swaying unsteadily, and to her shock she realized he only stood because of her support.

"Behind that hill are—there is a shelter," he said thickly. "You need rest, dearling, you are—"

He did not finish, clutching at her as his legs gave way. He

stared blankly at Dianna, his green eyes too wide open and
his face oddly pale beneath the tan. Now Dianna saw the dark
patches on his hunting shirt were blood, new blood, and not
all of it Mattasoit's. The hair over Kit's left ear was wet and
red, the curl gone limp.

"Nay, Kit, 'tis you that's wounded," she said as she struggled to keep him upright. Lord, why did she have to be so
small a woman in a world of large men? She lifted one of his
arms across her shoulder like a yoke and tried to lead him.
"Listen to me, love! We must get you to this shelter, but I'll
need your help. Nay, don't wobble on me now, Kit!"

Kit heard her voice from far away and smiled, wondering
why this pretty little woman beside him should accuse him of
wobbling. Wobbling was a damned foolish accusation to make
to a man. He was steady enough to dance, if he'd a mind to,
and mayhap with this very lass, if only she'd stand still long
enough for him to catch her. Her face spun before him, her
features crazily unfocussed. Silly baggage, to tease him this
way!

Somehow Dianna managed to lead him over the hill, not
even sure that the shelter he'd mentioned even existed. But
there beside the trickle of a nearly-dry stream were the bent
saplings of an abandoned Indian camp. The Indians had taken
away most of the woven mats that turned the sapling arches
into houses, but one little wigwam remained almost intact,
perhaps the last refuge of a villager too old or ill to follow
with the rest. It was empty enough now, smelling of musty
reeds and squirrels, and there were ragged holes in the walls
where the mats had fallen through. Yet the wigwam was better
than Dianna had dared to hope, and with one final effort, she
half led, half dragged Kit inside. He groaned, muttering something she didn't understand, and at last, his body gave way to
unconsciousness.

Dianna pushed her hair back from her face and tried to think
what to do next. With a quick glance at Kit, she ran back over
the hill to where the two dead Abenakis lay. First she retrieved
the basket she had been carrying, loaded with provisions Mattasoit had appropriated from the Pennacooks—two blankets, a

brass cooking pot, twice mended, smoked venison, parched corn, walnuts and a bark basket of cranberries that were only slightly crushed. Next she collected Asa's musket and Mattasoit's, too. For a long moment she stared down at Mattasoit's body, flopped on his side with his arms outstretched across the bloodstained leaves. Quickly, before she lost her nerve, she reached down and pried the tomahawk from his stiffening fingers and pulled the powder horn and bag of bullets and patches from around his neck. She did the same to Quabaug, shivering as she tried not to touch him more than she had to, and then, her arms full of all she'd gathered, she ran as fast as she could back to the house where Kit lay.

He had not moved, and Dianna wondered if that meant good or ill. She filled the brass pot with water in the stream and tore the last of her petticoats into strips for bandages. Nothing was as clean as it should have been—what she would have given for a cup of strong soap!—but she made a small fire in the center of the hut beneath the roof hole and balanced the pot of water over it to boil. Finally she knelt beside Kit and as gently as she could, pulled off his blood-soaked shirt.

One cut ran diagonally from his collar-bone, and another crossed his forearm. Neither was serious, and the bleeding had almost stopped. Her hands grazed the dark hair on his chest as she washed the cuts. She'd forgotten how powerfully muscled he was, and how, too, his body was already crisscrossed with old scars. Lightly she rested her fingers over his heart. The beat was steady and regular, as was his breathing, and satisfied, she turned to the cut on his head. This was the one that worried her and the one that bled the longest, each cloth that she pressed to it soon becoming soaked. Finally, by sunset, she was able to wrap her makeshift bandages around his head, had covered him with one of the blankets, and then sat back to wait. In the morning she would try to find the wild herbs to make a poultice to draw out the wound's poison.

She loaded all three guns and kept guard herself, wrapped in the second blanket with a musket in her hands. The night seemed very black to her, and very lonely, even with Kit lying beside her, unconscious or asleep she did not know.

She was far more frightened than she wanted to admit. Strong as he was, Kit's wound was still dangerous. She didn't know how long it would be before he could travel or how far they were from any English settlement. The Indians who'd abandoned this village could return. The Frenchmen Mattasoit had avoided might be searching for them, perhaps even Robillard himself. And Mercy, poor, innocent Mercy, could be a hundred miles closer to Montreal by now. Dianna placed another branch on the fire and huddled into her blanket. Last year in the fall she and her father had been in Paris, and she'd sung in the white-and-gold music room of the Vicomte de Thavenet…

It was mid-morning before Dianna awoke, with Kit muttering restlessly beside her. She followed Hester's receipt for the poultice, but by nightfall he was feverish and the head wound had become angry and swollen. He never seemed to know her, speaking disjointedly about his mother and father and other names she did not recognize. She cooled his fever with cloths soaked in the icy stream water, and tried to get him to sip the broth she'd made. She sang to him, too, for the sound of her voice seemed to calm him as gently she pillowed his head in her lap and stroked her fingertips across his forehead. No grand queen's laments this time, but old lullabies and wistful Scottish tales of forgotten lovers.

There was little more she could do, and she needed no great physician's skill to tell her that each hour he was drifting a little farther away from her and from life, nor did she need to be told what would become of her if the infection finally claimed him.

No matter where the dream began, it always ended in the same place, and in the same way.

He was on the old bay gelding, the autumn sun warm on his back. He had travelled this road to Wickhamton so many times that he and the horse could have done it blindfolded. As he rode he was thinking about a copper-haired tavern-keep's daughter in New London, and wondering if he could talk his father into letting him return downriver on business to see her

again next week. He couldn't quite remember her name—Nel
or Nan, he'd recall it soon enough when he saw her again—
but she'd been quite generous in her affections, and at twenty-
two, that was what mattered to him most.

Right before the bend in the road, low by the river, the horse
had shied skittishly, and he had swatted its rump and called
it a cowardly old noddy as they'd pushed on. And that was
when he saw the body of his mother first, her skirts snarled
against the red-and-gold berries of a bittersweet vine, and
then his father, face up and staring, surprised, at the cloudless
sky, and finally Tamsin, who'd run the farthest before they'd
shot her, too. There was a thin red line around her throat
where they'd yanked away her coral beads, and she still
clutched the arm of her calico doll, Sukey.

He should have been there to save them. That never
changed. Nothing he ever did could make it different.

He should have saved them...

"You saved me!" said Dianna hoarsely. "Without you I
would have died, and now, God forgive me, I cannot do the
same for you!"

Confused, Kit realized it was her tears that were falling on
his face. His mouth felt dry as a desert, but he forced himself
to form the words, to make her understand. "I—I should have
been with them," he said, half the words no more than breath
without sound. "If I couldn't have saved them, I should have
died, too."

"Nay, don't speak so!" she cried, her face close above his,
and he saw how her mouth twisted to keep from weeping
more. "You have been ill, and I thought—I was afraid—but
you've come back to me now, and you'll live. You *will* live!"

Gradually his thoughts began to untangle, and his eyes began to make sense again. And Dianna: he'd never seen anything dearer than her face, her dark brows drawn together with
concern as she watched him. But she looked too tired, bluish
circles ringing her silver eyes, her face thinner than he remembered, and on her jaw, the last yellow patch of a fading bruise.
She was the one who needed coddling, not him.

Gently she slid her hand beneath the back of his head and

ried to raise him so he could drink from the little horn cup he held to his lips. He scowled, irritated by his own weakness, and too quickly tried to raise himself. The rush-mat walls of the wigwam spun wildly, and he feared his stomach would rebel and shame him. Desperately he clung to his bent knees, willing his own body to behave, until at last, covered with sweat from the effort, he could take the cup from her hand himself.

"How long have I been ill?"

She held one hand up, the fingers spread. "Five days."

"Damnation," he said softly. He touched his face and felt the rough beard that confirmed what she'd said, and then the bandage that swathed his head. He remembered everything now, how he'd let that damned Abenaki take him down neat as a babe in leading-strings. Unbelievably, unforgivably careless he'd been, and his head throbbed as though it still had the tomahawk in it. "Sweet, holy, hellfire, *damnation!*"

She shushed him gently. "Don't vex yourself, Kit, you're still weak."

"You don't need to remind me." He spoke too sharply and saw the surprise and hurt in her eyes. He should be thanking her, not swearing at her. But he couldn't bear to see her face go soft with love again. He didn't deserve her or her love, not the way he'd failed again. "In fact you don't really need me at all, do you? I came to rescue you and ended up half-brained instead. You'd have done better to stay with the French."

"The French didn't want me, nor did the Indians. They only took me to get you." She ducked her head, feeling like a fool for wanting to cry again. Hadn't she wept enough for this man? She told herself that he was still in pain, that this wasn't really Kit talking to her like this, but his surliness stung, and so did the way he would not meet her eyes. "I told them you wouldn't come after me, but it seems they knew you better than I do."

"Aye, that's true enough," he said bluntly. If she knew what an incompetent coward he really was, she wouldn't have stayed with him a minute, let alone five days. He wondered why she hadn't realized the truth yet, when even the French

were mocking his weakness: a man who could not protect th
ones he loved most.

He saw Tamsin's plump little hand, never quite as clean a.
their mother wished, clutching at the chickweed where she'
fallen....

"Where's Mercy?" he demanded abruptly.

"A French priest took her away when we were in the vil
lage. I tried to keep her with me, I swear, but—"

"Asa was wrong to give the child to your safekeeping. No▪
that he's dead, she is my responsibility entirely, not yours."
He paused, and Dianna noticed how he clasped one hand s▪
tightly over the other that his knuckles showed white. "Yo▪
knew they killed him, didn't you?"

She nodded, but Kit's eyes were closed, his head bowed.

The still, small figure lying in the grass seemed more an
gular, was dressed more simply, and in place of the doll wa.
a small, white cat named Lily.

The image was so vivid, Kit sucked in his breath as h▪
fought it back, shaking his head fiercely with denial. No▪
Mercy, nay, not Mercy, too.

Fearful that the fever had returned, Dianna reached out t▪
calm him. "Nay, don't even think it," he growled as he shoo▪
her hand away, his eyes still tightly shut. "Don't even thin▪
it!"

Swiftly Dianna drew back and stared down at her hands i▪
her lap. He was right. She didn't know him, not when he wa▪
like this. When two days before she had found in his haversac▪
all the torn red rosettes she'd left along the trail, she'd seen i▪
as proof of his devotion. But now she wasn't so sure. Lik▪
too many other things he did, maybe rescuing her was simpl▪
one more test of himself, another chance to prove how in▪
valuable Colonel Sparhawk was to the people who depende▪
on him.

And not once in his feverish ramblings had he mentione▪
her name.

"Who is Tamsin?" she asked softly. "You called for he▪
often."

He started so visibly at the name that Dianna's heart sank

'Someone very dear and special to me,'' he answered un-evenly.

He'd grown pale again, his forehead glistening with sweat, and she worried that he'd faint. But she couldn't stop. She had to know. "You love her very much, don't you?"

"How could I not?'' His voice had dropped to a hoarse whisper. "From the day she was born she seemed like another part of me. And then to lose her like that— God, Dianna, she was but seven years old!''

Dianna stared uncertainly, her own doubts forgotten before his obvious misery. "Tamsin?''

He had not meant to tell her, for he didn't think he could bear her scorn when she learned the truth. But to hear Tamsin's name on Dianna's lips seemed to shatter the last boundary within him and he could not have kept back the truth had his life depended on it.

"They came after the last war, after the treaties, only three of them, Mohegans. They—they murdered my mother and my father and my sister Tamsin and took their scalps, and when I found them, it was too late.'' He was shaking, his eyes red-rimmed and staring as he saw it all again. "If I had been there, I would have saved them. But I wasn't, and they died. They died because of me.''

In horrified silence Dianna listened, and one by one, all the half-explained conversations and mysteries began to make sense. Asa and Hester and all the others had known. Only she, the one who loved him most, was left unaware of his suffering.

"Oh, Kit, my poor love,'' she murmured. "You should have told me before.''

He dropped his head to his chest. "I know, Dianna. God forgive me, I should have told you long ago. But I was so afraid I'd lose you, and now look what it's come to. I've failed you and Mercy, too, just like I did my parents and Tamsin, sweet, silly Tamsin.''

His voice broke, and Dianna realized that tears were running down his cheeks to tangle in his half-grown beard. She threw her arms around his shoulders and pulled him close, and he fell against her like a weary child.

"Never say you failed me, Kit," she said as she rocked him
gently against her, his face pressed against her shoulder as she
drew her fingers through the snarls of his hair. "Never say i'
and never believe it. You came and you found me, and if you
hadn't, I would have perished. And what of my uncle? If you
had not come to his house that night, he would have killed
me in his anger. I didn't think you were real, you know. You
were too perfect, like a magic prince in an old story. But you
saved me, and together, somehow, we'll save Mercy, too."

Kit listened without hearing what she said. The words didn't
matter. Only the peace that came with her voice was real, and
he didn't want it ever to end. She did not doubt him, did not
scorn him. She still believed in him. His arms went around
her waist and he clung to her in desperation.

"But think of what I am, Dianna," he mumbled against
her. He had forgotten how soft her skin was. "A sorry, foolish
creature who couldn't even protect his own family."

"Oh, Kit, I do not believe it," she said softly. "You always
put others before yourself. 'Twill likely be the death of you,
you know. To be the man you are, your parents must have
loved you very much. I don't think they would have wanted
you to blame yourself all this time."

He wanted so much to believe her. He had lived with the
pain for so long that it was part of him, and there was no way
he could simply let it go because she said so. But she was
offering a way to ease it, and maybe, given time, she could
help him forget. Why was it she was half his size, and yet had
twice the strength? "Don't leave me, Dianna. God knows I've
no right to ask you anything, but you can't know how I felt
when I thought I'd lost you, too."

"Hush now, love," she said as she feathered a kiss on the
top of his head. "I swear I'll not be going anywhere without
you."

But he was already fast asleep.

Chapter Nineteen

"Your woman tried to kill me, Sparhawk," declared Attawan indignantly as Dianna followed him to where Kit sat by the stream, her musket leveled evenly at the Indian's back.

"I doubt it's much comfort, but she's said the same of you," answered Kit, trying very hard not to laugh. He wasn't sure which one, Attawan or Dianna, would be more upset with him if he did, and besides, it would probably not help his aching head at all. But the sight of Dianna in her tattered dress determinedly herding a disgruntled Attawan with a musket that was nearly as long as she was tall, was almost too much for him. Lord, how much he loved her! "Lower your gun, Dianna. Attawan's the best friend we have in these parts, and I'd prefer to keep him alive."

Reluctantly Dianna uncocked the musket and rested it back onto her shoulder. She hadn't expected to find Kit awake yet, let alone dressed and washing by the stream, and she wished she'd had a comb or brush to make herself look more presentable. She'd grown so accustomed to him ill and unconscious that to see his green cat's eyes once again watching her so attentively was somehow disconcerting. Despite all that he had told her last night, or maybe because of it, she felt oddly shy around Kit this morning, almost as if they were beginning all over again, and she tried to hide her skittishness by concentrating on Attawan.

"I suppose, then, I should ask your forgiveness, Master At-

tawan," she said stiffly, "but my experiences with Indians a
of late have not exactly taught me to trust your people."

"Not *my* people. Abenakis." Attawan sniffed scornfully
confident that no more explanation was necessary. He touche
his fingers to the bandage on Kit's head as he sat on th
ground beside him. "Does your tiny woman carry a tomahawl
as well as a musket?"

"You can't blame the damage on her, Attawan, only the
healing." His smile flashing white against the dark beard, Ki
looked past the Indian to Dianna, and she blushed with pleasure at the warmth in his expression and looked down, self-
conscious in front of Attawan.

Attawan's eyebrows rose skeptically, not at all convinced
this woman was worth the effort she'd cost. "I hope she does
better tending your wounds than making your friends welcome, for you cannot linger here longer. Trailing that French
priest was easy enough, but you, eh, you hide yourself away
like a squirrel and I wasted three days finding you."

Anxiously Kit leaned forward, all trace of teasing gone
"Have you found Mercy Wing?"

Dianna rushed to Kit's side. "Is she well? They haven'
hurt her, have they?"

Attawan shook his head. "The fat priest and the soldier
brought her to the mission at Deux-Rivières, and left her there
with Père Vernet. They want her stronger before they take her
to Montreal, but I don't know when that will be. A week o
in the spring. They may have gone while I searched for you.'
He looked pointedly at Dianna, as if the delay were her faul
alone. "We cannot wait."

Kit stood unsteadily, closing his eyes until the dizziness
passed, and Dianna took his arm with concern. "You're not
ready to travel, are you?" she asked softly. "It was only yesterday that the fever broke."

"I have no choice, dearling." Kit patted her hand on his
arm to reassure her, but Dianna saw the strain etched around
his eyes. "I have to get Mercy before they take her north."

"The mission is only a day's journey, Sparhawk, not hard
travel for a strong man." Attawan studied Kit shrewdly. "But

will you be any use when you get there, eh? Will your aim be true, your knife sure?''

"It will be, my friend, I swear to it. I'll be ready. I must. We can't very well rap on the door and ask them sweetly to give up the girl.''

"Why not?" asked Dianna. "I'd think we'd have a better chance that way than to have you two go crashing in with knives and guns and God knows what.''

"We'll hardly go crashing in anywhere." Kit frowned. "Dianna, love, you don't know how these things are best handled.''

"Nay, you listen to me!" said Dianna urgently. "I'll tell them Mercy's my daughter, that Indians kidnapped her and I want her back. I'll pretend I'm French, and you can be my guide. I'll say the Indians set upon us, too, so that's why we look so shabby. With the beard, no one would ever recognize you.''

"True enough." Kit ran his hand across his jaw, thinking. He knew he'd be no use in a fight, but he hated to admit it, even to Attawan, and especially to Dianna. "I don't speak French, and they wouldn't understand why you hired an Englishman. Best I be your husband and Mercy's father. They can't quarrel with that.''

Dianna smiled shyly, equally pleased that he would listen to her and be willing, even as a ruse, to be her husband.

"And Attawan," continued Kit, "you'll stay outside to cover us or go for help if we don't come out when we should.''

"With the French, that's wise." Thoughtfully Attawan stroked his long scalp-lock. "Perhaps this woman of yours has merit after all.''

Dianna groaned with exasperation and stalked off toward the wigwam to pack.

Kit grinned and slapped Attawan on the arm. "Watch your back, my friend. She not only has merit, but she's the very devil with that musket.''

Uncomfortably, Père Vernet regarded the two people standing in the hall before him. Because the mission at Deux-

Rivières was so deep in the wilderness, Père Vernet often went months without seeing another white face. And here, in less than a week, had first come Monseigneur le Abbé de Saint-Gilbert and now these two, an English settler and his French wife. Even with her clothing shamefully torn, the young woman seemed graceful and modest, her genteel French a pleasure to hear, but the tall man was mistrustful, his hand never straying from the knife at his belt. So be it, decided the priest. If the sad tale they told of their missing daughter was true, the Englishman had reason to be wary.

Troubled, he thought of the child now sleeping in the kitchen. The monseigneur had described the girl's mother as a shrill, blasphemous Englishwoman, and Père Vernet had readily agreed to keep the child until she was well enough to go to the sacred sisters in Montreal. But the tears of the young woman before him touched his heart, and it would be clear enough if the child were hers.

Kit caught Dianna's arm as they began to follow the priest. "Has the little rascal admitted he's got Mercy?"

"He says there's an orphan in his keeping, and we must judge for ourselves," she whispered anxiously, chewing on her lower lip. "It must be Mercy, Kit. It must!"

"Attawan wouldn't have made that kind of mistake," he said thickly, hoping Dianna didn't realize how close to collapsing he was. Somehow he'd walked twenty miles this day, most of it hanging on to Attawan, and only sheer will and fear for Dianna and Mercy had kept him on his feet. "We'll take her from here as soon as you can make our thanks. I've no great taste for French hospitality."

The priest led them into the kitchen, where an old Indian woman with a conspicuous cross on her breast sat dozing over her knitting by the dying fire. To one side of the hearth was a small dishevelled pallet, and at once Dianna recognized Mercy's dark unruly hair poking from the mound of coverlets. With a little cry Dianna ran forward and lifted the sleeping child gently into her arms. Still too sleepy to comprehend, Mercy rubbed her hand across her eyes and muttered to herself before she slowly realized it was Dianna holding her, and Kit was there, too, bending over her. Without a sound she threw her arms around Dianna's neck and hung on as if she'd never let go.

Père Vernet wouldn't soon forget the sweetness of that reunion and the satisfaction of having done right by bringing it about. To witness such happiness, a child restored to loving parents, was a rare blessing, indeed. It had, then, been most unfortunate to see the poor father succumb to the shock of the ordeal and topple to the floor, his senses dead to the world.

Dianna undressed by the faint glow from the banked fire and climbed beneath the musty coverlet, being as careful as she could not to make the straw-filled mattress rustle and wake Kit. It had taken two of Père Vernet's Christian Indians to manoeuvre Kit's exhausted body up the narrow staircase to the mission's tiny bedchamber reserved for travellers, and he'd been asleep even before she'd stripped off his moccasins. Awkwardly she hugged the edge of the bed away from his body, listening to the even rhythm of his breathing. She had never slept with a man, and she wasn't sure what to do, whether to touch him or not. But it was cold, and slowly she inched across the bed and tentatively snuggled her body against his back.

He was instantly awake, every nerve and muscle acutely aware of her imprint against his. Gingerly her hand crept around his waist, holding him, and he couldn't help groaning.

"Oh, Kit, I've wakened you," she whispered with disappointment, and he felt her begin to move away. "Forgive me, but I was cold. Here, I'll move back."

"Nay, stay." His fingers tightened around her wrist as he pulled her back, wondering how she could be cold when it seemed to him the very mattress was on fire from her nearness.

With a contented sigh she eased herself against him, her legs curled into his and her cheek turned against the broad muscles of his back. Her heart fluttered faster as her skin touched his where her tattered shift pulled up, and she inhaled deeply the special fragrance that was his alone. Sternly she reminded herself of how weak he still was, but her hand seemed to be moving on its own wanton volition, her fingers trailing through the curling hair on his chest.

"Did I really swoon away like a weak-kneed maid?" Kit asked, his voice strained. She had come to him innocently because she was cold, and in return he was randy as an old goat. If she'd only lie still!

"'Twas not your fault, Kit. The kitchen fire was too warm, that was all, and you've pushed yourself too far. Père Vernet understood. And the other priest, the one who took Mercy, isn't due back here for a fortnight, so we're safe enough here tonight." Safe enough from Frenchmen, thought Dianna guiltily, but not from her. "I sent the old woman in the kitchen to tell Attawan we were unharmed and would meet him in the morning."

"You've taken care of everything, haven't you, sweetheart?" said Kit softly. He said it proudly, without blaming or faulting himself, and Dianna didn't answer, smiling to herself in the darkness.

"You sang to me when I was sick, didn't you?" he asked. "I only now remembered it. 'Greensleeves,' and 'Hangman's Tree,' and 'Pray, Fair One.'"

"Would you have me sing to you now?"

"Nay, Dianna. I'd have you marry me. Now, this night, if that priest below didn't believe us already wed, but as soon as we return to Plumstead, if you'll have me."

Dianna froze, positive she'd misheard. "You don't owe me anything, Kit," she said in a tiny voice. "Not this. Whatever I've done for you—I expected nothing in return."

With a swiftness that startled her, he rolled over and trapped her against the pillows, his face so close to hers, she felt the hot urgency of his words upon her cheek.

"Listen to me, Dianna," he said. "When I thought I'd lost you forever, that I'd never touch you again, I knew then I could not go on living unless I found you. I want you in my arms by night and at my side by day, and I wish never to be parted from you again. Never, understand? I'm offering you everything I have, Dianna—my name, my home, my heart—

d I pray to God it's enough. How I love you, sweetheart.
ow I love you!''

Dianna's throat constricted with emotion. ''And I you, Kit.
rom the first, I've always loved you. Forever and always,
it, my only love. Oh, Kit...''

She sighed his name as his lips met hers, a kiss that sig-
alled a reunion, a pledge, a future for them as one. He kissed
er tenderly at first, teasing with his tongue over the swell of
er lips until they parted with a tiny catch of desire. He had
orgotten how sweet she tasted, or maybe the velvety delight
f her mouth was simply beyond remembering.

Dianna pulled away, her breathing already labored. ''Your
ead, Kit,'' she protested weakly. ''The wound—''

''The devil take it.'' His voice was more a growl, deep in
is chest. ''I'd sooner die than not love you now.''

He pulled her shift over her shoulders, unwilling to have
ny barriers between them, and Dianna curled herself around
im, marvelling again at the differences between them. His
ody was so lean and hard where hers was soft, his strength
o visible in every muscle of his arms and back, and even
vhen the fever had held him, he still had a power, a physical
resence that she couldn't explain. He was unthinkingly con-
dent in a man's harsh world of right and wrong and sudden
eath. Yet behind it all was the gentleness that touched her
ow, callused hands that caressed her with the tenderness that
nade her feel cherished and special. Then the gentleness fled
efore the passion, and their bodies twined together, wildly
rching toward fulfillment. And when at last he cried out and
alled her name, she melted into him and knew such sweetness
hat she almost wept with the pure joy of loving him.

''In seven days by the river, we'll be home at Plumstead,''
e whispered happily as they lay still joined together. He
wept her hair back to kiss her ear, and Dianna felt a con-
entment she'd never known before. Home, her home, with
er love, her husband, her perfect Master Sparhawk.

The lantern's light was blindingly harsh as the door ex--
ploded open. The room seemed full of men, leering Indians
vith eyes like jackals, and Dianna shrank behind Kit.

"You see how completely these two sinners have sullie
your good hospitality, Père Vernet," said François Robillar
triumphantly, the curl of his mouth distorted by the lantern'
upward glare. "But I'll teach them the folly of their wicked
ness. Aye, they shall learn, and learn well."

Chapter Twenty

Restlessly, Dianna paced the narrow length of the bedchamber that last night had been her sanctuary and now was her prison. The double-planked door was locked from outside, and the diamond panes of the casements were too narrow even for her to squeeze through. She wore the simple gown that had been brought to her, coarse grey wool fit for a penitent. But Dianna was neither penitent nor ashamed of what she had done. Instead, she was furious with Père Vernet's betrayal and frightened of what had become of Kit when Robillard and the others had dragged him away.

She stopped near the window when she heard the heavy footsteps echoing on the wooden stairs, and she didn't turn when she heard the key scraping in the lock. Whoever it was, she wouldn't give him the satisfaction of a greeting beyond the straight, proud line of her back. Absently she scratched the frost from the window pane and noticed the snow that had begun to fall. October still, and yet winter had already come to New France.

"Look at me, *mademoiselle!*" ordered Robillard crossly. "If we are to be friends, *ma chère,* I expect to see your pretty face."

"Friends!" Now Dianna wheeled around, hands clutched tight into fists at her sides. "How could I ever be friend to a vile creature like you?"

The Frenchman's face grew mottled above the grimy lace

collar, his eyes narrowing into the pouchy folds beneath them
His expression was one that Dianna remembered well from
her uncle: hungry expectation, as if she were a sweetmeat to
be gobbled up in one sharp bite, changing to ugly belligerenc
with her refusal. Refusals were dangerous—she remembere
that from Sir Henry, too—but nothing could make her giv
in. She belonged to Kit, and to Kit alone.

"There are other words to call you if *friend* is too fine,'
snapped Robillard angrily. "*Bonne ami,* mistress, whore—
what you call yourself matters little. You *will* do whatever
ask, whenever I wish it. Why else would I have kept you here
warm and safe, instead of making you share the fate of tha
bâtard Sparhawk?"

"What have you done to him?" she demanded. "I swear
if you have hurt him—"

"Ha, and what would you do to me, eh? This time yo
don't have a gun to pretend you're a man." His laugh was
mean-spirited little bark. "Sparhawk is not so comfortable a
you, *non,* but he still lives."

"Wherever he is, I'd rather be with him than you!"

"That is unkind, *ma petite fille.*" Robillard shook his head
the cool morning light glinting on the single earring he wore
"Let me tell you my plans for him, and then you will perhap
change your mind towards me, eh? The Indians with me ar
Mohawks, and I've promised them Sparhawk for their villag
divertissement. Already they wager over how much pain he
will take before he cries out. They enjoy their torture, *oui*
Perhaps they'll burn him alive or cut out his tongue and mak
him eat it or slash at his belly until—"

"Stop it!" Dianna cried shrilly, her hands tight over he
ears. "I won't listen anymore!"

"Have you heard, *ma chère,*" he continued, smiling, "tha
the Mohawks eat the flesh of other men?"

"Nay, stop!" She was trembling with what he described
knowing none of it was exaggeration, and she could not bea
to think of Kit suffering that way. "Why do you hate him so
What has he ever done to you?"

The smile abruptly disappeared. "I hate him for what he is

mademoiselle, a Sparhawk and an *Anglais.* Sparhawks ruined me with their crops and their cattle and their little farmers everywhere I look. Sparhawks try to eat away at New France in the name of your fat Queen Anne, and Sparhawks drove the beavers away, and what did they leave me? An *indigent!*"

"That can't be so," said Dianna slowly. "Kit says there haven't been any beavers near Wickhamton for thirty years."

"Eh, what else would he tell you?" he asked furiously. "This Christophe is even worse than his father. He set the Pocumtucks against me and threatens me in my own house with his governors and soldiers. He won't even let me defend my honor and my name and fight me like a man, but insults me and then runs back to his grand manor house.

"But his fine living days are past, *ma chère.*" Robillard's smile returned, and he hooked his thumbs into the fringed sash slung low under his belly. Almost swaggering, he gradually closed the distance between Dianna and himself. "At one word from me, his blessed Wickhamton will be burned and looted like Deerfield. I will claim the Sparhawk house for my own and the Sparhawk land for New France."

Slowly he reached out to Dianna. He wore a gold ring on his middle finger, the knuckle swollen above it, and his nails were rimmed with dirt. "I know I will have these things of Sparhawk's, because already I have his woman."

"You don't have me," Dianna said with such vehemence that his outstretched hand froze awkwardly in midair, "and you never will, any more than you'll have Plumstead or Wickhamton or the rest."

Furiously Robillard jerked back his hand, using it to tug at the beard along his jaw. "Soon enough you will see how wrong you are, *ma fille.* When you hear the cries of the Mohawk braves as they drag your precious Christophe away, you will crawl begging to me."

Dianna drew herself up as tall as she could, folding her arms across her chest to hide the shaking of her hands. "I will never beg from you, *monsieur.*"

He scowled at her with disbelief. "Not even to save Sparhawk's life?"

"Nay, I would not." It took every shred of self-control to keep her voice from breaking beneath his scrutiny. "I would not because Kit would not want me to and because it would make no difference to you at all."

Robillard slammed the door without bothering to disagree and Dianna sank to her knees onto the bare floor. If there was a way out of this for her and for Kit and for Mercy, she must find it and soon.

Carefully Kit felt his way around the four stone walls of the cellar, trying in the darkness to make his fingers see what his eyes could not. Cold, damp stones chinked with earth and moss; a floor of packed dirt; stacked pyramids of hogsheads nothing unusual and no way out.

Discouraged, he slumped to the floor with his head tipped back against one wall, staring up at the faint square of light that marked the trap door. The thick hewn beams supporting the floorboards creaked with footsteps overhead, and Kit could distinguish the rise and fall of conversations, though not the words, of the people in the rooms above him.

Dianna's voice was not among them. He hoped that meant she was still upstairs, and he prayed that Robillard was leaving her alone. Kit had hated the way that the Frenchman had watched Dianna last night, ogling her so blatantly while she had scrambled for her clothes, and the image twisted like a knife in his conscience. She'd looked so small, her silver eyes huge in her pale face.

Kit had wanted to kill Robillard then, and would have if the three Indians hadn't held him back. He rubbed the new bruises on his arms, the only marks on him to show how hard he'd fought before the three had thrown him and his clothes down into this cellar. They'd been careful enough not to injure him. Though Kit had no delusions about their gentleness, he had no intention of ending his days in some Mohawk squaw's stew pot, either. *Damn Robillard!* It seemed that the man had been there all of Kit's life, an irritating annoyance, a coward and a bully, but nothing worse than that. He should have stopped the man the way Attawan had advised months ago when the dying trapper had named his attacker. But Kit had believed that talking would be enough.

He sighed restlessly, staring at the trap door. Sometimes it seemed his whole life had been nothing but wrong choices made, an endless list of "should have done."

With a groan, he buried his face on arms crossed over his bent knees and thought about Dianna. Last night he should have—*God, there was another one!*—he should have insisted they leave the mission. And yet he wouldn't wish away the magic of their lovemaking. Nay, that was the one thing he'd done right! *She* was right. He could breathe her scent still on him, a comfort and torment at the same time. What he felt for her went beyond love, or love as he'd always defined it before her. She was part of him, in his blood and in his heart so completely that he felt the separation as a physical pain.

Somehow he had to get back to her. Somehow he would steal her and Mercy away from Robillard and his Indians, and together they would go home to Plumstead, and they would wed, and they'd never be apart again.

Somehow.

Père Vernet sat across the wide table from François Robillard, his unhappiness growing by the moment. As more and more of the mission's carefully rationed burgundy had disappeared down Robillard's throat, the heavy-set man came to seem less and less the gentleman he'd presented himself to be, and the more, too, that the little priest regretted his hospitality.

"And I tell you, *mon père,* that Lieutenant Hertel de Rouville himself has an interest in this affair." Robillard was bragging yet again. "You wouldn't know the lieutenant's power or influence, stuck back here where you are, but believe me, in Montreal, he is a man others listen to. When he learns how I've destroyed Christopher Sparhawk and that all the Sparhawk land can now be claimed for New France, he will be pleased. *Non, non,* he will rejoice!"

Père Vernet studied his hands clasped on the table. "I am, as you say, only a backwoods priest," he said hesitantly, "but still, this man Sparhawk did not seem to me to be quite the villain you portray.''

''Then he has fooled you as he fools so many!'' cried Robillard, slamming the bottle down on the table for emphasis. ''He is *Anglais,* and that alone makes him an enemy of King Louis. But he is also greedy and cruel, with no morals. You saw how he pleasured himself with his woman even beneath your holy roof!''

Much as you would yourself, my friend, thought Père Vernet. For him the memory of the woman reunited with her child, the man bending tenderly over them, was a much stronger, much sweeter image than the one Robillard kept repeating. And although the priest had no first-hand experience with venal sins, he was astute enough to recognize them in others, and was certain Robillard desired the woman himself.

''His lands will all be mine,'' said Robillard with expansive satisfaction as he tipped the last of the wine from the bottle directly into his mouth. ''All of it mine, *mon père!*''

''Then you will benefit from the Englishman's misfortune, *monsieur?*''

''*Oui, oui,* and New France, too, of course!'' Robillard kicked the chair back from the table and rose unsteadily to his feet. ''But it's time I took to my bed, *mon père,* I've—''

But once Robillard let go his grip on the chair, he tumbled forward to the floor and stayed there, snoring open-mouthed on his back. Slowly Père Vernet came to stand over the man. The priest reminded himself that vengeance belonged to God, not lowly men. But this, perhaps, seemed more a case of righting a wrong.

Swiftly he called to the Indian woman, giving her orders in her own tongue, and then hurried up the twisting stairs. He tapped at the locked door even as he fitted the key into the lock.

''*Mademoiselle?*'' he whispered. The room was dark, no light showing beneath the door. ''*Mademoiselle,* are you awake?''

He opened the door and ducked barely in time to avoid the crash of the earthenware chamberpot. ''Stay back, *monsieur,*'' warned Dianna tersely, grabbing the slat-back chair she planned to use as her next weapon. "You betrayed us, and I'll have no guilt from serving you the same!"

Humbly Père Vernet bowed his head and nodded, acknowledging her reproof. "*Oui, mademoiselle.* I could beg your forgiveness, but there isn't time, not if you and your family wish to escape."

Dianna studied him warily. "Why should I trust you again?"

"Because you have no other choice?" asked the priest uncertainly. "Come, we must free your—your husband while that man Robillard sleeps."

Dianna didn't hesitate, but grabbed the blanket she used as a cloak and ran after the priest. In the hall she paused long enough to see Robillard stretched out on the floor, his mountainous belly gently rising and falling. How long would he remain like this, she wondered? With a shudder she rushed into the kitchen.

Père Vernet had already unlocked and lifted the heavy trap door, holding it open by its iron ring. Uncertainly he leaned over the edge, peering into the dark cellar. "*Monsieur?*" he called. "Monsieur Sparhawk?"

Suddenly Kit flew out from under the lip of the floor, attacking the priest like a great lion and rolling over and over with him in his grasp until they bumped into the trestle table. Kit grabbed Père Vernet by the throat, tightening his fingers while the priest began to gasp and clutch ineffectually at Kit's arms.

"Nay, Kit, stop it!" cried Dianna, grabbing Kit's shoulders to pull him away. "He's going to help us!"

"Dianna!" Abruptly he freed the priest and caught Dianna in his arms instead. "Praise God you're safe! They didn't hurt you?"

She shook her head. Briefly Dianna savored the comfort of Kit's embrace before she pushed back against his chest. "We must hurry, love, while Robillard sleeps!"

"*Ivre, monsieur,*" croaked Père Vernet, massaging his

throat as he pulled himself to his knees, and Dianna rapidly translated for Kit. "He's had too much wine."

"Then our lives may still be worth more than three hops of a louse!" Effortlessly Kit lifted the little priest to his feet and led him to a chair. "Forgive me, sir, I didn't realize—"

But Père Vernet waved his apology away. "It is no more than I deserved, *mon fils,* though I wonder that this man Robillard would dare to fight with you two. Your guns and other belongings are there on the chest." He shook his head sadly. "Such spirit, ah! No wonder you *Anglais* have prospered in this wilderness!"

Kit found his knife, his fingers tightening on the hilt in anticipation as he turned toward the room in which Robillard slept, but the priest called out and staggered to his feet. "In God's name, I beg you, no killing beneath His roof! That man has drunk enough to stop a bear. He can't harm you now."

Reluctantly Kit tucked the knife back into the sheath on his belt, and Père Vernet sighed heavily. "But you must leave now. Follow the river to the fork. There will be canoes waiting. You can trust the *sauvages* to take you back to your territory. And those Mohawks—they will bring you no trouble, either."

"If ever you are in New England, sir," said Kit, grasping the priest's hand, "you'll be welcome at my home. Farewell and many thanks." The old Indian woman appeared, leading Mercy, who ran to Dianna as Kit urged them both out the door and into the night.

The snow had begun again, or maybe it had never stopped; fat, lazy, wet flakes that barely covered the grass and fallen leaves. Because of the snow, the night sky was pale with a yellowish tinge, and the trail was clear, black trees outlined against the white snow. Although the journey before them— days in an open canoe in winter snow—would not be easy, Dianna couldn't help but feel elated, almost deliriously happy. They had escaped! Had Kit not ordered them to keep silent, she would have begun to sing, something triumphant, heroic perhaps, for Kit—

"You could not believe I'd let you go so easily, eh?" demanded Robillard, his voice booming in the cold air. His dark outline blocked the trail, and in the half-light of the snow, the pistols in his hands glinted ominously.

Instantly Kit determined his alternatives. He could stop one of the pistols, but not both, and he refused to risk the lives of Dianna and Mercy. "Let the women go," he said. "You have no quarrel with them."

Dianna stared up at Kit's impassive profile, the snowflakes clumping on the brim of his hat and in his hair. "I won't go," she said softly. "Even if he says we can, I won't leave you again."

Robillard laughed harshly. "Don't worry, *ma chère,* I intend to keep you here to watch me regain my honor, and deal with this *bâtard* as he deserves!"

Kit didn't move. "You're still drunk, aren't you?" he said mildly.

"Be thankful that I am, *Anglais,* for it improves my mood. I won't slaughter you at once, eh? Now throw your guns in those bushes, and the knife, too. I know your tricks. Go on, now!"

One by one, Kit tossed Dianna's musket and his rifle and knife away, carelessly, as if they meant nothing to him. "So is this how it will be, Robillard? You will shoot me where I stand, without even pretending to make it fair?"

"That is what you wish to believe of me, isn't it, Sparhawk?" asked Robillard almost forlornly. "You and your father before you, you never would treat me like a *gentilhomme,* like yourselves. You have stolen from me and turned others against me, and with your smug *anglais* face alone you have shamed my king!"

"And to ease your pride, you've bullied and harassed my people for twenty years," answered Kit warmly. He knew he had to control his anger, but when he thought of all the misery that had come from this one man, he felt the blood pumping hot in his veins. "You've had men murdered and families torn apart, houses and farms burned, and worst of all, you've always been too great a coward to do any of it yourself."

"We will see who is the bigger coward, Sparhawk." Robillard stuck one pistol into his belt, reached into the bag he carried slung over his shoulder and pulled out a broadsword wrapped in an old blanket. To Kit's surprise, Robillard tossed the sword to him, and then the Frenchman drew his own, leaving the pistols and the bag on a rock behind him.

"You see, Sparhawk, I will give you your fair fight," crowed Robillard, already waving his sword in the air before him with excitement. "I will give you the honor of dying like a *gentilhomme,* and then your woman and your lands will be mine."

Dianna laid her hand on Kit's arm. "You can't mean to do this," she said urgently. "He could kill you!"

"And *I* could kill him," said Kit almost cheerfully, testing the weight and feel of the sword in his hand. The hilt was wood, the guard as battered as an old pot, but the blade was well balanced. He'd never carried a sword himself, finding them cumbersome in the forest, but his grandfather's long-ago lessons were still with him, as much in his arm as in his memory. He kissed Dianna on the forehead and gently disengaged her hand, feeling strangely calm. "Go now, sweetheart, take Mercy and stand clear. This should not, I think, take long."

"Then you're as mad as he is!" Dianna cried as she pulled Mercy back to the edge of the little clearing. The girl was crying silently, the tears slipping down her cheeks, and Dianna bent to hug her.

"Kit will be fine, you know he will," she whispered. "He's younger and bigger and—and, oh, he loves us too well to leave us like this!" And, she added to herself, she intended to help him win, manly honor be damned. She had watched where Kit had dropped their guns, and she meant to retrieve her musket. Slowly she began edging her way around the clearing.

She hadn't expected the harsh, scraping sound as the blades struck each other and the grunts of exertion from the men. Panting and snorting like a bull, Robillard held his sword with two hands, slashing large arcs that Kit always met and deflected. Around and 'round they circled, the blades swinging, as snowflakes drifted past them. Both men grew warm from the fight, and the steam rose from their bodies in the cold air.

Suddenly Kit lunged forward, his blade slashing deep into Robillard's shoulder. The man howled in pain and clutched at the wound, the blood rushing through his fingers and dripping crimson to the snow as his right arm now hung uselessly at his side.

Kit paused and wiped the sweat from his face with his sleeve, expecting the Frenchman to surrender, but instead Robillard lunged forward with the sword in his left hand, his thrusts now wildly uncontrolled, his feet staggering. Kit realized the fight's end was near, and he raised his arm to finish it.

Robillard's face stared up at him for the last time, his features distorted by hatred, pain and fear. "Your father fought like this, too, damn his soul," he gasped, "yet he could not save his women either, not even the *jeune fille* who tried to run."

Paralyzed, Kit felt the old nightmare wash over him again. *Robillard had watched his family die. Robillard had done it, and all these years Kit had let him go unpunished.* Kit didn't feel the pain as the Frenchman's sword sliced across his arm or hear the gunshot that jerked Robillard's body like a puppet. All his consciousness narrowed to the faint whistle of his sword through the air and through the snow and deep into Robillard's chest.

Then Dianna was running toward him, awkwardly, sliding on the snow with the musket still in her hand. There were others coming through the trees, Englishmen, soldiers from the fort at Northfield, and there was Attawan with them, and Mercy hopping up and down with excitement.

Dianna's arms were tight around him now, and when Kit slipped his hands about her shoulders, he realized she was covered with blood, his blood, but she didn't seem to care, and neither did he. She was all he wanted, and she was here.

"It's over, my love," he said hoarsely as he stroked her head against his chest. "It's finally over."

Afterword

Plumstead
July 1705

"Before I cleared New London last November, I kissed your bride farewell, and now when I return, I'm to kiss your babe, too," declared Jonathan as he peered down at the baby in Kit's arms. "You've wasted no time getting an heir, dear brother."

Kit only laughed, glancing across the room at how pink Dianna's cheeks had grown, while Jonathan bent dutifully to kiss his new nephew. Propped up on a mountain of pillows in the bed, Dianna happily watched the two brothers, one fair, one dark, admiring three-day-old Joshua John Sparhawk. At the foot of the bed perched Mercy, with Lily beside her, the little cat, too, basking in maternal splendor with five kittens tumbling across the coverlet.

Wincing, Dianna eased herself up farther on the pillows. The birth hadn't been easy—Joshua already seemed destined to equal his father's size—but she'd forgotten it all the moment the midwife had handed him to her. And Kit—Lord, she'd never seen a man so proud!

Jonathan presented his finger to be squeezed by Joshua's tiny fist as the baby squinted seriously up at his uncle. "Don't let them landlock you, boy. You come to sea with me, and I'll show you the world.''

Kit snorted. "Ha, Jon, more likely he'll be leading you a merry chase for the wenches!" he scoffed. "Mark that hair! You can tell already he's a golden Sparhawk, and there's not a woman alive that can resist us.''

"Mind I was a tow-headed lad, Kit, and look how I turned out. Nor do the ladies complain, either.'' Jonathan bent closer to the baby. "Ain't that so, young master?''

The young master's face crumpled, and he began to yowl with a surprising volume for so small a bundle. Quickly Jonathan stepped back, and Kit responded with all the experience of three days of fatherhood: he promptly returned the wailing child to Dianna.

"It's nothing you did, Uncle Jonathan,'' explained Mercy philosophically. "He be hungry, that's all.''

"Then it's best we left him to his supper, poppet,'' said Jonathan heartily, relieved to have an excuse to flee. "Come, let's see if Hester's finished with those plum tarts.'' Eagerly Mercy hopped off the bed to join him, followed by Lily, her ears flattened at the baby's crying, and her kittens.

Clicking her tongue with sympathy, Dianna unlaced her gown, and soon the only sound from Joshua was a satisfied cooing. Kit sat on the bed behind her, and with her own sigh of contentment, Dianna settled back against his chest.

"Don't listen to Jonathan, Kit,'' she said softly, still in awe of her son's perfection. "Joshua's exactly in your image. He's got your hair and your eyes—or will have, once they change from blue to green—and even his ears look like yours. Though I believe the chin *is* mine,'' she added, touching a finger to the tiny cleft, now puddled with milk, that so mirrored her own, "and perhaps his brows.''

Lightly Kit kissed the top of her hair, his arms encircling her as she embraced their child. "He's quite welcome to your chin and your brows and whatever else he pleases, as long as your heart belongs to me.''

Dianna lifted her lips to his. ''Forever,'' she whispered, ''forever and always, my heart will be yours.''

* * * * *

TRAVEL TO A LAND LONG AGO
AND FAR AWAY WHEN YOU READ
A HARLEQUIN HISTORICAL NOVEL

If you enjoyed what you just read,
then we've got an offer you can't resist!

Take 2
bestselling novels FREE!
Plus get a FREE surprise gift!

Clip this page and mail it to The Best of the Best™

IN U.S.A.
3010 Walden Ave.
P.O. Box 1867
Buffalo, N.Y. 14240-1867

IN CANADA
P.O. Box 609
Fort Erie, Ontario
L2A 5X3

YES! Please send me 2 free Best of the Best™ novels and my free surprise
gift. After receiving them, if I don't wish to receive anymore, I can return the
shipping statement marked cancel. If I don't cancel, I will receive 4 brand-new
novels every month, before they're available in stores! In the U.S.A., bill me at
the bargain price of $4.24 plus 25¢ shipping and handling per book and
applicable sales tax, if any*. In Canada, bill me at the bargain price of $4.74 plus
25¢ shipping and handling per book and applicable taxes**. That's the complete
price and a savings of over 15% off the cover prices—what a great deal! I
understand that accepting the 2 free books and gift places me under no
obligation ever to buy any books. I can always return a shipment and cancel at
any time. Even if I never buy another book from The Best of the Best™, the 2 free
books and gift are mine to keep forever.

185 MEN DFNG
385 MEN DFNH

Name	(PLEASE PRINT)	
Address	Apt.#	
City	State/Prov.	Zip/Postal Code

* Terms and prices subject to change without notice. Sales tax applicable in N.Y.
** Canadian residents will be charged applicable provincial taxes and GST.
   All orders subject to approval. Offer limited to one per household and not valid to
   current Best of the Best™ subscribers.
   ® are registered trademarks of Harlequin Enterprises Limited.

BOB01   ©1998 Harlequin Enterprises Limited

In August look for

AN IDEAL MARRIAGE?

by *New York Times* bestselling author

DEBBIE MACOMBER

A special 3-in-1 collector's edition containing three full-length novels from America's favorite storyteller, Debbie Macomber—each ending with a delightful walk down the aisle.

Father's Day
First Comes Marriage
Here Comes Trouble

Evoking all the emotion and warmth that you've come to expect from Debbie, AN IDEAL MARRIAGE? will definitely satisfy!

MONTANA MAVERICKS

THE GUNSLINGER'S BRIDE

by *USA Today* bestselling author

CHERYL ST.JOHN

Discover the origins of Montana's
most popular family in the
MONTANA MAVERICKS
HISTORICAL SERIES

Outlaw Brock Kincaid returns home to make peace
with his brothers and finds love in the arms of an
old flame with a secret.

MONTANA MAVERICKS

RETURN TO WHITEHORN—
WHERE LEGENDS ARE BEGUN AND LOVE LASTS
FOREVER BENEATH THE BIG SKY...

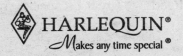

HARLEQUIN®

Makes any time special ®

Visit us at www.eHarlequin.com

HH577

New York Times bestselling authors

DEBBIE MACOMBER
JAYNE ANN KRENTZ
HEATHER GRAHAM &
TESS GERRITSEN

lead

TAKE 5

Covering everything from tender love to
sizzling passion, there's a TAKE 5 volume for
every type of romance reader.

Plus

With $5.00 worth of coupons inside each volume,
this is one deal you shouldn't miss!

TAKE 5

5 Quick Reads. *5* Great Escapes.

Look for it in August 2001.

Visit us at www.eHarlequin.com   HNCPT5R